Richard Herley was born in 1950 and has lived in England for most of his life. He read biology at Sussex University, and while there he gained his knowledge of the countryside where much of this story is set. He has devoted himself to writing since his graduation. *The Pagans* is made up of three novels: *The Stone Arrow*, w[...] Winifred Holtby Memorial Prize, *The Fli*[...]

THE PAGANS

'This novel deals [...]ulture. I read it with great [...]ery way a remarkable achievement'
Anthony Burgess

'To evoke such an ancient and alien world is a daunting task to any writer, and I congratulate the author straight away on having achieved so well a picture of man as still very much part of the natural world, in competition with other animals in a shared environment'
Stuart Piggott *Times Literary Supplement*

'The natural Darwinian world of which he writes with a blood-soaked passion left me gulping for air. Horridly imaginative, powerful in its refusal to avert its eyes from the results of violence, the book appeals to the blood lust in us all'
Glasgow Herald

'Takes neolithic genocide, incest, helotry and weaponry in its fine imaginative stride . . . the stark action and the snows and wolf-woods of a hostile landscape are powerful feats of description'
The Observer

RICHARD HERLEY

The Pagans

The Stone Arrow
The Flint Lord
The Earth Goddess

GRAFTON BOOKS
A Division of the Collins Publishing Group

LONDON GLASGOW
TORONTO SYDNEY AUCKLAND

Grafton Books
A Division of the Collins Publishing Group
8 Grafton Street, London W1X 3LA

This one-volume edition published by Grafton Books 1986

The Stone Arrow, *The Flint Lord* and *The Earth Goddess*
first published in Great Britain by
Peter Davies Ltd 1978, William Heinemann/Peter Davies
1981 and William Heinemann Ltd 1984

ISBN 0-586-06618-7

Printed and bound in Great Britain by
Collins, Glasgow

Set in Times

The Stone Arrow

Tagart came out of the woods and stood facing the broad downhill sweep of the cereal field. The feeling of openness seemed strange and sudden after the embrace of the trees; he sniffed at the smell of the evening, almost cloudless now after the storm, a soft wind coming off the sea, bending the stunted ears of barley, fluttering the leaves of hazel and whitebeam.

A hundred yards away the labourer stood upright and leaned on the handle of his mattock. He had only just become aware of another's presence; yet Tagart had heard the man at work minutes ago, from the depths of the wood, whose floor he had traversed without so much as the snap of a twig.

Tagart, or Tugart, or Tergart, was twenty-five years of age, tall and fine in the face, with dark hair and watchful brown eyes that knew the value of patience. His skin – for it was now the height of summer – was well tanned, his frame hard-muscled and long-limbed, with an economy of movement that seemed like slowness to those who had never been with him in the woods and tried to keep up. Chance had endowed him with stamina, and a wry intelligence which the teachings of his elders had turned into solid skill and a command of the necessary knowledge. Of all the young men in his tribe, it was Tagart who had been regarded as successor to the leader, Tagart who had taken the most beautiful bride, Tagart whose small son would in turn one day be chief; and Tagart whom the others were beginning to look upon with more and more respect and love as each season went by. But now, in the course of a single night, all that had changed: beauty made foul, cleanness made filth. Everything changed; everything raped and defiled.

Not quite everything. Tagart was still alive. He was still alive, and behind the grief he was still himself. The plan, flexible in detail but rigid in outline and purpose, lay like a cold network in his brain.

It was time to begin.

'I come in friendship,' he called out, leaving the protection of the trees and starting across the field.

The labourer made no reply. He stood shielding his eyes against the west, his body held nervously, right hand taking a firmer grasp on the polished ashwood haft of his mattock.

Tagart went on. In the edge of his vision he was making a second survey of the field, making absolutely certain that he and the labourer were alone. The farmers' village, which he had studied the previous day, was a cluster of stone and timber buildings inside a wooden palisade, hidden from this field by the rise of the land. It was only a quarter of a mile away, too close, asking for trouble; but then he'd had no choice. He had been forced into the open by the shape of the forest and by the way the fields sloped. Without revealing himself there had been no way to be sure that the labourer was alone; and to waste such an opportunity would be madness, so he had accepted the risk. But that did not stop the tingling between his shoulder blades, nor an almost irresistible urge to check more overtly behind and to the sides.

He halted just beyond the swing of the mattock, and smiled. 'The soil needs more rain than this. After the drought she drinks it like a pigeon.'

The farmer said nothing. He stood impassive, expressionless.

'I have come along the coast from Valdoe,' Tagart told him, speaking more distinctly. He indicated his leather pouch. 'My master wishes an exchange of barleys.'

The farmer's eyes flicked to the pouch, and back to Tagart's face.

'I see barley is your crop here on this acre.'

No reaction.

'I was told to ask for a man with no beard,' Tagart said. 'A man of importance in your village. Do you know him?'

The farmer grunted. There was no meaning in it.

'Is he your head man? Will you take me to him? I want to talk trade.'

The labourer took his hand from his brow and changed position so that he no longer faced the sun. He was a short, broad man, with stumpy legs and wide shoulders filling a stained and streaked doeskin jacket, with beaver leggings bound by thongs, and on his feet alder clogs carved with lines and circles. Round his neck was a talisman of some sort, a flat stone striped with bands of colour – cream, brown, maroon – hanging by a cord that passed through a hole drilled off-centre. Greasy black locks showed beneath a hare's-skin cap and hung in a tangle at his neck. Years of weather had left his skin leathery and his eyes wrinkled almost shut, yet his was a face devoid of animation or humour, the kind of face under a low forehead that frowns blankly as the brain behind it struggles to assimilate something new. Clearly the man was low in the order of the village, sent out to the fields to do some small task on his own. He had been digging up stones and heaping them to one side, making a tilth of what once had been a barren patch. This was the kind of work reserved for the losers, those at the bottom of the village hierarchy.

He nodded at Tagart's pouch.

'Seed barley,' Tagart said, holding the pouch forward.

The offer was disregarded. 'You say you come along the coast.'

'From Valdoe.'

'From Valdoe?' For the first time he showed a sign of interest. It was as if Tagart had not already mentioned the word. 'Valdoe? From Valdoe? Are you sent by the Flint Lord?'

'By my master, one of the Trundlemen.'

'And he sent you trading barley?'

'Yes.'

The farmer's eyes narrowed cunningly. 'You will know the flint sellers. They will be here soon with flints: it is time for their trade. Fallott, Bico and the rest.'

'My trade is not in axes,' Tagart said. 'It is in seed.' More mildly he added, 'There are many at Valdoe. A mere slave cannot know them all.'

'You are enslaved?'

'Building my freedom.'

'Why go back? You are far from the Trundle. They could never catch up.'

'That is not my way,' Tagart said. 'My master trusts me and I am grateful.'

The farmer forbore from comment. He turned and took a long look to the west, across the curving line of the field, beyond the distant green scrub on the clifftops, to the golden path where the sun was coming down on the sea. The wind pushed wisps of hair at the sides of his face. Tagart heard corn buntings and skylarks, and glimpsed the flash of a jay's wing as it emerged from and returned to the security of the wood. He swayed slightly. Exhaustion was threatening to overtake him. His body wanted to yield and sag to the ground. Sections of his mind were faltering, blinking on and off. He was aware that his strength was draining away; with its loss came the panic of realizing that he might be left with too little when the moment arrived. He had foolishly eaten nothing that day, and the day before he had felt too ill to contemplate food. His stomach had been emptied anyway, in the grey wet dawn with his arms and legs covered in ashes, slime and blood, the back of his throat burning and his eyes watering with each useless retch as he sprawled across their bodies on the riverbank.

His mind drew back suddenly. He must not think of them. Not of them, and not of the tribe. He must think only of the immediate, the practical, what had to be accomplished in each moment. Only thus could he see it through. Fleetingly the whole vista stretched before and behind. In a sense the end of it was hazy and unimportant, the rest of his life a mere contingency as long as he got through the next few days intact; there was no point considering a future which, whatever happened, could for him have no meaning or colour.

'You must talk to Sturmer,' the labourer said.

'Sturmer? Is he your chief? A man with no beard?'

'Sturmer does our trading.'

'Will you take me to him?'

'I will not. We have rules.' The labourer scratched his chin. 'You say you bring seed. What of it? Our barns are full of seed.'

'This is different,' Tagart said. 'My master wants a barley for the salt wind; the Flint Lord desires new ground opened up along the coast.'

'So you were sent to villages by the sea to trade. But why should we give our secrets to the Flint Lord? If he wants them he must pay, as we must pay for the tools his traders bring. Flints, livestock, clothes – these are the things we want. Of barley we have plenty.'

'No – this seed is different. It's special.' Tagart pointed out to sea. 'It comes from there, across the water. The yield is double.'

'Double.'

'That is what my master says, sir.'

'Not possible.'

'It must be possible or the Valdoe farmers would not sow it by the score of bags.'

'Show it to me.'

'There is nothing to be gained by that.'

'Show me.'

'My master said I was only to offer it in the presence of a head man. Take me to Sturmer. I will talk with him.'

'Show me.' The labourer stretched out a hand. 'Show me or be on your way.'

'I should not do this.'

The labourer moved his fingers impatiently. Tagart gave him the pouch, which was tied at the neck with a drawstring. Two hands were needed to get it open.

Seeing this, the labourer tried to loosen the string while keeping a grip on his mattock-handle, picking with a fingernail at the bunched leather, which Tagart had drawn especially tight before leaving the woods. After a few fruitless moments, aware that he would make himself look foolish by asking Tagart to open the bag, the labourer released the handle, lodging it in his armpit, and freed both hands for the job.

That was the instant Tagart chose to kill him.

Later, Tagart had time to wonder what went wrong. It may have been weariness, making him slow. Tagart was not sure. He knew only that the man had put up a struggle which made his end more protracted than it ought to have been.

When it was done Tagart searched the body for personal effects. With his flint knife he cut through the cord, releasing the talisman, and slipped the stone into his pouch. Tagart worked quickly, apprehensive now that someone might come from the village and discover him. The sun had dropped more to the west, going down over the trees, casting long fingers of shadow that advanced downhill in a hurry to be night.

A name formed on Tagart's lips, a word without bidding. Sturmer. He said it again. *Sturmer.* A name to go with the beardless face, the face in the firelight.

Picking up the mattock by its blade, he thrust the haft into the ground. Beside it he arranged lines of stones taken from the pile the labourer had made, forming an arrow pointing in the direction of the wood; he finished it with three stones for each barb, and grasped the corpse by its armpits.

It seemed much heavier than a man's body. Ideally he needed a sledge. He forced a smile. Ideally, he needed help for what he planned to do, the help of a hundred men. Or if not a hundred, then ten of his friends from the tribe, who were better than any hundred taken from these slab-faced peasants.

The tribe. He must not think of the tribe. Anger would only slow him down, ruin his chances. He held a duty in sacred trust: the honour of the tribe had devolved upon him and upon him alone. Nothing must be allowed to stand in his way. If he was to discharge his duty he could ill afford the luxury of rage.

But it was with a fierce renewed energy that he took up the corpse again, pulling it towards the forest.

Part 1

1

Sturmer opened his eyes and lay listening to the blood pulsing in his ears. The chimney-hole in his roof was blind, blocked for the summer: the blackened rafters travelled up and met in gloom. There were five, like the arms of a starfish, speared by the central pillar that held up his house. From them, on pegs and hooks, hung clothes, netting, tools, pouches of flints, water-bags; seed of wheat, corn, and a dozen other crops; jars of lamp-fat and bundles of rush-pith for lighting; baskets, cooking utensils, pots suspended in nets, leatherware muzzles and straps and tackle, fire-making kits, and all the other possessions that were better kept off the ground and away from the vermin and the village animals which ranged free in all the houses.

Sturmer's was the largest and best-appointed dwelling, with three other rooms besides this, where his children slept and he kept further stores. The doorway, which was low and broad and looked out across the village compound towards the Meeting House, gave on to a small area paved with stones from the beach. Behind the doorway and a short tunnel-like porch, which contained a miniature effigy of Gauhm set in a wooden casket, the passageway opened into a pebble-floored kitchen with a sooted hearth, above which was another chimney aperture. To the side was the room where the children slept; to the front another chamber, and beyond that the main room with the tall roof, which from the outside appeared as a cone of weathered timber, caulked with plant fibres and clay, in places tufted with burnt grass and clumps of weeds. The flat part of the roof towards the front of the house was turfed, on a base of planking, and the porch was covered with skins that could be drawn across the entrance. A few small windows – simple apertures – had been left in the walls, which were made of selected and interlocked stones, the gaps and chinks filled with pebbles and the remaining cracks plastered with clay.

Against the wall were piles of kindling-wood, logs, a wooden water-butt, a number of digging-sticks and mattocks, a stack of wattle panels used for temporary animal pens, and an old bench where the people in the house could sit in the evening and face the Meeting House opposite. It was here that Sturmer sat to answer informal questions and settle small disputes. He was head man of Burh village, and had been so for twelve years.

He was in his late thirties, of medium height and build, with unexpectedly soft features and a mild manner edged by the perceptive gaze of pale blue eyes. Sturmer kept his beard neat and favoured subdued clothing: pigskin and goatskin dyed with subtle patterns of yellow and grey. His hair, which was glossy black, he tied in a bun. Triple lines of blue tattoo ran the length of his right arm, flank, and leg, culminating in pentacles on his instep and the back of his hand: for he was also a priest.

He turned on his side and watched the contours of his wife's back. His eyes explored her shoulders and the tiny humps of vertebrae, and the light and shade and texture of her black hair, which he found girlish and endearing where it grew from her nape. He extended a forefinger and almost touched the bumps of her spine, moving his hand slightly to compensate for her breathing. It was no use making plans any more. The matter was out of his control; the spirits had taken over. The drought showed no signs of coming to an end. Starvation, the break-up of Burh, was beginning to look inevitable.

The previous winter Sturmer, like all the villagers, had become uneasily aware that too many dry days were following one another, and that the rain, when it did come, was light and sporadic. A single snowstorm in early spring, with a week of bitter frost, had been the only hard weather the whole winter, when usually Burh could expect heavy drifts and blizzards for days or weeks on end. And there had been no sign of flooding from the river: usually the farmers had to work through the night to protect their village. At the end of the spring and for the two months of low summer the clearings had been filled with blossom – of elder, blackthorn, whitebeam, hawthorn, cherry – to an extent which no one had ever seen before; many plants had gone on flowering through the winter, when normally there was no colour to be seen. Even the spring birds seemed earlier and more numerous than usual, supernaturally numerous, and the woods and grassland near the village and on the cliffs were alive with butterflies: blue, red, orange, yellow, white and brown, flying up in clouds from every bush and clump of nettles. The yellow lilies in the river bloomed profusely long before their time. The ditches and banks were choked with frog-spawn. One night they saw shooting stars over the sea, and Sturmer knew that Aih had been disturbed.

The farmers divided the year into six seasons, each of two moons or months, beginning on the shortest day with winter, followed by spring, low summer, high summer, harvest, autumn, winter again. It was now halfway through high summer, when the crops should have been making their fastest growth and all was to be got ready for harvest. Normally on such a morning Sturmer would long ago have been up and with the rest of the village in the fields. But today there was no work to be done. The crops were dying. For six weeks there had been no rain at all. That alone would have been enough, but Sturmer had other worries too.

During his tenure the village had enjoyed an increase in prosperity and population on an unprecedented scale. Apart from its thirty-three stone and timber houses, Burh now had a threshing-shed, granary, two silos and a general barn, bakery, a bear-proof palisade, and, to Sturmer's pride, a long Meeting House where met the village council. The most important crop was emmer, a kind of wheat that Sturmer had substituted for the old einkorn used by his predecessor. From corn and barley and honey they made ale; broomcorn millet and oats were grown partly as winter fodder for the animals – goats, cattle and sheep. Crops like lentils and broad beans, kale and rape, were grown in plots beside each house. The wealthier families owned pigs; most kept a dog, medium-sized hounds derived from the yellow hunting dogs such as once had been used by the nomads.

Sturmer had been having trouble with the land. He disliked burning the forest, and would have preferred to go on using the same fields for the village crops: long ago he had begun to guess at the value of manure, and now regularly changed the location of the animal pens. Some of the beasts were allowed to wander more or less at freedom, grazing on the wild leaves, bringing back their goodness to the village; he tried mulching with leaf-mould from the forest, and gathering seaweed from the shore, a mile to the south, and using that to enrich the ground. The Earth Spirit Gauhm, Sturmer knew, needed help if she was to deliver up her best bounty. But as the years passed it was becoming plain that the ancestors had been right: to grow good crops you must clear forest. Clear the forest, burn it, plant the ground, and move on when the goodness has gone. That was the old way. Sturmer's new way seemed to be wrong. He was disappointed to find it so, because what he yearned for was stability. With a stable village, more elaborate buildings would become possible, more children, more families in one place. More people could be freed from working on the soil. Goods could be fabricated, goods for sale to other villages, and possibly, one day, Sturmer might grow wealthy through trading, like the great Flint Lord at Valdoe.

The vision was moving further and further out of reach. In spite of all Sturmer's efforts quite large areas round the village, once excellent land, were useless and reverting to scrub.

Others in the Council, led by Groden, kept pressing for a return to the old order. They wanted wider forest clearance, a change of site for the village; more, not fewer, acres under cultivation. Sturmer felt it unwise to resist too strenuously. He was thirty-six – getting old. His position as leader was becoming precarious. It was only a matter of time before a younger man – and who else but Groden? – made a thrust and forced the issue, and Sturmer was not sure that Groden would not win. The younger and rasher men in the village supported him: they favoured an aggressive approach to the forest and the countryside.

This worried Sturmer in another way. As far back as memory would go, there had been a nomad summer camp by the river some three miles upstream, well inside the forest. The nomads were hunters, in winter foraging in the marshes to the north where they were guaranteed plentiful wildfowl and game, in spring coming over the downs to the forest by the sea coast. In some years they came not at all; in others they stayed a few days or weeks and moved on again. This summer, the nomads had been present all season.

They were rarely seen in person by the villagers. The odd goat or pig missed from its pen, and even tools and skins stolen from the fields, were never closely pursued. The farmers hated and feared the nomads, and they feared even more the magic the nomads controlled. Their god was Tsoaul, Spirit of the Forest. Through the nomads he worked evil on Gauhm; even now he was struggling to win back the village fields, as he always did, working stealthily and by degrees. First he rendered the land infertile for crops, making its cultivation pointless. Next he sent weeds. When these were established he sent hawthorn and birch, which soon became inpenetrable scrub. From scrub it was an easy step to forest. Not a square yard of the village was safe from Tsoaul's work; he infested good land as well as bad; he even wanted the very roofs on the houses.

Sturmer was worried because each tree that fell effectively brought the nomads a little closer. Every clearance fire reduced the extent of forest available to the nomads and increased the chance of trouble between them and the villagers.

In other summers there had been trifling incidents. A scarecrow was burnt. Excrement appeared on the Shrine at the cliffs. A pair of youths from the village went to the nomads' camp for a dare: both returned badly beaten and unwilling to talk. Nets had been stolen from the river; a coracle dragged downstream and left wrecked. A beacon fire, set up on the cliffs for the mid-summer festival, was prematurely burnt and the ashes thrown about.

But this year, in this strange summer, the nomads had been here longer, and there had been many more such incidents. Overshadowing them all was the drought.

Sturmer had gone to the Shrine, where the word of Gauhm was breathed. She told him in a dream of Tsoaul and his new onslaught. The drought was the nomads' work: obeying Tsoaul, they had seized advantage of the dry winter and spring, and by their incantations had awoken Aih the Spirit of the Heavens. Tsoaul had tried to persuade Aih to combine with him, that both might overcome Gauhm. Aih had refused, but said that during the contest he would not intervene. This had left the

Forest Spirit alone, goaded by the nomads into greater and greater feats. But in time Tsoaul would overreach and exhaust himself, and then Gauhm would collect her victory. The villagers were not to interfere: to meddle would upset Aih, and then the rain, which was under his control, would never come again.

Sturmer had explained all this in detail, standing on the steps of the Meeting House. It had done little to help. Was he not head man? Was he not supposed to be in Gauhm's favour, her priest, her chosen one? Surely if he were a better man the spirits could be won over, persuaded to end the drought.

Sturmer sensed that Groden might try to use the situation for his own ends. Everything depended on the drought. If it went on much longer, Sturmer's real troubles would begin.

He rose without disturbing his wife and pushed aside the flap of leather at the doorway. His eyes painfully adjusted to the light: the sun was already hot, the sky a white glare only two hours after dawn.

The previous afternoon there had been cloud, and the hope of rain; towards nightfall the air became very close and sultry, with thunder heard far away on the hills. It had seemed as if it must rain, but by dawn the clouds had gone and the emptiness returned.

Everything in the village seemed dusty and old, all the life baked out of it by six weeks of total drought. Since the longest day, over a month ago, the heat had intensified so that even the nights were unbearable. Most of the village had taken to sleeping out of doors, on the stones by the thresholds to their houses. There was even talk of sleeping on the beach, but no one dared to leave the palisade at night.

The water in Sturmer's washing-tub was warm and the colour of clay. Bits of straw floated on the surface. He bent and held his head submerged for a few seconds before straightening up, expelling spray and wiping his eyes. It was then that he noticed a party of people among the buildings, coming towards him, and for a moment, in spite of the sun on his body, and for no reason that he could understand, he felt cold.

They were walking slowly. In front was Hernou, Groden's

woman, slender and dark, with grey eyes in an intelligent face, her tumble of lustrous black hair drawn back and held by a wooden brooch. Once Sturmer had slept with her; she was only a few years his junior, much older than Groden, to whom she had borne a dead baby in the winter. She and Groden lived in a house by themselves, rather further from the Meeting House than their status and their ambition seemed to warrant.

Behind her came old men, women, some of the older children: twelve people in all. Sturmer folded his arms and stood with his body weighted on one side; he remained silent as the deputation stopped. Hernou looked up at him.

'Look what the nomads have done.'

She was holding out a dead dog for his inspection. Its jaws gaped, the side of the top lip folded back and glued to the gums by a frothy crust of dried saliva. A brown trickle of blood had caked hard on the fur from the nostril to the eye. Otherwise there was no sign of the damage done inside the dog's head by the hazel-shafted arrow, tipped with flint and flighted with mottled quail feathers, that slickly and with tremendous power had burst the animal's eye and tunnelled through bone, brain and muscle to come to lodge on the inside of the lower jaw.

With the tips of three fingers he stroked the quail feathers, making the dog's head move slightly against Hernou's wrist.

'The arrow need not be theirs.'

'The dog is Uli – my husband's dog.'

Sturmer acknowledged it.

An old man spoke up. 'What do they seek by this?'

'Tsoaul is getting stronger every day,' another said.

'They attack and we do nothing, we stand helpless.'

'Aih must let us defend the village, if nothing else.'

'We must do what was said by Groden in the Council.'

'No!' Sturmer said angrily. 'That was turned down by decision!'

'Decision? Whose decision? Yours?'

'Or Tsoaul's?'

Sturmer rubbed one forearm with the other hand. A suspicion was growing in his thoughts. 'Where was the dog found?'

'On the Shrine path, by the ash tree.'

'And when was it last seen?'

'Yesterday,' Hernou said. 'Yesterday night. We ate with Morfe and Deak. Groden threw it scraps.'

'And afterwards? Did you see Uli in the night?'

'I cannot say.' She bent and placed the animal at Sturmer's feet. Its head lolled on one side. Rigor had not yet begun.

'It is newly dead,' Sturmer observed. 'This morning, early.'

The dog had been shot either at very close range, or by an extremely accurate bowman. The arrow seemed to implicate the nomads, as did the place where the animal had been found, but something jarred, something was wrong. In all the past troubles with the nomads there had always been an explanation, however outlandish, for the things they had done. Sturmer might have understood had the dog been stolen, or even butchered and eaten. He might have understood had the dog represented any threat to the nomads or any conceivable symbol of trespass on what they regarded as exclusively theirs. But for the nomads wantonly to shoot an animal of any kind and leave it to be found, for them to indulge in casual and irrational killing – that went against everything Sturmer had learned about the people in the forest and their attitude to life.

There was only one explanation. Now Sturmer knew why he had felt cold. He opened his mouth and heard himself speaking the words.

'Where is Groden?'

2

Zeme was thirteen years old, one of the children who by miracle had survived, her open, questioning face partly obscured by the thick dark hair which fell across her shoulders in a shine, smelling clean from her morning swim. Like her sister Mirin she wore her hair loose. Her eyes were black, with a shy glance, the eyes of her ancestors. She loved the sunshine, this summer of perfect weather: for weeks there had been no rain, days on end filled with blue sky and light; and though she did not say it in words to herself, she loved the forest and the incredible plenty it so freely gave. The woodlands at this season seemed benign and calm, smiling on the nomads and the camp site, in graceful, patient acceptance as the preparations for the summer feast went on. To Zeme it was only natural that her sister should be the centre of the feast, the first woman of the new tribe, the chief's daughter, mother of his grandson: Tagart's woman.

Today was feast day. Zeme had been looking for flowers since sunrise; they had made fun of her at the camp because they said she was jealous of Mirin, so before dawn she had left to find flowers for garlands which would show them how she really felt. She knew all the flowers, and which were right for each occasion. This morning she had found many appropriate kinds: clary, milfoil, vervain and a dozen others.

Her arms were full of them as she passed under the trees, returning to the camp. Her sister was in her mind, and Tagart, and the funny things he said; the way he pretended to be solemn and talked in a low voice and then he burst out laughing and he'd been joking all along. She thought about him as a brother, and the way he hunted, with traps and spears and arrows. Tagart was the best marksman in the tribe. He had the straightest eye and the strongest arm. He could even impale a snipe as it zig-zagged up from some marshy patch, or bring down a speeding teal over one of the meres at the winter camp. His bow was so strong that Zeme could only bend it an inch. And his arrows, which he made with a flint shaver, he polished with tallow and fletched with goose quills to make them run faster. Sometimes, when preparing for large quarry, Tagart used wolf's-bane poison on his arrows, but he preferred more passive methods: he said that tracking was hard work. Tagart was an expert in strategy, in waiting. He knew precisely where to dig the pits with spikes in the bottom, where to place the beaters and fences in a drive, how to use the long soft ropes to make booby-traps and nooses that could suddenly hoist a stag from the ground and leave it dangling; he lived with the habits of the prey and could tell what they were going to do before they knew it themselves. Much, Zeme conceded to herself, he had learned from Cosk and the other elders, but now Tagart's word was always sought, his advice always listened to and acted on, his intelligence and inventiveness recognized for their constant part in keeping the tribe well fed and safe. Tagart had no fear of the aurochs, the wild oxen with their big horns; when they charged he merely seemed to dance round and round and they fell down dead. Nor had he any fears of the wild boars, nor the lynx, and he had no fear of the wolves, although he said it was wise to leave them in peace and they would do the same for you.

The only animals to avoid, Tagart said, were the brown bears. The bears were unpredictable, moody, and you were never to go near a bear or its cave, and never ever when there were young ones inside, because that made the bears fiercer than anything in the forest, or in the marshes, or along the white sea-shore.

Sometimes Zeme wished she could go out hunting with the men. It was unfair being a girl. Instead of hunting she had to go out with the women gathering plants. There was a lot to know. Even her mother, Sela, the chief's woman, said she was still learning and would be a pupil of the forest until the day she died. The women went out nearly every day with their hazel and osier baskets, collecting fruits, nuts, fungi, tubers, fleshy stems – whatever was in season. They knew the plants to pick for medicines that soothed pain and helped wounds heal. There were plants to know for dyes, for perfumes and essences, and for seasonings to add to meat and drink; plants to poison arrowheads and spears and spikes; plants to keep the shelters dry, to make a soft bed, to keep insects away; plants to burn for any kind of heat and flame; plants for charcoal, or carvings, or for making toys. Sela and the others had taught Zeme how to twist fibres into strings and ropes, how to peel bark, how to use plants to know where squirrels or jays had hidden their winter stores. The men had shown her how to read the ground by thc grasses and sedges that grew there; whether the ground was wet and unfirm, dangerous to traverse; when there had been a fire, even years before; what animal or bird had fed or left its droppings there. And Zeme was learning, like the others, the plants for decoration and for favourable omens and the plants for happiness and long life.

She came to a stream she knew and walked beside it, allowing it to lead her back to the river and her father's camp.

The nomad party had been together in its present form since the early spring, when the large camp in the marshes broke up into smaller units, the families staying together or regrouping as changes in friendship and loyalties dictated. Before the first catkins the nomads were beginning to leave, some spreading north into the great river valleys, others moving westward along the hills, eastward towards the low coast, or, like Tagart's tribe, south over the downs to the chalk cliffs and the vast oak forest which every year seemed to suffer further incursions from the farming people of the south. These were a different breed from the nomads, only partly native, with ideas and blood imported from across the sea. In the west at Valdoe was the largest settlement of them Tagart had heard of: a prison filled with slaves, commanded by one man who had established an army to protect his trading empire along the coast and far inland. The nomads knew of Valdoe because many of them had been captured to work there; a handful had escaped and told stories at the winter camp. The tales were worse than the imagination could make. Yet the farmers were pleased to trade with Valdoe and tacitly to accept the protection it gave them from the foreign raiding parties that would otherwise cross the water whenever the weather allowed.

Tagart's party was led by Cosk – which meant an owl, from the silent way he moved – a man of forty who had led the Owl tribe for ten years or more. This summer the Cosks were forty-one people: nine couples with fourteen children between them, two old men and three women beyond child-bearing age, a woman whose husband had caught a fever and died, and three young men of marriageable age. Cosk and his wife Sela were without sons, but their eldest daughter had brought them a boy, now three years old.

His name was Balan. In twenty years, after Tagart, if he survived, he might be chief. But, before then, Tagart's time was coming. In the years since his wedding to Mirin his acknowledged place as natural successor to Cosk had slowly been confirmed, and now it was certain. To Tagart and Mirin had gone the honour of the summer feast, a celebration of the forest, of renewal and the future. The preparations had been going on for weeks. Young bison were allowed to survive their parents in the hunt and were brought back to camp alive to be tethered nearby until needed. Hares, trapped along the field edges, were kept in cages made of woven sallow; larks, lapwings, pipits, wheatears, nightingales, finches and wagtails had been snared or limed or brought down by whirling lures and stoned with slingshots. In withy baskets in the water were frogs and newts, and writhing masses of fish: river trout, eels, mullet, perch, pike; and the skill of one boy, who seemed to have a gift for finding them, had brought in more than a hundred crayfish, which now crouched in baskets at the water's edge, their claws and feelers and eyes distorted by the ripples. Along the banks, in rows and racks and wrappers of leaves, were edible flowers: lime, elder, knapweed, hop, dog-rose; roots of reed-mace, rampion, parsnip, water-lily and flowering rush; stems of burdock and reed; leaves of dead-nettle, plantain, sorrel, comfrey and nettle; hazelnuts and pignuts; and fruit: whitebeam, redcurrant, blackcurrant, barberry, blackberry, raspberry, strawberry, sloe, crab-apple and cranberry. There were carved wooden boxes of beetles, lizards, caterpillars, shrews, voles, woodmice and moles; hedgehogs tied by thongs to stakes; slabs of honeycomb taken from the hive; mints, thyme, fennel and many other herbs; wooden and clay flasks of liquor steeped with crushed leaves of wormwood and cicely. From the beach and estuary the women had collected seaweed: dulse, kelp and bladderwrack; and shellfish in tubs of salt water: clams, cockles, winkles, and scallops. It had taken a fortnight to prepare the feast, and to build a new shelter, and to find all the flowers and leaves for dressing the couple and the camp. Now, at mid-morning. Emis and Varl were building up the cooking-fires with hornbeam logs; the clay ovens were being prepared, and into them went joints of beef, fillets of hare and venison. The heat of the fires made faces red; across the flames, the air shimmered and made people unrecognizable, trees and branches swirl.

Those who had finished their duties were getting ready for the ceremony, with dyes and pastes and special costumes which after the ritual would be consigned to flame. They wore leather and fur striped and studded, or tasselled and plumed in all colours, especially grey and brown and white. Blue streaks and chevrons on faces and backs, applied with meadowsweet and dog's mercury dye mixed with fat, were displayed by those sharing Tagart's blood, for he was derived from Waterfall people; Mirin and her family were decorated with ash-grey and black, with black and white capes and bunches of owl quills at elbow and knee.

Cosk, the chief, was dressed in a long cloak of owl feathers fixed to deerskin in exact rows that formed patterns in various ways: diagonals, rings, zigzags, verticals, stippled and mottled effects which had taken many hours of work to get right. He carried a carved and stained ceremonial mace, predominantly black with a crest of black feathers, which tapered and continued halfway down its length. Chalk-dust had been rubbed into his hair and beard, and all his skin painted white. He wore a beaked mask made of owl feathers, with tall plumes and a shaggy ruff that extended across his shoulders and blended with the cloak, and feathered footwear with three toes before and a spur behind, taloned like the feet of an owl; oxhide shinguards with the hair left on, dyed and patterned with angular streaks like those on an owl's legs; and a broad leather kirtle, white, radially marked from the belt with lines of dark-brown, ash, and black.

The others were dressed, some almost as elaborately, according to their family and tribe.

One by one they were emerging in the sunshine.

Groden halted, half turning and slightly raising his hand.

It was hot. Even under the green gloom of the trees the air felt stifling and oppressive. Ragged sunlight fell through the high canopy of leaves, sending coin-sized spots of light to the bracken and brambles on the forest floor. A blackbird turned over litter, making a furtive rustling sound. The silence was almost complete. No birds sang: the summer moult had begun.

The oaks here were old and massive. Great gnarled boughs turned this way and that. Here and there in the distance a tree had crashed, and in the space so formed saplings were thrusting upwards, greedy for the light. Their roots spread widely, wherever they could, worming through the soil, in places coming to the sides of a stream as it purled through the trees towards the river.

Groden listened carefully. He was twenty-two, lean and tall, with coarse swarthy features and blue eyes as cold as a gull's. He shaved his face, not just from vanity, but because he wished to mark himself out; he meant to be head man one day. Helped and advised by Hernou, he was already a voice in the Council.

He turned and looked at the others, young men like himself: his friend Morfe, Deak, Feno and Parn. They had covered more than two miles from the village and were far from the usual pathways, much deeper into the forest than anyone ventured in summer when the nomads were about.

'Do you hear anything?' Feno said.

Groden shook his head. The others were waiting, waiting for him to tell them what to do.

'We're too far into the trees, Groden,' Parn said. 'I think we should go back. If we go on we'll come to their camp.'

'Parn's right,' said Deak.

Morfe grinned, white teeth against his beard and the tan of his skin. 'If you're scared, go home to your mothers.'

'It's not that. You know it's not that.'

'Keep a still tongue then.'

Groden treated Parn and Deak to a moment's glance. 'We go on,' he said.

'Your hound is dead, Groden,' Parn said, 'and we know how you feel. But do you want our corpses added to Uli's on the Dead Ground? We're too close to the river. We've seen none of them. Let's go back.'

'We are only five,' Feno said. 'If they catch us we'll have no chance.'

'Cowards,' Morfe said. 'You talk like old women.'

'Come with me, or go back,' said Groden indifferently.

Parn and Feno and Deak looked at each other. They all knew that Sturmer would not last for ever. The question was – how important was this moment? It was impossible to tell from Groden's face. He kept his thoughts locked up; they came out only in actions. By then it might be too late to get back into his favour.

'Down there,' Morfe hissed. 'Something moving.'

'By the stream,' Groden said, in answer to Feno's questioning glance.

They watched. Coming between the trees, now visible, now obscured by piles of overtowering bracken, in and out of the sunlight, a small figure was following the line of the stream, a child, a young girl dressed in skins. She could not have been more than thirteen. In her arms she carried a bulky bundle of plants, stems and leaves and flowers of many colours.

'One of the nomads,' Feno whispered.

'Get behind her,' Groden told Deak. 'Parn, Feno, go ahead and close in. Morfe, across there.'

'What do you mean to do?' Feno demanded.

He was ignored. With Morfe at his side, Groden was already striding through the bracken, moving downhill to head the child off. For a moment the others hesitated, and they too set off as directed. The girl was less than two hundred paces away. A blackbird shrilled its alarm-call: the child looked up, her face changing to consternation as she saw them coming. She faltered in her step . . . looked from side to side . . . and the bundle of plants tumbled piecemeal from her hands. Some of the flowers fell in the stream and the current started bearing them away.

Groden and Morfe were running now. The child moved a few paces along the bank, saw Feno emerge and block her path, turned to go the other way, only to see Deak coming from behind.

Groden was beside her on the bank. Morfe at her rear had grasped her shoulders, and before she could scream his sweaty palm was clamped across her mouth.

Groden examined her closely. His eyes travelled down her body, lingering in places, returning to her face. There was no doubt of what she was. The nomads' camp was less than a mile away.

He nodded at Morfe, who took his hand from her mouth.

'Why did your people kill my Uli?'

The girl was too frightened to answer. Her black eyes darted from side to side; she was trembling with fear.

'Can't you speak?'

She opened her mouth. No words came.

'Why do you hate us? What do you hold against our village? Why do you plot with Tsoaul to withhold rain? Why do you blight our fields and make spells near our Shrine?'

'Let me ask,' Morfe said. 'I'll get it out of her.'

Groden nodded. 'In a while.'

The girl was trying to speak.'

'What was that?' Groden said.

'My . . . friends are coming.'

He looked at his companions in turn. 'She says her friends are coming.'

'Let's take her back to the village now,' Feno said. 'She might be telling the truth.'

'Which way are they coming?' Morfe said into her ear. 'And are they all as pretty as you?' He tightened his grip across her throat. 'Which way? Along the stream? From the ridge?'

'They – '

'Why take chances, Groden?' Feno argued. 'Get her away from here.'

'Which way?'

The girl cried out.

Groden watched, saw her skin, the shape of her thighs where they were exposed. He had originally planned to make a hostage of a nomad, to take one back to the village. But now he reached out and put his fingers to her neck, spread his hand and gently caressed the softness of her cheek.

'Which way do your friends come?' he asked her quietly.

'They – '

'Tell me.'

'They've been hunting . . .'

'Hunting?' His fingers explored the back of her neck, winding themselves into her tresses. 'Hunting what?'

'Boar. They're hunting boar.'

He yanked viciously on her hair and she screamed.

'Truth,' Groden said.

'Truth,' Morfe said. 'Tell us the truth.'

'Why do your people hate us and wish us dead?'

The girl looked from face to face. She seemed unable to answer. Morfe's hand slid down her belly, pressing her up against him. He bent his head; she turned and suddenly met his eye.

'Tell us the truth,' Groden said. 'That is all we ask.'

'This one is no use to us,' Morfe said, lifting her deerskin with his other hand. 'She can only speak lies.' Without warning he tried to rip away her dress and throw her to the ground, but before he knew what was happening she had sunk her teeth into his arm and blood was welling out. She wriggled past Feno and leapt across the stream.

'Catch her!' Morfe shouted.

It did not take long.

3

The Shrine on the cliffs had been made many years before, a dome of chalk with a central alcove holding the stone altar slab on which rested the carved stone figure of Gauhm, Spirit of the Earth. Only the priest was allowed to come here freely; only he was allowed to pray at the Shrine and listen to Gauhm's word.

It was early afternoon, two hours after the Council meeting when everything had started to crumble in Sturmer's life. Below the clifftops, far below, herring gulls swooped across the veins of foam on the green water as it swelled and smacked around the rocks. Their cries and yelps rose up the cliff-face. The air, hot and balmy, smelling of salt and iodine, felt soft on Sturmer's skin as he lay staring upward into the pink realms of his lids. He heard bees humming, and a faint breeze in the parched stems of grass, and the gulls against the waves below, and the sibilance of rock pipits as they flew from chalk ledge to ledge on the cliffs. From time to time a jackdaw called.

Sturmer was almost asleep, lingering on the border. Strange thoughts seemed normal. The sun on his face made him drowsy. He was enveloped by the sound of the bees, their transparent wings at work in the pink flowers of thrift.

He was thinking about what had been said at the Council. *Reckless to go into the forest, Groden. Reckless and stupid. But they killed Uli, Sturmer. They killed him and I was angry. No plan, nothing clear. Just angry. Yes, we were stupid, we were wrong.* But in his secret face, in the moment's flash of unconcealed triumph in Groden's eye, Sturmer saw that Groden knew. He saw that Groden was not stupid. He saw but he could not fathom the words to fashion an answer to turn the others from believing.

Morfe and Feno and Deak and Parn said the same.

Then they were coming out of the trees, Sturmer. Defending ourselves, only defending ourselves.

– But you killed one of them?

– We had to.

– Then you ran away?

– There was nothing else we could do. If you'd been there you would have seen it.

Groden's face; the circle of believers; the Meeting House closing in.

– You will bring disaster on us all!

– The nomads will call on Tsoaul to avenge the dead man!

Groden talking, reasoning. His hands outspread. Winning them over.

– We must act first and drive them out. For if we don't move quickly it is they who will strike first.

– But we are only farmers, Groden! They are killers!

– We outnumber them . . . if we can take them unawares . . .

In all the shouting was Sturmer's voice.

Now it was all over. Groden had killed one of the nomads. Whether his story was true did not matter . . . nothing mattered, not even that Gauhm had failed to appear to him as he lay here on the clifftop by the Shrine.

Perhaps she did not want to intervene.

He felt no excitement, no expectation. Gauhm was not coming.

Sturmer opened his eyes and raised himself on one elbow, looking at his fingers as they twiddled with a stem of grass. For a long time he gave his thoughts to his family and himself.

At last he brought his legs in to sit cross-legged, and then pushed on the outside edges of his feet, bringing himself in a single smooth motion to a standing position.

He addressed himself to the Shrine, bowing to kiss the edge of the altar slab, and spoke a soft prayer for the village, before setting off along the path and back to Burh.

Happiness had brought a marvellous radiance to Mirin's beauty. Her hair was black, almost blue, the locks wound into plaits which were held by a snood decorated with freshly picked speedwell. On Tagart's head was a garland of white roses woven among brambles. Little Balan, Tagart's son, stood between them, holding hands. He was only three: most of what was being said he could not understand, but he was aware that this was a day of importance, that he himself and his father and mother were important to the tribe.

In front of them, in the sunshine by the water, Cosk was speaking the words of the summer celebration. As he neared the conclusion Sela handed her daughter a bowl of essence of vervain and fenugreek. Mirin drank; Tagart drank; and leaving Balan they waded into the river. While the others watched they merged with the current and let the water wash away the white and ochre pigments from their skin, billowing downstream in a pale cloud.

Tagart took hold of Mirin's hands and looked into her eyes. Some of those on the bank were smiling, aware that Tagart was teasing them, keeping them waiting.

Giving no sign, he slowly kissed his woman, and as they kissed they sank beneath the surface.

An exultant shout went up. It was the signal to begin the feast.

Burh that evening was quiet, in the few hours before dark. There was no communal eating: everyone kept to his own hearth. In Sturmer's house the conversation was sparse and awkward. His children, three girls and a boy, sensed that it was better to say nothing. They ate their beans and oatcakes in silence.

Afterwards they were sent out to the river to clean the pots. Sturmer put his fingertips to his brow.

'I am afraid, Tamis.'

'Do you have to go with them?' his wife said.

He nodded.

'Is there no way to stop them?'

'No.'

'I know what you should do.'

'Send him away?'

'Send him away or kill him. He plans your end. It is only fitting that you should plan his first.'

Sturmer smiled ruefully. 'He has the Council on his side.'

'But Groden is a fool.'

'That he is not.'

She came and sat beside him. 'Only a fool goes into the forest in summer.'

'A fool or a schemer.'

'What do you mean?'

'He shot his own hound.'

'What?'

'Hernou knew it. I could see it in her face. Perhaps Morfe too.'

'But why?'

'He wished to start trouble with the forest people. By blaming them he could make a start.' He took her hand. 'If he succeeds and brings rain I am finished.'

'Do the others know about his hound?'

'Would they believe it? They want rain. Groden has promised it.'

'You must tell them.' She squeezed his arm. 'Tell them. You are head man.'

He snorted.

The sunset outside made everything blood-red. Pots and discarded tools threw long shadows; the river slid past the jetty, its surface in shade, dimpled by the beaks of the sand martins and swallows as they dipped in flight to drink. Swifts screamed among the barns and over the squat house roofs, chasing each other, climbing to altitudes where the sun was still hot on their wings; the coastline below stretched unwavering into the west, a thin ribbon of beach and cliff separating the sea from the dark shroud of the forest, which spread, faithful to the contours of the land, almost without pause to the very limits of vision.

4

The feast fires had nearly burned out, each one a bed of embers that occasionally popped and sent a mote or a wisp of smoke into the warm night air. The dancing and singing had gone on long after dusk. Zeme was missed at first, a half-serious suggestion made to find her and bring her out of her sulking. Everyone knew she had a crush on Tagart; everyone knew she was jealous of Mirin. But as the celebrations went on the awareness of Zeme's absence receded, even in the minds of her parents, whose other daughter was the proud focus of attention. No one noticed just when the clouds began to roll across the sky to blot out the moon and stars, or when the first low thunder came. For some hours now it had been coming intermittently. The air was humid and close, the darkness almost complete, the hot and sticky night smothering the camp.

The remains of the summer feast lay strewn about: dishes, trampled flowers and garlands, bits of food. For once the rule had been relaxed and the task of clearing up deferred till morning. Any scavengers within ten miles would have been scared off by the music and shouting – at least, that was Cosk's theory. Only the usual guard, one man, had been posted.

Now it was three hours before dawn, and Tagart and Mirin were alone.

A brilliant blink lit up the camp and the humped shapes of the shelters, making black shadow and ice-white of all the colours, jabbing splinters and fragments of light on the leather wall of his shelter. Below him was the pallor of Mirin's face, the vague expanse of her hair. He felt her hands on his shoulder blades, pulling him back to her.

'It was only lightning.'

The thunder came then, a double crash, followed by a long rumbling peal.

'The river sang differently,' Tagart said. 'I thought I heard movement.'

'Just a fish.'

'Fish?'

'A fish jumping. Nothing more.'

Tagart strained his ears, all senses taut. A wind was rising in the trees. Its hiss mingled with the river currents as rocks broke the surface, the liquid curling its way past twigs and debris, with the flow past stems and stalks, the small ripples against the muddy slope and the tiny beach of the bank nearest the camp.

The press of Mirin's body became more insistent. The bed was filled with her smell. Her mouth yielded, melding with his as her teeth opened. Tagart went further on the familiar exploration that had just begun, that now became more searching as he recognized the rhythm of her movements, the spread of her fingers on his back, her face against his. She spoke the syllables of his name as he kissed her eyes, her ears, her neck and throat.

Again.

She moaned as he broke away.

It was unmistakable. An unnatural sound in the water.

Tagart's shelter was new, built specially, and by chance the one nearest the river. It had no weapons inside, no food; merely a bed and flowers. Now he wished that he had heeded his intuition and left some weapons at the door.

'What is it?' she said.

'Keep quiet.'

She tried to pull on his shoulders again. Tagart resisted. His mind was no longer in the shelter. It was outside, imagining the river, the banks, wondering what might be happening. He tried to remember everything as it had been at the end of the feast: the position of the fires, the debris on the ground. He pictured the shelters and their relationship with one another and the trees.

Another peal of thunder, closer than the first. Tagart rolled to one side, crushing scent from the honeysuckle blossoms. Mirin sat up and softly he put his fingers to her lips.

Something was in the river.

It was too late at night for any of the others to be up, except Braul, who had been posted as guard. Guards did not leave their posts. Camp rules were inflexible on that point; a guard was only to leave his post once the others had been awoken, even if his relief did not come.

Tagart raced through his mental catalogue of animals large enough to disturb the water like that, and of animals that might be interested in the camp and its occupants: Tagart reminded himself that there was food lying about. Wolves? Too small. Pigs? No. A bear? There was a brood den some miles south-east, with a mother and two cubs and a nursemaid female; but that was too far away. The he bear? He was probably at large somewhere in this part of the forest, though as yet the tribe had encountered no definite sign of him. Was it the lone male in the river?

Tagart crawled to the entrance and looked out. He saw the feeble glow of the feast fires, and above them the faint distinction between sky and forest. All else was darkness.

If not a bear, then what? A man. Another tribe might have arrived in the region. But they would advance openly and exchange news, share a meal, not come in stealth by night. An outcast? Sometimes offenders were banished from a group. Such men lived the best they could, stealing when it suited them.

A bear, then, or an outcast from some other tribe.

A shape moved across the glow of the nearest fire, too quickly for Tagart to glean any information from the silhouette. He felt his ribs contract with fear. His hands became fists and slowly he revised the disposition of his limbs, ready to move. His heart was pounding and his eyes were wide. He wondered whether to alert Braul, and decided against it. Braul was certainly already aware of the newcomer's presence. To call out might lose them what small advantage they had.

At the crack of a twig some yards off to the right, Tagart jerked his head in that direction, staring hard into the darkness for some scrap of vision. None came. And then another shadow passed in front of the fire, and another, and another. A fourth, a fifth, and shadows were passing in front of all the fires. A wooden bowl was inadvertently kicked. It scraped and slithered into the ashes. Licking flames leapt at once. Tagart saw a reddish glow on legs bound with fur and thongs. An instant later a sheet of lightning lit the sky and the full extent of what was happening in the camp lay revealed.

'Braul!' Tagart shouted, coming out of the shelter unarmed, at a run, cursing the fact that he was naked, cursing everything that had conspired to bring this about.

As the thunder came he reached the nearest man, whose image he had glimpsed in the lightning and retained. He jabbed with straight fingers at where eyes should be. There was a squeal. Tagart gripped a handful of beard and tore it upwards and back; he brought his left arm in low, stealing balance by scooping behind the knees. As the man went down Tagart's punch missed aim and ploughed up into the solar plexus. He brought his heel up and to the side and rammed it into the screaming face. The jaw broke with a snap like an old branch.

Tagart reached down and armed himself with the fallen mattock, aware of something happening behind. The mattock blade hummed through the air as he spun round, legs flexed. The shock of the blade striking home numbed his hand and forearms, the impact running up the haft from the dead thump of the blade; and there was no time for a scream, or even a gasp: a body in which there would be no more life brought down the ruined head and hit the ground.

On all sides Tagart was reacting to shapes and faces, kicking and lashing out with the mattock, sometimes warding off a blow with his forearm. Any limb that was not his own could be attacked. The farmers, for that they were, were hampered by darkness and confusion. They were clumsy fighters. Frequently Tagart sensed that they had hit one of their own. He heard screaming and smelled the rush of blood, their protests and imprecations in his ears. He had been fighting now for twenty seconds. He marvelled that he had not been hit. Again and again he connected with faces, eyes, genitals, kneecaps, in a frenzy to disable as many as he could before the blow that would be his end. The feast fires, disturbed by the throng of men, flared as the embers came to life, outlining at ground level the tangle of arms and legs and waving weapons. Tagart saw the glint of saliva and a pair of terrified eyes, which involuntarily closed just as the mattock-blade struck home again, a stone cleaver powered by the whole swing and thrust of his strength; in a vile spray the blade and a section of the handle broke off, spun into the air, were lost. He trod on and seized a digging-stick, a heavy staff wedged into a ring of granite for weight, which, wielded like a sledge-hammer, sent down man after man. He became aware of a fresh attack from the side. He raised the point of the staff and hooked it into the oncomer's armpit. Tagart braced, hoisted, and the farmer sailed into the air.

Now the camp was coming alive. Now the men were pouring from their shelters, armed with clubs and spears. Cries of pain and surprise greeted them. Behind Tagart one of the shelters caught light, engulfed in flame from a blazing brand, casting more glow in which he could see. Other shelters were being fired, beside him, by the river, on the far edge near the forest, everywhere. The camp was burning. Tagart saw children running. He saw hair and clothes on fire, small bodies rolling over and over again in the dust.

He saw Balan. It was Balan, falling, and over him a man with a spear. As if casually, as if an afterthought, as if to be rid of an irritation the spear lanced down. In horror Tagart saw his son's last moment of life. And briefly he saw the farmer who had done it: a man as tall and wild as Tagart himself, a man with no beard.

Directly overhead the storm broke with a flaring crackle of lightning and an instantaneous explosion of thunder so loud that it left a ringing in Tagart's ears. One of the tall beeches across the river had been hit and was on fire.

The beardless man appeared again, behind Tagart this time. He had the advantage. Just in time Tagart dodged the spear thrust: the point buried itself in the ground. In the sudden torrent of sparkling rain Tagart fell backwards, rolling into sedges to one side, and snatched at ankles as the other man went past. The other man lost balance and fell. Tagart sprang, landing badly, and in an instant was on his back and the beardless man's hands were at his neck, encircling, strangling, the thumbs pressing into his throat. Tagart was choking. His eyes bulged. There was froth on his lips. The beardless man squeezed harder, his face wet and orange in the flames, his hair dripping rain and hanging forward.

Tagart brought his knee up and into the man's groin; he let go at once but doubled his fists and smashed a blow into Tagart's face. Tagart brought his knee up again, and in agony the other man rolled away. But he was lifting his legs, one across the other, and too late Tagart realized that his neck was between the ankles. Tagart's feet left the ground. With an emptiness in his stomach he saw the camp turn over; and he was coming down in the cold shock of the river, in the mud by the bank.

He watched the other man getting up, coming for him, wiping a hand across his mouth, and for a strange moment Tagart held the cold blue eyes with his own. But from another quarter he glimpsed something coming towards him, a weapon, too quick to see, and then his head was kicked a hundred miles sideways and he saw before him vast streamers of white starbursts, here and there red lights blinking, and his face was in the mud, the taste of it in his mouth. A roaring filled his brain. Long tunnels of pink hoops stretched away, gently descending into pink caverns where he wanted to run and hide. Above him the sky inverted, was sucked into a vortex that followed the tunnels down, leaving the blankness of a glaring white horizon, tinged with red as from behind spots soaked through, staining, haemorrhaging, spreading, sponging up his life as the redness dripped and became a trickle, a flow, a pouring race that rushed along the tunnel walls, carrying him before it. He could no longer breathe. His lungs were clamped flat, going under, arms helpless, borne along and downwards at avalanche speed. He opened his eyes and saw only crimson. The crimson darkened and the roar grew louder, many voices in the storm, and in the emptiness beneath him Tagart knew he was going to die. He knew he was going to die even as he struggled in the torrent like a wet insect doomed and drowning, but he was fighting, fighting to the end, swamped by the blackness and engulfed by its pressure as the roaring became louder and louder, a roaring too loud to bear.

The river had carried him a little way. He knew it could not be far, because he could hear voices, and when he looked up he saw faint firelight on the stems and drooping leaves of the sedges of the bank. His face was close to them: his eyes tried to focus, but would not.

He spoke to Mirin. She would not answer. He felt the rain on his body, the river lapping at his skin. He tasted the water and the slime of the bottom. Mirin lay on a bed of flowers. The honeysuckle twined about the white skin of her wrists and ankles, her hair had been spread out on a pillow of ferns, and she was smiling.

The rain was falling steadily, less fiercely than before, hissing into the fires. Tagart's hands found purchase and he began to drag himself further out of the water and a little way up the bank.

The effort was too great. He saw men going from place to place, turning over corpses with their feet. He saw axes and hammers raised, twitching legs become still, moans silenced. The man with no beard was giving orders. Behind him the shelters burned, and Tagart watched them through the sedges, moving against the glow. It was a long time before he realized that some of the women had been spared. Voices were raised in laughter and jeering. He saw Sela stripped naked and made to kneel.

Tagart tried to raise his head further, staring at what was happening. He was lying face down, his legs in the water. It pained him to keep his head up. The pain spread into his back as he watched them, along his spine and into his legs, becoming excruciating; but he forgot it as he saw Sela thrown sideways, and behind her, being brought forward, he saw Mirin. The beardless man shouted something and there was laughter. He pulled her to the ground and then he was on top of her, thrusting at her. She lay limp as he got up and another took his place.

Tagart watched the sedges. They were orange and black, curved and weaving with each other under the impact of the rain. He could not follow the beauty of their patterns; too many raindrops were falling.

He was drifting now, away from the screams of a voice he thought he knew, away from the shouting and laughter, drifting deeper, towards the centre where he could not see them, where he could not hear them, where what they were doing to his wife would not be true.

5

Three hours after first light, two hours after crawling from the sedges and on to firm ground, he arrived at a position overlooking the village.

He was familiar with its appearance, in keeping with a general knowledge of the terrain near the camp site, but he lacked the detailed information that only a thorough inspection could provide.

He was at the very edge of the forest, looking down from the top of an escarpment which abutted the village on its east side. Rain-flattened grass clothed the slope, with oak bushes and clumps of blackthorn which could provide good cover for an unseen approach. This, he had already decided, was the way he would come when he wanted to get into the village. At the bottom of the escarpment, where the gradient eased, were a few anthills of varying age. These too would provide cover. Beyond them, a patch of nettles and a thicket of briers and blackberry canes grew up against the structure of the palisade. This was the height of two men, a fence of stout logs buttressed behind with log struts. It enclosed the whole of the village, including several hundred yards of the river; the tops of the logs were sharpened to points. Without equipment it looked impossible to climb.

Tagart shut his eyes. His head ached very badly and the taste of vomit was still in his mouth. The back of his forearm was a mass of congealed blood: he had wound strips of soft leather from elbow to wrist. A dull pain filled his neck and left shoulder. One of his ribs felt as if it might be broken.

Somehow they had spared him. When he awoke he found himself lying half in the river, half in the vegetation of its bank. They must have taken him for dead; or, more likely, missed him altogether.

He allowed his face to rest in the wet, musty grass. His clothing was drenched and heavy; the leather glistened and bubbled where it creased as he moved. He groaned and let the ground receive the weight of his body, letting gravity take each muscle. Even though his eyes were tightly shut he could not stop seeing Zeme. They had raped her too. He had found her body by chance, not long after he had dragged himself from the riverbank and left the camp behind. He jumped into the stream and took her up in his arms. He did not know which way to turn with her.

Tagart jerked his head up and opened his eyes. Had he fallen asleep then? Had any time passed? The village looked the same. The rain was keeping them indoors, sheeting across the compound, drumming and splashing on the house roofs. To the south-west, over the sea, occasional bolts and forks of lightning danced. The wind was driving fast paler cloud below the cumulus, gusting and howling and bending the trees behind him.

He pulled his tunic closer to his neck. His hair was soaked and drops of water trickled from the tip of his nose, leaving a salty taste on his lips.

For a long time he lay studying the village. The houses seemed to have been built at random, arranged haphazardly, relying for defence on the palisade. The single thoroughfare was an extension of their path from the shrine on the cliffs. It passed through a gate, now closed, and widened into a rough oval bordered by a huddle of most of the thirty-three dwelling houses. Thirty-three: that meant between a hundred and eighty and two hundred people. The houses were tall, with conical roofs and narrow windows, built of timber and blocks of stone, with pavements to the front where they faced the oval. There were five larger buildings: a barn, bakery, threshing shed, and granary; the fifth was a Meeting House of the type he had seen in some of the more prosperous villages farther east: twice the height of the houses, long and broad, with a peaked roof and a wide doorway with a porch, from which a flight of plank steps led down to the village compound. The walls were of timber, faced with wattle and daub to keep out the weather. The floor was raised from the ground on massive oak piles about chest high. On the right of the Meeting House stood the barn and the bakery; on the left, the threshing shed and granary; behind them flowed the river. Between the granary and the palisade were two circular pits which Tagart took to be silos.

Now and then he heard a snatch of music and chanting, carried faintly on the wind, and it seemed to be coming from the Meeting House. He could see people inside.

The thoroughfare resumed its course between the Meeting House and the threshing shed, ran down to and crossed the river by means of a wooden bridge, built a little way downstream where presumably the bed was more suited to supporting the piers; nearer the village, next to the Meeting House, the path ran beside the riverbank, littered with upturned coracles and piles of nets. There was a landing stage, and a larger coracle tied to it riding the stream.

On the other side of the bridge the path left the palisade by another gate and disappeared westward into the fields. Much of the valley had been dug for cultivation, almost as far as the western slope, and southwards a long way towards the sea. A strip of heath remained between the fields and the beach, and more sparsely along the mouth of the river where it widened into a small estuary with a few shingly islets. Northwards the land had been cleared for half a mile, mainly on level ground by the river, but also on the north-eastern slope, where a large barley field had been made to catch the sun, or to escape winter floods.

The fields ended; the forest resumed. The line of trees snaked behind the barley field, south to the village and the escarpment, and then downhill, beside the river to the sea. East of the village the forest rose steeply, over the hill and towards the cliffs.

Tagart took his flint knife in hand and began the slow crawl down the escarpment.

At the bottom he broke from cover and with a crouching gait ran the fifteen paces to the palisade. Keeping it close by his right-hand side he set off to circle the village.

Whoever had built the palisade had been serious in his intention not to let anyone in. It rose above Tagart, the tree-trunks fitted tightly together, shaved at the top to slanting points. The gaps for the most part had been plugged with wedges and slivers of wood, rammed home and plastered with mud and clay. A few chinks remained. Through one of these Tagart had a partial view of the nearest house. He pressed his face to the rough bark. Water was cascading from the roof, splashing against the stone, soaking and making dark the already waterlogged timbers.

He went on until he came to the east gate. This was fitted with a heavy door, opening outwards on three hinges, secured by two great bars. Like the rest of the palisade it was topped by spikes. At ground level there was a gap of a hand's width, slightly more in the middle of the path where the passage of feet had worn a way; and now after some hours of rain the path was turning to mud.

The palisade continued, curving along the south side of the village, down the bank and into the river, the only concession to the water being the wider spacing of the logs; on the other bank it curved to the right and ran beside the river, enclosing a strip of ground ten yards wide. Now the palisade ran arrow-straight for a quarter of a mile, turned back into the river, crossed it, and, following the rise and fall in the ground, looped back to the escarpment and the east gate.

Tagart put his feet into the mass of sedge and yellow cress and went down the bank, let himself into the water. It was deep here, where the current behind the weir of logs had churned up and removed the bottom, and three steps from the bank Tagart was treading water. The river felt warm and soothing on his body, much warmer than the rain. For a while he rested, holding on to one of the logs. From the green and white stains on the palisade it could be seen that the level, although very low, was on the rise.

He dived and the noise of the rain abruptly stopped. Underwater he could see only green; he kicked against the current and felt the bulk of the palisade, slimy with weed. For a second his fingers were where the logs entered the river bed, before he was forced to surface for air. It seemed that the gaps between the logs were the same above and below the water: the wood had rotted hardly at all. He dived again and managed to explore more of the gaps. None was more than a hand's width. After many dives he satisfied himself that there could be no access here. He pulled himself from the water and climbed the far bank.

It was not going to be easy. He stood shivering in the shelter of the palisade. His arm was bleeding again. He held it up and saw the trickle of blood across his palm, running down the backs of his fingers.

He shook his head angrily and continued along the base of the palisade, still keeping it on his right. Through gaps he could see the river, and beyond it the silos, threshing shed, and granary. To the left of them, a little way ahead, was the bridge and, in line with it from this angle, the Meeting House. The music had grown more distinct. At one of the windows in the side wall he could clearly see signs of activity within.

A man staggered out on to the porch, his hands across his face, and fell headlong down the steps. Tagart craned his neck, trying to see. A moment later two middle-aged women, both naked, followed him from the doorway. They stooped and seemed to berate the fallen man. He lay face down in the mud, not moving, scarcely even breathing. Presently the women, after discussion, started shaking him by the shoulders, trying to make him get up, without success. The shorter woman went back inside and returned with a third. All three took hold of the man and carried him up the steps.

Still there was no sign of movement elsewhere in the village, no children, and no dogs.

He set off again. The second gate was much like the first, with a narrow space at the bottom – too narrow to get under. Tagart put his eye to the gap between gate and post. He could see no dogs, but something of more interest had caught his attention.

Beside the Meeting House, in a rank, had been laid the corpses from the previous night. There were twenty-six.

Then it struck him that the music inside the Meeting House might be something to do with the corpses, marking their transition from this life to the next. He knew little about the farmers' beliefs, beyond what he had heard in stories at the winter camp, but something of the sort seemed possible, for in the event it seemed their victory last night had not been without cost. Twenty-six. Tagart had not realized it was so many.

The Meeting House was less than a hundred yards away. He was standing at a point in the palisade almost opposite the jetty, from which, on a creaking painter, a large coracle rode the current. It could be of no use to him.

He continued along the base of the palisade, past the Meeting House, the barn and bakery, walking through the rain to the northern corner of the compound, where the palisade turned east and back across the river.

The water was shallower here, but still there was no gap wide enough to admit him. He came up for air again and again.

When he reached his starting-point at the bottom of the escarpment he sank to the ground and sat with his head in his hands, overcome by weakness and despair. He felt giddy and ill. The pain in his chest was worse, sharp and stabbing; blood soaked steadily into the bandages on his arm. Every few seconds he fought back an overwhelming urge to vomit, not that anything remained in his stomach.

There were three ways to get past such an obstacle as a palisade. Going through was out of the question: he had no tools, except a knife and his bare hands. Going over involved too great a risk of being seen, and anyway he had no means of climbing. That left going under, which meant a tunnel, and that would take too long; and even if he did manage it he might well emerge in full view of the farmers. The gates? Were they the weak point? Or the river – perhaps he should try again, search more thoroughly.

The ladder-marks: he remembered the ladder-marks.

He stood up and walked past the east gate, making his way towards the river again. With his eye to the top of the palisade, he stopped three hundred yards on. Sure enough, there were marks left by the harvesters' ladders on the spikes at the top. He found a gap and looked through it to confirm his position, moved four paces west, glanced over his shoulder and dropped to one knee. With his knife he scored out and rolled back a small trapdoor in the turf.

The soil was still relatively dry, black and loamy. He dug

with his bare hands, scooping the earth back like a dog. The palisade extended the length of his arm below ground level, no more; his fingers found and felt the bottom of the log where the wood had been shaped by adze to a rough four-sided point. The timber, although treated by scorching, was beginning to rot: decay would be more likely in this part of the palisade. Tagart dug deeper, below the points, resting from time to time to flex his fingers and rub the cakes of dirt from his hands. His fingernails were clogged; his arms were aching, the left forearm crusted with earth and blood, but he was starting to uncover what he had hoped to find: a panel of sticks set vertically, which went down as far as he cared to dig. An hour later he had reached a depth of three feet, not really enough, but it would have to serve. As it was he had displaced a surprisingly large heap of earth which would have to be disposed of when he finished. Sitting at the edge of the hole, he drew back his legs and kicked at the panel of sticks. It caved in at once, releasing a sickly sweet smell of ensilage. Tagart kicked again, and again, compacting the crushed vegetation behind the panel, making a hollow which he enlarged with his hands, punching and pushing at the dirty yellow straw. When he had hollowed out a space twice his size he climbed outside once more and, using his feet, pushed the spoil into the hole. The earth had made the turf muddy: that couldn't be helped. He hoped the rain would wash most of it away and leave the trapdoor all but invisible. He had strengthened the trapdoor with a pair of sticks, so that it lay flat.

With a final glance round he climbed into the hole and pulled the flap of turf after him.

Sturmer abandoned the last vestiges of inhibition and gave himself entirely to the fly agaric. The fire of the fungus at the back of his throat was a flame that filled his brain and made it huge. Unwittingly his tongue slid from the side of his mouth. A string of blackened saliva dribbled to his chest. He was not aware of the girl retching beside him, nor of the other people in the Meeting House. He was alone, swallowing the core of intense heat, fighting along the borders of self-control, tricking himself into ignoring the filthy taste, refusing to acknowledge nausea, making progress to the farther shore.

He reached it and in exultation he soared, borne upwards at tremendous speed: his body shrank to a point and vanished, leaving a tingling spot which glowed briefly and was gone.

He was master of the drug now, riding it, just as the others were riding it.

Occasionally someone screamed, clawing at his face, and fell sideways to lie unconscious on the floor. Others sat with heads hanging between their knees, while some shouted and argued and gesticulated. A few, those who like Sturmer were nearing the peak, sat entranced, rocking from side to side and quietly moaning. The women moved to and fro with bowls and drinking cups, waiting to collect urine from the men.

The fly agaric fungus, a toadstool with white stalk and gills and a scarlet cap, grew in many places round the village, and commonly in the forest where the ground was poor. It appeared suddenly in the middle of high summer after the rains, and went on until the end of harvest or into autumn. The fungus was a gift from Gauhm. It enabled the bereaved to go part of the way towards the Far Land of the Dead. The drug was sacred. It could only be gathered after special prayer, and was to be prepared only by the priest. First the stalks were discarded and the caps left to dry in the sun, after which they were placed in the Agaric Casket, a beechwood box kept next to the altar in the Meeting House. Its lid and sides were carved with figures of visions achieved under the drug; inside, the shrivelled caps were stored in layers of close-fitting trays, one lifting from the other. The trays were replenished each year at harvest.

The mode of using the agaric achieved the greatest possible distance along the road to the Far Land. The women, who were not allowed to eat it, took most of the taste from the caps by chewing them and rolling them between the hands. The pellets so formed were then given to the men to be swallowed immediately.

Ten pellets were enough to kill, and as one of the side-effects of consumption was a raging desire to eat more, the women strictly rationed each man's supply; experienced users such as Sturmer could eat fully nine pellets. Younger men were limited to three or four.

The drug seemed to pass quickly through the system, and the urine of the men, though less potent than the pellets, was carefully saved and drunk by the women. Meanwhile the musicians played, drums and flutes and pipes making a dirge. They would not eat the drug till later; they sat cross-legged by the window, their heads and shoulders outlined against the gloomy morning light.

Groden shouted out. Hernou lay beside him. In a while she would be ready to drink again.

In total darkness Tagart groped upward, his fingers feeling for the mat of sticks. Below him his feet found difficulty in getting purchase. The ensilage yielded to his weight, and he knew that if he did not keep moving he would sink to the bottom and suffocate.

His hands closed on the sticks and he pulled himself up. He dug his toes high into the hole he had made and pushed; the combined effort brought his head through the mat and into daylight. Momentarily he hung there resting, looking out across the village.

The silo through which he had burrowed, and the one next to it, had been positioned at the base of the palisade so that the haymakers could drop their loads from ladders instead of hauling them round through the east gate. The silos were largely hidden from the Meeting House by the threshing shed and granary. To the left a patch of waste ground led to the river; to the right and ahead were the walls and precincts of a single dwelling house. Others were nearby, near enough to entail danger of being seen, but then wherever he chose to cross the palisade there would be some risk of that. In all, this was quite a good place from which to approach.

Tagart raised himself up and out, sprinted the few yards to the granary, and to the threshing shed, where he stood breathing heavily for several seconds before, in full view of the Meeting House porch, he ran with everything he had down to the river, launched from his right foot, blurred over the soggy stand of vegetation, and with scarcely a splash plunged into the water.

He reappeared upstream, a few yards nearer the Meeting House, ducked, and swam again. Under the joists of the bridge he came up and clung to the timbers, glad to be out of sight. The water here sounded loud in the hollow space under the bridge; the ripples of his movements echoed back to him. He waded into the shallows on the village side and lay flat on the mud, resting with his eyes shut, listening absently to the current.

A long time passed before Tagart felt able to emerge from the bridge, a long time before he felt safe even to stand up unaided. But at last some of his strength returned; his heart-beat slowed; the pain receded from his chest, neck and shoulder. He raised himself to a sitting position and noticed that the dizziness was almost gone.

He came out from the bridge. Now he was ready to investigate the village.

Sturmer did not know how his eyes had become focused on the water falling from the Meeting House porch. Suddenly, he found it interesting. He studied the shapes, the crystals as they fell, the variegation of silver and blue, the exquisitely transparent drops. In them he saw distorted miniatures of the view outside, each one upside-down. He saw the forest on the escarpment, each branch, each tree, each leaf. On each leaf he saw the veins and lobes, the beads of water standing like silver spheres. The spheres were reflecting the forest, the sky, the village waiting below. With slow recognition Sturmer saw the form of a dark young man dressed in nomad's skins, pausing momentarily on the crest and looking down into the village with implacable eyes.

And then the crystal globe exploded on the boards of the porch, and Sturmer found himself searching desperately for another to take its place.

6

They had removed nearly everything of value from the camp. Fewer than a dozen coils of usable rope remained. All the furs, and all the better skins had gone, as had all the weapons except those stored in a shelter which, partly burnt, had not been properly searched. What food had not been carried away was spoiled and kicked into the mud. Baskets lay smashed, ovens and hearths destroyed. He had managed to find enough food for two or three meals, a pair of pigskin water-bags, five bows and seven arrows, a spear, a bundle of lime-bark twine, some tallow, two bags of flints which he emptied into a single pouch, a deerskin, and seven goatskins. That was all. These things, and a heap of indifferent ropes, were all he had to exterminate an entire village.

Despite the pain in his chest he was walking quickly. No direct rain fell under the trees, but the air was damp and water dripped steadily from the branches. A green twilight made a suffusion of the wet bracken and rain-sodden foliage; the acrid smell of disturbed leaf-litter rose from the ground as he made his way uphill.

There was a great deal yet to do. He had already been to see the bears' den, and he had been back to the camp four times so far to salvage what he could and take it the three miles south-east, about a mile east of the village, to the place where he had established his lair: an old yew tree on the slope of the hill, among dense broad-leafed forest. The ground under the yew's spreading branches was dusty and, even after the storm, quite dry. By rearranging and cutting the boughs Tagart had fashioned a hiding-place in the space round the trunk. Once inside he was able to close up the screen of branches, and his seclusion was complete.

The bears' den was about a mile to the north. Some days before, one of the best trackers in the tribe had returned with news of the spoor; he and Tagart and another followed the tracks into a part of the forest dominated by oak. One of the larger trees had fallen, and in the root-pit the she bear had burrowed out her den. Brief – and extremely cautious – observation revealed that two cubs were present, and a second, younger female which was acting as a nurse. As expected the male bear was not to be seen, though a few days later crunched mussels were found on the beach which were probably his leavings.

Today the bears were still in residence. Tagart had gone there and heard the cubs' cries. When he and the others had first visited the den the cubs were being suckled; now it looked as if the mother was beginning to wean them.

He was laden with ropes as he began returning to the yew tree once more. This would be the last trip from the camp.

From time to time as he walked he stopped and stood for several minutes squinting up at the trees. Once in every ten or fifteen stops he left behind a coil of rope; frequently he changed his mind, picked up the rope, and went on. The way they would come along this path had to be carefully anticipated; he could not afford to waste rope. Perhaps he should have taken some from the village that morning after all. Those nets by the riverbank would have been handy . . . he shook his head. That would have cost him his only advantage: the fact that they did not know he was alive.

For the twentieth time he wondered what they had been doing in the Meeting House. He had spied on them through a chink in the wattle, unable to understand what was going on. The men intoxicated and seemingly deranged; the women vomiting and drinking urine; twenty-six corpses in a row outside. While watching he had for a moment entertained the idea of bursting in with his knife. Certainly he could have killed many before he himself was brought down, but not all the men were incapacitated, and it was not unknown for women to fight. Even so, it might have been worth doing, were it not that he had taken a vow. He was going to kill them all.

From the Meeting House he had made his departure from the village, going out through the silo as he had come in; from there he had gone straight to the camp to begin work.

The last coil of rope was deposited; he returned to the yew tree. It was the end of the afternoon, towards an early dusk, and he had decided that there might be enough time to try for some deer. At this season the calves were about eight weeks old, large enough to accompany their mothers and the rest of the herd on the evening visits to the drinking-place: the shallows a mile downstream from the camp. The shore, muddy and churned, showed a multitude of hoof-slots. Tagart approached upwind, and with his best bow slung across his back climbed into an ivy-hung oak. He chose a bough commanding a view of the muddy area. Sitting astride it he took three arrows, nocked one, and rested the lower end of the bow on his instep.

He composed himself to wait, quite comfortable, motionless. By a trick he disengaged his brain and with his body completely relaxed let time drift over him, trusting his senses to alert him when the deer came.

The river gurgled and splashed; rain was still falling relentlessly. He was aware of the background of happenings on the riverbank, which taken together meant that all was normal, all was well. A water vole came diffidently to the water, and with yellow teeth gnawed at a plant stem held in its hands. The wet made its fur spiky and dark; its eyes, black and shiny as berries, blinked as it paused in its feeding and sniffed for danger with head moving from side to side. No untoward scent registered: the vole went on nibbling. Presently it discarded the last of the stem and slipped into the water, swimming with nose up and feet furiously paddling, its tail streaming behind. Overhanging leaves hid it for a moment; it reappeared with a length of cowbane stem in its mouth, held crosswise like a dog with a stick. The water thrashed: the cowbane bobbed to the surface, and there was a glimpse of the languid white belly of a pike. The ripples merged with the current; the pike lazily finned back into deeper water. The vole did not reappear.

The birds were making an end to their day. Blackbirds chuckled in the undergrowth; a willow warbler called from the base of an alder. A cuckoo flew low over the water, swooping, hawk-like, and came to perch, arresting its flight and swaying at the tip of one of the elder bushes lining the river.

As darkness approached the woodland grew quiet. The elder

bushes, some with a few white flowers remaining, assumed odd shapes and seemed to expand and contract under Tagart's gaze. The light was failing. Four or five large bats were busy with the insects over the river; from time to time he thought he heard the snap of their jaws. He watched them on their black wings, weaving this way and that, stopping short, going on, in concert with the rain scouring every insect from the air.

Imperceptibly Tagart braced himself and opened his eyes more widely. He was alert again. The herd was coming.

They came forward, one by one appearing between the trees. The leading hind paused by the water as the rest of the herd passed her by: six hinds with calves, four antlered stags, one of which was already stripping its antlers of velvet; and a hummel, a hart without antlers. The hummel was the biggest animal in the herd. Next down was one of the stags, perhaps a ten-pointer, though the light was too bad to be sure.

The muscles on Tagart's arm began to bulge as he slowly drew back the arrow. With his thumbnail resting on the corner of his jawbone, he made allowance for the drop and fixed his eyes on the hummel's flank. He had chosen the surest spot, just behind the foreleg where there was least chance of missing a vital organ. The light was playing tricks. The movements of the deer as they drank seemed jerky, their forms and the foliage round them took on a grainy quality: Tagart readjusted his gaze and with it automatically his aim and his fingers were opening and the supple slap of the bowstring sent the point of the arrow on its intended way.

Before it had arrived he was nocking the next arrow and taking aim at the ten-point stag. He ignored the hummel, concentrating on the second shot. It flew too high, missed the animals altogether, and he lost sight of it.

The deer were running now, in a frenzy scrambling to turn round and get out of the river. For a moment Tagart thought he had missed the hummel as well, but it was struck, struggling after the others. They were leaving it behind. The hummel bellowed after them, its head strangely twisted, looking down at the mud. He had hit it in the neck. With growing dismay he wondered whether it could still run, whether he would have to follow it, perhaps for miles before weakness overcame either him or it. The hummel was free of the mud now, still bellowing, charging dementedly forwards into an elder bush. It staggered wildly, and charged again, this time into a tree-trunk. Its hind legs gave way and writhing it collapsed to the ground.

Tagart joyously came slithering down the oak and ran to the wounded beast. The arrow had been driven further into the neck by its fall; the eyes, showing white, stared open; its breath panted past a lolling tongue. Rich blood started to ooze from the nostrils and mouth.

He worked at speed. With his knife he opened the skin at the anus and along the back of the hind legs. Gripping the cut skin he worked his blade beneath, severing connective tissue, and one by one allowed the hind legs to slip out to a quarter of their length, as far as their first joints, which he parted with a few skilled strokes. With more flints he cut through the rectum and behind the pizzle, and with the tail free began to roll the skin back along the body, turning the animal this way and that. The skin slipped free of the forelegs: he dragged it over the head, slit under the eyes and behind the lips, and stood clear.

Now, with the skin inside-out, he cut a strip from the head and tied it very tightly round the neck, below the hole made by the point of the arrow. He turned the skin back, right side out, and went with it to the water, where he allowed a quantity to flow inside. The skin took on the greatest weight of water that he could carry: he slung it over his shoulder and set off uphill.

As he laboured up the slope he decided to leave the meat where it was until morning. The bears might find the hummel: he did not care to compete with them in the dark. If anything remained in the morning he would try to get as much of it stored as he could. He did not know yet how long he would have to depend on his hiding-place at the yew tree; he needed a larder.

The darkness was almost complete when he arrived with the hummel-skin at a coil of rope he had deposited earlier in the day. Using his foot he picked up one end of the coil; spilling only a little water, he tied the rope to the open end of the skin, making use of the remaining bones in the hind legs, and, throwing the free end of the rope over a branch just above head height, hoisted the skin and left it dangling. He squatted and held his palm beneath the neck. It seemed to be watertight.

Tagart stood up. As he did so a wave of giddiness came over him. He put a hand out to steady himself against the tree, eyes half closed, jaw tightly clenched, but it was no good: he felt his stomach twisting inside him, being wrung out; he fell against the bark, the spasms coming in agonizing waves. Tagart slid down the trunk to his knees, sick with grief and horror and exhaustion and shock. He was wet and cold, weak with uncontrollable shivering; the thought of food repelled him, but he would have to eat, and get rid of his clothes, soaked and heavy with the rain and the river. He needed comfort urgently: warmth, dry clothes, food. If he did not get them he would be unable to stop the long slide downhill and, as Cosk might say, the forest would have him.

He wiped his mouth, stood up, and turned towards the yew tree. The forest could have him later.

The vigil over the corpses on the Dead Ground began at nightfall. The village square had gone from dust to mud; the rain seemed to be settled now, falling steadily hour after hour. Twilight had come early. Dark figures, some bearing hooded lights on poles, crossed and recrossed the compound, converging on the Meeting House.

Inside was a blaze of light, brightest at the altar, where Sturmer was making ready for the prayers and the token sacrifice to Gauhm. The yellow glow filled the room to the rafters and threw shadows from beams and projections and the moving shapes of those on the floor. No one spoke. The only sounds were of the rain, and the spluttering wicks in the lamps at the altar and in the sconces round the walls. Sturmer stood over the stone slab; the kid struggled in the crook of his arm and lay still.

The Meeting House was full. At this time yesterday there had been a hundred and ninety-six people in the village; now there were a hundred and seventy. The injured numbered forty or fifty, some with only mild bruises, but others with serious wounds or broken limbs, which meant more deaths to come, and permanent cripples among those who survived.

These men, like the widows and children of the dead, would be a heavy burden on the village.

It was a harsh price to pay for rain: Groden had been discredited, for a while at least. Sturmer decided not to accuse him of killing his own dog. There was no proof, and an unsubstantiated accusation might lose Sturmer some of the ground he had made.

He reverently placed the bowl of kid's blood on the altar-stone, spread wide his robes and raised his eyes in the chant. The others responded. Groden's bass voice, as feeling and grief-stricken as any in the room, was among them.

7

Yew-wood made the best bows, and the strongest spears: it was magic, protected by the Sun who gave everything, guarded for the hunters by the Sun's disciple the Moon. To keep animals away the Moon had rendered the shoots and berries poisonous; thus yew trees always remained well filled and dark, a safe place to hide in overnight, as the Sun had intended. The thick branches kept out the rain; the resinous, soothing balm of the leaves lulled and refreshed; and where the shed needles fell they made a soft-dry bed.

Sleep came to Tagart eventually. He had lain awake for a long time, sometimes speaking words aloud, his face hot and puffy with weeping.

When he awoke it was still night. The forest was silent but for the rain. He sipped from one of the water-bags, raising with himself and immediately rejecting the question of food; the previous evening he had tried to eat, but gagged and was unable to swallow anything. He felt no more able to eat now. Nevertheless, food remained his priority: he would go and see whether the hummel had been interfered with, cut whatever meat remained and bring it back to the yew where it was dry and the smell of food would less readily escape to bring unwelcome visitors. Possibly he would go to the trouble of finding some flat stones, build a hearth and risk a smokeless fire to cook it, risk a stray wisp being seen in the village. He changed his mind. Raw meat was just as nourishing, if less palatable.

He left the yew tree to relieve himself, came back and dressed in skins which had hardly dried overnight, and gave his mind to the morning's work. Dawn showed grey above the trees as he set off for the hummel.

A little while later he was back with fifty pounds of venison, sliced into strips and hung from either end of a hazel pole. The hummel had been a big animal, fat and well fed, three times

Tagart's weight: he had done well to kill it. A beast like that would have supplied the tribe for two days or more. But now he contented himself with the easy cuts and left the rest for the scavengers. One uncertainty had been resolved in his mind: he would not go hungry.

He finished tying the last strip of meat inside the yew. The rain had slackened slightly, strengthened, and slackened again. Each renewal of gusts dislodged a noisy shower of droplets. The wind had a cold edge; he found himself shivering again as he knelt down to sort through his meagre supplies. From them he selected what he felt he would need, packed everything into his pouch and one of the goatskins, and started out.

He went first to the place where he had left the hummel's skin, dangling from a branch.

He was grateful for the fact that it had not leaked. It hung there, a grotesque bulge, the curves of the animal's chest parodied by the swell of water, its flanks and haunches tapered to a creased apex, stretched tight by the weight. The tree to which he had fixed it was just off the farmers' path from the village to their shrine. He had chosen the spot because of a lime tree near the path, a hundred and twenty feet tall, with an unobstructed drop from one of the limbs at a height of ninety feet or so. There were many such trees at various points along the path: what made this one suitable was the way the holly-bushes grew below it. Not only did they cover both sides of the path, restricting its width, but there was a particularly stout plant – almost a tree – about twenty feet from the path and directly below the limb with the unobstructed drop.

Tagart set about this plant with his knife. First he stripped the branches from the stem and cut it to waist height, and with a new blade, sharpened the tip to a point. Just below the point he cut out a notch with its upper surface parallel to the ground, so that the holly stem looked like a harpoon with a single barb. From the discarded section of the stem he cut an identical harpoon: the two barbs fitted together, slotting into each other like two hands with bent fingers interlocked. Along the back of the free harpoon he scooped a longitudinal groove, deep enough to take the radius of his rope, which later he would need to bind on with twine, pulling every turn with all his strength, for the lashing would have to support the weight of the hummel-skin filled with water.

But for the moment he slipped the bundle of twine into his tunic, selected a piece of tallow, and climbed the tree. He edged out along the limb: the ground was a long way below, his tools, the skins, seemed tiny. If he fell now he would be impaled neatly on the sharpened holly stem.

He fastened a piece of flint to one end of the twine and lowered it gently to the ground. The flint swung backwards and forwards interminably as he adjusted the position of the twine on the limb. After many attempts he found the point precisely above the holly stem, with the twine hanging still and the flint just touching the tip. He marked the place with his fingernail and let the rest of the twine drop down on the other side.

With his knife he grooved across the mark he had made; when satisfied with its depth he rubbed the groove with tallow, again and again to smother the sticky lime sap and make a practically frictionless surface. The purpose of the twine hanging on either side of the limb was to give a lead with which to pull over the rope. He placed the twine in the groove and descended to the ground.

Alone, without the aid of other hands, the next part of the operation was more difficult. There was too much water in the hummel-skin. He emptied part of it out, into two goatskins. With twine and many knots he made the hummel's hind legs fast to the free end of the rope, and cutting it free from its overnight branch he hoisted the skin high into the lime, pulling hand-over-hand until the hind legs reached the groove.

He had judged it quite well: the weight of rope hanging down was a little greater than the weight of the skin; the rope didn't move as Tagart gingerly loosened his grip, and when he took his hands away altogether it merely eased slightly, pulling the skin upwards and against the branch.

He pulled the dangling rope straight and held it against the holly stem, and to it lashed the second harpoon. This he fitted into its sister notch on the stem and temporarily bound the two together with a few turns of twine. The rest of the rope, below the second harpoon, amounted to some ten or twelve yards. He began to lead it towards the path.

The dead-weight and its release were almost complete: he was ready to start work on the trigger device.

For this he needed two lengths of springy holly, one thrust into the ground at a shallow angle, and the other – which provided the power to work the release – a small sapling stripped and bent over in a loop, its tip shaped to hook into the tip of the first length, in principle like the interlocking barbs on the two harpoons of the release. Pressure on the first length would push it down, allowing the sapling to snap back, jerking with it a length of twine attached to the second harpoon. The two harpoons would then be pulled apart, allowing the hummel-skin to fall.

Whoever had applied the pressure to the first length of holly would find the end of the rope – which Tagart was now tying into a noose with a sliding knot – closing about his ankle. The water-filled skin had ninety feet to fall, on to the holly stem, whereupon it would burst. The victim, by now hoisted some sixty or seventy feet into the air, and no longer counterbalanced by the weight of the water, would do the same.

He had to clear two or three branches and sprigs before the trigger cable was completely unobstructed; and he had difficulty with the trigger pedal, for the ground was so dry that it was no easy matter to drive it in. But finally he was satisfied, and he went about with leaves and handfuls of earth to camouflage the noose and the rest of the mechanism. By dragging a small log on to the path he guided the footsteps of his quarry; he roughly guessed at the length of stride, adjusted the position of the log, stood back, made another adjustment, trying to plant the footfall directly on to the trigger pedal, in the centre of the hidden noose.

All that remained was to fill the hummel-skin with water. This he did by making several trips to the river with his goatskins, climbing into the lime tree and carefully decanting the water into the larger skin. The two harpoons creaked under the weight, but the lashing held firm. Tagart undid the temporary turns of twine holding them together and, with a stick, prised the harpoons apart fraction by fraction until the notches overlapped by no more than a finger's width.

A final inspection, a check that he had left the minimum slack in the trigger cable, that everything was hidden from view, the cut wood disguised with earth, that the noose would not snag at the critical moment; and the trap was ready. Part of the drop of rope was on view, and so was the hummel-skin, if anyone cared to look up, but he hoped it would not be noticed against the brown trunk.

The trap had taken a long time and a great deal of effort to make. He had never attempted one on his own before: normally there were others to lend a hand, three or four men to hoist the water-filled skin straight up to the branch and hold it there while the harpoon was lashed.

But, he had done it. He had done it alone, and as he stood looking at it some of his doubts began to dissolve. If he could make one trap successfully, he could make many, and if he could make many he would be well able to achieve what he set out to do, which was, notwithstanding how long it took, to secure utterly the total destruction of the village.

He gathered up his belongings and set off for the next tree. He had hidden the noose so well that he forcibly reminded himself where it was as he passed.

It would not do to tread on the trigger.

Tagart heard the clink of the mattock faintly on the wind and stood quite still, suddenly alert. He had just finished making a ladder, a kind of ramp fifteen feet long covered with brushwood, which he had left hidden at the top of the escarpment. Work had gone well during the day. The rain had stopped early in the afternoon, and now the sky was blue.

It came again. He had not been mistaken.

He was quite close to the fields here. The ground sloped down to the field-edge, which he could just see in places where the trees allowed. The barley showed rich brown and gold, lit by a brilliant evening sunshine.

He changed direction, moving swiftly and silently from tree to tree, getting nearer the origin of the sound. His feet were noiseless: by intuition he avoided crackling twigs and beechmast husks, rustling leaves, branches that were dead and would snap if trodden on. He stopped to listen. The mattock clinks came singly, intermittently, as if one man, working none too enthusiastically on his own, were digging the ground, bending, digging again. Tagart moved to the very edge of the woods and looked out across the field. The user of the mattock could not be seen from this angle: the sound originated away to the left, hidden by an elbow of trees. To come upon him Tagart would have to walk across open ground, between the forest and a shallow dip in which men might be waiting.

He was immediately on his guard. It was too easy, too neat, and much too soon after the raid for him to find a man out alone.

Had he been seen the previous day in the village? Was that it? Did the farmers now realize that someone had survived, were they trying to lure him into the open? They would surely know the futility of chasing a nomad through the forest. Their only chance of killing him, of preventing word of the massacre spreading to other tribes, would be to bring him on to open ground and surround him.

Or was he overestimating them, attributing to them powers of cunning which they did not have? They were farmers, men who lived by grubbing the soil and slaughtering captive animals; not hunters, whose living depended on foresight and strategy. Were they capable of such a plan?

He did not know. He was very tired, of that he was certain, and when tired he knew that judgements could be wrong. Everything in him urged him to go back into the safety of the deep forest, to feed himself and recuperate, to make more preparations before letting the farmers know that all was not to be well for them. He wanted to renew his supply of arrows and flints, establish another hiding-place in case the yew were found, replenish his ropes, rig more traps, attend to more of the pitfalls the tribe had dug earlier in the season . . .

But he was only one man, and men were not meant to work in the forest alone. Every hour that passed increased his chances of being injured or falling sick with no one to tend him, or of being overpowered and eaten by some animal larger and stronger than himself. And, however many preparations he made, he knew he would never be fully satisfied, he knew he would always need just one more trap or another quiver of arrows to help even the appalling odds against him.

He turned and went back into the trees, as silent as before, moving in a curve calculated to come out of the woods more or less opposite the labourer and his mattock. As he went he slipped his knife inside his tunic and, forming a makeshift plan, tightened the drawstring at the top of his pouch.

He stood beside fluttering leaves of hazel and whitebeam. At his back was the forest, his world. Before him stretched the alien fields. And there, across the slope, was a stocky man working on his own.

Tagart stepped into the open. The man with the mattock looked up suspiciously.

Tagart set his face in a smile and went on.

'I come in friendship,' he said.

Part 2

1

'It cannot be Tsoaul,' said Vude, a grandfather with white hair and walnut-brown face and arms, one of the elders in the Council and a supporter of Sturmer. 'It cannot be him. How can it when the nomads are all dead?' He turned his eyes again to the stone pointer, and to the mattock thrust by its haft into the ground beside it. The mattock looked like the one Gumis had taken the previous evening, and this was the place where Sturmer had told him to clear stones, but of Gumis himself there was no sign. He had not returned at nightfall, nor had he been seen at daybreak, which had come cloudy and cool, with pearly mists above the river and the rain-soaked fields.

When it was realized in the village that Gumis was truly missing, a search party set out: Sturmer, Vude, Domack the Tool-mender, Merth, Tamben, and several others. They had gone first to the top barley field and were mystified to find the stone arrow pointing towards the forest.

'It cannot be Tsoaul,' said Vude for the fourth or fifth time, but his voice lacked conviction.

'See the ground,' said Meed, a small, swarthy man with rounded shoulders and a way of twisting his head sideways as he spoke. 'Where is the struggle if Gumis was taken by force?'

Sturmer dropped to his haunches and minutely examined the soil near the arrow. The ground was too rough and stony to show much detail, but Meed's suggestion seemed logical: if there had been a fight it would show. There was no sign of a fight. Hence Gumis had gone of his own free will. It did not occur to Sturmer that the tracks might have been doctored by an expert hand.

'There was no forcing done here,' he concluded. 'We do not know why Gumis should have left his work, but he went in peace.' Sturmer stood up and allowed his gaze to follow the direction of the arrow. 'He left this marker to show us where he had gone.'

'Tsoaul enticed him away!'

'Tsoaul made the marker!'

'That cannot be!' said Tamben, a man of twenty-seven, fair-haired and quiet, who had been coerced into taking part in the raid. 'The nomads are all dead! How can dead men do his will?'

'Then explain why else he should go! There is no reason.'

'A game. He plays a trick on us to make us fearful.'

'If that is so he has already succeeded,' interjected Merth.

Sturmer bit his top lip. 'Gumis does not play tricks; he has no mind for them. He is interested only in food and sleep. He has no time for anything else.'

'Could he have been carried off by some animal?'

'A bear,' said Domack.

Sturmer rounded on him. 'Did a bear make this marker?' he demanded, trying to keep the mounting panic out of his voice. 'Did a bear post the mattock in the ground? Did a bear drag him off and leave no tracks?'

'Then it cannot be Tsoaul,' Vude said calmly. 'The bears are his servants, just like the nomads. The nomads are all dead; there are no tracks; it wasn't a bear. So Tsoaul was not involved. We are worrying for nothing.'

'But Gumis is not here.'

'He has been carried away and killed!'

'Tsoaul has acted to avenge the forest people!'

'No! Listen to me! Listen to me!' Sturmer raised high his arms and shouted over the others.

'He may have been taken by traders!'

'Taken to Valdoe and enslaved!'

'Would they have left a marker?' said Meed.

'Pointing in the wrong direction, just to confuse us!'

'Let Sturmer speak!'

Sturmer slowly rubbed his right forearm, moving his left hand up and down, something he did when nervous. He was glad that Groden was not here. That would have made a bad moment impossible.

Sturmer looked from face to face. There was no alternative. He would have to lie. Vude might have already guessed the truth, and one or two others, but he was counting on them to understand, to keep quiet, not to reveal to the others that a spirit need not necessarily work by agency, need not press bears or nomads into his service; that a spirit if outraged could become substantial and real and work directly on the world. Vude had told stories of his youth, of a day when Burh had been farther west, when the villagers witnessed Aih's descent from the sky like a ball of flame, like lightning in a ball no bigger than a man's head. He came into the compound and many of the villagers tried to touch him.

'My reasoning is this,' Sturmer said. 'First, the nomads are all dead. We made sure of that. Second, there are no tracks to show that Gumis struggled or was dragged away. Third, no animal could have done these things.' He gestured at the mattock and at the lines of neatly-arranged stones. 'Nor,' he said, looking directly at Vude, 'could a spirit, which can act only by agency.'

Vude was about to speak, but closed his mouth and gave an enlightened nod.

Sturmer continued. 'It follows that a man made the marker, and it makes no sense to say that man was anyone but Gumis. If it were traders they would just take him. There would be no reason for them to leave a marker, and besides, we should see their tracks. If – and this is only to complete my reasoning – if Gumis was killed by one of us in the village, the murderer would not leave such clues.'

The others started to protest. Sturmer cut them short.

'I say that Gumis made the marker. He heard or saw something in the forest, and went after it. To show us where, he left this marker, and to show us that it was not dangerous he left his weapon, the mattock, behind. Now, whatever he was following took him deeper into the trees than he had intended to go. He got lost. He is still lost. Unharmed, but lost. That is all. We must go after him and bring him back.' He pointed at the sky. 'It's cloudy. After nightfall and in cloud there is no direction in the forest. We'll find him somewhere walking in circles.'

'Gumis is not our greatest thinker,' said Domack.

The others seized on this explanation. They eagerly agreed, elaborating on Sturmer's theory, recalling past cases of villagers getting lost in the trees. Gumis might have seen a wounded deer and chased it; or he might have heard a strange bird calling and gone to find out what it was. A dozen similar suggestions were made.

'Whatever drew him into the forest, we will not find him by talking,' Sturmer said. 'We must follow the arrow and see where it leads.'

In better humour the villagers set off. 'We'll cut blazes on the trees to guide us back,' Sturmer announced.

Vude fell in beside him. 'You think it is Tsoaul,' he said in a low voice.

'I hope I'm wrong.'

'Will he act now, in the daytime like this?'

'I cannot say. He might. But what else can we do? We must try to find Gumis. He might just be lost as they believe.'

Vude shook his head. 'I have never known him to do anything on his own account. He would not follow a deer into the trees, even if it were already cooked and on a plate. And as for following a strange bird call, Gumis divides birds into two kinds: those that can be eaten, and those that cannot.'

'I know that,' Sturmer said.

'It may not be Tsoaul,' Vude said quietly, and just when Sturmer was about to turn in question he added: 'It may be Gauhm.'

'Gauhm?'

'Groden and the others acted against her wishes. She has been belittled and denied. Twenty-eight of the village, her people, are dead. More are dying even now. Do you think she will be pleased?'

Sturmer did not answer. Over his shoulder he called out, 'If we have not found him by noon we'll send back for help.'

They reached the edge of the field. A broken whitebeam twig, where the trees began, showed where Gumis had entered the forest. Below it a few bramble leaves had been crushed.

'There,' said Domack.

'What is it?'

The Tool-mender reached up and unhooked the talisman from the branch. He weighed it in the palm of his hand, the striped stone smooth against his skin. The talisman had been left dangling on a cord, in plain view at head height. Vude took it. 'This is his,' he said. 'It was made for him by Chal's wife. He wore it always.'

'His fortune stone,' Tamben said. 'I have one the same.' He brought it out of his jerkin and held it up for the others to see.

'Proof he was not taken by force,' Sturmer said. 'It's another sign to us, like the marker. I expect we'll find others. Come.'

They moved forward, filing uphill, through the dense foliage of oak and hazel. It was obvious where someone had passed the night before, the swath of undergrowth crushed and broken down. A few paces on they found a shred of hare's-skin, which someone said came from Gumis's cap. The shred, like the talisman before it, was suspended from a branch and clearly was meant to be noticed.

'Make the first blaze,' Sturmer said.

They went on.

Even at this short distance from the fields it was easy to see how a man might find himself lost inside the wild tangle of vegetation, the unruly hazel, elder, and honeysuckle bushes pressing and twining from all sides, the brambles snagging at shins and forcing frequent detours which rapidly dulled the sense of direction. Above, the ponderous oaks crowded together, the leaves and branches intermingled and forming a dense barrier to all but the feeblest green light. Pigeons exploded from the tree-tops as the men pushed and hacked a way forward.

The ground levelled and dipped, rose again, and again began to fall. Still the crushed path led them on. They found more shreds of his cap, hung on branches like the first. More blazes were cut; soon nobody had any sense of north or south. It seemed they were moving away from the village, and generally downhill, but whether inland or towards the sea they could not tell; though as yet they had not crossed a regular pathway, only the narrow, well-defined courses of badger trails.

'Look there,' Meed said, pointing to a long tatter of doe-skin hanging in the fork of a rowan sapling.

'A piece of his jacket!'

Sturmer took down the strip of leather. 'There is nothing to fear,' he said as the men crowded round to examine it. The strip passed from hand to hand.

Vude said, 'For Gumis to take off his jacket the prey must have been a stag at least.'

'Or a beautiful wood-nymph.'

'Perhaps it was her singing that lured him away.'

'Should we go on, Sturmer?' said Domack with a wink. 'Will she thank us if we find him?'

Sturmer smiled. 'Let us see what else he has taken off.'

Presently, in several places along the way, they came across the rest of his jacket, and then his beaver leggings torn into shreds. Their good humour was beginning to evaporate: the ground was sloping noticeably downwards now, and a sinister change was coming over the woodland. The increasing dampness of the ground was reflected by the character of the trees, younger and less massive, oak giving way to oak mixed with birch, and in the undergrowth there was less holly, less hazel, but more elder. They were being drawn down into the valley, towards the river. They were being drawn towards the nomads' camp.

When they found the clogs, lying casually on the ground ten yards apart, Tamben and several others wanted Sturmer to send back to the village for help.

Sturmer refused. He told them again that there was nothing to fear, that they would doubtless find Gumis a little way ahead; probably dead drunk in the undergrowth with a pot of corn liquor stolen from the Meeting House. Privately, Sturmer could see no reason to endanger extra lives. If they were going to be attacked by a spirit better that a few should die than many; not that he seriously felt there was any real risk. The evil had been done the previous night.

For almost half a mile there was no further clue to the way Gumis had come, except for the crushed vegetation and broken twigs. They came to a stream and crossed it.

The stream marked a more profound change in the quality of the forest. The soil here was black. Alders lined the stream. Beyond it the woodland was mainly birch, with stands and thickets of willow. In places the ground seemed to have collapsed and there was standing water: stagnant pools covered by a bronzy scum over which clouds of gnats danced. The bird sounds were different. The ground was strewn with rotting logs, some half in the water; marsh gas was in the air. Sturmer, leading the way, broke through the old dead branches of willow, the noise of it filling the woods.

He stopped dead.

His eyes did not move.

For the moment he forgot the men behind him, forgot his feet slowly sinking into the boggy ground. He forgot everything. There was no past or future, only the present. Only the present in which the forest was a sepia blur, a background to the place ahead, framing it, the place where a man's five-fingered hand had been speared on a stick and the stick thrust upright into the ground, in plain and intended view.

Sturmer forced aside the last of the elder bushes and at the edge of the clearing stood looking out across the nomads' ruined campsite.

Tamben and Merth, despite his orders, had panicked and turned back, leaving only nine men to follow the trail that had been made of the organs of Gumis's body. Draped over branches or merely thrown down, the signs came at closer and closer intervals. Everyone knew they were being drawn towards the camp; those who were not already armed took up heavy branches and held them like clubs.

They had seen the smoke first, curling upwards through the trees, a single hazy plume of blue woodsmoke which Sturmer could now see was coming from a cooking fire.

With a harsh chatter three magpies, white and green-black, rose from the riverbank and on short round wings fluttered to safety. Simultaneously there was the sound of something falling, crashing through foliage to the ground. Sturmer looked up to see, on the highest branch of a tall oak, the uncertain wavering of a slim, mottled bird of prey as it flexed and unflexed its legs, leaning forwards and backwards, as if deciding whether to leave or stay. A moment later the kite opened its wide wings and with a plaintive cry was sailing away, over the treetops.

Sturmer turned his eyes back to the clearing. It seemed

different by day, larger and more open than before, the surrounding trees farther away. The river had risen. For most of its length through the clearing it was fringed by vegetation, except on the bank nearest the shelters, which was of bare mud leading straight into the water like a beach.

Sturmer had not seen the final devastation of the camp; sickened, he had left when the last of the hunters was overpowered and clubbed down. He had felt no desire to participate in what Groden had planned for the surviving women. Leave no one alive, that was all he had said.

Little of the shelters remained intact: the skeletons of spars and frames, burnt black like charcoal; charred leather; scorched bedding which had escaped being consumed by flame. Broken baskets and other remnants of human occupation had been kicked here and there.

These things Groden had done. But he had not built the cooking fire.

The smoke issued from the middle of the camp; a small heap of sticks smouldered quietly under a spit with a joint of unidentifiable meat. The smell of it on the breeze was like pork. Seated round it, shoulder to shoulder, with eating bowls in their laps or by their feet, were thirty or forty people. Some held their heads erect, others were bowed to the ground. Their eyes looked dark and hollow, their cheeks sunken, their bodies mutilated and disfigured, the colour of decay. They were sitting in a ring round the fire, at a feast. Above them buzzed a multitude of flies.

Domack screamed and ran past Sturmer into the open, brandishing his axe, and the others were running too, yelling and shouting, and Sturmer was among them. One of the feasters fell sideways and lay still. Sturmer raised his mattock and brought it down, opening dead flesh, hacking, slashing. The bodies rolled and yielded to every indignity, every blow, passively accepting, not disapproving, until under the blizzard of axes and clubs and mattocks the dead nomads had been mangled, destroyed, and completely rendered unrecognizable.

But even before they had finished Vude was shouting, pointing into the air and across the river.

On the far bank was the beech tree that had been struck by

lightning in the storm. The heat of the strike had boiled the sap within, sundering the trunk from top to bottom; the foliage hung tattered, shrivelled and scorched. Many of the boughs had been peeled of bark, giving the tree an odd skewbald appearance.

From one of these boughs a curious shape dangled, like a man but then not, slowly turning in the soft breeze, coming to rest, turning in the other direction. It had no hands, and its chest had been opened from throat to navel and roughly cobbled back with twine. One leg was missing below the knee, and with a rush of comprehension Sturmer knew the nature of the meat on the fire.

Domack climbed into the tree and worked his flint blade through the rope. The dummy thumped to the ground.

He had been skinned. Cleanly and expertly, he had been skinned. To give it bulk the skin had been stuffed with leaves and twigs; as it struck the ground they saw something moving in its chest, crawling and glistening brown. Ants were crawling out. They were boiling over the sides of his chest. An ants' nest had been put inside him. They were already everywhere, all over him, his body, in his nostrils, between the taut lips. The skull had been left in. The features of the face, though sunken and changed, could be those of no one else.

It was Gumis.

2

Not long after the farmers left, taking the skin of their comrade with them, Tagart came down from his vantage in a low branch of a durmast oak and stood surveying the mutilated bodies of his tribe.

He was past anger, for he had ruined it. His trap had worked to perfection, precisely to plan: the men had been open targets, so easy to get in four or five quick shots while they were running amuck among the corpses. Five shots, five dead farmers, and he would be down the tree and vanished into the forest before they had time to react: that was his plan, but he had ruined it, in the most simple, stupid and infuriating way possible. He had dropped his arrows.

It happened when the magpies woke him, for he had drifted off to sleep again despite all his efforts to stay alert. As he awoke he started and knocked the quiver from the branch. It fell, the strap slipping away before he could grasp it. One of the farmers seemed to have heard it, but his attention was drawn by a kite which evidently had dropped in to take a closer look at the camp and its occupants.

Thereafter Tagart had been forced to sit quietly, watching impotently from his tree.

But in a way the trap had not failed utterly: he had managed to frighten them, and he had shown himself that he could draw them out of the village, manipulate them into situations of his own choosing; it was a disappointment that the chief, the beardless man, had not been among the search party – not that Tagart would have killed him. He was reserving that task till last.

Tagart collected his arrows and left the camp behind at once, determined never to go back. The bodies of the tribe meant nothing to him, not even that of Balan: they were mere objects, the spirits within having departed long since, but the place itself held memories and he did not want to see it again.

* * *

The rain came and went during the afternoon, in the wake of big piles of cumulus cloud drifting along the coast from the ocean and the west. Towards evening the cloud thinned, became patchy, and occasional shafts of sunshine glanced across the treetops. Smoky white vapour edged the areas of blue which slowly proceeded east.

Tagart emerged from the yew branches and sat cross-legged on the ground, chewing a strip of venison, a water-bag at his side. He felt much better for the food and for his afternoon sleep, spent in the cool half-light under the yew. In his mind he was at peace for the first time since the raid, for Mirin was gone and could never come back. Their life together was over. He had been robbed of her touch, her softness. And he had been robbed of his son. But as he ate he filled his void with peaceful thought, the only way to keep himself calm and level, and consciously, studiously, he kept his mind from the chilling prospect of what he had decided to do next. His arm was healing, the pain in his chest less. His rib, he was sure, had not been broken after all. Strength was returning. He straightened his legs and appraised the muscles, relaxed his calves and felt them loosen completely, then flexed them and they were as hard as wood. He was aware of his body, his sense of speed and balance, and he was glad, glad that he could run as fast as any.

A final strip of meat, a final draught of water, and he chose three blades from his flints, hitched his pouch to his belt, and left the yew behind.

To get downwind of the bears' den he made a long detour, circling back uphill through the oak trees and the thickets of hazel. It took him a long time to cover silently the half mile of final approach to the root-pit where the she bear had given birth to her litter. The hearing of a bear was said to be phenomenal, second only to its sense of smell. In the tribe it was said that a bear could smell fear. If that was so, Tagart told himself as he gingerly moved branches aside, he had doubly good reason for keeping leeward of the den and its mouth.

The den was on a slight gradient, sloping downhill from west to east. It was situated in a glade of large oaks with ground cover of holly, bramble and dog-rose. Two hundred paces from the root-pit Tagart halted yet again to listen. He heard nothing of the bears. He went on, halting, going on again, until he reached the place where he had hidden before, with the others of the tribe, that day when they had kept watch on the den and its occupants. He climbed into the tree they had used, stopping when he was near the top, forty feet from the ground.

He looked down. The ground rose from thc base of his tree, foreshortened from this angle, sloping up to the den, which was twenty-five or thirty feet below the level of his vision. His view of the entrance was obstructed partly by the uprooted trunk of the oak, partly by intervening vegetation; but he could see well enough to know when one of the bears came in or out.

From within came the faint cries of the cubs. Tagart composed himself to wait.

Bears were the masters of the forest. They hunted anywhere, indifferent to day or night: nothing threatened them, nothing could bring down an adult bear unless it was sick or wounded. Bears in open country were big enough, but those in the forest attained almost unbelievable size through easy living. Females of four or five hundred pounds were commonplace, and in the densest regions lived males which might reach six hundred pounds in the rich months of late summer and autumn. Yet in a run the bears belied their size, and in staying power and resistance to fatigue and pain they were superior to the aurochs which could run for days though mortally wounded.

Their only real enemy was the cold, which they detested, and when winter began to bite they sought out caves and other natural hollows which afforded shelter. It was during competition for these shelters that most fatal encounters between men and bears took place, for, though extremely daring and expert hunting parties – usually spurred by hunger – could exceptionally trap and lance a bear, men were with good reason afraid of the bears and left them severely alone. Trackers of the tribe would find and mark out the breeding sites: and from then on, during the summer's stay, entry to those parts of the forest would be forbidden. Only a madman ventured near a bear's den, and only a man who no longer wished to live went near to or made the merest or most tentative threat to anything that had the remotest connection with their breeding and their young. And inside that hollow under the oak roots were not only two helpless bear cubs, but two fully-grown females, one a nursemaid having all the attributes of the mother except that it was smaller and even faster and would catch hold of and devour Tagart even more quickly, for its jaws were just as strong, its claws as sharp, its devotion to the cubs and fierceness in their defence just as well developed.

He would be killed. He knew he would be killed. It was suicide to remain a moment longer. He would jump down from the tree and run. Run from the she bear, a carnivore, an omnivore, the forest's chosen one, ultimate receiver of all its bounty, its most perfect design for killing: three times his weight, a mountain of brown fur over driving muscle that could power a single lazy slash of her huge front paw to scoop out hearts and lungs and viscera, in her jaws a glistening crowd of sharp white teeth which were there for nothing but ripping flesh, stripping bones, grinding pelvises and shoulders and heads. He prepared to move, to come down the tree and be on his way, to abandon this madness and think of some other plan.

But even before he could release his grip on the branch the mother bear came out. As she emerged from the den she rose up to her full height, and on two legs towered for a moment before dropping to all fours. She looked from side to side, and then, seeming to scent something, took on immediate purpose as she looked straight ahead, directly at him.

Tagart remained absolutely still, praying that what he had been told by the elders was true, praying that their lore still held. For what he knew of bears had been told him by others. They had told him that a bear could not take his scent from this position; that he would betray himself only by movement, and only then if the movement were pronounced, because a bear's eyes were weak and poorly suited to recognizing shapes alone.

The other female came up out of the hole behind her, a

smaller animal, with paler fur, her ears flat against her head. The mother turned to greet her, and then the nursemaid was leaving on the hunt, going past the roots of the fallen oak, trotting south among the holly, along the line of the hill. The outline of her rounded, brown body appeared and reappeared among the trees, merged with the vegetation, and she was gone.

The mother bear irritably shook her head as if to dislodge a fly. She seemed in no hurry to leave, if indeed she were going to: she might have been hunting during the afternoon. Again Tagart heard the mewling of the whelps. The she bear went partly back into the den, and it seemed as if she meant to bring the cubs outside to play in the dusk. But she turned and came out alone, and once more reared up with crinkled nostrils. Something was worrying her.

The sun had gone behind the hill. Deep shade filled the forest. A long way off to the south a nightjar was churring, keeping to one note, changing up, changing down. It too would be hunting soon, wheeling and zigzagging over the bracken, snapping and gaping its wide bill at the moths and dor-beetles as it flew.

The light was deteriorating: Tagart refocused his eyes a little to one side of the she bear so that he could see better. She had dropped down again and was washing, licking her paws with a long pink tongue. He fancied he could almost hear the rough skin rasping against her fur.

The she bear finished her toilet and yawned, revealing for the first time her rows of murderous white teeth.

Without warning, she was leaving. Tagart watched in consternation as she started downhill towards his tree. He had foreseen the possibility, but it had all been part of the risk and he had not considered it further. He was considering it now. What if she scented him or his trail? What if she scented him and climbed into the tree? If she made a little spring from the ground and her claws took purchase, and with terrifying rapidity passed branch after branch on her way up the trunk towards him; driving him higher, higher, until there was no height left and she had hold of his legs . . . The wind had not changed: it was blowing steadily from the west, but inside the forest anything was possible, even with a steady west wind. The trees could take a current and break it up, scattering scent in all directions; they could even reverse it. What had been a remote and theoretical problem now took on new significance as the she bear approached. He heard the crush of sticks and undergrowth, and as the distance reduced he made out her eyes, nose, the features of her head; the rolls of fat at her neck; the curve of her claws as her feet, slightly turned in, came padding forward.

The bear was yards from his tree. If she chose to stop and look up she could not fail to see him. His bowels felt loose as he looked down. He clung desperately to the branch, holding his breath, holding himself in, not daring even to think in case she heard.

A moment later her broad back was passing below. She trotted on, downhill through the holly and hazel, each step taking her further below Tagart's level and away from the stream of his scent. He turned and watched her go. She went under the trees, and in a matter of seconds Tagart had lost sight of the bear, of her huge haunches swaying among the undergrowth. She had gone.

Now was the time to get down, to get away. He had been wrong to refuse himself help: he would leave at once and find another nomad group, and with them return in strength to the village to carry out his vow. That is what he should have done from the start; that is what Cosk would have done. Tagart had let his pride take him too far, and as a result he had nearly killed himself for no reason.

With almost no concession to silence he scrambled from branch to lower branch, not caring how badly he might bark his knees or scrape his arms. He paused at the last ten feet and dropped noiselessly on slack knees to the ground.

It was almost dark. The nightjar had stopped singing. Tagart glanced at the fallen oak.

Suddenly he found himself running uphill.

Running uphill, his hand reaching into his pouch to free his knives from their soft wrappings of leather. The yards were behind him: he was standing beside the roots at the mouth of the den, by the mass of soil and stones that had been dragged up by the tree's fall. Before he could change his mind he was stooping, scrambling down into the fetid warmth of the den, a flint blade in his hand.

The bears had tunnelled some way into the earth under the root ball. He could hear the cubs at the end of the tunnel, a few feet ahead. He could see nothing: the only light was a dim greyness from the entrance behind him. The smell of the bears, rich and gamey, almost choked him; the cubs' high-pitched cries reached his ears. His head struck the earthen roof of the tunnel and dislodged a crumble of soil. He reached down and felt warm, coarse fur. He had hold of a cub. It struggled half-heartedly as he lifted it by the loose skin at its neck; but then, realizing that it was not a bear who held it, the cub squirmed strenuously and its cries became louder and more urgent. Tagart felt for and with his left hand clamped the jaws shut. The cub was still small, and no match for him in strength, but its milk-teeth were sharp. The other cub was alert now, snapping at his ankles. He kicked it aside, turned, and, bending double with the cub tucked under his arm, he started along the tunnel to its mouth and freedom.

As he came into the open air he changed his knife from his right hand to his left, and without stopping slashed the blade across the cub's neck. The blood welled, dripped to the holly and the ground. After a moment's resistance the cub went limp in his arms and it was dead.

He ran as he had never run before, away from the den, away from the directions taken by mother and nursemaid, caring nothing now for wind or scent, plunging through the forest and the growing night, exultant, alive, set free. Power, triumph, intoxication possessed him as he ran. In his arms he carried a few pathetic pounds of lifelessness: fat and muscle and unformed bone.

But it was more than a dead bear cub he carried. It was the means to draw out the beardless man, the means to draw him out and kill him.

3

The death of Gumis had thrown a shadow over the village. What remained of his body was laid on the Dead Ground; later, it would join those who had died in the raid, buried in the village mound on the western side of the valley. The dead man had no wife and no real family in Burh, and few people whom he had called his friends.

For some reason she did not care to fully understand – she did not admit to a feeling of guilt – Hernou put herself forward as the first watcher in the vigil over his body. She stationed herself beside him, close to the Meeting House, a cape over her shoulders, for the evening was cool. The sun lingered on the hill beyond the palisade, a trembling globe of fire that bulged and became misshapen as the earth drew it down. The underbellies of the few high clouds were lit with orange; the rest of the sky was without feature, a greyish blue turning steadily violet. Over the forest the first stars of the constellations showed as tiny points.

The sun went below the horizon, filling the west with red light. Hernou felt the breeze stir on her cheek. She clasped her arms about her knees and gently rocked from side to side. Across the compound, lamps were coming on one by one. Normally the evenings saw eating outside, in groups of ten or twenty, but tonight each family kept to itself. Behind her in the Meeting House Hernou heard footsteps and voices, and lights were being lit there too. From its windows a yellow glow came over the Dead Ground and the collapsed and empty corpse, making Gumis one colour, a drab brown with deep folds and shadows of black. He was still being discussed inside the Meeting House: his death and its implications were keeping the inner circle of the Council late in session.

Groden was not part of the inner circle, not yet, and he had gone to the house of Morfe to eat. Groden had acquitted himself well in the Council that day, Hernou told herself. How could anyone have foreseen that Tsoaul would act without agency to avenge the nomads? For that was the explanation given by Sturmer and Vude for the disappearance and death of Gumis. Knowing that Tsoaul himself was involved, no one in the village but Sturmer harboured any longer even a slight resentment against Groden for the outcome of the raid. The rain had come, as Groden had promised. He could not be blamed for Tsoaul's intervention.

Vude then related a tale of his boyhood, when Aih had appeared in the compound like a ball of flame. The head man, Vude told them, had offered a sacrifice to Gauhm and Aih did not return. If Gauhm could do that, Vude reasoned, could she not do the same with Tsoaul? So during the afternoon Sturmer, the Council, and the whole village made prayer at the small shrine in the Meeting House – they did not dare venture into the forest to attend the shrine on the cliffs – and three lambs and a calf were killed and their blood allowed to run into the ground as an offering to Gauhm, in hope that she would be able to appease Tsoaul on the villagers' behalf.

Hernou brought the cape further round her shoulders and shivered. With each passing minute fewer people were to be seen. The ground was losing heat. On her right she heard the murmur of the river. From the outskirts of the village came the hard, sharp barking of a dog fox, and with it the shrilling of a blackbird flushed from its roost, somewhere near the east gate.

The lights went out in the Meeting House and Sturmer and the others came down the plank steps.

'Till morning then, Sturmer,' came Vude's distinctive voice.

'Till morning.'

Hernou glanced to her left. Sturmer was crossing the open ground to the big house nearby.

He stooped and went through the flap of leather at his doorway, and for a brief and painful moment she glimpsed the picture of warmth and cosiness within.

The ladder Tagart had fashioned the previous day was where he had left it, hidden in the undergrowth at the top of the escarpment. It was fifteen feet long, more a ramp than a ladder, covered sparsely with brushwood to keep its weight low. The thing had been heavy and unwieldy enough in daylight, but now it was almost impossible. Tagart was making so much noise dragging it down the escarpment that he was sure he would be heard in the village. He did not really care. Being captured by the farmers would be a hundred times preferable to what would happen to him if he took too long in getting the ladder to the bottom of the escarpment.

He tripped on an anthill, lost his footing, and fell for the third time. The ladder came down heavily on his leg. A dog fox was barking nearby; as Tagart fell he disturbed a roosting blackbird from the brier patch. He breathed a curse and struggled to his feet.

There were lights in the village, and food smells on the wind. Tagart hauled the ladder over the anthills. No sound of alarm had yet come from the other side of the palisade. He got under the ladder and raised it, positioning the top against three spikes. The slope was steep – too steep. And would the brushwood stand the load? He did not think so, but there was no time to consider it. He freed the dead cub from where he had tied it, at the end of the ladder so that it dragged along the ground, and, holding it to his chest, climbed the brushwood rungs.

His head came level with the top and he looked into the village. The lights in the Meeting House had now gone out. Lamps flickered elsewhere in several windows of the dwelling houses with their conical roofs. It was too dark to see properly: he could not tell whether there were any people in the compound.

A dog started barking. He dropped the cub over the palisade and climbed over the top, turning round and gripping the spikes, lowering himself as far as he could before letting go and dropping the last six or seven feet to the ground. He landed well, next to the cub.

Taking the cub by a limp hind leg, he dragged its muzzle through the grass as he ran, half-crouching, along the line of the palisade. The houses were on his left, passing him by. Still he saw no one, but more dogs were barking and he expected trouble from them at any moment. He reached the bakery, the last of the buildings before the river, and paused. Beyond the bakery loomed the Meeting House, its walls and stilts and steps silhouetted by lights from the large dwelling house on the far side. This house, Tagart knew, would be that of the chief: that of Sturmer, the beardless man. His eyes glowed. She might be in there at this very moment, Sturmer's woman, the one he had seen at the ceremony. He had seen her well and marked her features as she lay naked, drinking the beardless man's urine from a wooden bowl. He hoped he would be able to restrain himself when the time came to take her into the forest. To kill her too soon would be a tragedy. And he prayed he would not come face to face with Sturmer himself, not yet.

He left the cub by the bakery wall and ran to the river. He slipped into the water, which flowed with sparkles of starlight on green and black and closed over his head without a sound; he dived and wriggled into the slime, came up for breath, dived again, feeling and then not feeling its subtle touch on his skin. Bubbles of methane wallowed up to the surface and broke about his head. He dived three times in all, ridding himself of all trace of scent of bear-den and blood, masking his own odour with the sulphurous smell of the mud on the river bottom. Letting the current float him, he drifted past the jetty, past the roof of the Meeting House, black and angular where it shut out the stars, and came to the timbers of the bridge.

He clung to them in the middle of the river, his hair wet and the gritty taste of the river mud on his lips. The water flowed about him with small throaty sounds. His eyes were near the surface, below the rise of the banks, which were blacker than the river and sky, tall with vegetation. Above him the bridge was utter darkness. The hollowness underneath it amplified the river noises, and Tagart strained to listen. He wanted to hear what was happening, away from the river, far away on the other side of the village.

With his chin in the water, he waited.

He did not have to wait for long.

The bear came at speed down the escarpment, in her anguish paying no attention to the obstacles in her way: brambles, briers, oak bushes, tussocks, the anthills at the bottom. Without pause she scaled the ramp of brushwood and, merely noticing the eleven-foot drop on the other side of the palisade, gained entry to the village.

She had followed the scent of the he cub from the den, each drop of its sweet blood glowing like a marker in the dark. Mingled with the trail she caught the sickly musk of human feet, and long before the circuitous route began nearing the village she knew that the he cub had been taken by men.

The smell of them was everywhere on the inside of the palisade: their bodies, their animals, their cooking fires and the things they ate. She found the scent of the cub at once, leading beside the palisade towards the smell of water. On her left she was aware of lights, and a throng of barking dogs, and she was aware of the fire she feared, coming from the houses; and as she lumbered towards the river she heard for the first time men's voices raised in alarm.

Hernou stood up as she heard the shouting. Her first reaction was disbelief. The cries of Bear made no sense. The village was bear-proof; everyone knew it. She ran from her vigil-place to the corner of the Meeting House, by the steps, where there was a better view. The disturbance was on the far side of the village, by the palisade. Figures of men and dogs were outlined in the light of torches and burning brands. And then she saw the running bulk of the bear as it appeared between two houses, and she knew the inconceivable had happened.

The nightmare of a bear loose in the compound, with nowhere for her to hide, nowhere safe, had come true.

Sturmer, alerted by the shouting, armed himself with a spear and came out of his doorway. Hernou turned her head as the flap raised and lowered, revealing the light inside.

'It's there!' she shouted at him.

'Get inside! Get under cover! I want no one loose!'

She held on to the beams of the Meeting House, numb with fear. The other men, and many of the women too, were appearing at their doorways. Sturmer did not stop to argue with Hernou further. He was yelling orders, trying to organize the villagers, hoping to pin the bear inside a semi-circle backing on to the palisade, where it could be held at bay with torches and in time wounded with enough spears to immobilize or even kill it. But the bear had already broken through the line and was running towards the bakery, away from the palisade. Two villagers had been cuffed, another seized and worried in its jaws. The screams of the dying were lost in the confusion of shouting and yelling.

'Force it into the river! Deak, Tamben, Domack! This way! Over here!'

Hernou did not wait to hear any more. She thought of hiding in the Meeting House, but its doorway was wide enough to admit a bear. The nearest safety was Sturmer's house. She ran across to its threshold and pushed aside the entrance flap, scrambling through the porch into the kitchen.

Sturmer had been interrupted at his meal. In front of the hearth were wooden platters, clay spoons and bowls, and cowhorn cups in wooden stands, left half full of food and drink. Hernou passed through the kitchen into the central chamber, and through that into the main room with the tall roof. Here Sturmer's wife Tamis and her four children sat in the rumpled bed of fur and skins, huddling together for protection and comfort. The younger children were crying; the eldest looked up fearfully as Hernou pushed her way into the room.

'Your house was the nearest,' Hernou said. 'Sturmer told me to hide myself.'

Tamis nodded. 'Have you seen it? Where is it?'

'By the bakery.'

Tamis shut her eyes.

'They can kill it,' Hernou said. 'I know they can.'

'We must pray for our lives. Tsoaul has sent the bear; only Gauhm can save us.' She looked with hatred at Hernou, at her grey eyes, her hair, her smooth brown skin, the body that the men still found attractive, watching her deliberate walk as she crossed the compound. Tamis knew that Sturmer had once made love to her – and she knew that Hernou wanted Sturmer back. 'You and your Groden have brought this on us. You have brought evil to this village.'

'That's not true!'

'Then how did your husband's dog die?'

Even with lights and spears and arrows the villagers had been unable to force the bear into the river, where it would have been hampered by the water and mud. Instead it had stopped by the bakery wall. At its feet they saw it had brought a dead cub with it. Raised up on hind legs, the bear slashed out wildly with its forepaws. In the flickering torchlight it looked brown and shaggy against the wood of the wall.

Groden hit it with yet another arrow in the throat and the bear began a strange, piteous wailing. It stumbled blindly forward and lunged with a wide paw, catching Meed a blow that sent him flying. The bear checked its lunge; lashed out again, missing Morfe by the width of a hand. He did not move: he had armed himself with a felling axe, and in the torchlight his eyes glittered and his teeth showed between his lips.

'The snout!' Sturmer screamed. 'Hit the snout!'

Morfe took no notice. He knew what to do.

He had positioned himself for just this blow, and as the bear wagged its head from side to side the axe-head came sailing down, and, judged by Morfe's mad, cold, calculating eye, the stone struck its muzzle and it had a muzzle no more.

The bear gave a bellowing squeal and again raised itself up, but it went too far, staggering on its hind legs, and then it was toppling, falling backwards, and more arrows and spears were raining into its belly and chest. Its head and shoulders hit the bakery wall and broke through the planking, splintering the wood and leaving fresh white break-marks. The villagers ran forward and thrust spears into its belly. The legs thrashed; twitched; and lay still.

It was only then that they realized a second bear, bigger than the first, had got into the compound.

No one saw it clamber over the palisade and run along the line of scent. The mother bear was upon them from behind even as Morfe dealt the nursemaid its death-blow.

Left and right the second bear bowled villagers out of the way with swingeing forepaws. Skulls, rib-cages, pelvises were fractured and crushed. Faces were trodden into the ground by huge hind-paws. A woman was taken up in the mother's jaws and her waist almost bitten through before she was flung aside.

Sturmer and Groden were frantically pulling arrows and spears from the carcase of the first bear as the mother turned on them, scattering weapons and lights, pawing and swiping and striking down man after man. The mother turned to her side, selected Domack's wife, ran her down and with bared jaws grabbed her shoulder; now on hind legs, now on all fours, the bear dragged her along, let her drop, reared up with a roar.

'Get back!' Sturmer screamed as he saw Tamis running across the compound. 'Get back! Get back!'

She had left the house when she realized there were two bears to be killed, knowing that everyone would be needed, every hand. She had argued with Hernou, but Hernou had refused to help and had stayed behind.

Hernou could hear the screaming and shouting, the cries of the wounded and dying, the injured and destroyed, and for the first time she began to fear that there might not be enough people left to deal with the bear. It might win. And if it won, it might in its systematic plunder of the village come here and seek her out. She thought of placing Sturmer's children at the entrance, as a decoy, so that if the bear came it would take them and not her. But what if the children served only to attract the bear to this house above all others? Surely it was better for her to wait in the entrance herself, where she could see what was happening. If the bear came, she could run into the bedchamber and escape through the window, while it forced its way into the back of the house and was delayed by the children. That would give her the best chance of making a run for the gate. And if it did not come here first, but went to the other side of the village, she needed to know the best time to escape: she needed to be able to see.

'Stay here quietly,' Hernou told the eldest child. 'Your mother will be back soon.'

Hernou briefly wondered about Groden. He was fighting the bear, she assumed. There was nothing she could do to help him.

She moved aside the flap of leather into the middle chamber, and crawled through it into the kitchen. Here the lamps were still flickering, giving an unsteady light, smoking and giving off the smell of burning fat; but with this smell was the smell of wet leather and mud, and before Hernou could turn and run into the bedchamber there was a rustling in the porch and she was looking into the eyes of a wild-haired and mud-streaked man, a man she had never seen before, not of the village, but dressed in skins like a nomad. His high cheekbones and wide, tall forehead, and the hard line of his chin, gave him under the matted tangle of his hair and beard the semblance of a demon, and Hernou knew she was looking upon the spirit of the nomads in human form: she was looking upon Tsoaul. She was looking upon the Forest God, who had brought down a plague of bears on Burh and would destroy every man and woman and every thing in the village, who was coming for her now because she had incited Groden and it was Groden who had led and engineered the raid on the nomads' camp.

'Cry out and I'll kill you.'

She could make no sound, and feebly submitted as he grasped her arm and pulled her towards the entrance. She preceded him, crawling through the porch and into the open air.

In a daze she stood up. The Forest God came behind her, and he stood up, much taller than she. Across the village the screams were undiminished; Hernou could see lights dancing, the rush of people as the bear changed direction, dark and formless in the light.

The stars were overhead: she felt only the wind from his fist as Tsoaul struck her. She saw a waterfall of colour, and heard a thin, high keening, and then blackness overtook her and she knew nothing more.

Tagart caught her as she fell and hefted her on to his shoulders. She was not heavy, and he ran between the houses of the village, gained the thoroughfare, and in a few moments reached the east gate. He threw down his load and impatiently wrested aside the heavy oaken bars. The shouts and cries far across the village seemed to indicate that the mother bear had been hit – he could not tell how severely. But if she had been mortally wounded and the fighting was coming to an end, there could be no more time to lose.

He swung the gate aside. No one but Sturmer's woman had seen him so far, of that he was certain. In his desire not to reveal his existence he had been almost too cautious, leaving it to the last minute before coming out of the river and crossing the compound to the head man's house, the house of Sturmer, the beardless man, where Tagart hoped and prayed he would find the woman he had seen at the ceremony. And indeed he had almost left it too long. He had almost missed her.

Tagart tore off the woman's doeskin dress and dropped it on the ground by the gate. There was no time for subtlety: he had to leave a clue, a pointer, something to tell the farmers that she had not merely run away, that they were to follow and try to get her back.

He slung her body round his neck and in the chilly summer night, crisp with the first hint of autumn, started for the forest and the yew tree where he had made his lair.

4

Already the summer was dying, spent and overblown. The breath of decay blew through the forest, on old leaf mould, on fallen logs and the dead branches of diseased trees: the rains in their wake had brought the first flush of fungi. From their underground threadworks of mycelium they groped upward: shaggy caps, opening like feathered parasols that softened into dribbling slime; autumn morels, white and grey and rust; blushers, which stained cut-red like flesh where they were bored and nibbled by beetles; fairy clubs, tiny white antlers powdered with spores; troops of wood mushrooms, as wide as umbrellas or small grey-white bulbs; stinkhorns that smelled of carrion; wood woollyfoots, yellow stainers, puffballs, earth stars, brackets, champignons, chantarelles; boleti which appeared suddenly among the grass-blades; and the edible grisettes, opening from papery white flasks, just like the others of their tribe which were not edible: fly agaric, red and white-spotted, the fungus gathered by the farmers for their casket; the panther, a poisonous kind; and, on bad ground, the destroying angel: beautiful, a white apparition, with a slimy, shining cap, a poison so virulent that a single specimen in a basket of mushrooms was enough to bring horrible and agonizing death. And there was a fourth kind, more poisonous still, growing under oak trees and beech, coming with the first summer rains, in shape and size like a small blusher, but its cap was a dull and inconspicuous olive-green. It resembled a wood-mushroom, and when it was no more than a button could be mistaken for one, but never by the nomads, who knew the death cap and what it would do.

Autumn was in the air. The small birds of the forest had finished their breeding and the tits, nuthatches and tree-creepers were coming together in groups and family parties that would swell and become roaming bands; the robins and redstarts and thrushes, tailless and moulting, skulked in the tangle near the ground; from their eyrie high in the branches of a dead tree, the young goshawks were making their first tentative flights; cuckoos, whose call had not been heard for weeks, were moving south, towards the sea; and the swifts, climbing on their black sickle wings with feeble screams, revelled in the banks of cloud and would soon be leaving late young to starve.

The aurochs, too, were on the move, each bull with his cows. At night their bellowings sounded far through the wooded valleys. Tagart heard them as he lay resting and waiting on his bed of yew needles, in the middle hours of darkness long before dawn. Beside him was the woman, taken from the village earlier that night, now tied at wrists and ankles. To keep her warm Tagart had covered her with skins. He would feed and water her too, to keep her alive.

It was still dark when she regained consciousness. Tagart heard her breathing change, and smiled to himself as she cunningly made her breaths longer as if she had not awoken at all.

'What is your name?' he said.

She did not reply. Tagart knew she had heard him, and he knew she had understood. They both spoke the same tongue, and although the farmers' dialect was thick and guttural, closer to the language of their ancestors on the mainland across the channel, during thirty generations of slave-raiding and intermarriage the old language of the nomads had been lost.

'Tell me your name, woman.'

Still she did not answer. He sensed that her eyes were open in the dark, that she was afraid. The resinous smell of the yew needles filled the air. The woman forgot to regulate her breathing: it came more quickly, and Tagart could almost hear the beat of her heart.

'Tell me your name. I will not hurt you again.'

'You . . . you know my name.'

Tagart frowned into the dark. The woman's quiet, fearladen voice came again.

'You killed Gumis as a sign to us, and you sent your servants the bears to avenge the forest people. You have chosen me because of my husband and I know I am to be sacrificed. I am Gauhm's sacrifice to you.'

Tagart's frown deepened. 'Not if you tell me what I wish to know.'

'But you are Tsoaul and know everything.'

He widened his eyes with new interest. Tsoaul? Who was Tsoaul? 'That is true,' he said. 'I am Tsoaul. But if you are to be spared I must hear these things from your own lips.'

She was silent.

'You must tell me what I wish to know.'

'Yes.' She almost whispered it. 'Yes.'

'First. Why do you call me "Tsoaul"?'

'You . . .' She seemed confused. 'You are the Spirit of the Forest . . . that is your name.'

'I am known by many names.'

'Forgive me.'

'Next. Do all the villagers know that I, Tsoaul, have done these things?'

'Yes. They all know it. They are all afraid.'

'They know that I caused Gumis to die?'

'Yes.'

'And that I sent my servants into your village tonight?'

'They know that also.'

'And do they know that it is in my power to destroy the village?'

She said nothing.

'Next. Tell me of the ceremony in the Meeting House.'

'I . . . I do not know . . .'

'No harm will come to you. Tell me about the ceremony.'

'Which one? There are many ceremonies . . .'

'The morning after the rain returned. Tell me what you were eating in the Meeting House.'

She hesitated, anxious to give the right answer, still not quite sure of the question. 'We eat from the Agaric Casket to go with our dead to the Far Land.'

'To go with their spirits when they die?'

'Yes.'

'Tell me what you eat.'

'A toadstool, prepared by the priest. He calls it "agaric".'

'Explain. What does it look like and where does it grow?'

'It has a white stalk and a red saddle with scales of white. The priest finds it in the woods.'

Tagart nodded to himself. The nomads called it by another name, but he knew it well. 'How is it prepared?'

The woman described the drying process, how the caps were placed in the casket, where the casket was kept. She told him how many caps could be eaten, and she told him the stories the men had recounted of their visions. She said that whenever the agaric was eaten the musicians played, so that the real world could be found again by its music.

'Who is your priest?'

'He is called Sturmer.'

'Sturmer? Your husband?'

'No. My husband's name is Groden.' She bit her tongue. Had she offended her listener? Did Tsoaul know that she had once shared Sturmer's bed, could he look into her heart and know secrets?

'What is the name of the man in your village with no beard?'

She hesitated. 'Groden.'

'And you are called by what name?'

'Hernou.'

'Hernou.'

'Yes.'

'And is your husband head man?'

'No. Sturmer is head man. He is head man and priest too.'

'Sturmer is bearded.'

'Yes.'

'But Groden is of importance in the village?'

The coldness in the question chilled Hernou and made her afraid for Groden. But Groden was in the village and Hernou was here in the forest with Tsoaul and now she realized that she put her own life before Groden's and she answered:

'Yes.'

Drizzle came from the ocean on a warm wind, bringing back summer to the sea cliffs and the line of endless forest. Heavy clouds rolled in the night above the trees. Cold air worked on the clouds and made them rain; the sea broke muddy and listless along the beach, lifting and dropping lines and fragments of black weed, too feeble to make a roar of the shingle drag, and where the waves slopped on the white rocks below the seven striding cliffs the water swirled endlessly and made no spray. At the mouth of the estuary, on a long shingle spit barely emerging from the sea, black-backed gulls stood in roost and waited for first light. Thirty wing-beats away the river debouched into the tide race: its flow was swollen with rain, winding and meandering through the Burh valley. The valley basin was wide and flat, hemmed in by steep forest to the east, and more gently rising forest to the west. In a past age the river had broken through one of its own meanders, leaving stranded an oxbow lake which had become a calm lagoon. From it rose the voices of wildfowl in the dark: mallard, teal, wigeon, shoveler.

Farther up the valley, lights showed from a village of houses overhung by an escarpment, and sometimes the wailing and cries of grief were taken with the smoke and sent by the wind among the trees.

The bodies of the bears had been dragged into the middle of the compound and set on fire. The smell of burning belched into the rain; meat slowly burnt back from skulls and paws, revealing scorched bone.

It was no recompense. They had killed thirty people. Another twelve were dying; fifteen more were maimed. Fewer than a hundred uninjured people were left, the majority of whom were women and children. Forty-three able-bodied men remained. Not many wished to respond to Groden's appeal for help. His wife had been taken: her dress had been found near the east gate.

A path led from the east gate, past the escarpment, rising south-eastwards into the forest. It wound and climbed through the trees; here narrow and closely pressed by undergrowth, there open and wide passing through woodlands of old beech where the death cap fungus grew. Over a dry gorge the path became a wooden bridge, under which Tagart had hung with his flints and bow-drill in the first hours of loneliness after he had been down to the village and watched them in the Meeting House. Concealed ropes led away into the brambles.

Other ropes lay in readiness elsewhere in the forest, other traps. Deadfalls, dug by the Cosks, had been cleared of debris and restored, the spikes made needle-sharp and coated with wolf's-bane. Weights and counterweights waited high above the ground. Snares and loops, nooses and treadles and triggers: one had been fired by a badger, which with the speed of reflexes and impulses running along nerves had leapt clear just as the whip of ropes ripping from the ground signalled the crashing fall of a water-filled skin, straight on to a barb of sharpened holly. The hummel-skin exploded in a drenching gush; the water flooded the ground and slowly drained away. The badger caught the taint of human scent on the crumpled skin and ran off the path into the deeper forest, where soon it was unearthing beetles, the incident forgotten.

Grey dawn had appeared in the east and the inside of the yew tree became less than black, a gloom in which vagueness could be discerned. Hernou watched the features of the young man taking form, and as she watched her suspicions grew stronger. This was no spirit. Would a spirit ask such questions? Would a spirit be wounded and cut about the arms, bruised and dirty? And would a spirit talk in the accents of a nomad?

In repose, his face seemed almost gentle. He looked a little like Groden, but his expression differed and was more like Sturmer's. His brow was tall and delicate. In the line of his jaw and high cheekbones she saw the nomad face, and in the blackness of his beard and glossy hair, and in the texture of his skin, she saw the old complexion, found only in those village-dwellers whose blood was close to the native stock. She noticed his hands. They were scratched and torn, calloused and grimed: strong hands for strangling and punching, gripping weapons.

Hernou was afraid. The nomads were killers. It was the way they lived, by hunting and killing. They thought no more of blood and murder than did the farmers of soil and harvest. The harsh forest life streamlined their tribes and made them strong and ruthless, like the animals they sought for their prey; their discipline, their life, were impossible to understand. For them to swim free in the seasons, not to have precise tasks for each week and day, but to wander the land by whim, thrust the nomads far beyond comprehension. Even after all these generations the farmers still felt themselves to be strangers, foreigners. Their true home lay across the sea. The only true natives were the nomads.

Across his shoulders and the top of his chest she saw the form of bones and muscle, rising and falling as he slept. In the crook of an elbow she saw his sinews; his legs were relaxed, the great muscles at ease, and his feet, with their hard soles which never knew clogs, lay to the side. An old white scar ran the length of his calf. At his belt he wore a pouch, and an empty sheath for blades. His garment was a tunic of thick leather, its sleeves held by stitched thongs of seal-hide. The tunic was too small: it didn't look as if it had been made for him. Hernou thought of the things Groden had plundered from the nomads' camp. There had been several such tunics among them. Perhaps the one this young man was wearing had been overlooked, just as he himself must have been overlooked by those who Groden said had gone round with axes, making certain. Below the tunic he wore a breechclout of soft doeskin. That too looked as if it had been made for another.

Everything Hernou saw about him, everything she thought, hardened her conviction. This was no spirit.

He awoke with a blink, as if he had felt the touch of her eyes on his face. For a moment he said nothing, and Hernou's heart hammered more violently. She was helpless; she could not move. Her hands were bound behind her back, and her shoulders ached. The nomad had tied her at ankles and wrists and lashed the bonds to the yew trunk.

He sat up and turned to one side, away from her. 'Do you want something to eat? Water?'

When she did not reply he stopped busying himself among the provisions and looked back at her face. She nodded.

'If you wish to shit, tell me so. I do not want this place fouled.' He put a rib of venison before her. 'Now I will free your hands to eat.' He went behind the yew trunk and untied the lashings; she rubbed each wrist in turn, soothing away the chafing and trying to bring back circulation.

'I beg you, free my ankles.'

'Why? Do you want to go outside?'

'My ankles hurt.'

He considered briefly, and did as she asked. She gratefully massaged her ankles. She was naked under the skins the nomad had provided; the skin covering her shoulder slipped, but she did not trouble to restore it. Hernou looked surreptitiously from under her brow. He was watching.

'Eat,' he said.

She diffidently picked up the rank venison. It smelled bad, but out of fear she tried to tear off a piece and chew. The taste made her gag. She felt her gorge rising, and for a moment thought she would be sick. The nomad was already swallowing; he caught her eye and seemed amused. He passed her a waterbag. She pulled out the wooden bung, and although the water was musty and stale she drank deeply, for her mouth was dry.

'Rain again,' the nomad said, gesturing with his piece of meat at the forest outside, where the water dripped from the trees. 'That is good. Good for me, bad for them.'

'What does Tsoaul plan?' she said. The beating of her heart filled her head. She was near to panic, hysteria, but she knew she had to say something or it would be too late.

'Don't worry. You will be safe. Do as I say and you will be safe.'

The skin covering her shoulder slipped further, revealing her breasts. She did not take her eyes from his face. The nomad was watching her, no longer chewing, his eyes in shadow. She reached down and slowly took the leather in her fingers and pulled it aside. Her hand opened and let it fall. Inch by inch, she stretched out her arm to touch his hand with her own.

Still he did not move. The water dripped among the foliage outside. She felt her fingertips meet the warm skin of his hand.

He gave his head a dismissive shake and drew his hand away.

His voice came then, heavy with contempt. 'Now I understand why they rape children and women who do not love them.'

'I – '

'Get dressed. We must be leaving now. Tie back your hair.'

She did as he had ordered; the nomad tied her up again,

tighter than before, and between her wrists he tied a longer piece of rope, a halter so that she could be pulled along. He picked up three bows, and from the ground collected a number of things to go into his pouch.

'It is time to leave,' he said.

5

The search party filed through the east gate, passing over the spot where Hernou's dress had been found, walking in pairs, armed with hammers and axes and bows and spears. In front went Sturmer, beside him Ockom, a tall man dressed in black skins. Morfe and Groden came last. As they left the protection of the palisade those staying behind swung the gate back and dropped the bars into place. Fifteen men had been left to defend the village, too few, against Sturmer's better judgement; but at length he had given in to Groden's persuasion. The village had lost enough people. They had to try to get Hernou back for this if no other reason. The search party was selected and armed, twenty-eight men, and set out at once, barely two hours after dawn.

Few of the men had not lost someone the previous night. Sturmer had been spared: his wife and children were safe, but some men had seen two or even three members of their family killed or maimed.

The path from the east gate – for surely that was the one Tsoaul had meant them to follow, just as he had laid signs to Gumis – was well known by all the villagers. They walked it regularly. It led generally south-east; after skirting the escarpment it rose by a series of swings into the forest. A thousand yards on, at the halfway point, it crossed a dry gorge by means of a cantilever bridge, built to save a long detour. The gorge walls, sheer and white where the chalk was exposed, or rubble-strewn and grown with rough brambles and shrubs, dropped to a fern-filled bottom. Beyond the gorge the path turned south, and then east, coming out by the sward-covered cliffs and the sea, at the Shrine to Gauhm.

The men had come a long way into the woods by now, moving forwards cautiously, stopping when Sturmer raised his hand. On either side the rugged trunks of oak and hornbeam were streaked with rain; under the trees the light was bad.

The path turned once again to the left and opened out into a small clearing by the bridge over the gorge. Sturmer signalled a halt.

The gorge, which at one time had carried a stream down to the sea, was part of a long rift which gradually widened and formed the separation between two of the seven chalk cliffs, on the fifth of which stood the Shrine. The rift carried back into the forest for a mile north of the bridge. One of Sturmer's predecessors had built the bridge, thirty feet wide, a long platform of oak logs buttressed into each side of the gorge with oak and beech. Below it the gorge fell away sharply, thirty-five feet deep, its walls partly clad with the roots and twisted branches of stunted shrubs, growing badly in the subsoil. Brambles and tufts of male fern grew among and across the chalk rubble at the bottom.

Sturmer turned to Ockom. 'Do you think it's safe to cross?'

The bigger man bit his lip, his eyes, normally wry and humorous, now dull and flat. His brother had been mauled by the bears. Ockom was reckoned the best man in the village for fieldcraft. He knew the different animal tracks, the names of all the trees and plants that had names to know. He said, 'There has been no sign of her this far. I see none now. I think it is safe. But send Groden across first – it's his wife we're risking ourselves for.'

Sturmer addressed Groden. 'We fear an ambush. You cross first.'

Groden seemed reluctant, but slowly he ventured out across the clearing and on to the logs of the bridge, testing each step, with both hands gripping the rails. He looked over his shoulder. 'Nothing!'

'Cross to the far side!'

Groden did so, jumping the last three feet on to solid ground. He dropped to his knees and as best he could inspected the timbers of the bridge, stood up, and waved the others on.

They crossed singly, Sturmer going last, standing by the lip of the gorge, vigilant for unusual sounds. There were none. The file reassembled on the far side, and, still watching for tracks, Sturmer and Ockom led off.

Sturmer began to wonder whether they had taken the right

direction from the village. They had merely assumed that Hernou had been taken along the Shrine path.

The ground, level for a quarter of a mile, now started sloping down into a shallow dry valley. There had been no evidence of activity anywhere along the path this far: the mud of the path was unmarked by footprints. As the search party descended into the valley Sturmer's doubts deepened. Perhaps Tsoaul had tricked them. Were they going the wrong way? Perhaps Hernou had been taken in an entirely different direction.

He frowned and turned to Ockom. 'Do you see tracks?'

Ockom opened his mouth to speak but then Sturmer flinched as in a rush of wind he heard a loud bang and felt a spray of blood on his face. As Ockom's two hands came up Sturmer could see the arrow where it had struck, in the centre of the upper lip, smashing through the front teeth and emerging at the back of his neck. Sturmer saw the grey goose quills, and all he could think was that they were not quail feathers, they were not like the fins on the arrow that Groden had shot at his dog Uli . . . they were goose quills, on a polished hazel arrow that had come from among the trees and passed a handsbreadth from Sturmer's face and turned Ockom's head into a screaming mass of flesh and pain and teeth.

The second arrow hit the line of men farther back, thudding into Holmer's kidneys even as Ockom, dead in his black tunic, went down.

The file broke loose in pandemonium. A third arrow slithered across the path and into the undergrowth. It had come from the left, and a little ahead: Sturmer marked the place, and shouted to the others to follow.

They plunged into the forest, branches whipping at their faces, their weapons tangling as they ran. Ahead, Sturmer could see little: oak trunks, the branches above, the bushes of holly and hazel at eye level. There were no silhouettes against the sky, no archers hiding in the trees in the place he had marked.

On his right he heard a shriek and turned in time to see Parn and Coyler, with arms upraised, disappear into the ground, something giving way under their feet. They were out of sight, in a hole in the ground. Sturmer ran to their screams and the edge of the pit. They had fallen on serried wooden spikes, fifteen feet below ground level: Parn face-forward, so that he was partly spreadeagled, partly crushed against the earthen wall of the pit; and Coyler to one side, so that his face was upraised.

'Sturmer!' His features twisted with the new realization of what was happening to his body beneath him. 'Sturmer!'

Sturmer had been joined by Boonis and Morfe. 'Get them out! The spikes are poisoned! Get them out!'

'We've got no rope!'

'The poison! You can see the poison! Pull them off the spikes!'

It was too late. Coyler's face as he looked upward was a mask. His hands groped for help. His eyes filmed. Already his legs and waist felt dead beneath him. There were faces in the rectangle of light. Faces, and the leaves of trees. Patterns. Waving. Rain coming in. Beside him Parn was on the spikes. Making a tiny sound. The faces in the rectangle would not be able to hear. Coyler shut his eyes.

All but two of the search party were standing helplessly at the edge of the pit. Sturmer barked orders: in the brambles nearby they found a long stout branch. Boonis and Groden lowered it into the pit, and the bodies of the poisoned men were brought out and laid on the ground, among the briers and the wet leaves.

Tamben and Domack, who had run farther into the woods, returned and joined the rest. They had seen and heard nothing of the mysterious bowman.

'It is Tsoaul!' Dopp said. 'He will take us all in this vile place!'

'He will deal with us as he has dealt with Gumis!'

'And Ockom!'

'And Coyler and Parn!'

'And the victims of the bears!'

Sturmer shouted angrily for silence. 'We must think what to do!'

'We'll be killed!'

'Let's go back to the village and get away while we can!'

'What if Tsoaul drew us here to keep us from the village while he attacks!'

'Let's get back to the village!'

'No!' Groden screamed. 'We must go and find Hernou!'

'You bastard! She can protect herself!' Dopp shouted in his face. 'You and she brought this down on us – now she must fend the best she can!'

'What did you say?'

'She's a slut, a whore! If she's dead we're well rid of her!'

Before Sturmer could intervene Groden had struck the smaller man in the face: Dopp staggered, and would have fallen into the pit had not Domack and Tamben caught him in time.

'Stop this!' Sturmer shouted. 'We must think ahead if we are to survive!'

'The village is cursed!' said Munn. 'I am taking my children away! The bears came and killed their mother and sister; Tsoaul shall not have their father too!'

Several of the men seemed to be in agreement with him and were backing away.

'No!' said Sturmer.

'Stay and fight, cowards!' Morfe shouted.

'Scum!' Groden screamed. 'Filth! Cowardly filth!'

'I am still Gauhm's chosen one!' Sturmer shouted above all of them. 'I am her priest! Any who leave us will have their ground blackened by Gauhm wherever it may be! You must fight for her if not for your own village!'

'We'll take our chances with Gauhm!' Munn said. 'She did not mean us to go through this!'

'He's right!'

Morfe jumped forward with his axe. 'Leave if you wish, but you must pass me first.'

For an instant it looked as if Munn and the others would attack Morfe; but they turned away. Morfe lowered his axe.

'Nothing can be done for these two,' Sturmer said, gesturing at Parn and Coyler. 'We'll return for them later. Now we must go back to the path.'

'But we cannot fight Tsoaul! It is death to fight a spirit!'

'We are defenceless against him!'

'Back to the path.'

Sturmer did not know what to do. He considered returning to the village to fetch some more men, and some of the women too. Was it wise? He did not know – but he had no other plan. A plan of sorts was better than no plan at all.

They came out on the path a few yards from Ockom's body.

In panic Sturmer turned his head this way and that. A rising terror seized him. He was a fool! A fool! He looked along the path, uphill and down, among the trees. Blandness: mud, rain, leaves, trunks, branches. Just woodland. Nothing else.

'Where is he?' Sturmer shouted desperately. 'Where is he? Where's Holmer?'

Holmer, the wounded man, had disappeared.

They found his body in the brambles just beside the path. When they saw what had been done to it there was time for no more words.

They ran.

Even if they had looked, or known how to interpret it, they would have been able to make no sense of the churn of tracks on the path towards the village. Sticky mud sucked at their feet as they ran, obliterating a set of barefoot marks. A stitch was rising in Sturmer's side. Overhead the trees made a smear of grey and green and spidery brown. The faster runners – Morfe and Groden and Boonis – were fifty paces ahead, and even Munn was in front of him, getting farther away. Sturmer realized he was being left behind, dragged back by his age, his years, too many years. Domack overtook him. They were on level ground again. Sturmer reached for the effort to try and keep up, the stitch twisting in his side. He saw Morfe turn a bend and become hidden, then Boonis, Groden, and the others.

Sturmer's toe hit an exposed root and he fell headlong into the mud. He struggled to his knees and to his feet, and with both hands clutched to his side ran on.

He came out on the clearing by the gorge and its bridge. Immediately he saw that the others had stopped, uncertain whether to go on or turn back. On the far side of the bridge, a few yards from the edge of the gorge, stood a slim, dark-haired figure. It was Hernou. She had been bound at ankles and wrists; a tight gag drew back the corners of her mouth. Otherwise, she looked unharmed. She was alive.

'It's a trap!' Sturmer shouted, as he saw Morfe taking the first stupid step on to the bridge, on to the logs above the buttressing.

'We can't go back!' Morfe called out. 'We've got to go on and get her safe!'

'No! Come back!'

Morfe ignored him. He continued across the bridge. Then others watched as he gained firm ground and turned to them. 'See! It's safe! None here but Hernou!' He ran to her to untie her bonds. She was shaking her head furiously.

Sturmer watched in disbelief as Boonis and Tamben went next on to the platform, followed by Emetch and Haukan. Groden ran from the back of the group and shouldered Dopp aside to get on to the bridge. 'She's my wife! Let me pass!'

Just as Groden set foot on the bridge he became aware of ropes rising from the ground and tautening on the far side, heavy weights plunging in the trees; and there was a jagged report, a splintering sound, and with a roar the buttressing was coming away from its joints with the platform and the logs were rising and twisting and giving way. The bridge was collapsing.

Groden leapt back. Haukan, the last across, was unable to scramble to safety and Groden saw him falling with the bridge and into the gorge. An oak beam, spinning in the air, caught Haukan with its tip and he was pulped against the rocks.

As he looked up Groden saw Hernou and the four men on the far side; and, from nowhere, from the branches of a tree, from the sky, dropped a white and scarlet creature, an apparition, a god, plumes of white feathers on its elbows and knees and head, taller than a human being, much taller, its face hideously striped with white and scarlet. Tsoaul's teeth showed yellow as softly he hit the ground.

Emetch and Boonis were backing away in terror. Tsoaul suddenly crouched and Groden noticed he was holding a spear, a god's spear with tufts of white feathers. He jabbed it in their direction. Emetch and Boonis turned and ran, across the clearing, to the edge of the gorge, and into space, their legs running in nothing as they fell for a few seconds, shouting as they went, and vanished into the rocks and ferns at the bottom.

Now vicious Tsoaul turned on Tamben. He stood frozen, mute, unable to cry out, unable to react: and in dreamland Tsoaul thrust muscled arms with the spear and Tamben bent his head and saw the blue and cream scalloped blades of its point.

Only Morfe retained presence of mind. On its length of sweat-polished ashwood he swung the head of his felling axe and Tsoaul ducked under its hiss, lunging from below with the bloodied point of his spear, glancing off Morfe's chest; but the power and momentum of Morfe's own axe swing took him off balance and Tsoaul looped the end of the spear forward and snagged at Morfe's heels: Morfe lost balance and fell.

Tsoaul seemed shorter and more man-like as he dropped to one knee, a knife in his hand. In the blink of an eye he had drawn the blade across the big tendons at the back of Morfe's knees. Morfe had been hamstrung.

'Shoot at it!' Sturmer screamed, remembering for the first time that they were armed with bows. 'Shoot!'

But before they could fit notches to their strings the apparition had melted away into the trees, leaving Hernou standing, Tamben dead, and Morfe writhing on the ground.

The bridge had been wrecked, ruined. There was no way to cross. To reach the survivors they would have to detour to the head of the gorge.

'Stinn, Mastall!' Sturmer shrieked at two of the men with bows. 'Stay here! If Tsoaul returns, shoot him! The others, come with me!'

They broke into the trees on the right of the path, running uphill and to the east, keeping the gorge beside them on their left, hands up to ward off branches tearing at their faces and necks, and Sturmer, driven on by blind dread, dread of what would happen to Tamis and his children, the village and himself, had lost count of the able men destroyed: Ockom, Gumis, Emetch, Holmer, Parn . . . the victims of the raid . . .

Coyler, Boonis, Haukan crushed by the timbers in the gorge . . . the victims of the bears, Tsoaul's bears . . .

At the head of the gorge the soil was leached and poor and it was here that the briers and brambles grew in greatest profusion. Sturmer reached the first of the stout loops of rust-coloured stems with their red and green leaves. He did not feel the barbs at his legs; but there was something wrong with his shins and his feet were not working properly and he was falling, crashing with the shock of lost momentum into needles and thorns and prickles. Red appeared everywhere in spots and lines across his forearms and face. He ripped himself free and stood up. Domack was running past him, managing to avoid the briers, skirting the densest patch and left and right things were happening in the trees and Domack was upside-down and being hoisted from the ground at unbelievable speed. Struggling and screaming he was lifted impossibly high into the loftiest boughs of a giant beech: a cluster of bags glimpsed coming down against the light struck a spike and white chalk-rubble spewed forth. Now Sturmer raised his eyes to see Domack seventy feet from the ground, eighty, reaching the height of his rise, hanging motionless, suspended in the forest ceiling: straight and vertical the rope hung to the ground.

It quivered, and Domack began to make his fall.

The ending of his screams left a vacuum. High above the ground the empty counterweights had come to lodge against the branch. They moved once or twice as the weight at the other end of the rope settled itself, and then, were still.

Sturmer struggled free of the brambles. Groden, Feno, Munn and the others started walking forward, not taking their eyes from the place, the one place. The one place ahead.

'There may be more traps!' Sturmer warned them.

He had broken the silence. They passed Domack's body.

'Here!' Deak shouted, ten yards to Sturmer's right. By a tall tangle of briers, between it and three hazel bushes, he had found thin branches laid side by side, covering an eight-foot square loosely disguised with litter.

Groden took a piece of wood and prodded at the covering. It gave way at once, and when they saw the spikes below they cleared the rest of the branches aside. The spikes waited, in uneven ranks and files, their tips soaked and dark, made so by the coating of wolf's-bane. Sturmer looked down into the pit. He thought of Parn and Coyler, of Coyler's hands reaching up.

'Fill it in,' he wanted to say, but he remembered Hernou and why they had been running, and grimacing turned aside and motioned that the others should follow.

Mastall and Stinn, the men left on guard with bows, had fled. As Sturmer emerged from the trees he saw that Hernou had gone too; and Morfe, previously lying on his face, was now supine with his arms spread wide. With a cry of anguish breaking from him Groden pushed past the rest of the group and ran to his friend's corpse. Groden went down on one knee and lifted the dead shoulders, cradling Morfe's head against his arm. The eyes stared vacantly. There was blood on the teeth. And, round the neck, was the ragged wound where Morfe's throat had been cut.

Something in the grass caught Sturmer's eye. He stooped and rubbed the white-stained blades between his fingers, and, holding his fingertips to his nose, smelled the gritty white paste. He tried to think what the smell could be. And then it came to him.

Chalk.

Fallott grinned, despite the driving rain and the filthy grey mud. Pode and Bico came behind him, leading the team of goats with their wicker panniers, and in the rear the boy Bewry toiled and struggled to keep up. They were walking men, men who could cover a dozen miles a day, or sixty on the Flint Lord's roads that went out like the arms of a spider's web from Valdoe and penetrated far into the coastal strip and the flat country north of the downs. Bewry would have to learn to walk too if he wanted to be a trader.

Fallott turned and caught Bico's eye. They had made Bewry walk behind, where the mud was worst. The seven goats, each with two panniers, were heavily laden with flints and tools: knives, axes, arrowheads, scrapers, and blades of all kinds, already pressure-flaked by the Valdoe craftsmen; and the weight of them made the goats' hoofs sink deeply, turning the trackway to mire.

On their right the trees opened to give a glimpse of grey-green ocean flecked with white. Fallott scanned the expanse of scrubland as by instinct, scarcely seeming to move the eyes in his head.

'Two miles more,' Bico said over his shoulder to Bewry, who was hot-faced and near to tears.

'We may go on to Hooe,' Fallott said, naming a village twelve miles farther east.

Bewry said nothing. He knew that Fallott was lying. Fallott had been told to go to Burh: he would not dare disobey. Bewry hated Fallott. He hated Pode and Bico too, and he hated the overseers and the soldiers, but most of all he hated the Flint Lord, who had taken him and his sister and murdered their parents and tribe, and whose men had told him his sister would be given to the miners if he did not behave himself on the road with Fallott's team.

Fallott drew up his sheepskin. He was a tall, hard, heavy man with watery blue eyes and lifeless brown hair tied in a topknot. The fingers and thumb of his left hand had been smashed and badly set, and under his clothes a white scar showed where an arrow had punctured one of his lungs, the injury that had ended his days in the Flint Lord's garrison and brought him by way of the armoury to take charge of a trading team. He was a veteran of three expeditions to the foreign coast for slave-trading. At that time he had been younger and stronger, but even today he was with good cause shown deference by those in his control. Bewry, a thin child with brown hair and eyes, and an open, small-featured face, was twelve years old. His sister was sixteen and had been showing reluctance to settle with the reality of her new existence; thus the boy had threatened to prove a nuisance. Putting him on Fallott's team had been deliberately done.

The ground rose into a grove of blackthorn. Fallott spoke an order and the pace of the team increased.

Soon they would be arriving in Burh.

6

After finishing the man he had hamstrung, Tagart put the woman over his shoulder and made his way north-east through ankle-deep wet leaves, uphill and towards the yew. He covered a wide curve, avoiding a thicket of old hazel where the fallen branches lay in a tangle, festooned with lichens and grey mould: such woodland was impossible to traverse in silence, at least when carrying a load. Instead he kept to the open forest where ground cover was sparse. On the way he collected the rope he had saved from the hummel-skin trap – the one that earlier he found had been sprung by a badger during the night – and picked a tree suited to his purpose: an oak, squat, densely foliaged, on one of the thicker slopes, less than two hundred paces from the yew.

He dumped the woman and, taking one end of the rope, grasped a low branch and pulled himself up. He climbed into the middle of the tree, where the trunk forked into five boughs, and fed the rope over a lesser branch a little higher up.

Over the gag, the woman's eyes regarded him fearfully as he climbed down and jumped the last few feet to the ground. He knelt beside her and tied one end of the rope between her ankles, knotting it to the ropes forming her fetter. She began to struggle desperately as without a word he hoisted her into the tree, pulling smoothly arm-over-arm on the rope, scarcely slowing as she came into contact with the great bole, slid past it and ascended to the lesser branch. She hung there, bound and gagged, head downward, in the centre of the tree. Her arms, tied behind her back, hung a little away from her body: the weight of them would become a strain that would get worse as each minute passed, within an hour a torture. Tagart was not concerned. He let out a little of the rope and she awkwardly came to rest upside-down in the forking of the boughs; for the second time he climbed up, pulling the free end of rope after him.

'I'll be back later with food and water,' he whispered, and hoisted her again so that she hung freely. Upside-down, her eyes and face looked peculiar, as if a mouth should be across her forehead. She made noises of protest under the gag. The skins Tagart had tied to her body hung in loose folds: with a curious delicacy he rearranged them, tucking a flap between her thighs.

He made the rope fast and descended to the ground.

At an easy pace he trotted downhill towards the river. He was still daubed with chalk paste, parts of it dyed scarlet with blackberry juice, and he was going down to the river to wash. That was his immediate task.

But afterwards?

He had a hostage, and she could be used in a variety of ways; and he had taken a useful idea from the details of the ceremony she had so foolishly described; but now his larger plan had run out and he did not know how to proceed. With some surprise he realized that he had not expected to survive this long. He had disposed of more of them than one man acting alone had any right to. The labourer; two shot in the dry valley; three in the gorge; one speared; another with his throat cut. Twenty-six killed in the raid; an unknown number killed and injured by the bears; and perhaps others in the deadfalls, and in the hoist-trap at the head of the gorge. Thirty-four certainly dead. The true total was probably double that. But how to proceed? So far he had applied the laws the tribe had taught him, for hunting and luring and waiting. He had observed that the farmers were slow-witted and easily driven to panic. As individuals, few or even none of them were his superior. That was the conclusion he had reached. He was wary of under-estimating an adversary; but he was just as wary of under-estimating his own powers of observation and deduction. From the things he had clearly seen, from the ludicrous and cowardly way they had reacted to his attacks, he felt safe in discounting any spark of resourcefulness or ingenuity in those who had by virtue solely of their greater numbers massacred his wife, his child, his family, and his tribe.

Again he felt the tide of revulsion and weariness rising in his mind, and furiously he again forced it back. His resolution had not failed him yet – and it would not do so until he had finished. He knew he was pushing himself on, fighting himself on two fronts, refusing to acknowledge any of the new thoughts that threatened to weaken him and make him give up. But with every act of violence, with every man killed he found it harder to maintain that pitch of loathing which had spurred him to go alone into the den of a mother bear. He did not think he would be able to do the same thing again.

He wished he had someone to talk to. He wished he could ask Cosk what to do.

But Cosk was at the camp with the kites and magpies and buzzards.

He reached the river and slipped into the water to wash. Several times he plunged his head beneath the surface to get the chalk from his hair. The river was swollen and he could taste fresh mud in its currents.

The rain. It had been raining for four days. Was it too long?

He stood up, water draining from his body. It might not be. The wind was in the west, and even though the crops had been soaked the ground was still dry and once the flame got hold the corn would burn. If he fired the fields west of the river, the flames would not be able to spread to the east bank, and the forest and he himself on that side would be safe. In his imagination he saw the western part of the palisade consumed, leaving that side of the village open. He saw the farmers showing themselves, putting out the flames, and he saw himself waiting.

He strode from the river and ran along its bank. There were many preparations to be made.

The fly agaric ceremony came to an end at midnight, leaving the village quiet and sorrowing for ten more men lost. Only seven of their bodies had been brought back: Sturmer had not tried to recover those in the gorge. Mourners with torches sat in vigil over the Dead Ground.

Inside the Meeting House the boy Bewry lay awake and unable to sleep. His mind was alive with the sight of all the corpses and with the stories the farmers had told, of the Forest God and the disaster he had brought. One of the village women, the wife of Groden, was still missing, and Groden and his friends were going to search again tomorrow. They had asked Fallott to help.

'That cannot be done,' Fallott said carefully. They had been sitting in the Meeting House, eating the food the villagers had provided on their arrival. It was late morning, raining hard outside. The flints were laid out on the floor for the farmers to make their choice. Bewry was sitting by himself, leaning against the wall, a beaker of water at his knee. He was slowly getting through the gruel of lentils and beans. He could scarcely taste the food: he was just grateful to be still, no longer walking, for his feet were blistered and his whole body ached. He was too young to walk so far.

'That cannot be done,' Fallott said. 'We must leave at dawn for Valdoe. The team has other walks to make.'

'But you are a soldier, Fallott!' said the head man, named Sturmer. 'With your help we can fight Tsoaul and get Groden's woman back!'

Fallott corrected him. 'I was a soldier. I am a soldier no longer.'

'Then leave us Pode or Bico. They know the methods of the Flint Lord and how to fight.'

Pode and Bico glanced at each other in amusement, before going on with their gruel.

'Pray to the Earth Mother,' Fallott said earnestly. 'She will bring you out of trouble.'

'No,' Groden said. 'This time we must fight. I beg you, leave us Pode or Bico.'

Fallott held his spoon on one side and carefully considered his words. There were many farmers, and, discounting the boy, only three in the walking team. 'They are with me because we need three men,' he said. 'It's not safe to walk with less; most teams have more.'

'Seventy-seven villagers have been killed,' Sturmer said. 'Another twenty lie maimed or dying in their beds. You have seen them. You have heard them. Now you must help. Were it not for Burh and villages like us Lord Brennis would have no trade. Will he stand by and watch us all murdered? Will he do nothing to stop it?'

'Why should he?' Bico said curiously.

'Because from us he grows wealthy!' Groden shouted.

Bico shrugged. 'Keep soldiers like he does to protect yourself from the heathens and the demons. Feed your own barracks. Work hard. Build a fort. Look after yourselves. He has no duty towards you.'

'That's enough,' Fallott said, and Bico fell immediately silent.

Fallott raised a hand. He spoke placatingly. 'You mistake us, Sturmer. We would help if we could, but we cannot. Our orders are strict. If we broke them the Flint Lord would be angry.'

'Then can you plead for us? Get him to send soldiers?'

Fallott shifted evasively.

'Will you ask the Flint Lord to send soldiers?'

'It is not usual.'

'Unheard of,' muttered Pode.

'My wife is still with Tsoaul,' Groden said, near to despair.

'And mine lies outside with her face bitten through,' Stinn said, and all those who had been bereaved began to plead with Fallott for his intercession.

Again Fallott held up his hand. 'You say you have seen Tsoaul himself.'

'He came from the trees. It was Tsoaul.'

'Then you will need many soldiers, half an army.'

'Will you ask, Fallott?'

Fallott hesitated. 'I will,' he said.

'It is enough,' Sturmer said. 'We know you, Fallott.'

'Depend on me. When the soldiers come I will take charge. We will sweep the forest clean.'

Soon afterwards the fly agaric ceremony had commenced. Now the Meeting House was empty of villagers, and Bewry was lying awake. He could hear Bico snorting in his sleep, and the drone of Pode's snoring. The light from the watchers' torches danced on the ceiling and made flickering patterns; Fallott's body was a huddle, his sheepskin pulled up to his ear.

Bewry did not know how much time had elapsed when Fallott sat upright and rose to his feet.

'Two hours to first light,' he announced, kicking Pode and Bico awake.

Bewry stood up himself to avoid being kicked.

'Better not piss on their Dead Ground,' Fallott told him. 'Do it by the steps.' He turned to the two men, who were sitting up and complaining. 'Bico, go and get the head man up. Pode, you make sure we eat a good breakfast. We've a fifty-mile walk today. Bewry, see to the goats.'

Fallott, rubbing his hands, went to the nearest window and inspected the sky. Stars remained unblinking behind wisps of thin moving cloud. 'Rain this morning before Whitehawk,' he said, as Pode and Bico went out of the doorway and down the steps, with Bewry coming respectfully behind.

Tagart struggled through the silo, groping for the covering of sticks. His fingers found them just as he felt his body being sucked into the ensilage, and he drew himself up and into the fresh windy night, pausing with his head and shoulders above the ground while he checked the village.

Torches burned beside the Meeting House, and in their light he saw the mourners sitting by what he knew would be bodies. The rest of the village was in darkness.

As before he heaved himself out of the silo, ran to the granary, the threshing shed, and down to the river, where he leapt from the bank and into the water. He swam underwater for three strokes, took breath, and crossed to the far bank to make his way upstream and past the bridge.

In his pouch, wrapped in a square of tallowed skin, were the pieces of death cap fungus which he had prepared during the preceding day. He had found the toadstools growing in many places between the river and the yew, and in the beechwoods near the gorge, in ones and twos and small groups. With meticulous care not to put his fingers to his mouth or eyes or any part of his skin which was not whole, he collected every cap he could find, numbering three hundred and six. In the valley north of the yew he gathered twigs and bents and shavings and in a three-sided oven of flat stones built a hot, smokeless fire which he buried in pebbles. On the bed of pebbles he gently heated the fungus, taking off each cap as it shrivelled and dried. They were small, smaller than fly agaric caps would be, but they looked sun-dried and in his memory they matched closely enough the caps described to him by Hernou – closely enough to pass without suspicion. By nightfall he had finished. At dusk he fed and watered Hernou – whom he had allowed to sit on the ground during the afternoon – and hung her up again in the tree for the night. He slept then, for his normal term: the next day he would need all his alertness and strength.

Two hours before dawn he had come down the escarpment to the village, and now he was inside the compound, wading through the shallows by the riverbank.

The Meeting House showed as an angled bulk against the compound with its scattered houses contained by the spike-topped palisade. On the right-hand side of the Meeting House he saw the seated mourners, their torches thrust into the ground in front of them. He waded farther upstream. He knew he would have to get inside the Meeting House silently, find the Agaric Casket, exchange the caps, and get out again without alarming the mourners. That was counting on the fact that the Meeting House would be empty; otherwise, he would have to wait his chance, or even give up the idea altogether.

Making small ripples he swam to the village-side bank and stealthily climbed into the sedges. The rear wall of the Meeting House was directly opposite, thirty feet away. Tagart shook the water from his limbs, squeezed his hair and beard, and one by one took off his garments and wrung them dry before replacing them. He came further up the bank. The sedges rustled as he left them and darted to the Meeting House wall. For a long time he leaned against the wattle, listening. No unusual sounds came. He put his ear to the wall and could hear nothing from inside. The building appeared to be empty. He edged to the corner, away from the Dead Ground, and gingerly put his head round. Nothing. The barn and bakery were in full view, as were nine or ten houses; but it was dark and moonless and if he were observed he would be no more than a faintness against the river behind. The only danger came from the mourners' torches. The glow among the network of piles and crossbars beneath the Meeting House floor would show the movement of his legs. If he was going to be seen from the bakery side, that would be the cause.

The risk had to be taken. Pressed against the wall, he worked his way along to the first sizable gap in the wattle, wide enough to see inside. He looked. The interior was much as he remembered it: the wooden floor, the altar, the windows and walls, the doorway at the far end through which he could glimpse more of the village.

The room was empty.

He made his way to the first window. The ledge was eight feet above the ground: he jumped and grasped the timber of the frame, hanging for a moment as he listened for a reaction. None came. Gradually he pulled himself level with the ledge and climbed over. He landed soundlessly on the smooth boards of the floor; his feet left slight damp stains as he crossed to the altar. In the uncertain light of the mourners' torches he found the Agaric Casket Hernou had spoken of, a cubic beechwood box the width of his forearm, furnished with a lid that opened with a soft gasp as he swung it on its hinges. The casket had been superbly made. It was airtight, the back, lid, front and sides carved into panels of stars, clouds, comets, mythical beasts, the deities of Earth, Forest, Sky and Sea, the sun and wind, and the fly agaric toadstool itself, growing under birch trees by the gates of the road taken by the dead to paradise. Ten trays inside fitted one upon the other, each scrupulously polished and fashioned.

The top three trays were empty. Tagart removed the other seven and tipped the fly agaric caps into a heap on the floor, replacing them with the caps from his pouch. He did not have quite enough: he made up the deficiency in the bottom trays with fly agaric caps, and put the rest of the trays back into place. He shut the lid and positioned the box as he had found it, and scooped up the fly agaric from the floor to pack into his pouch. A few crumbs he scattered by blowing this way and that on the floor.

There was a noise at the doorway.

Someone was coming up the steps.

Tagart stared terrified past the altar and into the darkness at the end of the room. Thoughts flooded his mind. He could not attack, for the mourners outside were too close and he would be heard. He could not jump out of the window and run: it would take far too long to burrow into the silo, or if he ran to the path, too long to get the gates open. He could not fight them all. And he could not hide here in the Meeting House, for whoever was coming up the steps would already have seen him.

It was all over.

He stood up and turned and saw that it was worse than he had thought. There were two of them, at the top of the steps, men outlined in the doorway, coming inside.

It was all over. They would kill him.

The two men came farther into the room. Tagart stood quite still, oddly peaceful now that he knew it was coming to an end at last. He did not care. In his heart his life had no value and he did not care.

'Good day to you,' one of the men said.

Tagart croaked.

He started walking towards them.

The man on the left caught him by the arm and Tagart tensed.

'Have you seen Fallott, friend?'

'No,' Tagart brought himself to say.

The two men seemed to lose interest in him. He edged past them to the door. From the corner of his eye he saw one kneel and begin tidying a pile of bedding by the wall.

Tagart hesitated in the doorway, in full and heady view of the whole village, and casually he was descending the flight of plank steps, the mourners' torches behind him and to the right. He reached the ground without challenge, and, still forcing himself to go slowly, turned left and sauntered towards the bakery and darkness. Shortly he turned left again, strolled by the side of the Meeting House, and retraced his steps to the river.

The water was his friend. It was warm and buoyant and smelled of the forest. Its broad surface curled and gurgled and carried him past the bridge, past the lights of the mourners, and to the bank beside the threshing shed.

Moments later he was in the silo and pushing open the trapdoor of turf.

A small bundle lay next to the trapdoor: his bowstrings and fire-making kit. He took it up, with his quiver and bows, and ran beside the palisade back to the river, which he swam with his arm high in the air holding the bundle clear, gripping the bows and quiver with it, making deep strokes with his free hand and frog-kicking at each threat that he might go under and risk getting his tinder damp. It was not easy, and he came to the western bank a long way down from the village. A moorhen squawked as he crashed a passage through the flags and sedges.

Tagart gained solid ground and stood facing the fresh west wind. Ahead, the low shape of the hills. Behind, the river and the forest, the trees heavy with summer coming almost to the water. To his left, the widening mouth of the estuary. To his right, acre upon acre of corn and barley.

He turned his face to the north-west and set off across the fields.

Sturmer preceded the trading team across the bridge and opened the gate for them. Daylight was just showing above the forest behind the village; the air felt chilly and smelled damp from the river.

Most of the farmers were out of their beds and had come to see the trading team leave.

'Have you all you want of our wares?' Fallott said routinely as he let the goats pass him by.

'We have.'

'Good.'

Sturmer stepped forward. 'You'll not forget us, Fallott?'

The larger man slapped him on the back. 'My word is on it. Lord Brennis will be your saviour if I am worth anything at Valdoe.' He glanced at Pode and Bewry, chivvying the goats through the gate and on to the road. The animals' panniers were loaded with grain, skins, cuts of meat: mutton, goat, pork, and the stringy beef of the semi-wild cattle that served the village as milk beasts. 'We must be gone,' Fallott said.

Sturmer stood back.

'Come on there, Bico!' Fallott called out. To Sturmer he said, 'In a few days, then.'

'In a few days.'

The gate swung shut and the flint-sellers heard the oak beams being dropped into place. Fallott quickened his step and caught up with the end of the team, where Pode was prodding the trailing goat with an elder switch.

'Lord Brennis their saviour,' Pode said with a grin.

'Did you want to be held there by force?'

'True enough, Fallott. There was nothing else to tell them.'

'They were desperate.'

'What if the Forest God comes down and kills them all?'

'We strike Burh from our list of walks,' Fallott said drily, and Pode gave a short, harsh laugh as his leader moved to the front of the team. 'Bewry go behind.'

Resentfully Bewry dropped back. The path was still bad, very muddy, and today the team had to cover the whole distance to Valdoe by nightfall. The goats' hoofs churned the track, making small deep holes which immediately filled with water. Already Bewry was struggling to keep up, his night's rest counting for little.

On either side was the expanse of the farmers' arable; in the dawn light the barley looked bracken-brown, paler and darker where the storms had beaten it flat. The path led through the fields for half a mile from the village, and at their edge wound through a spinney of maple and oak. Beyond the spinney spread a gentle incline of short grass kept neat by the villagers with flint sickles. Ordered lines of small chalk boulders marked out a large rectangle, in the centre of which was the village burial mound: six feet high, fifty feet long, twenty wide, looking like a black upturned barge. The farmers kept it free of weeds; at its base were posies of red campion and corn chamomile, laid for the newly dead. Here the trading team had seen fresh earth the previous day: the graves of those killed in the attack on the nomads' camp.

For protection and other purposes on the road, the flint-sellers went armed. Fallott wore an axe in his belt, and in his pouch ready to hand was a sling-shot and a supply of pebbles which he could propel with speed and accuracy over a distance of forty yards. Also in his pouch he kept a set of bolas, two fist-sized stones sewn into leather coverings connected by a long thin strap. This when thrown at a fleeing deer would wrap itself round the animal's legs, entangling it and bringing it down.

The team came out of the spinney.

The man was walking along the top of the burial mound. Bico saw him first. He was dressed in skins, without shoes, a tall and powerful figure moving with noticeable fluidity and grace, unarmed, a quiver of arrows and two unstrung bows leaning against the base of the mound.

The man looked up suddenly, as if he had been disturbed in deep thought.

Fallott had seen him too and was already unfurling his bolas. He moved clear of Bico and began to swing the leather-covered spheres, feeding out the strap as he did so.

'You there! Wait!'

The man leapt from the mound and scooped up his quiver and bows and started running.

The doubled thong of the bolas hummed loudly as Fallott worked power and momentum into the swing: the balls blurred into a perfect circle, precisely horizontal.

Fallott was waiting.

At first the fugitive had put the mound between himself and the team, but as he climbed the slope he came out of cover and his legs were revealed. He was eighty paces away when Fallott let fly.

Unerringly the bolas snapped out of orbit and raced after the running man, whirred over the mound, and before he had taken another five steps the balls were spinning past each other in opposite directions and the strap was winding itself again and again round his knees. With a shout of dismay he flung his arms wide. The quiver and bows were thrown into the air; he left them behind, falling, sliding on his face to a tangled halt in the dew-wet grass.

Before he had even a chance to sit up Fallott was standing over him with his axe. The man looked round, took in Fallott's form, and turned his eyes to the ground.

Bico joined his leader.

'A bonus for us,' Fallott said. 'How much do you think he'll fetch?'

'A walk saved or two days with the whores for each of us,' said Bico with enthusiasm. He cautiously circled the prostrate figure. 'He looks well fed. Too well fed to be a farmer. Do you think he's one of them?'

Fallott shook his head. 'I know them all by sight. This is a stranger, a nomad I think. A wild man.' He prodded Tagart with a foot. 'You. Where are you from?'

'I am from Highdole,' Tagart answered. 'I have journeyed to see my friends at Burh.'

'Alone?' Bico said to Fallott. Fallott smiled.

'And is this how you pay respect to their dead? Walking along the barrow?'

Tagart said nothing.

'Let's go back to the village then, and see if they know your face.'

Tagart looked round again and held Fallott's eye. 'They will tell you I am their friend. Untie my legs and we can go.'

Bico was frowning with recognition. He squatted and took hold of Tagart's hair, wrenching his head back to see his face. 'I know him,' he said to Fallott. 'Pode and I saw him. We saw him this morning in the Meeting House.'

'Of course,' Tagart said evenly. 'I slept at Burh last night. I am the guest of Sturmer. I am here for a week to help with harvest.'

'What is your name?' Fallott said.

Tagart did not hesitate. 'Meker.'

'You say you come from Birdbrow.'

'Highdole.'

'What is the name of your head man?'

'Foss.'

Fallott laughed. 'A good try, my friend. You forget we are a walking team. I know them all.' His expression changed and he jerked his head at the goats. To Bico he said: 'We're wasting time. Cut a yoke from that spinney. We must be on our way.'

Part 3

1

Tagart's wrists were tied above a stout oak branch across his shoulders, his ankles fettered with a short length of rope. He could walk, but no more, and if he did try to escape he would not be able to get far before the oak branch snagged and barred his way. As extra insurance Bico fixed a sliding noose round his neck, and at the end of this halter, Tagart began the long walk to Valdoe.

Their progress was slow. Fallott found the delay irksome. On many occasions Tagart stumbled and fell into the mud, only to be kicked and again dragged to his feet. Before long there was no part of him that was not spattered with grey slime. His shoulders were burning centres of pain; all sensation had gone from his hands and forearms, and where Fallott's kicks had struck his kidneys he felt a dull, hard ache. From time to time the boy Bewry wiped his face and gave him sips of water. The boy did not speak, but in his eyes he was sorry for Tagart and Tagart's mind began to work.

'Come on, Bewry!' Bico shouted.

The team followed the road, up the western side of the valley away from Burh, and along the slope of the chalk hills which, half a mile to their left, became white cliffs above a shingled bay. Spectacular cloud formations were building up in the west: purple, black, lead-grey, green; cold, sudden showers came and went, the rain making clean streams across Tagart's skin.

They descended into a wide, flat valley filled with an expanse of reeds, broken up by wind-ruffled lagoons and meres over which flights of wildfowl made straggling chevrons. A black, oily path led through the reeds, between the walls of rustling stems. It came out on a rough grass marsh where the sky was reflected in ribbons of water. On the far side the spread of a grey river crawled towards the sea. A line of posts stood across its width; weed-hung rope looped from top to top. Fallott and

Pode went out on the shingle by the water's edge and righted some of the punts that had been left there beyond the tide's reach.

After the crossing they turned south, in the shelter of bramble-clad cliffs of crumbling chalk, and by a steep path climbed the headland where wizened shrubs bent before the salt spray.

As the team emerged from the lee of the headland the sea wind struck them. Below, beyond the cliffs, white crests showed against green swell, in irregular patches deep blue where cloud shadows were passing. Puffins whirred overhead. Terns, delicate grey and white, patrolled offshore, plunging for sand-eels; a pair of black skuas, heavy and sinister, selected one and chased it, relentless, twisting and turning, along the surface, gaining altitude until they were high specks against the sky: at last the tern could take no more and disgorged the contents of its crop. The skuas dropped back, and with easy, tumbling flight caught the fish-mash as it fell.

The road along the cliffs was firm and the team made better progress, and in an hour they had covered more than four miles. Soon afterwards, three hours after leaving Burh, Fallott ordered the first rest stop. The panniers were taken off the goats, which grazed quietly on the clifftop turf; Fallott, Bico and Pode took out the ale and bread given them in Burh, and at Bewry's suggestion the slave's wrists were temporarily untied from the yoke.

Tagart fell back on the grass and shut his eyes. He heard the voices of his captors, talking as they ate. One of them laughed, the sound of it swept away on the wind. Bewry said something. There was an indifferent reply; a few moments later Tagart became aware that the boy was shaking his shoulder.

'Some food,' Bewry said.

Tagart sat up and accepted the proffered bread. It was unfamiliar to him. He sniffed at it, tasted a corner, bit off a mouthful.

'These men,' Tagart said in a low voice. 'You do not wish to walk with them.'

'I have no choice. I am a slave. At least I am too young for the flint workings.' Bewry glanced over his shoulder. The three were taking no notice. 'That is where they're taking you, to the mines.'

Tagart nodded.

'What tribe are you?'

'The Cosks,' Tagart said.

'I am of the Guelen. Guel was my father's brother. We were on the beach at Lepe, by the big island. Then they came with dogs and spears. They chased us into the salt-marshes. Some of us drowned. I got stuck in the mud with my sister and my parents and some others. The soldiers killed many of us there, on the saltings. They killed my mother and father. Guel was killed too, and the rest of the tribe killed or taken for slaves and sent away. They took me and my sister Segle. If I do not do as they wish, Segle will be put into the whores' place where the miners go.'

Tagart looked into the boy's open face. 'How old is she?'

'Sixteen.'

Tagart had never heard such despair in a child's voice.

'She is the niece of a chieftain,' Bewry said. 'And they make her serve swill to the mine slaves.'

Sixteen. Two years younger than Mirin. 'I can help you,' Tagart said. Bewry looked up. 'I will get your sister out of Valdoe if you help me to escape.'

Bewry's eyes widened.

'We are not meant to be slaves,' Tagart said.

'What are you whispering there?' Fallott shouted. 'Give the slave a drink and get away from him!'

The rest stop lasted five minutes more. Even as Bico came to pull Tagart to his feet, Tagart was toying with the idea of jumping over the cliffs. It would be better than Valdoe. There was no real chance of escape: Fallott was a very different man from Sturmer and Groden. The only chance, if chance it was, lay perhaps with Bewry.

They did not stop at Whitehawk fort, one of the Valdoe outliers. It passed them to the north, its forbidding black palisade topped by ramparts where Tagart glimpsed the movement of men. Fallott kept to the cliff road. He was forcing the pace, making up for lost time, and as a concession to this

Tagart's wrists were fastened below, not above, the yoke. Soon Whitehawk was far behind.

Six miles on, at the approach to Thundersbarrow fort, the road swung inland, north-west and into the hills. The chalk track climbed at a gruelling rate up the lower slopes of Thundersbarrow. Rain was blowing off the sea as they came within sight of the fortifications; Tagart felt his stomach fill with sick fear as the faces of the guards by the gate became discernible.

Fallott was recognized and the team admitted for fresh pack-animals and a meal. Tagart had never been inside a fort before. Compared with the Trundle, this was nothing; but he stared despite himself and the yoke, marvelling at the timbers of the palisade, the earthworks, the buildings, the horn and leather armour of the soldiers.

'More Valdoe meat?' one of the guards said as Fallott came through the gate.

'Fallott has a talent for it,' said another with a grin.

'Serve as I did on the slave runs and you will learn it too,' Fallott answered. He crossed the inner compound to the door of the mess room, looked round once, and went inside.

Pode and the guard exchanged glances. 'He does not like delay,' Pode said.

'Or anything else.'

Pode smiled agreement. 'Food for the boy and slave,' he said. 'Keep them apart.'

The team did not remain long. Less than an hour later they were on the move.

To their left, seemingly tilted towards them, spread the expanse of grey sea. The track, glaring white against dark-green scrub, dipped and rose with the land, past a small village on the hill next to Thundersbarrow where the farmers paused to gaze at the prisoner as the team went by.

The few huts of the village dwindled; ahead and below, a mile away, wound the course of a lead-coloured river. At its mouth it became lost in the waters of a glittering estuary, protected from the breakers by a long fawn shingle-bank mottled green with seablite. Westward along the coast rolled marshland as far as the eye could see, with scattered lagoons, salt creeks, and mile upon mile of reeds, the plumes in mass making the horizon purplish-brown. The line of hills rose again from the river a mile or so inland, running slightly away from the coast. Parts of it were covered by forest, parts by old farmland turned to scrub; but with each mile nearer Valdoe more of the landscape came under cultivation.

Fallott led the team down into the valley and across a flooded field. The water came to their knees; they splashed and waded through the shallows, the grass green at their feet. Strands of hay-coloured seaweed drifted on slight currents, and under the water they could see drowned thistles and clumps of burnt ragwort.

The river was too wide and too frequently crossed to depend on punts. The Flint Lord had built landing stages on either bank, and a ferry station to house the men who worked the raft. The ferry station, with stone walls and a plank door, stood on raised ground between the river and the flooded field. Beyond it the river slopped and slapped against the logs of the raft as it rode its moorings. The sun showed behind the clouds and lit up the hills on the far side, then the flooded land at their base, the river, the ferry station; and the sunlight moved on towards Thundersbarrow.

'More rain coming,' Pode observed.

Fallott merely grunted and climbed the steps to the threshold. Before he had a chance to knock, the door was pulled back and a tall, red-haired man appeared. He was dressed in armour like the soldiers Tagart had seen earlier. With a glance at the other members of the walking team he said something over his shoulder and two more men came out, both dressed in soldiers' clothes, with oxhide greaves and vambraces, helmets and cuirasses of thick leather, and mail made of linked ovals of deer-horn. On their feet they wore thick-soled boots in pattern like the fur-lined walking boots issued to the team. Their belts, studded with bone, carried sheaths to take knives, and axes with sockets cushioned by cartilage; in addition they carried spears fitted with elliptical tangs of the very finest ground and polished flint.

The red-haired man smiled at Fallott. 'You have found us more work,' he said, a reference to Tagart.

'I would like to stay and talk, Gane, and even drink your filthy ale, but as it is we shall not be making Valdoe by nightfall.'

Gane, the red-haired soldier, shrugged and walked along the duckboards to the landing-stage, followed by his assistants. 'Bring the beasts on first!' he called out.

While Bico and Pode helped Fallott usher the goats on the raft, Bewry stood next to Tagart, pretending to keep guard. Tagart, weak with exhaustion, watched the farce of loading the seven animals on to the raft, no expression on his face.

'I will help you,' Bewry said.

Tagart slowly turned.

'I will help you escape. If you promise to free my sister, I will help.' Bewry looked at Fallott. His back was to them. 'Do you promise?'

'Very well.'

'Tell me what I must do,' Bewry said.

Tagart struggled to think. His mind refused to respond. He could think of nothing but the raft, the goats, the drab river and the silvery light in the droplets of spray. He saw the wicker panniers filled with provender, the goats' backs, Bico striking them with his elder switch. Gane had grasped one animal by the head and was dragging it bodily from the landing-stage on to the raft.

'At the next rest stop,' Bewry said, 'shall I help you then?'

'Yes. Help me then.'

'If he lets me take your yoke off I'll steal a flint from the panniers and give it to you with the bread. You can cut your fetter and run.'

Tagart nodded wearily.

Bewry bit his lower lip. 'You must run hard, and if they catch you say you had the flint in your clothes. My sister is in the slave quarters, by the gate. She serves in the kitchen there.'

'Yes.'

'You'll want to know what she looks like.'

'Yes.'

'She is beautiful. Her hair is dark brown, to here.' Bewry indicated the nape of his neck. 'Her eyes are brown. She has a soft voice. She wears a deerskin tunic with a circle on the back.'

'And her name is Segle,' Tagart remembered.

'Everyone knows her.'

Again Tagart nodded.

'You promise to help her?' Bewry insisted.

'I promise.'

'Fallott will thrash me if he finds I helped you escape.'

'We will be careful.'

The last goat was aboard; Gane's assistants went to the mooring lines and untied them. Pode shouted to Bewry, telling him to bring the slave. Tagart preceded Bewry along the duckboards and on to the undulating deck of the raft. For a few seconds the men were busy shoving off, Gane and the two others bending poles against the bank, while Fallott, Pode and Bico drew in the mooring lines and made sure of the goats. Bewry examined Tagart's face anxiously, beginning to doubt whether he could be trusted.

Tagart noticed and looked into the child's eyes. 'I keep my word,' he said quietly.

The next stop came eight miles farther west.

From the valley they had climbed to the ridge of the hills and followed it, through scrubby woodland where the wind groaned and made dead branches squeak, and onward to the fields of the open settlement by Cissbury fort. A flock of sheep with wooden bells scattered in their path, and the shepherd with a hand to his brim acknowledged Fallott's nod. Dogs barked as the team went by; one ran out and snapped at Tagart's ankles until Pode growled and struck it with a stick. They went on, skirting Blackpatch Hill and the small flint mines at Findon, and, leaving the fields, entered a belt of oak forest.

The road became a leafy ride, the grass still lush under the trees despite the summer's drought. A mile into the wood the ride opened into a glade, hemmed in by piles of bracken, shaded by the quiet branches, and here, beside an old fallen oak tiered and clustered with brackets of brown fungus, Fallott decided to halt for rest.

He and Pode unpacked the last of the route-victuals, while Bico went into the bracken to relieve himself. Fallott instructed Bewry to give food and water to the slave.

The sun had gone behind cloud; the air was grey. Early afternoon in the wood was silent, with no birds' song. Hoverflies, striped yellow and black, hung momentarily like little wasps in front of Tagart's face before darting away to investigate something else.

He was sitting alone, a little apart, leaning on the fallen trunk. His wrists had been untied and the yoke left lying on the grass nearby.

He stared at the ground. The whole of his body was a mass of tiredness. The yoke had seemed to drain all feeling from his hands and arms, and as he sat there he slowly clenched and unclenched his fists until a trace of sensation returned. Where he had stumbled his feet were raw; criss-cross lines showed where brambles had torn his legs. Dull bruises covered his thighs and body, bruises from being punched and kicked or from falling helpless to the ground, unable to put out his arms to shield himself. His left eye had turned red and puffy; he could no longer see from it. Dried blood was crusted in his beard and top lip below and to the side of one nostril.

Tagart looked up into the network of leaves and light above. He was thinking of Burh, wondering how soon he would be able to get back there and finish what he had set out to do.

'Take it,' Bewry hissed. 'Quick before they see.' He was pressing something cold into Tagart's palm. 'Take it.'

Tagart turned and came face to face with Bewry, and he remembered what they had arranged earlier. He was to cut through the fetter. Bewry was going to help him escape.

'Take it.'

'Yes,' Tagart said. His fingers tried to close on the flint. It slipped from his grasp.

'It's on the ground,' Bewry whispered. 'I cannot reach it yet. Fallott will see.'

'I'm sorry. My hands are slow. I'm tired . . .'

'Drink.'

'Those bastards have done for me.'

Bewry had positioned himself between Fallott and Tagart so

that nothing suspicious could be seen. He raised the water-bag to Tagart's lips. From time to time Fallott glanced in their direction: Bewry and the slave had been whispering at the first rest stop and it seemed prudent to watch them, not that there was any serious danger of trouble.

'The flint is by your leg,' Bewry said as he corked the water and broke off a piece of bread.

'I know.'

'Can you reach it unseen?'

'If I reach it I will still not be able to use it. I have no strength to cut my fetter.' Tagart put his hands to his face. 'Leave it till later.'

Bewry looked over his shoulder. It was a mistake. Fallott noticed and with a frown got to his feet. 'What are you doing there.'

'The slave is eating bread.' As he spoke, Bewry sneaked his hand to the ground, and changing his mind did not palm the flint but pushed it under Tagart's thigh.

Bewry's manner made Fallott narrow his eyes. 'Show me your hands.'

'Just bread, Fallott.'

Fallott's gaze revealed no feeling as he saw the opened hands. It went to Bewry's face, to the ground, to the slave's bent head. 'Move aside that water-bag.'

'I was giving the slave bread as you ordered,' Bewry said as he lifted the bag. There was nothing underneath it.

'You. Slave. What were you whispering?'

The slave mumbled.

'What was that?'

'He was giving me food.'

Fallott glanced round. He had an audience: Pode was watching; Bico had returned from the bracken and had found himself a piece of bread.

'I asked you what you were whispering, nomad.'

'He was giving me food. He asked if I wanted more. I said I did.'

Fallott was unconvinced, but he didn't know why. He was on the point of turning away when Bewry said, far too quickly, 'The slave is exhausted, Fallott. Leave him alone.'

'And why should I do that?'

'If he dies he'll be worth nothing to you when we get to Valdoe.' There was a tremor in his voice.

'What has the slave been saying to you? What do you care if he lives or dies?'

'Nothing. I care nothing.'

Fallott's frown deepened. 'You care nothing, but you whisper to him at every stop.'

'At the ferry station too,' Bico called out.

Bewry shook his head. 'He's said nothing to me, Fallott. Nothing at all.'

Fallott could see the boy was terrified. He wanted to know why.

'What are you hiding there?'

'Nothing. Nothing, Fallott. I'm hiding nothing.'

With the sole of his boot Fallott thrust against Tagart's shoulder and pushed him aside.

His eyes fell on the flint.

He bent and picked it up. 'Nothing, you say. A sharp nothing from our panniers. Is this why we haul a slave across the country, so you can cut him free with a knife stolen from your masters?'

'It was my plan,' Tagart said weakly. 'I made him bring it.'

For an instant Fallott contemptuously studied the slave before turning back to Bewry.

'No,' Bewry said, backing away as Fallott advanced.

'Nothing, you little heathen. Nothing, you say.'

Now Pode had risen, worried for the first time that Fallott was losing his temper.

'Get to your feet!' Fallott shouted at Bewry.

'It's nothing, Fallott,' Pode said. 'Forget it. Forget it and we'll be on our way.'

'Get to your feet!'

The boy put his hands against the fallen tree. He could back away no further. With his eyes fixed on Fallott's face he seemed to shrink against the bark, as if he would melt into the wood itself.

Fallott drew back his hand.

'No!' Bico cried out. 'Don't hit him!'

The Brennis Gehans had made the beginnings of Valdoe over a hundred years before. The flint mines, discovered at first and tentatively worked by local people, lay on the southern slope of a commanding hill, its summit six hundred and seventy feet above sea level. The presence of the flint mines, the configuration of the landscape – not least the proximity of a system of saltmarshes and creeks and natural harbours – and the high quality of the local forest, had all persuaded the first Lord Brennis that Valdoe would make a suitable base for his operations in the island country. He was not the first colonist: for eight hundred years ships had been coming from the German homelands, and most of the coastal farmers shared his ancestry; but the Gehans were something new.

On his arrival the hill had been in the possession of a group of natives, brigands who lived by raiding the villages in the region and pressing their inhabitants into labour in the mines. The brigands had built for themselves a kind of fort, levelling part of the summit.

The Gehan force swiftly overwhelmed the hill fort and dealt with its occupants. Slaves were seized from the surrounding countryside and the building of the Trundle began. This was to be the heart of Valdoe, an impregnable fortress. Further levelling of the summit took place, forming a plateau of roughly oval shape, some fourteen acres in extent. A ditch nine feet deep was dug round the circumference, and inside the ditch was erected a burnt oak palisade twenty feet high, with elevated guard-towers at intervals of sixty or seventy yards. Two gates, at south-west and north-east, gave ingress and egress. A second ditch and palisade, with a single heavily reinforced gate, enclosed three acres in the centre of the main enclosure, and here Brennis Gehan First (the first Gehan who ruled over the island country) established his residence and the barrack to house his personal guard.

The main barracks were built in the outer enclosure, in two sections, one by each of the gatehouses. Other buildings and structures, including dwellings for craftsmen and overseers, store-houses, animal sheds, an armoury, two brothels, reservoirs for ten thousand gallons, dewponds, hawk mews, kennels, and a prison, were set out close inside the main palisade, leaving an open space and parade ground by the inner palisade. Quarters for slaves and miners were erected outside the defences.

Meanwhile the hill itself was cleared of whatever timber remained, and strip-fields dug on the lower slopes. Roads to Eartham in the east, Bow Hill in the west, and Apuldram Harbour in the south, were pushed through to form the basis of a road system.

Soon the investment of time and effort began to pay. A stream of trading vessels from the homelands docked at Apuldram, where a quay and worksheds were under construction. Ships from the home yards were paid for with exported flint of the best grade, manned with soldiers, and sent on slaving sorties to the Normandy coast, for local labour could no longer supply the ambitious programmes of road-building and mining. Freemen at home, dazzled by the tales of wealth and plenty, eagerly applied to the Gehans for permission to make the sea crossing, and within five years the slopes of Valdoe Hill supported the largest single community the island country had ever seen: there were soldiers, farmers, and friendly natives too, derived from those tribes which over the years had intermixed and provided petty traders, itinerant workmen wandering from village to village and harvest to harvest. At the age of forty-two the first Lord Brennis returned home, leaving his nephew in charge.

The initial impetus did not continue. The second Lord Brennis had failed to inherit his uncle's particular talents, and the rate at which Valdoe annexed new tracts of land became slower. A policy of exterminating the native nomad stock was allowed to fall into decline, and in consequence their numbers again built up in the densely wooded region north of the downs. Domination of the coastal villages was relaxed. The secondary forts at Butser, Harting, Whitehawk and elsewhere became weaker and in some cases were abandoned altogether, as were the small mines at Findon and Cissbury and Raven Hill.

It was not until the advent of the fourth Lord Brennis that the Gehan attitude was reasserted. Now the mines were vastly extended, the secondary forts refurbished. The number of slaves was doubled, then trebled and quadrupled. Military and naval strengths were stepped up. French and Cornish raiders, who in the past had made heavy depredations among the slow-minded farmers of the coast, now met a different reception as their ships were seized and their crews taken prisoner and enslaved. During this period certain coastal villages, such as Burh, were becoming more settled, and the fourth Flint Lord tried a system of direct extortion rather than troubling with trade, but soon this was given up: it was easier and more productive to control the slaves at Valdoe than the scattered population along the coast. Plunder and pillage were in future reserved for the settlements across the sea. To enforce the revised discipline tough new recruits were brought from the homelands and trained, and with their help the boundaries of the Valdoe empire began once more to expand.

Now the fourth Lord Brennis was dead. His son remained. At the age of twenty-nine, he had been in command for six years, in control of all the soldiers, the ships, the craftsmen and overseers, the slaves and miners, and in control of the Trundle, the unassailable fortress built by his ancestors on the top of Valdoe Hill.

2

The next day Tagart was put into the mines. He was given no chance to recover from his journey, for on their arrival long after midnight Fallott informed Bewry's overseer that it was Tagart who had struck and broken the neck of the boy, and the other slaves heard the news.

The fertility of the mines – the richness and extent of their flint-seams – was influenced by Gauhm just as the fertility of her fields; effigies of the Earth Spirit in chalk, together with chalk phalli, were enshrined at the entrance to each shaft, and in alcoves underground. Ladders went down from the surface to the galleries, leading off from the shafts at various levels and in various directions, up to seventy feet below ground. The slaves worked by the light of oil lamps, roughly hollowed in small lumps of chalk. To remove flint from the rock-face, they were issued with picks made from the antlers of red deer. The points of the picks were hammered into the chalk and the flint-bearing rock levered out and broken up, the rubble being pushed back with shovels made from cattle shoulder-blades lashed to a handle. The shafts and galleries, from two to six feet high, were shored up with oak planks and props; these frequently failed and collapses were common. When this happened no real attempt was made to rescue the trapped men, for they had been claimed by Gauhm and were regarded as her right, an offering, payment for the flints extracted from the soil. The dead were only slaves, easily replaced – especially if not too many had been lost. A simple shrine would be made at the entrance to the fallen tunnel, to remind Gauhm of the sacrifice that had been made.

Throughout the mines a system of ropes and leather bags brought the newly dug celts to the surface, where they were sorted by specialists, ready for transmission to the knappers' and blade-makers' workshops inside the Trundle. Here the raw flints, first split along lines of natural weakness to make two or more implements from each, were shaped by simple chipping, or, for axes and tools of a better and consequently more expensive grade, the flints were subjected to pressure-flaking: a highly skilled technique in which the pressure of a hand-held stone, applied at precisely the right spot, forced away flakes of flint to leave a sharp and durable cutting edge. The blades were then ground down by rubbing on a slab of wetted sandstone. In this way an axe-head could be produced that was capable of felling a hundred trees before it dulled, and with which one man could clear fifty square yards of birch forest in under an hour.

Tagart did not see Segle, Bewry's sister, until work finished that night. She was serving food in the slaves' quarters, in the refectory, passing bowls of porridge from the ladlers to the man at the head of each bench. An inclined head, a pointed finger, and Tagart was brought to her attention.

Tagart was on the verge of collapse, from lack of sleep, exhaustion, and from the punishment he had received on the walk and since his arrival. During the day, in the mines, he had been kicked and shoved and deprived of his lunch-bowl. He'd had no sleep: word quickly reached the sleeping quarters that he was responsible for Bewry's death; supervision there was less rigid than in the mines, and he soon learned that the overseers were prepared to ignore peccadilloes which if noticed and acted on might incite the majority of the slaves to more general trouble. They had done nothing while he was being beaten up.

During the day he could barely summon the strength to move; his partner, the man allotted to work beside him in the gallery, had been compelled to push Tagart up the ladders in order to get out himself.

Together with the rest of the day-shift, some ninety men in all, they had been marched from the flint workings to the slave quarters, a collection of leather tents and canopies enclosed by a tall wooden cage in the shadow of the south-west gatehouse. The quarters were partitioned into refectory and sleeping areas, the sleeping area enclosed by an inner cage with a roof of tattered skins on a grid of poles. The refectory, next to the kitchens, was formed by four large canopies over eight long wooden tables flanked by benches. It had just been vacated by the outgoing night-shift: the dirty bowls cluttered the tables.

Tagart's partner, Boak, was a heavily built, doleful man with black eyes, wide lips and nostrils, and an overlarge square chin showing under a sparse black beard. He was handing dirty bowls to Tagart, who in turn handed them to the next man, up the table to kitchen-slaves who took them to the ladlers. The long wooden ladles dipped again and again into the smoke-blackened clay cauldrons, emptied their steaming contents into the bowls, and other slaves, including the girl, distributed the filled bowls among the tables.

'That's the sister of the boy you said you did not kill,' Boak said.

Tagart looked up. He saw the circle on the back of her tunic, just as Bewry had described. She turned from the cauldrons with two bowls. In broad cast of feature she resembled her brother; but where Bewry had been ordinary, she was delicate, and even now, begrimed and oppressed by her existence, Tagart could see that in the forest, clean and free, she would be very beautiful.

'Pretty for a kitchen slave,' Boak said. 'It won't be long before they move her to more important work.'

'More important?'

Boak smiled, showing yellow teeth in a weary face that had seen too many people degraded and destroyed.

'She is not yet ready,' Tagart said.

'Tell that to the brothel Trundleman.'

'What is a brothel?'

Boak explained. 'Blene has an eye on her,' he said.

'Blene?'

'You saw him today. In the lynx jacket. He wants her out of the kitchens; come Crale Day he'll have the first taste. When he's finished she'll go into the Trundle, for the soldiers I expect.'

With his baton the nearest overseer warned the two men to stop talking.

Tagart was seated third from the end of the table. The dirty bowls were cleared; full ones were being given out. Gradually each man was served. When Tagart's turn came, he saw that the bowls were being brought by the girl.

She paused at the head of the table, and for a moment stared with hatred at Tagart, a bowl in each hand, steam curling upwards. She gave one bowl to the first man, who passed it to the second, who passed it to Tagart. He slid it in front of Boak, whose meal it was.

Segle stood holding the second bowl, the one destined for Tagart. All eyes were turned. The overseers watched. Everyone in the refectory knew who Tagart was, knew what Fallott had told the supervisor.

Segle drew her arm back and with all her strength threw the bowl at Tagart's face.

The boiling gruel seared his face and neck; the bowl struck his temple and clattered to the table. He sat unmoving.

There was a murmur from the slaves. Tagart gripped the edge of the table, eyes downcast; three of the overseers stepped forward, and the murmur ceased.

The meal resumed in silence. Boak shared his gruel with Tagart, giving most of it away. At first Tagart protested when Boak offered him his bowl; but Boak from the corner of his eye noticed the overseer and by a quick lowering of his head warned Tagart to be quiet.

After the gruel the kitchen-slaves came round with water-bags and baskets of the coarse brown bread baked in the camp ovens. Segle came to the table once more and Tagart seized his chance. When she put down the baskets he lunged across the two men beside him and took hold of her wrist; she tried to pull away as if his touch were poison.

'Listen to me,' he said, as at arm's length she struggled to free herself. 'Your brother died for you. Before Fallott killed him I made Bewry a promise.' Tagart noticed the overseer stepping forward, pulling his baton from his belt. 'I promised I would get you out.'

'Hands off,' the overseer said, prodding the back of Tagart's neck. 'In two weeks she'll be promoted. You can have all you want then – if you wait your turn.'

Tagart released her. Segle drew away, nursing her wrist.

'What were you saying to her?' Boak whispered.

Tagart ignored the question. 'Why are they waiting two weeks? What happens then?'

'In two weeks is Crale Day.'

'Crale Day?'

'The first day of Harvest. High Summer comes to an end. Crale Day is a feast. We're given ale, food fit for a human being, and a visit to the Trundle. I told you she was too pretty for the kitchens.'

When the meal was over the miners were herded into the sleeping cage, moving in single file through the wicket while the overseers watched and counted heads. In the brownish light of the oil lamps Tagart shuffled behind Boak. He passed the overseer by the wicket.

'Sleep well, nomad.'

Inside the cage the smell of sweat and excrement was stifling, despite the fact that it had just been sluiced down and besomed by other slaves, cleaning up after the night-shift. Tagart, knowing that he could expect a repetition of his previous night's treatment, tried to find a position close by the wooden bars in one corner.

'Stay with me,' Boak urged him, stepping over those who had already staked places on the floor.

They sat down in the corner, Tagart with his back to the bars.

The enclosure was full; the overseers shut and secured the gate, and the miners were locked in until mid-morning when the night-shift would return to take their place. For a while longer the glimmer of the lamps lingered on the dull leather awnings, the bars of the cage, the limbs and bodies and heads of those within, and then the overseers withdrew, taking the lamps with them.

Boak formed his words distinctly, so that all could hear.

'Any who strikes Tagart will have to strike me too. He's had enough.'

'He killed Segle's brother,' came a voice on their left.

'For that we have an overseer's word,' Boak retorted. 'Tagart says he didn't do it. I choose to believe him.'

'And if we do not?'

‘Then you are insulting me and I must act accordingly.’

The others objected, but did nothing to approach. Tagart remained unharmed.

‘I am grateful to you,’ he said to Boak.

‘Don’t be. Like it or not I have been burdened with you as partner. If the roof falls in tomorrow I depend on you to pull me out.’ He spoke more quietly. ‘Whether you killed Bewry or not, I don’t care. My only interest is in a partner who is strong and well.’

‘That I can understand. But for my sake I will tell you again: Fallott killed the boy. He hit him in a fit of rage and broke his neck. Fallott blames me for it because a slave’s word here is worthless.’

‘I have only heard of this Fallott,’ Boak said, ‘but as he leads a team you may even be telling the truth. That’s how I came to be here myself – a walking team caught me. They took me from the fields while no one saw.’

‘How long have you been here?’

‘A long time. I cannot remember. Some have been here all their lives.’

‘Do you ever think of escape?’

‘Of course.’

‘Have you tried?’

‘It’s impossible. You will learn.’

‘Has it been done?’

‘Only in rumour,’ Boak said. ‘Once a man was brought back who they said got away. A nomad, like you. They made us watch what they did to him. If you’d seen it you would not be asking these questions.’

Tagart lowered his voice still further, in case they were overheard. ‘You’ve given up all hope, then.’

Boak did not answer at once. ‘Life is sweet,’ he said at last. ‘Even for a worm.’

‘But not at Valdoe.’

‘Even at Valdoe.’

‘No.’

‘You’ll find out.’

‘I would rather be dead.’

‘You are young and know nothing.’

'I know I must get out.'

'Those men in armour today, did you think they were shadows?'

'Not shadows. But not gods. They are men, mere men. Cut a soldier's throat and he will bleed to death like anyone else.'

'That is what the other nomad thought, the one they brought back.'

In the morning the slaves were counted out of the cage, fed and taken downhill to the mines. The older men, or those who had found favour with the guards, were given light work such as rubble-clearing, hauling up the leather bags of flints, fetching and carrying water and food. Others were formed into details to replenish the heaps of struts and planks used for shoring and shuttering below ground. The rest of the slaves were counted down the ladders and sent into the galleries.

Tagart and Boak and two more descended the creaking ladders to one of the deep seams off a minor shaft. The first man down carried a light, a small flame in a chalk lamp which served to do no more than throw confusing shadows. His partner carried a bundle of fifteen or twenty deer-horn picks. Boak wore a leather pouch with supplies of lamp fat, hammers, and a water-bag, while Tagart drew down the ropes which would be used to bring out the flints. As they went deeper the air became cooler. The chalk, brown and dirty white, came off on their clothes and knees; in other places the walls of the shaft were unstable and had been shuttered with planks. They passed the entries to several galleries before reaching the one they had been told to work.

It was low and constricted, narrowing from the entrance, turning slightly from side to side as it followed the flint seams. At its end, twelve feet from the shaft, there was not even room to move on hands and knees, nor was there enough room for a light, and Boak was compelled to work blind. He levered out the chalk blocks with his pick and with his fingers, passing them back to Tagart farther down the tunnel. Tagart passed them back to the third man, who broke up the blocks and pushed the rubble aside. The flints went into the leather bags, which when full were dragged out of the gallery by slaves on the surface. The fourth man went up the shaft with the bags to bring them back; while they were being filled he fanned a panel of laminated reed-leaves stuck with glue, in an attempt to bring fresh air to the gallery mouth. But it had little effect. With the lamps lit, and four men working in a restricted space, the air in the gallery rapidly became foul. Sweat ran unceasingly into Tagart's eyes; the chalk dust clogged his nose and mouth and turned his hair and beard white. Every few minutes the four men changed places so that none should have to spend too long at the end of the gallery. Boak took the brunt of Tagart's work.

The hours fell into a numb, deadening routine. The leather bags came and went. Faintly through intervening rock Tagart could hear other picks at work. At long intervals an overseer climbed down the shaft to supervise progress.

Halfway through the shift a wooden gong sounded at the top of the shaft: the signal to break for food. An old man brought them bread, and bowls of boiled meat or beans and lentils. The same gong sounded at the end of the day when the shift was over and the miners were marched up the grassy slope of the hill, past piles of timber and white rubble, to the canopies and poles of the slaves' quarters.

Bewry was dead; Segle knew that her term in the kitchens would soon be coming to an end. Luckily Blene, the mines Trundleman, had no direct authority over her, but she had seen him watching her as she worked, and now that Bewry was gone and they no longer needed a lever to make him compliant, there could be no reason to deny Blene's request much longer.

It made no difference to her, not now. Her life, the tribe's honour, had finished. They had finished at that moment under the cliffs at Lepe when the soldiers appeared. She remembered the look of the sea, green waves blending to grey in the strait, foam crashing on the shingle as the tribe wandered the tideline. In pairs and threes oyster-catchers, black and white, piped from their red beaks and fought the wind in the troughs, flying just off the beach. Over the drab expanse of saltings and samphire to the west she remembered the wild cries of the curlews and godwits; the distant noise of the gullery where the

Guelen had spent a week living on eggs; and she remembered the smell of the marshes, of brine and rotting weed, the air somehow making your skin more smooth, and when you licked the back of your hand it tasted of the sea. And she remembered another sound, urgent and dangerous, emerging from the roar of surf: hounds.

The soldiers had outmanoeuvred them, coming from the east along the shoreline. Others were appearing against the sky on the clifftops. There was nowhere to run but into the mud.

Segle emptied another bag of oats into the cauldron. Now Bewry too. She was past tears; she thought of his small body lying somewhere in the bracken and a little more of the light went from her eyes.

At first she had believed the story, that the nomad had killed him, but now she was not sure. She did not know. Boak, she had heard, had defended him last night. Did that mean anything? And what had he said to her about a promise? She could think now of nothing but the strength of his grip on her wrist. His words had escaped her. But his eyes had not, nor had the sound of his voice. In them she had recognized her own kind.

'More beans here!'

Segle pushed the hair from her brow and went to obey.

'So from what you have told me,' Tagart said, 'there can be no escape from the cage, nor from here. That means we must wait our chance and break from the bathing party.'

It was the fifth day: Tagart and Boak were working alone in a minor gallery at the bottom of the main shaft. Tagart had recovered much of his strength. The cuts and bruises sustained on his walk had almost healed, his eye had opened, and regular food and sleep were bringing back tone and balance to his muscles and limbs. Work underground was arduous and unpleasant, but he was young. The output of the other slaves was well within his capacity, and he saw no reason to extend himself. For long periods when lightly supervised he and Boak sat and rested, taking up their picks and hammers when they heard the creak of rungs which meant an overseer was descending. The overseer in charge of the main shaft, named Stobas, was a broad-faced man with pale blue eyes and straight black hair, shoulder-length, tied into a pigtail. Like all the overseers, he was himself a former slave who knew no other existence but Valdoe.

'He's coming,' Tagart said, and crawled into the end of the gallery, where he began to hammer conscientiously at the chalk.

Stobas appeared at the mouth of the gallery, swinging himself off the ladder and into the tunnel. He carried a lamp with him, and in his belt a blackthorn cudgel fitted with a wrist-strap.

'Work is slow here,' he said. 'You're slacking.'

'The seam is harder at this end, master,' Tagart said.

Stobas briefly examined the rock face. He scratched it with his thumbnail, wiped the chalk off with his index finger. 'More bags or you'll both be beaten,' he said tersely, returning to the ladder.

'Yes, master,' Boak said.

Stobas paused. 'Didn't you hear the gong? End of shift. Get above ground.'

At the top of the shaft, in a wide cavern, the ladders became a permanent staircase of worn and chalk-stained planking which led up into a sloping tunnel with daylight at its end. Tagart and Boak emerged with eyes squinting against a red sunset.

'Full count!' another overseer cried out as Stobas stood surveying the ragged ranks of slaves, three deep, thirty yards long.

'To quarters!'

The men wearily turned and started up the hill, closely guarded by the overseers and the squad of soldiers sent from the Trundle at times of shift change. Other soldiers kept watch during the day and night at each exit from the mines, armed with spear-slings and bolas; and, following a mass break-out some years before, the watch on the slaves' quarters had been reinforced. A system of head-counting at shift change, meal times and on entering and leaving the sleeping cage reduced still further the opportunities for undetected escape. Similar vigilance attended the details formed for timber cutting, water haulage, and the like, or when, twice a month, small groups of slaves were taken down to the river to wash and have the lice removed from their bodies. If a slave did manage to escape, his chance of remaining free was almost nil. Teams of tracker dogs with their handlers could be despatched from the Trundle within minutes.

The men of the night shift were counted out and passed down the hill to the flint workings; Tagart and the others were counted into the refectory and in silence sat down to their meal.

Bewry's sister was there. On several occasions over the past four days Tagart had met her eyes; but since the incident on the first evening they had not spoken, for by chance he and Boak had always been seated well away from the cauldrons. But tonight, as they had been the last in line, they were put at the end of the table nearest the big clay hearth. Segle moved to and fro; Tagart watched her, and with a pang realized what he had not admitted to himself before – that she reminded him in her movements and attitudes of Mirin.

'What is it, my friend?' Boak said.

Tagart shook his head.

Warily Boak kept an eye on the overseers. 'What's troubling you?'

Tagart could not tell him: he did not know how to put his feelings and longings into words. How could he explain what his life had been; how could he describe what they had taken away?

'I do not take to captivity,' Tagart said at last.

'Then are you serious about escape? Or was that just talk?'

'You said you'd changed your mind today. If you want to come with me, I plan to break from the bathing party.'

'We'll never do it. They bring the dogs down to the river.'

The overseer passed behind them. Tagart continued handing dirty bowls to the serving-slaves; Segle was two tables away, not near him. He looked at her and she half turned, and Tagart knew that she was aware of him as he was of her.

'You've never been in a bathing party,' Boak hissed. 'I know what to expect. There must be another way.'

'How did the other man do it? The nomad.'

'No one knows.'

'Then it must be the bathing party. When are we due to go?'

'The day after tomorrow.' Boak sneaked a glance over his shoulder at the overseers: their attention was elsewhere. 'It's too dangerous,' he whispered to Tagart. 'Even if we get away, where can we go? Where can we hide?'

'In the forest. No one can catch me there. If you come with me you will be safe too.'

Boak bit his cheek.

Tagart shrugged to himself. He needed Boak, or at least he needed someone who knew the routine. But once on the loose Boak might well prove a nuisance. 'Decide tomorrow,' Tagart said.

Boak nudged him to silence. An overseer had come to stand by the cauldrons, idly watching the ladlers at work. Now the freshly filled bowls were being given out. A grey-haired woman had been serving Tagart's table; Segle spoke a few words to her.

Deliberately Segle came over. Her presence beside Tagart was almost tangible, and even before she opened her mouth and spoke he sensed something shared, wordless, a sensation he had only known once before. But her face was hardened by determination and as she slid the bowls on to the table she spilled a little of their contents and he saw that her hands were trembling.

She looked straight into his eyes. 'Did you kill my brother?'

Tagart slowly shook his head.

'Then was it Fallott?'

'Would I kill a future hunter, one of my own?'

Her expression softened and Tagart knew that he had been believed, that she now regretted her first feelings; he felt an urge to touch her hand with his own and make contact, physically to confirm what had passed between them in looks, but Segle was already moving away, back to the cauldrons.

3

The following morning dawned windy and grey; spots of rain began to fall as Tagart and Boak stood in line, waiting to be ordered underground.

Blene, the Trundleman in charge of coordinating the mines, a man of forty, unapproachable and fastidious, appeared from the Trundle and at his leisure made his way downhill. His black hair was cropped very short, close to his scalp, and twice a day he scraped off his beard with a flint razor and seaweed mucilage as soap. His eyes, pale grey, missed nothing: no detail of the mines was beneath his attention. Today he had discarded his lynx jacket in favour of a sealskin cape fixed at the throat with a cherry-wood clasp.

He arrived. 'Six more for the west workings,' he said crisply. 'Take them from the main shaft.'

With jerks of his finger Stobas indicated the six slaves who were to be reallocated. He chose carefully. If productivity in his section fell he would lose privileges, but if he gave Blene men who were obviously old or infirm he would incur the Trundleman's disfavour. He picked one old man, a youth with scarcely a beard, two brothers who were well known reliable workers, and, smiling inwardly, Stobas indicated Tagart and Boak. At his command all six joined the remainder of the day shift for the west workings. This was an old part of the mine, nearly exhausted now, providing flints that were only barely superior to those that could be picked up off the ground anywhere along the downs; the shafts had gone as deep, the galleries as far, as the flint seams and the difficulties of ventilation allowed. Blene was anxious to complete work there and make a start on new excavations farther down the hill.

'Have you decided on escape?' Tagart said to Boak as they waited. 'Are you with me?'

The other man looked at the ground, unwilling to meet his eye. 'The bathing party is tomorrow,' he said.

'What of it?'

'Tomorrow is too soon.'

'Not for me.'

'We must prepare. Let's go tomorrow just to look.'

'No.'

'Why?'

'I must get out.'

'Leave it another half month till the next bathing party. We can do it then.'

Tagart was adamant. He refused.

'But why?'

'Crale Day.'

Further conversation was impossible; Tagart and Boak were teamed with the old man, Maphen, and a dark, quiet foreigner named Chorn, issued with lamps and picks and a water-bag, and sent down the ladders to a wide gallery thirty feet below the surface. For much of its length its walls and roof were boarded and supported with oak planks and struts. Broken picks littered the floor. Maphen set lamps in crevices and alcoves and Chorn started work on the rock-face even before the rest of the shift had finished climbing down past the gallery mouth. Tagart and Boak exchanged glances; Boak wagged his head in mock amazement.

At a lower level men were shouting orders and responses. Boak explained that the gallery below theirs was being closed: the six extra slaves had been needed to help reinforce the shuttering, retrieve the ropes and bags, and dismantle the ladders.

'You still have to answer me yes or no,' Tagart said, shovelling rubble back. The work was beginning to make him sweat. Chorn, the foreigner, hacked at the chalk as if he bore it a grudge. 'You must tell me if you are coming.'

'I know.' Boak felt himself standing on the edge of a precipice. But realizing it, he already knew he was falling.

'What have you decided?'

'Let it be tomorrow.'

'And are you with me?'

'Yes.'

The attempt was doomed, Boak knew it as well as he knew

his own name, but he no longer cared. He had been affected by what Tagart had been saying day after day. At first he had refused to listen. Boak knew the boy's words for what they were, facile and immature; he knew the hard reality. A slave at Valdoe could not get away. They would both be caught. But he also knew that even if they were seized the first instant of escape, even if they were, like the nomad who had tried it, tortured and put to death as an example, even then he would have made an attempt, a gesture, futile perhaps, but he would have been free for a few seconds, no longer in bondage, no longer in the service of those who had made themselves his masters. He would have shaken them, brought a moment of uneasiness to the Lord of Valdoe, a man he had never seen, a man who despised him as a slave. It would be worth it for that alone.

The first gong sounded. Work in the gallery ceased. Stew was brought down the shaft in leather satchels and given to the miners in the wooden bowls left in each gallery for the purpose.

'Stew good,' Chorn said. He was sitting with his back to the shuttering, picking fragments of meat from the bowl, raising his fingers to his open mouth, head tilted back.

'Make you work faster,' Tagart told him.

'Ya.' Chorn nodded. He noticed Maphen. 'Old man,' he said. 'You don't eat. I eat for you.'

Maphen waved his words away. He was tired. The lamps were spluttering. He shut his eyes and rested his head against the boards.

Tagart finished his stew. It left an oily taste in his mouth. 'Pass me the water,' he asked Chorn.

Chorn did not understand.

'The water. Give me the water.'

Comprehension came across his face. 'You want water.'

As he handed Tagart the leather bag there was a low, barely perceptible vibration, a kind of distant groan, in the strutted roof above them. The boards at Maphen's back moved slightly. Tiny streams of dust showered down. Then from a much deeper level a loud, dull booming rose up the shaft and was followed by a series of percussive cracks as if structural beams were breaking. Behind Tagart the boards rattled and jolted and two of the lamps tumbled from their alcoves.

'Get out!' Boak screamed. 'Get out!'

But even before they could scramble to their feet the ceiling props were no longer vertical and in the moment before the last lamp went out Tagart saw broken boards collapsing and the shape of boulders and dust and slabs of chalk falling in a solid roar, burying Maphen and Chorn in ton after ton of crushing pressure, catching Boak as he struggled towards the mouth of the gallery, and Tagart himself was being buried, struck by the fall, pounded across the shoulders and back, on his head, his legs, pinned to the floor by the intolerable weight of rock above him. He was unable to breathe, unable to move, utterly caught, his face being forced with increasing insistence downwards. A little longer and he knew his cheekbones would fail. They would give way under the unbelievable weight and his skull would be pushed in from behind. But the ground had not yet stopped moving: it was still shifting, grinding, settling, filling in from above and at random the vacancy of galleries and shafts tunnelled out below.

He lost consciousness. The voices woke him.

At first he had tried to accommodate them in his dreams, but the voices resisted, growing louder, intruding, annoying him: he wanted only to be left in peace. The voices made him frown. He was made to listen as his warm landscape dissolved and he became suspended in blackness and cold.

'Is anyone left alive?'

'Knock if you can hear us!'

Silence.

'You slaves, dig there and see how far in it reaches. There may be a pocket.'

He heard rocks being pulled aside, dull and hollow.

'Is anyone in there?'

'It is Gauhm's will.'

Tagart remembered what had happened.

The voices were not far away, three feet at most. Tagart raised his head and found it free. He could move his arms also. He felt them. They were not broken. He put his fingers to his face and discovered blood.

'Gauhm has taken them in this gallery too. Back to your labour.'

The blood was in his beard; he traced it back to his nostrils and the warm ooze was slippery on his fingertips. From his nose he ran a finger along his teeth. One at the front was broken. The rest were intact. He probed them with his tongue. The taste of more blood. His hands were shaking.

'How many lost in all, master?'

'Overseer?'

'Seven below and four here, Trundleman Blene.'

Pain sliced into Tagart's chest at each intake of breath. The bruising felt as if it extended down both his sides and into his buttocks.

'Eleven men lost in all, then.'

'It might have been worse, Trundleman.'

'Shall we make the shrine here, Trundleman?'

'Below. Make it below where most were lost.'

A long time later Tagart realized the voices had gone away. Vaguely he could make out the sounds of activity at different levels, and when he heard the gong it was not long before the ladders creaked close by and he knew the day-shift men were going above ground.

There were varying weights on his lower back and legs. His feet seemed to be splayed at an odd angle and he hoped they were all right. He was trembling, shivering with the cold, yet there were chilly points of sweat on his forehead. With care he began turning his back, putting more weight on his right side. Lumps of chalk rolled off him. He turned completely and realized he was no longer trapped: his legs, like his body, were bruised but otherwise undamaged, and all he had to do to free himself completely was pull them out from beneath the pile of rubble.

Boak's voice, feeble and hoarse, came from the darkness behind him. 'Tagart? Tagart?'

'Boak?'

'I can't move.'

Tagart reached up and his fingertips sculptured the outlines of the crossed struts that had fallen against each other in the cave-in and spared him the full force of the final collapse; the floor of the gallery had shifted sideways and down, forming a small chamber where he and Boak were left alive.

Boak was in pain. He said, 'I'm cold.'

'Keep still.' On hands and knees Tagart crawled towards Boak's voice. His hands lit on the water-bag: he felt it, the leather, the bung, the strap, acknowledging what it was. 'Are you thirsty?'

Boak groaned. Tagart reached him and quickly found his face. There was something slimy over it. Boak was lying on his back, breathing quickly. He coughed. Tagart felt his jaw, his nose, behind his head. Much of his scalp had been torn off. Lower down, at the nape, Tagart touched something hard, wet, and strange, gritty with dust, the place where his neck was broken and his spine exposed.

'What are you doing to my feet?'

Tagart held the water-bag to Boak's lips. He kept knocking the spout against Boak's teeth: for he was trembling very badly. A trickle came out. Some of it found its way into Boak's mouth. He retched and coughed and Tagart took the water away.

The rocks under which Boak had been buried were too heavy to shift. For a moment Tagart had been able to clear Boak's mouth and nose so that he could breathe more freely. That was all. He knew that Boak was already finished. Even if they were rescued, even if Boak were given the best treatment with comfrey and splints, he would never survive. A broken arm might be cured, with luck; perhaps even a broken shin. But not a broken neck.

'I'm cold,' Boak said. 'I'm cold. I want to be in the sunshine.'

Tagart sat rocking from side to side with eyes closed. His chest hurt. He hugged himself, trying to ease the pain of bruising.

'Boak?' he whispered.

No answer came. Boak was dead.

Tagart crawled to the other end of the chamber, to the place where he had heard the voices and put his cheek to the rocks. Sounds of picks and hammers reached him, faintly, from another level. He moved his face from side to side, listening, watching, and tried to catch a glimmer of light. There was none.

Tentatively he explored the pile of rubble in front of him, desperate not to make a sound. It was composed mainly of small fragments of chalk, distinguishable by its greasy texture, some larger chunks, and a few flints. Here and there he felt broken planks and spars, and the shapes of wooden pegs and rope, and leather bindings that had burst from their brackets.

Piece by piece, he moved the rubble behind him.

The major obstacle was a pit-prop, wedged at an angle across the blockage. Even if he could have managed it, removal of the prop would have brought down the rest of the gallery about him and summoned help – the last thing he wanted. He was forced to work round the prop. The necessity for silence slowed his digging still further, but the blockage was less than four feet thick and his progress towards the other side was sure.

He had actually pierced the blockage, made a hole large enough to put his arm through and feel air, when the gong sounded and he thought he had missed his chance.

But instead of the night-shift men coming up the ladders, he heard the descent of the meal slaves with their bags of stew. And in spite of everything he grinned with delight. At last fortune was beginning to go with him again.

He continued to pick at the rubble, making the hole wider, wide enough to get through, and then he put some larger lumps back to fill the gap and settled down to wait and to examine himself properly, to take stock.

He had not suffered any internal injury, of that he was fairly sure; but the pain and bruising in his chest was very bad and spreading further, into other regions, especially down his left side. The trembling in his hands had scarcely improved. But his limbs were intact, especially his legs, for which he was glad: whether or not he had received a concussion, he could still run, and for the moment he could think. There in the complete darkness of the collapsed gallery his thoughts ran clear and cold, uncluttered in a way he had never known before. He felt he could see into the future, if he wanted. He knew what was going to happen. It was no mistake that events had fallen in the way they had.

For him it had all been a lesson. The forest, impersonal, indifferent to him in his time of need, now promised to take him back. He saw the pattern. He saw the end, his release from the acrid loneliness that had been with him since Balan died.

He waited, as if he were waiting for deer, exploring his thoughts. The water-bottle lay at his side. No mistake. Fifty miles to Burh. He could not risk using the Valdoe roads. A forest route, then. Twenty miles a day, his usual speed, might be too much for him in his present state. Fifteen, then. Allow three days. Four at most. He would have to feed himself on the way. Burh in four days. Four back to Valdoe. That left two spare days before Crale Day.

It could be done. He could get the girl out somehow.

He gave his mind to luring the head man from the village. Among the trees, he wanted him among the trees. Easy.

Everything easy, falling into place . . .

How to deal with Valdoe afterwards, how to bring Segle out, as he had promised her brother by the ferry station with the clouds blowing over Thundersbarrow and the spokes of sunlight across the river, giving the weight of his honour; and, because he was the one chosen to be left, the weight of the tribe's honour, given to a small boy struck dead later that day because he loved his sister more than his own life.

Valdoe would not be so easy, not so easy as the village, but in his delirium Tagart knew he could do it too.

At the second gong Tagart was ready. He pulled the lumps of chalk from the gap, and, before the first slave had started up the shaft, he was squeezing through the hole and into what was left of the gallery. He lay there momentarily, overcome by the excruciating pain in his chest, forcing himself by an act of sheer will to do what he had planned next.

The ladders were creaking with the weight of men passing upward by the time he had finished it, the painstaking task of filling the hole in. He waited his chance in the darkness near the gallery mouth, and, the water-bag thrust inside his tunic, he swung himself on to the ladder and joined the exodus.

A rainstorm was blowing above ground. The guards and soldiers wore glistening sheepskin capes and shouted to each other against the howl of wind. Tagart was the sixth or seventh miner to emerge blinking in the morning light; he turned with a comment to the man behind him.

'I hope they plan something better for us than the mid-shift meal.'

'At least we can drink with it.' The other man nodded at the rain, pelting the ground, driving in sheets across the face of the hill, obscuring and then revealing the shape of the fortress at the summit.

All the miners were filthy, grimy with chalk: Tagart's appearance excited no interest or comment, for he had cleaned most of the blood from his face and beard. He moved forward, covertly glancing at the piles of timber newly removed from the west workings. The others, twenty-seven in all, came behind.

Tagart traded remarks with his new-found friend, establishing himself, he hoped, as a member of the night shift.

'Quiet there!'

More men were appearing at the entrance of the other shafts, while the soldiers watched and the overseers shouted orders, marshalling the slaves into a rank. The soldiers and overseers looked cold and wet. Some of them had been standing in the open all night, and would get no shelter until this shift was safely behind bars.

Tagart heard Stobas's voice issuing instructions. The rain blew in curtains across the workings, streaking chalk on the miners' faces, plastering hair to heads. Tagart felt his clothes increasing in weight.

The line of men was moving too fast, too far away from the pile of timber Tagart had chosen; he stopped and pretended to see something in the grass before shuffling on. The man with whom he had spoken went ahead.

'All up!' shouted the overseer from the west workings, and one by one the others reported the same.

'All up!'

'All up!'

Tagart felt a flood of gratitude. The weather was doing it for him. The weather.

From the back of the rank he glimpsed the overseers standing tall, moving their hands edge-on, counting off slaves in threes. The first had finished his count and was frowning slightly. He started to count again.

On either side of Tagart the slaves were looking straight forward. One was a thin, spare man who looked like a farmer, the other was a shorter man who could have been a foreigner like Chorn. Neither seemed to have noticed him particularly. Like the others, like the guards, they were keen to get the count finished and hurry back to the building for shelter.

The back of the rank was being observed by at least three soldiers. From the rank to the pile of wood he thought it twelve or fifteen paces, too many to cover undetected with the soldiers watching, even in this rain.

A hundred or so heavy struts made up the pile of wood, laid parallel to the line of the rank. Just beyond it lay other piles of wood, and a series of white chalk spoil-heaps discoloured by top-soil, leading downhill and away from the fort. The ramparts were nearly a mile off. In this weather there was no danger of being seen from the Trundle.

'One over!' the first overseer shouted, and for a moment all heads turned.

It was enough. Tagart, backing gingerly at first, cleared the rank and ran to the pile of wood. He glanced behind. Everyone, mildly curious, was listening to Stobas ask how ninety-three could come out when only ninety-two had gone down.

Everyone except one man, the farmer who had been standing next to Tagart.

Tagart met his eye.

The farmer smiled, glanced sideways at the soldiers, and turned back with every sign of renewed interest to watch the dispute between overseers.

'One over!' the second overseer shouted.

'Check count!' Stobas ordered. 'Rank form into pairs!'

But Tagart had already found a place to hide in the middle of the pile. He crawled through a triangular gap, constricting his chest again, pushing with the heels of his hands on the rain-soaked timbers. The pain of working himself past the struts threatened to make him cry out. But his chest was through and he dragged himself further inside, into a space lower down. Vision fuzzed by pain, he forced himself into it, and, just as the rank reformed and the soldiers again began their supervision, his feet and then his toes slid through the triangular entrance to his hiding-place and disappeared from view.

4.

The oak tree in which Tagart had hung the woman grew on the slope above his yew tree, less than two hundred paces east, but it was not until some while after his return that he was able to focus his mind on his hostage and what he had done with her.

His journey had taken five days, the first being spent in hiding under the heap of struts. The worst moment came after the completion of the check count. Stobas became suspicious, and considered sending a man to the Trundle to advise Blene; but for the weather, and the fact that the check count gave, after all, the right total, a search might have been ordered, and perhaps the dogs brought down. Tagart tried to draw himself further into the pile of timber. He was hungry and very tired, suffering the symptoms of shock, and mild concussion, and the pain of the bruises on his body was turning steadily worse. Later in the day more timber was flung on the heap and Tagart feared that he might not be able to get out. But at nightfall, when the shifts had long since changed and the soldiers were least expecting anything unusual, he silently crawled out and hobbled into the darkness unobserved.

That night he made only five miles, stopping in the early hours to rest and await the morning. Any exertion made the discomfort worse. His sleep, a few minutes together, was coloured by nightmares that seemed to persist in his waking thoughts. The same dream repeated itself. Segle was with him in some unfamiliar place, a lake in a clearing. He knew they were safe, a great distance from Valdoe; they were beside the water, drowsy in the afternoon sun. Tagart had shot a wild-cat and they were roasting it over a bed of embers. Beside the lake stood the brown stems and umbels of chervil and keck. Creamy blossoms of hemp agrimony billowed pink across the water, in line with the course left by the passage of their bodies through the weed. They had been swimming, out through the frog-bit and into the centre of the lake where from a deep spring the water welled limpid and cold. The girl was naked, her hair wet and lying close, revealing the shape of her brow; but as he looked into her eyes her face became a grinning skull. He ran to the water's edge and knew what he would find. She was floating just beneath the surface, white and swollen.

There were other dreams, all involving the girl. Frequently he shouted himself awake and sat up, shivering and trembling. At last he got to his feet. The strength had gone from his legs. He found it hard to keep moving, even from tree to tree: he was bone tired. Full daylight was coming on. He ate a few berries, felt slightly better for them, and in the dry leaves below the bushes discovered a hedgehog, curled up and asleep. As he had no knife or handaxe he urinated on the animal to make it uncurl and killed it by pinching the snout. With a broken pebble he did his best to skin it, and ate it raw. A little later he came across a wood-pigeon's nest in the ivy against an oak and gulped down the contents of both eggs.

He was travelling north-east, into the deep forest behind Eartham Hill, keeping well away from the coast and the danger of open ground. The sky cleared gradually and by the time he reached the first of the great rivers there was intermittent sunshine. The sun stayed with him on most of the following days, days of slow progress and weariness. Increasingly he found it hard to think straight, to remember details; his thoughts were sluggish, and his body refused to respond properly. The second day was the worst. After that he began to improve; he was able to cover more ground. On the third day he came across the remains of a temporary camp, vacated less than a week earlier by a tribe whose bark-cut signs he identified as the work of the Jays – people he knew. Not for the first time he considered seeking help. But he had no time to spare. The Jays had gone north-west and might be days ahead, and he was on his way to Burh.

On the fourth night, under a gibbous moon that made the marshes silver and black, he came out of the forest and used one of the punts to cross the wide river in the reeds, the last great river before Burh. And on the fifth day, at mid-morning, he found himself once more in sight of the village.

He had been absent for twelve days. Outwardly, there had been little change. From the escarpment he saw people in the compound and on the steps of the Meeting House; work had resumed in the fields, which now were markedly greener. After a while he made out the beardless man, Groden, working with several others, cutting hay from a field by the river. Tagart wondered if his hole in the silo, his entry and exit, had been discovered.

He could not find the yew tree straight away. It had been concealed and camouflaged too well, and his memory deceived him: the tree was more to the north than he remembered, and it looked different in shape. But even if he had been unable to know the place at all, his attention would have been drawn by the carrion flies and the smell of putrefaction. The strips of venison had turned. A fox had taken many of them. The rest were crawling with maggots. Tagart carried the strips beyond the yew and flung them far into the undergrowth.

He checked over what was left of his stores. A few flints, three bows lacking strings, an arrow, short lengths of twine and rope, two water-bags, and the bottle he had brought with him from the mines. He would need to arm himself before going back for Segle. The village: they would have weapons down there; and he would have to have clothes and clogs to get inside Valdoe. Those too could be found in the village.

Yes, he knew the way it was all going to unfold.

He shut his eyes and covered his face. His hands were still trembling: they had not stopped, not completely, since the cave-in. He felt as if he were burning his reserves at a profligate rate, fighting alternate waves of chill and heat. Still his thoughts were not normal. There were blank spots, areas of impenetrable and hazy memory, moments of lucidity followed by a kind of delirium in which his mind raced extravagantly, inconclusively. The toll of the past weeks was catching up with him. Physically the bruising on his body had begun to heal: yellow, green, purple. He undid his tunic and examined himself again.

He told himself that he had been in low states in the past, and he had suffered bruising. He had been hurt before. This was nothing new. The exhaustion and fever, the delirious thoughts, these were nothing new. He tried to console himself.

But in his condition he had no defence against mistakes.

He pushed the thought aside, fastened his tunic, stood up, and went outside to find food.

Only in the late evening, after he had slept, did Tagart remember there was something else in his camp that he still had to investigate. He found the oak tree after a short search, and climbed into it.

Hernou was still there. Hanging upside-down, the blood had drained into her head and the upper part of her body. From the contortion of her features he gleaned an idea of the circumstances of her death. In her throes the rope had been worn almost to its last fibre wherever it rubbed on bark. Tagart undid the gag. Her face seemed barely recognizable. She had been dead about eight days.

He cut the body down.

He was trying to think. How could he have forgotten?

How could he have forgotten such a thing?

No answer came. He put her over his shoulders, and, remembering what he had planned to do, gasped and struggled with her weight on his way towards the escarpment.

Sturmer paused in his work and stood upright, pulling back his shoulder-blades and stretching his spine. Stooping no longer agreed with him so well. In his right hand he held a sickle, a yard of blackthorn with a steam-curved end in which were set half-a-dozen flint chips to form a cutting-edge. With it he had been swinging gradually along the riverbank, cutting down the tall bromes and meadow-grasses for winter silage, in line with thirty others. Between them they had cleared most of the river-field since daybreak. Now, at mid-afternoon, women and children, and those who could no longer do full work, came behind collecting the cut grasses into sheaves ready to be bundled and dragged back to the village. The old men, supervised by Vude, trimmed the hay-sheaves to size, ready for packing in the barn.

This task would not normally have fallen to the old men; but the population of the village had been almost halved, with the worst losses among the young, those whom Burh could least afford to be without. The crippled and maimed numbered more than twenty, and they, like the orphans and widows, would have to be fed.

Most of the surviving young men wanted to leave. They were afraid that Tsoaul had not yet finished. Fallott had failed to come with help, and for that Sturmer had been partly blamed; but he had reasoned with them, and begged them to wait. Since the new moon the forest had been quiet. The trouble was over. Tsoaul had taken Hernou and would not be back. Why allow themselves to be driven out? Why throw away years of work for nothing? Why face the danger and hardship of founding a new village when their true home was here in Burh?

The Council decision on the matter had been inconclusive. The older men felt that Hernou had been taken because it was she who had been to blame for the killing of the nomads, and only right that she should be sacrificed for the common good. They said she had plotted to attack the nomads, blinding Groden and those round her with her beauty, an evil and poisonous influence. Now that her influence had gone, there could be no more risk; and even Groden had given up hope of finding her. The younger men argued differently. The only reason, they said, that no one had been abducted since Hernou's disappearance was that no one had left the village, except in parties of a dozen or more, and no one at all had ventured into the trees. Tsoaul was still in the forest, waiting his chance.

Sturmer had been unable to convince them. In deference to the elders, and for that reason alone, the young men had reluctantly agreed to stay.

Now their fears had been eclipsed by the urgent need to make a harvest. The prospect seemed bad. Even though there were only half as many bellies to fill, there would not be enough food to last the winter. The drought had persisted too long. The barley crop was all but ruined; the wheat down by three-quarters; the millet by half; and the oats had failed completely, the panicles stunted, crumbling to dust when rubbed between the fingers. To save feed, all but a few of the animals would have to be slaughtered. Some could be sustained on the rougher ensilage that usually was not even harvested, which included the bromes and meadow grasses.

Sturmer returned to his cutting. The line of men moved steadily forward, in a rhythm with the swish of sickles and the soporific chuckle of the river as it went on its way to the sea. Behind them the slain grasses lay strewn across the field.

The women had not been gathering for long when Sturmer heard his name called out from the village. He looked up. Vude, white-bearded, his bald head hatless, was hurrying towards him along the river path.

'Sturmer!'

'What is it?'

He went forward to meet the old man. They came face to face, twenty yards ahead of the line, and Vude bent and leaned on his knees, breathing with difficulty. He turned his face. 'You must come, Sturmer. They're in the barn. They haven't seen it yet.'

'Seen what?'

'Come quickly.'

Vude led him back to the village, through the east gate. On the far side of the compound they saw the women, on ladders leaning against the palisade, dropping bundles of hay to the old men waiting below. Another group of old men trimmed and shaped the sheaves, while a third carried them into the barn and packed them crosswise and lengthwise, making a solid rick.

'This way,' Vude said, branching left from the thoroughfare and leading Sturmer between the houses.

At the base of the palisade he stopped. 'I came to see how much of the trimmings we could save. I took off the covers. Look.'

A tunnel had been burrowed through one of the silos. Its cover, a mat of interwoven sticks, showed holes and signs of damage.

'The tunnel is large enough for a man,' Sturmer observed.

'It joins up with a trapdoor in the turf on the other side. I thought you alone ought to know.'

'So you have guessed the truth too.'

'Not before now.'

'I told Groden to make sure none remained alive,' Sturmer said.

'You should have seen to it yourself.'

'I think it was only one.'

Vude nodded. 'Any more and the ambush would have been different.'

'That is how I reasoned it.'

'Do you think he's still up there, in the forest?'

Sturmer squinted up at the escarpment behind them. 'There's been no trace of him for a fortnight. He must be ill, or dead. If he'd gone for help it would all have been over for us a week ago.'

Vude agreed. The nomads could signal each other, by magic, over great distances. One survivor of the massacre, if he had sought them, could have brought many to attack the village.

'You did well to tell me first,' Sturmer said. With his sickle he rearranged the silo to hide the tunnel. 'I must have your silence, Vude. If the others hear of this, the young men will prevail in the Council.'

'But suppose the nomad is still alive? Suppose he has gone for help?'

'He hasn't.'

'I trust you, Sturmer. I believe what you say. But the young men . . . they're saying you're not what you were. They say you're too old. Groden . . .'

'Groden is disgraced,' Sturmer said curtly, standing up.

Vude let the comment pass.

'If you doubt me,' Sturmer said, 'tell the others. Tell them an army of nomads is coming and Sturmer is too stupid to admit it. Tell them and kill the village yourself.'

'All I say is that you must take care.'

'I shall.'

'Then you have my silence, head man.'

Tagart shifted sideways, throwing the woman's body from his shoulders. She rolled a little way down the escarpment and came to rest, arms and legs at strange angles, her face bloated and stretched, as tight as a drum. Tagart came after and shoved her with his heel. She turned over, twice, three times, and came to rest again.

The village lay in shadow; from up here the last wash of sunset could be seen. The moon, almost full, rode in the sky among the trees. Already its shine outdid the dusk: he could see it on the roofs and palisade, and on the curves of the forest across the valley, where the evening star burned steadily in the west. A heron flapped its way inland, like a pale grey wraith following the reflections and rushes of the river, neck curled back, legs outstretched behind, still dripping the water of the estuary. Over the village it uttered a single harsh cry.

Tagart rolled the corpse most of the way down the escarpment, stopping well short of the palisade for fear of alarming the dogs.

He dragged the body upright and manhandled it over to an oak bush, resting it against the drought-scorched, premature brown leaves. It slid rustling to the ground. He hoisted it again, positioning it another way, and another, until it remained, spread-eagled, in full view.

With many pauses to catch his breath, he turned and climbed back to the forest.

5.

By early afternoon the next day Sturmer knew that to save himself and the village only one course of action remained. His special knowledge, shared with no one but Vude, made the decision easier to take, for it promised him the recapture of the support he had been losing throughout the day in Council. But the courage he needed did not come easily and in the floating unreality of the Meeting House he almost left it too long. His announcement, that he alone would go into the forest and fight Tsoaul, drew gasps of disbelief, amazement, and then admiration.

The hours of the day had begun rapidly. His bed was still warm when he heard the news; and then Deak and Feno brought the corpse into the compound and he saw it for himself. The thing laid in the dirt before him had at one time been Hernou. It had housed her spirit, long sincc fled. He himself had, many years before, slept with it, made love to it, even once thought it might mother his children and be his wife. In those gaping orbits, eyes had sparkled. Tsoaul, the young men were saying, had finished with her and flung her back: an omen, a sign of hostility renewed. In the early half-light, made chill by mists from the river and fields, Groden came at a run from his house and thrust his way among the villagers gathering round the body. He broke through to the inner circle and stood transfixed, staring at what had been his woman.

His face twisted; he took a step back. His mouth seemed to fill, and he turned away.

An abomination sprawled there, a body with no soul. Without prayer, without the necessary repose on the Dead Ground, her spirit had been driven out, forced to wait too long alone in a disembodied state. Her soul had been lost for ever to the demons and the wilderness. They could not give her a place in the burial mound. She had become part of Tsoaul's works, like the bodies of the bears.

But they did not burn her. At Sturmer's order, with Groden's acquiescence, she was taken to the beach and left for the ebb tide to carry out beyond the river mouth and on to the shoals, where the surf would pound her to fragments.

They returned to the Meeting House and sat in session all day. Every aspect of the omen was discussed. It meant further violence, further deaths. It meant plague and murder and terror. Tsoaul had not finished with them. There could be no mistaking his intent. In the voting and arguing the young men now held firm majority. All those with families wanted to pack their belongings and leave; and many of the old men were changing their minds and voting to join them. Vude stood out against the many.

'Where will you go? And what of those you leave behind? The old, the sick, the orphaned?'

'They can come with us or starve!'

'It's all the same to us!'

'We've seen enough of crippling and killing!'

'Time to leave while some of us can!'

'To go is to stay alive!'

'No!' Vude shouted. 'To go is to be defeated!'

'Easy for you to say, old man!'

'Where were you in the fighting, old man?'

'Listen to Vude!' Groden said, and Sturmer for the moment could not understand what was happening. 'Listen to him! He's right! Where will you go? No other village can take you. You will have to start anew. And how long will it take to build another Burh? Five years? Ten? How many will die before you can finish a new palisade? How many will the wolves come for? How many the bears? Do you think Tsoaul's hand can't reach wherever you go? This is our home! Our lives have gone into these fields! Nothing, not even a spirit, must be allowed to drive us away!' He turned to Sturmer. 'This fool denies the truth! He refuses to face it! He still tries to tell us Tsoaul has gone! Well Tsoaul threw back my woman and any man who says not is no longer fit to lead us!' He thrust an arm towards the forest. 'Tsoaul is there! He's there but we can fight him and we can win. We can win and we can stay!'

'I'll fight,' Feno said.

'And I,' Deak said.

'Who else will show himself a man?'

But before anyone had a chance to reply, Sturmer rose and told the Council what he meant to do.

High above the village, well into the forest, Sturmer thought he heard something.

He listened, turning his head, holding his breathing.

The random sounds of the forest at night came to him: the squeak of dead branch on dead branch, a low hiss of breeze.

He cupped his hands to his mouth and shouted again.

By day or by night, he'd had to make the choice. He knew the nomad was ill and alone, no match for a fit man. But in the forest a nomad would have all the advantages of woodcraft and silence. Night among the trees held many fears, imaginary as well as real, but Sturmer had witnessed the nomad's skill at shooting, and only darkness would rob him of it. To kill him Sturmer's best hope would he to come at him face to facc and attack with a spear; and a hope was all it could be, even though one man, sick and alone, made a very different adversary from the Spirit of the Forest. So Sturmer had chosen night. He waited and listened on the path, sick with fear.

The promise of a return triumphant, boasting that he had personally slain Tsoaul, now shrank in importance in his eyes. Again he wondered whether to go back to the village and disclose what he and Vude had found, to take a group of the better fighters with him. But then he would never be able to flush the nomad out. He had to go on his own, to entice the nomad from cover and into a position where he could be seen and attacked. If he were to disclose what he knew his advantage over Groden would be reduced still further: and how much longer then would Sturmer be head of Burh, even if there were a Burh left to be head of? Self-preservation, more than bravery, or any desire to spare the village, kept Sturmer standing there.

'Come out! Come out! I am your friend! I mean you no harm!'

Far off to the left he heard the sound again, the rustling that had made him stop and listen before.

He put one foot off the path.

'Show yourself!'

The branches swayed a little in the breeze; the multitudes of leaves gently moved and returned, moved again. The wind had freshened. Sturmer looked up. Behind the sparse, high cloud, moving like fish-scales across the sky, he saw the faint disc of the moon.

'I wish only to talk! Come out!'

No answer came. Sturmer stepped back on to the path and took a few paces along it, towards the gorge and its ruined bridge. The clearing there would be a good place to wait; he had already decided as much. The danger of traps in the clearing would be less than under the trees, for on the day of the ambush the nomad himself had walked freely to and fro across the clearing and presumably would not have rigged it since.

The cloud thinned and the moon appeared briefly, misty at its edges, casting a faint bluish light down the length of the path.

For less than a second, in less time than it took an eye to blink, Sturmer glimpsed someone moving ahead, glimpsed the movement of limbs, sensed rather than saw a sunken face in shadow; and the hazel branches by the path had opened and swallowed the figure up. He barely heard the scrape of leather on bark, circling him to the left; but it was as loud to him as any sound could be.

'I wish only to talk!'

The nomad had halted.

'Show yourself! I mean you no harm! Come out and we can talk!'

The soft crush of a foot on dry leaves reached him, and hesitantly, another. He caught the judder of bramble hooks across leather, the tiny snap of a twig. And he realized the nomad was moving away, leaving him.

'Come back!'

But it was no use. The nomad obviously suspected trickery, or else was too timid to show himself. Sturmer listened closely and heard another twig break, deeper into the trees.

He looked up and down the path, not sure whether to follow. Was he himself being lured on? Was he being led into a pitfall or a hoist-trap? Or was the nomad merely afraid?

The spear he carried bore a short shaft, so that it would be less likely to catch in the undergrowth. He slid it into his belt and stepped off the path. As he put down each foot Sturmer made a conscious effort to avoid breaking dead wood, felt with his hands for sprigs and branches which might whip back. The woods here, hazel under oak and hornbeam, lay deeply littered with dead leaves and he could not prevent them from rustling, seeming to him to be making much more noise than his quarry. He stopped to listen. A little way ahead he caught a faint scratching, and then it was as if the nomad had stopped to listen too.

'I must talk to you! I mean you no harm! I can help you! Answer me if you hear!'

The given reply came as a loud snap of old wood. The nomad was going on. Sturmer followed. They were climbing slightly, across the side of a slope.

Behind them the cloud went past the moon's face, becoming patchy, showing deep-black fields and ribbons of clear sky with stars. When these crossed the moon its circle stood sharp and flooded the trees with light, sliced to chequers and lozenges and black shadows by the leaves and branches, and Sturmer was able to see that he was being led into a grove of older hazel. He waited for the moon to be covered, and went on. Something like confidence began to encourage him; he could hear the nomad plainly now, breaking a way forward. They were entering the grove. In places the rotten hazel sticks lay this way and that, some caught up in the living bushes, others on the ground, half buried in the leaves. Lichen, pale in the weak moonlight, festooned the sticks and bushes.

Sturmer took his spear from his belt as he heard the nomad stumble. He quickened his step, no longer caring how much noise he made, snapping off projecting stubs, treading on dry branch after branch. He was gaining on the nomad, whose progress seemed to be slowing, growing weaker, the attempt of a sick man to get away unheard.

After three paces more Sturmer realized that the grove had fallen silent. The other man had stopped.

Gripping his spear with both hands, he warily turned from side to side. In the stillness following the crashing trail of the preceding minutes, he strained hard for a sound of movement or life.

Sturmer bent and listened, a frown on his face. He could hear nothing. Nothing at all.

The moon sailed from the clouds and illuminated the hazel grove. He stared at the place where he thought the nomad might be. Perhaps the nomad had fallen; perhaps he was injured, wounded, even dying.

Sturmer opened his mouth to call out, but another thought checked him. He looked round. He had allowed himself to be drawn into the middle of the hazel grove, a natural sounding-box strewn with dead branches and obstacles, from which, whether he chose it or not, he could not hope to extricate himself without revealing his exact whereabouts with every step he took. The nomad had stopped making a noise; but had he stopped moving? Could he pass quietly where a farmer could not?

Suddenly Sturmer felt oppressed by the trees, isolated, confined in a place where he neither belonged nor had any right to be. He was a trespasser here. A hostility seemed to come at him from the forest itself, as if it somehow knew that he lived by the axe, cutting fields and clearings where green had reigned, the village an intrusion, the palisade and all the stolen timber, the trees uprooted and shorn of their branches a crime, an act of sacrilege.

Behind him, where no sound should have been, a spray of leaves rustled as if deliberately shaken. He whirled round to see its source, but cloud once more obscured the moon and the grove darkened.

He began to back away, his hands shaking and his mouth dry. He trod on a stick and broke it, turned, and with his forearm held high he plunged through the grove. A forked branch snatched at his spear. He let it go, too frightened to stop.

He ran straight into it. The force of the blow knocked him off his feet and flung him sideways, and he was landing hard and badly, smashing through dead wood, slithering into the carpet of leaves and rotting sticks. His fingers stretched out and the violence of his fall drove them into the ground. Dazzling numbness flared into pain in his neck and shoulder and jaw where the club had struck him.

He looked and against the sky saw the shape of his killer with arms raised, club held high for the finishing stroke.

Tagart's eyes opened at the scream. He had been almost asleep when he had heard it, a little way off to the south-west, a man's scream, ended abruptly as if by death.

He lay there listening, wondering if he had imagined it. His condition had improved a good deal in the day and a night since putting the woman's body out on the escarpment. But he was still not right; for long periods he had lain motionless under the yew, his mind invaded by irrational plans of revenge and strategy. More than once he had been determined to set fire to the village, or to build a dam and divert the river, or to lie in wait forever if need be and shoot the farmers one by one. But when the delirium receded he remembered Segle and Valdoe and he was unable to think of anything but getting back to her. At dusk he had checked the village again. He knew that he must wait for the music to come from the Meeting House, the music: he kept that in his mind, centrally, and even when he could not remember why he was waiting for the music he knew that it was important and he could not make a move before it came.

At nightfall he had returned to the shelter of the yew to sleep, to recover more of his strength; and then, some hours afterwards, had come the scream.

He sat up and pushed himself to his feet.

Broad white moonlight bathed the forest outside the yew tree. Tatters of cloud drifted overhead; away from the moon's glare a rich haze of stars filled the sky. Tagart looked up and found the constellation of the Giant, a bowman with arm outstretched and one foot crushing the head of the Snake. The third star of the Snake's tail, between the Ladle and the Bear, marked due north. Taking his bearings, he set off to the south-west, downhill, frequently breaking the run of his progress with the heel of his hand against a branch or trunk, not daring to risk a fall by going too fast.

Groden untied the end of the twine from the bush and wound it round his hand, making a neat hank which he pushed into his pouch. The trick had worked well, just as he had intended. And now Sturmer had atoned for Hernou's death: for it had been Sturmer's fault that the bears had found a way into the village, Sturmer's fault that Morfe had been killed, Sturmer's fault that the village was dying and all the families planning to move away. But Groden had long ago suspected him of worse than just poor leadership. His opposition to further clearance of the forest, and his unwillingness to fight back at the nomads who infested the trees and made spells against the village and its crops: all this had made Groden suspicious, adding to his fears about Sturmer's secretiveness and his pretence of introducing new methods and crops. Over the months a pattern had begun to make itself clear, and in the days before the raid, while the sun steadily baked the fields to rock, the truth emerged. Sturmer, for months or even years, had been in league with Tsoaul. And when, in Council that afternoon, Sturmer had offered to go into the forest and fight its Spirit, Groden suddenly knew he had to stop him before he had a chance to make a new pact with Tsoaul and finish the village altogether.

His suspicions had been completely vindicated as he followed Sturmer from the village and heard him calling, trying to lure his evil master from the trees. Groden's last doubt evaporated: he went to the hazel grove and put into effect the plan he had made, to draw Sturmer there, and with the twine to deceive him and throw him off guard.

Now it had succeeded. He pulled Sturmer's body through the thicket and towards the path. He did not trouble to retrieve the broken branch he had used as a club. He had no further need of it. The corrupt head man had been disposed of. With his going the canker that had rotted the village would go too, and Tsoaul would once again shrink away before their axes. When Burh became strong again, with time to heal the damage Sturmer had done, Groden would tell them the truth. But for now such revelations could serve no purpose; they might even prove dangerous, for Sturmer had so warped their minds that they could not see. For the moment Groden decided to pretend that Sturmer had fallen in battle with Tsoaul. After the change of leadership he would take a fighting party and go deep into the forest to challenge Tsoaul, and the matter would be resolved. He knew that Tsoaul would be afraid to come forward: Gauhm's power was too great. With her help, and the people of the village, Groden would work to make Burh new again.

He reached the path and put the body over his shoulders.

Tagart kept his distance, following Groden, the beardless man, down the path to the village. In the moonlight Tagart saw that he carried a corpse: the owner of the scream. He had not imagined it.

Tagart badly wanted to attack, to kill the beardless man, but he hung back, slowing when Groden slowed, forcing himself on when Groden went faster, not sure what to do. He wished he were armed.

They were getting near the village. Tagart had left it too late, even had he wanted to make a move; but his curiosity had been aroused and it impelled him to follow.

Groden turned off the path, to the right, and through the stand of oaks which gave on to the top of the escarpment. He passed among the black trunks and the moonlight, bearing the weight of the body easily, one of its arms hanging loosely and swinging as he walked. Tagart left the path and in utter silence passed over twigs and brambles.

At the edge of the escarpment Groden let himself down and on to the steepness of the slope, taking it sideways, faltering a little now. Halfway down he stopped and let the body fall from his shoulders, just as Tagart had let Hernou fall; Tagart drew back into the shadows in case Groden were to look up.

When Tagart stepped forward again the body had been

leaned against an oak bush, and Groden was crossing the escarpment, descending as he went, making for the east gate. At the bottom he merged with the total shadow of the palisade, and Tagart lost sight of him.

The gate opened slightly and effortlessly, as it had been left unlocked for his return, and Groden slipped into the compound. Tagart did not hear the two wooden locking bars being eased into place, but he saw the gate drawn shut and a few moments later Groden's figure on the village thoroughfare, walking towards the cluster of houses.

6

Sturmer's body lay, covered with flowers, on the Dead Ground. His common clothes of pigskin and beaver had been removed and consigned to the altar flame, and in their place he had been dressed in a chief's grave-robe of ermine, the hood drawn up and showing only the oval of his face with beard and moustache and eyebrows shorn. Beside him lay everything he had owned, everything that would go with him into the burial mound. His wife Tamis knelt weeping at his feet. Their four children, also dressed in white, stood nearby and watched. The youngest did not understand.

The villagers climbed the steps of the Meeting House one by one. Nobody had yet challenged Groden's sudden promotion to prospective leadership of the Council, for at the meeting that morning, held to discuss the finding of Sturmer's body, no other suitable candidate had emerged. The new head man would have to be formally chosen tomorrow, by Council vote, or by trial and contest of strength and wisdom if Groden were challenged; but today they mourned Sturmer. He would be buried at sunset, after they had tasted the agaric and joined him on the road to the Far Land.

As they passed into the Meeting House they left their clothing by the steps, a mark of purification, and naked crossed the floorboards to take up their positions in the circle of village hierarchy. By the altar sat Groden, at his right Vude, the oldest man on the Council, friend of Sturmer the priest, in whose hands now rested the health and spiritual guidance of the village until a new head man should be chosen. Beside Vude, in their order from high to low, sat the members of the inner Council, on their right the other Council men, followed by the wealthiest of the ordinary villagers, decreasing in power and importance as the circle curved round towards the altar; and on Groden's left squatted the lowliest man in the village.

The women came forward and took their places behind the

men, ready for their part in the ceremony, each holding a wooden bowl or drinking vessel.

Vude arose, his hands under the Agaric Casket, and turning towards the Dead Ground inclined his head and reverently slid the casket on to the front of the altar, in line with the small flame flickering there, which represented Sturmer's soul.

'We take this hour the gift,' he said, and waited for the congregation to speak the words of response.

'The gift of the Earth Mother.'

'On eagles' wings we go with our loved one.'

'Borne in peace along the road of the dead.'

'We see the gates of the Far Land and the journey safely done.'

'We turn back.'

'And in sadness and in joy come home again.'

The musicians took up their instruments and on pipes, tam-tams and flutes opened the dirge. Vude went on reciting the phrases of the Agaric Chant, and as he did so pulled back the lid of the casket and removed the trays. The first three were empty; he put them aside and handed the caps from the fourth to the woman behind him and to his left, who passed them round the circle. The chant finished: the women put the caps on their tongues. Vude lowered himself to the floor and sat cross-legged.

When the women had fashioned the caps into pellets, rolling them between their palms, squashing the fungus in their mouths to take away the taste and rolling it again, the men reached behind and took the pellets with their fingers, opened their mouths wide and thrust the pellets to the backs of their throats, and swallowed.

Chal's wife came to the altar and spoke quietly into Vude's ear. 'Something's wrong, Vude. The taste is not the same. It tastes like . . . like pepperwort. Usually it burns like fire and makes us sick.'

None of the women were showing any sign of nausea. Vude glanced at Groden, who opened his hands slightly, able to offer no explanation.

'The caps must be old and weak,' Vude decided. 'How long have they been in the casket?'

'I cannot say,' Groden said. 'Did Sturmer replenish the whole casket every autumn, or just the empty trays?'

Vude did not know.

'What is it?' Feno said from across the circle. 'The pellets aren't working.'

Others spoke up to say that the fungus tasted different, that it was having no effect.

'Then let us eat more,' Vude said, and gave out more caps, from each of the trays. He himself tasted a cap from the bottom tray. At once the fierce burning flared in his mouth and he spat the fragment out. 'This one has not lost its power,' he said, holding it up for all to see. He turned to the girl behind him. 'Chew this for me, child.' To the others he said, 'Taste the caps until you find those with strength.'

But although they found many caps which still seemed potent, most had lost their vigour and there were not enough good caps to make a ceremony. As Chal's wife had said, the stale caps tasted peculiar, peppery, and the men as well as the women ate several of each, hoping without success to produce some of the effects of fresh fly agaric, even in a diminished form.

Not long afterwards they came out into the compound and, taking their clothes from the pile by the steps, walked slowly to their houses to prepare for the funeral of their chief.

Across the river, in the sunshine, blue cornflowers and scarlet poppies made colour in the drab fields extending to the edge of the valley. Rooks flapped in the haze above the ground, pitching unhurriedly here and there in small groups to dig at the soil and turn over clods; from the estuary came a faint skirling of terns, and the piping cries of the wading birds as the tide went out and the rich grey mudflats appeared. A warm sea wind blew across the village, carrying before it a few husks and wisps of barley, gently knocking a loose plank on the bakery roof.

The west gate opened. Tamis and her three daughters, keeping near the palisade, stooped and picked bunches of corn chamomile, which together with red campion would make their simple wreath for Sturmer.

Tamis had decided to leave the village, with the sick who could walk, the children, and the animals. The others had been persuaded by Groden to wait, to remain behind while he challenged Tsoaul anew. And when Groden triumphed the animals would come back, and the children, and even the sick; but not Tamis. She meant to take her children back to her home village, where her mother was still alive and the children could be raised in peace and safety. In time the grief of Sturmer's death might recede; until then she would go on in her numb state, stunned, doing what was best for her family. As was the custom, she had not taken part in the fly agaric ceremony and she had chosen to stay outside on the Dead Ground with the body of her husband.

Just before sunset his funeral began.

Vude led the villagers over the bridge, through the west gate, and along the narrow, dusty path across the barley field. Groden came at the rear. Six men carried Sturmer's body, on white leather straps passed beneath his ermine grave-robe.

At the spinney on the far side the path curved between the trees and Tamis looked over her shoulder for a last glimpse of Burh. She would not be seeing it again. Chal and Hombeck were to escort her that evening after the funeral on the nine-mile walk to Highdole, where her mother lived.

The procession left the spinney and halted on the close sward of the burial ground, outside the line of chalk stones containing the earthen barrow where for many years the dead of the village had been interred. This evening a chief was to join the ancestors. Part of the barrow at its head had been freshly dug away, ready to receive him.

Vude spoke the incantation. In the long shadows of sunset, and then the grey light of darkening dusk, the corpse in its robe and the dead man's possessions were covered with earth and filled in, to begin by their decay to dust and fragments the slow return to the place from which they had come.

Over the escarpment the moon appeared above the trees.

Tagart stared into the space below the yew branches and tried to remember: how many days? How many days had he been here waiting his chance? How many days before the Crale

Festival and Segle was taken from the kitchens and put into the Trundle?

His thoughts swirled. He would need weapons, concealed weapons, and clothes from the village. And if he wore clogs and looked enough like a farmer he could use the coast road and pass the forts unchallenged to reach Valdoe in a single day. In darkness, with ropes and grappling hooks, he would make himself find a way to scale the ramparts and get inside; and somehow he would find Segle and bring her to the gates and they would be free: free to run into the marshes and reed-beds along the coast and hide where the Valdoe dogs could never find a scent. And after that, when he had kept his promise to Bewry, he would ask Segle to stay with him and travel north-west, away from the coast and the farmers and the acres of land by the sea they had befouled and laid waste. And together they would search for the Waterfall people, his old blood-tribe among whom his father had been born.

He sat up. Tomorrow. He must attack tomorrow. He was well enough; he had recovered much strength. His bruising was better. He could walk, and he could run, and he tried to tell himself that his thoughts had cleared and that he was planning lucidly again for the first time in days.

But with the fever of ideas in his mind it was a long time before he closed his eyes and allowed sleep to come.

Before dawn he had settled on a scheme to finish the village. By appearing on the escarpment he would draw them after him, south through the forest and down to the beach. There, in the corner of land between the estuary and the sea, he would trap them while the forest burned and the wind spread the flames east and south. At high tide there could be no escape under the cliffs, nor along the beach of the estuary, where the scrub grew close on the shore. Those who could not swim would be burnt alive; and of the others many would drown in the tide race out by the shoals. But he would have a coracle waiting, and if any of the farmers tried to swim towards land he would chase them and club them in the water with the paddle.

This was his plan. To enact it he needed a coracle. He knew

there would be coracles at the village, some left outside the palisade.

The moon had set when he arrived. He skirted the village to the south and came to the river. Two coracles had been left upturned on the bank; he holed one by thrusting his heel through it, and launched the other. At once the current tugged at the painter. He walked beside the bank, letting the river carry the coracle along, easing it round clumps of sedge, and led it downstream into the tidal reach. Jumping over channels and runlets, or walking ankle-deep in mud, he brought the willow and leather craft to the edge of the estuary, where the broad water of the river merged rippling with the sea. Here he dragged the coracle on to a narrow strip of shingle and left it hidden by the bushes.

From the shore Tagart turned back into the forest and climbed uphill, reaching the edge of the gorge and following it past the wreckage of the bridge and on to the path. East of the village, a quarter of a mile behind the escarpment, he knelt and nurtured the first fire, knocking flint against flint until the sparks ignited dry grass stems. Carefully he held them to thicker dry stems, blowing gently, to brown bracken, to thin twigs broken into lengths, and blew to make the flame dance. Bitter white smoke curled: the twigs burned. He put them against a small cone of dry sticks, and when they had caught he brought larger branches and heaps of bracken until the pile burned orange and strong. Ash and glowing charcoal began to fall into its heart. The encircling ground slowly grew hot; the grasses and twigs withdrew in a scorched circle, elongating on the leeward side, and suddenly the neighbouring bracken was alight.

He waited until silver rectangles appeared on the end of a charred branch, lifted it from the fire and checked that it went on burning alone. Taking this brand he laid a trail of fire south-east, coming after half a mile to the hazel thicket, which he fired in three places before throwing the burning brand into its centre.

For a moment he watched the shimmering farther up the slope, behind the trees, his eyes smarting and his face grey with dust and ash. The fire had not yet taken off, even though the wind had picked up and he felt a push of heat on his face.

He lingered there, overcome by fascination for the flame, seized by a desire to see it all burning, the sky on fire, the wall of flame racing through the forest and destroying everything in its path. All his life he had been ruled by fear of flame, scrupulously dousing camp fires, obeying the elders, never allowing flame to get out of hand. But now he was watching it develop its full glory, growing and feeding, demanding and consuming, towering into the sky and across the land. It carried for him a lesson of vitality, power, singleness of mind; and it reminded him that the village waited below, ready for his arrival.

Along the ridge of the forest columns of pale smoke stood in similar and parallel shapes against the sky. They seemed to be truncated, the white pillars cut off sharp where the rising sun shone on them and made the smoke invisible. The forest was burning.

Vude waited no longer. No more could be done. There was no cure. As priest, doctor, he had remained till now, going from house to house, trying to make them comfortable. He had wanted to bring himself to kill them, to end their misery, but he could not.

In the early hours the first terrible herald of death cap poisoning had announced itself, arriving without warning, taking with sudden and violent abdominal cramps all those who had tasted the peppery caps at the agaric ceremony. One by one the symptoms visited each house, coming again and again as if the stomach were being wrenched to a hard knot and released, only to be racked more tightly and viciously than before. No one escaped, save the wounded and the crippled in their beds, and the women who had been tending them, and Vude, who by chance had not eaten any of the strange caps.

Now the victims lay past vomiting, weak with watery bowels, cold sweat on their bodies. Some had crawled into the compound trying to find moisture to slake their thirst.

Vude knew they would be like this for two days, growing steadily weaker, until the pain abated and they were able to rest for a few hours before the cramps and the sickness returned with a venom that would make the first attacks seem mild. Disintegration of the vital organs, and seizure of the limbs, would lead into a long period of madness and repulsive visions, relieved at last by coma, collapse, and finally death. Those who had eaten several caps might suffer for three days; those who had tasted only one might last for ten.

Vude, his spare clothes and belongings on his back, hesitated by the bridge. He was the last to leave the village who could.

He saw Feno crawl from the doorway of the threshing shed, his face twisted and alien, the eyes sunken, streaks of filth in his beard and hair. Feno opened his mouth to cry out but made no sound. His lips and tongue were the colour of sand. His head fell forward and he stretched out one arm, the fingers clenching and unclenching in the dust.

Vude turned and went out by the west gate.

7

Tagart could see no movement in the village. He came farther out on to the escarpment and shouted at them again, hoarsely, sick and grey and tired. Sweat lined the dust on his forehead and round his eyes. His clothing, crusted and dirty, bore gashes which revealed grimy skin and, below his tunic, the ugly bruises on his left side. His hair and beard were matted and tangled, and his teeth, when he drew back his lips to shout, showed yellow and broken. But his eyes, though rimmed red and stinging from the smoke, shone clear.

'Bastards! Bastards! Come out!'

He half ran, half jumped, a dozen yards down the slope and shouted again.

From the compound came no response. He ran stumbling to the bottom of the escarpment, through the anthills, through the nettles, and with his right hand fending along the rough bark of the palisade logs, arrived at the east gate. It would not open. They had tried to lock themselves in. He struck it with his fists, shook it until the latches and hinges rattled, and turned away. With the fields on his left he ran beside the palisade, down the bank and into the river.

The west gate swung freely. He flung it open and entered the village.

It was deserted. They had gone.

Only then did he see the man writhing on the ground, face down in the dirt by the threshing-shed door; and he saw that there were others, here and there across the compound. He crossed the bridge and with a fork-tipped pole taken from a stack leaning against the threshing-shed, cautiously prodded at the man lying there. A bearded face, tormented and disfigured, lifted to look at him, pleading without words, begging for release.

Tagart frowned and went further into the village, unable to understand what had happened. The others in the compound were the same, women as well as men, all seemingly poisoned. It made no sense.

Inside the houses he found more victims of the poisoning, sprawled on the floor or in reeking bedding, groaning or silent, but all with the same look in their eyes, the same twisted faces. In the second house, in a cramped chamber noisy with blowflies, he found, as well as a poisoned man, two women with sheepskins drawn over their bodies. The stench of gangrene made him cover his nose and mouth. He lifted a corner of one of the sheepskins. Part of the woman's body was not there. He realized she was watching him; he let the skin fall and staggered outside into the morning sunshine.

Arming himself with an axe from the porch, he went from house to house, searching for the beardless man.

He found him by an upturned water-butt, behind a house on the far side of the compound. Groden moved feebly in protest as Tagart's shadow fell across his eyes. He groaned and Tagart heard the voice again, the voice he heard in the rainstorm by the burning shelters. He thought of Mirin, her face beneath his own, soft in the honeysuckle scent of his shelter; and then her face in the mud and slime on the riverbank, the story of her agony in her eyes, what they had done to her, what they had singly and together made her endure. He thought of the lightning and the ranks of men coming into the camp. And he thought of Balan, his death, and he remembered the man who had done it, a man with no beard.

And in glimpses and fragments Tagart remembered Hernou's voice in the darkness of the yew, and he saw again the preparation of death cap he had made, and then he knew the nature of their poisoning and how it had come about.

He took Groden by the ankles and dragged him on to open ground, and left him there. It was enough. He could do no worse to Groden. To torture him now, as Tagart had intended, to hasten his death, would be a crime against Balan and his mother and the tribe of hunters Tagart had once loved.

In a house nearby he discovered a leather sack with an osier carrying-frame to fit the shoulders and back, fastened with straps and wooden toggles. Into it he bundled a selection of clothes to make him look like a farmer: clogs, jacket, leggings, a badger-skin toque, wristbands. From a kitchen he chose food for two days, to save him the time of catching his own. Discarding his flints, which were blunted and virtually useless, he took the best he could find from the farmers' supplies, and put them in the sack, together with baling twine, a length of rope, and a grappling hook made from fire-hardened blackthorn. Across the top of the pack he laid a pair of short axes with new blades. He carried the sack into the sunshine and beside it laid a full water-bag.

Tagart crossed to the Meeting House, an unlighted torch of bundled kindling in his hand. At the far end stood the altar as he had remembered it. A flame burned there, a wick held in a bowl ground from the stone and filled with oil.

8

Behind the escarpment and down to the sea the smoke made a mountain, black and white and grey. The roar of crackling and exploding branches, fanned by the wind, merged with and engulfed the crash of falling trees, their trunks and skeletons showing black among the flames. As the fire moved on to fresh forest, boiling sap whined and hissed; green leaves scorched and curled and passed through brown autumn to become traceries of veins that glowed and burned instantly to nothing. In its path the fire left black ground: cleansed, purified, ready for new growth.

On the far side of the barley field, by the spinney of maple and oak, Tagart paused and looked back.

For the gangrened and dying, the wounded and the mauled, for those he had not dragged from their houses and into the open, the end would be swift. He had set fire to the village.

It was achieved. Against even his own expectations, it was achieved. Tagart had overcome all obstacles and discharged his duty to the tribe. He had reached his goal, using only the forest to help him; its animals, its plants, the weapons it provided. With these and with his own strength and singleness he had realized his ends. From within himself he had drawn on reserves that perhaps not even Cosk had possessed. And now the village was finished. He personally had destroyed it. One by one and in groups he had executed its inhabitants and swept away their houses and the things they had made. In a matter of months no trace of them would remain. The forest would take over; the fields would become overgrown, unrecognizable, and then indistinguishable from the virgin woodlands that had stood unchanged for centuries.

By all the rules, by the code of his tribe, Balan had been avenged. This should have been a moment of sweet triumph.

But Tagart felt nothing of that. He felt only bleakness, desolation, and a vast grey weariness that no sleep could ever assuage. His one goal had been reached. All his strivings were over. He had spent himself, he had succeeded; and been left with nothing. Those corpses lying in the compound, those people: what did he care about them? They meant nothing to him; they never had. What were they? Could anything about them, least of all their destruction, bring Balan back? Or Mirin? Or the joy he had known with the tribe? Tagart had failed, bitterly and completely, to achieve anything of value or importance. What had he brought himself? Not the taste of vengeance, or satisfaction, but vileness, misery, and three weeks of the worst privation he had ever endured.

Yet out of those three weeks one glimmer had emerged. Without it there could be nothing to relieve the emptiness of his future. It provided a chance, no more, but from chances he knew he could make much. And most of all it provided hope. The days were too fleet to be spent with a dead spirit. There was one more promise to fulfil.

Tagart stood and watched the village.

Swirling, making the sunshine brown and the grass on the slope dark, the billows of smoke and ash drifted towards the forest, particles returning to their birthplace, from five buildings and thirty-three stone and timber houses that rippled and belched an orange blaze and one by one disintegrated, the beams falling inwards with showers and flurries of sparks. In twenty places the palisade was down or had burnt away. It would not remain standing much longer.

The roof of the Meeting House collapsed, too heavy for its weakened supports; the stilts and rafters and walls twisted sideways, and the whole structure fell in flames to a mass of burning wreckage on the ground.

Tagart entered the spinney. On the other side, in its neat enclosure of white stones, the head of the barrow showed newly dug earth. He took some in his fingers and crumbled it. At his feet he noticed a wilted wreath of campion and chamomile. He stooped and held it to his face. No hint of scent remained.

Tagart stood up, and hitching the pack on his shoulders, let fall the wreath and set his face towards Valdoe.

Part 4

1

Too quick for the human eye to follow, Blene's tiercel hobby swept into the twittering flock of migrating martins and came out on the other side. As it flew it bent its head and tore a morsel from the prize that Blene saw it now held in the clutch of one foot.

The mines Trundleman was out alone, two miles from Valdoe. He could see the black walls of the Trundle encircling the crown of the hill across the valley. The unmarked pennons of the Flint Lord flacked and strained at their masts above each guard tower and barrack house. Smoke from many fires was scattered by the wind. The gates stood open to admit the traders and itinerants: the preparations for the Crale had begun. In the valley below, the river looped and showed dark blue in a green pasture, among the nodding foliage of alders and willows. This was the last afternoon of High Summer, the eve of Harvest, and though the sun was shining brightly a chilly breeze turned the white undersides of leaves and made the trees along the field edge sigh.

Blene whistled. On rapid, shallow wingbeats the tiny falcon climbed to turn, and with the glare of both eyes directed at its master described a low glide that terminated in a jangle of bells as its talons took purchase on the gauntlet. The martin, white feathers bloody, fell to the turf; the hobby, sleek and unruffled, opened its beak and panted, riding Blene's wrist as he secured the jesses at its legs. He had trained the bird himself, and it was his favourite, his usual companion on these daily walks. It served no practical purpose, it caught nothing for the table, but to see it killing was to Blene a thrill incomparable to anything that the hawk mews in the Trundle could provide. Sometimes he took out one of the austringer's goshawks, for hares; in the winter perhaps a gyrfalcon for wildfowl; or perhaps an eagle to run at deer. Most of the

Trundlemen favoured peregrines, with their faultless control of wind and sky, but Blene liked his little tiercel.

It was late. Much remained to be done; Blene gave his thoughts to getting back. The reports from Stobas and the other day-shift overseers would have to be heard, and there was the season's tally to complete before its presentation to Lord Brennis the following day. After that, work could be forgotten, for a while at least. He smiled to himself. Even Trundlemen looked forward to a holiday.

The Crale Festival, marking the beginning of Harvest, was second in the calendar only to the first day of Winter, the new year. To people whose survival depended on their crops, on the abundance of the harvest, the ceremonies and sacrifices of the Crale meant everything. This was the time of adoration and prayer, litany and chant; in every village and settlement was heard a petition for Gauhm's continuing beneficence during the two crucial months of the harvest. She had allowed the wheat to grow: let her now permit it to be gathered in, before the rains of autumn beat the fields and spread the grasses flat. The Crale was also the time of renewal, when the last of the year's stocks were almost gone. What remained would be replaced by the new and would otherwise be wasted, so for once even the thrifty could afford to be prodigal, squandering all in a few days of eating and drinking: an act of faith, a demonstration to Gauhm.

Both inside the Trundle and out, the feasting would begin at nightfall. The oxen had already been turning and sizzling for two days; scores of pigs and sheep had been slaughtered. For the soldiers and overseers there would be liquor and free access to the brothel. For the miners and field-slaves there would be extra meat and half a gallon of beer apiece, and the next afternoon a visit to their own brothel in the outer enclosure. The older and more tractable slaves might be permitted an escorted walk through the Crale Market. Tents and awnings now going up in the shelter of the palisade held booths and stalls where the soldiers and farmers would be tempted to make bargains with those who had come from farther afield, bringing pottery and imported wares, toys, sweetmeats, beard-scrapers, talismans and periapts, wooden combs, needles, bone awls, carved and leather work, ornaments, effigies in stone and wood, miniature axe-heads of polished white marble, foreign woven goods, bundles of ash-wood handles for every kind of tool, ropes, twines, and leather by the strip and in pelts, furs and untreated skins. Under the south-west gatehouse, next to the slave quarters, the animal market had already been assembled, with pens and stalls for cattle, swine, sheep and goats. Other stalls were piled high with wildfowl and game, and animals and birds for pets: goldfinches in sad little cages, badger cubs, squirrels with their hind legs tied. Brisk interest surrounded the traders of grain and vegetable seed.

The refreshment stalls stood nearby, laden with clay dishes of blackberries, sloe and crabapple jelly, elder and parsnip wine in jars, fruit liquors, corn liquors, and ale and bread and cold meats.

'What is this?'

Blene had paused by an open table on which strange little bottles had been arranged in rows. The old woman behind it, a crone with stooped shoulders and swollen knuckles, had averted her eyes at the approach of a Trundleman and now scarcely dared look up.

'Rosewater, master.'

'What is it for? Perfume?'

'Yes, master.'

Blene could have taken the bottle without payment, but the idea of the perfume amused him and his sensibility would not allow him to confiscate it. 'Four scrapers,' he offered.

'Yes, master. Thank you, master.'

'Are four enough?'

'Yes, master.'

Blene dropped the flints on to the table and passed through the crowds to the gate, between the sombre walls of the south-west barrack house. The shadows had grown perceptibly longer. The afternoon cast a dusty, golden light on the outer enclosure, on the craftsmen and soldiers and freemen moving to and fro among the sheds and dwellings; a hundred paces away across the parade ground, the sunlight made the burnt oak of the inner palisade look more brown than black. Here, standing just outside the ditch, and facing south across the parade ground, had been built the Trundlemen's quarters: long and low, a single storey divided into many rooms and suites, roofed with planks, the walls half-timbered and finished with clay and flints. Blene threaded his way among the openings which appeared for him and crossed to the main entrance, which led through a tackle room where outdoor clothing and equipment could be stored. Beyond it a long, dark passage, decorated with the heads and hides of trophies, allowed access through skin-draped doorways to the common room, refectory, and through hinged wooden doors to the Trundlemen's various private quarters. Once inside his own suite, Blene handed the hobby and gauntlet to his attendant and went into his chamber to bathe and change.

Leaving the bottle of rosewater standing on a low shelf by his bed, Blene reappeared, freshly attired, in the sunshine, and strolling towards the mines to complete his day's business there, first stopped off at the slaves' quarters and spoke a few words to the overseer of the kitchens.

Moments later, a hand on Segle's shoulder marked the end of her employment at the cauldrons.

That she had not been taken from the kitchens before was to her a source of dull surprise, for when a Trundleman, especially the Trundleman in charge of the mines, made even a mild request, the request was that in name only. But Blene seemed more distant, less imperious than the others, and it was not as if a kitchen-girl alone could serve his needs or ranked high in his preference. Each of the Trundlemen already kept several women. Some had wives here at Valdoe, even families. Segle guessed that Blene's interest in her would not be sustained; it was a whim, a small pleasure, a moment's gratification.

Whatever his attitude, it was of no consequence to her. Whether she was violated in Blene's chamber or in the soldiers' brothel, Segle knew that what little remained to her was about to be finally taken by Valdoe, taken and ground underfoot. She tried to think bravely, to compose herself for the ordeal; but as the women slaves bathed and dressed her ready for the Trundleman's presence she was filled with a blind terror and for the first time in her sixteen years fervently and truly wished herself dead.

Tagart walked through the massive framework of the gateway and found himself inside the Trundle.

Beside all the elaborate plans, the devices and stratagems he had invented on the length of his journey from Burh, this was the only, the single possibility he had not considered, had not even thought of: that the gates would be standing open without the slightest challenge to his entry. The whole feel of the place had changed. Soldiers and strangers alike were passing in and out as if the Trundle were not a fort at all. There were silhouettes in the guard towers; and Tagart had been given a desultory scrutiny by sentries on the road up the hill and by the gates; but since entering the boundary limits no one had spoken to him, asked him who or what he was, where he had come from, or what he was doing at Valdoe.

It had taken him over two days to make the walk. The heavy exertion of the journey had left him weaker, with constant pains in his chest, and aching feet, legs and back; but in his mind he had begun to improve, to plan more clearly. The delirious, dreamlike periods had grown shorter and less intense, and now he was almost himself again.

He had kept to the roads, making detours into the trees only to avoid the ferry stations, swimming the rivers using the inflated water-bag to help float his pack and clothing. West of the Arun he had caught up with and, at some risk, joined the tail of a party of itinerant pedlars, chapmen on their way to the festival. In his speech and manner he found no trouble in joining them, for chapmen were usually descended quite closely from the nomad tribes: people who retained a wandering existence, working where they could, selling what they could, hawkers and petty thieves, despised and avoided by nomads and farmers alike. And in appearance Tagart was not out of place among them, and prompted no undue interest: after swimming the river he had cleaned himself up as best he could, washed his farmer's clothes, and forced his feet into the unfamiliar clogs. The chapmen, a dozen or so men with their families and flocks, questioned him briefly but seemed inclined to accept that a lone traveller would prefer to walk in company. In a group there was less chance of being captured and taken for a slave.

As payment for this protection, their leader demanded the whole contents of Tagart's pack. Tagart tried to bargain. He told them that he too was a pedlar, that he had come from farther east, and that he was searching for his family, from whom he had become separated at one of the villages where there was only enough harvest work for himself. He said he thought they might have stopped at Valdoe or be there still; he was hoping at least for some word of them. He could not spare his belongings: they were his livelihood, the tools of his trade. The leader insisted. After much argument he relented and accepted a compromise, and Tagart parted with all his spare clothing, most of his flints, his rope, twine, grappling-hook, and one of the axes.

It was extortion, but it provided a safe passage through the most dangerous part of the journey: the last few miles to the fort. Tagart fell to the rear of the line, walking beside a youth whose sullen capacity for conversation soon became exhausted, enabling Tagart to withdraw into his own thoughts and plans.

They passed through Eartham, below its fort, and Tagart traded a few flints for hot gruel and bread at the settlement there. Keeping his adopted companions in sight, he left the shed where gruel was being sold and sat down in the shade of a beech tree by the road. With the silvery trunk at his back he dipped his bread into the bowl. Above him the sky showed blue; the wind hissed in the beech-leaves; the branches swayed. The road here was wide and well trodden, an important route. It ran between an avenue of beeches, not planted, but two uneven and inconsistent rows of trees which had escaped the axe only because no one had seen any reason to cut them down. The houses and huts of the settlement, encircled by a palisade, stood on the south side of the road and backed on to a system of barley and wheat fields which sloped gradually downhill into a belt of woodland. Beyond this, just visible from the village, spread the low coastal marshes of reedbeds and saltings known as the Rifes, having their beginnings at the Adur in the east, and running for mile upon mile along the coast below the hills, below Valdoe, to Apuldram and Itchenor in the west.

Tagart finished his gruel. There were other travellers on the road, some stopping for refreshment, others going straight on, covering the last few miles to Valdoe. Most seemed to be pedlars of one sort or another, with bales and bundles for sale at the Crale Market, or animals led on ropes and halters. He saw a few soldiers, some in armour, and here and there a group of more prosperous-looking travellers: wealthy farmers or priests from the villages. A small crowd had gathered by the gruel shed, and by another shed where meat and fruit were on sale.

Tagart stood up. His companions were leaving.

A few hundred yards west of the palisade the avenue of beeches came to an end. On the right was the scrub- and tree-clad steepness of the hill, leading up to open ground and Eartham fort. On the left were the village fields. With Tagart again at the rear, talking to no one, the chapmen followed the road through fields and scrubland as it curved first one way and then another, accommodating itself to level ground beneath the hills. Less than an hour from Eartham, in the late afternoon, they came within sight of the Trundle.

Tagart's main worry was a fear of being recognized. He had worked at the flint mines and might be known, and although he half consciously pulled up his jacket to cover his neck and the lower part of his jaw, he put his trust in the anonymity of a slave. His features might cause a twinge of memory; he might be half remembered; but it was unlikely. An overseer took little note of a slave's face, caring only about the number of flints he could produce in a day. And out of the mines, in farmer's clothes, among the crowds, there was still less chance of being recognized. Nonetheless Tagart watched warily as he went, walking self-confidently as if he were a freeman and not a fugitive, with a ready rebuttal and feigned resentment on his lips if he were to be challenged.

On the outskirts of Valdoe the group was closely questioned and searched for weapons. Tagart repeated his story, the one he had told the chapmen. It was accepted without demur. The soldiers opened his pack and took the remaining axe, and he was allowed to pass on.

Tagart accompanied the chapmen for most of the way up the hill, past the slaves' quarters, and leaving them, went on alone through the timber framework of the gateway and into the Trundle.

'Give me one of those,' Tagart said, pointing at a leg of bustard on the stall in front of him.

'Five scrapers.'

Tagart did not know that he was expected to bargain. He nodded and reached into his pouch. His flints were almost all gone, but he was hungry. Over two hours had passed since his arrival, and he had yet to be sure where Segle was. He had loitered for as long as he thought it safe, watching the kitchens at the slaves' quarters. There had been no sign of her. He saw the day-shift miners brought in for their food; he saw them led out again and into the cage for the night. Meantime, round the walls and inside the Trundle, the preparations for the feast were coming to a close. Tagart heard shouts and music, and one by one more fires were being lit. The sun touched the horizon and sank beneath it; the breeze dropped; and in the kitchens the overseers had departed and the slaves were beginning to clear the tables for the holiday. Desperately he wondered whether he could afford the risk of an inquiry. He decided he could not; but there was no other choice.

There was no other way to find her. He approached the edge of the kitchens and called to one of the women there, and asked for Segle.

'Who are you? Why do you want her?'

'I am her friend.'

The woman, middle-aged, with lank brown hair, stood closer to the bars and looked from side to side.

'Blene has taken her,' she said. 'The mines Trundleman.'

'When was this?'

'Today.'

'Where is she now?'

She could not tell him, nor could she speak longer. The

kitchen overseer from his corner had seen her slacking and called her back to work.

From the slaves' quarters Tagart had made his way to the stalls.

Tagart paid for the roast leg of bustard and tore off a mouthful of the rich, dark meat. 'Do you know anything of the Trundle?' he said, as casually as he could, to the man behind the stall. 'Do you know which part is which?'

They were standing near the gate; the parade ground and much of the outer enclosure were visible. A great bonfire had been torched by the knappers' shed, in the middle of the enclosure, well away from the palisade, and its flames threw an orange light on the crowds.

The stall-holder was a short man with fair hair, dressed in beaver and doeskin: a sleeveless jerkin, leggings formed of spiral strips sewn with seal-hide. He was a fowler, a freeman who traded with the consent of Valdoe, giving a tithe for its protection.

'Why should it interest you, friend?' he said affably.

'I have never been here before. I would like to know. Where is the house of Lord Brennis? Where do the soldiers sleep?'

The stall-holder, aware of an opportunity to impress pointed out the various features: here the barracks, there the deep ditch which had taken hundreds of slaves to dig, there the inner palisade surrounding the Lord's Enclosure, where only Lord Brennis was allowed to enter freely.

'And the Trundlemen? Where do they sleep?'

'See there,' the stall-holder said, indicating a low building next to the inner palisade. 'Their quarters.'

'Do all the Trundlemen live there?'

The stall-holder frowned. 'You seem strangely interested.'

Tagart made himself smile. 'All those who know me say I am too curious.' He finished the last of the roast meat. 'You cook this well,' he said.

'My woman does it.'

Tagart dropped the bones into a butt provided for the purpose. 'I wish you good fortune in your trade,' he said, moving away into the semi-darkness, but the stall-holder was already attending to another customer.

In the west, behind Bow Hill, the last of the day had become a mere paleness. Smoke from the bonfires and cooking fires and from the torches which had been set up on top of the walls, and smoke from all the night fires of the temporary settlement, the fair, rose into the darkness. Tagart turned towards the Trundle. From the high ramparts came a squeal of pipes and a loud, wild, rhythmic thumping of drums which persisted through and overcame the cheering shout of the crowd; instantaneously burning brands were held to a huge heap of brushwood and timber on the southern slope of Valdoe Hill, and the beacon fire caught light. An orange twinkling appeared on Bow Hill to the west, and Eartham Hill to the east, and on along the coast, one after the other, on every hilltop where there was fort or settlement loyal to Valdoe and the Gehans.

The door of the bedchamber shut with a clatter of pegs locked into place, and Segle was alone.

She looked round the room. The women slaves had conducted her here, into the Trundlemen's quarters, down a dark passage, and into Blene's suite. Light in the room issued from wooden lamps – clips holding rush-pith dipped in beeswax – standing variously on shelves, by the bed, on a table by the window; as they burned they cast weird shadows and made prancing shapes of the curtains and hangings on the walls. Under her feet she felt soft matting. A smell pervaded the room, a smell of rosewater.

Outside, she could hear shouting and music and the noise of the feast. She stood in the middle of the room and clasped herself, and, no longer wishing to witness any part of the bedchamber or its furnishings, closed her eyes.

Segle opened them again and looked up. A curtain was drawn aside: Blene came in. In the uncertain light she saw that he was wearing nothing; she forced her eyes not to drop, not to look down, to keep to his face. Blene came and stood behind her. She felt his fingers on her neck.

'You're trembling.'

Segle said nothing as she felt his body pressed against her own, moving her towards the bed.

2.

Tagart elbowed and shoved and shouldered aside the jostling crowd of people and pushed a passage across the parade ground to the door of the Trundlemen's quarters, his mind working at furious pace, not knowing what he was going to say or how he was going to get in. He had wasted too much time, hesitated too long, been too cautious, too timid; nightfall had come, and with it the Crale feast had already started. Segle was inside with the mines Trundleman.

As the pipes on the ramparts shrilled and the hard patterns of the drums grew faster, Tagart forced his way through the last of the throng and found himself in the main entrance. He was in a tackle room, hung with nets and bows, ropes, outdoor clothing and gear.

A man came from the side, out of the shadows and into the lamplight. He was more than forty, grey haired, less tall than Tagart, with a thin doeskin jacket and leggings – an attendant of some kind.

'Who are you? What do you want?'

Tagart looked past him and into the dark doorway that led further inside, and unbidden the right words came to him and he was speaking them. 'I bring an urgent message from Stobas at the mines. I must see Trundleman Blene.'

'Has there been an accident?'

'I must see Trundleman Blene, in person. Immediately.'

'He cannot be disturbed.'

'Where are his quarters?'

'He cannot be disturbed!' The attendant stood barring Tagart's way.

Tagart thought of striking the man, of knocking him aside, but changed his mind and checked his hand. There would be other attendants.

'I would not be in your place when he discovers you've

stopped me,' Tagart said. 'A year's work is in peril. The main-shaft struts and shutters are in danger of collapse. We're rigging jury props but even those are breaking up under the strain. We must have Blene's word. Only he knows what to do.'

Faced with a dilemma, the attendant seemed to waver. 'Blene is in his chamber with a girl. My orders are strict. I daren't disturb him. I daren't go in.'

'Then let me. If he's angry I'll take the blame. I'll say you tried to stop me.'

The attendant bit his lip.

'Which is Blene's door?'

The attendant hesitated, but then pointed at the opening to the passage. 'Through there. Follow the passage to its end. You want the last door. Knock before you enter; he's alone with her.'

Tagart was not fully aware of pushing past the attendant. He was in a dark passageway, moving down it towards a glimmer of lamps and the shapes of wooden doors. His hands fumbled with catches and the door was opening into a dimly lit room. Making big shadows he crossed it and thrust aside a curtain and there before him was a bedchamber and in the corner a bed and a smell of rosewater; Tagart saw a girl's fingertips touching the rush matting, fingers spread wide in an agony of revulsion and submission, and in them and her slender arm he remembered Mirin and the burning shelters and the rain and Segle's beauty. Even as in alarm the man on the bed realized that something was wrong and began to rise, Tagart's double fists came down on the back of his neck and broke from him a low grunt: Blene's muscles went limp and he slumped, a dead weight that Tagart rolled aside and on to the floor.

Tagart looked down. He sat on the edge of the bed and in the feeble light of the rush lamps took Segle's small, pale hand. Her hair, soft and dark, framed a face made unfamiliar by strain, her eyes and lips shut tight. Tagart whispered her name; again. She opened her eyes.

'I am Tagart,' he said gently. 'Sit up. You will be safe now.'

She could not speak; she could not raise her head from the

deep fur covering the pillows. She watched Tagart without recognition.

Beside Tagart, Blene stirred. On the table Tagart found a roll of legging-straps. He tied Blene's ankles and wrists, and pulled them together from behind. With another strap he tied a gag into Blene's mouth. Blene lay defenceless. Tagart told himself that he should kill him for what he had done; he should kill a man who lived by enslaving others, who had no conscience about robbing them of their life and liberty.

But Tagart could not bring himself to strike. There had been enough killing; and there would be no more.

Segle slowly sat up, in a daze. Tagart wanted to comfort her, to reassure her, to put his arms round her shoulders and draw her to him; but after what she had been through it would be wrong; and there was no time. 'Where are your clothes?' he said. 'We must be gone.'

Still she was unable to understand. Tagart noticed her clothes on the floor and crammed them into his pouch. Taking one of Blene's capes, he pulled it round her and helped her up, over to the window. He ripped the kidskin curtain from its bar and caught a glimpse of the view outside, the fires and lights in the outer enclosure.

Segle would not respond to his voice. With a hand on each side of her waist he lifted her over the ledge and let her down on the other side, then climbed through himself.

'You were killed,' she said softly. 'They said you were killed in the mine with Boak and the others.'

'Can you walk?'

'Yes.'

Tagart guided her away from the wall of the Trundlemen's quarters and into the crowd, the bonfire somewhere on their left, its glare rising into the sky, carrying up smoke and heat with burning twigs and glowing bents of straw. On the wind was the smell of roasting meat and cooking, and the smell of ale spilled on clothes. 'Keep by me,' Tagart said, and held fast to Segle's wrist as he drew her towards the south-west gate.

It would be at most only a few minutes before the attendant went in and found Blene. Tagart knew that he and Segle would have to make the most of their start. He thought of taking a straight run for the forest. At night there, alone, he could not be caught. But with Segle it was different. She would slow him down; and from her things at the Trundle the hounds would hold a scent so strong that in dry woodland there could be no escape.

Close by the wall of the barracks, they came out of the gate and into the stalls and stands of the fair. He looked over his shoulder. Life was returning to Segle's face.

'This way,' he said, taking her behind the fowler's stand, round it in a loop, under a tent where cooked venison was being sold, through a narrow gap between two tables piled high with the dead plumage of mallard and quail and snipe, and, coming out of the fair, he led her downhill, due south, past the throng of people round the beacon fire, following the road to the mines where many people were passing back and forth, talking, strolling. The crowds grew thinner; beyond the fires there was darkness. The moon, a perfect circle, hung in the glare over the fort.

With Segle's warm hand in his own, Tagart left the road and started across rough ground, scrambling down the slope of the settlement fields. They were trampling the crops. Vaguely the huts and houses passed them in the moonlight. The slope steepened and they were among hawthorn scrub. Twice Segle slipped and fell; twice Tagart pulled her to her feet and drew her on, putting distance between them and the summit. They reached a level on the hillside and Tagart halted on an empty path, unfamiliar to him, that ran to left and right, with more scrub leading down on its farther side, towards the marshes and the coast.

He glanced uphill at the Trundle. He saw the slaves' quarters illuminated by the firelight of the beacon, he saw the palisade and ramparts, the framework of the guard towers, black and linear against the smoke and an orange sky. He saw the loose awnings and canopies of the fair, the people and animals, the cattle in pens; he heard their voices and the music, and above them he heard the hounds give tongue and the shouts of their handlers as the teams came straining through the south-west gate.

Even as Tagart pulled Segle across the path he heard the

shouts become angry and the hounds' voices become yelps as they tangled their leashes with the stalls: tipping over tables of venison and game, their muzzles confused and over-busy with the strong scents of quail and snipe and mallard. The pack was already broken in purpose, not fifty yards from the gate, the hounds running against their collars, eager to find the trace; the handlers dragged them to, and held for them again the bedding from Segle's quarters and the bottle of rosewater given by Blene. But still the course through the stalls and crowds puzzled them and Tagart heard more yelps.

The delay gave him no heart. He knew that dogs trained to hunt human beings were of a special kind. They would not be among the stalls for long.

'You must run with me,' he told Segle. 'When I am not carrying you, do as I do. Plant your feet in mine. We're going into the Rifes.'

3

Between Valdoe and the sea lay three miles of unroaded waste: reed-marsh and lagoon, wet thicket and underwood, acre after acre where the drainage of the hills merged with the wash of surf and the sluggish leak under an unstable beach. At night it was a dangerous place, a wilderness of water sounds, of sudden deep channels and rotten islands, and beyond them sparkled moonlight on ripples and the mace-swamps, and the open streams that twisted and turned and became choked and lost among shattered willows and decaying leaves. Where the rivers grew brackish the reed-beds began. For nearly two miles they stretched towards the coast, giving way at last within hearing of the beach, becoming a muddy creek and a line of saltings. After that, there was only shingle: pebbles, foreshore, stinking weed, breaking froth, and the open sea.

A mile ahead of their pursuers, two figures waded the last of the freshwater marsh and appeared in the moonlight by the beginnings of the reeds. Tagart had used all his knowledge to slow the dogs, and Segle, who knew wet ground better than he, had guided them through the worst of the willow swamps and osier beds; but from the hounds' voices they could tell that the gap was closing quickly, perhaps too quickly, and they knew that if they misjudged and blundered in the reeds they would stand no chance. By now they were both naked, covered in mud, their limbs bleeding and torn from brambles and broken branches. For some of the way Tagart carried Segle. Times beyond count he had fallen; they had both fallen; or sunk to their thighs in ooze and struggled clear.

There were three dog-handlers. The break handler controlled the leading team, and two brace handlers came behind. They were soldiers, experienced men who had served on slaving trips, both from the Trundle and abroad; each lived with and looked after four hounds, big, heavy animals chosen for their endurance and strength, trained to obedience.

The dogs knew the marshes. They knew the sounds of splashing, of breaking wood, and the sound of breeze in the reed stems. They knew the bird cries, and the smell of eels. By their breed and training they could taste scent as it lingered on the surface of the water, or in the filling footprints across an oily mud-bank. A trail which had long since scattered among the spikes and fluffy heads of the reed-mace could with a few stray molecules be regained and held and followed with renewed baying and hauling at the leashes.

Behind the handlers came four ordinary soldiers, cursing the way of the scent, south through the scrub and towards the swamps. They had been held up for a long time among the stalls of the fair: the dogs had lost the scent completely, not once, but six or seven times. At last they had found it again just off the road, in the barley field.

They passed the deserted boundary line and followed the trace across a scrubby heath which dipped in slow stages to the lower road from Eartham. On the other side the heath became one with a dense stand of birch and oak, mingled with elms where the trees bordered the Apuldram road.

The dogs massed here in the moonlight, their noses close to the ground. The line of scent had been drawn beside the road for a hundred paces. Halfway along it, the trace of rosewater abruptly stopped, where Segle had climbed on to Tagart's back. But the hounds had already owned Tagart's personal odour: the vegetation by the road held it strongly and they followed without difficulty. The scent crossed the road, recrossed it, wandering and broken among the foul stench of the wayside hemlock, and turned back under the elms and through a broad bed of nettles that stung sensitive muzzles and eyes and flews. From the stamens of the male flowers powdery pollen got in the dogs' noses; the leaves and the ground smelled of dry hemp. The leading hound, a big black bitch, turned in bewilderment with her tongue held low. The scent had died. The other dogs came up. One sneezed; another whimpered. The brace teams spread through the nettle bed, searching from side to side.

'Where's it? Where's it? Where's it?'

The handlers spoke to the dogs, and to each other.

'Where's it, girl? Where's the line?'

The black hound sniffed at a particle, a hint, her wet tongue sliding at something in the air . . . roses; not roses . . . rose-petals. She drew in air again, across damp membranes, but no fresh nerves fired: she had used up all the scent.

'Back it on! Back it on! Turn it!' the break handler shouted, anticipating by moments the black hound's own conclusion: that the prey had doubled back.

'Back it on! Back it on!'

They raced back to the roadside and the stink of hemlock. The hounds ran about, loose on their leads. Within moments they had regained the taste of Tagart's musk. And, ten yards on, at the place where Segle had climbed down, it was rejoined by rosewater.

The trail led due south. In full cry the hounds ran straight through the trees and after it.

They were checked by the first water of the marshes, at a stagnant ditch, a natural drain rank with willowherb and flags. To cross it in the easy wake of the scent they were awaiting the handlers' word – the dogs never went leashed where the handlers could not follow. The black bitch whined impatiently as the leading handler probed the ditch with his staff.

It was safe, waist-deep, and the dogs thrashed across. The water stank; smelly mud rose to the surface. The quarry had smeared themselves, to no avail. Their scent, barely disguised, appeared strong and sure on the other bank.

The soldiers crossed the ditch and dragged themselves clear.

They were in the marshes now: it was time to change the mode of chase. There were firm places for dogs that would not take human feet, short-cuts made obvious by the wanderings of the scent.

The hounds yelped and strained in excited frenzy to be free. Fingers worked at straps and buckles, and twelve collars were unleashed.

Before them reached wet woodlands of sallow and willow, with open ground among the islands of trees and fallen trunks.

Mud-spattered and sweating, the men ran behind, skirting ditches the dogs had crossed, negotiating streams the dogs had leapt. With every yard the trail grew stronger, newer, fresher.

As the dogs sensed it the pack's stride lengthened and its speed increased.

Just ahead of the black bitch the leading runner squealed. In the moonlight and darkness it made a clumsy, tearing somersault and slid limp-backed into the leaves. It had run on to a broken stake, hastily angled and thrust at dog's-head height into the ground.

The pack faltered. The black bitch smelled suddenly opened flesh and heard the handler's rage.

'Leave him, girl! Leave him! Go to!'

She turned and the dogs ran on, less one, the stream of rosewater growing. Together in a scramble they entered and swam a black pool; on its far bank they trod on thorns and tasted Tagart's taint. Snarling, growling, worrying what they had found, tearing it to pieces, they dragged something free, the strongest scent yet, rammed into the space below a rotten log.

The handlers came up.

It was Blene's cape, the one that Segle had worn.

'What do you think?'

'They're slowing. They must be tired.'

'We're nearly on them now.'

The hounds whimpered and panted. Some shook fur and made spray.

'Go to! Go to! In the water! Go to!'

Another black pool; a tangle of willow branches and old trees lying drowned and quietly rotting in the water with their limbs submerged. The trace wandered at its edge, and moved uncertainly, then went in. The quarry, both together, had swum the pool, so recently that the trace lingered in the air as well as on the film, destroyed by the hounds as they plunged and splashed, whining with frustration: for in deep water the scent went under, below the rise of a floating trunk, where the dogs could not follow. Wet pads and claws, legs not meant for climbing, scrabbled at rotten willow bark. The dogs found no purchase and fell back, unable to climb over the obstacle, unable to swim under. The brace hounds paddled to the sides, exploring the tangle of old branches and withered leaves, looking for a way through. It was no use.

'Turn it! Turn it! Turn it!'

'Come out and turn it!'

Reluctantly, paddling, the hounds came out, while the handlers struggled to catch up and tried to find a route which circled the maze of streams and pools, to get to the other side of the floating trunks, to search among the osiers and willows for the line of scent that somewhere had to resume its course.

Pushing the reeds down flat, using the stems and leaves to help support their weight, Segle led Tagart first in one direction and then another, pushing southward in a passage of rustling and crushing and sucking. She carried a light pole, a broken sallow branch two yards long. By the feel under her feet, by the subtle changes in the rate at which the mud threatened to give in, Segle sensed her way along the seams of older and firmer ground: a skill she had been taught in the tribe, demanding speed, nerve, and experience. To stop once, to hesitate, would allow the mud to open and swallow them up.

Above the noise of their progress Tagart tried to listen, to ascertain how long the pursuit had been delayed at the pool.

It came again, the terrifying music of the hounds. They had crossed the pool and regained the scent.

In one hand Tagart carried a pole like Segle's. In the other he carried the bundle of his clothes – leggings and a farmer's jacket. Before entering the reeds he had taken them off. When Segle gave the word he was to drop them, leave them for the dogs to find; because once the dogs had stopped in their course to investigate, the handlers would do the same.

'Now!' Segle called out.

Tagart let the clothes fall.

In the brief freedom since leaving the fort, Segle had already recovered herself. From incredulity that Tagart had come back from the dead, and wonder that he had managed to overpower Blene, Segle had marshalled her feelings and now it was she who was guiding Tagart, using her knowledge of the reeds to help them both. And in the few words and tender gestures they had exchanged he knew that he was no longer alone; his empty days were over.

Suddenly there was no support for his feet and Tagart was

sliding into the mud, slime rising past his calves, his knees, his thighs, towards his waist. Somehow he had lost his grip on the pole. Instinctively he threw his arms out and tried to grab handfuls of reeds: Segle heard his shout and turned to look. Without seeming to pause, she turned her pole horizontally and allowed herself to fall, spreading her arms and legs to distribute her weight.

'Lean back! Lean back and keep still! Struggling gets you in deeper!'

Tagart felt the mud rising over his waist. The reeds towered above him, the seed-heads pendulous and heavy, obscuring the bright circle of the moon. In the clear space overhead the night sky was filled with stars. Before him was utter blackness; on the mud, bluish glints.

Segle, using the pole for support, crawled towards him. 'Lean back! Lean back!'

He heard the hounds coming closer. By the change in their voices he thought they were entering the reeds.

'Lean back!'

Tagart tried to do as she asked. The fierce suction below fought him, dragging on his legs, refusing to let go. He was going in deeper.

'Lean back!'

Contrary to its every instinct, he forced his body to respond. He forced it to yield, offering more of itself to the mud; and as he leaned back he found his feet rising slightly and became aware that he was no longer sinking so fast.

'Spread your arms and pull on the reeds. Let the mud float you like water. Don't struggle against it, let it help you.'

With agonizing slowness Tagart tried to obey, to drag himself backwards out of the mud. But now he felt his head sinking into the slime. He heard the dogs' voices become dull and faint as the slime filled his ears, its coldness rising up his face. Despite himself he knew that he was very near to panic; he knew that once he felt the mud closing over his nose and mouth he would thrash and flounder and be unable to stop himself from going down, on his back, with no hope of getting out.

The dogs were coming. He was trapped here, and they were coming.

He spoke, and his voice sounded strange to him; he heard the words filling his head.

'Leave me here. I can't move. Leave me here.'

Not a word of Segle's reply reached him.

The soldiers splashed and waded knee-deep through the last open channel before the reeds. From the osiers and sallows they had each taken poles.

The brace handlers had called their dogs in and directed them after the break team, into the corridor of reeds broken down by the prey. There was no longer any need of scent. The trackers could see where the quarry had gone.

One of the soldiers carried a bundle of thin rope; he took it from his shoulder and passed the end along the line, linking the men together. If one went down in the mud, the others should be able to pull him up.

'Go to! In the reeds, girl! Go to!'

The black bitch, her feet sinking in the ooze, her tongue hungry for confirmation of the wide trace shown by mere eyesight, led the hounds into the forest of stems and along the zig-zag of reed swath made only minutes before.

Below his head, Tagart felt a gentle pressure. Segle was lifting him so that he could breathe.

His fingers found something hard and relatively unyielding, out of place in the sea of slime and reeds. It was his sallow pole. Segle had found it and put it within his grasp.

Using the support of the pole, he began to win. Slowly, he freed more and more of himself from the mud. Beside him he was aware of Segle's help, her support, lifting first his arm, trying to raise his body, his legs; and then all at once the mud had released him and he was able to move.

Segle was speaking, her words unable to penetrate his deadened hearing. He pressed his fingers to his head and cleared some of the mud from his ears. At once he heard the hounds, three hundred paces away, less, drawing nearer through the reeds, and he heard the soldiers' shouts.

'Try to stand on the pole. Try to stand up.'

Segle had risen to her feet, balancing on the precarious support of her own pole as it gently sank deeper into the mud. She extended a hand. With a slippery grip Tagart took it and he too was rising. His feet found the pole, ankle-deep in slime.

'Follow me!'

They had made a mess of the reeds and mud where Tagart had foundered, churning the mire into a black and watery bog. But Segle managed to pass it, and Tagart, covered in mud, placed his feet exactly where hers had been and once again was running through the reeds.

Almost as the fresh reeds opened for them, the dogs ran down the reek of Tagart's clothes.

The break handler shouted. 'Go to! Leave it!'

'Go to!'

'Leave it! Go to!'

But in their excitement few of the hounds heard. Too late he shouted again; too late the other handlers shouted. Only the black bitch had heeded and gone through. The others, growling, gnarring, tussled with bared teeth for the jacket and leggings; and as they fought for them their feet began to sink deeper and deeper.

'Go to! Go to you bastards!'

'Don't let them stop!'

'Go to! Go to! Go to! Go to!'

The break handler tried to change direction, to avoid the pack of dogs in his way. With his pole held high, unthinking, he faltered, stumbled, and in the softest mud at once sank to his waist. The water soaked his jacket, his chest, covered his chin. He sensed the suction beneath him, all around him. The mud was almost a living creature. And as the break handler tasted swamp he knew the mud wanted him.

Another of the handlers hesitated, was made to turn; his left leg slid into the mud to the knee, and then the right. Behind him two of the soldiers were going down. The other men laid their poles and spread themselves flat as Segle had done, holding fast to the rope. One of them, desperate, threw himself on to the heaving backs of the dogs. They were sinking too; as he hit them they turned and snarled and tried to bite him. But their bodies were giving him support, keeping him clear, and however many dogs suffocated it did not matter.

The break handler felt the water rising over his forehead. He screamed. They did not hear it. The scream was the last of his air, his life, a silver bubble which wriggled its way to the surface and broke. His body involuntarily prepared to make another scream but as his chest expanded for it his lungs drew only mud.

The black bitch ran on alone, through the reeds, dipping her nose low. Her tongue touched the water and lapped the scent she had pursued all the way down from the fort. From the strength of it she knew the prey were only yards ahead, and she knew that she was gaining. She could think of nothing but the quarry. Her handler's voice had given an order: until countermanded it would push all else from her brain.

The scent-stream turned and rose on to firmer ground, away from the soft mud. The reeds parted in front of the black bitch and her eyes dimly discerned running shapes against the moonlight and the night blue of the coastal sky. She heard them shout with fear. Power bursted to her muscles and sinews and with her feet leaving the ground she sprang, throat-high. In the instant of her flight she tasted rosewater and then the full weight of her body struck and was bringing the human down.

Her training was not to bite the quarry, not to attack unless it showed resistance. She was merely to subdue and hold it until her masters came. But as the girl beneath her struggled and screamed, the black hound felt other hands closing below her jaw and the back of her head and she knew she was fighting for her life.

A strength like that of no human she had ever known jerked her head upwards and back. Before her neck broke she saw white and smelled the welter of her own scents and those of the marshes and the prey. Vertebra parted from vertebra; her spinal cord tore and leaked fluid. Damaged tissues fired a blizzard of faulty impulses to her brain, fading, quickly going dark, and she received no more.

4

Segle held closely to Tagart, her face in his shoulder.

'Are you hurt? Did it bite you?'

She shook her head.

In the marshes at their backs they could hear the calls and shouts of the soldiers. The plan seemed to have worked – the hounds had come across Tagart's clothes. But whether they had been stopped or merely delayed, there was no time to waste. Other teams might be dispatched from the Trundle.

'We must keep moving,' Tagart said.

He helped Segle to her feet and pushed the lifeless body of the dog aside.

She touched his arm. 'Listen.'

Away from the shouting and the soldiers, to the south, sounded the distant crash of breakers on a sloping shore.

It could not be much farther to the sea.

They went on; and now it was Tagart who led the way.

The ending of the reed-beds was signalled by the fluting cry of a curlew disturbed from its feeding in the creek. For several seconds it had stood with head bobbing in uncertainty, alarmed by the approaching noise of rustling stems; and when Tagart and Segle came out of the reeds it saw them and took wing, twenty feet over the glittering mud, passing in front of the moon. Other birds in the creek and in the saltings heard its cry and shared the alert: red-shanks, whimbrels, oystercatchers, and their own distinctive voices were added to the curlew's as they too opened their bills and flew up.

'The tide's out,' Segle said.

They left shin-deep footmarks across the width of the creek and entered the saltings, among the glasswort and sea-purslane, stepping over gullies and gutters of wet mud. The glasswort gave way to seablite which scratched softly at their legs. Before them was the rising slope of the beach; behind them was silence, and no sound of pursuit.

Their feet crunched on shingle, climbing to the low crest of the moonlit shore; and there from west to east spread sparkling sea, the waves angled in broad sweeps and tumbling into surf, almost luminous where the foam broke and slid back into the oncoming crests.

Tagart wearily took Segle's hand and led her down to the water. Their scent could still be traced, even across the pebbles. It was time to make sure they would be followed no more.

It was time to slip into the sea, swim beside the beach, to come out where it was safe and sleep an untroubled sleep; and afterwards, with the sun on their bodies and the wind blowing subtly along the shore, to find food and clothing and make a start on all the questions.

The water was warm. A wave slapped at their knees; they went in further. Wordlessly they drew together. With the friendly sea swelling to their waists they let the water wash away the black mud from their skins, the filth of the marshes, clean and healing, gentle, soothing, billowing in a dark cloud, merging with the currents until all trace of it was gone.

The Flint Lord

Part 1

1

Fodich felt his fingers move. He touched the hard spikes of gorse. He closed his hand and made it bleed.

He was alive.

He was cold.

Needles of rain hurt his back where the flesh was open, rain in the wind like the soldier spikes in his palm.

Fodich was hallucinating. They had nearly killed him, tied him to a ladder and rendered him useless, and thrown him away to die. Night had come, yet in his brain it was still morning and he was at the ladder. That first moment had not ended. All day it had been with him, receding, coming back, filling his mind. In his mind he was still hanging by his forearms, and it was as if he had lived no other life but this, known no sensation but pain; seen nothing but the wooden rung before his eyes. The whole of his existence had become this silent, dreaming agony after the lash. He luxuriated, spread his wings, drifted in the mist, and heard his screams as at a distance.

Far above him, Brennis Gehan Fifth came to the window. He pushed aside the shutter, opening it into the wind, and looked down into the outer enclosure of the fort, beyond the spiked top of the inner palisade which surrounded his own residence.

He tapped his fingernails on the rough wooden sill. At the new year, a month away, he would be thirty, but he looked much older: a man of middle height, strongly made, his blond hair left uncut since the summer. Where his beard ended, flecked dark and light, the form of his cheekbone angled into a plane which changed shape as he opened his mouth and revealed his teeth. But it was not a smile. As he stood watching, dressed in sealskin and lynx, the soft leather of his tunic flapping at his neck, only his eyes showed that thoughts were passing. His eyes were luminous, clear, and grey; and they saw everything that was happening below.

A man was being flogged. That was the source of the screaming that had brought Gehan to the window. The man, stocky, in his early thirties, had been tied to a ladder against one of the workshops. Two overseers were beating him, watched by an ordered crowd of two or three hundred people: men, women, children, dressed in animal skins and tatters, none properly clad against the blusters of rain-bearing wind driving in from the marshes and the sea. They were slaves, and they had been brought to watch. Many of the men were still grimed with the chalky soil of the mines.

The slave receiving punishment had been stripped to the knees. His back was being flayed. With each new blow he writhed as if he would break the ladder, only to sag in the moment before the next stripe was made.

Brennis Gehan, the fifth Lord of Valdoe, studied the progress of the punishment with a detached interest. He observed particularly the reactions of the other slaves: those who watched, mulishly or in sympathy; those who turned away; the faces of the children.

A girl's voice came from the chamber behind him. 'What is it?'

'A slave. Nothing to worry about.'

She came and joined her brother. She was eight years younger, with waist-length blonde hair tied at the neck. In texture her hair was like his, but it was paler, and in the regularity of her features could be discerned a resemblance, of attitude rather than shape: her eyes were bluer, her mouth softer, her brow more sensitive; but, unlike her brother, she had allowed her face to remain expressive and alive. He was intellect; she was emotion. She drew her furs to her chin and watched without speaking.

A heavy man in sheepskins was supervising the punishment, arms folded. From time to time some of his words reached the window.

'. . . see Fodich now. He did not even reach the trees . . . away from the hill . . . and the hounds . . . let this serve you all . . .'

The girl seemed to shiver.

Gehan turned. 'Do you like to watch it, Ika?'

'Who is the man?'

'Just a slave.'

'Why is he being beaten?'

'The overseers say he tried to escape.'

'And did he?'

'They say he will not work. In the mines he causes only trouble. It is salutary to the others to provide an escaper now and then.'

A less pensive light entered Ika's eyes as the man's screams ended and he hung limply at his bonds, unconscious and bleeding. Ika took her brother's arm. Her fingers felt the strength beneath his sleeve and moved among the sensual warmth of the lynx fur there. Something flickered about her lips, almost pleasure, perverse and incomprehensible: the overseers were not stopping. Each by turn, the two men with whips continued to step forward. The sound of it was the only noise above the wind.

'Horrible,' she said. 'They are beating him to death.'

'It is cold here, Ika. Let us go back inside.'

The Trundleman noticed the shutter closing. Under his breath he began to count the blows, almost as if its closing had been a cue, a sign of the all-seeing approval of Lord Brennis, as if the remaining supervision could be delegated now that the chief effect had been secured. The Trundleman understood. The beating needed to be severe to have any purpose. Fodich, the slave, had turned out lazy and, worse, dangerously uncooperative. The overseers had tried to make his life easier. They had given him warnings, repeated warnings which no sane man would have disregarded. Yet still he had refused to work. And then, one afternoon a week previously, he had threatened to be violent.

. . . Nine, ten . . .

'That's enough,' the Trundleman said.

They cut him down and threw a bucket of water over his back. It made him cry out. Whimpering, he tried to crawl away.

The Trundleman bent at the waist and with hands on knees examined the slave's wounds. Fodich's hair was gripped and he tried to see the face looking into his own. He tightened his grasp on the soldier spikes. His mouth was open against the ground. In his hallucination a whole day had passed, a morning and afternoon, reduced to nothing. In his crawling downhill he had forced his head sideways: there was no Trundleman's face to see.

'Take him on to the hill.'

They carried him from the fort. He was not worth keeping – it would take too long to make him better, and even then he would not be able to work as they wanted – and it was unlucky for him to die inside the fort. He was a savage, a wild man: better that his spirit should be released in the open. Two soldiers in leather tunics took his wrists and ankles, and with his head hanging back and his jaw open, carried him across the waste ground that once had been fields. Halfway down the hill, on a rough scarp of broken soil and brown winter grass, they stopped. This was far enough. They let him fall and turn back up the hill towards the fort.

It was midday. Under a grey sky Fodich opened his eyes and saw the black branches of a thorn bush straining in the wind. He rolled on to his stomach and fainted with pain: a hundred grass stems had torn open congealed blood.

Some time later he was conscious again, in the afternoon. He knew he had to get out of the wind. Shelter first, always shelter. The soldiers had given him his freedom: he would not waste it. He would not die alone, an empty soul without ancestors or tribe, without a place among his people. He thought of his children and his woman. They did not even know he was still alive; they did not know he had been captured and taken to Valdoe. By now they would be at the winter camp. He knew the way there, the old routes followed by the nomads since the world began. He would be with them again soon. Was he not Fodich, a hunter, resourceful, provider of plenty?

He raised his face and saw the gorse bushes a long way down the hill, dark green, almost black, pinstuck with yellow flowers in defiance of winter, offering shelter, making dense shambling screens of warmth. He estimated the distance he would have to crawl and did not think it could be done. If he kept still the pain reduced slowly to a constant level; otherwise it became unbearable, worse than it had been at the ladder. And to cover the rough ground of the hillside would cost him too much in movement. Each tussock would be an agony to get round. But he knew he had to do it, to find a calm place out of the wind. If he stayed in the open much longer he knew he would go to sleep and not wake up.

He shut his eyes, just for a moment, very close to peace. At once it drew nearer, blissful and warm, enticing him down.

No. He would not rest. He willed himself to think of the morning, the ladder, the ragged crowd of onlookers, the overseers. They had cut him down and thrown icy water on his back. It had hurt. It had made him crawl, like an animal at first, and then like a broken man, down the hill, among the thorns and tussocks, knowing he had to want the pain to come back.

He opened his eyes and the grass-blades were different. They had changed. He must have been moving. He must have been moving and he did not even know it. He crawled like a broken man. The Trundleman gripped his hair and looked into his face; he tried to stare back, his head forced sideways in his progress down the hill. The whole day a dream, a cry of pain, darkening to dusk as the afternoon waned.

It was dark. There was something sticky in his palms. Blood. His own blood. He squeezed the vicious spikes again. Fresh blood.

Lie in this darkness and the pain will go away. A route passes a few miles from the hill. Tomorrow, or the next day, or the next, you will be strong enough to find it.

With bleeding hands he dragged himself out of the wind. He listened to the noises above him, fluted spikes on shaggy branches in the wild stream of night, pelted with rain, gusting harder; he smelled dryness and an odd scent of woody green stems, and just faintly an aromatic sweetness of the small yellow flowers he had seen so long ago.

Fodich realized he had reached the gorse bushes.

2

Tagart listened again, his head averted and his eyes unfocused on the ground, using all his concentration to filter the sounds of the forest at nightfall. The branches overhead, bare or with a few sere leaves remaining, gave no hindrance to the rain which was falling steadily from a windy sky. And as the light slowly failed, the tree trunks lost their colours: shades of green or grey migrated to dark and pale, and the shapes of unsuspected patterns emerged.

Crows were roosting somewhere far away to the south. Their raucous chorus suddenly went quiet, and started again with a few isolated cries. Tagart frowned. He was beginning to doubt what he thought he might have heard.

Tagart was carrying a bundle at his side; over his tunic he was wearing a fur stormcoat, and below it leather leggings fixed with tasselled straps. Segle had made these things and her own; he had caught the animals which provided the skins. His feet were bare. When winter came he would wear boots, the leather worked with tallow to make it waterproof. Later he would need a leather mask too, to protect his face from the wind, and mittens, and a fur cap to pull down over his ears. The stormcoat was fitted with a hood: this he had pushed back, the better to listen.

'Did you hear it?' Segle said. She had been with him constantly since the end of the summer; together they had travelled the country looking for Tagart's blood-tribe, his father's people. They had gone as far as the mountains in the north, and turned back down the east coast, through the fens and inland to the south-west, but of the Waterfall people they had found no trace. Tagart knew that he would be sure to find them at the winter camp: as the autumn had begun to fade he and Segle had started eastwards, along the south coast and towards the routes leading to the camp.

'Did you hear it?' she said.

He had not. 'What about you?'

'I might have heard voices again, just faintly.'

'Which way?'

'I couldn't tell.'

It was late. They had to find somewhere dry for the night; they had to build a fire.

But – if there really were a fire nearby, if they really had heard voices, then shelter, food, and company too, all would be freely given. And what if by some chance the tribe proved to be at last the Waterfall people – what if its leader were Shode, the man who with Tagart's father had taught him almost everything he knew? What if it were Shode up ahead?

'We'll go and look.'

They pushed forward, between the branches of leafless bushes on each side of the path. It was hard to see detail now. More than once a branch slashed back into Segle's face. She said nothing to him; if it were not for Tagart she would be a slave still, at Valdoe, where she had been taken by the soldiers who had killed her family and friends. She would be a slave still, or dead.

The path began to climb. After a hundred paces they breasted a ridge. The faint course of the path crossed the ridge and followed the slope down. Below the tangle of undergrowth the rusty leaves of hornbeam trees lay in shallow drifts.

A hint of cooking came on the wind.

'Down there,' Tagart said, and through the moving branches Segle saw a twinkle of firelight. A moment later the smell of roasting meat came more strongly, borne on a gust of wind that blew rain from the trees, and with the wind they heard voices and the sound of wood being cut.

Tagart squeezed Segle's hand and drew her on.

Near the bottom of the slope the path opened into a small clearing, and here, beside a stream, surrounding a pile of glowing logs, were eleven hump-shaped tents made of leather and fur. People were making ready for a meal; four women and a boy were splitting wood with flint hatchets.

A man stepped on to the path, holding a spear. It was nearly dark and nothing could be seen of his face, but he was dressed like Tagart, in a stormcoat, and when he spoke his voice was harsh.

'What people are you?'

Tagart told him. 'We heard you from the other side of the hill,' he added. 'We're on our way to the waterfall camp. My father was in the Shoden.'

'The Shoden.' The man with the spear seemed satisfied. He looked over his shoulder at the fire. 'We also are going to the waterfall camp. We are the Ospreys. Come. You're welcome to eat with us.'

Brennis Gehan Fifth was alone with his wife.

He had left all the lamps burning in the chamber. The servants and body-slaves were elsewhere; the dishes and trays of the night meal had long been removed, but the odours of the food lingered in the room. Outside, the wind pleaded with the walls and sent rattles of rain to add to the undersong of creaking timber. At night it could be heard most plainly, even in the wind: the structure of the fort was never silent. Gehan had learned every subtle component of its groans: the weight of logs settling, expanding and contracting in damp air or dry; the movements of joists and floorboards and rough-hewn woodwork; the cracks and stutters of suddenly released tensions. Gehan's ancestor, the first Lord Brennis, had built the Trundle over a hundred years before, and it was still alive – the oak piles and beams were still a part of the climate and the land, and in their movements it seemed as if they yearned to go back to the forest in which they had seeded and grown.

Gehan could not sleep. He lay with his eyes open, listening to the gale. There had been four Flint Lords before him, all with the same name – Gehan, the name of the family in the homelands that had grown to power through trading and ruthless elimination of its enemies. The first Flint Lord had opened Brennis, the island country, to profit and exploitation; but lesser men had succeeded him, fed on the proceeds of his vision and energy, and almost squandered his work. He had dreamed of autonomy: freedom from the taxes and imposts of the mainland Gehans, the chance to expand and take, eventually, the whole country for himself. The dream had not been realized. In the years of the second and third Flint Lords the Valdoe domain had remained subservient to the mainland, its lands restricted to an eighty-mile strip along the south coast.

Only with the advent of the fourth Flint Lord, Gehan's father, had matters changed. After twenty years of work and planning he had seized independence, facing its dangers in return for its advantages: and the advantages were enormous. At the end of his life he had begun to plan for expansion of the domain. And now, Gehan knew, it was his duty to continue and fulfil what his father and Gehan First had started. It was his duty and his destiny to make the vision real.

The first Gehan had found Brennis a wilderness of trees with isolated farming villages near the shore. The farmers, like Gehan himself, had come by sea from the German homelands. The villages he encountered were poor and badly organized, at the mercy of raiders and brigands who came either in ships and rafts from Normandy and Cornwall, or from inland strongholds to the north and west.

One such stronghold was Valdoe Hill, thrusting nearly seven hundred feet above the marshes and the coast, thickly wooded, its crown cleared by the brigands to make a fortress. On the southern slopes they had discovered rich seams of flint. Prisoners from raids were made to dig, in shallow pits at first, and deeper, until the pits branched underground and became mines. The true wealth of Brennis was its fertile land, from which grew villages of farmers who could be subjugated and exploited; but flint was wealth too, for it supplied the means to exploit: weapons tools, ready fire. Without flints, man could be little more than an animal. With them, he could cut down trees and clear a forest, harvest his crops, kill beasts and dress their skins to wear. He could kill other men more easily and take what they had made for himself. He could win freedom from hunger, freedom from toil, by making others feed him and build his shelters.

The best flints were to be found along the chalk hills of the South Downs, and of these the flints at Valdoe were the finest.

Under the direction of Brennis Gehan First, the brigand fortress was razed and its site levelled to fourteen acres, an oval plateau circumscribed by a ditch nine feet deep. Just inside the ditch, forming a palisade twenty feet high, and three-fifths of a mile in length, were erected oak trunks preserved by scorching, each the thickness of a man's chest: the product of two thousand trees, cut from the forest and dragged to the summit with ropes. Protected by this palisade, construction of the Trundle began.

In the following years the fort was completed and then improved, and smaller, secondary forts were built in a chain along the downs – at Butser, Harting, Bow Hill, Eartham, Cissbury, Thundersbarrow, Whitehawk. More of the country was taken under control, more villages and their produce secured for the use and profit of Valdoe and the Gehan family. In return the farmers received a measure of protection from attack, and a village was established at the foot of Valdoe Hill.

In the hands of their new masters, the farmers began to thrive. New villages, new communities, sprang up along the coast, peopled by settlers from the homelands. To feed them, new fields were required. Mile after mile of oak and beech forest fell before the axe, more every year. The life of any one field was short. Without proper management, of which the farmers knew little, the ground soon became exhausted. Once exhausted it was abandoned and left to become scrub, and more forest was cut to take its place. Villages shifted their sites, leaving destruction behind. Deeper and deeper incursions were made into the forest. The smoke of the clearance fires, the smell of newly hacked woodchips, the belching pyres of mangled trees moved farther and farther from the coast. Always the domain of Valdoe was on the increase, powered by the personality of one man, the representative of the Gehan family in the island country: the Lord of Brennis. His flint seams provided the axes; his artisans fashioned the tools that could be exchanged for food and skins and lumber; and his forts and soldiers watched over everything and allowed it to proceed.

With increasing prosperity, increasing boundaries, there was more to protect. The barracks at the Trundle were enlarged, and the slaves' quarters too: more labour was needed, to build roads, to dig, for every menial task. Soldiers were sent across the sea, to prey on the very communities which in other days had sailed against the farmers. The slavers came back with dark-haired, brown-eyed people, in complexion and temperament like the brigands, the original masters of the coast, whose immediate threat had now been broken and whose clans had been disrupted and enslaved.

Besides the brigands there were other natives, more elusive, with far older traditions. These were the savages, who lived by hunting and gathering, travelling the forests by routes which had not changed for hundreds or even thousands of years. The coming of agriculture, of the foreign farmers, had eroded their hunting grounds and forced them to restrict their wanderings. It was from a few such tribes that the brigands had arisen, in response to the presence of the farmers on the coast.

The savages made slaves of indifferent quality. And each time a new inroad was made into the forest there was trouble: sabotage, ambush, open attack. Every tribe was a source of delay and expense. Once deprived of its territories, if events were allowed to develop, a tribe of savages would become a horde of brigands.

During the summer the savages were scattered throughout the country, in the hills, along the river valleys, from the flat eastern coast to the mountains in the north and west; but when cold weather came they congregated at winter camps, traditional gathering-places. The tribes in the south, those which caused the trouble, used a camp some eighty miles north of Valdoe, in a valley near a waterfall.

With the aid of surprise, the soldiers of the first Lord Brennis marched on this valley and purged it. The problem was solved.

The first Lord Brennis grew old and tired; other men took his place. His policies were no longer so rigidly observed. And, as one symptom of the decline, the savages began to come back.

For many years there was no real clash between them and Valdoe. Forest clearance had slowed down anyway; old fields had reverted to woodland. What small friction there was between native and farmer was of little concern to the Flint Lord: Valdoe's interests were rarely threatened. Gradually the savages ceased to be important. Even as slaves they were negligible, of no value. They were just denizens of the forest like the other creatures there, nothing more; and like the other creatures they could sometimes be a nuisance, occasionally stealing livestock or damaging crops.

Gehan's father, the fourth Flint Lord, had restored the ideals of Gehan First. In his lifetime he had remade much that Valdoe had lost; and he had won independence from the mainland as a first step in the establishment of an empire in Brennis, but he had died before the work was finished, leaving his son to take over.

At his father's death Gehan had been twenty-three. Now he was nearly thirty. In those years he had upheld the old spirit, the spirit of the old Valdoe, of his father and of Gehan First. The consolidation was complete: expansion had once again begun. In three years, seventy thousand acres of land had been reclaimed or freshly burnt. Next summer there would be more, much more. There would, in ten years, be fields and villages beyond the Weald, thirty, forty, fifty miles from the coast. The land would be stripped of timber, the marshes drained.

There was only one obstacle. Last summer there had been a resurgence of trouble from the savages. In the north-west of the domain, they had repeatedly harried the forest clearance teams. Farmers had been captured, tortured, put to death. Stores had been stolen and befouled at a dozen sites. A unit of soldiers, twenty-five men, had been routed. And in the east, one of the most prosperous villages had been sacked and burnt to the ground.

The records of Gehan First had been preserved in stories and paintings. The young Gehan had known them from his earliest days, taught by his father to revere the daring of Gehan First, the ancestor who had come to a fierce land and stolen it from the brigands. Recently the stories had been coming again to his thoughts, and with them an uneasy feeling, a foreboding, vaguely recriminating. Yet he knew there could be no guilt in his mind. What he was planning was no more than a military prerequisite of expansion. The savages were an obstacle to the smooth extension of the domain: it was his duty to remove that obstacle. He was going to march on their winter camp and destroy them.

At the latest estimate of his scouts, there were something

like three hundred savages either on their way to the camp or already present. The number of soldiers that could be safely mustered, leaving enough to defend the coast, was numerically only equal to the enemy, and heavy losses could be expected in even the best-planned onslaught. There was also the difficulty of the season. The camp would not be full, and an attack would be less than completely effective, before the end of autumn. The solstice, Goele, marked the first day of winter and of the new year. Goele was the prime festival of the calendar. For religious reasons there could be no departure in the week of the festival. By then, however, it was almost certain that the snows would have started. In mild years the snow would not be too deep; sometimes there was even a thaw for a week or two, but normally the ground was frozen till spring, when the camp would quickly disperse, too quickly to risk leaving the attack until then. It would have to be made in the snow. Gehan had consulted his Divine: she had forecast a bitterly cold winter, with heavy drifts. Marching in such conditions would require many men.

The forces of Gehan First, it was said, had outnumbered the savages by three to one. They too had marched in deep snow. The extra soldiers had been brought from the mainland: the same would have to be done again. But such reinforcements took time and great expense to arrange, and the problems of transporting, feeding, and sheltering them were not easily dealt with. In winter especially, the channel between Brennis and the mainland was rough and dangerous. Weeks might pass before a calm day allowed a crossing. The number of craft available was limited; and they were small and slow, capable of carrying only a few men at a time.

However, it would be done. Even now there were ships across the channel, waiting for the swell to ease.

The alternative to an all-out assault on the savages' camp – piecemeal extermination, tribe by tribe, using soldiers already available – was tempting to consider. Not only would it be cheaper and require fewer men, but it could be carried out in favourable weather. The previous summer it had already been tried; but only when there had been no chance of a survivor carrying word to other tribes. None the less, there had been several escapes, and Gehan's advisers had warned him to stop. The capacity of the various tribes for working together was unknown. Given warning by a consistent series of massacres, a force of savages might form and descend on the coast, a force perhaps of daunting size. Such an enemy would be impossible to defeat without help from the homelands, for although the Trundle itself was impregnable, and the contingency of a mass attack had been well foreseen by its designer, supplies of water inside the fort were finite and a protracted siege could not be defended.

Given all this, a sudden advance on the winter camp was the only way. Using surprise and vast numerical superiority, the savages would be dealt with once and for all, and the peaceful work of expansion would again be allowed to proceed safely and profitably. Villages beyond the Weald: that was the dream. To attain it Gehan would need all his ingenuity and courage. The details of the campaign had been crystallizing in his mind; he examined them endlessly. They brought him alive, excited him, kept him from sleep, and as the season turned and the weather worsened the anticipation had begun to consume and torment him.

He could share none of this with Altheme, his wife. Only Ika, his sister, his own flesh and blood, could truly understand. Only she knew what their heritage was.

Tonight a storm was blowing. But tomorrow it might be clear. It might be calm. Ships might be launching.

Under the bedding he put his hand on Altheme's smooth skin. She stirred drowsily and half woke, still asleep as he pulled her towards him.

Her eyes opened fully and she tensed. She seemed to draw back from him bewildered, afraid.

'What do you want?'

Gehan said nothing. He moved on top of her, not looking at her eyes, the dark eyes that were nothing like his own. And her hair was the darkest brown before black; every night she sat combing and brushing and brushing it, no longer speaking to him; and when she undressed, she turned her back and quickly took the wrapper held up by her body-slave, before her husband could see. She had given him no children, no son.

Gehan ran his hands under her thighs and pulled them apart. She resisted, in silence. Always in silence now, for months, even long before Ika had come. At one time, in the middle of the day, he had found her weeping, sobbing, her face in her hands, wet with tears. She would not tell him why. Moving inside her, she would not tell him why. He tried to kiss her, to find her tongue with his own, forcing her against the pillows, his hands gripping her wrists. She went limp and the tenseness had gone. Not melted, but gone. She looked past him. Outside the gale was streaming the shutters with rain. Gehan saw her dark hair on the pillow, moving more quickly now, loveless and violent. In the channel the seas were mountains. They were keeping the ships on the beach, pounding the shingle, scouring spray along the shore, a wet night, utterly black in the sandhills where men were waiting. Breakers smashed on the line of coast, hurling weed and wood. Solid water fell on the beach and drowned the marshes beyond, reaching toward the homelands, toward Valdoe, reaching toward the hill. And despite the storm the ships were launching. He wanted to shout a warning to the men with ropes. But they couldn't hear. The ships were breaking up, the boards splintering, the sails ripped away downwind. Men were in the sea, heads and hands visible, shouting, swimming, trying to cling to wreckage. On the sloping walls of waves he saw them. They were drowning, all of them. And as they went down their hair was no longer dark. It was golden; it was fair, forming whirlpools, going under, going down.

Gehan did not know whose name he had spoken, but as he slumped across her Altheme heard it and she felt her heart flood with coldness and fear. It was true, what she had guessed, what she had known. It was true. It was true and now there could be nothing more.

'Damn you,' he said. 'Bitch. Damn you.'

She shut her dark eyes and listened to the wind.

3

Tagart found the man first, half dead, in the mud of the path, his eyes open to the rain.

He and Segle had been walking with the Osprey tribe since the previous day. Their route had curved away from the coast and passed through hilly forest, on the outskirts of the cultivated land controlled by Valdoe. Early in the morning they had crossed a system of fields and then the Flint Lord's road between Valdoe and Bow Hill, following the course of an old trackway which turned north to find a gap in the downs: this was one of the established routes to the waterfall camp.

The rain had not stopped. Everything seemed to be soggy; everyone was miserable and bad-tempered. For much of the time two families had been arguing. Tagart had been glad when Visar, the leader, had told him to take his turn and go on ahead, to make sure of the way.

For a moment Tagart thought the thing obstructing the path was a rotten log, or a curious lump of earth or stone with pink showing. He did not associate it with human form. It was utterly motionless. Then he saw that it had arms and legs and a head.

The man's beard and nostrils were the colour of mud; his hair was matted and knotted with it. From the abrasions on his skin it could be seen how far he must have crawled and how many times he must have stumbled and fallen. Tagart closed his fingers on the man's wrist and bent to listen to his heart. He was barely alive.

'What have you found?' Visar said, pushing a way forward.

Tagart looked up at him mutely and turned back to the man on the path.

Only when they tried to lift him did they see the furrows on Fodich's back. Blood and mud had commingled and congealed. Rain dripping from the trees made watery streaks which revealed the rough edges of the wounds, from neck to buttocks and to the backs of his knees.

The fortress at Valdoe was less than three miles away. Tagart himself had once been a prisoner there; he had once laboured in the mines. He had been given first hand experience of the brutality of the guards; he had been forced to breathe the atmosphere of corruption and despair in the slaves' quarters. The place itself was evil, the very ground infected by the man who remained unseen and for whose personal benefit so much suffering was endured. Evil: there was no other way to think of the raw force, almost tangible, which the Trundle and its master seemed to generate. It had crushed and defiled Segle, and she would never fully recover from her experience there. The Flint Lord had killed her brother and parents and every member of her tribe. And, when she had been the only one left, a Trundleman had raped her, deflowered her on the night she was due to be put into the soldiers' brothel.

A sudden constriction grasped Tagart's chest, rage and sadness, too intense for tears or words. He found it impossible to breathe. He wiped the grey mud from the man's face and cradled the back of his head as other hands lifted him from the path. Tagart stared at the inanimate features. From many small clues he already knew that the man was a hunter like himself. At some time their lives would have been almost identical – even to the point of enslavement. But there things had changed. Tagart had been able to escape intact, unmutilated. This man had not.

'It's Valdoe,' Tagart said. 'The Flint Lord has done this.'

The women carried Fodich to the bracken and washed him. They smeared his back with herbal salves; clean, soft leather was applied to his wounds and bandaged in place. The men cut poles from the woods to make a stretcher. Shortly before noon, the Ospreys were on their way again.

Tagart offered to help carry the stretcher. Fodich lay on his front, without speaking, occasionally turning his head and grimacing when the roughness of the ground made the stretcher jolt. His eyes were open: he watched the passing leaves and mud. Towards dusk he slept.

He was strong, otherwise he could not have survived. Tagart

thought he knew his face from some past winter camp. The features were square and resolute, the eyes gentle, filmed with pain. His limbs were powerful and his body well muscled. In age he was between thirty and thirty-five.

During the night Tagart and Segle sat with him, in one of the leather shelters. They gave him a little broth, in sips from a wooden bowl. He tried to clasp the bowl with clumsy fingers and spilled it on his chest. Segle eased his head back. He fell asleep again, woke, drank water, fell asleep. In the early hours he awoke sweating and retched; afterwards he seemed to feel better.

He was lying face down, his head on one side.

'Can you understand me?' Tagart said. 'What tribe are you? What is your name?'

He tried to speak. Segle brought the lamp closer and took his hand.

'What tribe are you?' Tagart said.

Fodich's mouth opened, wet with dribble. Slowly he turned his eyes and took in Tagart's face.

'I'll tell you,' he said weakly. 'But first I'd like some more of that broth.'

By dawn, Fodich had finished his story.

Tagart rose. He was deeply troubled, not so much by the account of Fodich's punishment, but by everything else he had said. 'This is too important to be kept,' Tagart said. 'I must go and tell Visar.'

Three days later the rain had gone. The wind had veered to the north, bringing clear sunshine and the first real chill of the winter. At sea the waves were muddy and discoloured, crested with foam. White gannets rolled with the swell and followed the coastline westwards, appearing and disappearing in deep troughs, occasionally flapping higher, gliding above a horizon of rough water.

Inland the trees had been stripped of their leaves. The hues of autumn had become drab; the forest canopy was now a skein of empty branches. The rivers ran cold and dark, full of rain. A keen wind blew through the hawthorns on scrubland where old fires had destroyed the trees. Straggling flocks of winter thrushes descended on the bushes to eat the berries: redwings and fieldfares, still travelling southward in the face of the coming season.

The path into the Shode Valley, after crossing the scrubland, slowly descended between the trunks of beeches and oaks. Along this path had come most of the three hundred people, in nine tribes, who had been arriving steadily over the past weeks.

The camp lay in undulating countryside eighty miles from the coast. This was a region of dense woodland and marshes with open pools full of game. Three rivers turned southward among the hills and discharged into the marshes where the three valleys merged. In the western valley, two miles above the confluence, the river was swift and at a hardening of the rock became a noisy waterfall, from which one of the tribes had taken its name.

The Shoden, the Waterfall tribe, held first place among the people who used the camp each year. The camp had been in use for many generations: nobody knew how many. It was situated on sloping ground a mile above the waterfall, in a clearing beside the river. A few trees had been left standing, and these served to define the invisible boundaries which divided the camp into areas for each tribe. Yet at first glance no such segregation could be seen: the children ran about as they wished, the huge heaps of firewood and the cooking areas were communal, and the shelters seemed to be sited at random.

The soil in the clearing was relatively soft and easily excavated to make pit dwellings. Bundles of reeds were thatched on a hazel framework to make a thick and largely impervious roof, completely waterproofed with layers of holly and yew. An opening at one corner allowed access to the interior, which was insulated with bracken and lined with skins and furs. The opening served to ventilate the pit. It remained open in all but the worst weather; with people inside, a pit rapidly became warm.

There were about eighty such dwellings in the waterfall camp, some cleaned out and used year by year, others abandoned and used as middens, others dug afresh. No cooking was permitted inside. All food brought to the camp was to be shared at the fire, which burned continuously through the winter and was flanked by awnings to keep off the rain and snow.

Klay, the chief's son, was sitting in the sunshine by the fire, with a bone needle making repairs to a boar-net. He was wearing a disagreeable look: he disliked such tasks. He was the son of Shode, leader of the Waterfall tribe. Eventually, when Shode died or decided to step down, Klay would take his name and become chief in turn. Not everyone welcomed the prospect. Something in Klay's character made him unpopular. He was twenty-four, at the peak of his strength and resilience, and just entering that state in which the older men could tell him no more about the forest and hunting. His eyes were burning and intense, his jawline hard and bunched. He liked action, sudden decisions, violence in the chase and, although he knew well enough that net-mending was important, it irked him to sit still and listen to the gabble of the old women. To make things worse his two small daughters and his wife were at his side.

There was to be no hunting today. Other men and their families were cutting shafts for new arrows, holding them up to judge them true, selecting goose, quail or swan quills for the flights and flint chips for the heads, or making bindings with twine and fish glue. Others were trimming stakes for use in fences to drive game, or with the women were helping to twist rope from untidy bundles of lime-bark fibre. Shode said that it was essential to keep ahead with such work. Later on, depending on the severity of the weather, food would become scarce and poorly kept equipment might cost hardship or worse.

Shode was seated near his son, working too, discussing with Klay the change in the weather and the effect it would have in the coming days. As chief of the leading tribe of the camp, Shode controlled all hunting, allotting to each tribe its share of opportunity. Often two or more tribes hunted together, but everything had to be agreed by Shode. He was quietly spoken and introspective, his hair turning grey. In his movements could be seen the control and coordination that thirty years of the hunting life had brought. Even among the others, Shode was still a strong man. Although in his middle forties and not quite as fast as the younger men, he could run as far, work as hard, and go without sleep for as long as any. He rarely insisted on taking every privilege that was his due, but when he made a ruling his word was final. He had become chief not by inheritance, but by challenge, twenty years before. Since then there had been scarcely any threat to his leadership, and none at all in recent years. He was acknowledged to be the best man in the tribe; the best man to lead the Shoden and to give unity to all the tribes of the winter camp.

Behind him the breeze hissed in the trees, and poured clean air through the valley. The sky was perfectly blue; the late morning sun still held a trace of warmth.

Shode was joined by a bulky, bearlike man, the leader of the Bubeck or Beaver tribe.

'We'll try Yote Wood again tomorrow,' Shode said to Klay. 'The pigs will have taken themselves in there by now.' He turned to Bubeck. 'Are you with us again tomorrow?'

Bubeck grinned his assent, exposing gums and broken teeth. He was almost a giant, a head taller than Klay, and supremely ugly. In his boyhood he had been caught by a brush fire and horribly burnt: his face was a scarred mask, his left eye pulled outward and down. His left ear had gone, and what remained of his hair and beard grew in feeble tufts.

The Bubecks and the Shoden often hunted together. Like most of the tribes that used the camp, they were of the same lineage, tracing their descent from that part of the Sun's creation ruled by the spirit Water. Even in summer the two tribes had sometimes travelled together. They were closer to each other than the others of the spirit – the Ospreys, Dragonflies, Otters and the rest. Bubeck was also related to Shode by marriage. Despite his appearance he had taken the most desirable woman in the tribe as his wife. The chief and the chief alone had this right, taking if he wished the wife of another man; for Bubeck was leader because no one dared to challenge him. In the winter camp he was second only to Shode. He had been a part of Klay's earliest life. From Bubeck, his 'uncle', Klay had learned how to shoot, how to make a trap, how to wait in silence, how to read a trail, how to follow like a shadow for mile upon mile. With Shode and Bubeck and the boys of his own age Klay had killed his first roebuck and skinned it, and been shown how to use every part of the animal, to waste nothing. From those early years Klay had spent his time with another child, a boy two years older, the son of the man who had then been chief of the Waterfall tribe. Tagart – the other child – remembered little of his father's death. A broken leg, gangrene, his mother weeping. The outcome was what Tagart's father might have wished: his friend defeated the others and took the name Shode to become the new leader of the tribe.

Tagart continued to learn in company with Klay, to be taught by the elders, and by Shode in particular. Yet even as a child of six, Tagart sensed that everything had changed. It was now Klay who was to inherit the name of Shode; Klay who received the best instruction; Klay for whom the leading beast was reserved; Klay who was expected to excel in all things. Eventually Tagart left the Shoden and married into the Owls, a tribe of the Air spirit. From then on he saw Shode and Bubeck and Klay only occasionally: the Air tribes wintered at another camp, in the east, and the Owls rarely spent any time in the south.

Klay looked up from his work, squinting. On the far side of the river his father's name had been called. He saw that a column of people was arriving, preceded by Edrin and Wone, two men from the Shoden who had been posted to watch the bank path and the bridge of logs, fixed in place like stepping-stones, which joined it to the camp.

Edrin raised his voice again. 'Shode! Shode! A new tribe!'

Shode stood up and shielded his eyes against the sun. 'Who are they?'

'The Visars!'

When Klay reached the river he was among a jostling crowd welcoming the newcomers, taking loads, helping to carry the heavy packs and frames, the bundles of furs and skins and shelter-poles. In a line the Visars came over the bridge, stepping one by one on to firm ground to be greeted and divested of their loads.

It took a while for them all to cross – the Visars were a large tribe, of more than forty people. Towards the back of the line a stretcher was brought across, on which Fodich of the Dragonflies had eased himself up so that he could see. Word was sent to his woman, and almost at once he was reunited with his family.

Over the heads of the crowd Klay looked at the remaining people on the far bank, where Edrin was waiting to be the last on the bridge. Beside Edrin, in easy conversation, he saw a face he knew.

Tagart was carrying a heavily laden frame, his thumbs tucked in the straps. Somewhere on his walk with the Visars he had found, or someone had found for him, purple knapweed flowers to tie in his hair. *His walk with the Visars*. The Visars. Not the Owls. Klay was suddenly apprehensive. His eyes searched for the necklet of bones which he knew all members of the Owl tribe wore. Tagart no longer had one. Then he was no longer in the Owl tribe; nor was he wearing any emblem of the Visars.

A girl preceded Tagart on to the logs, a girl with purple flowers in her hair, and all else fled from Klay's thoughts.

Her name was Segle. She was seventeen and very beautiful. Later Klay learned that she was one of the Terns, a tribe now dead. She had been imprisoned at Valdoe and made to work in the slaves' quarters. Tagart had helped her to escape. Now she was his wife.

After dark they were sitting together by the fire as Tagart again told the story of their escape, their subsequent wanderings; he described the things he had seen and heard at Valdoe, and the way they had found Fodich.

Fodich was still very weak, but he had been brought to the fire to repeat what he had told Tagart and Visar. It was something to do with the Flint Lord and rumours at the fort. The talk registered only slightly with Klay; he did not bother to follow what was being said. He was watching Segle. Once she looked his way, once only, and again he told himself that she had sensed it too. He knew what she wanted. He knew what they both wanted. He had never spoken to her directly, never seen her before today, but were it not for Tagart, not for his own woman and his family, he would get up and go to her now and take her down to his dwelling.

Klay remembered that he was the chief's son. The talk seemed to be important. It would be as well to pay more attention.

'The snows are a month away,' Shode said. 'We have time to send scouts to confirm what you say. Much as I trust you, Visar, and Tagart and Fodich too, it goes against all our interests to act rashly.'

'Mild words,' said Bubeck. 'I think they're mistaken. The Flint Lord has never dared move his men in winter before. Why should he do so now? Has he gone mad?'

'It is possible,' Fodich said. 'Some say he has been visited by demons. Others say the farmers' gods have deserted them. Their fields are failing and the villages are going hungry.'

'We've seen no sign of it,' Bubeck said angrily. 'Do you want us to risk the winter just because of a few rumours in the slave pens?'

'I repeat only what I have heard,' Fodich said.

'The drought was bad this year,' Shode said. 'We saw ruined crops.'

'And my wife will testify that the Flint Lord had already begun killing us,' Tagart said. He was becoming heated. 'Didn't he murder her whole tribe? What more do you want: I suppose you won't be happy till the soldiers are here.'

Shode held up his hands. Tagart, who had been newly welcomed into the tribe, was losing his sense of respect for Bubeck, a chief. 'This is what we will do,' Shode said calmly. 'Before committing ourselves we must know how many soldiers the Flint Lord has assembled.' He turned to Chenk, leader of the Kingfisher tribe. 'I want you to lead the scouting party. Each tribe will give the man with the best eyes and the fastest legs. Leave in the morning; go to the Flint Lord's landing-place, to Valdoe and all his other works. If you see the truth of what Visar and Fodich have said, the elders will convene and we shall decide what to do.'

Tagart pleaded to be allowed to go with the scouts. Shode refused. 'From this tribe I give Wone.'

The other chiefs began to nominate their scouts.

Klay sat studying every detail of Segle's face. She was sitting in profile, her eyes downcast. She seemed to turn too frequently and attentively to Tagart. Klay watched her tiny movements and her self-conscious gestures, missing nothing; her shins were bare to the firelight.

'I beg you, Shode,' Tagart said. 'Let me go. I've been inside the Trundle. I know the other forts too, and the mines, and the landing-place.'

Bubeck said, 'Slavery must have rotted your brains.'

It was then that Segle stole her glance at Klay.

He knew at once that she had been expecting him to be looking elsewhere, at Bubeck or Tagart. She was momentarily caught out: her feelings lay revealed. She wanted what Klay wanted. Her glance faltered and she looked away.

Tagart was standing with fists clenched. Bubeck had insulted him in front of the whole camp.

But Bubeck was a chief, and this was the day Tagart had been allowed back into the Waterfall tribe; and Bubeck was Shode's close friend. Tagart sat down.

Bubeck, sprawling on his couch of skins, held Tagart's eye for a derisive moment before he turned to Klay and grinned.

But Klay did not see. He saw only Segle, at her place by the fire.

4

Bugling and whooping, nine swans flew southward along the valley, their plumage white against the grey sky above the water. Yellowed reeds stood swaying in the ripples; and in the centre of the mere, flocks of waterfowl showed as dark patches.

The morning was intensely cold. It was three days before the winter solstice – over three weeks since Tagart had returned to the Shoden: in that time there had already been snow flurries and twinkling nights of hard frost. Now a sleeting north wind was blowing, numbing the face and fingers and finding a way through every layer of clothing.

Tagart and Klay heard the swans go over. They could not see them – they were crouching inside a makeshift hide of bundled reeds, watching the flooded land where since dawn the clapnets had stood open and ready to be sprung. All morning the mallard and teal had been flighting above the osiers and islands. Some had joined the coots and wigeon on the floods, grazing by the water or sleeping, heads on backs, white eyelids closed, shedding occasional feathers that the wind snared among grass-stems and dead thistles. The wildfowl slept lightly. Once a falcon appeared in the sky, drifting west, showing no interest, yet the ducks left the ground in a storm of wings and circled for a long time before returning. As they came back in pairs and parties they redistributed themselves and some chanced to come nearer the nets.

The work of waiting was made more tedious by the cold. The catch today would be consumed as part of the solstice feast, a celebration to mark the start of the new year. Most of the hunters had gone ten miles down the valley to try for a specially large boar, but Tagart had opted to work the duck traps, and he had asked Klay to join him.

The trigger-cords from the nets entered the hide and lay across a branch, ready for use. In the cramped space the reeds smelled musty. Tagart put his face to the slit and peeped out.

More wigeon had ventured out of the water. The grazing birds were now all round the nets; three or four were even inside.

'Not much longer,' he said to Klay.

Klay grunted. Tagart regarded him for a moment before turning back to the slit.

The change in Klay's manner had not escaped Tagart's notice. The reason for it was not hard to guess. In Tagart, Klay plainly perceived a rival. Until Tagart's arrival, it seemed, Klay had seen no threat to his future. There had been no other likely successor to the name of Shode, from within the tribe at least. But Tagart was certainly Klay's equal in strength and skill, and if there were a challenge these qualities would be put to the test.

Chenk and the scouts had still not returned from Valdoe. They should have been back within a fortnight at the most, and yet Shode seemed content to wait. 'We'll give them two more days,' he had said that morning. Tagart thought they might have been captured; he could not understand Shode's attitude. In time, the matter might cause trouble with Visar and the other chiefs, many of whom shared the strong views of Tagart and Fodich. Bubeck, though, did not share these views. He openly ridiculed them. Shode was non-committal; Klay had been influenced by Bubeck.

Discord over such an important issue might precipitate a challenge for leadership of the camp, and perforce of the Shoden too. But, whatever happened about Valdoe, Klay would know that when the day came, perhaps years from now, when Shode died or became too old, he could no longer be so sure of succeeding his father.

Tagart felt he understood this. It explained many things. In the past, with Tagart in another tribe, Klay had always been friendly. Now he was resentful; and his manner towards Segle too was peculiar.

And Bubeck had been hostile from the moment of Tagart's arrival. He had no son himself: Klay was his favourite. Possibly he nurtured a hope that, after Shode's death, the two tribes would merge and that he would become the chief, working through Klay.

Tagart sat looking out across the bleak marshes of the valley.

The bad weather had started. Soon the meres would be solid. In some years even the rivers froze. Such times were rare, every ten or twenty winters, often following a hot summer; and last summer had been the hottest anyone could remember. The old men were already saying that a cold winter was on its way.

He opened his mouth to speak, but closed it again, not sure how best to frame his words. Out on the floods the duck were still feeding. The cloudy day made the colours of their plumage dull, blending with the grass and the thistles. Beyond them the water of the mere was blown into tiny waves; the wind flicked droplets from their peaks and drove them on the shore. The nets had almost filled with birds.

'Get ready to pull,' Klay said.

'You know why I asked you to join me here,' Tagart said. 'I want to talk. I want to make things plain.'

Klay did not look at him. He watched the nets instead. 'Go on.'

'I have no wish to be chief.'

'If you had no wish to be chief, you would not be able to say such a thing.'

'I want only to live in peace.'

'You mean you are not at peace already.'

'How can I be? You and Bubeck will not let me.'

Klay's hands tightened on the cords. 'You seek to make trouble here. Why did you come back?'

'The Shoden are my tribe.'

'No longer. You left us and went to the Owls. They are dead. You are tribeless; you have no ancestors. They died with the Owls. It would have been better if you'd died with them.'

'My ancestors are here.'

'You do not deserve to be welcomed back.'

'That is for Shode to say. What would you have us do? Spend the winter with the wolves? Die without ancestors?'

'There are other camps,' Klay said.

'Where I have no friends.'

'You have no friends here.'

'My father was once "Shode".'

It was useless. Tagart had achieved nothing; less than nothing.

Klay put his face closer to the slit, cutting the conversation off. The nets were waiting and open, the cords stretched tight. Ducks had filled the fatal space: wigeon, pintail, mallard, teal.

'Pull!' Klay shouted, and they yanked the cords back.

Like folding wings the nets closed in. A teal escaped; the rest were pinned to the ground by the meshes. The other birds on the floods went up in a roar of alarm. Klay was the first out of the hide, splashing through the sleet and floodwater, a cudgel in his hand, ready to dispatch the birds they had caught.

In the late afternoon Altheme came down to the quay to watch the soldiers landing. She stood alone, almost unnoticed in the shelter of the worksheds, her hair drawn back with a carved brooch of jade and ivory. She wore a small jade earring, and a necklace of worked scales of nacre and lapis lazuli. She pushed her hands farther into the pockets of her sealskin coat, which was made of the pelts of unborn pups. Like nearly everything she owned, it was the gift of her husband, the Lord of Valdoe.

She gazed at the landing stages and the wooden vessels bumping there. Her thoughts were confused. It was three weeks and six days since the night of the storm. She tried to argue with herself: in all the years with Gehan she had conceived not once. Why then should she do so now? She was worrying without reason. It made no sense. A child would not fit the pattern, the destruction of their happiness and their life together. It could not fit: it was too grotesque.

But the night of the storm would not leave her thoughts. That was the last time they had been together. She could not forget the rain and wind on the shutters and the groaning timbers of the fort. She kept seeing Gehan above her; she kept hearing the name he had breathed. *Ika, Ika.*

The afternoon was turning to dusk. Drops of rain began to fall.

The soldiers had arrived two hours ago. The men were ashore, already finding their quarters in the Trundle four miles away. Now slaves were unloading the rest of the weapons and equipment, packing sledges to be drawn along the road that led from the quayside and the creek.

The landing stages stood near the head of the creek, accessible at all but the lowest tides. Across the water were saltmarshes, and here and there on higher ground were clumps of scrub. That was where the savages, the spies, had been captured, a week or so before.

Altheme left her place by the corner of the worksheds and slowly walked towards the water. The ships, like all that was most costly, drew their design from the mainland, and ultimately from the east. The prows reared up, the heads of monsters carved and inlaid, from flat plank decking smoothed by the adzes and sandstones of craftsmen in the homelands. From stem to stern the largest ship was twenty-nine feet. The larger vessels had two deck-houses, the smaller only one. Low masts carried leather or fabric sails, now furled with white ropes. Shipped oars stood pointing skywards, like the rays of fish-fins. Hatchways lay open as the slaves passed up bags and bundles to those above.

This was the eighth or ninth such landing in the past three weeks. The number of extra soldiers was steadily growing.

'What are you doing here?'

At the sound of Gehan's voice Altheme took her hands from her pockets and turned. 'I wanted a change of air, my lord.'

He was not pleased to see her. He had been speaking to the harbour Trundleman, arranging for another landing stage to be built. 'How did you get down from the fort?'

'An empty sledge.' She bit her lip. 'I meant no harm. They were bringing it down anyway.'

'And how do you propose to get back?'

'I didn't think.'

'You never do.' Gehan beckoned to a man nearby: the overseer of a team of slaves. The overseer hurried across the quay and inclined his head. 'Unload that sledge and take Lady Brennis back to the Trundle,' Gehan said. 'Make haste before it gets dark.'

The road up to the fort had become a quagmire. The slaves hauled at their harnesses and struggled to keep the sledge

moving. Soon they were under the trees; reaching branches made a tunnel of the road. The sledge turned a corner and the flickering lamps of the worksheds were left behind.

Gehan that evening arrived late for the meal. Altheme had bathed and changed, and for a long time sat alone in her chamber. She had dismissed her body-slave: she wanted to examine her thoughts.

She heard the voice of the man to whom she had given herself for so many years, the man who had changed so much. He was outside, in the vestibule, taking off mud-spattered clothes.

Her thoughts returned to their first encounter, all those years ago. She had been eighteen and Gehan twenty-two. Her father, a merchant, had brought her to Brennis on a visit to see his friend, the fourth Lord of Valdoe. She remembered her first sight of the crude, wild coast of the island country; the sinister ramparts of the Trundle on the top of Valdoe Hill; the docking of her father's ship; and the sharp premonitory pang she had felt with her first step on the strange soil. She remembered a formal young man with sun-bleached hair and solemn grey eyes who had walked with her by the willows, trout dimpling the river. In him she had recognized the complement of herself. His strength of will had overawed her; but more striking had been his gentleness and his capacity for understanding. He knew her perfectly – in his company she needed no pretence.

Seven years ago. A month after their wedding his father died and Gehan became the fifth Flint Lord. At once their happiness began imperceptibly to dissolve. Gradually, over five years and more, she realized that in her inexperience she had made a mistake. His power in this country was frightening. It had invaded his sanity: it was driving him mad. His idealism had become something else.

She knew she should go, escape to her father, anywhere. That was her urge, but there was nowhere safe. She could not go home. The trade with Brennis had become too important. Even if she did try to escape, she would be sent back. Outside Valdoe she had no acquaintances, no one to whom she could turn.

Altheme rose from her couch and entered Gehan's chamber,

the room where they ate and slept. His sister was seated on the bed, cross-legged, her blonde hair hanging loose.

Ika looked up. 'Did you hear? The other savage died this afternoon.'

'I suppose you went to watch.'

'For a little while.' In Ika's lap was an oval box. It contained the dried female flowers of hemp, a plant brought to the homelands by traders from the south and east. Ika took some and packed it into a narrow-bowled pipe with a long, curving stem. 'Pass me a taper, Altheme.'

She held the taper to the nearest lamp and lit the pipe, inhaling deeply, holding the smoke in her lungs till it had lost its blueness and become brownish grey; and exhaled. She had been using the drug throughout the day. 'For you?'

Altheme shook her head.

'Perhaps you should.'

'No.'

There was a draught as the door opened and Gehan came into the room. He went to a table by the window and poured a beaker of milfoil essence.

'Did you see the savage die?' Ika said.

'I was there, yes.'

'Did he say anything?'

'Not a word.' Two savages had been caught near the landing-place. They had been lying in the bushes, watching the quay. According to Gehan's advisers, it was rare to find such men away from their tribes at this time of year. The clear implication was that the landings had already attracted attention and that the two were spies. When interrogated, though, neither had so much as admitted that he could understand the questions. One had been pressed to death in front of his companion. The sight had produced no effect. He had given nothing away. The guards had then exercised their skills on him, to no profit.

The incident was puzzling, even worrying. If the two men were nomads, as their appearance suggested, their presence at Valdoe might or might not indicate that news of the campaign had reached the winter camp. But if, as was possible, they were merely a couple of outcasts, or pedlars, or wanderers from some place beyond the domain, then the matter was not worth further consideration. Gehan tried to put it out of his mind.

'No guests tonight,' he said. 'We're eating alone.'

He turned to the door and called for the night meal.

5

Tagart shouldered two more bundles of stakes and balanced them. His fingers felt cold under his mittens; his breath fumed as he stood waiting for Edrin to finish sorting through the heaps of gear. Since first light they had been working with the others, carrying bundles down the valley and into the marshes. The previous day the hunters had been unsuccessful in their attempt to catch a suitable boar for the solstice celebrations; it had been decided to try again, in a place called Yote Wood.

The Yote Oak, a hollow tree from which the wood was named, stood in the middle of an island of high ground among the marshes, an eyot which the river had not yet worn away. The island was long and narrow, clothed at its edges with dense tangle. Farther in there were beeches and oaks, and it was these that brought the wild pigs to feed.

Bristly and squat, burly and dark, the pigs dug with tusks and pushed with snouts, and made small contented sounds of feeding. Their hoofs printed cleft tracks in the mud. At one end of the marshes they had made a wallow and rubbed the bark from a nearby tree. The boars were solitary, nocturnal, lurking by day; the sows travelled at night too, with their piglets, continually chiding them. In the easy soil of the marshes they uprooted tubers and insects, found and ate toadstools of many colours and kinds. Their hours were spent in continuous eating, wandering the lakesides and woodlands. Autumn was the time of feasting. And when the frosts came and the mud froze, the pigs turned to a diet of acorns and beechmast.

To catch them the hunters used various techniques. Most efficient, where the terrain permitted, was a line of beaters moving towards a funnel of wattle fencing. At the end of the funnel, catchers would be waiting with netting and spears. The placing of the wattle panels, their precise configuration, was a matter of extreme skill – a boar could weigh as much as three hundred and eighty pounds. Armed with powerful tusks, spurred by fear, such a beast could not be stopped by a fence of flimsy wattle. The fences did not prevent the animal's progress: they directed it, subtly, from clump to clump and copse to copse. Only towards the mouth of the funnel did the fences become more substantial and uncompromising. Then the posts were driven in with heavy hammers, the panels reinforced to withstand demented barging and butting. The final corridor towards the netting was made of solid stakes.

These stakes were made of the strongest oak, and were six and a half feet long, trimmed at one end to a point. They lay at the camp in bundles of six, beside the pile of wattle panels, the netting and hole-borers and the rest of the equipment.

'Which are the new nets?' Edrin said irritably. He was thirty-six, small and slight, with keen brown eyes and a sparse beard. He rarely smiled or spoke idly. He was humourless and ambitious, but he had no presence and commanded little respect. None the less he held a special place in the tribe, which he had earned by his closeness to Shode, by his advice and experience in matters of the chase: his gifts in tracking and deduction were uncanny. From a blade of grass and a broken twig Edrin could compile a story, detail after detail, rejecting the irrelevant, picking out clues that anyone else would have missed. What he lacked in physique he made up for in resource and cunning. He was a man of subtle motives. A member of the Waterfall tribe all his life, he had at one time wanted to be its chief. But now all that seemed to be forgotten. Now he appeared content merely to advise Shode, to be one of the elders. He had sided with Bubeck and Klay on the question of the Flint Lord, and privately regarded Tagart and Fodich as scaremongers.

'Are these the new nets?' he said, turning the heaps over. 'Klay said something about repaired nets and new ones.'

'We should make sure,' Tagart said. The weight of the stakes was beginning to hurt his shoulders.

'It's that pile there,' said Berge, a man of twenty with wild beard and hair.

'Are you certain?' Edrin said.

Tagart said that he recalled having seen Klay with the nets earlier. Berge was right.

This was to be the final trip down to the marshes and Yote Wood. The rest of the gear had already been deposited there. During the afternoon it was to be assembled in preparation for the drive the following day.

Tagart, Edrin and Berge set off, downhill, leaving behind the untidy, expanse of the camp, the fires and shelters, the dwellings with their roofs of piled branches. The river flowed quietly among the bridging logs. Tagart felt a melting on his nose and looked up.

'Snow,' he said to Edrin. 'It's already starting. But where are the scouts? What has happened to Chenk?'

'He'll be here soon enough.'

Tagart noticed Segle across the river, working at rope-making with the other women. He called her name, but she did not acknowledge: perhaps she hadn't heard.

Edrin, observing, said, 'There are troubles nearer home than Valdoe.'

'What do you mean?'

'It is not my place to say.'

'Say what?'

'What you are the last to know. But gossip means nothing. The women have too much imagination.'

At once Tagart understood and was angry. True, since coming to the camp it had been different between him and Segle; alone with her in the forest he had been sure of her, but here, surrounded by new influences, everything had changed. Yet she was his woman and Edrin had no right to make such remarks. Tagart's first impulse was to strike him down.

Suppressing his rage, Tagart said 'What do the women imagine?'

'I cannot say,' Edrin said. 'Just remember the penalties.'

Tagart checked his reply. Among the nomads the marriage bond was held sacred. It was the foundation of the family, the tribe, the spirit group, and hence the foundation of Creation itself. Only a chief, whose actions were divine, could choose his woman as he pleased. For the rest, the laws were harsh. Those aggrieved by adultery could insist on severe punishment: for the man, castration and banishment; for the woman, death by burning. After only three weeks in the tribe, Tagart did not feel confident enough to challenge an elder, nor did he know exactly why Edrin had spoken as he had.

Edrin glanced sideways at Tagart and saw that he had achieved the desired effect.

They continued in silence. Berge, walking behind and whistling, had heard nothing of the conversation.

The snow shower did not persist. By the time they reached the marshes it was over.

In Yote Wood, near the big oak tree, they found Klay and Bubeck. This was to be another joint venture of the Waterfall and Beaver tribes. In consultation with Edrin and the other expert trackers it had already been established where the ending of the funnel was to be sited, here by the oak tree. They were hammering in the posts as the three men arrived.

The ground was hard with frost, but despite the cold Klay had taken off his stormcoat. He was sweating as his hands took a firmer grip on the haft of the long stone-headed hammer and he swung again, smacking the top of the post held upright for him by another man.

The corridor of posts was almost complete. It curved slightly to the right, terminating in a gap just wide enough to admit the flanks of an adult boar. Behind the gap was a framework of poles. Over this the netting would be laid, loosely, so that the animal's progress would not be halted too quickly, but quickly enough to ensure that it would be entangled in the meshes quite safely before a spear-stroke brought about its end.

Tagart set down his burden.

'Take the hammer,' Bubeck said.

'Yes,' Klay said. 'I'm sick of this.' He stood back, wiping his nose on his wrist, and let the handle of the hammer fall. It hit the ground at Tagart's feet.

Frequently in the past weeks Bubeck and Klay had singled out Tagart for the unpleasant or arduous tasks. But Tagart did not belong to the Bubecks: their chief had no power to give him a direct order.

Tagart turned to Edrin, an elder of his own tribe. Edrin gave a nod: assent to Bubeck's order, turning it into a mere proposal.

Bubeck sneered.

'Let me take the hammer,' said Berge, picking it up, and the moment passed.

They finished the corridor of stakes and arranged the netting on the framework. By early afternoon, work on the entire funnel was complete. Everything was ready for the drive next day; the men withdrew.

At the meal that night the Shoden, twenty-one people in all, ate as a group. They sat close to the flames, warming their hands, sheltering from an east wind. The leather awnings flapped and whipped as the wind blew the fire to life and threw sparks beyond the guy-ropes and into the night. Tagart watched Edrin, who was eating assiduously, occasionally speaking to his woman and to Shode. He watched the other men in the tribe: Orick, Berge, Grisden, Phale, each with his family. He watched Klay sitting with Yulin, his wife, dumpy and dark, made drab by child-bearing, her brown eyes withdrawn and resigned. More than once she glanced at Tagart and Segle. She gave food to her daughters, two small girls who clung to Klay. Klay was speaking, boasting of all the pork they would be bringing tomorrow from Yote Wood.

He noticed Tagart watching him and seemed to avoid his eye.

'This way!' Bubeck shouted. 'This way! Keep him this way!'

The boar, disturbed from sleep at the very feet of the beaters, was one of the biggest they had ever seen. It had burst from a brake of rotten brushwood as the men moved forward, shouting and screaming and banging with sticks.

The men were running now, leaping through the undergrowth, trying to keep up with the boar as it crashed first one way then another, guided by the wattle panels on its headlong passage through the woods, gaining speed, its snout held low; they glimpsed its yellow tusks, the hackles of coarse bristle on its back and abruptly it had vanished in a holly thicket, the glossy foliage slapping back to hide the place of its entry.

It was the first drive of the day, under a sky that looked full of snow. Tagart was near the middle of the line. They had managed to keep the boar well inside the funnel. The holly thicket was one of a number of such sanctuaries along the course where a quarry might go to ground – unavoidable hazards which the siting of the fences had kept to a minimum.

'Careful now! He might break anywhere! If he comes too fast let him go!'

The animal was too big for them to take chances. They had not seen it properly yet, not in the open, but it stood easily three feet high at the shoulder. If it chose to come out of the thicket where it had gone in, if it chose to run back down the funnel – as some old and wily boars might – it would be far too heavy to stop.

'There he is!'

'He's coming this way!' Tagart cried.

For an instant the boar, head down, was tearing through the brambles directly towards him. It had emerged from the holly at a gallop, close to the place where it had entered, almost as if it had sensed a weak link in the line of men, a slight gap between Orick and Tagart on his left. But Tagart was moving sideways, closing the gap. The boar came nearer: twenty paces, ten, and, with two sudden steps, jolted to a halt. It took breath, eyeing Tagart. He met its eyes: they were very dark, nearly black, with rims of white showing at the bottom, bloodshot and rheumy. The pig was looking at him. And then it turned its head and was running again, away from Tagart and the others, more desperately than before.

It skirted the thicket and plunged along its ordained path toward the corridor of stakes.

'Keep him straight! Keep him straight!'

The final screen was behind; the funnel walls were narrowing. The boar, terror-stricken, was running much too fast to take the curve of stakes and its flank barged into the left wall, robbing it of speed, but it kept on, goaded by the yelling and screaming and suddenly the stakes opened and there was freedom and it was fooled, meshed in a tangle of netting that brought it in a slithering crash to the ground.

Men were ready with spears. Klay thrust first. The blade snapped and he shouted an oath. He drew back; Grisden stepped forward. The boar rolled its eyes, blood dribbling from its mouth, and with a convulsive spasm got to its feet. Grisden raised his arms and stabbed, badly, too quickly, goring the flank, unleashing a paroxysm of thrashing and bucking and squealing. Shode gave an angry cry and jumped forward to finish it, to end its pain; but then, impossibly, the netting was somehow coming apart as the boar wrenched its head from side to side and one foreleg was free. Then the other foreleg came free and the netting was being dragged behind like an old skin. Teeth chattering with pain and rage, the boar twisted sideways and ran straight into Shode. Its right tusk jabbed upwards and pierced his groin. Tagart saw the boar give a frenzied jerk of its head and Shode was flung down and pulled along the ground.

Other spears were plunged into the boar from behind. In a moment it was dead.

Shode was shouting, shouting through all the woods with unhuman cries, a beast in slaughter. The trees, the sky, the ground – everything seemed to Tagart unreal, from some other world where emergency waited to break through. And it had broken through. What had happened so swiftly and easily could not be grasped, could not be believed.

Klay fell to his knees beside his father.

Among others, Bubeck and Edrin jumped the line of stakes, screaming orders. They dragged the carcase of the boar aside and cut away Shode's clothing.

'Hold him still!' Bubeck growled.

They stared, aghast.

'Better take him back.'

6

The solstice symbolized rebirth. It was the first day of the new year. On the morning of the Creation, after the Sun had vanquished the Ice God and exiled him in the far north, the four spirits were born, released from the Sun's dazzling body in an endless stream, each separate, each remaining a part of the Sun. The spirits were a family. Together they made Light, the essence of the Sun, returning to him, coming forth. The father of the family, Fire, warlike and proud, was sent north and charged by the Sun with keeping the Ice God a prisoner. The daughter, Water, peaceful and passive, was given the south. The son was Air, whose domain was the east; and their mother, Earth, dwelt in the west.

The Moon had betrayed the Ice God and ingratiated herself with the Sun, who made her his acolyte. To her were entrusted the seasons, and each winter, when the Ice God tried to win her back, her allegiance was put to the test. At the solstice she renounced him and turned back to the Sun. It was the Moon whose slender fingers had taken the Sun's needles and sewn the threads of light he had provided: from light, from the four spirits, in greater or lesser proportions, everything was made, and, having been made, assigned its place in the world. Thus the eagle was a blend of Air and Fire, and was traditionally governed by those spirits; the bison belonged to Earth, the otter to Water. The creation of man was more complicated. His body was composed of all the spirits, but his soul was imperfect, lacking one or more of the elements that would allow him to achieve perfection or Light. He spent his life trying to repair the deficiency. If he lacked Fire, he would go to live in the north, and the totem of his tribe would be chosen from one of Fire's creatures.

There were four spirit groups, each with its winter camp in a different part of the country. Sometimes these camps split up, changed sites, fell into disuse, and then there might be five, six or even more.

Each spirit group was led by one tribe, known as the First. The Firsts, alone among all the tribes, took their names not from a creature but from the direct manifestation of each spirit: Crase, Lightning; Shode, Waterfall; Sare, Cloud; Omber, Mountain. Their totems – lizard, salmon, peregrine, ox – were secondary symbols which none the less possessed great power, for each was the purest totem of the spirit.

Most tribes belonged to two spirit groups. Their summer hunting grounds, although never precisely defined, were usually adhered to and each tribe had its customary territory and rights. The Dragonflies mainly wintered in the north, at the Lightning camp; but because the dragonfly was a creature of Water as well as Fire the tribe sometimes used the Waterfall camp instead. Occasionally, finding themselves in autumn in the west or east – perhaps deliberately, for most marriages outside the tribe were arranged in winter – they might stay as guests in the camp of another First, just as the Wolves, the Bisons, and the Martens were this year wintering in the Waterfall camp.

Shode died from his wounds at nightfall. The loss of blood was too great, the damage too horrible for any hope of recovery. Yet the priests chanted through the hours of waiting, and sprinkled mineral earths on the fire, causing many-coloured sparks to rise into the grey afternoon. They made prayer to the Sun, to the Moon, to the four spirits. To Water they addressed a continuous and dreamlike hymn: as chief of the Water First, Shode was the embodiment of the spirit among the nomads. There would be no rest until another had been found to take his place.

Even as they had carried Shode back to camp the speculation had begun. With such injuries they knew he was already finished. It was time for a new chief to take over. Klay's time had come.

Below ground, the Waterfall priest, Phale, spoke his prayers while Shode's woman held her husband's head in her lap. He had lost consciousness.

Shortly before dark there was a cry from the river. Chenk and the scouting party had returned. Nine men had left the camp three weeks ago; only seven crossed the bridging logs to be greeted with the news about Shode.

Chenk took the remaining chiefs, eight including himself, and gathered them together under the awnings at one edge of the cooking area. He was exhausted, filthy, dispirited; the scouts had covered the distance from Valdoe in two days. Normally it took at least twice as long to traverse, on overgrown paths, eighty miles of forest and marsh. Chenk sat down and for a moment put his face in his hands before speaking.

'Fodich is right,' he said.

He described how the scouts had divided in order to survey all parts of the Flint Lord's domain. 'We saw ships landing, soldiers moving from fort to fort, supplies coming from the villages. You've never seen such things. Wone and Trander are missing. They must have been taken by the soldiers.' He explained that Wone and Trander had been sent to Apuldram to watch the landing-place. All the scouts had been due to rendezvous on the way back; when Wone and Trander had failed to appear, Chenk himself had gone to Apuldram to find them. 'There's no cover. To get close to the worksheds they must have risked being seen. We waited two days for them; we even questioned a field slave on the outskirts of Valdoe Village, but he could tell us nothing. Then we came back.'

Four of the chiefs – Osprey, Dragonfiy, Heron, and Kingfisher, Chenk himself, agreed that there should be an immediate convocation of the elders, not only of this, but of the other winter camps. The remaining chiefs were divided. Bubeck and Marten were still sceptical; Bison and Wolf wanted to leave the decision to Shode or his successor.

Their argument was interrupted by the arrival of Phale, the priest, tall and sharp-faced, his beard and hair almost wholly white. He was leader of the elders in Shode's absence.

'Come at once,' he told the chiefs.

Klay appeared at the top of the ladder from Shode's dwelling. He stood looking round the camp for a moment before stepping forward. People began rising to their feet; the compound fell silent.

'My father is dead.'

Phale pushed his way forward. 'A new chief must arise!' In his right hand he was holding aloft a long staff, a carved mace intricate with flowing patterns which culminated in a leaping salmon, symbol of aspiration and the Waterfall tribe.

At his elbow, Tagart felt someone stir. It was Yulin, Klay's wife. Segle had become separated from him in the crowd.

'Who is there with strength?' Phale cried. 'Who is there with strength to carry the Mace?'

Klay responded. 'As my father's issue I put myself forward by choice of the spirits. Render the Mace to my charge!'

Klay's woman was standing on tiptoes, speaking into Tagart's ear. 'He wants your wife,' she said. 'They have already known each other. If he is chief he'll take her. You will be abandoned, and so will my children, and so will I.'

Phale turned to the assembly. 'Does any man stand against Klay?'

'You will be cast out,' Yulin hissed. 'You will be tribeless. It's true. I saw them in the woods.'

Tagart could not absorb what she was saying. He could not think.

'. . . in the woods,' she whispered again.

Murmurs were rising around him. A name was being repeated over and over again. Edrin, Edrin, Edrin.

'No!' Klay shouted. He shot out an accusing arm. 'It was he who killed my father! It was Edrin, Edrin and Tagart, and Berge. They brought the old netting on purpose! It was Tagart! Tagart and Edrin!'

Edrin came forward. 'I challenge his fitness to lead.'

'Yes! We want Edrin as chief!'

'Klay is unworthy!'

'He cannot lead us!'

Phale raised the Mace for silence. 'Klay, will you defer to Edrin? Or will you accept the challenge?'

'Do I have any choice?' He wiped froth from the edge of his mouth. 'It was a plot by Edrin and Tagart to kill him!'

'That's enough.'

'Murderers! Murderers!'

Phale restrained him with the Mace. 'Enough, I said!'

Tagart perceived that Edrin was the choice of the majority, of all who opposed Klay. But he also perceived that Edrin was too old to challenge a man like Klay. Edrin would have better fieldcraft, no more, and in the forest, especially in winter, that was not enough. Klay would win and become chief. And if what Yulin had said were true, he would take Segle and drive Tagart out. Tagart would have to leave his blood tribe and his ancestors and never return. He would have to leave Segle, leave her with Klay . . .

'Edrin is old and weak,' Yulin said into Tagart's ear. 'Only you are strong enough to challenge my husband.'

Earlier Tagart had seen the arrival of the scouts and he had already heard rumours of what they had found. At the back of his mind was something larger and far more important than Klay and Segle and his own life.

Yulin was still speaking, in a low, insistent voice. Tagart sought Segle's face but couldn't find it.

A huge man was moving through the crowd, pushing people out of the way. 'Let me through,' Bubeck said. 'Let me through.' He reached the fire and addressed Phale.

'I too challenge Klay's fitness to lead.'

There was uproar.

The Shoden objected, because Bubeck was outside the tribe; they said he could not compete.

'Not so,' said Phale with regret. 'The Beavers are of our spirit. Their chief, and the chief of any tribe of the spirit, may challenge. 'This is lawful.'

Bubeck grunted. 'The Shoden have become too few,' he announced. 'They need fresh blood. Our blood. Our tribes will merge. The Bubecks and the Shoden will become one, a great tribe, the first tribe of the spirit!'

Tagart observed that Klay did not seem upset by Bubeck's challenge. He realized what it meant. It meant Edrin would stand no chance at all. Not against two.

Tagart heard his voice speaking, as though it were not his own; the words he uttered were squeezed from him by the press of people, by the firelight and the night, by Klay and Edrin and Bubeck, and Yulin, by the long hours of torment waiting for Shode to die. They were uttered for Segle, anguished and desperate words, but most of all they were uttered through the memory of Fodich lying in the mud, through terror: of Valdoe, and the carnage that would surely come if the Flint Lord remained unopposed.

Tagart faced Phale and the whole assembly.

'I too challenge,' he said. 'I challenge Klay's fitness to lead!'

The laws of challenge had their origin in the mists beyond memory. Their object was simple: to find the best man to be chief. In the process no one was to be killed, unless by misadventure, for no face was lost by defeat and a fair surrender was held to be honourable. In this way valuable men were not wasted, and the man who was strongest and cleverest would succeed.

Phale, as leader of the tribal elders, broke the Mace into five pieces. The uppermost fragment with its salmon emblem was retained by him. The other fragments, one to each contestant, were given to Klay, Edrin, Bubeck and Tagart. Contestants were allowed their choice of clothing, a pouch, and, through some tradition whose purpose was obscure, a coil of spear-binding twine eleven paces in length. They had no food, no weapons, no fire-making kits.

The challengers were then to be banished from the camp, in accordance with the laws. The one who came back with all the pieces of the Mace, to match the emblem and make it whole, would be recognized as the new chief.

If a man sought or accepted the help of another, or if he destroyed or lost his fragment before it could be taken, or if he returned to camp before his part of the contest was resolved, then that man would be tried by the elders. If found guilty he would be executed and all his family cast out, left to wander without tribe or ancestors, without hope of the afterlife. In winter such expulsion meant virtual death, from hunger and exposure or attack by wolves.

There were no other rules. Nothing mattered except that one man should demonstrate his superiority by finding, and having found, taking – by violence, stealth, or persuasion – each and every fragment of Mace.

The four men were separated, searched by the elders, blindfolded, and sent out secretly, each in a different direction, chosen by lot. Because they were four, each had been assigned a cardinal point. Tagart had drawn North; he had then been conducted to the edge of the camp. Only then had the blindfold been removed, so that he would not know which directions the others had taken.

No stars showed: under the trees everything was dark. Tagart made his way uphill, towards the burnt-out heath where he had decided to wait till daybreak. Brambles snatched at his leggings. Branches broke under the heavy soles of his boots. He was leaving a plain and easy trail, but that could not be helped. At night, the others would be doing the same.

He had already shaped the outline of a strategy which depended upon no one but himself. That was the only way to succeed – if he tried to be too subtle, to anticipate what the others might do, he knew he would become confused and failure would inescapably follow.

It would be simple to hide among the trees, to wait, to let the others fight each other first and thus reduce the odds. But he had neither food nor fire, and what if they too were planning to hide? What then?

He knew he had to start at once, and the man to start with was Edrin. Edrin was past his best, and, though he was not to be underestimated, he would be the easiest of the three.

Tagart was afraid. Klay and Bubeck were working together, and he would have to take them both at once. They would try to kill him. They could not risk his return to camp, his testimony that Klay had been helped. So they would kill him in the woods and hide his body. And afterwards Klay would take Segle and become leader of the Shoden. Disaster would come to the tribe and all the tribes of the south, for, whoever won the contest, only Tagart recognized the threat from Valdoe.

He tried to push aside all such thoughts and thoughts of Segle too, but she was with him constantly, a dull, bewildering ache. He refused to let himself believe what Klay's woman had whispered, refused to connect it with what Edrin had so maliciously said or with what he knew in his own heart.

There was no time for her now.

At first light Altheme was standing alone at her window, looking south. She kept her eyes above the tent-filled enclosure and the spiked wooden walls of the fort, above the rough steepness of Valdoe Hill falling to bleak marshland and the sea. The sky was grey. From it, even as she watched, single snowflakes began slanting down.

It was the day of Goele, the winter solstice, a feast, and not yet sunrise, but Gehan had been up and working for three hours, leaving Altheme to listen to the sounds from the adjoining chamber.

Gehan's sister Ika was in there with a girl and a youth. The youth, Gehan's food-taster, had recently been a nightly visitor to the chamber. He was tall and languid, with red hair and pale skin and green eyes. The cast of his features was beginning to betray the decadence of his life in Gehan's retinue. It was a life devoted to luxury, pleasure, sensation, with women or with men, Gehan's guests, and sometimes with Gehan himself. Altheme knew this. She was aware of her husband's tastes, the changing favour with which he viewed his other women, and the way he regarded his wife. The knowledge disgusted her. And it disgusted her to listen to Ika with the food-taster and the girl. The girl was innocent, a child barely eleven years old. She had been summoned from the slaves' quarters during the night. Altheme had heard her frightened pleadings silenced; and now, at dawn, the noises were beginning again: the creaking bed-frame, growing moans, stifled cries of pain.

Altheme turned quickly from the window. By the doorway she paused to take a robe from her clothes-rack. The first to hand was pale brown, embroidered with flowers and ferns of yellow, pink, lavender and green. It flowed behind her as she left the chamber and crossed the gallery, from which a twisting flight of stairs led to ground level and the Flint Lord's day rooms.

Gehan was there, in the main chamber. The ceiling of this room was low, scarcely above head height. Polished oak boards, gleaming in the lamplight, covered the floor. The walls were decorated with panels of painting, some of extreme age, others quite recent: scenes of symbolism and history, depicting demons, flames, men in battle, winged creatures spewing swarms of insects. Three wide windows overlooked the inner enclosure. Each was provided with a heavy shutter closing from within, for defence, and the door, which was made of thick elm, swung on oiled oak hinges and was fitted with four stout locking-bars. A yew-wood cradle held heated rocks, renewed every hour by slaves. There was little furniture in the room: a few small chests, a kind of low bench on which stood burning oil-lamps, and some leather cushions scattered on the floor. On one of these Gehan was seated, cross-legged, studying a sheet of wood marked with daubs of ink. The daubs represented hands. A hand was five: five men, a team. Five teams made a unit. Other marks separated the daubs or joined them together. A square represented the Trundle; triangles the secondary forts; a wavering line the Brennis coast.

In normal times he maintained a force of nineteen units. Seven were under the command of the General of the Coast, one unit being deployed in each of the secondary forts. Six remained permanently at Valdoe – one to guard the mines, two to guard the other works outside the Trundle, two on duty inside the fort, the sixth kept in reserve. The remaining units made up deficiencies in the secondary forts, helped with road and bridge building and repair, escorted trading teams when needed, and composed the slaving parties which made regular crossings to Normandy and Brittany.

'We must draw twelve teams from the secondary forts,' Gehan said.

There were two men with him, also seated on cushions. One was fat and soft, dressed in dark grey and fox fur, with curious pink eyes, white hair, lashes, and wispy beard: an albino named Bohod Zein, agent for the forces in the homelands. Through this man, Brennis Gehan Fifth had paid in flints and goods for ships and reinforcements.

The other was General of Valdoe, a former commander from the mainland called Larr. Like Bohod Zein, he was dressed in the dark grey of the Gehans; over his garments he wore a military tunic of plain hide. A white scar marked his forehead, an old axe wound. His eyes were black and penetrating, his face fleshless and hard. In the army of the Gehans the ranks were few: soldier, team-master, unit leader, commander, general, lord. Larr had begun as a soldier at the age of ten. In twelve years' slaving he had advanced to team-master, unit leader, and commander. Under Gehan's father he had been brought to Brennis and then, at the age of thirty, had been made general, one of two in the island country.

'My lord,' said Bohod Zein; 'if you take so many from the General of the Coast, will your forts there not be weakened? I can respectfully arrange for three more units to be sent, trained men, all experienced, at a price scarcely greater than that negotiated before.'

Gehan considered. At this moment over three hundred men were waiting across the channel, consuming food and supplies. Two hundred more had already landed and were overcrowding the barracks. The expense of the campaign so far was giving worry. The output of the mines for the next three years had been mortgaged. If the weather worsened and the crossings were impeded, the expense would become ruinous. But he knew that the agent was right. To leave the secondary forts under strength would be dangerous.

'Arrange it.'

'As to price, my lord – '

Gehan arose as Altheme entered the room. Larr stood too, lithe and controlled. Bohod Zein struggled to his feet.

'My lady,' Larr said.

Bohod Zein eagerly stepped forward and took Altheme's hand. 'My lady.'

His familiarity far exceeded the bounds of etiquette. Gehan observed Altheme's uncertain glance, noted the lingering clasp of Bohod Zein's fingers. With a courteous smile she drew her hand away.

'I am sorry, my lord,' Altheme told Gehan. 'I did not mean to disturb you here. But have you seen outside?'

Already there were white ridges on the roughness of the inner palisade. Gehan strode to the nearest window and looked out and up.

The air was filled with tumbling feathers and stars, multitudes and multitudes coming from a darkening sky.

The snows had started.

7

Klay heard the camp coming awake. From his perch in the boughs of an old beech, he looked across the river towards the compound and tried to see movement, but too many winter branches were in the way.

He took off one mitten and held up a licked finger. East, the wind was coming from the east, and when he studied the sky he saw that it was sliding majestically, a dense, almost featureless mass of cloud tinged with yellow that meant snow for certain.

He replaced his mitten and started down the tree. In snow they would be able to find Tagart very quickly; and then, when the first of Shode's murderers had been dealt with, he and Bubeck would go after Edrin.

Edrin would already be in hiding, somewhere safe, somewhere impossible to find for Edrin was the finest tracker and his woodcraft was too good for any of them, even for Klay himself. To search for him would be wasted effort. Better to let hunger bring him out. Meanwhile, they would find Tagart and kill him.

Klay wondered what Tagart was planning, and how far he had managed to think things through. He was stupid: he would not have guessed that Edrin was in hiding. But then . . . was that really what Edrin was doing? Was it safe to presume anything? Suppose Edrin weren't in hiding at all. Suppose he intended to find Bubeck or Klay and keep his distance. Suppose he saw what they did to Tagart and went back to the camp to tell Phalc. Or suppose he joined forces with Tagart. Suppose . . .

The confusion in Klay's mind multiplied. He did his best to sweep it away. One thing, at least, could be depended on.

In the lottery for direction, Klay had drawn West. He had left the camp under the eyes of the elders and disappeared into the darkness. Two hundred yards from the edge of the compound he had halted and climbed into the beech tree. There was no sense in going any farther. In the morning he knew he would be meeting Bubeck. He knew Bubeck would be nearby, because this was what they had arranged in whispers. Together they would circle the camp and find Tagart's trail, leading in one of the two directions that they themselves had not drawn. There would be little doubt about whose trail it was: Tagart was taller and much heavier than Edrin, and, unless Edrin went to immense and improbable pains, that could not be disguised.

Klay reached the ground and looked about him. Bubeck had instructed him to walk sunwise, following its circle. Bubeck would walk the other way, and in this manner they would quickly meet: so close to the camp it would be unsafe to linger. The solstice feast had been cancelled, and for the duration of the contest there would be no hunting excursions; even so, now in the gloom of first dawn, there was a risk of being seen by someone in the camp.

Klay set off. The ground was hard underfoot from days of frost. When he came to the gurgle of the river he waited near the bank, reluctant to go in. The water would be very cold, and he would have to cross with bare skin, for contestants were allowed no spare clothes. The river flowed south-eastwards; Klay had drawn West. Bubeck, not knowing – their whispering had taken place before the lottery – had told him to walk sunwise.

Klay nipped at his cheek-lining. One or other of them would have to cross.

Suddenly there was movement on the far bank, among the thicket of elder and dogwood that grew right to the water's edge, the branches in the twilight overhanging the swift current. Klay drew back in alarm.

'It's me!'

Bubeck broke the branches aside. He was clad in a bearskin stormcoat, shaggy and dark, tied with a horn-buckled belt, and his leggings, also of bearskin, were tucked into high leather boots. On his head was a peaked fur cap with flaring flaps, and his hands were protected by fur mittens. He brought them together with muffled claps, then swung his arms in the cold. 'Come out of there, Klay!'

Klay appeared, glad to be alone no longer. Bubeck hissed the good news across the intervening yards. 'Tagart drew East. He's left a trail like an aurochs'.'

'You've already found it?'

'Yes. Come on. Get across the river and we can start.'

Klay hesitated. The water here was deep as well as cold.

'What did you draw?' Bubeck said.

'West.'

'That means Edrin drew North. I drew South.'

'You've already crossed once?'

'On the stepping stones at the waterfall.' Bubeck gestured impatiently. 'It's not that cold. Get your boots off.'

'It looks difficult here. I want to try further up. At the swamp.'

'Don't worry,' Bubeck said. 'It's shallower than it looks. You can cross all right.'

'I'm not sure about it, Bubeck.'

'I've done it myself here. Come on. You're wasting time. If we're not quick we'll lose him.'

Reluctantly, Klay undressed. The air was so bitingly cold that his teeth began to chatter at once. The water would be worse. However, he would soon be across and back in his dry clothes. Shivering uncontrollably, he squatted naked, bundling his stormcoat and wrapping it round the pouch and the rest of his things.

'Heave them over,' Bubeck told him, and Klay did so.

Klay neared the water's edge.

'Hurry up! What are you waiting for?'

When Klay's foot touched the water he gasped. Water of such intense coldness was not possible. With his right hand he was gripping a branch. He let it go and gingerly put his other foot forward, probing for the river bed.

It was not there. The current was strong and fast and had cut deep. The water seized Klay's foot and pulled at it like a playful animal. It was scalding his calf, his knee. How much colder would it be on his thighs, on his genitals? Too late, much too late, he realized he wanted to change his mind and he scrabbled for the safety of the branch, but he was losing his balance, his left foot slithering: he knew his equilibrium had gone and he was falling. He shrieked and hit the water with a clumsy splash. At once the grabbing, caustic pain clawed at his skin: in an instant all sensation had been destroyed. He was nerveless, dead with grinding cold. He thrashed his arms, but could not stop his head from going under and the river was dragging him with it.

Numb feet found the bottom and he managed to stand up, against the flow. He had been carried some yards downstream. He opened his mouth, gaping for air. His thorax seemed to have collapsed

Something hit the water in front of him: a bundle of clothing and a pouch. The pouch had been plundered. The fragment of Mace was missing. And when he looked towards the bank, so was Bubeck.

Tagart frowned. Someone had been in the river here, less than an hour before. He plucked a blade of meadow-grass from the tangle of vegetation on the north bank where the man had pulled himself out. The grass, bright green even in winter, was freshly bruised.

Tagart stood up, with a practised eye examining the faint impressions in the ground, the disarray of twigs and leaf-litter, the clues which seemed to lead toward the camp. He turned his eyes to the far bank, trying to see where the man had entered the water. There. Upstream.

He worked his way along the water's edge. Opposite the spot he found new damage to the elder branches. From the number and thickness of split fibres which had so far resumed their shape, he deduced that everything here must have happened at about the same time. The man in the water and the man on the north bank had been here together. Tagart pictured the scene, a grim smile growing on his face. It seemed that Bubeck hadn't been planning to violate the laws of challenge after all. And how did this affect Tagart's quarry – how did it affect Edrin?

At dawn, Tagart had come down the hill to quarter the eastern side of the camp, searching for a recent trail. Those who had drawn West and South would have started from the other side of the river.

So near the camp there were many confusing signs of coming and going, but all were at least a day old. It had not taken Tagart long to find tracks that were unmistakably recent, and from the stride and weight of the man who had left them, he concluded that the trail was Bubeck's and that it was Bubeck who had drawn East. That meant Edrin must have drawn West or South and would be on the other side of the river. If Edrin had gone to earth, that would be where the contest would be resolved. Tagart would have to cross. There were not many places to cross safely, and at any one of them an enemy might be waiting. Tagart, despite his decision to start with Edrin, had to know what Bubeck was doing. He had followed Bubeck's trail to the river, where he had found what he took to be Klay's trail, leading out of the water and towards the camp: the trail of a beaten man.

Tagart resumed his pursuit of Bubeck's trail. It ran generally beside the river, heading upstream. At times it made detours, favouring the easier passage away from the thickest undergrowth. Tagart followed. All his senses were alive; but the woods seemed empty and reassuring.

The wind was keener now. The sky was dark. Soon snowflakes were falling one by one. As they touched the water they vanished and were carried onward. A mile or so above the camp, the river curved away from him and became a wandering stream in a rushy swamp. The snow was falling more quickly. Snipe, harsh-voiced, sprang from the frozen rushes as Tagart approached; they flew up in towering spirals, calling incessantly.

He found the spot where Bubeck had removed his boots and did the same, placing his bare feet in the marks that Bubeck had left, paddling through the icy black mud and into the stream. The water was painfully cold. There was gravel underfoot and between his toes. Tiny fish, black in the pellucid water, streaked away from his feet. The water came to his knees; he crossed as quickly as he dared, afraid of losing his footing, afraid of an ambush, knowing that he was vulnerable here.

On the other side of the swamp, where the ground began to climb, Tagart pulled on his boots and found Bubeck's trail again. It led south – to Edrin.

Tagart stopped on the rise above the valley and looked back. Over the landscape and down into the grey, leafless woods, the sky was shedding snow.

The flakes softly found their way through the branches and, no longer melting, began to settle on the forest floor.

Klay knew the dangers of what he was doing: if he were caught, both he and his family would be tried and punished. His wife and two daughters would be made tribeless, and he would be disembowelled, the manner of execution reserved for the lowest criminals, those who had betrayed the trust of the tribe.

But, however great the dangers, they could not compare to Klay's rage.

Yulin was still asleep when he came down the ladder and into his dwelling. He was certain he had not been seen. His dwelling was near the edge of the camp, and by crawling and rolling he had reached the ladder unobserved.

His immersion in the river had left him weak and chilled, but his furious resolve had given him new strength. Bubeck, the man he had followed and respected always, was now revealed, laid bare. His treachery was like the eruption of some obscene fungus that had finally reached its season and burst. So Klay had retrieved his clothes from the river and put them on. In his wet stormcoat he had made his way to the camp and to his ladder and had climbed down it.

Yulin awoke as he pulled off his coat and threw it into the corner. 'Hide this, and the rest of it,' Klay said. Above him in the camp, he could hear someone talking. Soon the first meal would begin.

He gestured at the two small girls curled up together in their bed of furs. 'Keep them quiet,' he said. 'I want dry clothes. My second stormcoat. And food. Plenty of it.'

Yulin looked at her daughters in the half-light of the pit. They were wide-eyed with fear. She enjoined them to silence with a finger on her lips, and from the travelling bags unpacked fresh clothing for Klay. She knew better than to speak.

'Get the food, woman! Hurry!'

'I'll have to go above ground.'

'Then do it!'

She moved toward the ladder, urging herself to betray him, for then he would never be chief and her daughters would never be without ancestors: they would never be expelled and made tribeless.

'Let no one suspect!' he said, seeming to divine her thoughts.

'No one,' she said, and climbed out.

Klay's eyes seemed to be burning in their sockets. His fingers were tingling. Impatiently he turned out Yulin's pouch – he had no other – and started to cram it with weapons and supplies. First, a fire-making kit in a wallet of tallowed skin. A leather purse with a dozen bowstrings. From pegs on the wall he took down his best longbow. This was not a toy for killing coots, not for hares or squirrels: this was for felling big animals. He unhooked his quiver and filled it with suitable arrows, each one tipped with flint. Lastly he took down his prized hunting spear.

The weapon was heavy with magic. It had impaled many beasts. Its tang was still strained with dried blood; the shaft was of flawless yew, shaped and tapered to take a perfect trajectory from Klay's arm. His rage blazed more fiercely. The spear had been made for him alone, a coming-of-age gift from Shode. It was the work of a master weaponer, now long dead, a man from the Eagle tribe whose very name meant Spearmaker. The grip was bound with coloured twine, making a herringbone pattern of yellow and brown. This spear was a javelin, designed purely for flight; in its making Spearmaker had breathed his spirit into it, and now it had its own life and its own desires, seeking the heart of its prey. Bubeck's heart.

'I want you to look outside,' he told Yulin, once he had packed the food she had brought down. 'Go up the ladder and look. If it's safe I will leave.'

Yulin had come close to giving him away. At the fire she had almost spoken to Phale's woman; but she was afraid of Klay.

'Please, Klay. You have been defeated. There is no dishonour. Tell Phale and let the others fight among themselves. Your place is here with us.' She drew in her breath, frightened that she had dared to speak her mind. 'Please, Klay. Please.'

He studied her contemptuously. At another time he might have struck her. 'Get up the ladder.'

She obeyed and urgently beckoned. For a moment the way was clear. Using every inch of cover, he darted from the ladder and ran, bent almost double, to a fallen log, to the trunk of a tree, to a pile of firewood, and in moments he was out of the compound and running into the forest.

When Bubeck saw smoke rising from the hillside below him, he knew why the fire had been lit.

After taking Klay's fragment he had followed the river upstream, in order to cross safely at the swamp. It would have been quicker to circle back and cross at the waterfall, but he had already found Tagart's overnight trail and he knew that Tagart would be returning to the vicinity of the camp at dawn to look for signs of the other contestants. Bubeck did not want to come upon Tagart unexpectedly; he also wished to leave him a plain trail to follow.

But that trail had been quickly obliterated by the snowstorm. By mid morning, after two hours of heavy snowfall, the wind had freshened to a blizzard and Bubeck had been forced to shelter in the lee of some bushes. Later, looking for traces of the others, he had wandered south-eastward, near the river. From there had climbed to the highest slope of the valley and into the top of a beech. His view, of undulating hillsides covered in trees, was grizzled by the continuous falling of light snow. Since noon the light had steadily got worse. It was now too drab to pick out moving figures: Bubeck had searched the valley for minutes at a time, his eyes watering in the cutting east wind. He had almost given up hope when he saw the thread of smoke.

He tried to fix the position of the fire in his mind and came down the tree.

For most of the day he had managed to keep moving, to keep warm, but even so his hands and particularly his feet were suffering. If he were hiding somewhere like Edrin, not daring to stir, he knew he would be afraid of frostbite.

But he also knew that Edrin would have anticipated this thought. And he knew that if Edrin wanted a fire, he could make it burn perfectly well without any smoke to give his position away.

That meant the fire could have only one purpose. It was a signal: an invitation, an admission that the snow had made tracking a matter of chance and not skill. Above all, in this dangerous weather, it was a ploy to hasten the end of the contest. Whether Edrin would be nearby was doubtful. He would be elsewhere, safely awaiting the outcome of whatever encounter his fire produced.

Bubeck started downhill. His feet crunched and creaked and crushed snow into the mouldering leaves and litter of the forest floor; his breathing, wet and warm, returned to him in the confines of his mask.

He stopped to listen.

The silence was not encouraging. The hairs on the nape of his neck began to prickle. He waited a very long time; snow accumulated on his hat and shoulders, on the sparse and disordered tufts of his eyebrows. He licked meltwater with a small, furtive motion of his tongue.

The fire could not be seen from here, but he knew it could not be very much farther down the slope. He looked in vain for the smoke. Sky and snow had made it invisible.

Finally, measuring each footfall, he continued downhill, stopping every few yards. The woods here were of oak and birch; clumps of brambles were tangled and clotted with white. He sniffed. A faint tang of woodsmoke met his nostrils. Another dozen steps. He could see the fire, a mound of sticks whose centre had collapsed to leave a bed of embers. The bracken round the fire had been roughly cleared.

He whirled round, but no one was lurking among the trees. Perhaps he was the first to get to Edrin's fire.

In a conversational tone he called out: 'Who's there?'

No answer.

Resisting the impulse to retreat, Bubeck went forward to the fire. He looked round uneasily and squatted to make a rapid study of the half-burned sticks. Judging from the embers, the fire had been burning for two or three hours.

He stood up and yet again looked round, sensing the presence of something malignant. The wind moaned. Grains of snow flittered to the ground.

Bubeck examined the bracken round the fire. After missing it twice, he found the first of what looked like a series of footmarks, a pocket of crushed bracken shaped like a bird's wing. He took a twig and disturbed the snow in the pocket. Its surface was powdery and new, but, underneath, a thin layer of snow had been compacted by a man's weight. The thickness of the powdery layer told him that perhaps two hours had elapsed since the footmark had been made.

His eye followed the line suggested by the mark and found another mark, and another, making a trail. The gaps between them were not great: they had been left by a man of less than average height – Edrin!

He stood up. He had two choices. He could wait here in the hope of catching Tagart unawares, assuming Tagart would be drawn by the smoke: this was obviously what Edrin was hoping for. Or, he could follow the trail to Edrin and the third fragment of Mace.

The decision was easy to make. He had anyway decided earlier to leave Tagart till last.

Placing his feet in the marks – just to puzzle Tagart – Bubeck set off. He had not doused the fire: he wanted Tagart to come after him.

He followed the trail downhill and towards the river. More than once he became confused, only to find the trail again by dint of patient searching. The whole of his attention was given to the ground ahead. He was ill-prepared for the blatant message that had been strewn so carelessly across his path; it took him momentarily by surprise. Human urine had been splashed in a place where the footmarks had become vague, near the base of a sturdy durmast oak.

Bubeck had just enough time to look up, half knowing what he would see.

Falling from the height of a bough, plunging towards him,

accelerating, came the boot-first weight of a man in a stormcoat, a man who had been waiting up there for two hours.

Tagart took the impact in his knees. His boots struck Bubeck in the throat and chest, and his hands, gripping each end of the piece of Mace, brought it down with a dull crack on the upturned mask. It hit the bridge of Bubeck's nose, and with an odd quiet grunt he collapsed.

Tagart was thrown to one side. His piece of Mace spun away and landed in the snow, making a slot of itself.

He lay on his back, dazed, his eyes wandering in the pattern of twigs and branches above. He remembered building the fire, and he remembered working and working his makeshift bow-drill, in his palm a concave pebble to press down on the spinning stick: the first miraculous wisp when friction made smoke, renewing his efforts, blowing on the spot, until the flame caught and burned in the dry punk-wood he had scooped from a rotten birch. From the fire he had left a trail with deliberately shortened strides, and climbed into the oak to wait for Bubeck.

None the less it had taken him a moment to adjust to the shaggy presence of the man below who had stopped to peer at the ground.

Then he had launched himself.

Bubeck lay groaning. His groans ceased and blood oozed from one corner of his mask, staining the snow.

On unsteady legs Tagart got up and stood over him. Bubeck's breathing was laboured and hoarse. He had fallen on his pouch. Tagart knelt down in order to roll him out of the way and undid his mask to help him breathe.

Tagart could scarcely believe his luck. After the blizzard he had been forced to give up hope of finding Edrin; instead he had been made to concentrate on Bubeck. And now by this simple ruse of the fire he had given himself a huge advantage. He was three-quarters of the way to victory. All that remained was to find Edrin.

Bubeck was heavy, like a dead thing. The strength had gone from Tagart's arms and he feebly and repeatedly tried to push Bubeck off the pouch and roll him aside. It was no use.

He found the strap of the pouch and tugged. The pouch came free at last: Tagart delved into it and brought out the two fragments of Mace. The wood had been varnished by the handling of years, but the splintered ends were newly white. Tagart tried to fit them together. As he did so he sensed movement in the field of view beyond his hands. He looked up.

Klay was a hundred paces away, approaching at a trot, following the line of footmarks from the fire. He was fully dressed in dry clothing. A bow was slung across his back, an axe dangled from his shoulder, and held to the ready was a hunting spear. At the sight of it, Tagart began to rise.

He had not noticed Bubeck's eyes opening.

Bubeck's kick caught him in the side of the head and sent him sprawling. The two fragments of Mace were flung from his fingers. His shoulder struck the bark of the durmast oak and he tumbled into the snow, face up. Bubeck was on him at once. The weight of his body crushed Tagart against the ground. Bubeck's hat had gone; his eyes were mad gleaming points in smudges of shadow. A choking stench of sweat, foul breath, and stale fur caught at Tagart's throat as Bubeck raised his fist to deliver a single tremendous blow.

With a hiss the spear sliced under Bubeck's arm and carried something with it. A fine red spray hung sprinkled in the air: the point of the spear slammed into the tree, penetrating to the heartwood before its flight was arrested with a loud and plangent humming of the shaft.

Bubeck stared at his forearm, at the inexplicable red flow that was gleaming and welling across his sleeve, and as the humming died he turned to see where the spear had come from.

Axe in hand, Klay hesitated a moment longer. He had missed, and in his panic he saw what he must do. It meant leaving the spear behind, certain evidence of his return to the camp, but he did not consider that. He saw only that he had missed, that Bubeck and Tagart were unhurt, that they were two to his one; and he saw that three pieces of the Mace were lying in the snow, waiting for him.

He snatched them up and ran.

8

Bubeck got to his feet and chased him, shouting abuse. Fifty yards from the oak tree Bubeck tripped and fell. Tagart ran past him carrying the spear, its flint tip broken, but Bubeck's kick had left him weak and dizzy and Klay easily outdistanced him. He saw Klay disappear into the trees.

Tagart looked back. Bubeck was on his feet again, clutching his arm, approaching with lagging steps. 'He's been back to the camp!' Bubeck called out.

Tagart began to retreat.

'No! Tagart! Stay! I want to talk!'

Tagart smiled inwardly; Bubeck hurried his pace. Snow was still falling lightly.

Tagart knew Bubeck. He had already guessed what was coming, but he did not want to seem too eager to listen. However, the contest had taken a new and desperate turn. Klay now had at least three of the four fragments. If he had already taken the fourth from Edrin, or if he did so before Tagart, the contest would be over and Tagart would have lost. By the laws of the challenge, it was true, Klay had cheated, but Tagart did not know how much credence the elders would give to his accusations, especially if, as seemed possible, Bubeck were to refute them for reasons of his own. Even the spear could doubtless be explained away.

Tagart's best hope was to get to Edrin first: this would be true no matter what Bubeck was about to propose. And it was no more than a hope. Klay may well have got there already, something which would soon be confirmed if his trail were seen to lead directly back to camp. But it seemed likelier that Klay had simply been drawn by the beacon fire after a morning of aimless wandering.

A race was on to find Edrin. If Klay won the race, he would also win the contest. If Tagart won the race, the contest would be prolonged and he would have a chance of taking the rest of the Mace from Klay.

Where was Edrin? More than elementary woodcraft would be needed to sniff him out. But he would not have made his hiding-place impossible to find. The cold would tell on him more severely than on the others, and he would scarcely want to prolong matters needlessly. Some process of deduction, then, should give the key to finding him.

What was more, Tagart knew that Edrin would not be simply waiting to be found. He would be busy making preparations for the arrival of his visitors. The nature of those preparations would, ideally, need to be revealed by some third person.

Bubeck, breathing hard and warily eyeing the spear, stopped a few paces short. His stormcoat was badly bloodied, the bear-fur caked and white where he had been rolling on the ground. One of his leggings had worked loose and hung at the top of his boot. The flow of blood from his nose, where Tagart had hit him, had ceased and congealed in his beard; he was still nursing his wounded arm.

He nodded in the direction of Klay's tracks.

Tagart prepared to listen.

Towards mid afternoon the snowfall stopped altogether. Bubeck and Tagart were following the river south towards the marshes. Beyond Yote Wood it broke into several streams; the valley floor was filled with beds of sallows, osiers and reeds. On slightly higher ground were open leas, profuse with low growths of annual plants and with close clumps of grass which could withstand months of submersion. With the rains, the ponds and puddles of the leas coalesced to form small meres.

Bubeck was leading the way, his arm bandaged with a spare boot-lining. He was continuously aware of Tagart behind him with the spear, but he felt hopeful, for once Tagart had been persuaded to listen, it had been easy to dupe him into apparently joining forces to find Edrin. Tagart had agreed to Bubeck's proposal almost at once; he had even fallen for his glib reply to the question of which of them would keep Edrin's fragment. 'We'll worry about that later. For now, we must reach him before Klay.'

So far Bubeck had scrupulously observed the rules of the contest. He had arrived alone at an idea of where Edrin might be: he had neither consulted Tagart nor asked his opinion of the idea, though Tagart had expressed his doubts about its logic.

Bubeck did not share them. It was plain that Edrin would have picked a hiding place that could be found by inference rather than tracking. As a result of his seemingly casual questioning of Klay at the river, Bubeck had deduced that Edrin had drawn South. Thus Edrin was probably somewhere south of the camp. But where? He might be waiting by one of the established paths in that area; or he might be waiting close to the camp. Or if there were a hunting shelter, he might be waiting there. But there was no hunting shelter. The only shelters for miles were those actually inside the camp – and it was forbidden for him to hide there.

Then it had come to Bubeck. It was so obvious that he marvelled he had not seen it before. There was only one man-made structure outside the camp. It lay on the south side of the river. It would offer Edrin protection from the weather, and moreover it would allow him to sleep, for no one could approach without giving warning by the crash of breaking ice. Lastly, and Bubeck saw this as the finishing touch of ornament on his theory, the structure's name proclaimed the purpose to which Edrin had put it.

The hide was near the edge of the marshes, on the western side of the valley, overlooking a sheet of water three or four acres in extent. Behind it was a channel of the river and a gloomy copse of alders. A makeshift log bridge spanned the channel, leading to a causeway of broken branches which had been strewn in the mud along the fifty paces to the hide. The hide was the height of a man's chest, large enough to seat two, made of reeds bundled on to a crude framework of poles, the joints lashed with strong cord.

Tagart and Bubeck came to the copse of alders. The channel here was eleven feet wide, bridged by the log. Stubs of broken branches projected from it: one trailed in the water, slitting the surface and sending a wake of ripples downstream. A crust of snow covered the log; it had been disturbed during its formation by the passage of feet. Edrin had been here. At the end of the causeway the shape of the hide was visible.

'He's done something to it,' Bubeck said.

Many of the reed-bundles had been untied and the framework looked lopsided. Too much light was showing through. The front of the hide had been removed.

'What do you think?' Bubeck said.

'He may have wanted the lashings.'

'Let's look.'

Tagart glanced round uneasily. This was a good place for an ambush.

'You're armed,' Bubeck said. 'You check the hide.'

It was too late for Tagart to argue: possession of the spear had trapped him. Bubeck was using him in just the way he had meant to use Bubeck.

He went out on the log. It was precariously balanced, and the snow made it more dangerous still. He cautiously reached the other side and started along the causeway.

Bubeck stood watching. The light was failing and he did not notice the heavy, water-logged willow bough that came drifting downstream, gaining momentum. Behind it stretched a long tail of thin twine – spear-binding twine. Ahead, the bough was overtaking yards of sodden, knotted cord which preceded it to the bridge. The bough barely broke the surface of the channel; it passed under the log without a sound and travelled onward. Ten yards from the bridge, the cord tightened in a straight line under water. Its end had been tied to the projecting stub of the log, the one that had been partly hidden by the current. As the cord tightened the log jerked and slewed and was gently dragged into the channel, and at a distance followed the willow bough as it resumed its stately journey downstream.

The bridge had gone. Tagart heard the splash and looked round. He and Bubeck had been separated by the width of the channel, a width too great to leap unaided.

Tagart checked his shout of warning and allowed Bubeck to be taken unawares. Behind Bubeck Edrin came at a run from the copse and with a grunt brought down a length of broken branch on his head. The power of the blow struck Bubeck squarely on the back of the skull and he staggered. With the second blow he went down on his knees. Edrin hit him again. He pitched forward and lay still. Edrin dropped to his knees and tore open Bubeck's pouch.

Tagart sprinted towards the channel. Edrin rose to his feet and made for the copse. His movements were stiff and slow: he had been waiting all day for the arrival of his adversaries.

Tagart was three yards from the bank. Barely slowing, he planted the tip of Klay's spear next to the water and hoisted with all his strength. The vaulting motion carried him almost across the channel; he smashed into the ice and slime on the far side and at once felt the disastrous soaking in his boots, and, tangling with the spear, slithered on the snow as he pulled himself clear and tried to stand.

Edrin had vanished. His feet already freezing, Tagart ran after his tracks, past Bubeck's slumped form and into the alder copse.

He saw Edrin then, climbing the slope among the trees, struggling in the snow. Edrin was running as if wading. He looked over his shoulder and redoubled his efforts.

Tagart caught him fifty yards on, by a bramble patch. He seized Edrin's shoulders and dragged him down, punched him in the face, and Edrin gave in. Tagart ripped open his pouch: the piece of Mace was not there.

He turned Edrin on to his stomach and forced his arm up against his shoulderblades.

'Where is it?'

'I wasn't . . . expecting a spear . . . You've cheated . . .'

'Where is it?'

He gasped with pain. 'Klay took it!'

Tagart, already tired, cold and hungry, was beginning to lose his temper. He shoved the arm further and felt something tearing. Edrin screamed.

'By the waterfall! In the poplar! In the poplar! I hid it in the poplar!'

'The hollow one?'

'You've broken my arm!' He screamed again. 'Yes! The hollow one, the hollow one!'

Tagart considered this reply before easing the pressure. Although he was disinclined to believe anything Edrin might say, the words had sounded convincing enough. It made sense that Edrin would hide his fragment somewhere.

Using the strap from Edrin's pouch, Tagart bound his wrists.

'What are you doing?' Edrin said in alarm.

'I want your boots.' Tagart took them off, removed his own and tossed them aside. With his spare linings he dried his feet as best he could before pulling on Edrin's own, fur-lined hunting boots.

'I'll lose my toes!'

Tagart did not bother to answer. He added his spare boot-linings to those already in Edrin's pouch. 'Put your feet in there.'

When he had done so, Tagart tied his ankles with twine and tied the bindings at wrists and ankles together. He left Edrin lying in the snow and went back to the alder copse and the channel.

Bubeck was unconscious. Even his thick skull had been unable to withstand such an onslaught of blows. When Klay eventually found him he would be in no state to defend himself. Edrin too would be helpless.

That was a matter for Klay's conscience. Tagart trussed Bubeck and tied him to the bole of a young alder.

Taking Klay's spear, Tagart set out. By the shortest route, across the hills, the waterfall was three miles away at most; but he would lose his way under the trees. If he wanted to travel by night, under cloud, he would have to follow the riverbank and let it guide him along the trail he and Bubeck had already made. At the confluence of the first tributary – the one that came down from the camp – he would branch left and keep with it till he came to the waterfall.

But he managed to cover only half a mile. At first the remnants of dusk had enabled him to proceed, but soon all trace of daylight had gone. Everything had been reduced to black and greyish white, the snow picking up the faint and general luminescence afforded to the clouds by the stars behind. It was too dark to see the way.

This was the second night Tagart was going to spend in the open, and the prospect worried him. He had not eaten since the previous day, and he badly needed warmth, but with Klay searching for him he could not risk lighting a fire or being found asleep.

Nearby was an old willow with a big spreading fork fifteen feet above the river. Tagart climbed into it, refastened his mittens and made sure that the drawstrings at his wrists, neck, waist and legs were tight. He pushed the edges of his mask deeper into the sides of his hood, which he drew down over his brow, leaving just a slit for his eyes.

Through it he could barely discern any variation in the quality of the darkness. The cold was getting worse.

Hugging himself more tightly, Tagart prepared to wait out the night.

During the afternoon Klay had followed the trail of Bubeck and Tagart, down from the woods and along the river as far as Yote Wood, where failing light had forced him to stop. He had sheltered for the night inside the Yote Oak; at dawn he woke and emerged from the tree.

He returned to the river and was perturbed to find a new set of footprints heading towards the camp. They were indistinguishable from those Tagart had left yesterday.

'He's passed me in the night,' Klay said aloud.

He took another piece of hardtack from his pouch and chewed it, trying to understand the meaning of the new tracks. Had Tagart returned to camp? Had he been beaten? It seemed likely, for if he had been seeking Klay, he would surely have followed his tracks to the Yote Oak and surprised him there – unless it had been too dark for Tagart to see tracks when he had passed. Perhaps Tagart had beaten the others. Perhaps he had the fourth fragment and had gone to Phale to accuse Klay of cheating. Or perhaps he was searching for Klay despite everything.

Klay placed his hands on the three fragments of Mace protruding so reassuringly from his pouch. He needed only one more. Then he would be chief, and not only of the Shoden, but of the whole camp. His first act would be to put Tagart and Edrin on trial, and Berge too, for the murder of his father. All would be disembowelled; he would do it personally. Bubeck would then be tried and found guilty of conspiring with Tagart in the contest – their tracks had crossed and recrossed; they had been together. Bubeck would be stripped of power and shamed, and the Beavers would become part of the Waterfall tribe. And then, once the spirits had been appeased, Klay would take Segle for his wife. He would be divine, a demigod, almost one of the spirits himself. Did he not already feel greatness? Had he not already shown himself superior? Had he not won three of the four fragments?

He wanted the fourth. He had to know whether Tagart had it.

Klay started north, his axe in his belt, his bow across his back. For part of the way along the river, as far as the place where yesterday's tracks came down from the woods, Klay's own tracks of the previous evening were plainly visible. They had been ignored – or missed. Beyond that place, Tagart's trail continued alone, through virgin snow, still keeping by the river.

Klay forced his pace. He was beginning to feel warmer. He had breakfasted well, on nuts and dried fruit and venison hardtack, and now the loneliness and discomfort of the night were receding and he was becoming eager to make an end to the contest.

At the tributary, Tagart's tracks turned with it, still heading for the camp. The footprints went on and on, keeping with the river path, through the alders and crack willows, leading Klay between the steeply rising sides of the valley.

After another mile he stopped to listen. He was getting near the waterfall. A little way off he could hear its roar, churning the grey morning air with subtle variations in pitch and volume.

He was about to continue when he thought he glimpsed movement among the trees ahead. His heart suddenly pounding, he stared at the spot; trunks and branches of hazel and alder impeded his view.

He unslung his bow, nocked an arrow, and went slowly forward.

9

The waterfall was two miles above the confluence. Green water slid over the lip and tumbled in a dense sheet to explode on the pebbles in roils and froths of white which curved in on themselves in standing waves that dragged the river bed. A few yards on, the dazed current recovered itself and continued downstream. Spray from the fall had accrued as grotesque icicles on either bank; withered curls of hartstongue had been frozen solid and encased.

A line of stepping-stones crossed the river just above the waterfall. On the north bank stood a hollow poplar, old and gaunt.

All sound lost in the din of falling water, Klay drew back his arm and took aim. The dark barbs of the flight quills scraped his cheek as he readied himself for the shot, eyes focused with deadly purpose on the air slightly ahead of Tagart's moving profile, his wrist and arm smoothly travelling with Tagart's progress across the river from right to left. Tagart seemed to be knee-deep, walking in the waterfall, but that was just the angle of view. The range was about a hundred and ten paces, and still Tagart had not noticed him. Klay's vision became a lucid tunnel. His whole will and intent slowly merged with the arrow's flint tip. He wanted to strike Tagart's skull, to burst his brain in a flurry of blood and skin and hair. He waited for Tagart to gain solid ground, one heartbeat, two, three, four, and when the arrow could go nowhere but down the axis of the tunnel the string was no longer in his fingers and the shaft had been released.

But Klay, contrary to the teaching he had received, had left his bow strung overnight. Away from its protective envelope of leather, the string had become slightly dry. The constant tension of the bow had stretched it and impaired its elasticity. And, during the night, he had leaned against the quiver in his sleep, crushing some of the delicate barbs, unhooking the tiny barbules that linked to make a smooth vane for flight. These imperfections took expression in the arrow's path and it flew six inches wide.

Klay saw Tagart jerk instinctively back as the wind from the arrow raked his face. Klay reached over his shoulder for another arrow.

Tagart recovered his footing and for the first time seemed to see Klay. He ran down the rough slope beside the waterfall, coming straight for Klay; his pouch fell to the ground behind him and with his right hand he took a throwing grip on the javelin.

Klay aimed again, more rapidly. He tried to concentrate on the shot: this was just an animal running towards him, not Tagart, not Tagart, just a large animal, sixty paces away, fifty: Klay let fly.

Tagart dodged and in a single fluid sweep the spear was in the sky, flickering against the branches, curving down, plunging so rapidly that Klay had only time to turn. The broken tang struck him as he was turning, a hammer-blow at the base of his neck. Something heavy exploded inside his head and his mouth was full of sharp, granular snow. He was on the ground. A merciless weight was crushing his spine: he could feel Tagart's knee in his neck where the spear had struck. This was a pressure point, a death-place. Tagart was shouting. Klay could not understand the words: his ears were filled with a roaring like the centre of the waterfall, the centre of the world. Through a carmine fog he saw Tagart's wolfskin mittens gripping either end of a piece of Mace, forcing it upwards across his throat.

The pain had become a single continuous blare louder than anything he had ever known. His neck was breaking. If he did not give the sign now he knew Tagart would pull with one more ounce and he would die.

He beat his hand on the snow.

The pressure relented. Tagart was still shouting.

'Shode's death was an accident! Say it!'

Klay croaked.

'Say it! Say it!'

'Accident.'

'And what will you call me? What will you call me? What's my name?'

'T . . . T . . .'

'What's my name?'

Then Klay understood. Tagart had the whole Mace. He had all the pieces. He had got them all.

'Shode, Shode,' he said.

'Again!'

'I . . .'

'Again, I said! Louder!'

'Shode! Your name is Shode! Shode!'

Klay remained for a long time with his face in the snow, listening to the waterfall, before he realized that Tagart had gone away.

Part 2

1

'What is it, my lady?'

Altheme shook her head, too sick to speak, and though nothing more would come she leaned over the bowl again and retched. On waking she had felt nauseous, but it had not been until she had sat upright and put her feet on the cold floor that she had lost control. Rian, her body-slave, had come running into the room with an empty wooden laver.

Rian had borne three children. She knew well enough what was ailing her mistress.

'Let me help you,' she said, putting her arms round Altheme's shoulders and easing her backwards against the pillows.

Rian summoned her under-slaves and quickly the room was fresh again. The floorboards were scrubbed, the bedclothes changed, and the heated rocks renewed. Altheme was washed and, after she had been wrapped in clean marten furs, looked gravely at Rian and spoke in a low voice. 'Sit by me, Rian.'

Cracks in the shutters admitted slits of grey light; the draught toyed with the flames of the rush-lamps burning by the bed.

'There can be no more doubt,' Altheme said. 'I am going to have his child.'

Over the past few days she had confided her fears to Rian.

'You should be glad. Perhaps this will change everything.'

'No. It has come five years too late.'

There was no bitterness in her voice, but she could no longer conceal the extent of her misery. To the older woman, Altheme looked like a child, a pale child, ill and overwrought. Rian had been serving her for two years. Her predecessor, for some reason that had never been divulged, had been dismissed by the Flint Lord himself. Rian was almost twice Altheme's age. She had been a slave all her life.

Altheme took her hand and held it closely. Shadows covered the ceiling and walls. The doorway was in gloom; beyond it, down the stairs, were men's voices. From outside, from the enclosure where many soldiers' tents had been erected, from the overcrowded barracks, came ceaseless shouts and the sound of work.

'How many soldiers are outside, Rian?'

'Too many for me to count, my lady. I hear the landings are half done. More ships are due when the snow stops.'

'They say there will be six hundred foreign soldiers here soon.'

'Yes.'

Rian noticed sparkles of light at the corners of Altheme's eyes. Tears slowly welled and ran down her cheeks.

'You must tell him, my lady.'

'I cannot.'

'You must.'

'And have him change towards me just because of the child?'

Rian had already had this conversation with her mistress, but there was a new firmness in Altheme's voice as she added, 'The baby is my only weapon.'

'But he will find out soon enough.'

'Let him.'

'I beg you – '

'I will dress soon,' Altheme said curtly.

'You are too ill to rise.'

'There is nothing the matter with me. And I have instructions for you. Tonight I want no slaves near my chamber. Not even you.'

'As my lady wishes.'

Altheme squeezed her hand more tightly. She studied the bedclothes, unable to look Rian in the face. 'There is a man,' she said presently. 'There is a man called Bohod Zein. I must . . . Your master says . . .'

Rian stared at her. She had seen the agent from the homelands, Bohod Zein, a fat, white-haired albino, and she had seen his pink eyes following her mistress, but she could not believe what was being said.

'Gehan has no more flints,' Altheme went on. 'He has promised them all away, and still he wants soldiers. Bohod

Zein is rich. In the homelands he has twenty villages. He owns ships and many cattle. And he . . . he wants . . .'

Rian opened her arms as Altheme broke down and wept. Eyes closed, Altheme crushed her head against Rian's breast and allowed herself to be comforted. Rian gently stroked her hair. 'You must tell my lord about the baby,' she said. 'He will never permit it then.'

Altheme shook her head and began to sob. Rian felt her shoulders heaving and tried to calm her with soothing words; but then she too was overwhelmed and began to grieve, not only for her mistress, but for her own plight and the plight of every slave. Through her tears she brushed her lips against Altheme's cheek to give her a child's kiss, and, as on the vulnerable skin of a child who has been ill in the night and washed by its mother, Rian tasted but did not mind the musty, bittersweet odour she found there.

Envoys to the other winter camps were sent out as soon as Tagart had formally received the Mace and the name of Shode.

On returning from the waterfall he had given the broken pieces of Mace to the elders, as tradition required. Everyone was summoned to watch Phale as he crudely repaired the Mace and matched it to the tribal emblem. Tagart was prepared for the ceremony by the other chiefs: no women were allowed to witness his ritual washing or the slow process of dressing in robes and mask. Dyes and daubs were applied to his skin and hair, in cream, white, pale-blue and green. He sat as if numb, elated and exhausted. He was to be the chief and leader of his own blood tribe and the winter camp, first man of the spirit. Upon him had settled the divine choice of the Sun: he was to be Shode.

Dragonfly and Heron reverently unpacked the striking and beautiful salmon mask with its glossy eyes and hooked lower jaw, each scale of its skin cut from mother-of-pearl and left the native colour, or stained and finished with crimson and olive green like the skin of a living salmon. In the compound, the sacred foods were nearly ready.

Meanwhile men had been sent to find the other contestants. Edrin was unhurt but, like Bubeck, badly chilled. Bubeck had been concussed, though not seriously, and he seemed to bear no grudge; indeed, he had trouble in dissembling his admiration of Tagart's victory. Klay, on Tagart's instructions, had been brought back to the camp in a hood with his hands tied.

At last Phale gave the signal and Tagart was conducted into the open.

The ritual of making a new chief was an occasion of urgency and awe. There was rarely time to prepare elaborate costumes such as were seen at other ceremonies during the year. The chief of each tribe wore his mask and robes; the others wore the best they had. There was no feasting, nor was there music save the measured speech of the elders. This was a time when the spirits were very near. As if to acknowledge their presence, the trappings of the ritual were both simple and powerful. The holy, magic, forbidden wood of the spindle-tree – from whose branches the Sun had fashioned needles to sew the threads of his Creation – was gathered and used to heat the morsels of dried man orchid that conferred divinity on the new chief. With them, because this was the Waterfall tribe, a few scraps of salted salmon, the sacred food of the water spirit, were also made ready and heated on a flat stone.

The whole camp had assembled. It was about noon when Phale began to speak. In a freezing wind, under heavy cloud, the river flowed past; the snow on its banks were packed hard. Here and there across the compound were small movements: the motion of smoke, a hanging strip of leather.

Watched by the people of nine tribes, and eight chiefs in bird, beast and insect masks, Phale held the pieces of orchid to Tagart's mouth.

'This becomes your flesh.'

Another elder recited a prayer and brought Phale the platter of warm salmon.

'This becomes your spirit.'

Tagart ate. It was very salty; a fine bone stuck in his cheek.

The fish mask was placed on his head.

'Your tribe calls you.'

One by one, everybody in the Waterfall tribe walked past and spoke the name 'Shode'.

Last but one came Tagart's woman. Through the apertures

in the mask, he saw on Segle's face mixed apprehension and hope; and she had passed.

Now Phale stood before him again. As he spoke the name he gave the Mace into Tagart's hand. It had been repaired with twine and leather: a new Mace would be carved soon. As Tagart's fingers closed on the knots and twists of the binding and felt the firmness of the wood beneath, he sensed for the first time the reality of what had happened.

'You are the holder of the Mace. You are our chief. You are Shode.'

After the ceremony he called all the chiefs together. Chenk, the leader of the Kingfishers, the man who had been sent as a scout to Valdoe, and the other chiefs who previously had been in favour of a convocation to discuss the Flint Lord, with Tagart's new authority managed to persuade Bison, Wolf and Marten, the doubters, to join their view. Bubeck alone resisted for a while; finally he agreed that envoys should be sent to the other winter camps.

'But not for a convocation,' Tagart said. 'It is too late for that. We must call for help.'

'Shode is right,' Chenk said. 'I have seen the soldiers. Talk will waste time. We must defend our lands; we must ask for warriors to join us.'

Eventually even Bubeck consented. Token tributes of flint spearheads and presents for the chiefs' women were got ready, and Tagart chose three pairs of envoys, each pair led by a man who had himself seen the preparations at Valdoe. Men were picked from the Herons and Beavers, and from the Dragonflies went Fodich, who was now almost completely fit. They were accompanied by men from the Wolf, Marten, and Bison tribes – tribes which did not belong to the water spirit but to the spirits of the other camps: in the north, east, and west.

'Tell them what you have seen,' Tagart said. 'Tell them we must fight together or be driven out.'

The envoys left in the afternoon, in the middle of Klay's trial.

The trial was over by nightfall. Testimony was heard from Tagart and Bubeck. Yulin was interrogated, and the clothes and weapons he had unlawfully used were held up and displayed to the camp.

In turn, Klay accused Tagart and Bubeck of cheating: he said they had colluded to find Edrin. But Bubeck said that Tagart had offered no help in finding Edrin; he had merely used Bubeck and his ideas, and so had exercised nothing more than the 'stealth' that was permitted under the rules. Edrin confirmed that Tagart had made no attempt to help Bubeck.

Phale pronounced sentence. Klay's woman and children were to be expelled and made tribeless: when at last they died, of cold or hunger, or were eaten by wolves, their spirits would be unable to join the ancestors. It was a terrible punishment. Yulin sagged and collapsed. The penalty for Klay himself was that which was always paid by those who had betrayed the trust of the tribe.

Final authority rested with Tagart. He was sitting in the middle of the line of elders, stroking his beard, studying Klay, Yulin, and the fire. At his side was Bubeck. They briefly conferred. Tagart glanced at Segle, and looked again into the fire.

'Sentence will be deferred,' he said. 'At the next moon, the elders will reconsider.'

Klay, who was still bound at the wrists, stared impassively forward.

Tagart arose. There was one more matter to be resolved.

He left his place by the fire, took Segle's arm, and pulled her towards their shelter.

2

Six miles north-west of the Trundle, on the highest point of a five-peaked hill, the secondary fort of Harting dominated the sweep of the downs and the fertile plain to the north. Between Harting and its companion fort to the west, Butser, lay some of the richest farmland in the Valdoe domain. At the base of Harting Hill was the village of Fernbed, which, in a sheltered valley, cultivated acre after acre of barley, wheat, oats and millet.

Gehan's sledge passed a snow-whitened clump of gorse and Harting fort came into view, a black palisade on the distant hilltop. Behind it, in contrast with the snowy landscape, the sky was solid and grey. Colder than the snow, an east wind blew behind the sledge and piled drifts against the gorse bushes and the roadside banks. It beat against the leather hood of the sledge and left stray draughts of exhilarating air in its wake.

Ika turned to him and laughed. She was excited to be making such an adventurous journey in the snow. The business to be dealt with, Gehan had told her, would be unpleasant; the journey, and the overnight rest at Harting, would not be comfortable. But in the sleigh it was warm enough under the thick furs, and Gehan took pleasure in the proximity of her body on the padded seat. The wind had brought a high colour to Ika's cheeks. Her eyes shone. In this severe winter light, her blonde hair just showing beneath a fur hat, she seemed more beautiful than ever. 'What is the name of this village again?' she said.

'Fernbed.'

'A lovely name.'

Gehan nodded and, reminded of the destination, went back to his thoughts of the difficulties in hand.

In some ways he saw himself as the expert husbandman of a complicated and volatile herd. The beasts of the herd were the farming villages in his domain; his muzzles and harnesses were the soldiers and traders who enabled him to maintain the balance that produced the heaviest yield of profit. There were over a hundred villages, stretching seventy or eighty miles along the coast and up to twenty miles inland. A few were prosperous, with palisaded compounds, wood and stone houses, granaries; most were squalid collections of huts whose inhabitants lived in constant fear of starvation. Over the centuries these people had come to the island country to escape oppression in the homelands: it was important to ensure that things did not get so bad that any were tempted to return. It was important, too, to allow them a measure of hope, for this was a most effective stimulant to hard work.

The farmers depended for their implements on flint. At one time it had been possible to gather good quality flints from anywhere along the surface of the downs. No longer. Today, they had to be mined. Most of the mine-workings were in the region of Valdoe Hill and on the hill itself; all were the exclusive property of Brennis Gehan Fifth. The flints, cut and ground by his craftsmen, were taken by trading teams to the villages, and there exchanged for food and goods.

The price exacted by the traders was carefully regulated. In years of bad crops, the price went down. To prevent retailing between villages, the price at any one time was fixed throughout the domain; but the larger and more successful villages, those which were able to acquire a surplus, were subject to a harvest impost determined by inspectors from the forts. Attempts to bribe or deceive the harvest inspectors were rigorously punished; failure to pay the imposts likewise brought soldiers. Such punishment was rare – the harvest impost normally took no more than two thirds of the surplus. Despite complaints, the village head-men felt this was not only reasonable, but, considering the power of the Flint Lord, almost generous.

In times of very great hardship, Valdoe sometimes waived all taxes and distributed free tools, even free seed-corn, to distressed villages. Conversely it occasionally made an additional levy for special purposes.

A levy in respect of the campaign against the savages had already been made. From each village an amount equivalent to half the harvest impost had been assessed by the inspectors, and from every fifth family the eldest son had been pressed into non-military service. The preceding summer had given a poor harvest because of drought: fewer villages than usual had managed a surplus, but some, like Fernbed, had done well and had been assessed for the impost. The levy should have left Fernbed with enough food to last the winter, and with seed to sow crops the following spring, but with no more.

However, an informer from a neighbouring village had been to Harting to tell the unit leader of a secret storehouse in the forest outside Fernbed. Here also the eldest son of the head man was in hiding, avoiding his duty to Lord Brennis.

A unit of twenty-five men was stationed at Harting. Fifteen had accompanied their unit leader to investigate these charges. They had found the storehouse, cunningly camouflaged in the woods: it had been in use for years, and it held several tons of first quality grain.

Duplicity of this kind so close to the fort had enraged the unit leader. Some of the blame would attach to himself, for it was his duty to make regular searches of the countryside for just such caches. And, in view of the orders from Valdoe, evasion of service by the head man's son could only be seen as a direct challenge to his authority. He had wanted to execute the youth and his father at once; but permission for executions had to be obtained through his superior, the commander of Harting, Bow Hill, and Butser, who in turn had to petition the Flint Lord himself.

On receiving the request, Gehan had taken advice from the General of the Coast before issuing his personal instructions in the matter of the head man and his son.

Yesterday the signalmaster at the Trundle had read a message from Harting, relayed by the intervening fort at Bow Hill. In dark and light smoke the message had slowly taken shape. *The . . . punishment . . . at . . . Fernbed . . . ordained . . . by . . . Lord . . . Brennis . . . has . . . begun . . . We . . . await . . . his . . . illustrious . . . presence.*

Gehan's sledge, drawn by ten slaves in harness, flanked by guards, passed through the open gate of the palisade and into Fernbed. It was early afternoon: the journey from Valdoe had taken four hours.

A crowd of over two hundred people parted to let him through. The sledge stopped by the head man's house and Gehan alighted. The commander, a heavy, grey-bearded man named Awach, came forward and saluted. It appeared that, like the crowd, Awach and the soldiers of his units had been waiting in the snow for some time. Their armour of horn and leather, overlaid with winter dress of fur capes and leggings, had been meticulously cleaned.

Gehan looked about him. The village had changed little since his last visit. The palisade enclosed a compound of twenty or thirty dwelling-houses built round a small open space. Two low barns stood behind the village pond, where a few ducks, their feathers ruffled, huddled on the bank beside the ice; another building, a bakery, occupied a slight rise near the north gate. There was no meeting house in this village. Instead the head man's house was unusually grand, with a long extension on one side into a chamber for public meetings.

The village showed unmistakable marks of prosperity. Most of the dwelling-houses were made of stone and timber, with pitched roofs clad in boards or turf and window apertures shuttered for the winter with planks. Some of the houses had integral pig-sties; many had two, three, or even four rooms. The head man's house seemed to have at least five rooms besides the public chamber. A paved precinct by its entrance had been brushed free of snow. Part of the precinct was sheltered by a wooden portico supported by two great posts; as he passed between them, Gehan paused to notice the carvings, of twining barley-heads, that climbed the posts from floor to roof. A boss in the lintel depicted the Earth Mother, serenely guarding the doorway.

The entrance gave directly into the public chamber. This was twelve paces long and half as wide, floored with boards of pale beech which had been finished with beeswax. The walls were rendered with clay, smoothed and then whitened with lime. A simple and elegant system of beams held up the roof. At the far end of the room, below an open window, was a stone altar. Beyond it the window looked out on the whiteness of Harting Hill. Gehan could hear the cawing of crows. That, and the screaming from the compound, were the loudest sounds in the village.

In front of the altar, geometrically arranged on the polished wooden floor, a repast of many small delicacies had been surrounded by an oval formation of leather cushions. Gehan motioned that Ika should be seated. He sat down next to her.

During the meal, Awach nervously gave an account of the events leading to his request for execution of the head man and his son. Awach also confirmed that all instructions from Valdoe had been followed. A priest or the head man from each and every village in the domain had been commanded to present himself at Fernbed, to witness the punishment. Today was the fourth day of the Goele festival, when it was considered unclean to travel: a fact sure to impress still more deeply on the villagers the significance of the occasion.

'And what is the name of this old woman, the head man's wife?'

'Lythou, my lady.'

'She is the son's mother?'

'Yes, my lady.'

Ika accompanied them when they went to watch. Smoke was rising from the open ground faced by the houses. A scaffold had been erected there. Below it, a clay cauldron of water was being gently heated. Lythou, the head man's wife, was naked, suspended on a noose under her armpits; the rope ran over the top of the scaffold. Since yesterday she had been repeatedly immersed in warm water and raised into the wind.

She made no sound: she was nearly dead. The screams were those of her husband and son, who had been locked in two pillories close to the fire. They had not been physically harmed.

Gehan felt Ika moving nearer. Her hand discovered his.

By her touch she had joined him in the invisible radiance that set him apart from all others. From villagers and soldiers alike Gehan sensed a surge of hostility and outrage, but it was inextricably mixed with cowardice and he knew he was safely in control. He had judged them accurately.

With a glance from Gehan the commander began his prepared remonstration with the villagers, while his men brought bundles of brushwood which had been stored nearby. Lythou was raised clear of the cauldron; the soldiers started to build up the fire, heaping bundles against the pillories. Three of them fanned the flames with boards until, unable to bear the heat, they had to move back.

The head man and his son were silenced. Their charred corpses, still kneeling at the blazing pillories, began to burn alone, without aid from the brushwood, sending fierce flames above the general fire. Awach, without pause, continued to harangue the people of Fernbed and to warn the others of their fate should they seek to deceive the inspectors. He said that the Flint Lord, benefactor of all the villages, had ordered the special levy for a secret purpose that was vital to everybody. The conscription of eldest sons was a part of this purpose also. Those who tried to evade it were traitors to the common good. In view of events here at Fernbed, a second, voluntary, levy would be accepted by Valdoe until the new moon after next. The source of any goods so received would not be investigated; but, after the period of amnesty, deceit would be shown no mercy.

The water in the cauldron was boiling as the speech came to an end. Gehan gave a curt nod and the rope was released. Ika tightened her grip on his hand; Lythou fell into the water. A moment later the cauldron cracked. It broke into clumsy earthenware pieces and drenched the fire in a rush of steam and smoke. Ika's hand relaxed. With wide eyes she watched the aftermath of the punishment, her hand lingering in Gehan's own.

That night Gehan was again unable to sleep. The hours since Fernbed had passed with a curious, heightened awareness: the journey up to the fort, the inspection, the meal, the entertainment. Awach had provided dancers, girls from his villages, accompanied by three musicians. One had played a flute; another had kept time on a little drum. The third had used his voice in a song without words, droning, repetitive, weaving and looping through the rhythms of the dance.

Gehan was lying in the chamber usually occupied by the commander. He stared into the darkness, his thoughts coloured by the musician's song. The room had been refurbished for his visit, and he could smell some indefinable herbal redolence in the luxurious coverings on the bed. It was a scent from his childhood, an old-fashioned perfume that evoked a pang of memory just beyond reach.

The door opened from the next room. Before it closed again he saw Ika's silhouette. She moved across the floor to the bed and sat down beside him.

'Can you sleep?' she whispered.

'No.'

'I keep thinking of that fire.'

He tried to make out her face, but the room was too dark. Hesitantly, timidly, she shifted her position on the edge of the bed. It was as if she were gauging an unknown resistance, waiting for a sounding before daring to proceed.

The silence was total. Ika's fragrance was beginning to reach him, from her skin and hair, from the folds of her robe, from her breathing. It mingled with and overwhelmed the herbal scent and entwined the musicians' song.

'It was a nightmare down there,' she said.

'Are you afraid to go to sleep?'

'Yes.'

Her next action seemed inevitable, like the succession of time, like the pervasive rhythm of flute and voice. She slowly bent over him.

He had abstained from drink during the evening; she had tried several essences. A rich, decayed sweetness remained on her breath. He tasted it as she hovered over him. They were separated only by the last remnant of her uncertainty, a narrow stream of darkness that was part of the larger night: secret, private, utterly quiet.

Trembling slightly, she touched his lips. The pressure of her flesh, miraculously subtle, was such that he could not tell precisely when the kiss had begun: he knew only that it was happening. As she became more confident her mouth opened a little; yet still she hesitated before crossing the last shred of darkness. Gehan hesitated too. Above all else he wanted to succumb, to ackowledge that he and Ika were of the same. She was perfect, golden, immaculate. She had, in the village today, glimpsed the frontier of the will, the vision of Gehan First, the frontier beyond which stretched the limitless sea of absolute freedom. She alone was worthy to join him on that awesome beach where he had dwelt in solitude for so many years.

He felt her hair fall across his face. In the villages, anywhere else, it would not matter that they were brother and sister. But he was the son of Gehan Fourth: he was the master of Brennis, the Flint Lord. And this was weakness.

He pushed her away. 'Go back to your room.'

'What is it?'

'This is wrong.'

'No, this is right.' She leaned forward again and whispered. 'We can do anything we want to. You proved that today.'

'Go.'

'Let me rest beside you, if nothing else.'

'You must go.'

'You want me to stay.'

'I want you to go.'

When she had returned to her room, Gehan tried to compose himself for sleep. Again he breathed the herbal scent. And suddenly he saw an image of sun-coloured flowers and smelled pungent green leaves, and he recalled that in his boyhood the house-slaves had hidden sprigs of tansy among the most valuable heaps of pelts and fleeces. It was supposed to deter insects. He strove to recall more clearly the clusters of flowers like little buttons, the spreading fernlike leaves; and he saw again a bright windowledge, a lonely playroom, and a barren view of hillside and sea. Ika had been a mere baby. At the age of six she had been sent to the homelands: Gehan's days had been shaped to some other purpose, filled with discipline, schooling, instruction; somehow, standing on tiptoe and peeping out, the empty vista beyond the playroom window had contained no explanation of it at all.

In the early hours, resigning himself to another night without sleep, he went to the shutters and opened them. The night was hard and freezing. Over a mile away to the south-west, and two hundred and fifty feet below his window, he saw a solitary twinkle of light. It disappeared and returned, disappeared and returned, sometimes disappearing for such a long period that he thought it had gone out. At this range the buildings of

Fernbed could not be distinguished, but among them somewhere a fire was still burning, and he knew it was not the pyre his men had made, but a memorial flame at the altar. The priest would have lit it to mark the mourning of the village and the passage of three more souls to the gates of the Far Land.

Gehan barred the shutters and rested his head against them. He stood like that for a moment, turned, and went back to his bed.

3

The snow deepened; for fifteen days the sun was not seen. Everyone in the camp who was not hunting was put to work, mending, sewing, making boots and mittens and clothing, cutting pelts and curing skins to make water carriers, packing food, binding spears and axes and hammers and knives, shaving arrows, carving bows and spear-slings. All spare leather and fur had been commandeered: those who stayed behind would be cold as well as hungry.

From nine tribes Tagart had selected a hundred men of fighting age and forty women who wanted to join the march to Valdoe. Only the very old and the very young, or those who could not be spared, had been forbidden to go.

Each day he calculated again how many people he might expect from the other camps, and when they would arrive. Sometimes he felt there would be none, that the envoys would fail; at other times he thought they would come, but too late. He counted the days needed for the envoys to reach the camps, to persuade the chiefs, for the preparations to be made, for the journey to the Shode Valley, added time to allow for the difficulty of travelling in the snow, subtracted it for the loyalty of this or that tribe which he knew to be friendly and helpful, added it again for those chiefs who were said to be uncooperative or who were likely to be indifferent to the troubles of the tribes in the south; and each day arrived at a different answer.

His strategy would depend on the amount of support he received. As his estimates varied so did he evolve and discard a dozen battle-plans, retrieve some, examine them afresh, and then in a fit of doubt or depression reject them all. At such moments he wondered whether perhaps Bubeck was right. Tagart would be committing all his people to fighting something that might not be killed by spears alone. He had been to Valdoe; he had seen what sort of men were there; he had seen the villages along the coast. Thousands of farmers relied on the Flint Lord: if they came to his defence there would be no hope.

But, on the fifteenth day after the envoys had left, a hundred and nineteen people arrived from the Cloud camp in the east. The next day Fodich arrived. He had brought nearly a hundred and fifty from the Lightning camp in the north: all that remained was the arrival of those from the Mountain camp in the west.

Tagart sent for Klay. Since his trial he had been given lowly duties and kept within the boundary of the camp. As Tagart revealed to him what his part in the march was to be, Klay saw why he had been reprieved. He listened with growing dismay to Tagart's detailed instructions. This was worse than the original sentence. He was given food and appropriate clothing and allowed to make his farewells to Yulin and his children. If he carried out his mission with honour they would be pardoned. They would no longer be considered tribeless, and his own sentence would be rescinded in full.

But it was with a heavy heart that Klay crossed the bridging logs and left the camp behind.

The stone bowl, supported by three squat legs, was half filled with charcoal which sent smokeless heat up into the rafters. Lamps burned on poles set round the bowl. They projected distorted shadows of the Divine as she finished her prayer.

Gehan watched from the darkness. Thille, the Divine, had read the sky that day and from the flight of crows had discovered that portents for the campaign had changed. All six hundred soldiers had been landed; the army was ready to leave. But the omens were bad. For confirmation, the Divine had taken a dry briar branch and on it, with a magpie quill, had inscribed seven runes.

'Fire, fire, speak to Thille! Fire, fire, do thy will!'

She threw the briar branch into the bowl. It lay on the charcoal, stubbornly refusing to ignite. And then at one end spitting flame crackled and scorched some of the runes. 'Aih has been burned,' said the Divine. 'The weather will hold.' The flame cleft into prongs and spread along the branch, wavering and fluttering, while the Divine studied its progress, circling the bowl. Her feet shuffled on the stone floor. Next to Gehan came the asthmatic breathing of Bohod Zein.

Bohod Zein leaned towards him. 'Your Divine would be prized in the homelands,' he said. 'Is she a native?'

'The daughter of a slave, born here in my grandfather's time.'

'She has a gift.'

'She has second sight.'

'Is she ever wrong?'

Gehan shook his head.

The briar branch had been consumed, reduced to a worm of grey ash. Taking a linden spoon, the Divine scraped it up and deposited it in a small leather pouch. Her attendant came forward and covered the bowl with a heavy stone lid; the Divine arranged on the lid a precarious tripod of three bone wands, their feet in some secret pattern that only she could memorize.

The attendant lit the rest of the lamps in the divination chamber.

'My lord,' said the Divine. Her robes were green; she wore yellow slippers. She was old and bent, but her eyes were direct. 'My lord, the fire has spoken. The flame was slow: there will be delay, and this is propitious. It will avoid disaster. Aih was burned first: the weather will aid you. Tsoaul glowed strangely and was enwrapped by blue flame: your enemy will be strong, but you will surround him. Gauhm burned yellow and will take no part. The briar crackled, and so the fighting will be very fierce. For every crackle a man will be slain. This was foretold by the crows.'

'But what will be the outcome?'

'In our question to the fire we spoke only of the savages. The answer is confused, as though you had another enemy, a more powerful one. There will be much killing and suffering. Order will be overthrown. By the shape of the ash and the burning of the four outer runes, the portent is very bad. The fire begs you to think again. No purpose will be served.'

'But you say the savages will not defeat me?'

'There is neither defeat nor victory here, my lord.'

'There will be no defeat?'

'Not at the savages' hands, my lord.'

Bohod Zein turned to him. 'If there is no defeat there must be victory.'

'I agree,' Gehan said, 'since we are to take the offensive. There must be some slight confusion in the ash. Is this possible, Thille?'

'Perhaps, my lord.'

'You speak of another enemy. Who could this be?'

'I cannot say, my lord. It is . . . forgive me, my lord.'

'It is what?'

'It is as if the enemy were yourself.'

Bohod Zein whispered in his ear. 'Preposterous!'

'What does the fire tell us about the delay?' Gehan said. 'Will it be long?'

'It urges you to wait till the moon wanes.'

'The full moon is seven days hence,' Bohod Zein said.

'We have been delayed too long already.'

'There will be certain disaster if you start in a waxing moon, my lord.'

'Of what sort?'

'On the march. There will be disaster on the march.'

'Does the fire say any more?'

'It speaks of the sea, my lord. I do not understand it.'

'The sea? The question has nothing to do with the sea.'

Bohod Zein revolved the white marble ring on his forefinger. 'The prophecy seems somewhat nebulous and inconclusive,' he said to Gehan. 'You say she is never wrong. Could it be, Thille, that we posed our question wrongly?'

'I cannot say. I speak only of what the fire tells me, and the fire gives a bad omen. I must repeat, my lord, that order will be overthrown.'

'A matter of opinion,' said Bohod Zein with an incipient smile, which died the moment he saw Gehan's face.

'Leave us, Thille,' Gehan said.

She bowed and, taking the leather pouch of ash, was followed by her attendant from the room.

Gehan rubbed his forehead. 'Another seven days! I must speak to Larr.'

'The delay is probably wise, and the General will concur,'

said Bohod Zein, thinking of the extra rations the soldiers would consume, and wondering how much might be charged for them. 'The Divine was quite specific on that point. But as for the rest of it . . .'

Gehan stood up; Bohod Zein did likewise. 'There is nothing ambiguous in Thille's words,' Gehan said. 'As a child she taught me how to view a prophecy. If you do not understand it at first, you must let it soak into your thoughts. Intuition will give you its meaning.'

Bohod Zein hitched his robe over his shoulder. 'Our divines in the homeland are much less reticent.'

'And much less accurate.'

The albino stepped aside and allowed Gehan to be first through the door. It was after dusk; stone cressets, set in the walls or suspended from roof-beams, gave their dismal glow to the next rooms. These were hawk mews which, together with the divining chamber, an office for the astronomer priest, and a room of maps and charts, made a single block set inside the main palisade on its northern side. There was only one exit: to reach it they had to pass through the mews.

One of the falconers was present, attending to a sea eagle, a huge bird which sat hunched on a padded perch, its head covered with a plain hood. As Gehan and Bohod Zein entered, the falconer saluted.

Gehan stopped to exchange a few words with him. 'Is that Larr's eagle?'

'Yes, my lord.'

'Is it ill?'

'He is hunger traced, Lord Brennis.' He gently indicated the folded wing.

'Let me see,' Gehan said, but even as he reached out the eagle unfurled vast wings and from the hood came an anguished cry. Its wings flapped once, twice, thrice, and the pressure of wind lifted it from the perch. Leather straps arrested its ascent; it fell forward and dangled by its legs, shrieking and twisting its head. The great wings hung awkwardly, brushing the flagstones, and three dark pinions broke away and fluttered to the floor.

Gehan and Bohod Zein departed at once, to leave the man and his charge in peace.

'It means nothing,' said Bohod Zein, unnerved by the incident and by Gehan's glowering silence. They were crossing the outer enclosure towards the inner palisade and Gehan's residence. 'A sick bird, my lord. An eagle in a rage.'

'A sea eagle,' Gehan said strangely.

On all sides they were being hailed and saluted. The enclosure was crowded with leather tents, each occupied by five men waiting their turn to go inside the barracks to be fed. Every foot of space in the Trundle was full: the two barrack-houses, the armoury; soldiers had been billeted in the dwellings of the craftsmen and in the overseers' quarters; vacant animal sheds had been taken over; even a spare cell in the prison had been appropriated. Some of the mine-slaves, whose cages were always kept outside the Trundle, had been taken from the chalk face and put to work in teams, helping the soldiers to carry skins of water up the hill from the river, for the reservoirs inside the fort were inadequate to the needs of a thousand men. Other slaves stoked cooking fires, stirred cauldrons, carried trays of steaming coarse bread; and others yet dragged sledges up from the sheds at Apuldram, where the rest of the stores and supplies had been unloaded.

The Trundle had been designed as two separate forts, one inside the other. The outer palisade, twenty feet high, with its guard-towers and ditch, carried a parapet from which projectiles could be rained upon rebellious slaves or besieging brigands. The gallery below this parapet was used to store a variety of ingenious equipment, some of it dating from the first days of the Trundle and conceived by Gehan First himself. The two gates of the fort, at north-east and south-west, swung on armoured hinges and were barred with enormous beams of oak, to which could be added sloping buttresses fitting into oak-lined pits. Constant vigil was kept from each of the sixteen guard-towers: Valdoe Hill had been cleared of trees, so there would always be ample warning, in daylight at least, of approaching danger – even in the extreme and unlikely circumstances that neither of the neighbouring forts at Eartham and Bow Hill was able to send signals or render support.

The inner fort was the Flint Lord's residence, enclosed by another palisade of greater strength than the first. It had one gate, and a single wooden building on two storeys – three, counting a platform for the signal-station. Part of the building formed the barrack for his personal guard, trusted men who received double pay and the best rations. The rest was divided into chambers for sleeping and eating and storage, on the upper floor; and much of the lower floor was taken up by one large day-room. There were side chambers for stores of emergency rations, a small armoury, and a cistern of drinking water which was renewed by rain-pipes from the roof.

In theory the gate of the inner enclosure was to be kept open whenever the Flint Lord was not present, and locked when he was inside; in practice it was locked only at night.

None of the Trundlemen, the freemen who managed the various workings of Valdoe – the mines, the slaves, the harbour, the fort itself – slept in the inner enclosure. Their quarters were situated just outside its gate. Apart from his retinue, bodyguards, and members of his family, only the General of Valdoe was allowed free access to the Flint Lord's residence. Even guests were expected to sleep in the main enclosure, although in the case of important visitors such as Bohod Zein an exception was occasionally made.

He had been given the principal guest chamber, a room four yards by three, furnished with sumptuous hangings of umber and scarlet. Above the bed was a mural on whose cracked surface a family of seals, hauled out on a sandbar far from land, basked in peaceful sunshine that had been faded by age.

After a long evening in the company of Lord Brennis, Bohod Zein retired for the night. He was washed and changed by the two women who had been appointed as body-slaves for the duration of his stay. The women finished tying his robe and left the dressing room; Bohod Zein fastened the catch behind them and passed into the sleeping chamber.

Altheme was already in bed. She had entered by another door; earlier in the evening Bohod Zein had intimated to Gehan that her presence would again be welcome.

'I hoped you would come,' Bohod Zein said. He put out all

the lamps except one at the bedside and pulled back the covers.

She was lying supine, staring fixedly at a point on the ceiling. To Bohod Zein it seemed that her pale skin and abundant dark hair had been invested with a new and healthier beauty, as if the past nights, when she had manifested signs of revulsion and repugnance, had after all secretly pleased and agreed with her. If it was possible, she had become even more desirable: not only was she the wife of the most powerful man in the island country, but now she was beginning to respond to his expert nocturnal tutoring. Suppress it as she might through pride – and he found her feigned contempt a source of additional stimulation – the evidence was in her face. Soon she would yield openly, willingly; what passions might then be released? At bottom, like all her kind, she was a harlot. When at last the floodgates opened, he knew his teachings would be richly repaid.

With a pleasant feeling of flattery and anticipation, he snuffed the remaining flame and climbed in beside her.

4

Ika had been out on Valdoe Hill with a party of servants and villagers, among them the head man, who owned the dogs with which they had been coursing hares. At mid afternoon, being near the village, the head man had invited her to his Meeting House for refreshments.

Rald, the food-taster, was at Ika's side as she sat sipping a hot barley tisane. It was spiced with thyme and cicely, and their flavours rose in the steam and mixed with the smell of hemp smoke: Ika and Rald had been sharing a pipe.

The village council had gathered in Ika's honour. The Meeting House, open at one end, was warmed by a log fire. The floor gleamed with polish; the walls were panelled with rush matting to keep out the draught. Ika, inwardly amused by the deference the villagers were showing her, had shocked them all with her open and brazen intimacy with a menial, a food-taster, a person of lowlier rank than anyone else in the coursing party. Insulted and outraged, the council men had done their best to hide their feelings, for she was the sister of Brennis Gehan Fifth. None the less, the conversation in the Meeting House was stilted and contrived, and at the sound of a commotion in the village compound the head man seemed grateful for a chance to leave the room and investigate. Presently he returned.

'What was it?'

'Nothing of importance, my lady.'

'Tell me what it was.'

'Merely a runaway, my lady. Some of my people caught him on the outskirts of our village. He claims to be a wandering pedlar, but we know him for a slave and, his lordship your brother permitting, we will present him to the fort.'

'At a price.'

'We must cover our costs, my lady.' He snapped his fingers

at a girl who was waiting meekly with a wooden jug. 'Will you take some more tisane?'

'Let's see this runaway. Bring him in.'

'He is uncouth and smells foul, my lady.'

'Bring him in.'

With a resigned glance at the other village elders, the head man went to obey.

The main intake of labour at Valdoe was supplied by slaving sorties to the mainland, when ships would bring back twenty or thirty or more captives to work in the mines, in the Flint Lord's fields, in road-gangs, or in the forts. Rarely did a month pass, though, without at least one native addition to the slave quarters. Most often this would be a farmer luckless enough to be out alone and caught by a trading team, who would be paid a bonus for their enterprise. Anyone alone and defenceless was deemed fair prey. Occasionally savages would be taken; occasionally a wandering herdsman or pedlar.

Ika put her hand on Rald's leg as the slave, hobbled with rope and with a line binding his wrists, was led into the Meeting House. His clothing was rude, grimed with mud and travel. He had apparently been subdued with plentiful blows about the head: a rivulet of blood had dried on his temple, and his cheekbone was bruised and swollen. But he was unbowed and he returned Ika's appraisal with defiance. Tall and dark, he was about twenty-five. Ika found him striking. Something in his primitive, uncompromising bearing excited her and she leaned closer to Rald, squeezing his thigh.

'Do you think he's interesting?'

Rald gave a cryptic smile.

The head man jerked the slave's chin aside. 'Show respect!'

For reply the slave spat in his face. The head man struck him; unable to retain his balance, he toppled to the floor.

'How quaint!' Ika whispered. She moved her hand higher, watching as the slave pulled to his feet. 'Do you find him beautiful, Rald?'

'We will take him away now, my lady,' the head man said.

'No. Not yet. I think Rald would like to know him better.'

Impulsively she stood up and started towards the slave. She

sensed the disapproval of the room: the air had become charged. For the first time today her boredom was forgotten.

'Be careful, my lady.'

'He won't hurt me.' She reached out and ran her fingertips across his lips. 'See? He didn't bite.'

The head man massaged his hands nervously. 'It is nearly time to go back to the hounds, my lady, if we are to have any more sport today.'

'We have sport enough here.' She beckoned to Rald.

The slave was slightly taller than the food-taster, and in every way quite different. Ika was thrilled by the contrast between the two men, in manner as well as appearance: one civilized and refined, with all the merits that culture could bestow, the other a rough bumpkin, a clod, an animal from the wildwood. And yet . . . there was some fire, some spark in this clod that Rald had lost. Rald had never looked at her like that. She stood back while Rald studied his face. Rald too reached out and touched his mouth, palpated his bruised cheek, and then, entering into the full spirit of his mistress's game, and with a conspiratorial smile for Ika alone, he began to walk round the prisoner, examining him from all angles.

Rald completed the circle and looked her way. Some subtle signal passed between them: Ika grew more animated still.

'My servant and I wish to speak to this fellow in private,' she said to the head man. A flush was rising in her cheeks; her eyes seemed to have grown wider.

'The council will withdraw, my lady,' the head man said.

'Are there blinds to close the doorway?'

'There are.'

'Then bring them.'

'Of course, my lady,' said the head man in bewilderment.

'And we shall want a knife. And some fresh rope.'

'What does my lady plan?' He indicated the altar. 'I . . . I must remind you . . . this is a sacred place . . . my village . . . the elders cannot . . . they cannot permit . . .'

'You'll have your price for him. Do as I say! He won't be killed.'

'That is not the point . . . we cannot permit . . . we cannot permit . . . sacrilege, forgive me, my lady . . .'

One of the older men stepped forward. 'We give allegiance to the Flint Lord, my lady. This is Valdoe Village: what we have belongs to him. It is so with this runaway. The slave is Valdoe's now and of course you are free to dispose of him as you would of any slave. We make no claim on him at all.' He paused. 'But our head man is absent-minded and has forgotten that a council meeting is due to be held here in a short while. Might my lady care to conduct her conversation in some other house? Perhaps in the head man's house?' – he glanced for confirmation at the head man, who nodded reluctantly – 'His dwelling is nearby, warm and comfortable, screened and shuttered for privacy. Here I am sure my lady would feel more at ease.'

Ika assented. At her direction, the slave was bathed. He shouted and struggled as six of the villagers tied him face-downwards on a bed, spreadeagled by taut ropes from his wrists and ankles to the pillars of the room.

The head man tried to conceal his dismay. He was the last of the villagers in the house.

'One more thing,' Ika said. 'Post some men by the door to see that no one enters. Give them weapons. If he becomes troublesome I want help at hand.'

The head man nodded. Rald blew out one of the lamps.

'Now go.'

The head man backed away. The doorway was low and led into a tunnel porch: he crawled into it backwards. As he lost sight of the room he heard Ika say something hoarse and unintelligible, and he saw Rald beginning to disrobe.

Nearly four hundred slaves spent their lives, by day or by night, in Brennis Gehan's mines. About thirty were stationed at the small workings at Findon, a similar number at Blackpatch nearby, and forty at Raven Hill. At Bow Hill, three miles west of the Trundle, eighty miners occupied the slaves' quarters below the fort. The rest, some two hundred men, were prisoners at Valdoe.

The mines here were the most productive and yielded the best flints. They lay on the southern slopes of the hill, just under a mile from the fort itself. The vegetation had long since been burned off, and only coarse turf and a few thorn bushes remained. The area was strewn with spoil heaps of stark white chalk rubble, piles of timber, and was crisscrossed by muddy paths. Plank structures, roofed with skins, protected the mine-shafts from the rain, and a small shed gave shelter on site for the mines Trundleman, a man named Blene. He was forty, with pale grey eyes and close-cropped hair. Born in the homelands and of a wealthy family, Blene held the most prestigious non-military post in the island country: he was responsible for all flint production in the Valdoe domain. From the aspect of a hill, from the way the land was shaped, he could guess where the flint seams were likely to run. At his word the overseers would direct the probing gangs to their work. Ropes and flags would be used to mark out the test pits, and samples of stone and soil would be taken back to the Trundle for examination. If all was auspicious, a shaft would be started, driven up to seventy feet underground, and from the shaft a radiating system of galleries would be dug. It was here that Blene's real genius displayed itself. He was an artist in the manipulation of loads and pressures and thrusts. As if by instinct he knew when a tunnel had gone far enough, and at the moment of imminent collapse work in the gallery would cease. By inspired use of timbers he kept shafts open long after they should have fallen in; and by means of his own inventions – rope transport and movable ladders – he ensured a smooth flow of work inside the mines. Sometimes there were failures: sometimes a few slaves or even an overseer would be lost in a cave-in, but this loss was small compared with the gains from Blene's efficiency. It was Blene who had been instrumental in helping Gehan to summon his present military strength: Bohod Zein had to be paid in flint.

Blene took an acute interest in the quality of workers provided for him by the slaves Trundleman. Most were 'Valdonen' – men who had been born in slavery or who had spent all their lives at Valdoe. From these the overseers were recruited, as were most of the skilled men – the carpenters, joiners, probers, and ropemen. The unskilled force, with the exception of a few who performed surface duties, worked at the chalk face, in pairs, eleven hours at a stretch. After each shift they were marched uphill to their quarters, a compound enclosed by tall incurved palings.

Shifts were changed at mid-morning and in the evening. The outgoing shift would be woken and fed an hour beforehand, and locked in a holding cage just outside the compound. A flag or flame signal would then be made to the mines and the other shift brought above ground. Only when the incoming men were safely locked in the compound would the holding cage be opened and the new shift released.

The compound covered a third of an acre by the south-west gatehouse. Inside the palings were leather tents and shelters for the overseers and guards, canopied kitchens and an eating area with benches and long tables, and an inner cage for sleeping. This had a wicket gate and a wooden floor, sloping slightly downwards to a shallow gutter, and a roof made of poles and skins. Above waist height the walls were open to the weather: the bars, vertical and horizontal beams of ash, allowed nowhere a gap of more than a hand's width. While the incoming shift ate a meal of beans, lentils, meat and bread, and while they used the troughs and latrines, women with brooms and buckets sluiced the cage; and then the miners were counted through the wicket and locked up.

They were thinly dressed: in winter they shivered. The floor was always damp, often icy, and there was little protection from the wind. Sometimes during the long nights one of the older slaves got so cold he did not wake up. For this reason it was considered lucky to be a night-shift man: underground, below a certain depth, the temperature varied little.

'It is not my fault,' Klay said to the man who was to be his partner, a thin, grumbling foreigner called Wouter. Wouter's partner had broken his leg. As a result Wouter had been moved from the night-shift and teamed with Klay, who, having been examined by the slaves Trundleman, had been approved for duties underground and put in the sleeping cage some time before midnight.

'Filth. They're filth,' Wouter said. He was grey, no longer young, stoop-shouldered, with tiny veins in his nose and in his watery brown eyes. His beard was lank; his joints and knuckles were red and swollen with rough work and the cold. 'Anyway,' go to sleep,' he said wearily. In the faint lamplight, Klay watched him lean back and find a space on the floor. His eyes closed at once and his mouth sagged open. In a few moments his breathing became a snore.

The moon had risen. Above and beyond the high bars of the cage, beyond the compound, Klay could see it drifting mysteriously behind scant, luminous cloud.

With misery in his eyes he watched its passage in the sky. He could not forget what had been done to him, there in the village at the bottom of the hill. Afterwards the villagers had dressed him and taken him up to the Trundle and he had not seen the green-eyed youth again, nor had he seen the blonde woman who at first had merely watched, urging the youth on, and then, slipping off her clothing, had participated. At the depth of his shame Klay had shouted out in humiliation and pain. With vile clarity he now recalled each detail, the first touch and the weight of the youth on his back . . . he clapped his hands to his face and sharply breathed in: he wanted to be sick, to vomit, to expunge from his thoughts all evidence of what had taken place in that loathsome room; but he knew that even if he could scrub his mind clean, he could never rid his body of its sense of dirt and violation. Tagart had not warned him of their customs; he had told him nothing of this. One more grief to add to Tagart's score! And that score would be settled – on the way south, trudging alone through the woods, Klay had vowed it. Tagart had cheated in the contest, Tagart had treated him unjustly and cruelly. His honour had been impugned, his family and ancestors belittled before the whole camp. The threat of banishment still hung over Yulin and his children, and he, Klay, a chief's son, true heir to the name of Shode, had been given an impossible mission as an alternative to public execution. Plainly Tagart had hoped he would fail. Well, Tagart would be disappointed! He would not fail! He would redeem his honour and restore the name of his family, demand a retrial, demand another contest, and this time the laws would be properly observed by all! And at last, Klay would depose the strutting impostor who had usurped his birthright, taken over his blood-tribe, shamed the memory of his father; and he would choose with dignity the woman he wanted for his wife. Yulin and her children would be well cared for and respected as members of his family, and he and Segle would govern the Waterfall tribe and all the tribes of the winter camp. This was the future: he would not fail it.

He looked up again. Most of the miners were sleeping. Grunts, sighs and moans broke from the huddle of men. Behind him, from the corner, came the sound of someone defecating. Klay tried to ignore it. For a while he studied Wouter. In ten hours or so they would be going underground, he had said, and Klay wondered when the best time would be to break his silence. He surveyed the sleeping men. They were ignorant of his identity; they had no idea why he had come; they were completely unaware that in a matter of days the secret he had brought would change their lives for ever.

He sat thinking for a long time, but he supposed later that he must have fallen asleep during the early hours, because he felt Wouter shaking him and opened his eyes to find that it was day.

'Come on,' Wouter said. 'Come on if you want to fill your gizzard.'

The miners were being counted out of the cage and were passing into the refectory, where they seated themselves at the tables. Serving women were already ladling stew.

'Over there, to the left,' Wouter hissed, pushing him from behind. 'We want to get on that table. She gives you more.'

They were beaten to the coveted places by the other men.

'No matter,' Wouter said. 'We'll be quicker after the shift.'

Klay squeezed in beside a middle-aged foreigner with greasy black hair. Across the table every face was turned towards the cauldrons: eyes watched and gauged the movements of the ladlers, counted heads to see where a bowl would end up. Some of the men drew shells or wooden spoons from their clothing.

Klay ate with his fingers. The stew tasted unpleasant: it was thick with strange vegetables; globules of pallid fat floated just below the surface. The meat, which Klay could not identify, was stringy and almost inedible. When he had chewed the last piece he followed Wouter's lead and drank the rest of his stew straight from the bowl.

Women circulated with osier baskets, handing out wads of loam-coloured stuff. Klay had never seen its like before. He could only compare it to fungus or rotten wood. He touched it with his tongue, licked it, bit some off.

'The bread's always stale,' the foreigner whispered. Talking was forbidden: he glanced warily at the nearest overseer, who stood swinging his cudgel on its strap. 'Give it here if you don't want it.'

'Silence!'

This man, who was called Gabot, was assigned to the same part of the mine as Klay and Wouter. After the meal, they and the rest of the shift, having been given a few minutes at the latrines, were counted out and, in their pairs, ordered into the holding cage. This was another enclosure of wooden palings, with a tall gate locked by a bar. Gabot and his partner were almost the last pair through. Wouter pointed Gabot out.

'Don't trust him,' he said. 'He's an informer. He sleeps in the cage and works at the face and pretends to be one of us, but he's been seen coming out of an overseer's tent.'

'Do they give him extra food?'

'No one knows.'

'He seems hungry just now.'

Wouter shrugged. 'Perhaps they've got his woman in the Trundle. They do that sometimes. A woman, or a child.'

The holding cage was secured; the chief overseer of the day-shift called to a soldier on the battlements, who waved a flag. Farther down the hill the signal was relayed by another soldier. At the mine-workings a gong was sounded above each shaft and the men came to the surface. They were counted and checked, and each was given a load of stone to carry to the Trundle.

Half an hour later they were locked into the compound. To Klay, watching through the bars of the holding cage, the night-shift looked more like walking cadavers than men: they were slow, haggard, whitened by smears and dust of chalk. Some were bleeding from cuts and grazes.

The sight of them gave form to Klay's dread of the coming day. The holding cage was crammed with men. Suddenly he could no longer bear to be trapped; but already the chief

overseer had removed the bar at the gate and the day-shift were leaving the cage.

'What's it like?' Klay said to Wouter. 'What's it like in the mines?'

'You'll find out soon enough.'

5

At the start of his second day underground, Klay and fifteen others, who yesterday had been working as a team, were kept waiting in the cold while the Trundleman, Blene, discussed something with the chief overseer.

The men stood in a line on the white ground, shivering and stamping their feet. Klay embraced himself and buried his chin in his shoulder. The wind was blowing at his back, flinging sleet across the face of the hill from the north-east. Far away to the south the hill ended in a belt of aspens heaped with drifted snow, beyond which, spreading three miles to the sea, were white, yellow and dun marshes, reed-beds, tidal flats. The sea was the colour of flint itself; sluggish waves pushed at the snow on the beach.

Gabot, the foreigner, was standing next to Wouter. The previous day he had made a point of eating his mid-shift meal in the same place as Klay. It was as if he had been told to make a report on the new man. During the night, Klay had awoken to the sound of faint whispering. Through his lashes he had watched Gabot conversing with an overseer through the bars of the cage.

At last Blene concluded his talk with the chief overseer and the slaves were told to collect their tools. Yesterday they had been set to deepening the shaft. Klay, Wouter, Gabot, and the rest of the unskilled men had taken turns to dig out the chalk and haul it to the surface, while three pairs of carpenters and joiners had cut and fixed new ladders and shuttering to support the walls. Today they would be doing the same.

Gabot went first, carrying an oil lamp. His partner was to have gone next, but Klay jostled him aside and grabbed his load, a bundle of antler picks. The partner said nothing and took a second bundle. It made little difference who went down first or last, as all the unskilled jobs were rotated throughout the day. The worst job was perhaps digging at the very bottom of the pit, where a persistent foot or so of water seemed to collect and form a creamy slurry with the chalk despite all their efforts at baling.

Klay ducked through the shaft-head shelter to see Gabot starting down the first ladder. Gabot's lamp dimly illuminated the shuttering, lit his face and chest; but below was unfathomable darkness overlaid by the darkness of his own shadow. The bottom of the shaft was at least forty feet down, and presumably the night-shift would have taken it even deeper.

Holding the lamp in his left hand, Gabot began to descend. Klay climbed on to the ladder, the bundle slung across his shoulder.

'Not so quick,' Gabot said. 'You nearly trod on my hand.'

Klay's face was level with the top of the ladder; he checked that Gabot's partner had not yet entered the shelter.

'I can't go so quick, fool!'

Klay rapidly moved down two rungs more and felt his foot crushing Gabot's fingers. He pushed with all his strength downwards. Gabot cried out and dropped his lamp. It fell, still burning for a moment before going out. There was an appreciable interval before it splashed into the slurry below.

Gabot clawed at Klay's ankles with his free hand. Keeping his right foot firmly in place, Klay descended another rung and lashed downward with his left heel. It struck Gabot in the mouth. At that instant he released Gabot's fingers.

Gabot fell. He scrabbled for the rungs as he lost balance and tumbled backwards, striking his head on the shuttering. Limply and clumsily he dropped into the shaft. There was a splintering noise near the bottom and Klay heard him hit the slurry.

'What's happening down there?'

Klay looked up to see Gabot's partner, a hand on either rail of the ladder, outlined in the twilight of the shelter. He was moving his head from side to side, trying to see.

'Gabot's fallen!' Klay answered.

Weak groans were coming from below: he was still alive. Without waiting for the overseer's interference, Klay hurriedly continued down the ladder. Gabot's partner was shouting something. Klay ignored him.

Near the bottom of the shaft, Klay reached the place where

Gabot had smashed the ladder in his fall. His foot failed to find a rung, and in the blackness he crouched down and fingered the jagged edges of the broken rails.

'You down there! What's going on?'

The overseer, leaning over the ladder, looked very small. 'He's hurt!' Klay called up the shaft. 'I must help him!'

Gabot's groans had become quieter. It was hard to tell how far away he was. Klay looked up again to see someone climbing on to the ladder. There was no time to lose: Klay jumped.

He was surprised to find that the bottom of the shaft was only two or three feet below. He landed on Gabot's legs and stumbled against the chalk wall.

Gabot gasped with pain and feebly snatched at Klay's clothing. Klay kicked his arm aside and got one leg across his chest; his hands found Gabot's forehead and forced it down. The injured man resisted for a few seconds. With a supreme effort he arched his back, gurgling as his face came clear of the slurry. Klay pushed harder. He felt the slime closing over his wrists, rising toward his elbows. Gabot relaxed.

Presently the overseer, bringing a lamp, reached the bottom of the ladder. 'He made a strange noise,' Klay told him. 'He made a strange noise and then he just let go. I think he had a fit. When I got to him he was already dead.'

The overseer gave Klay his lamp to hold and pulled Gabot's head and shoulders toward the light. Gabot looked like an effigy of himself in wet, white stone, but his tongue was partly pink and his teeth were brown and black. The overseer scrutinized Klay.

'It's just an accident, boy. Don't worry about it.' He glanced up the shaft. 'Wouter! Wouter!'

'Yes, master!'

'Send down a rope!'

Klay fastened it to the dead man's ankles. Using the fixed pulley at the top of the shaft, the other slaves drew Gabot to the surface and laid him in the snow outside the shaft-head shelter.

They gathered round the body.

'His little girl is in the Trundle,' one of the carpenters said. 'I'll pass the message on somehow.'

'All right,' the overseer said. 'We've wasted enough time here. Let's get to work.'

Valdoe Village, where Klay had been captured, was sprawling and prosperous, with many wood and stone houses, two granaries, several barns, and a large variety of sheds and workshops. The Meeting House was the finest in the Flint Lord's domain. The aesthetic pitch of its roof, the sweep of its eaves, proclaimed from a distance the extravagance of materials and virtuosity of craftsmanship that had been expended on its construction. The proximity of the Trundle did away with the need for a palisade round the village, and it was as if all the cost and labour saved thereby had been lavished on the Meeting House: its architect had been the chief builder in the service of Gehan Third, a man who, like many of the Trundle officers and craftsmen, had kept a household in the village for his family, away from the military atmosphere of the fort.

This custom was still maintained, and of the seventy or so houses in the village fewer than fifty were inhabited by those who held no direct post under Lord Brennis. These were freemen following every conceivable trade, all of whom paid a tenth of their earnings to the fort, with an additional annual tax reckoned proportionately to the harvest impost. The village fields belonged to Valdoe and were worked by slaves who lived in a small settlement on the outskirts.

The village lay in the valley between Valdoe and Levin Down, a hill whose summit was two miles from the Trundle and a hundred feet short of it in height. The southern slopes were partly under cultivation, but the rest of the hill, especially on its north side, was covered in thick woodland or scrub. Where the soil was poor there were patches of gorse; farther up were stretches of dogwood and buckthorn. These gave way near the summit to mixed woodland and coppice of ash, oak, beech, rowan, whitebeam, with occasional stands of pure oak and here and there a yew tree. Some of these yews were very ancient: the largest had a girth of ten yards and had been standing for as many centuries, during which it had become hollow. Over the years the hunters, farmers and soldiers too had cut wood from it for bows and spears and tools; at one time or another all the hill had been visited for timber. Many of the trees had been felled a hundred years before, during construction of the Trundle, but the old hollow yew had escaped.

A raven, perching on the topmost spray, craned its neck in alarm and then took wing; in silence it slid over the treetops and across the hill, away from danger and the approaching sound of men.

From his time as a slave, Tagart had learned that the Gehans had placed their forts on the most strategic, and usually the highest, points on the downs. The forts communicated by smoke signals, were connected by roads that remained passable throughout the year, and were each occupied by a unit of twenty-five men. He had also learned that the Flint Lord lived inside the Trundle and very rarely ventured beyond Valdoe.

Due west of Valdoe, three miles away and within signalling range, was the fort at Bow Hill. There was another fort, Eartham, south-east of the Trundle, also within range; but the road between Valdoe and Eartham ran through open farmland and provided little cover. The road to Bow Hill, however, passed for much of its length through deep forest.

Tagart knew the landscape of the downs, and his plan depended on this knowledge almost as much as on the three separate forces of nomads, each more than a hundred strong, that had converged on the Shode Valley from the other winter camps. Some had never been so far south before; others Tagart knew personally. Almost every tribe was represented, every totem: the camp was overcrowded and overstretched. Old animosities were laid aside, feuds tacitly forgotten, and under Tagart's leadership the strategy for killing the Flint Lord was explained.

They had left for the coast in two forces. The first, sixty experts in trap-building led by Tagart himself, had left two days after Klay's departure. A day after that the main force, four hundred and eighty-three people, had started, led by Bubeck. He was to take them as far as the Rother, a river in the south of the Weald. Here, well away from the villages and the Flint Lord's roads, he was to await further orders.

The march from the winter camp had taken Tagart and his men six days. Bubeck's force, travelling more slowly, would take seven to reach the Rother, which gave Tagart two days in which to make the necessary preparations in the countryside near Valdoe.

Most of Tagart's men had already gone on to the woods near Bow Hill. Tagart himself, Fodich, and six others, taking cord, axes, and hatchets, had hidden their packs in the undergrowth at the base of Levin Down and clambered up through the snow-covered scrub, cutting bundles of gorse which they had dragged to the top of the hill.

With his hatchet Tagart moved aside a branch of the old yew tree for a better view of the Trundle.

Sleet was falling across the hills and into the valley. They could make out the black timbers of the fort, the pennons flapping on their staffs above each guard-tower. Fodich pointed out the slaves' quarters, just visible at the right-hand shoulder of the hill. Winding past them, issuing from the south-west gatehouse and coming down the vast white flanks of the hill, a line of posts marked the descent of a trackway, four hundred and fifty feet to the village below.

'That's Valdoe Village,' Fodich said.

'Let's start,' said Tagart.

They arranged their bundles of gorse around the trunk of the yew. On the bundles they heaped twigs, bark, sticks, larger branches, and a layer of wet leaves that reached well above the lowest boughs of the yew. From his pouch Tagart brought out a pocket of tallowed leather and checked its contents – it was a fire-making kit, which he hid under a piece of bark.

They were three-quarters of a mile from the village and hundreds of feet above it, and the wind was blowing hard: there was little risk of their hatchets being heard below. They lopped a few branches from neighbouring trees and trimmed the undergrowth near the yew to improve the flow of air.

'No more,' Tagart said. 'We don't want anything to be seen from the village.' He turned to the man whose duty it would be to light the beacon. 'Can you remember this spot?'

'I think so.'

'You must be sure.'

'I'm sure.'

Tagart was satisfied. With a last look round, he led the others back the way they had come. They collected their packs and started south-westwards, towards Bow Hill and the rest of Tagart's men.

'Why did you kill him?' Wouter said to Klay.

Klay poked a piece of bread into his mouth and chewed it. There were no galleries yet in the shaft: the overseer had ordered the sixteen men to the surface to eat their mid-shift meal. Klay and Wouter were sitting a little apart from the rest.

'Why did you kill Gabot?'

'He fell and drowned in the slurry.' Klay pulled his tunic closer to his neck. 'It's cold out here.'

'His partner says you kicked him down the ladder.'

'He fell. He had a fit. Who cares?'

Wouter mopped up the rest of his stew. 'They might put me back on the night-shift,' he said hopefully. 'You could team with Gabot's partner.'

They sat for a while in silence. Klay squinted at the sea. Keeping his profile to Wouter he said at last, 'Have you heard these rumours about a rebellion?'

'What's that you say?'

'Someone in the cage told me. They said the fort was going to be attacked and we can be set free, if we play our part.'

Wouter looked round for the overseer; he was out of earshot.

'There will be smoke on Levin Down,' Klay said. 'That's the signal. When we see it we're to open the gates from the inside and let these people in.'

'How can we open the gates from here?'

'Word has to be sent to the slaves in the Trundle.' Klay looked Wouter in the eye. 'Do you think that could be done, Wouter?'

Breaking from the disbelief and fear in Wouter's mind came a sudden gleam of hope. 'This man in the cage,' he said. 'Your friend. When did he say these people were coming?'

'Soon. In a few days.'

'Do they know about the army? Do they know about the foreign soldiers?'

'That's what it's all about.'

Wouter's insides were churning. He had been a slave since the age of eight. As a boy he had often dreamed of escape – they all had. During the passing years he had thought of it less and less often. Now he was not sure if he wanted it any more.

But then he remembered that the meal break was nearly over. Soon they would be going back to work. There could be no question of choice.

Wouter saw again Gabot's white corpse lying in the snow. He thought of what the carpenter had said, that Gabot's daughter was in the Trundle. It explained why Gabot had spied on his fellows; it explained what had happened to him in the shaft. Wouter felt thankful and relieved that he had chanced to mention Gabot to Klay. If he had kept silent he might have jeopardized the only hope of freedom he would ever have.

'We must keep these rumours from the guards,' Klay said. 'Can everyone be trusted?'

'Yes,' Wouter said. 'They can be trusted.' He looked over his shoulder at the overseer. 'I think even he could be trusted. He'd take his freedom if he thought they wouldn't chase him and bring him back.'

'But you won't tell him.'

'No. Of course not. Of course I won't tell him.'

'This man in the cage told me we should all pass the message on.'

Wouter looked levelly at Klay. After his first excitement he was beginning to have doubts. 'Where did you come from?' he said. 'What are you?'

'A pedlar.'

'We have them here sometimes. You're not what you say.'

'It doesn't matter who I am.'

'Then who are these friends of yours mad enough to challenge the Flint Lord?'

'Just remember the signal. Smoke on Levin Down.'

Wouter was growing suspicious. He wanted to ask more questions. But he had no time: the overseer decided that the break had ended, and for the rest of the day there was no safe opportunity to talk.

Gongs sounded: the shift was over. The slaves, about a hundred in all, were brought above ground and formed into ranks.

After the first count the chief overseer, accompanied by another overseer carrying a torch whose flame was blown about by the wind, came and stood next to Klay's rank.

'Which man here was on the ladder when Gabot fell?'

'I was, master.'

The torch was put near Klay's face. 'What is your name?'

'Klay, master.'

The chief overseer studied him with experienced, sceptical eyes. Wouter watched. Throughout the afternoon his thoughts had been consumed by wild and changing moods. He had tried to keep calm, but it had been impossible. Talk of escape on its own would have produced no effect on him – he was too wise, too much a slave. No, it had been the circumstances of Klay's arrival that had given some credence to the talk; and then, and then, the blinding realization of what Klay had done to Gabot and why!

Of course, it was probably all nonsense! For some reason Klay had been trying to impress him. Or perhaps they had found out that Gabot was known as a spy. What more convincing way for a replacement to establish himself than to kill his predecessor?

But still . . .

The chief overseer plainly suspected Klay of something. This was no act. Wouter's heart soared.

'I'll be watching you,' the chief overseer said.

A second count was made. Tailed, flanked, and led by bobbing torchlight, the miners were taken uphill once more to be fed and locked in the compound for the night.

For the first time in over forty years, Wouter was looking forward to going into the cage.

6

The army was now complete. Twenty-four units of foreign soldiers had been acquired through the mediation of Bohod Zein and brought, twenty or thirty at a time, in ships from the home port. Twenty of the new units had come directly from the Gehan's barracks; of these, eighteen, the last to arrive, had been drawn from the Vuchten, the 'shock-squad', an elite body that gave fanatical allegiance to the Home Lord. Others were rougher and cheaper recruits, from as far east as Greifswald on the Baltic and as far south as Giessen, soldiers of the Felsengehans; from the Frisian Islands came mercenaries who spoke a harsh dialect and who wore no armour save crude tunics of sealhide and fur. Among the more outlandish recruits was a man of indeterminate age, hairless but for a small waxed topknot, his nose cosmetically removed – the practice of his western tribe – and the two nares forming the centres of whorls of tattooing in green and blue, which descended to his throat and spread out in fans across his chest. Another, dressed wholly in black, was a deaf-mute who conversed in a fluent and eloquent sign-language, refused to eat any food of vegetable origin, and insisted on sleeping in the open, even if snow were falling.

These men were arranged into teams and units and were issued with armour and shields. Over leather tunics they were to wear coats of mail made from horn cut into ovals; over this fitted thick leather plates at breast and back. They were given shinguards and armguards and helmets of plain, gleaming oxhide. The helmets of the team-masters were differentiated by a ridge from front to back, those of the unit leaders by hackles of feathers, the colour and shape identifying the unit. For protection from the cold, they were issued with fur-lined boots, mittens, masks, and fur or sheepskin stormcoats.

The Vuchten wore different armour and clothing, darker,

giving a more unified appearance, with helmets fashioned into hideous faces designed to frighten the enemy.

They held themselves aloof from the others and trained apart, spending long and gruelling hours on the hill. Their weapons practice was always attended by an audience, drawn by displays of strength, speed and accuracy in spear-throwing, archery, and combat with axes and hammers.

It was by now common knowledge among the slaves that the Flint Lord's army would be leaving on the morning after the next full moon, two days hence. The craftsmen, the overseers, the traders and tradesmen who came and went, all knew in lesser or greater detail the plans for the campaign. Some had sensed a strange expectancy among the slaves. Blene, the mines Trundleman, felt that the slaves were hoping for Gehan's total defeat.

There were ten Trundlemen. Their posts varied in importance between that of Asch, in charge of brothels, and that of Blene. In status Asch was equivalent to a unit leader, Blene to a general.

Blene and the Trundlemen for roads, trade, ships, and slaves, had been summoned to a conference in the main chamber at the residence. It was late afternoon; a young girl was lighting the lamps as another slave closed the shutters.

The Trundlemen were seated on cushions facing the windows. Lord Brennis was speaking. On his right sat Bohod Zein, who tomorrow would be taking ship and returning to the homelands; on his left was Larr, General of Valdoe. Beside Larr sat Hewzane, General of the Coast, a taciturn, pale-haired man of thirty.

Lord Brennis was describing the final plan for encircling the savages' camp. The army was to be led by Larr. Under him would be eight hundred and fifty men, most of them foreign.

Larr was of low birth – it was even said there was a slave or two somewhere in his parentage – and lacked the refinement of his fellow general Hewzane. Blene came from a family even better than Hewzane's, and of the two men he preferred Larr, whose exalted rank had been earned by hard years in the teams as well as by ruthless leadership and intelligence. Hewzane appeared to lack all humanity. Blene had heard that it had been upon his advice that Lord Brennis had specified the unnecessary cruel form of punishment at Fernbed. There were many other stories from the outer forts, most doubtlessly embellished, and tales of an atrocity at a village in the west. In mitigation it had to be said that Hewzane's task, maintaining the cohesion of the domain, was scarcely suited to a weak or pliable man. He had held his generalship for two years, having been purchased directly from the service of the Home Lord.

Blene, who was ten years older, remembered Hewzane's predecessor and regretted his absence. Perhaps this whole campaign – which Blene and, he suspected, a number of his fellow Trundlemen secretly regarded as unjustifiable, even foolhardy – could have been averted. Lord Brennis, who had only just turned thirty, might have been deflected from this lunacy by a few timely words; yet Larr, under whom in normal times were twelve units, seemed to have less influence with him than did Hewzane, who controlled only seven.

'Only two units will remain here,' Gehan warned Blene and the slaves Trundleman. 'Your overseers must be specially vigilant. I suggest extra food and perhaps beer for the miners, but postponement of rest days till we are back to strength. We must give them no opportunity for revolt.'

At last the conference came to an end. As Blene was leaving, he passed by Lord Brennis. 'Will you be supervising the attack, my lord?'

'Of course. Larr may be the general, but I am in command.' He took Blene's elbow. 'Come. Let us walk together. We haven't talked for weeks.'

Blene suddenly saw him not as Brennis Gehan Fifth, not as the Flint Lord, but as the boy of twenty-three newly bereaved by his father's death and burdened with crushing duties, someone in need of friendly understanding and advice. Blene felt impelled to risk a reprimand and voice his doubts about the campaign: perhaps even now Gehan could be persuaded to reconsider; or at least to refrain from exposing his person to danger. As they reached the doorway, Blene resolved to speak his mind.

But Hewzane was approaching. 'My lord!'

'Tomorrow,' Gehan said to Blene. 'We might have time to

speak then.' He turned to Hewzane and together they left the room, already deep in conversation, and Blene was left to reflect how much change the last six years had brought.

Gehan woke long before dawn and spent the morning with the provisioners and the quartermaster, making sure that nothing would be lacking the next day. Before lunch in the barracks he inspected the Vuchten, and after it the rest of the men, who were paraded by their commanders on the hill. At mid afternoon Bohod Zein took his leave; despite Gehan's express instructions, Altheme was nowhere to be found when it was time for the sledge to take the agent down to Apuldram and the turning tide.

For the rest of the day Gehan conferred with Larr. The Vuchten would lead the attack; Gehan would travel with the units of his own men.

Late in the evening a final divination was performed by Thille. And last, as a formality, the astronomer was sent for. He confirmed that the moon was about to achieve its perfection: in three hours it would be on the wane.

Gehan looked up at it as he passed through the gate. The sky was clear, another good sign.

He decided to bathe. Upstairs he was received by his body-slaves, who removed his cloak and leggings, his tunic and underclothes, and washed him with unguents and hot water. When he was dry they brought a clean new house-garment and helped him into a marten robe. With soft fur boots on his feet, he was ready for the night meal.

'Where is my wife? Bring her here.'

'She has already eaten, my lord, if it pleases my lord, and she has told her slaves to make up a bed in her own chamber.'

'Bring her to me!'

'It's all right. I'm here.'

She came through the doorway. With a motion of his fingers Gehan dismissed the slaves. He waited impatiently for them to leave. Altheme stood by the doorpost. She was wearing a maroon robe. Close to her throat was a necklace of small jade beads.

Gehan hit her across the face with the back of his hand. The necklace broke, scattering beads; Altheme fell against the wall, a crimson patch rising on her cheek.

'That is for eating without me and for leaving my chamber without permission,' he said. 'If I wish you to sleep elsewhere I shall say so. Get up.'

He had never been angrier. This was the eve of the most important day Valdoe had known since Gehan Fourth had won independence from the Home Lord. He had wanted to savour these hours. At dawn tomorrow would begin the fulfilment of his destiny in the island country, the fulfilment of all his father's dreams. He, her husband, had worked for months – years – to bring this about. Not once in all that time had she offered him the slightest support, nor had she shown the slightest interest in the campaign that was to herald the new empire. She was unworthy of him. Even this afternoon her indifference had disgraced the Brennis name and embarrassed him in front of the central figure in the negotiations with the homelands.

'I suppose you know how deeply you have offended Bohod Zein.'

'My lord, I was ill.'

'How dare you absent yourself against my orders?'

'I was ill, my lord, and – '

'That's enough, you whore!'

'If I am that,' she said quietly, 'it is what you have made of me. Don't you think he had already seen enough of me?'

'You are a whore,' he said, 'and good for nothing else. Where is my son? Where is the son you promised me? Where is the son to carry on the Brennis line?'

Her eyes flashed. 'Here! It's here! Here in my belly!'

'You're lying, you foul slut!'

'What do you think made me ill today?'

'Get out!'

When she had gone he put his fingers to his brow. They were trembling. She had implied that Bohod Zein could sire a son and he could not. She had called him sterile. And it was true. In all his liaisons he had never once fathered a child. Sitting on the edge of the bed, he shut his eyes and buried his face in his hands.

The room waited, utterly indifferent: the bed with its soft mattress and its covering of ermine and marten, the hangings of dyed and embroidered cloth, the shuttered window overlooking the enclosure, the six oil lamps on their turned poles. A slight draught was blowing in from the door; the flames by the window fluttered like moths' wings.

When he looked up, he saw his sister standing at the doorway.

'They are waiting to bring your meal,' she said.

'Have you eaten?'

'Not yet.'

'Then call them.'

She did so, crossed the room and seated herself on the end of the bed. Her skin seemed very delicate, translucent; the cloth of her pale grey robe was stretched by the swell of her body and revealed her ankles, forearms, and neck. Gehan noticed that her eyes, usually so blue, had been all but taken over by the large, black pupils. Briefly their intense, receding reflections contained minute images of himself; and she looked away.

The aroma of hemp-smoke still clung to her clothing and to her hair, which, in the lamplight, was densely composed of tints tending towards gold; where it was drawn up at the back of her head, the lines of tension seemed to draw their direction from the rise of her shoulders. It was held in place by a single ivory pin, like a trigger ready to release its charge.

The food-taster and three girls entered with trays of steaming vegetables and meats, cheese and bread, and placed them on the eating-dais. The girls adjusted dishes, spread face-cloths and trickled clear water into wooden bowls.

They began. Rald seated himself just behind Gehan. The girls withdrew to the floor and squatted on their heels, watching.

Once Rald had approved it, Gehan poured cups of essence for Ika and himself.

'To tomorrow,' she said.

'To tomorrow.'

At the end of the meal neither she nor Gehan had eaten very much. Rald appeared distant and withdrawn as he helped the girls to collect the dishes and load the trays.

'You may all retire,' Gehan said.

They watched the slaves go. Rald turned to shut the door, looking back into the room. His face was expressionless.

'It is too early for me to sleep,' Ika said. 'Are you tired?'

'No.'

'Is the moon full yet?'

'Nearly. Very shortly. Perhaps even now.'

'Can you tell when it's full?'

'The astronomer takes measurements. He could tell you.'

All through the meal he had felt their speech becoming stranger and less natural, and now it had become drained of any but a kind of brittle, superficial meaning.

'Shall we look at the moon?' she said.

He went to lift the locking-bar from the shutters.

'No, wait! Let's open them together.' From the wall she took down the snuffer and put out the lamps one by one. 'It's too bright in here,' she said. 'We must do this properly.' As the last lamp went out the room went black. In the swirling, particulate darkness Gehan slowly made out the dimness of the doorway and, turning, he saw the vertical filaments of silver where the shutter-boards did not quite meet.

Ika put her hand on the locking-bar. He did the same. Their fingers were almost touching.

'Together,' she said.

He was acutely aware of her presence so close beside him. He could hear her breathing; some heavy reluctance was preventing him from lifting the bar. It was affecting her too. They seemed to be waiting for the moon to complete its orb, synchronizing their heart-beats so that, at the precise moment, they could throw wide the shutters and let perfect moonlight flood in. But the moon was outside, high over the sea, and he and Ika were here, behind the shutters, standing next to each other.

He recalled the night at Harting Fort, her fragrance as she had hovered over him. He had despised himself then, but now he knew he had been wrong. This was not weakness. This was strength. At last he would no longer be single, cold, remote. With her he would be safe.

He put his warm hand on hers and took it off the locking-bar.

7

The road from the Trundle to Bow Hill was three or four miles long, a track wide enough to take six men walking abreast. It came down the long western slopes of Valdoe Hill and turned slightly to the south, avoiding high ground, before resuming its westerly course. A mile from Valdoe it entered the forest. Some way farther along it began to climb, and it was here, on a curving two hundred yard stretch, that Tagart and his men had concentrated their attention. With relays of lookouts protecting either end of the chosen stretch of road, and more lookouts in the surrounding woods, the intricate work had begun.

They had been interrupted frequently by false alarms, and more often by small parties of soldiers or farmers using the road. The delays had been agonizing. Tagart's scouts had counted almost a thousand men exercising throughout the day on Valdoe Hill: the Flint Lord's army would soon be leaving. Perhaps too soon. Again and again Tagart had wanted to ignore his own imperative of caution, to return more recklessly to the work after each false alarm; but he had not dared. If the Flint Lord got wind of anything untoward, the whole plan would be ruined.

And so they had taken nearly three days to do what should have been accomplished in one. Four tall oaks had been selected, like two pairs of gateposts, one at each end of the stretch of road, and interfering boughs and undergrowth skilfully cut away. Two hornbeams, partly rotten, had been felled and hoisted into position fifty feet above the ground and fifty feet back from the verge. A ditch had been dug on the south side of the road and lined with angled, sharpened stakes.

By late afternoon on the third day it had all been done. The road looked as it always had: a peaceful stretch of woodland track over-arched by the graceful branches of lofty trees. There were no unusual footmarks in the snow, no furrows to betray the heavy hauling that had taken place, not a splinter, not a shaving. All freshly hewn wood had been smeared with earth; the ditches had been disguised with brush, and everything given a seemingly artless sprinkling of snow.

Only at the ends of the traps might something have been noted by a suspicious eye. Between each pair of oaks, fifty feet up, a stout rope passed across the sky and on into the woods to the place where a long and bulky mass had been suspended in the treetops.

Tagart and all but two of his men withdrew to wait for morning.

The two he sent to the camp at the Rother, nine miles away, carrying orders for Bubeck.

Bow Hill was a long hump of land, rising as high as Valdoe Hill, three miles due west of the Trundle. The fort stood at the highest point on the hill. Near its gate were the miners' quarters, and, a few hundred yards away on the slopes, were the spoil-heaps and shelters of the mine workings. Three shafts were in use. Bubeck could hear voices below the ground, picks and hammers and shovels, the slow creaking of ropes.

The moon had set, tired and yellow, but there were so many stars that it was easy to see the way. Bubeck came up on the guard from behind. He had no time to make a noise. He dropped his spear and fought with insane strength to tear away the constriction at his throat, a loop of rawhide, knotted in the middle, its ends bound to a pair of wooden handles.

Steadily Bubeck continued opening his arms and the knot crushed the man's windpipe. His struggles became feeble. He slid to the ground.

Bubeck looked once again towards the fort. It stood as before, silent, unroused: nothing had been heard.

The other guards were dead by now. There were five, all strangled by Bubeck and his men. Behind Bubeck, in the hawthorn scrub, were twenty-five more hunters. He motioned to them and they arose and came forward, dividing into three groups, one for each shaft.

Bubeck led his group to the nearest shaft. It was covered by a wooden shelter, a leather curtain across the entrance. Lamp-light showed at its edges.

Bubeck ducked under the curtain. A man with curly hair and a thick beard, dressed in a ragged doeskin tunic, his legs bound with scraps of old fur, was pulling something up the shaft on a rope. Next to him stood an overseer in a sheepskin jerkin.

'Greetings,' Bubeck said, before the overseer had time to react, and thrust a spear into his heart. With all his strength Bubeck shoved him against the wall of the shelter.

The slave stared in horror. He let go of his rope: the load fell with a rasping hiss, and from below came a cry of anger and dismay.

Bubeck's companions laid the overseer on the floor of the shelter.

'Is there another one down there?' Bubeck asked the slave.

He was unable to reply.

'Is there another overseer in this shaft?'

'No.'

'Then tell your friends to come up. You're free.'

A second overseer was found in another shaft and killed; in a few minutes the whole of the night shift, forty-two men, had been brought to the surface and armed with spare weapons brought for the purpose. In the first light of dawn the whole force of seventy advanced on the slaves' quarters.

Bubeck and, in his planning, Tagart too, had underestimated the effect that sudden liberation would have on the slaves. Most of them seemed maddened, intoxicated. They smashed the palings of the slaves' compound and breached the sleeping cage, freeing the day shift. One of the guards managed to escape; the rest were cut down in a frenzy of axes and hammers. Despite Bubeck's shouts and the efforts of the other nomads, the miners pulled the cage to pieces and carried one of its sides to the palisade to serve as a scaling ladder.

The fort, like all the outer forts, had been made with a single enclosure and a single gate. Its palisade resembled that of the Trundle: a high fence of oak trunks, sharpened at their tips, set firmly in the ground and surrounded by a ditch.

The attackers were repulsed at the ramparts by soldiers with battle-hammers. Several were dragged over the spikes and clubbed to death. The soldiers' forked siege-poles thrust aside the makeshift ladder and its burden of screaming men; marksmen started to shoot. By the time the slaves fled there were twelve bodies in the ditch.

The survivors joined Bubeck's men and the rest of the slaves, who had been positioned just out of bowshot in the thorn and tussock scrub on either side of the road, commanding the gate. None of the nomads had been hurt.

Bubeck was watching the fort. A soldier had appeared on the platform at the top of the main building. He busied himself with bundles of wood and a firebrand and shortly a wisp of smoke appeared.

Most of the slaves seemed undecided whether to run or stay. Several had been wounded in the skirmish at the palisade; one man, an arrow in his leg, was groaning as a woman, a kitchen-slave, tried to help him. Those who had not been wounded were arguing and shouting about the bodies in the ditch. After a while they chose a leader, a man of about fifty who had been prominent in the assault on the ramparts. He was sallow and swarthy, a foreigner. At his approach Bubeck stood up, rising to his full height. The slave was tall, but Bubeck was taller.

'We want to get into the fort.'

Bubeck returned his stare.

'We're going to kill them all.'

'And end up like your friends in the ditch?'

For support the slave looked over his shoulder. The others averted their eyes.

'If you stay with us and do as you're told,' Bubeck said, 'you can have something better than killing a few soldiers.'

'What do you mean?'

The wisp had become a stream of white smoke gushing into the sky, rising for thirty or forty feet before beginning to drift downwind. As they watched, it changed colour from white to blue.

Bubeck turned and pointed to the Trundle and the east.

'My lord! My lord!'

Gehan opened his eyes, woken by his body-slave pounding on the door of the bedchamber.

'My lord!'

'What is it?'

'An urgent message from the signalmaster, my lord! Bow Hill has been attacked by brigands and the slaves are loose. General Larr has already stopped the departure, but he is awaiting your consent to answer Bow Hill's request for aid.'

'I'll be with him as soon as I'm dressed.'

'Shall I assist you, my lord?'

'No.'

To judge by the intensity of light at the shutters, it was almost sunrise. He had wanted to be up much earlier, to see off the first units, and at another time he would have been angry with his body-slave for letting him oversleep. However, Gehan told himself that his presence at first light had not been essential. All the preparations had been made.

He had changed. He felt he was no longer the indecisive coward who had permitted himself doubts about the glory of the future. Ika had guided him to that summit, that vantage, from which all was visible and all attainable. She was beautiful. She had shown him, more clearly than he could have dreamed, the boundless territory that was their birthright. It was the legacy of a supreme and masterful genius, of Gehan First, a man who had transcended mortality to seize the very flower of the gods themselves.

The body-slave's knock at the door had woken her too. She was regarding him calmly, triumphantly, her head on the pillow. 'Lord Brennis,' she whispered. He leaned over and kissed her on the mouth. She responded at once, drawing him closer, pressing her body against his; Gehan felt her leg sliding across his own and she was on top of him.

The bedcovers slipped down her back as he measured her waist in his hands. His thoughts returned to the night, marvelling at the softness of her skin and the lightness of her touch. Now at dawn she wanted unmistakably to begin again that rhythmic, mystical climb.

'I must speak to Larr,' he said.

'Soon.'

Gently, reluctantly, he pushed her aside. 'Now.'

* * *

The last group of soldiers had almost crossed the line traced by Tagart's eye from tree to tree. He turned in his seat, held up his hand, and signalled to Fodich.

Fodich was twelve yards behind him and to the left, astride a low fork. A harness was strapped to his chest and shoulders, attached to a rope. The rope led upward and was lashed to a branch, fifty feet above the ground, whose end had been carved into a hook-release for the suspended weight: a ton of hornbeam trunk, connected by two thick cables – one stretched tight and the other loose – to the two oak trees on either side of the road.

A similar arrangement and a second man in harness were waiting two hundred yards farther on towards Bow Hill.

The sun was rising among the trees. Here by the road the forest was still in blue shadow. The snow, crisp after the night's frost, sounded icy under the soldiers' marching feet.

Tagart had counted a hundred men in armour, led by a young man in a fox fur cape and hat. Their arrival and their purposeful pace towards Bow Hill showed beyond doubt that Bubeck had been successful there.

A hundred men. A tenth of all the Flint Lord's army.

Tagart brought down his hand: Fodich jumped.

The great hornbeam trunk creaked and cracked and was set free. Smashing aside the few branches still in its way, it charged downwards and swept into the body of soldiers. At the far end of the trap the second hornbeam trunk was released.

They had been penned in.

Their commander, the man in the fur cape, was already dead. He had been hit by the second tree-trunk and crushed against the ground, but one of the three surviving unit leaders, a plume of ochre feathers on his helmet, took command, yelling orders. Each man unslung his axe.

Before they could group properly the first volley of arrows whirred from the trees on the north side of the road. Many soldiers fell: another volley thinned those still standing. In the wake of the arrows a double rank of women and warriors stepped from the forest, spears held ready. For every soldier there were at least five nomads.

'Give ground! Give ground and regroup!'

They ran in terror across the verge, away from the oncoming spears, straight on to the spikes concealed in the undergrowth.

When it was over not a soldier remained alive. Two nomads had been killed and eighteen wounded. While they were being cared for and taken away, a group of men removed the hornbeam trunks. The rest, working in pairs, quickly cleared the road of bodies.

The commander had not yet been moved. Tagart put his toe under the commander's chin and turned his face to the light.

'He's young,' Fodich said.

'He's also dead.' Tagart let the blond-bearded face fall. 'You can send the runner to Bubeck now.'

The distress signal from Bow Hill had been received simultaneously by Harting and the Trundle. From Harting no reinforcements could be spared, but from the Trundle four units, Gehan's own men, were dispatched within a few minutes and their young commander, Chanvard, was given orders to investigate and render assistance.

The departure of troops for the savages' camp, already under way when the signal came, had been stopped. The eighteen units of Vuchten had left the Trundle long before dawn. Six had gone too far to be readily called back, and runners were sent to catch up with them. The other twelve returned to the Trundle.

Gehan slammed his fist on the windowledge. This signal had thrown the campaign into turmoil. While the trouble at Bow Hill was probably purely local, it was essential to halt everything until the matter had been dealt with. Any rebellion by slaves had to be quickly and firmly suppressed: to have them at large, in a position to reach Valdoe, would be very dangerous. The ratio of guards to slaves, not only here but at all the mines and works, had been carefully calculated. If the balance were upset by an onrush of insurgents the whole force of slaves might be set free, with formidable results.

But the signal had also mentioned brigands. This was the first time they had dared to attack a fort. That such an attack had occurred in winter, and only three miles from the Trundle, was deeply worrying. And then – were they brigands, or were they more primitive savages? Were they perhaps the nomads whose clans Valdoe had begun to destroy the previous summer? Gehan recalled the spies who had been found at Apuldram.

Larr was doubtful. 'We must not overestimate the savages, my lord. More pressing is the news from Bow Hill. Chanvard should have reported by now.'

'I agree,' Gehan said. 'I'm going up.'

They climbed the staircase and threw open the door to the roof. The signalmaster and his boy were at the smoke station; the fires were burning.

The signalmaster did not salute them. He was staring continuously westward to Bow Hill. Gehan looked and could discern little but the black shape of the fort: his eyesight could not match that of the signalmaster.

'Was that a double white, boy?'

'Single, master.'

The smoke station consisted of three shallow stone hearths, each about two yards square, and a wooden shelter for fuel: wood chips, dried dung, leather scraps, wet leaves, and the like. Plank covers, operated by pulleys, could be raised or lowered over the hearths. For complex messages three fires were lit, generating pure white, blue-grey, and dark smoke. Over the years, using combinations of colour and interval, a large and subtle vocabulary had been amassed.

'What are they saying?' Gehan demanded.

'They want to know if we have sent the reinforcements yet, my lord.'

He looked at Larr. This should have been a matter for Hewzane: it involved one of his forts. But Hewzane was at Eartham and there had not yet been time to summon him.

'What do you suggest?' Gehan said.

'We sent a hundred men,' Larr said. 'There are already twenty-five in the fort, not counting the slave-guards. That should have been enough to deal with thirty brigands and a rabble of slaves.'

'But if Chanvard has not yet arrived, he must have been waylaid.'

'My conclusion.'

'Then we must send more units. Five more. And this time we'll send Vuchten.'

'That is the best plan, my lord. But before committing more men and upsetting the departure further, we should have confirmation of Bow Hill's message.'

'Get it,' Gehan told the signalmaster.

The reply came, slowly and painstakingly pieced together.

'*Repeat . . . No . . . units . . . arrived . . . Enemy . . . laying . . . siege . . . We . . . are . . . alone . . . and . . . urgently . . . repeat . . . urgently . . . request . . . aid.*'

8

From the site of the ambush to the Trundle, by road, was a little over a mile and a half. The two routes that Tagart had chosen to convey his forces to Valdoe were longer, curving through the forest. One turned north-east, skirting the rise of the hill to emerge at the base of Levin Down, at Valdoe Village. This was to be the destination of two hundred and thirty-four of the nomads, who, together with the slaves from Bow Hill, were to be led by Bubeck in a raid on the village.

The other route, the one that Tagart and the rest of the nomads were now following, struck out south-eastwards and approached Valdoe from the seaward side, by means of the flint workings.

They were nearly there. Behind him, coming through the woods, were people from twenty or thirty different tribes, from every winter camp. Compared with the Flint Lord's soldiers they were ragged and undisciplined. The men and most of the women were armed with spears, axes, and bows. Some were carrying coils of rope and grappling hooks. All were laden with back-packs of food, clothing, bedding, and spare weapons.

Tagart felt physically sick with dread. He was trying to walk confidently, Fodich beside him, Segle just behind, but with each step the illusion became harder to maintain. The slaughter of the soldiers had left them all subdued; Tagart sensed that he was not the only one who was afraid. He knew he should try to break the mood; but he was too gravely occupied in thought, for now, too late, he feared that he had placed too much reliance on exact timing, exact coordination, and that it would all fail. And if it failed, he alone would be responsible for the destruction and death of the largest and best part of his own nation. If it failed, the nomad tribes might never recover.

The final plan had been settled the previous night, when his scouts had brought word that there were still a thousand men in the Trundle and that they were showing no signs of leaving.

The essence of the plan was the diversion of soldiers from the Trundle. While Bubeck's force attacked the village and drew most of the soldiers down from the fort, Tagart would advance on the flint workings and set the miners free. By that time the beacon on Levin Down would – if Klay had done his work – have signalled the start of the rebellion inside the fort itself. If all went to plan, the gates would be opened from within, Tagart's force would find and kill the Flint Lord, set fire to the Trundle, and escape before the soldiers could get back from the village.

A thousand men in the Trundle. A hundred had already been killed. When Bow Hill reported to the Trundle that these reinforcements had not yet arrived, more would presumably be sent, perhaps as many as two hundred, which would leave seven hundred or so in the fort. The second group of reinforcements would be well along the road to Bow Hill when Bubeck's force, almost three hundred strong, attacked the village. It seemed likely that the Flint Lord would send most or all of the remaining seven hundred to its defence.

Valdoe Village was over a mile from the Trundle, reached by a track which zigzagged at least half that distance again. In altitude the village was four hundred and fifty feet below the fort – a long and steep return climb for men who had not only already run down the hill in full armour, but who had chased an exasperating crowd of attackers from the village compound and into the trees: for Bubeck had orders to offer no resistance to the soldiers, but to retreat into the forest and try to lure them on, wasting as much time as possible before they realized the Trundle itself was under threat.

The timing of the raid would be controlled by the beacon on Levin Down. Its smoke would signal both the start of the slaves' revolt and Tagart's advance on the mines and Trundle. The man in charge of the beacon, who was already in position, had instructions to light it only when the soldiers from the fort had descended two-thirds of the way to the village. This would give Tagart a margin of some minutes to allow for unexpected difficulties – but now, as he led the way out of the forest and into the aspen break at the bottom of Valdoe Hill, the nature and number of those difficulties had swollen and multiplied in his mind with terrifying speed.

They prepared to wait. Nobody spoke. The Trundle could not be seen from here, but through the branches the terraced diggings and heaps of the mines, half a mile up the hill, were easily visible. The shelters and spoil-heaps were being patrolled in a bored manner by ten or twelve soldiers, who occasionally paused to chat with each other, stamping their feet, before resuming their walk. The soldiers could be told by their helmets and fur capes. The other figures on the hill, scurrying back and forth, could not be so readily identified. Tagart knew that most of them would be slaves, hauling stone up from the shafts, moving timber about, running errands for the overseers.

The sight of the mines brought a quick and repulsive vividness to his memory. The ground had been green then, it had been summer, but the rest of it was the same, the servitude, the grinding labour and hopelessness of the slaves, and, worst of all, the confinement in dark holes and galleries of men who worked drenched with sweat, breathing foul air and chalk dust. Sometimes he had coughed until he had seen bursts of light under his lids, and always he had felt trapped by the closeness of the rock and the weight of earth above him. At this very moment there were men down there, labouring by the light of smouldering wicks, digging with deerhorn picks, with scraps of wood, with their fingers, to extract from the depths of the hill the flint that gave strength to their master, their owner, the man who lived in the Trundle, the man who was planning to exterminate all of Tagart's race.

'There!' cried Fodich, pointing through the trees.

On the eastern edge of the hill, among the thorn scrub, there was the movement of a leather flag being waved. Orick had been waiting there, watching for the smoke on Levin Down.

The smoke had come. Bubeck had attacked the village and lured the soldiers down from the fort.

Tagart's mouth was dry. He unfastened his axe from its sling, summoned a shout, and at a run led his people from the trees and on to the hill.

* * *

Coming down the track from the north-east gate, Gehan was appalled and fascinated to see that the brigands had now set fire to the Meeting House. Black billows were rolling from the roof and pouring into the compound, giving a hellish, otherworldly tinge to the scenes of murder and pillage that were being enacted from house to house. Dozens of other buildings were burning too. Both granaries, many of the workshops, the leather stores, four large barns, and at least a score of the best and most luxurious houses, among them those of the quartermaster, the roads Trundleman, and even the fine and stately residence of General Larr: all were ablaze. Flame had engulfed the three great ricks of firewood, sending intense heat downwind to melt the snow from long, oddly shaped tongues of grey mud. Steam was rising from the mud to add to the smoke and ash, slowly climbing into and sullying the sky. The village had been turned into something unreal, fiercely set apart from the rest of the landscape. As he descended towards it, Gehan heard its noise growing louder: the combined shrieks and yells of the brigands, the screams of the wounded, of the scorched and impaled, of those with their hair and clothes alight, the frantic squealing of pigs and goats and cattle trapped and burning in their stalls.

There were at least three hundred brigands. Such a large and audacious force had never been envisaged by those who had built the village, those who had decided that no palisade was necessary; and the delay between the alarm being given and the dispatch of help from the Trundle had allowed the fires to take firm hold. Where the brigands had come from, why they were attacking the village, why they had attacked Bow Hill: these were mysteries that Gehan and Larr had been given no time to discuss. A message had been sent immediately to Bow Hill, recalling all reinforcements. Larr had been left with fifty soldiers, the civilians, and command of the Trundle, for Gehan had decided, on an impulse compounded of anger and a need for action, to take personal charge of the defence of the village. Of the twenty-one units remaining in the Trundle he had chosen nineteen – four hundred and seventy-five men – and brought them at battle-pace out of the north-east gate.

Gehan was in the centre of the column, surrounded by his

customary bodyguard of ten men. Behind him was one of the commanders, whom he had appointed as his lieutenant, a blond, spare-limbed man of thirty-five named Irdon.

At the bottom of the hill, three hundred yards from the Meeting House, Irdon shouted an order and the soldiers spread out across the rough, snow-crusted ground. In a few moments they had formed a huge half circle. All movement stopped.

'Spears!'

In exact unison they presented their spears, a long, curving rank of aligned and identical shafts, pointing inward to the centre of the half circle – the village.

Some of the brigands had already run away. Others were following. The compound was littered with their abandoned spoils and with bodies sprawled in grotesque attitudes or lying more or less normally, on the open snow, in burning doorways, on the steps of the Meeting House.

Irdon gave his instructions. The manoeuvre to be performed was a standard part of the soldiers' training. They were to pursue the brigands from the village and on to Levin Down, which, having a diameter at the base of only half a mile, was small enough to be encircled, the gap between each man being seven yards at most, reducing continuously as they climbed and drove the enemy to their deaths at the top.

'Vuchten Red Unit: take six prisoners! Hunt the others to the death!'

Gehan and his bodyguard were left behind. He watched the chase, his view partly obscured by burning buildings and drifting smoke. The brigands, women as well as men, were fleeing in a mob, being herded by the soldiers towards the trees. On the far side of the compound was an arable field, its clods and withered stalks unevenly covered by snow. Beyond this, across a frozen brook, many of the brigands had already reached the edge of the woods, which rose almost without a break up the steep scarp of Levin Down.

'My lord,' said the leader of the bodyguards. 'They've got a fire up there.'

It was so. White smoke was rising from the top of the hill. A camp? Some sort of signal? Gehan could not tell. This was another mystery that the six prisoners would explain.

The uneven surface of the field had delayed a few of the brigands; one had twisted his ankle and fallen. The soldiers killed him where he lay and ran on. At the brook three Vuchten had caught up with and speared a pair of women. Yet more soldiers were spreading along the base of the hill and disappearing into the woods.

Keeping well clear of the worst fires, Gehan walked into the village to look at the damage. Larr's house had been reduced to a stark framework of charcoal spars bathed in racing flame. The wood had burned away in cracked, reticulate patterns, leaving rows of squares and oblongs, like runes which were continually visited and abandoned by the caresses of the fire; even as Gehan paused to watch, the key beam gave way and the structure collapsed into the blackened rubble of stone and ash which had been rooms, bedding, clothes, the furniture of Larr's domestic life. There were no bodies to be seen here, but in the next house, also burning, he saw two dark shapes with spindled limbs and heads, shrunken as if by tremendous age. It seemed that most of the younger and more agile villagers had managed to escape, for the infirm and old accounted for a disproportionate number of those lying dead or pleading for help.

'Do something for that man,' he told one of the guards, and walked on, brushing soot from his shoulder, until he reached the eastern edge of the compound, farthest from the cries of the wounded and of the trapped beasts. Smoke was pouring overhead in great surges, as if generated behind him by the sound of the fire. He looked out across the fields. The chase had by now passed entirely into the woods, and from the slope above him and to his left could be heard, faintly but regularly, the shouts of the soldiers keeping contact. It would not be much longer before the brigands were brought to the top.

Hazy smoke under the morning sun spread thin, moving shadows over the flat fields in the valley ahead of him, fields bisected by a winding track which eventually joined the road to the north – along which his troops had that morning passed and repassed. Gehan wondered whether the six units of Vuchten, recalled by runners, had yet returned to the Trundle.

On his right, on the south side of the valley, rose the fields that had been made of the face of Valdoe Hill, and above them, where the ground was impoverished or the gradient too great, was the scrub of tussock grass and thorn that reached all the way up to the fort.

Casually his eye took in the distant form of the Trundle, black against the whiteness of the hill: the timbers of the palisade and guard-towers, the jutting framework of the north-east gatehouse; he even looked away again before realizing that something was amiss. At a mile's range it was not immediately obvious that the pennons had been struck and replaced with strips of sheepskin, nor was it easy to see the continuous, white plume of distress that was rising from the signal station.

It was being carried strongly eastward by the wind at the summit, quickly evanescing, becoming one with the sky, and though it left no trace of haze it was being blown by the same impulses as the smoke from the ruined village down here in the valley, keeping company with it as it moved towards the forest and disappeared.

The Trundle was being attacked.

Klay saw the blonde woman run into the hawk mews. He broke away from the fighting and followed her.

He reached the door and barred it behind him. The uproar in the enclosure outside had upset the birds: the owls, falcons, hawks and eagles. With piercing screams they were treading their perches; the more highly strung had already bated and were hanging head downwards with wings and tails in a broken tangle.

Klay looked round. The far wall was divided into alcoves by wooden partitions from floor to ceiling. Each alcove held three padded perches at chest height, above which were shelves laden with boxes, bags, tackle, bundles of twine and cloth and leather. Below the perches were lockers. They were too small for her to hide in.

His heart was thumping. He had lost all sense of time. He felt elated, drunk on the blur of events. At the mines he remembered spearing two men at least, seeing their faces, and in the fighting by the south-west gate he had taken three more.

Tagart's plan had succeeded. The nomads had stormed the

hill and cut down all the soldiers and overseers at the mines: the miners had come above ground as Klay had arranged, already armed with shovels and picks and lengths of wood. The slaves' quarters had been broken open and everyone there set free. Klay had been in the middle of the throng of slaves and nomads heaving against the ranks of oak logs that made up the gates. Almost at once the gates had opened inwards, released from inside by the slaves in the Trundle, and the crowd had surged forward and into the enclosure.

At the start of the rebellion, when the signal from Levin Down had been seen, there had been about fifty soldiers and thirty civilians in the Trundle. The civilians were craftsmen and free-men and overseers in the various workshops and buildings in the enclosure; working with them had been about forty slaves. When the smoke had come these slaves had attacked their overseers. Many of the other civilians had tried to run and hide, and the soldiers had been divided between fighting the slaves and making the fort secure – for they had already seen Tagart's force advancing up the hill and towards the mine workings.

Once the gates had been opened, the few soldiers remaining in the guard-towers and on the battlements had been pulled down and put to death; Klay had been among the fighting there. Other slaves and many nomads had already spread out across the enclosure, rampaging through the sheds and buildings in their search for overseers or soldiers left alive. Tagart and a group of more disciplined warriors had broken into the inner enclosure with ropes and grapnels, looking for the Flint Lord; it had been then that Klay had seen the woman, running towards the hawk mews. Somehow she had been flushed out of the inner enclosure. She was barefoot, wearing a thin white dress. And now she was somewhere in this building.

Klay noticed for the first time that he had been gashed in his right forearm. Spots of blood fell to the flagged stone floor as he passed from the hawk mews and came to the next room, a seven-sided chamber with a high, raftered ceiling. In the middle of the room, surrounded by a tier of seats, was what he took to be a cooking-pot or cauldron, a stone bowl on three legs, covered by a circular lid upon which was arranged a curious tripod of three bone needles.

He listened. Behind him was the screaming of the hawks, and outside, fainter now, deadened by the walls, he could hear human screams above the shouting of the slaves.

Klay's eyes jerked to the left. The wall there was covered by a curtain of dense woven stuff, yellow and white and black, hanging by a line of horn rings from a carved wooden pole. He had heard something: a moan, a low and involuntary whimper of fear.

He ripped the curtain aside. She was there, crouching in a niche, making herself as small as she could, tightly clasping her shins, her blonde head bent low to show the nape of her neck.

He had not been mistaken. This was the same woman, the one in the village, the one who had encouraged the green-eyed youth . . . Klay's hand trembled as he reached out his middle finger and allowed a drop of blood to splash on her neck. Her shoulders squirmed and she whimpered again, unable to deny to herself any longer that he was there.

Klay grasped her wrist and dragged her from the niche. She made no resistance and allowed herself to be pulled across the floor to the stone cauldron.

'I have jewels,' she said, barely able to speak.

Still holding her wrist, made slippery by his own blood, Klay reached out and took one of the bone needles from the tripod. With a dry rattle the other two fell to the stone surface of the lid.

'Look at me,' he said.

'I'll give you anything – '

'Look at me!'

Slowly she turned her head and raised her eyes. They were blue: foreign eyes, cold eyes, the eyes of the farmers and the land across the channel.

'I am going to keep you in this room and lock the door,' Klay said. 'I will visit you every day until you die. Until then, I want you to remember my face.' He gripped the bone needle and began to raise it. 'Remember me well. Mine is the last face you will ever see.'

9

He had gone.

Ika felt the coldness of the stone floor against her shoulders and knew that at last she had become still. She had taken her hands from her face and she was silent, even though it had seemed impossible, in the worst moments when she had confirmed with her fingers what had been done to her eyes, that her screaming could ever stop. And yet it seemed not to have stopped. It was continuing somewhere, somewhere else, somewhere beyond . . .

She was blind. She had been blinded. With a brutal hand clenched in her hair he had wrenched back her head and put out her eyes. She knew what had happened, and yet she refused to accept it. Nothing was permanent. Her eyes would heal. She could see something even now: the blackness that surrounded her was not complete. It was tinged with colour. Red, it was tinged with red, almost as if that were the colour of pain itself.

And as if to ward off the weight that was threatening to crush her into the floor she sat bolt upright, her hands came to her face and she was screaming again.

He had said that he would be coming back. The slaves had taken possession of the fort and he would come back day after day with new tortures until she was dead. But worse than that, she was already robbed for ever of her sight and her face and fingers were sticky with blood and everyone had been murdered and even Gehan could not help her because she was alone in this excruciating darkness where there was only Rald's voice and someone shaking her shoulders, shaking and shaking, hurting her, slapping her face, and to make it stop she cried out and was no longer screaming.

'Get up! Get up!'

'Who is it? Rald?'

'We must get out before they seal the gates!'

'Rald?'

He had helped her to her feet and they were leaving the divination chamber and coming into the hawk mews, into the banshee screeching of the birds, the screaming that she had thought might be her own.

'Rald! Where are you?'

'Here, my lady.' He touched her arm. 'We must cover your robe or they'll see you. At first they went mad. General Larr is dead, and all the soldiers and overseers. But now they're taking hostages.'

'Are they in the residence yet?'

'Yes. Quickly, my lady.'

He had found some coarse, musty cloth among the falconers' lockers. Calmly she allowed him to drape it over her shoulders. He led her towards the door.

'I was nearly killed myself,' he said. 'The others hate me. I was searching for you, my lady. Then I saw him coming out of the hawk mews.' He guided her to the left. Cold air and a change in sound told her that they had left the doorway. 'Now we must be careful. Say nothing. Walk slowly as though your legs are hurt and I am helping you towards the barracks. That's where they're taking their injured.'

Rald was keeping close to the line of workshops, making for the north-east gates. The slaves had opened these too, though it had been on the far side of the enclosure, at the south-west gates, that the worst of the fighting had taken place. Ika could hear voices, both near by and far away, but the frenzy of the initial onslaught was over, and where there had been horrible cries of suffering there were now coarse shouts and even laughter. On her right, from the middle of the enclosure, came sounds of destruction. They were ransacking the Trundlemen's quarters and the Flint Lord's residence.

'The gates are still open,' Rald whispered. 'Not much further.'

The pain in Ika's eyes had started growing.

'I can't go on . . .'

'You must.'

To be challenged now, as she was certain they would, to be taken and killed before they reached the gates, would be a kind of release: for she had thought that the first pain, soon after he had stabbed her, was the worst that could be imagined; but it had been a mere prelude to the remorseless, solid growth that was spreading into her skull from the unendurable points that had been her eyes.

'I can't, Rald. I can't.'

His hold on her arm tightened. 'We're coming to the gates now.'

She could scarcely understand him. Her feet slipped on the ice and she staggered, but Rald was supporting her and would not let her fall.

'We're through! Keep walking! We're through!'

Distantly she heard him speaking again. She was nearly unconscious and could recognize meaning only in the eager tone of his voice. Groping to comprehend, she retrieved the word *Vuchten*, sensed that it meant safety, salvation, vengeance; and then the rest of his words pierced her mind and before she collapsed she knew that he had said:

'*Lord Brennis is coming*.'

It had gone wrong. The rebellion had worked, and Klay had done his part, but the rest of the plan was in ruins. Once inside the Trundle, the slaves and nomads had been impossible to control. Even people from Tagart's own tribe had ignored his orders and joined in the massacre of soldiers and civilians. The whole structure of his carefully thought scheme to find and destroy the Flint Lord was on the verge of being swept away. He had arranged for a systematic search of the fort to be carried out: it had not been done. He had arranged for the north-east gates to be kept sealed: they had been opened and left unguarded, as had the south-west gates. And now, unless the Flint Lord was up here, hiding on the roof of his own residence, Tagart would have to face the fact that his quarry had escaped and that he had thrown away scores of lives for nothing.

The door to the roof had been locked from the outside. It was at the top of a steep staircase which, dark and cramped, rose from the landing connecting the bedchambers. Fodich had ripped a length of rail from the wall downstairs, but there was not enough room to use it to lever off the hinges, nor could two men stand side by side to break the door down. The angle of the stairs prevented the use of some heavy article of furniture as a battering-ram. They had tried to split the panels with stone hammers and failed. Now Fodich was hacking at the hinges with a felling axe.

The upper hinge and its cover had been reduced to a fibrous pulp. Chips and splinters of flying flint rebounded from the panelled staircase walls with each new blow and Tagart covered his eyes with his forearm.

Suddenly Fodich's axe hit the exact spot and the lower hinge parted from the frame. He kicked at the door: it twisted sideways and the upper hinge yielded.

Freezing wind and daylight filled the staircase. Fodich was first on to the roof followed by Tagart, Berge, and a man from the Martens named Porth.

They found themselves on a gravel-lined platform, thirty feet square, edged by a low wooden parapet. The main part of the platform was taken up by three stone hearths and a sort of shed. Tagart saw at once that this was the signal station: from each of the hearths there issued a column of white smoke.

The fires had been fed with wet leaves by a small boy and a man of middle age with a bushy black beard, his hair plaited into a pigtail which hung to his shoulders. To judge by his horn and leather jerkin and fur leggings, he was not an ordinary soldier but held some official post. Tagart took him to be a signalman. He had armed himself with a pole and, the boy taking refuge behind him, was standing his ground on the snow-covered gravel near the edge of the platform.

No one else was here. The Flint Lord had eluded them.

'Put it down!' Porth growled. 'Put it down or we'll throw you into the enclosure!'

The signalman laid down his pole. The boy clung more tightly to his jerkin.

From below rose the sound of the slaves running wild, wantonly breaking down doors, wrecking furniture, pulling down and fouling shelves and stores in the workshops, the barracks, the armoury. And the Flint Lord had gone: it had all been for nothing. With his army and his network of outer forts, he could afford to vacate the Trundle if he wished and retake it at his leisure. But even that would not happen. The Trundle had not been abandoned; the soldiers had simply gone to defend the village, and nothing remained for Tagart but to make an ignominious retreat before they had a chance to get back.

He went to the parapet. This roof was the highest point on the Trundle, which itself occupied the highest part of Valdoe Hill. On his left, to the south, spread a descending panorama of white and grey, running out four miles and more to meet the broad stripe of grey-green ocean. To the west he could see Bow Hill, to the north the wooded slopes of Levin Down and, in the valley at its foot, over a mile away and hundred of feet below the Trundle, the eloquent smoke that described Bubeck's work in the village.

In a tingling premonition of horror Tagart's gaze flashed from the village, farther to the right, and there, flowing up the road that zigzagged to the summit, already two thirds of the way to the Trundle, he saw a dark column of men: five abreast extending like a vast snake hundreds of yards long, sinuously winding up the zigzags, and as he listened he could hear their chanting and the crash of their boots on the hard-packed ice of the road.

'Shut the gates!' he yelled down into the enclosure, and cupping his hands he yelled again. 'Shut the gates! Shut the gates!'

Fodich and the others rushed to the parapet.

'Porth! Berge! Keep shouting! Tell them to shut the gates! Fodich, come with me!'

Tagart paused before jumping through the doorway and down the stairs. 'Keep that signalman! We may need him!'

Gehan was at the head of the column, separated from the empty road and the unguarded fort only by a line of body-guards. He was carrying no pack or weapons, but otherwise was keeping up exactly with the relentless pace set by the Vuchten at the rear. Behind him, powering him forward, he sensed the outrage of his men and heard it take form in the exhilarating battle chant that was made of the two syllables of his name: *Ge-han Ge-han Ge-han*, and he forgot that this was also the name of the Home Lord; it was his name alone, shouted by these men with their life's breath, shouted in the rhythm of their feet as they surged up the hill and towards the fort, towards total and devastating revenge on the vermin of slaves and brigands who had breached the Trundle and profaned the sacred territory of Brennis Gehan Fifth.

On seeing the white smoke from the Trundle, Gehan had sent Irdon, his lieutenant, on to Levin Down to recall the soldiers. The slaughter at the summit had already taken place. A few brigands had escaped the closing circle; the rest, numbering about two hundred and seventy, had been caught and killed. A hundred and three soldiers had been lost. Irdon regrouped the remaining men and, together with six captive brigands, started back down the hill.

During Irdon's absence five units of Vuchten appeared from the west, drawn to the village by the smoke. These were the second set of reinforcements that had been sent to Bow Hill; their commander reported that the first, four units under Commander Chanvard, had been ambushed and exterminated on the road. The Vuchten had continued to Bow Hill, found that the brigands had departed, and at a forced march had returned to Valdoe.

Under Gehan's personal supervision the men were marshalled and the race up the hill began. Their goal was the north-east gatehouse; the gates yet remained open. Once inside they could sweep through the enclosure and if necessary pursue the enemy out through the south-west gates to carry on a running fight on the southern face of the hill.

During the marshalling of the men, the captive brigands had been made to talk. In the brief time before the column set off, Gehan was apprised of the nature and size of the enemy: he could not bring himself to think of them as other than brigands, yet it appeared that his advisers last summer had been correct. The fort had been attacked by savages.

The gatehouse was drawing nearer. Gehan was by now feeling the strain of the run from the village. His legs were aching; his brow was hot and wet. He grasped at each breath; the air scraped his lungs as he pushed himself on. He could not stop. The Vuchten were behind him. He hurriedly wiped sweat from his eyes and saw that he had not been mistaken – beside the road, blurred by his own movement, he had seen two figures, one a woman lying in the snow among the tussocks, the other a man kneeling by her, now rising and running forward to meet him.

Gehan broke free from the column and allowed it to continue rushing past him, a stream of men still chanting his name. They were less than three hundred yards from the gatehouse, from the high black walls of the palisade; beyond the bobbing river of heads and weapons and armoured shoulders he was aware that the space between the gates was starting to narrow; and he was aware of Rald's outstretched arm, but brushed it aside and went to the woman. To Ika. Somehow the final safeguard of the inner enclosure had betrayed him: the sanctuary of his residence had been broken open and defiled, and from the filth and chaos of the fort everything he loved and valued had been vomited forth. As he came to her he saw for himself what had been done. Stunned, disbelieving, he fell to his knees beside her.

And looking up, wide-eyed, his knuckles in his mouth, he saw the slit of daylight vanish as the giant gates slammed shut.

Part 3

1

Both gatehouses had been made to the same plan. With slit windows and raised roofs thickly guarded with spikes, flanked by shielded walkways which gave access to the rest of the battlements, each gatehouse overhung a pair of massive doors composed of ranked oak logs set in ponderous frames. These swung inward and were secured with a grid of locking-beams, which rested in sockets in the jambs as well as in rabbets cut from the timber of the frames. The grid could be hoisted clear with pulleys operated inside the gatehouse. And as a final precaution, oak buttresses could be slotted into special pits and jammed against the gates in times of siege.

By now it was well past noon. The locking-grids had been in place for over an hour, ever since the Flint Lord had returned from the village. Finding both sets of gates shut, the army had withdrawn to the south-western side of the fort, a bowshot from the palisade. Fifty soldiers had been detached and sent down the hill; they disappeared into the aspen break, the nearest group of standing trees of any size.

Tagart could guess what they had gone to fetch. He was keeping watch from the signal station, not only on the soldiers but on the ominously quiet woods and fields round the village. The houses down there were still burning. He could just make out figures against the snow, approaching the compound in small groups, and from their behaviour it was obvious that they were villagers. Of Bubeck and his whole force of slaves and nomads there had been no trace.

Tagart was desperately trying to suppress his fears. Without Bubeck there would be no chance of leaving the Trundle alive. Sixty of Tagart's force had died during the assault, and a hundred more were too badly wounded to fight.

He looked down into the enclosure. The arrival of the Flint Lord had quickly sobered the slaves and those nomads who had disregarded orders during the assault. All the soldiers in the fort, including an important one called Larr, had been senselessly killed. So had many of the overseers and other civilians. The survivors had been spared only by the intervention of the chief of the Crows, who had locked them all in one of the barracks.

Even with the Flint Lord at the gates it had taken time to establish some semblance of order, and it was not before an hour had been wasted that a slave was found who knew something of the Flint Lord's army.

His name was Correy. In his early twenties, with wide-set brown eyes and a fleshy, slab-cheeked face, Correy was even dirtier than most of his fellows, who were washed and deloused only in summer. His beard was dark brown, somewhat lighter than his hair, which hung in ill-smelling locks about his neck. There was a boil beside one lobe of his nose, and another was visible through his beard, distending the line of his jaw. His remaining teeth were black stumps, and when he spoke Tagart tried to avoid his breath. But he was articulate and voluble and had worked both in the weapons shop and on a maintenance team.

Within a few minutes he had expounded the functions of the fort and the distinction between ordinary soldiers and Vuchten, whose darker uniforms could clearly be seen from the signal station. Tagart had estimated the total number on the hillside at five hundred and twenty, of which two hundred and ninety were Vuchten. It had been from the Vuchten that the tree-cutting detail had been taken: shortly after Correy had arrived, the men had reappeared, trotting up the hill, bearing something long and heavy which proved to be the trunk of a large aspen, newly felled and shorn of its branches.

Tagart and Correy went down to the enclosure. Slaves had lined the battlements, striving for a view of the Flint Lord. On Correy's advice the slaves were cleared and replaced with the best archers among the nomads, for whom extra arrows and bows were brought from the armoury.

Tagart climbed the ladder into the south-west gatehouse, Correy behind him. The trapdoor opened into a plank-lined room three yards by five. The room was in semi-darkness. In the rear wall, overlooking the enclosure, was a narrow window beside which stood the stocks for the pulleys and tackle of the locking-grids: ropes passed down through neat ovals cut in the floor. On the outward wall were four slit windows and a larger, central, aperture, two feet square, provided with a hinged shutter. Hanging on brackets above it, running the length of the room, was a trough-shaped board; below this was a curious device, a pair of wooden handles five feet long, attached to the wall with pivots and supporting a shallow basket fashioned from heavy osiers.

'That's the hoist. Those hooks in the ceiling are for the chute guys.'

At floor-level was a horizontal slit a few inches wide and about four feet long. 'What's this for?' Tagart said.

'The hose.' Correy indicated the shutter. 'You work it from there.'

Tagart opened the shutter and looked out. The soldiers were so close that he could hear their voices. They had spread out on the hillside, with an order and regularity which were themselves intimidating, just beyond the furthest bowshot. In the middle of their ranks a tent, taken from the mine-workings, had been pitched, and next to it a fire, the largest of the several fires they had lit, was being fuelled with pitprops by half a dozen men.

The tree-cutting detail had not yet reached the main body of troops. Tagart turned to Correy. 'You don't think they'll try it in daylight, do you?'

'I do.'

'They'll be shot. We'll hit them as they come.'

'They have good armour.'

Hanging just by the shutter, on a loop of cord, was a broad-mouthed cone about a foot in length, made from reed-leaves pressed together and laminated with glue.

'What's this?'

'A shouting-cone.'

Tagart took it down and examined it. 'By what name should I call the Flint Lord? Lord Brennis?'

'Yes. But he won't answer.'

Tagart put the smaller end to his lips and leaned forward. 'Lord Brennis!' The sound was amplified by the reed-paper trumpet and it seemed no longer to be Tagart's own voice. He shouted again. 'Lord Brennis! Lord Brennis! I am the chief of the Shoden! I wish to talk!'

The soldiers were behaving as if nothing had happened. No one made a move towards the tent, and no one appeared at its flap.

'To speak to us would be to admit that we have taken the Trundle,' Correy said.

Tagart tried again. 'Lord Brennis! We must talk! Lord Brennis!'

For reply came a few terse commands and responses; the aspen trunk had been made ready, with twenty-five equally spaced slings of rope. Fifty Vuchten went and stood by it. Two hundred of the other soldiers strung their longbows and formed into four rectangular squads, each five men wide and ten deep. These four squads now set off towards the gatehouse, flanking and keeping slightly ahead of the men with the tree-trunk. The first assault had started.

Behind Tagart, four nomads climbed through the trapdoor and took their places by the slits. Tagart looked impotently from side to side, at the approaching soldiers, at Correy: and suddenly Correy seemed seized with fright. He rushed to the ladder and scarcely touched the rungs as he slid to the ground. Tagart heard him shouting. 'The buttresses! The buttresses!' and, with the soldiers less than two hundred yards away, saw him directing a group of slaves as they manhandled across the ice, two for each gate, sloping frames made of oak beams.

Although the gates had been correctly closed, the locking-grids alone were not meant to withstand a battering-ram. Most of the slaves had known what was being prepared; all those on the battlements had seen the aspen trunk being brought up past the mines, seen it being brought ever closer to the Flint Lord's position, seen it being rigged with rope; but it was a measure of the confusion and indiscipline inside the fort that not one, not even Correy, had thought to mention to Tagart, or to Fodich or Crow or any of the other established leaders, the existence and purpose of the siege buttresses. Only now had Correy remembered them, and without reference to anybody he had taken men from their posts and was shouting orders at them as they tried to drag the unwieldy frameworks into place.

Fifty yards from the palisade the two hundred longbowmen, still in formation, had stopped to take aim and shoot, protecting the men with the battering-ram, who were keeping on, increasing their speed.

Tagart dodged aside as the soldiers let fly a howling volley of arrows, fanning outward on spinning vanes to cover the whole defended width of battlement, ending in shrieks and screams and a sudden loud crepitation against the logs of the gatehouse wall. Beside him one of the arrows had found a slit, found it and gone through, and the man standing there had been punched backwards, his throat pierced, his hands clutching the arrow and already bloodied as he fell against the pulley stocks and crumpled to the floor.

The Vuchten with the battering-ram had kept on, and when Tagart glimpsed them in foreshortened view, fifteen feet below, it was as if he was seeing one creature, with one brain, blind, insane, a tree-trunk for its body, horn and leather legs propelling it forward in a writhe of glinting grey and black, but each leg was a man, a human being, faceless behind an ugly visor, each one different, deformed, carved in the guise of nameless beasts and Tagart saw them no more and was thrown as the head of the creature struck its first tremendous blow. The whole gatehouse lurched. He grasped the shutter and pulled himself up. As one, with inhuman precision, the Vuchten had dropped the trunk and turned, ready to retreat for a second strike; but, ignoring the dense covering fire of the longbow squads, the men on the battlements had bent their bows and leaned into view. They let fly: a hailstorm of shafts and feathers converged on the Vuchten. Half fell dead or mortally wounded. Those who had not been hit tried to lift the battering-ram; others, with arrows sticking from their limbs, bodies, necks, added their ebbing strength and the tree-trunk actually moved a few inches. But the trunk was too heavy, they could not manage it, and with each moment more devastation was threatened from the battlements. The order came for retreat. Leaving their dead, they dragged the wounded to the cover of the four squads, whose men, shields held high to deflect the nomads' arrows, were slowly backing away.

They reached the main position and were absorbed into the general body of soldiers.

Tagart could see the casualties being attended to by their comrades, and from the tent appeared the figure of a man in a fur cape of the palest grey. As he passed among the men he was shown the greatest deference; he cursorily inspected the wounded and from his impatient gestures seemed annoyed by what he saw.

This surely was the Flint Lord himself. Under his cape he was wearing a high-necked tunic of what looked like ermine, leggings and knee-boots of sand-coloured hide, and gull grey gauntlets; on his head was a black or dark grey stormcap with ear muffs and neck flap. Beside most of his soldiers he was not tall, but even at this distance his bearing and carriage could be seen to mark him out from all the rest. Tagart found himself staring at the man, despite the need to leave the gatehouse to discover what losses had been inflicted on his own people. And at the back of his mind Tagart was trying to assess the chances of making a run for safety. The north-east gates, perhaps deliberately, had been left unguarded by the Flint Lord. It was as though he were inviting Tagart to try. Tagart's fighters were women as well as men, slaves as well as nomads, undisciplined, uncoordinated, lacking all training in warfare. Pitched against them were five hundred soldiers, awesomely well prepared and equipped. The odds were hopeless. But staying in the Trundle would be death. Before long, even more soldiers would arrive, from the outer forts. They would help the others to erect a temporary village and keep warm by burning timbers from the mines, and in a week, a month, supplies of food and water in the fort would run out. For a while those inside would eat snow and go hungry, but, when the last dog had been eaten, they would start eating each other. The dead first, then the nearly dead, then the weakest of those left alive.

The Flint Lord knew this. He had come to the forefront of the ranks and stopped, alone. Behind him was the movement of his men, the bright fluctuation of the fires; but he was motionless. To Tagart his stillness seemed uncanny, the product of an anger so deep and unforgiving that it wore the appearance of patience and calm, and at its centre was his gaze, fixed on the fort, on the gatehouse, on the open window, on the face and eyes and soul of his adversary. Tagart took an unconscious step backwards and his heel touched the paper cone, which had fallen to the floor. It rolled aside with a resonant scrape, and Tagart, who minutes before had been eager to use it, to bargain his way out of the trap into which he had sucked all the nomad tribes, now felt himself unable even to bend and pick it up, still less put it to his mouth and attempt to communicate with such a man.

Tagart made himself break the spell and look away. He had resolved to act, whatever the cost. He could no longer afford to wait for Bubeck: it was beginning to look as if Bubeck would never come.

Pushing back the conclusion of this thought, he glanced out again for a last glimpse of the man in grey.

He had disappeared. Something had drawn him back into the assembly. Tagart saw what it was.

Over to the right, climbing nearer through the thorn scrub on the western face of the hill, giving the Flint Lord complete superiority of numbers, was a column of a hundred and fifty men wearing the dark armour of the Vuchten.

There would be no escape.

Tagart left the gatehouse and in a daze went down into the enclosure.

There was a quality about the woman that preserved a part of her dignity even now. Like the Flint Lord's spotless and luxurious personal clothing, like the lavishness of his chambers and the costly contents of the chests and cupboards that had been emptied and looted by the slaves, she was of the best and most expensive breed: precisely the consort that a man like Brennis Gehan would take. Her face was grimed and bruised, and she was holding the torn flap of her robe to her neck, both to keep herself distanced from Tagart and to cover the flesh that had been exposed when the slaves had tried to rape her. She was exhibiting this rare pride, yet the manner in which she had been found, crouching in the bottom of an empty cistern, spoilt it all, and in her brown eyes it was easy to discern the terror that paralyses someone facing imminent death.

'Take her upstairs. Give her new clothes and a private room. Her own room.'

'The slaves want to kill her,' Fodich said.

'Keep them away. Keep them away from this building at least.'

Lookouts had been posted in the guard-towers and on the

signal station, but still there had been no trace of Bubeck or any of his force. Half an hour had passed since the attack on the gates. The aspen trunk was still lying outside, surrounded by the bodies of twenty-eight Vuchten. They had been sacrificed, perhaps merely to establish whether or not the buttresses had been erected, and any further attempt to breach the fort before nightfall seemed now to have been abandoned.

Three nomads, including the man in the gatehouse, had died in the attack; several had sustained serious wounds. They had been taken, with the rest of the wounded, to the barracks by the north-east gates, where women had been appointed to look after them.

The nomad chiefs were beginning to impose basic order. A handful of the most violent and uncontrollable slaves, most of whom had found jars of beer and liquor, had been bound hand and foot and locked in the prison.

Klay was alive; so was Segle. Tagart had been with her in the enclosure when word had come that the Flint Lord's woman had been found hiding in the residence.

He watched her being escorted to the stairway. She, perhaps, was the reason for the reckless savagery of the attack on the gates. And perhaps her presence in the fort explained the terrible gaze that had held Tagart helpless at the gatehouse window. For the nomads she represented hope: she was the key to deliverance.

Then there were the other hostages. They would add to Tagart's bargaining strength.

He left the day-room, Fodich at his side. It was already getting dark. Cloud had spread across the sky: more snow was on its way.

In the gatehouse, Tagart picked up the paper cone and went to the window. The scene on the hillside had changed little. Other tents had gone up, and men were bringing more timbers from the mines.

The fire by the Flint Lord's tent was still blazing.

'Brennis Gehan! Brennis Gehan!'

At first, as before, there was no reaction. Then a man came out of the tent. It was the Flint Lord.

'Lord Brennis! We have your wife! We have her! She's alive!'

The Flint Lord seemed to be deaf. He turned and spoke to one of his soldiers.

'Lord Brennis! Lord Brennis! We have your lady! We have other hostages! Let us go and they will be spared! Lord Brennis! Give some sign that you hear! I am Shode, chief of the Waterfall tribe! We must talk!'

The Flint Lord had by now turned his back and was in earnest discussion with the soldier. The soldier pointed towards the mines and the Flint Lord nodded agreement. With that, he went back into his tent.

Tagart shouted until it was dark.

The tentflap did not move again.

2

Hewzane, as General of the Coast, divided his time between the seven outer forts. In winter he travelled from one to another by dog-sledge, which, although considered slightly indecorous, was quicker, safer, and capable of covering greater distances between rests than the usual slave-drawn sledge. There were ten dogs in the team: sturdy, rough-haired animals bred for stamina and docility in harness. They pulled in a single long file, all but the leading dog wearing a withy muzzle, while Hewzane, seated in comfort under warm furs, flicked his whip and guided the light, elegant framework of the sledge in a path that left two endless lines in the snow. On each side ran a pair of bodyguards; a fifth man went ahead of the dogs.

For the period of the campaign against the savages, Hewzane had opted to remain at Eartham, the first fort to the east of Valdoe. The demands of the campaign would weaken the Trundle; Lord Brennis had agreed that Hewzane should be on hand.

Soon after observing Valdoe's signals for Bow Hill, Hewzane had indeed been summoned to attend Lord Brennis and give advice, for Bow Hill was one of the outer forts and its defence the proper province of the General of the Coast.

On his way, Hewzane had seen with his own eyes the distress smoke coming from the Trundle. It had both alarmed and puzzled him, and, arriving among the soldiers on the hillside, he had been astounded to learn what had happened and to find Gehan in charge of a rash attempt to get back into the fort.

Gehan's mood had been such that Hewzane had felt it better not to criticize, and the attempt, predictably enough, had failed, whereupon Hewzane, after hasty consultation with the senior officer of the Vuchten, had offered his assistance. Using timbers from the mines, work had begun on a toster, or protective roof, which would cover the men when next they used the battering-ram.

Among the survivors of the uprising had been the mines

Trundleman, Blene, who had managed to hide in one of the galleries. Blene was an expert, if not a genius, in the craft of joinery, and his flair for improvisation made him ideal for the work in hand. Hewzane had left him in charge, and gone to sit with Lord Brennis in his tent.

Gehan was distracted with grief and rage. He sat holding his sister's hand. She had been given a camp bed; her face, which Hewzane had formerly conceded to himself as pretty, even lovely, had been wiped clean of blood, leaving her complexion pale, blotched, and ugly. Her hair hung in damp strings. She fretted at her bandages, fidgeted continually, and was overcome by frequent fits of sobbing. As the day faded she grew quieter and more resigned and expressed a desire to sleep: Hewzane left the tent, to be followed shortly by his lord.

The Trundle, viewed for the first time from the outside by one denied access to it, seemed to Hewzane both magnificent and frightening. Set against the grey-blue of the snow at dusk, behind it the sweep of a louring sky, the dead weight of its walls and towers soaked up the last vestige of daylight and gave back nothing. Here and there, glimpsed through cracks in the palisade, were twinkles of firelight, but they served only to emphasize the oppressive bulk of the fort, this structure that had been built to dominate an entire foreign land and bring it under control. That was the meaning of the word *Gehan*: control, continuing manipulation, exploitation; the Trundle, straddling Valdoe Hill, looking north to the vanquished land and south to the sea and the homelands, was the symbol and the embodiment of the Gehan name.

The soldiers had begun to settle the details of their comfort in this unexpected bivouac. What tents there were had been brought up from the mine-workings, from the wreckage of the slaves' quarters and from the smoking ruins of the village. There were only enough tents for the officers, though, and no timber could be spared. As a result the men were even keener than their leaders to breach the gates. The alternative was a freezing night in the open, hard enough when on the march, but intolerable when warm barracks were only a bowshot away. Meat, some of it already grimly roasted, had been brought from the village, and cauldrons and cooking utensils had been salvaged from the slaves' kitchen and put to use, but there was not enough food to share among six hundred men, and Hewzane saw that many had already broken open their pack rations.

He removed, finger by finger, his kidskin gloves, and stood warming his hands at the fire. Beyond the flames, in the middle of the assembly, a space had been cleared for Blene and his carpenters, recruited from those soldiers who knew a little woodwork. With adzes and other tools rescued from the mines, they had prepared the members of the toster and now tenons and mortises and halving joints were being cut and tested before fitting the framework together. When finished, the toster would be twenty yards long and three across, a long, slightly pitched roof. Under it would be four files of men, to carry the battering-ram and the toster itself.

Hewzane pulled on his gloves: Gehan had emerged from the tent.

'How much longer, Hewzane?'

'An hour or two. Perhaps more.'

Gehan looked exhausted. He had been chewing his lips; his cheeks were hollow, his eyes sunken, but Hewzane sensed that these personal and outward signs of distress had been occasioned solely by the harm done to Ika. As her brother, he was grieving and his anger was open. As Lord Brennis, the merciless extent of his rage had, by strength of will, been contained and kept ready for controlled use on those who had taken the fort. He had, it seemed, regained himself since the heated madness of the first attack on the gates.

'Come along,' he said, and a way opened before them as they went to inspect the carpenters' work.

'Tell me about him.'

'He is my husband.'

'And you are carrying his child?'

Her eyes dropped.

'Why doesn't he care whether you live or die?'

She made no answer. Tagart studied her face; she was softly spoken and he had to strain to catch her replies. Her body-slave, a motherly woman named Rian, seemed divided in loyalty between her mistress and the success of the rebellion.

She had disclosed that Lady Brennis was pregnant, which made the Flint Lord's behaviour even more difficult to understand.

Tagart had taken over the largest of the ground-floor rooms in the residence. Food had been brought and the lamps lit.

With the coming of night, he had shed the defeatism that had made his despair insufferable. The change had come suddenly. He had been talking to Correy, giving instructions for fires to be kindled and certain stores broached, when he realized that he had allowed himself to become diverted from his first aim. His experience in the gatehouse had unnerved him and made him less than himself, but now he was glad there had been no response to his shouts. He had been willing then to bargain with the Flint Lord, to exchange hostages for mere freedom, when what he truly sought was nothing less than the man's death.

Once this had been secured – though Tagart as yet had devised no way of bringing it about – there would be time enough to worry about Bubeck and about getting the rest of the slaves and nomads safely away from the fort. Perhaps, with their leader dead, the soldiers would lose both their direction and their taste for fighting. He did not know. Nor did he know anything of the habits and temperament of the man he had decided to kill, and that was why he had sent for Lady Brennis.

She was sitting on a cushion, her hands in her lap, her legs tucked inside the voluminous folds of a finely woven robe, pink and grey, the narrow edging down one breast embroidered white on black in an abstract pattern of birds and grasses. A ribbon of the same design held back her hair. She was wearing no jewellery; it had all been taken by the slaves.

'I am sorry if they hurt you,' Tagart said, and she looked up defensively. 'You must understand what this means to them.'

Altheme said nothing. The bruises on her face were not serious. Only her composure seemed to have suffered, and she was doing her best to repair that. She had not deigned to ask Tagart who he was: she was trying, not very expertly, to give the impression that she regarded him, his questions, the rebellion, the whole upheaval of the Trundle, as impertinent vulgarities unworthy of her attention. Tagart felt himself losing patience with her. He had never encountered such a woman before. She bewildered him; he was unable to guess at, still less pursue, the line of interrogation that would tell him what he wanted to know.

'If you do not talk we will have to torture you.'

She gave him a reproachful glance.

'In your place I would be worried,' he said.

'In your place I would die of self disgust.'

He stood up, exasperated, and went to the window. If she were his woman, in the woods, at the camp, he would soon get the information out of her. These foreigners evidently allowed their women abnormal licence: he could no more understand it than he could fully take in all the marvels of the Trundle and the Flint Lord's residence. The paintings, the furniture, the simple fact that this was a shelter that went up in the air, the casual, easy mastery that was manifested in every incomprehensible joist and panel: it was all beyond him; he had no words for it. Compared with this one room, the whole of his culture was clumsy and pathetic. And this woman was unlike any he had ever met. He tried to imagine her in the company of the Flint Lord, serene, languorous, amusing. And yet she was not a foreigner in appearance, for she was dark, like a nomad.

He put his hand on the windowframe. The shutters were open, and he could see past the gate of the inner enclosure to the battlements, where two big clay cauldrons were being heated on beds of glowing charcoal.

'Has he always lived here?' Tagart said, without turning round. 'Or did he come from across the sea?'

'He was born in this house.'

An answer at last. 'Has the Trundle ever been taken before?'

'Perhaps.'

'In his lifetime?'

'I have never heard of it.'

'Does he have another woman he likes better than you?'

'You are impudent as well as stupid.'

'Then tell me why he does not care if you are killed.'

'I see how little you know about the Gehans,' she said, with every appearance of pride, but Tagart knew his question had touched a raw place. 'If Lord Brennis himself were your prisoner his men would ignore your demands. If they did otherwise he would kill them himself at the first opportunity, just as he is going to kill you tonight when he breaks down the gates, you and – '

Tagart did not wait to hear any more. Correy had called his name from the gatehouse: the second attack was about to start. Tagart snatched up his stormcoat and, pushing his arms into the sleeves, ran outside into the newly falling snow.

Soon after dusk one of Irdon's unit leaders, protected by a specially large shield, had tied the end of a long cable into a noose and dragged it to the aspen trunk. The savages had shot many arrows, at him and the cable, but he had retreated unharmed and the trunk had been safely and easily retrieved.

Gehan took a meal with Hewzane, Irdon, and a Vuchten commander, the senior man, named Speich. Now in his late forties, Speich kept his ash-blond beard and hair closely shorn. In the presence of superiors he was studiously correct, and allowed no expression of disapproval or disagreement to escape his lacklustre, pale blue eyes. He had achieved renown among his men for his surgical, mechanical fairness: they feared and loved him in equal parts. He belonged to the 'Garland', the inner circle of high-ranking officers whose loyalty to the Home Lord was beyond question. For the duration of the Brennis campaign he had been given charge of the whole Vuchten force.

'It will be as my lord desires,' he said.

Persuaded by Hewzane, Gehan had decided to keep the Vuchten in reserve from now on and use ordinary soldiers to breach the fort. There was no possibility of failure: the toster would be effective, but there would perhaps be further casualties and the Vuchten would be better employed in rounding up and dealing with the enemy once the gates were down.

Irdon glanced at Speich and for an unguarded moment compressed his lips in annoyance.

'Yes, Irdon?' Gehan said. 'Is there something you wish to say?'

'No, my lord.'

'Then let us go and see how quickly we can be back in our beds tonight.'

Gehan stood up and the meal was over. He led the way out of the tent – Ika had been moved to a warmer, more commodious shelter improvised from mine spars and skins – and saw the toster standing ready, sixty feet long, roofed with bark-clad planks, supported by twenty-five pairs of poles like the columns of a miniature but elongated pavilion. Blene had worked with impressive accuracy and speed. From conception to completion the toster had taken less than eight hours.

Snow was falling in small, busy flakes across the firelit clearing. Behind him Gehan was aware of, but did not turn to see, Ika's shelter. He clenched his fists and felt a shiver ripple through him as Irdon shouted orders and the harsh responses came. Gehan had found his love too late and she had been snatched away. What they had left him only mocked her former self; golden Ika had been smashed and trodden into the ground. For her and for what he had missed his grief was a gulf that fifty lifetimes could not fill. All his work had been undone. The campaign, the months and years of planning, his enormous debts to the Home Lord and Bohod Zein, the memory of Gehan First, of his father, the hopes and aspirations, the sense of destiny that had burned in him with a clear flame, everything, everything had been turned to dross. Even the fort had been entered and violated, and with his own men he was going to do it further damage. And yet, far down in the abyss of his suffering, he felt the glow of an illicit twinge of excitement. It was as if, by losing everything, he had moved closer to the brink, the edge of the sea that had tempted him all his life.

The men had taken their places.

Irdon shouted 'Forward!' and the unit leader at the head of the trunk repeated the order, using it to initiate the accelerating rhythm that would coordinate the men.

'For-*ward*! Ge-*han*! Ge-*han*! Ge-*han*!'

Gehan felt his blood stir as they all took up the chant and moved forward, away from the glare of the fires. He could still see the white-sprinkled roof of the toster and the men running beneath it, dark against the ground, heading for the greater darkness of the palisade. Beside him Hewzane said something he did not hear, for he felt himself being carried forward with the motion of his men. They were nearly at the gatehouse. Their chant had built into a run of irresistible speed: the end of the battering-ram would strike at the centre of the gates with a momentum that nothing could withstand.

Above them an illuminated rectangle, window-size, suddenly appeared. A wooden chute was thrust forth, and behind it some wide-mouthed object was steadily being raised.

'The cauldrons!' Hewzane said, but his words were buried by the crash of the impact and Gehan saw for himself the torrent of boiling lamp fat as it spewed from the chute and on to the men below. With the first screams of the scalded, a blazing brand was tossed from the window and the fat erupted in a writhing sheet of yellow flame that lit up the whole façade of the fort and residence: the palisade, the guard-towers, the battlements crowded with white faces. The front of the toster had collapsed. It had been let down with buckled knees by burning men, men in flames, and he saw them trying to crawl out, trapped underneath by the weight of timber and the trunk itself, drenched with fire. So many had fallen that those behind could no longer manoeuvre the toster. They were unable to move, unwilling to come out and show themselves, for arrows were already thudding into the planks above their heads. Some of the soldiers at the front, their clothes in flames, had pulled themselves free and were rolling in the snow, away from the inferno of burning fat. As they came into view of the battlements they were shot, each man, with one, two, or at most three, powerful and accurate arrows.

Gehan stared at the debacle. Lurid flame illuminated the gates and he could see now that the battering-ram had made scarcely any impression on them. The fort was intact, invincible, unassailable, as conceived and constructed by Gehan Brennis First. The savages had discovered its secrets, found out how to work it, even down to the siege weapons, to the chute that carried boiling fat safely beyond the cauldron-window and prevented the gatehouse from catching fire. They had, in the prescribed and regulation manner, delayed a few seconds before igniting the fat, thus giving it time to soak into the timbers of the toster and to liberally splash the soldiers' armour and clothing. They had turned the human and wooden debris under the gates into a hideous sort of wick. And they were still shooting his men.

'Withdraw,' he said to Irdon. 'Withdraw,' and there came to

his breath and almost found utterance a foul curse on Gehan First, on his father, even on himself, on all the Lords of Valdoe and all the Gehans of the Brennis line.

They had built the fort too well.

'Lord Brennis! Lord Brennis!'

'He won't answer,' Correy said.

'Lord Brennis!' Even in the open, here on the battlements, the stench of the fat-smoke was overpowering and Tagart had to pause to wipe his eyes before shouting again. 'Lord Brennis! You are the man we want! No one else! Come to the gates and surrender by dawn or we kill the hostages one by one! Starting with your wife!'

Below them the last of the soldiers had fled from the wreckage. The ground, dimly white, was strewn with bodies, the newly dead and the Vuchten who had perished in the first attempt, and among them were men who were still half alive, abandoned by their comrades.

'Lord Brennis! Listen to me!'

'He'll no more answer than he'll come at dawn,' Correy said.

'What then?' Tagart said. 'What will he do?'

'Let the hostages die. They expect to die anyway.'

'And then?'

Correy shrugged. 'He might try to make us waste our water with fire-arrows, that is if he doesn't care about burning down the gatehouse. Or he might decide on a tunnel. Or he might just do nothing. He can get all the supplies he wants from the villages.'

Tagart looked out across the spiked tops of the palisade logs to the Flint Lord's position. The fires were still burning; the army was still waiting. In the clearing where they had built the shield, Tagart could see new activity. More timbers were being brought. He saw a soldier kneeling on a trestle, his arm rising and falling with the blows of a carpenter's hatchet, and, lagging behind each stroke, the sound of chopping reached the battlements.

'What are they doing now?'

Correy could not say.

3

The rasping and hammering continued into the night. As far as could be seen from the battlements, the Flint Lord's carpenters were assembling some sort of framework. It seemed to be about fifteen feet long, built of rectangular-sectioned timbers from the mines. No one knew what it was for, though a few of the slaves said it was an earth-moving machine for digging a tunnel. Others thought it was a winch to pull down a section of the palisade. Others said it would be mounted on rollers and moved up to the gates, and in its shelter – the roof, if there was to be one, had yet to be fitted – soldiers with axes would cut through the hinge-posts, fix cables, and back away, dragging the gates with them.

Tagart was by now entering a high, giddy state of exhaustion. It was as if he had been awake for ever; he could not remember when last he had slept.

But he could not hope for rest just yet. First, an exact inventory of the food supply had to be taken. Closely rationed, there was enough to last for a month at most. Tagart ordered all the food and live animals to be brought to the residence and its grounds and placed under guard. Next he inspected the reservoirs. There were six, wooden-sided pits lined with clay and covered with boards. Each held seven or eight tons when full, but in the last few days, the slaves had told him, the supply had been allowed to run down and now perhaps ten tons remained in all. In addition there were two dewponds, now frozen, and butts fed by pipes from the roofs of the larger buildings. Several of these butts had been smashed by the slaves. Those still intact were emptied and their contents added to the reservoirs, which, like the food, were put under guard.

Next, with Fodich's help, he arranged a rota dividing his force into three equal shifts which would take it in turn to sleep. That done, he made sure that at all times, and at both gates, cauldrons of lamp-fat would be kept heated in readiness for further attacks. Finally he organized lookouts for the guard-towers, and, as a last act before going to the residence for a meagre meal and sleep, he put a man on the signal station to watch for Bubeck.

Bubeck had been separated from the other five prisoners and left in the snow, his ankles tied to his wrists. It was night; he was behind some tents or shelters and could not see the Trundle from here.

The other five were all slaves. At the village they had told the soldiers everything they knew. He himself had kept silent.

The massacre on Levin Down had been so rapid, so controlled, that nobody had known what to do. He and the rest of the force had counted on hiding in the woods. They had thought they would be safe.

He could not rid his mind of the pictures of irresistibly advancing armour and the beast-faces of the soldiers' masks. They had seized him and dragged him to the bottom of the hill where the Flint Lord had been waiting.

Since then he had been tortured twice. He had refused to agree to their demands. They had beaten him and he could no longer feel anything below his waist. His right wrist was broken. His breath was sliced into narrow gasps and he knew a splinter of rib was making him bleed inside. And now the soldiers were untying his bonds again and he was being helped along, his bare toes scraping the ice, through a corridor of tents and men and casually inquisitive glances.

They brought him to a warm fire by a tent where, seated on an upended log, was the General, Hewzane, the thin, fastidious man who had questioned him before. Snow was hissing into the flames; in the background were sounds of scrapers and sandstones.

Bubeck fell when the soldiers let him go and lay with his face near Hewzane's boots. One of the boots slowly came towards him and touched him on the collarbone. His shoulder was grasped and he was turned so that he could see Hewzane's patient, mock-benevolent smile.

'Have you reconsidered?'

At once Bubeck remembered his disdainful voice, associated it with the pain he had received.

'Will you speak to Shode and tell him to surrender?'

Bubeck shook his head doggedly.

'He must open the gates eventually. The longer he refuses, the harder it will go with him. You will be doing your people a service.' He smiled. 'I have heard they are counting on you to save them.'

He stood up and passed out of sight, walking round Bubeck in a circle. 'Do you hear the carpenters? At daybreak we shall take the fort back whether you cooperate or not. If you do as we ask, you will save the lives of your friends. If not, they will die. Which is it to be?'

Hewzane resumed his seat on the log and waited, the fingers of his left glove beating a slow tattoo on his knee. Behind him, beyond the tent, the carpenters were still at work. Bubeck did not know what they were making. He could hear a voice issuing instructions, a voice like Hewzane's, foreign, effete. None of the words could be made out.

'Are you sure you have nothing to say?'

Bubeck remained silent. For the first time, he knew that he was dying. General Hewzane, the fire, the sound of the sandstones, were receding; his thoughts were already far away, in another year, in a summer under the trees when he had been young and had known nothing about the world. When the soldiers had dropped him he had felt a great pain in his chest and now his life was leaking away. Nothing Hewzane said was important. He heard him speaking again, and the anger in his voice was no longer concealed.

'As you prefer. You have two hours to change your mind.'

And then, addressing his men, he said: 'Take him away.'

Tagart was asleep at last. He dreamed he was walking by the stream with Bubeck, but this was a Bubeck whose face was whole and unscarred. Tagart advised him to cross. Bubeck stepped on to the bridge and suddenly the water reared up. The water was fire and Bubeck was trapped and drowning in its centre, his features melting. Tagart shrank back towards the alder copse, unwilling to help him, afraid for his own safety, and he saw Bubeck's head and body become a blinding glow of light, brighter than the sun, unbearably brilliant.

Tagart woke up, shivering, feeling empty and sick. He

remembered where he was – on the floor of the Flint Lord's own chamber, lying on rush matting, Segle beside him. They had tried the strange, elevated bed, but found it uncomfortably soft, so had removed its covers and made their bed on the floor.

A lamp was still alight. The shutters behind it were of pale wood which cast a yellowness into the room, softening Segle's face. She was sleeping soundly, her mouth open a little, an arm thrown across his neck. Her lashes were long and thick, her nose small, her ears neatly formed and part hidden by her hair. Tagart caught himself studying her critically, comparing her with the Flint Lord's woman. In colouring they were alike, but Lady Brennis was older by a few years, more sensuous, and, about the eyes, she gave evidence of an understanding that Segle would never attain.

Gently he took Segle's arm from his neck and covered it with the furs. He shut his eyes. He had to rest, to refresh himself. Dawn was an hour away, perhaps less. With daylight there could be some fresh and more terrible onslaught. He would need to be alert.

Despite everything that was crowding his mind, despite his dream of Bubeck, he made himself relax, made himself shut down his thoughts and allow sleep to come. He was conscious of his woman's breathing, sharing her body-warmth. Except for the gentle and random creaking of timbers, the fort was quiet. From time to time there was a sound from the enclosure, a goat's bleat or the lowing of cattle. Occasionally voices could be heard. Tagart began to grow drowsy. He had left a guard by the door, and from the landing came a few words spoken in low tones: the guard had changed.

Tagart drifted towards sleep. He did not hear the door slowly opening, nor did he hear the careful footfalls on the rush matting. But he sensed the pressure of a man's weight on the floorboards and felt air currents moving, and it came to him that there was no cause for the guard to change, and with the thought he was rolling aside. Klay's axe, a full-sized felling axe swung from the shoulders, flashing downward in a powered arc, missed his temple by a finger's width and slammed into the crumple of bedding.

The force of the stroke caught Klay off balance. Tagart

grabbed hold of his leggings at one ankle and pulled with all his strength, reaching out with the other hand for the axe. Klay fell backwards and struck his head on the sharp corner of the dais.

Segle was awake and screaming as Tagart, still acting as by reflex, took firm hold on the axe-handle and rose to stand above Klay.

Although dazed by his fall, Klay knew enough to hold up his hands to ward off the blow. Anger filmed Tagart's vision and surged into a contraction of his muscles. Impervious to Segle's screams, he went up on his toes to give the axe its swing. All the weight of the preceding weeks and days and hours, like the weight of an immense stone blade, were bearing down on the flint edge, a hairline of intolerable pressure that could only be released in one place: in the head of his betrayer.

But, with the axe at its height, Tagart tottered and arrested his swing. He had overcome himself, and slowly he let gravity bring the axe to earth.

Then he saw that Klay was no longer holding up his hands. The eyes were blank: the sight had gone from them. Tagart let the axe go, knelt and lifted his shoulders. A wet gleam in his hair showed where the corner of the dais had split his skull.

Segle's screaming had become hysterical. She scrambled free of the bedding and put her head to Klay's breast, listening for his heart. She kissed his face again and again, prostrated herself across his chest, embraced him, put her face next to his, sobbing and calling his name.

Segle and Klay. The stories had been true.

For the moment Tagart could not absorb what Segle had done to him. On top of everything else, this was a trifle, unimportant. In a world where only fears came true and hopes were never realized, it was almost to be expected, of a pattern with the rest of it. But even as he stood watching them, he knew that, like bodily pain, this pain would not start with the making of the wound. It would come later.

She did not look up as he gathered his boots and stormcoat and went to the door.

'Take his body away,' he remembered saying to someone on the stairs.

As soon as he stepped outside, he realized that the hammering from the hillside had ceased.

Overnight snow had lined the enclosures and laid a fresh mantle along the roofs and palisades. Snowflakes were still floating down in the twilight before dawn. It had become very much colder; Tagart's mittens stuck to the rungs as he climbed the ladder to the battlements.

'They've moved it from the clearing,' said Correy, who was among those watching.

'I see it,' Tagart said.

'Are you ill?'

'No.'

The east was already pale, the ground beginning to brighten. At the front of the Flint Lord's position, a high scaffold or gantry could just be distinguished, its spars emerging from the night.

'They built it on its side,' Correy said. 'Now it's standing up.'

'What is it?'

No one knew. Gradually, under their eyes, the growing daylight showed them what had been made: a framework of timbers, somehow reminding Tagart of a huge stick-doll such as children played with in the camp. It was a puppet, a man, facing directly towards the south-west gatehouse. He was seated on the ground with his knees bent, his head and body leaning back at an angle. A concave seat or basket gave him what seemed to be a face. Connecting the flanks to the thighs were what appeared to be bundles of ropes. The knees were joined by a stout crossbar, and the base of the framework had, by the use of a roller, been made adjustable for rake. The whole construction was fixed to the ground with eight heavy piles.

Two soldiers went to the rear of the machine where, set on the frame, was a windlass with a four-spoked handle on either side of the drum. They set to work. One whole section of the machine, the part corresponding to the man's head and body, slowly tilted farther backwards and, when they had finished turning, came to rest in a nearly horizontal position, the basket-seat almost touching the drum of the windlass, which the soldiers locked in place.

The bundles between flanks and knees were not ropes at all. They were tendons, now stretched almost to breaking point by this act of turning which had reminded Tagart of drawing back an immense bow.

'It's a weapon!' Correy shouted.

'To your stations!'

Four more soldiers were approaching, carrying a man's body slung between them. They lifted it on to the seat; a block of wood was inserted between the windlass and frame, held there by the tension on the rope.

The corpse was that of an unusually large and heavy man. It hung there limply, head lolling back, arms loose, legs splayed. The darkness at the pubis formed an odd pattern and, even at this distance, Tagart could see that the corpse had been emasculated. He felt a foreboding of recognition. The chin was raised; the face was at an angle and could not be clearly seen, but he knew then that it would be scarred and misshapen, the left ear missing, the hair and beard tufted and sparse.

The Flint Lord came out of his tent, his breath like smoke. He was wearing the same grey cape, the same immaculate gauntlets and boots. He strolled to the machine. A soldier in dark grey took up an axe and went to stand by the windlass, awaiting a final order.

Standing beside the Flint Lord was another man in a fur cape. Tagart saw him raise a shouting-cone to his lips, and, in crisply enunciated words that penetrated the walls of the Trundle and reached the ears of those within, he delivered the message that was the prelude to the end.

'Slaves! Savages! We send you your saviour!'

Rising smoothly to his toes, the soldier with the axe paused at the height of his swing to confirm his aim, and swiftly and resolutely brought the blade down on the block.

The flint edge cut cleanly through the rope. The tendons, released from their torment, contracted so quickly that the uprights could not be seen in the moment before they slammed against the crossbar. The basket's load was ejected with a bang. It sailed upwards and towards the fort, a man's mutilated body, slowly turning, arms and legs flung wide. Tagart watched it clear the spikes on the gatehouse roof and saw it crumple against the ground, thirty yards inside the enclosure.

This too was a dream. It could not be true.

But the visage of the corpse, twisted by chance towards him, wore a death-grin that was too real for any dream.

And now, as the corpse lay in the enclosure, there was no reassuring white light to consume the horror of Bubeck's death. This flesh, propelled over the battlements as a grisly and symbolic warning, this was how the Flint Lord dealt with a man who had been revered, a chief, the choice of the Sun; and by this act he had announced the same summary fate for all those inside the fort.

4

The second projectile followed in a few minutes, when the cut end of the rope had been refastened and the drum rewound; but this time the load was the body of a living man, who survived just long enough after impact to gasp some unintelligible phrases. Four more living men followed one another at short intervals, thrown by the machine in paths of varying accuracy. One fell short; one struck the palisade and tumbled back into the ditch; two found their way over the battlements. Then, after a delay, corpses, both of men and women, the naked bodies of those slaves and nomads who had died on Levin Down, were hurled into the enclosure.

There was pandemonium. As each new body landed there were fresh cries from the slaves and many of the nomads, who had deserted their posts and wanted to risk their chances on the hill. However, as soon as Bubeck's body had been thrown over, a large contingent of soldiers had taken up a position on the north-east side of the fort, commanding the other gates. Despite their presence, a mob of slaves tried to open these gates anyway, and were only dissuaded by the rest with the use of force. And unknown to Tagart, a party of seven slaves on the eastern battlements found some rope and lowered themselves to the ground. They were seen, chased by three teams of soldiers, and clubbed down among the thorn scrub. Then their bodies were added to the pile waiting to be loaded on to the machine.

Besides the hostages and the hundred wounded in the barracks, there were just under three hundred people inside the fort. Over half were nomads; those from the Water Spirit were the most loyal to Tagart, who was doing everything possible to bring the slaves back under control.

They were going wild. Word had spread that spells had been cast on the bodies, that they were diseased, and, such was their fury to get out, a prolonged struggle took place at the south-west gates, directly opposite the Flint Lord's main position. The buttresses were thrown aside; the slaves clambered into the gatehouse and raised the locking-grid. They were fighting to open the gates themselves when it was realized that, for some time past, the bombardment had ceased.

Someone called out from a guard-tower. The machine had broken down.

'How long will it take to repair?' Hewzane said with acerbity. The whole effect of the bombardment, which had been his idea, was threatened by the incompetence of Blene and his gang of bunglers.

Blene was working with his men. He did not trouble to answer.

'Answer me or Lord Brennis,' Hewzane said. 'How long will it take?'

'Not long.'

Blene jumped down from the vurfer. One of the six great bundles of tendons had snapped near its point of insertion in the fixed part of the frame. As Hewzane watched, Blene's men continued to strip the broken bundle and prepare another.

'It's the cold,' Blene said, pulling on his gloves. 'We did our best to keep the tendons warm.'

The design was Blene's: he had based it on those he had seen in the homelands, siege-engines for flinging rocks and fireballs. But here, Hewzane had no wish to do needless damage to the fort, and so he had hit upon a novel way of achieving his ends. Gehan had readily consented, leaving Blene and Hewzane to work out the details.

From the five prisoners who had talked, Hewzane had ascertained that the savages in the fort were relying on the chieftain, the sixth prisoner, to save them. This man had been apprehended, partly by shrewdness, mainly by luck, in the thick of the fighting on Levin Down. He had expired under interrogation. After his body had been suitably prepared and thrown over the palisade, he had been followed to the vurfer by the other prisoners whom, as punishment for their loquacity, Hewzane had left alive.

During the night, teams of soldiers had brought the corpses from Levin Down. Other teams had been sent to local villages to procure, among other things, a supply of long tendons.

The vurfer's propulsive force, Hewzane admitted, had been estimated with commendable skill, but Blene's performance had otherwise left much to be desired. His shooting had been deplorable. To panic the slaves still more, Hewzane had wanted all the bodies landed in the same spot, on the roof of the little altar-house where the Trundle slaves were allowed to hold their services. None the less, the exercise had almost succeeded, as shown by the attempted escape of a few defenders from the eastern battlements, when, infuriatingly, this interruption had come.

'You'll pay for this, Blene,' Hewzane said, and returned to the shelter, where he had left Gehan sitting at Ika's bedside.

They both turned towards him as he entered, Ika with the uncertain expression and raised face of the newly blind, Gehan with an almost furtive look that Hewzane had never seen before.

'Well, Hewzane?' Gehan said, naming him for Ika's benefit. He rose to his feet. 'Well? What was it? What made them stop?'

Hewzane explained.

If not quite pleasing to Gehan, the news did not upset him greatly; it seemed instead to confirm him in some other course which he had already been considering eagerly. 'Come with me,' he said, taking Hewzane's elbow. Once outside, he began talking rapidly. He expressed the view that the bombardment could no longer succeed. Now that it had been interrupted, he felt, the savages would be able to recover their morale. The cumulative effect had been lost. Other tactics would be needed to get them out of the fort and avoid the deadlock of a siege. He suggested calling to their leader, Shode. The soldiers would offer to withdraw, and would indeed do so, allowing the defenders their freedom. Having left the Trundle, hindered by their wounded, they would of course be pursued and overtaken. Those who were able-bodied would be captured and returned to the slaves' quarters; the rest would be dispatched as worthless.

The idea, although dishonourable – in that it recognized the savages as equals who could be petitioned – was interesting, but behind Gehan's words Hewzane sensed something more.

It was as though his concern for the fort had been subordinated to an ulterior purpose. And so it proved.

'I want the man who blinded my sister,' Gehan went on. 'A slave. She doesn't know his name, but he was a pedlar, taken in the Village just after Goele. Rald knows his face. If they give up the man, we'll say the rest can go free.'

Hewzane was nonplussed. The implacable will that Gehan had displayed only the previous evening, the ability to keep his emotions in check, had, it seemed, been dealt a decisive final blow by the incident of the toster. During the night, Hewzane had watched his grasp on reality weakening still further. Over the past months he had become increasingly irrational. He had been subject to violent fluctuations in mood. His attention to detail had at times become obsessive; at other times he had maintained a lofty indifference to particulars, leaving his officers to arrange everything, careless of the extravagant cost of importing mercenaries from the Home Lord's army. The signs had been there, long before the campaign, even long before Hewzane's commission, and they had been observed not only by Hewzane, but by those abroad who were students of the island country and the wealth it promised, students who viewed with disfavour the independent turn taken by Brennis Fourth. Then there was the question of Ika, the unhealthy rumours that had been circulating. Since her arrival, Gehan's sanity had been eroding ever more quickly, and now, perhaps, with the events of the preceding day, he had come to the very borders of madness.

'See to it, then, Hewzane.'

'Very good, my lord.' He signalled to a man nearby. 'You! Fetch me the shouting-cone!'

Lady Brennis shuddered and tried to avert her face.

'Tell me!' Tagart said, and turned her chin so that her eyes were looking into his own. Her whole body was trembling; her composure had crumbled at last, unable to withstand this latest blow.

'Yes!' she cried. 'They slept together. He's in love with her and he's insane!'

They were upstairs in the bedchamber where Lady Brennis and Rian, her body-slave, had been confined. Tagart had run to the residence from the crowd in the outer enclosure. Although no one there knew anything about the Flint Lord's sister, Klay had been recognized from the General's description as the man the Flint Lord wanted. But Klay was dead and his body wrapped in furs, and no answer had yet been given.

Tagart went downstairs and started across the enclosure. Since the first hours of the siege, since fearing that Bubeck might not come, his mind had been almost permanently engaged in trying to solve the intractable problem which had its roots in a single fact: by shutting the gates, the nomads had cut themselves off from the outside world. The soldiers were free to draw on the resources of the countryside around them; they could change their position as they wished: they had no fixed or vulnerable point. In order to get at and kill the Flint Lord, these circumstances would have to change.

Tired and dispirited, he had tried again and again to arrive at a plan that might work, and every time he had failed. But he had never given up a glimmer of hope that Bubeck might come after all, and so the bleakness and finality of his failure had not confronted him in all its force. Only when he had seen Bubeck's body had he been compelled to accept the truth. It had shaken him and left him unable to think.

Tagart climbed into the gatehouse and took up the paper cone. The General was still standing by the machine, awaiting a reply.

This was the nomads' first and, perhaps, only chance. If Tagart wasted it, if the siege were allowed to develop to its inescapable conclusion, he knew that he and he alone would carry the blame: he alone would have committed the whole nomad nation to oblivion. It had given him its best warriors, the young men and women, and he had brought about their downfall. Half were already dead, heaped there in the enclosure or by the Flint Lord's machine. Those who had not joined the fight, those who had stayed behind in the winter camps, were the dependants, the children who could not look after themselves, and the old people who would be unable to breed a generation to replace the one he had destroyed. Unaided, they would linger for a time, like the prisoners in the fort, besieged by the forest, and one by one they would die. And although some of the children might survive, there would not be enough of them to maintain the old ways, and they too would eventually disappear.

Their future rested with him. If he ruined this chance, as he had ruined everything till now, it would be the end.

In all his life Tagart had never before recognized defeat. The elders had taught him their version of courage, a blend of tenacity and honour. He saw now that they knew nothing. They were innocents, like himself. The scale of their code was dwarfed by what was happening here; the Flint Lord was not an enemy that they would understand. He was a colossus, beyond evil, beyond humanity, beyond even the brain and body of one man. Somehow, among the villages and their fields, a monster had been spawned that might never be stopped.

His men served him, not for love, not for the respect that was all the reward the hunters ever craved, but for payment. If he was challenged by a man who could pay more, they would transfer their allegiance without a qualm; and, if that new master fell sick and died, they would go to whoever could pay them, and spit on his memory. These were the men who had built the machine, who were fitting new tendons, and one of them, their general, was standing there and waiting for an answer.

Tagart raised the cone. 'General! General! It is Shode!'

'Do you have the culprit?'

'We do!'

I fear treachery,' Gehan said. 'If I do as you suggest, there will be three of them, counting the prisoner, and two of us. I shall be in danger.'

The savages' leader was insisting on several conditions before giving up the guilty man. He had asked for the soldiers by the north-east gates to be recalled to the main company, and this had been done. He had then stipulated that the man was to be received by Gehan himself, alone and unarmed. He would be brought by the leader in person, also unarmed.

Gehan had refused this condition; it could have no object but to expose himself to attack. He had consulted Hewzane and Speich, the Vuchten commander. Hewzane had suggested a compromise: that each principal should be accompanied by a deputy. Gehan's would be Speich, an expert in close combat.

They were standing at the edge of the camp, the vurfer behind them; Blene had finished the repairs.

Impatient as Gehan was to apprehend the man who had blinded Ika, he had yet to lose either his caution or his common sense, and he found Hewzane's attitude quite inexplicable. They were very much in control: he saw no reason to yield to the savages' demands.

'But, my lord,' Hewzane said. 'If we refuse them this, they will not give up the man and your strategy will fail.'

Gehan studied him, and Speich. It was almost as if they wanted him to put his life at risk.

'Your argument is absurd,' he said. 'Tell them to send the man at once or the offer is forfeit.'

Gehan could see faces at the battlements, in the gatehouse, and someone was in the nearest guard-tower, leaning on the parapet and looking down. They had all been watching. Two of the savages had lowered a rope ladder and brought the guilty man across the snow, leaving him at a point that was out of range of Gehan's and their own archers. Two soldiers had then gone to collect him.

Gehan would give them no mercy. Their insolent presence on the battlements, the proprietary way they had taken over the fort, affronted him beyond measure. The Trundle was his inner house, and they had besmirched it, smashing and wrecking and killing like the animals they were. These alone were crimes enough; but they shrank to nothing beside what had been done to Ika. And now this. A corpse.

'He is the man,' Rald said.

Gehan tried to calm himself. 'Hewzane,' he said. 'We have wasted enough time on these vermin. We must get back into the Trundle.'

'I agree, my lord. We'll withdraw at once and allow them to escape.'

'No!'

'They have kept their part of it, my lord. We can pretend to do the same.'

'Their chief has shown himself a liar. He cannot be trusted. They will leave the fort on my terms, not his.'

'But – '

'Blene. Can you make fireballs?'

'We have enough netting,' Blene said. 'And some straw.'

'Lamp fat?'

'Pig fat. We got it from the villages last night.'

'Send for boulders. We'll burn down the gates.'

'Yes, my lord,' Blene said, and made as if to leave.

'One moment.' Gehan gestured at the body of the pedlar. 'This is to be our first fireball.'

Gehan went to Ika's shelter and let the entrance flap fall behind him. She turned her face; he crossed to the bed and reassured her with a touch of his hand. She put her own hand on his and held it to her breast.

'Stay with me.'

'Just for a little.' He sat down.

'Have you got him?'

'He's dead.'

'Dead?'

'Listen to me, Ika. We're going to take the fort back now. It may not be safe here. I want you to take Hewzane's dog-sledge and go with Rald to Eartham. Will you do that?'

She nodded.

'I'll send a man to bring you back.'

She transferred his hand to her lap and made a chaplet of it, counting the fingers over and over again as if they were the prayer-beads the villagers used in their supplications to the gods of earth and sky. Her head was wound with a new sheepskin bandage; her mouth, still the soft and voluptuous mouth he remembered, was moving in a silent petition. Was it only two nights ago? How different she looked now! And yet, the savages could not take away what had been. He had filled her; their union deserved to bring forth golden offspring. A son, a child to vie with Gehan First!

'What will you do with me?' she said.

'What a strange question!'

'Will we be together again?'

Gehan extricated his hand and began to rise. 'We will be together always.'

'As we were?' she said, anxiously lifting her face.

He kissed her lightly. 'I must go now, Ika. Don't be frightened.'

5

Ten tons of water: at two pints a day each, the supply would give out in less than a month. And each bucket being poured into the leather tank, bucket after bucket brought by human chain from the reservoirs, held one man's water for a week.

Everyone knew it. Very soon, the chain would break and the slaves would try to get out again. They had been quiet for a time, pacified by the hope that the Flint Lord would keep his promise to withdraw, until Klay's body had been set on fire and thrown from the machine. He had hit the gates and lain there, burning.

The slaves' panic had then been rekindled. Even before the first fireball landed there was yet another attempt to break out, restrained by violence. Then the slaves had been made to join the nomads in the work of preventing the gates from catching fire.

The ditch surrounding the palisade was nine feet deep: the two gatehouses were the prime targets for fire attack. This had been foreseen by those who had equipped the Trundle, and among the siege-goods stored under the battlements, Correy led Tagart to a contrivance which consisted of a collapsible frame supporting a large tank made of waterproof ox-hides sewn together with sealskin. A leather hose led from the front of the tank, near the ground, and to this fitted a pan-shaped box drilled on one face with many small holes.

When assembled, the tank occupied the best part of the floorspace in the gatehouse. The hose, fed out of the slit in the wall, could be manoeuvred by means of a hinged rod. Where the hose joined the tank there was a tourniquet to shut off the flow of water.

Tagart had left Correy in charge of directing the spray on to each fireball as it arrived. Made of chalk boulders covered with netting and stuffed with straw and wood and fat-soaked leather, the fireballs were coming at regular intervals, loaded with smooth efficiency on to the machine. The axe fell; the throwing-arm slammed against the crossbar; the blazing ball was launched in a roaring trajectory and fell against the gates, or against the palisade, rolling back into the ditch where it burned uselessly, or fell among the wreckage of bodies and timber left by previous attacks.

It was inconceivable that the Flint Lord was unaware of the low state of the water supply inside his own fort. As Correy had said, one of the purposes of a fire attack was to make the defenders waste their water and shorten the period of the siege. In effect the Flint Lord was saying to them: 'Either let the gates burn or yield to me when you are dying of thirst.' The slaves understood this only too well. At the rate at which the precious water was being passed up to the gatehouse and poured into the tank it would not be much longer before they abandoned their places in the chain and made a final effort to break out. Once the chain was broken, the fire would take hold, and the nomads would have no choice but to follow the slaves.

Tagart had not believed the General's offer to withdraw. He had known it for what it was, and had tried at all costs to keep the gates safely shut. But with the rejection of his conditions and the failure of his attempt to get within reach of the Flint Lord, he had, after considering whether to send an imposter or to go himself, decided he had little alternative but to give up Klay's body in case the offer was, after all, genuine.

If the soldiers had withdrawn then, he would have risked trying to run. But the whole army was still in its original position. What was more, none of the soldiers had returned to the north-east gates. In this Tagart saw not an oversight, but the shape of the Flint Lord's plan to recapture the fort. He was leaving the way clear for a breakout on the north-east side. Once it had started, he would move some of his men round the palisade and pursue those who had escaped, while other soldiers would enter the enclosure and chase those still within out through the gates and into the main position.

Tagart was in the day-room, discussing this with the other chiefs: they were agreed that the slaves would eventually succeed in breaking out. Unencumbered, making a break and trying to outdistance the soldiers was now the best and only chance of survival; but there were more than a hundred wounded to consider. Of these almost half were nomads. Some of the chiefs were in favour of taking the wounded nomads and leaving the wounded slaves, since their able-bodied comrades would have deserted them. Crow said that, if the breakout came as Tagart anticipated, there would be no hope of taking any wounded. Every man would have to escape the best he could: better that some should live than all should die. Any who could not walk, or run, for themselves would have to be left behind. With luck, they might be allowed to live as slaves. No more could be hoped for them.

Tagart wanted to, but could not, refute this appalling and ruthless reasoning. He had become numbed by the horror that bludgeoned him on all sides. After the meeting had broken up and the chiefs had gone back to the enclosure, he stood for a moment at the window, staring through the gateway of the inner palisade at the double line of people, one line passing full buckets forward, the other line passing them back, empty, to the reservoirs.

There were footfalls on the stairway behind him. Lady Brennis and her body-slave were coming down. Tagart had removed the guard from the door of her chamber: the man had been needed in the line.

She raised her eyes and glanced at him as she stepped on to the floor of the day-room, turning slightly to allow a bag, which was slung over her shoulder, to clear the staircase wall. She had changed her clothing. Instead of house-robe and slippers, Altheme was now wearing a thick fur jacket, hat and mittens, leggings and snowboots. Rian was also dressed for travel, and, like her mistress, was carrying a bag.

'May she fill it with food?' Altheme said.

Tagart nodded: Rian left in the direction of the kitchen.

'Do you want our help with the water?' Altheme said.

'No. Thank you.'

She looked anxiously outside.

'Where will you go?' he said.

At that instant there came shouts from the enclosure. Women were screaming. Tagart saw slaves throwing their buckets aside, running to catch and overtake the first few who had seized the initiative and begun the rush to the north-east gates. And with them, among the stampede, he saw nomads. He began to recognize some of those who had been defending the gate-house; and, as Rian returned from the kitchen, he saw Correy and then Crow running past.

He grasped Altheme by the wrist and followed.

Speich, the Vuchten commander, stood at the fore of his personal Grey Unit and felt his stomach fluttering with the old sensation he knew so well. It never changed. From the day of his first battle at the age of eight, through forty years of bloody campaigns and slave-raids in the glorious service of the Home Lord, this feeling was the truth and constant in his life. His palms were sweating; he tightened the bone-studded fingers and knuckles of his right gauntlet on the haft of his axe and prepared to meet the exhilarating moment when he and his men would be working as one.

The fire attack had succeeded in flushing the savages out of the far gates. Four hundred and seventy-five men, in two contingents of twelve and seven units each, had encompassed the walls of the Trundle and converged on the open gates; the larger contingent, led at his own insistence by Lord Brennis himself, was at this moment running down and recapturing the escapees. From here, where three Vuchten units had remained to guard the south-west gates, little of this battle could be seen, but flag signals were coming from the lookouts and keeping Speich informed.

The second contingent had fought its way into the enclosure and now, as Speich watched, the south-west gates opened and a stream of slaves spilled forth. They were scrambling over the smoking debris of the toster, the corpses, the battering-ram, the heap of burned-out fireballs, being chased by the soldiers, driven out of the fort and into the crescent-shaped formation which had Speich at its centre.

The slaves were coming closer.

'Units!' Speich shouted. 'As ordered and detailed! Pre-pare!'

After the losses at the village and in the attacks on the gates, Hewzane had given the commanders orders to regroup their teams and units. Fifteen units of Vuchten and seven of other men remained. The heaviest casualties had been among the common recruits from the homelands, then among the men of the Brennis barracks. The Vuchten had escaped lightly. They now outnumbered the other soldiers by more than two to one.

Along the curve came the soft sound of visors shutting.

'Ad-vance!'

The slaves, with a few savages, comprised mainly the old, women, and the walking wounded. They made little resistance. In a short time, all had been captured and bound hand and foot, strung together ready for sorting. Some would go back into the slaves' quarters. The rest would be destroyed. Meanwhile, the fort had been made secure and the Flint Lord's pennons were again raised into the wind.

Irdon, the Brennis commander, his breastplate smeared with blood, took off his helmet and put his hand to the back of his neck, twisting his head from side to side. He had led the seven units, four of them Vuchten, which had cleared the slaves from the fort.

'What are our orders now?' he asked Speich. 'Do we go back into the Trundle? Or do we support Lord Brennis on the hill?'

According to the flagmen, Lord Brennis had nearly finished and did not need support. Speich gave Irdon a long, calm look. His stomach had not stopped fluttering: this was the moment. It had been delayed, delayed again, by the sea, by the snow, by the superstition of Brennis Fifth and his soothsayer, and by the wholly unexpected invasion of the fort. Since yesterday the plan had been restructured, the details revised, Gehan's inclinations kept on course, guided by the sure, lucid logic of Hewzane's mind. The numbers had been carefully estimated, the casualties monitored and taken into account. On the hillside with Lord Brennis were eight units of Vuchten and four of his own men. The ratio here, at the main position, was the same: six to three. And it was a Vuchten unit that had stayed behind in the fort to secure the gates.

Irdon was waiting for an answer.

'You are my prisoner,' Speich told him quietly.

'In there! In there!'

Half running, half kicking their way downhill through the snow, they were trying to reach a broad, piebald expanse of gorse. They had been seen by the soldiers and were too far from the bottom of the hill to do anything now but hide and wait for night.

Fodich had nearly reached the first bushes.

'Into the middle!' Tagart shouted.

Beside him, just keeping up, were Altheme and Rian. They were at the rear of the group of eight or ten who had managed so far to evade the organized, systematic pursuit which had already claimed at least half of those who had escaped from the fort. Tagart had seen Crow being run down and killed, and he had looked back to see Segle captured and led away.

The soldiers, three hundred of them, had divided into a dozen parties. Each party, alone or in conjunction with others, had concentrated on one part of the hill, for the escaping nomads and slaves, on leaving the gates, had fanned out. Most had gone directly north-east, making straight for the forest. Few of these had succeeded, for they had attracted the largest number of soldiers. Tagart himself had turned left at the gates and started westwards.

The wind had strengthened and a near-horizontal blizzard was blowing from the north-west. Far below, in the safety of the valley, the fields of the settlement were blank, immaculate, their boundaries traced by white-drifted lines of spidery hawthorns. Between the fields and the fort, descending by steep scarps and slopes, the hill was patched with scrub.

Rian stumbled and as he helped her Tagart looked back once again. The soldiers were less than three hundred yards away now, a party of twenty-five in the brown armour of the Brennis barracks, carrying spears and axes. Behind him he thought he glimpsed ten or a dozen more, clad in black.

'Quickly! Into the middle!'

Heedless of the sharp green spines, they pushed branches aside and plunged after the others. The bushes were old and thick, in places towering above their heads, grudging, obstructive, barring their way with strong, springy arms densely dressed in painful prickles. Near the ground, where they had lost their needles, the branches were bare and peeling and snagged at their feet.

'Spread out!' Tagart cried. Ahead of him, the others had broken a passage through the gorse. They were making it easy for the soldiers to follow.

After struggling another fifty yards or so he judged that they had reached the middle of the thicket. In one hand he was holding an axe, which he had snatched up as he had left the fort. With the other hand he took hold of Rian's sleeve. 'Get down on the ground. Down there. Don't move.' He went on another few yards and called to her mistress, a little way to his right. 'Now you! Get down!' He found a place for himself. 'Everybody! Get down!'

As far as he could tell from their voices, the soldiers had stopped at the edge of the thicket and were debating what to do. He clenched his fists and shut his eyes, praying that they would be called away to search some more profitable spot. It was after midday. In two or three hours darkness would come and they would be safe.

One of the voices was raised in a shout.

'Altheme! Altheme! Altheme!'

'It's him!' she said. 'My husband!'

Tagart knew then that the soldiers would not be leaving. Others would be called; they would surround the thicket and move inwards. He had exchanged one trap for another, the Trundle for the gorse.

But, in making the exchange, he saw that he had suddenly earned the chance of one last, desperate attempt to achieve his goal, to redress in some measure all that had been sacrificed. His own life was now finished. It had finished with Bubeck, with Klay, with Segle. He would die here on the hill. But the manner of his death could redeem the futility of what he had done to his people. If he remained strong, if he took his chance and got close enough, he might yet kill the Flint Lord.

'Altheme! Altheme! Come out!'

Tagart crawled among the branches until he could see her face. 'You must go back to him,' he said. 'There is still time.'

'Altheme!'

'Do you order me to?'

'I cannot,' Tagart said. 'You are free to choose.'

'Then I choose to stay.'

'You know what will happen to you?'

'Yes.' She turned toward the place where Rian was hiding. 'Rian! There is no need for you to die!'

'No, my lady. I am free now. I'll stay with you.'

'Altheme!' the Flint Lord shouted. 'Altheme! We are going to burn the gorse! I have sent to the Trundle for fire! Come out while you can!'

Despite the snow, the bushes and the ground beneath were like tinder. With the wind blowing so strongly, everyone in the thicket would be burned alive.

'Would he burn his heir?' Tagart said.

'He thinks it is not his.'

Tagart met her eyes. 'What do you mean?'

'It does not matter now.'

'Tell me.'

'If you wish.' Quickly she explained about Bohod Zein, the agent from the homelands.

'Yet you were with child before then?'

'I was.'

'Could he be convinced? Could Rian convince him?'

'It is possible.'

'Then she must try.'

6

'And he says she will be released after dark, my lord, and allowed to go back to the fort, if you withdraw now.'

'Has he threatened to kill her?'

'No, my lord.'

'But he might, if I make a move. Is that it?'

'I cannot say, my lord.'

Gehan was torn between anger and concern for the child Altheme was carrying, a child which Rian had halfway persuaded him might be his own. A son! He remembered the moment in his chamber when he had struck Altheme. She had told him then, and he had not believed her.

He cared little for her any more; but if it were true – if she were bringing him an heir – he could not risk her life.

'What made her go with the savage?' he said to Rian. 'Why was she running away?'

'He took her hostage, my lord.'

'And you? Why did you run?'

'I am my lady's body-slave.'

With a curt gesture at Rian, Gehan turned to the leader of his black-armoured bodyguard. 'Tie her up. When we've finished here, she can go back to the slaves' quarters.'

'But my lord!' she protested. 'He said I was to – '

She was silenced; Gehan stood glaring at the thicket. Anger had made him take personal charge of his men to pursue the savages on the hillside. It was his first reaction now. He wanted to fire the gorse; but he allowed to himself that Altheme might get caught in the flames. The savages had, by implication, threatened to harm her if he sent in soldiers to drive them out. But the alternative, conceding to their demands and leaving, could not be tolerated. Besides, the word of the savages' leader meant nothing. If Gehan withdrew, he would never get Altheme back. She would be killed and left here.

He had no choice.

'Flush them out,' he said to the unit leader. 'Kill any you find, but bring Lady Brennis to me.'

The gorse thicket, sloping down in two directions across a crumbling scarp, was about a hundred and fifty paces across at its widest part, with an irregular outline like the coast of a dark, rocky island in a sea of white. At its edges were smaller islands, smaller clumps of gorse, but beyond them the ground was open, the surface of the snow humped with the suggestion of the tussocks below. The search had led Gehan and his men to the western part of the hill; the road to Apuldram and the south-west, its banks heaped with frozen slush, ran across the shoulder of land a little way above them.

'Look, my lord!' the unit leader said, before he had had time to act on Gehan's order. He pointed up towards the fort. Two units of Vuchten were descending. 'Shall we wait for them, my lord?'

'Yes. We'll surround the gorse and close in.'

Gehan watched the approaching Vuchten with satisfaction, his anger abating. Across the hillside, the exercise to catch the slaves and savages, which he himself had commanded, had been expertly and cleanly brought to its conclusion. Doubtless one or two slaves had managed to take refuge unseen; doubtless, in the zeal of the chase, one or two useful creatures had been inadvertently killed. On the whole, however, the invasion of Valdoe had been successfully dealt with, the rebellion quashed, the savages eliminated, the slaves restored to their proper quarters; and now the fort was again firmly in good hands.

Gehan smiled to himself. It seemed that the savages' force had consisted of the pick of the tribes from several, if not all, of the winter camps. The loss of these men would weaken for ever the tribes of the whole country, and not just those in the south. There was every chance that here in Brennis, as in the homelands, the savages could be permanently stamped out.

Tomorrow, he decided, he would rally his men and march north as planned. Undefended, its warriors' bodies here on the hill, the waterfall camp could be completely annihilated. From there, if the weather and supplies allowed, the army would continue to the eastern camp and destroy that, and perhaps the western and northern camps also.

He reflected that, in some ways, the turn of events had proved more satisfactory than the original plan. Although the fort had been damaged and four whole units had been ambushed on the Bow Hill road, other casualties among the soldiers had been no worse than might have been anticipated in a straightforward campaign. Among the Vuchten, particularly, losses had been slight, which would reduce the burden of wound-fees and death-sums payable to the Home Lord.

From the military viewpoint, Gehan had turned the invasion to his advantage. The savages, the object of his campaign, could now be wholly exterminated; the work of forest clearance and expansion could begin unimpeded in the spring, and proceed without a check until the whole island was under cultivation and under his control.

These thoughts had occupied only a moment; but his mind darkened as he realized that not once had they dwelt on Ika. Compared with her loss this reckoning of wound-fees was shameful and petty. Yet he saw now that this was the way he had been trained. Since boyhood he had been forced into the rigid military ideal, forced to dissociate himself from weakness, from his feelings, forced to prepare for the day when he became the Flint Lord. He had accepted the burden, embraced it, discharged his duty with diligence and skill, and in so doing had become a man split in two. His destiny, the heritage of Gehan First, called for single-mindedness; and he had striven continually and at great cost to himself to conform and to yield that which his duty demanded. He had left his feelings behind, drifting farther and farther from ordinary humanity. He had made himself deaf to the tiny whispering doubts which once had plagued him. Altheme was the personification of those doubts. In rejecting her and reaching for Ika, he had tried to close the chasm inside himself by denying its existence. But now Ika was destroyed and his need of her was over. He had transcended his dilemma: he was free. He was the master of himself, strong, enduring, like the hill, like the landscape and the climate of this land he had once imagined he could possess. He felt again the thrill he had known when watching the toster, and now realized that this was the most important part of him. It was the truth. It told him that the world, and all that was in it, were valueless compared with the reality and growth of his own spirit. To be free to cast away his heritage and all that was precious, to see it trampled and befouled, and not to care: this was a luxury sweeter than could be imagined.

His vision had suddenly cleared: he saw everything as it was. No longer would he be a slave of Valdoe. He would use Valdoe, as it deserved to be used, as an adjunct to himself. His duties would now be self-determined; no more would he chase the impossible phantoms conjured up by the memories of his father and Gehan First. Because it suited him, he would continue as Lord of Valdoe, and, if Altheme gave him a son, Valdoe would be bequeathed to Brennis Gehan Sixth.

She was in the gorse with the savages. He would get her out, with the help of the Vuchten units: they were now only a hundred yards away, approaching at battle-pace.

Gehan stood his ground, waiting to speak to their commander.

Tagart had known from the first that the Flint Lord would not accept the terms he had set. He had wanted Rian's message only to delay the search and to stop the soldiers using fire, and to give himself more time to reach the edge of the thicket undetected.

His face was bleeding, jabbed and scratched again and again by the fierce spines. In his flight from the fort he had left his mittens behind, and his hands too were bleeding, making the axe-handle sticky.

Close by, in the sound of the blizzard, he could hear voices. Each prick of the gorse, each moment spent negotiating a branch that had blocked his passage through the thicket, had spread fear into his body, and now he had to force himself inch by inch to crawl forward.

He moved aside another branch and saw that he had come to the last bush, exactly opposite the Flint Lord. For a few seconds Tagart watched him through the dark network of the gorse, his cape cloud-grey against the rising snowfield of the hill. He was not five strides away, and the way was open. The men in black armour, his bodyguards, were beside him, and Tagart was close enough to see their eyes and hear one of them hawk before spitting sideways into the snow. If Tagart moved now, if he burst through the last branches and ran, axe high, he would be able to fell him: with one blow he could kill the Flint Lord before his bodyguards had time to react. The Flint Lord's back was turned: he was looking up towards the fort.

Tagart edged forward to see what had attracted his attention. It cost him his chance; he had delayed and let the moment slip, for as he saw the Vuchten coming, the bodyguards moved stiffly into formation, a three-sided box surrounding their master and open at the front, and the back rank was between the Flint Lord and Tagart.

He watched the Vuchten drawing near. Again he saw the grotesque and sinister forms of their masks – their visors had been lowered and they were coming at speed, spears held ready. From the Flint Lord's men came a shout of recognition and welcome, and for that instant Tagart shared their belief that the Vuchten had come to help in the search for Lady Brennis. But before Tagart's dread had taken shape, his belief, like theirs, was twisting aside. The charcoal-grey breastplates and vambraces, the fur capes and leggings, the snow-caked combat boots kicking powder in the mechanical unison of their run: these were a preordained force, like an avalanche that could not be stopped by mere words and a shout of appeasing welcome. Their spears were not being lowered. They were coming on, ten yards from the Brennis soldiers, five, and from the expressionless beast-faces came a chant, a blood-chilling double chant of *Ge-han Ge-han Ge-han*, and then the Vuchten were colliding with the brown-armoured men in a confusion of spears and screams. Grey and brown armour thudded together; spears were locked and raised to the sky, falling, drooping, as brute strength overpowered brute strength or from behind came an enemy's crippling thrust. Axes were being brought into use, and stone hammers with flailing heads on loose thongs. Tagart saw a man's helmet struck and stoved, his skull smashed. He saw a grey soldier run through, the flint spearhead puncturing his cape and backplate with a creaking report and bulging the leather at his breast before the point broke through, bringing with it a vivid gush as from a burst bladder. Where the browns were alone they were falling one after another to the greys, the Vuchten, who in numbers alone overwhelmed them; but where they were mingled with the blacks, the

Flint Lord's bodyguards, wielding black-bladed axes and black spears, the fighting was so ferocious that even the Vuchten were intimidated, and grey after grey was going down.

Vainly Tagart searched among them for a glimpse of the man they were fighting over, but it seemed he had disappeared, swallowed up by the blizzard and the battle, the shouts and screams of pain and the clashing of wood and horn and stone. Then Tagart looked uphill and to the right. The Flint Lord, in his grey cape, holding a spear, had passed unnoticed between the fighting and the gorse and was now fleeing, staggering and struggling through the snow, putting yards behind him, making for the Apuldram road.

Before he knew what he was doing, Tagart had left the thicket and was running too, past the fighting men and on to the open hill. He felt the wind stinging his face. On his right was the darkness of the gorse; on his left the whiteness rising steeply to the fort. The battle was behind him. He fixed his eyes on the single figure ahead and with new resolve forced himself upwards through the fresh furrow of the Flint Lord's tracks.

The snow here was deep and crusted and dragged at the legs, hampering progress, giving Tagart the advantage. He quickly began to gain, and as he gained he felt the shape of something evil inside him and the promise that it could be set free. His fear was forgotten. He let his axe swing wildly in compensation as he ran, keeping his balance, his boots finding the very pockets of snow and shade that had just been trodden by his prey: for this had become for Tagart a chase, the most important of his life, an ecstatic hunt to catch and in a frenzy of blood and elation to find release from the monster he had vowed to destroy.

The road was still a hundred yards away; the Flint Lord was labouring towards it as if towards an unattainable summit, every fourth or fifth step using the spear as a staff. In his movements he appeared to be stunned, uncoordinated, fleeing from the incomprehensible forces that had been unleashed below. He was veering away from the stench of betrayal that hung over the fort; he was toiling towards the road that Tagart knew would lead him to his ships. His army and power had been stripped from him, and now just his own flesh and sinews and a hundred yards of Valdoe Hill lay between him and the way to safety.

He paused to glance back at the battle and noticed Tagart for the first time, ten yards from him, following his tracks. He turned and half-heartedly made as if to climb again, seemed to change his mind and turned back, spear in hand, to face his pursuer.

Tagart sensed weakness. He was aware of the spear, but did not slow his pace. He prepared to swing the axe for the first disarming blow, to knock the spear aside, and in a rush, in a single impression before the collision, he saw the Flint Lord in close detail, his blood-blotched ermine tunic, his cape in the wind, his blond beard and dishevelled hair, and his eyes: grey, remote, contemptuous, and in them alone Tagart saw that the weakness had been no more than a feint. And in a masterly, graceful movement, the exposition of years of weapons training and practice, the Flint Lord was floating backwards and to the right. The axe missed its target and sliced into the snow, pulling Tagart forward. He tripped and went down, his face ploughing into the crust of ice.

The spear hit him with the impact of a heavy inconceivably thick bludgeon, in the back, below his left shoulderblade. It cut deep into his body before the blade twisted and was wrenched away.

His hands outstretched, his face rigid, Tagart rolled on to his side. He looked and through his agony saw the Flint Lord receding. He wanted to crawl after him, but everything tilted and ahead there was nothing but a grey sky streaked with snow. The streaks made the sound of the blizzard, piercing and cold, the remorseless breath of the Ice God, demanding Tagart's warmth, and slowly he felt his fingers taken by the snow and turned to crystal as a gift for the Moon. The winter was filling his body, pouring in through the breach in his back. He opened his eyes and was under water, under a white, limitless sea.

Then he raised himself above the snow and saw the cloud-clad figure of the Ice God, clambering over the wall of frozen slush at the roadside.

Tagart cried out and let his face fall forward.

7

During the retaking of the Trundle, Hewzane had followed Irdon's units to the north-east gates. There he had lingered, at a distance, until the fort had been cleared and made safe.

From the roof of the residence he had watched Speich capturing Irdon's men. He had also watched the progress of Gehan's exercise on the far side of the hill. Gehan himself had been lost to view when Hewzane had judged that most of the slaves and savages had been killed or returned in bonds to the Trundle, enabling the signal – green pennons hung from the guard-towers – to be given for the Vuchten to attack the Brennis soldiers.

Two Vuchten units, led by the commander who was second in authority to Speich, had been briefed to shadow Gehan and wait for the green pennons. The other Vuchten were to take their lead from these two units. Their orders were to capture rather than wound, and wound rather than kill, all the Brennis men, except Gehan's bodyguard and those soldiers actually with him at the time of the attack. Gehan himself was to be unharmed: the Home Lord wanted him alive.

With the attack under way and the outcome assured, Hewzane went down to the main enclosure to inspect the captives. They had been tied together and herded into four groups in the shelter of the north-western palisade. The snow-storm had worsened. Hewzane fastened the collar of his fur cape as he crossed the enclosure, Speich at his side.

Even this part of the operation had been meticulously planned by Hewzane and, in accordance with his orders, Speich's men were already processing the largest of the four groups, the slaves and miners. The healthy ones were being stripped, searched, and conducted to the slaves' quarters, which had been temporarily repaired. The injured were being assessed by the unit leaders and their fate decided. If they could walk and lift a small boulder they were deemed healthy. The rest were dragged or carried to the north-east gates, where, in full view of the other captives, they were being brutally dispatched by Vuchten with axes.

The second group, those savages who had either been left behind in the fort or brought from the hill, would be carefully examined and any potential slaves picked out. The third group, the Trundle freemen who had survived the rebellion, would be closely questioned. Any who showed a trace of loyalty to the Brennis Gehans would be put into the mines.

The last group, almost as numerous as the slaves, consisted of the vanquished and dejected Brennis soldiers. Those who could not be trusted would provide a useful source of further slaves; and the men of Hewzane's old command, in the outer forts, would be brought to the Trundle by false signals and given the choice between service in the barracks or at the chalk face.

Many slaves would be needed in the coming months. The Bow Hill workforce had been lost. The Trundle had suffered much damage. The mining schedule was behind: hundreds of essential timbers had been wasted and would have to be replaced. Tree-cutting in midwinter was a hazardous and time-consuming operation. Then, when the thaw came, there was a variety of other works to be put in hand, in accordance with the Home Lord's wishes. Concurrently with the programme of forest clearance, new outer forts would be built, and these of course would need new roads, bridges, ferry stations. The villages could supply some of the labour, forced if need be, for the laxity with which the farmers had been treated hitherto was now a thing of the past.

So too with the savages. In a way, their unexpected appearance had not been entirely unwelcome to Hewzane. They had spared him the unpleasantness of executing Larr, his fellow general, who would doubtless have remained loyal to Gehan. They had also, albeit, unwittingly, speeded the outcome of the Home Lord's design to win back the island country.

The original plot, known only to Hewzane and then to Speich, had planned to use the attack on the savages' camp to deplete the number of Brennis men. Then, on the return journey, well away from the Trundle and the outer forts, the Vuchten were to have turned on the other soldiers and killed them. In this way not only would Valdoe have been taken with the minimum disruption, but the lesser problem of the savages – rightly seen by Gehan as an obstacle to expansion – would have been solved at small cost, for Bohod Zein, who was not a party to the scheme, would be free to apply to Gehan as vigorously as he wished for the recovery of his debts. Bohod Zein's interests on the mainland were anyway too large for him to risk the displeasure of the Home Lord. The mortgages would be revoked, and Valdoe given a clean start.

The Home Lord's plan had been upset by the arrival of the savages, but his larger design had remained unhindered. Valdoe had been seized, the resident army crushed, and now, after the loss of so many warriors, the savages' camps were ideally vulnerable. In the next few days, Hewzane would launch a heavy force against them. The vermin, as Gehan had so aptly termed them, would be stamped out in their winter nests and never allowed to infest the island country again.

Of the sorry examples standing before him, in the second group of captives, Hewzane could see few who would make suitable slaves. Their leader, Shode, was not among them. Presumably he had been killed by Gehan's men. But Shode's woman, a girl of perhaps twenty, perhaps less, had been pointed out to the soldiers by some of the more garrulous and contritely toadying slaves.

'Bring her forward,' Hewzane said.

Cleaned up, she might be amusing, and for a moment Hewzane toyed with the idea of sending her to the residence. But then, remembering what she was, a faint shiver of repugnance passed through him.

'Take her for your men,' he said to Speich. 'And pick out any others you think might be suitable.'

The Vuchten continued with their work. Just outside the gates, the pile of bodies was growing. They would be taken down the hill later and left for the ravens.

The scene at the gates was having its expected effect on the other captives. Most of the freemen had renounced Brennis Gehan and were vowing undying devotion to the Home Lord who, through the heroic bravery of General Hewzane, had released them from lifelong and grinding tyranny. But some were silent, and among them Hewzane caught sight of Blene, one of the few Trundlemen to have survived. Blene's eyes were not drawn to the gates: they were instead following Hewzane and Speich as they moved along the line. Their expression bespoke hatred of Hewzane and loyalty to the old order. Hewzane sighed inwardly. Although, as a man, he disliked Blene, his talents were undeniable and would have proved useful in the months to come.

'That one,' Hewzane said, pointing him out, 'is to join the mine slaves.' The thought of Blene toiling in the galleries tickled Hewzane's sense of irony and he smiled thinly. The smile vanished: Blene's technical knowledge would present a continuing risk of sabotage which could not be suffered to remain.

'No,' Hewzane decided. 'Take him out and kill him.'

'Look there,' said Speich, inclining his head toward the gates, where a Vuchten unit leader, one of the men detailed to capture Gehan, was making his way into the enclosure. He was alone. His weapon, his helmet, even his cape had gone; there was blood on his face.

Anxiety gripped Hewzane's heart. He and Speich went to meet the approaching man.

'I make no excuses,' the unit leader said, when he had finished his story.

'Are you wounded?' Speich asked him.

'No, sir.'

'Then go back and help your men.'

Fifty Vuchten had been sent to capture Gehan, and they had failed. Forty-three, including their commander, had been killed or incapacitated in the battle with Gehan's bodyguards, who, together with a unit of Brennis soldiers, had allowed Gehan to make good his escape. All the bodyguards and soldiers had now been killed, but the damage had been done.

Gehan had been glimpsed running for the road to Apuldram, something which Hewzane should have foreseen and provided against: for there were loyal Brennis men at the worksheds and two ships in the creek, both seaworthy, and now, at mid afternoon, the tide was high and on the turn.

Five of the Vuchten had already gone in pursuit. They would not be enough.

'Speich,' Hewzane said. 'Take your Grey Unit. Bring him back.'

'I will,' Speich said, and, scarcely pausing, he added: 'My lord.'

Plastered with snow on its windward side, the figurehead of the *Kormoran* nodded and rolled with the glossy black waves which, spumed and threaded with white, were being driven by the blizzard to break about the waterline and send spray over the deck and the icicle-hung rigging. The ship had turned into the wind: snow-blind, the jet and ivory head of the cormorant, fantastically styled with arched neck and hooked bill, had come to face the rough width of Apuldram Channel and the wintry saltmarshes beyond. At the next mooring, riding its cable with the same measure but to a different time, a larger, less elegant vessel, the *Empire*, kept parallel company. Thirty yards of cold water separated them from the landing stages, where a big upturned coracle waited to be launched.

A wisp of smoke showed from the roof-hole in the main workshed. Everything seemed to be normal. Gehan hesitated no longer. He went to the door and threw it open.

Two men were inside, cross-legged on the floor, engrossed in some gambling game played with bone counters. They struggled to their feet and saluted him.

'Where is the harbour Trundleman?'

'Asleep, my lord. Our work is finished for today. We – '

'Get him at once.'

The older man hurried outside. Gehan followed him to the door and yet again scanned the road from the fort. It emerged from the trees two or three hundred yards away and to the left, and in a gentle curve arrived at the precinct of the worksheds. The main shed was nearest the water, with removable panels along one wall to give access to the repair shop and storage loft. Next to it was a general storehouse, a seasoning shed, a boat-building shed, and, at the edge of the little group of buildings, stood the sail tannery, which smelled of rotting fish and urine and gave Apuldram its own peculiar odour.

The road was empty.

'You,' Gehan said to the other man. 'Come here. If you see anyone on the road, tell me immediately.'

Gehan wiped his brow, took off his cape and, though he wanted nothing more than to sit down and rest, went to a trestle table where the two men's afternoon meal was half finished. He ate without knowing that he was pushing into his mouth, bread, salt fish, cheese honeycake, indiscriminately mixed with beer drunk straight from a wooden jug. His heart was still hammering: he had run and slithered more than three miles without a break, not knowing how close pursuit might be, not even knowing if Apuldram would be safe. He was not used to heavy exertion. He found his hands refusing to respond properly; and he felt as if a broad strap were being tightened about his chest.

'Lord Brennis!'

As Gehan turned he clumsily knocked over the jug: beer flooded the table and dripped to the floor.

The harbour Trundleman, Tain, moved through the bluish rectangle of the doorway, a man of forty, bald and grizzled, wearing a fur and sealskin jacket with sheepskin lining and leggings. Like the men who worked under him, maintaining, repairing, building, and often sailing the Valdoe ships and boats, he was of a breed drawn from those coastal villages which fished as well as farmed. He had lived with the sea all his life; he knew every yard of coast for a hundred miles to east and west. At a glance he took in Gehan's appearance, the abandoned gambling-game, the beer dripping to the floor.

'Is the *Kormoran* ready for sea?' Gehan said.

A look of alarm crossed Tain's face. 'Not in this wind. It would not be safe.'

'But is she ready?'

'She can be made so in a few minutes.'

'Then do it. Quickly. And I want you to scuttle the *Empire*.' Now the Trundleman was openly astonished.

'Sink her. Do it now.'

The rest of the harbour men, half a dozen in all, had gathered meanwhile outside the door. Most were middle-aged or old like Tain, with sheepskin or doeskin jackets and capes. One had lost a hand, another walked with a bad limp, but all were skilled men. Tain sent them to their work.

'Do you keep snowshoes here?'

'Yes, my lord.'

'I want a man to go to Harting fort with a message for Commander Awach.' Again Gehan looked out of the doorway towards the empty road. 'The message is this. There has been a mutiny at the Trundle. The Vuchten have attacked my men. Awach must signal all the western forts, including Bow Hill. On no account are any instructions from the Trundle to be heeded. The secondary forts are to be kept sealed until my orders come. These orders will be coded with the word . . . cormorant. Is that clear?'

The Trundleman repeated the message without fault. 'I have just the man to send, my lord.'

'The rest of you will come with me. We'll sail east and beach below Cissbury fort.'

Outside, in the creek, axes were sounding in the hull of the *Empire*. The coracle's painter had been tied to the sternpost; the men had already freed the *Kormoran*, which was being drawn on a long cable towards the shore. Plaited rush fenders crushed and squeaked against the frozen timbers of the landing stage, and the hawsers were looped and knotted round two oak bollards.

The youngest and fittest of the harbour men, given a storm-coat, backpack, and snowshoes, set out for Harting and Commander Awach. For the first half mile he was to follow the edge of the creek, leaving no tracks.

The *Empire* started to list. Two men appeared on deck, clambering free of the fountains of dark water gushing in from below. They let themselves down into the coracle, cast off, and paddled back to help their comrades carry sails and essential gear from the sheds to the *Kormoran*.

In his haste to be gone, Gehan joined in the work, with numb fingers helping to rig the mainsail and raise the boom. He scarcely looked at the *Empire* as it upended and, in a boiling rush of bubbles, sank into the mud at the bottom of the creek. Briefly its prow reared into the air for the last time, high, defiant, hovering uncertainly between life and death. The figurehead, the emblem of the Gehans, a lavishly carved serpent picked out in scarlet and green, stared indifferently into the blizzard and began its slide to oblivion.

'My lord! Look! The road!'

Five men with spears, a team of soldiers, Vuchten, had appeared between the trees, and were running toward the worksheds. A team of Vuchtėn against five old men: Gehan would stand no chance.

'Get aboard!' he shouted to the three who were still by the sheds. They dropped their bundles and ran to the ship. With the Vuchten less than two hundred yards away, they freed the hawsers and scrambled up the gangplank, while the others, Gehan included, found poles and tried to push the *Kormoran* into the current, against the full force of the blizzard.

But the wind was in the north-west, blowing onshore. Like a sentient, malevolent being, it was keeping the ship pinned to the landing stage. A strip of water appeared below Gehan's pole, narrowed, widened, narrowed; he looked up and saw the Vuchten almost at the main shed.

As they reached its precinct, Gehan heard a violent commotion above and behind him: the sound of tearing ropes, a sudden cascade of opening leather. There was a bang, a squeal of sheets running in their blocks, and with a jolt that shook the whole fabric of the ship the boom swept the afterdeck and was checked. The mainsail had come undone. Instantaneously the wind surged against the expanse of russet leather; the *Kormoran* heeled over against the landing stage, water flooding over the gunwale and rising up the deck. Gehan clawed at the shrouds to stop himself from falling. There was screaming below him, to his left. The Trundleman had been hit by the boom and knocked overboard, trapped between the hull and a pile of the landing stage. And, despite its list, the *Kormoran* was slowly moving forward, timber grinding on timber. Gehan saw Tain being rolled and crushed into the weeds and barnacles before his body was released and floated into the water with the motion of the ship; and they were beyond the landing stage, out of control, veering with the wind and running diagonally across the few yards that separated them from the shoals at the creek's edge.

The *Kormoran* ran into the stones at speed. The port bow crunched and splintered. The shrouds sliced into Gehan's fingers: he lost his grip and was flung forward, his feet fouling something on the deck.

The water hit the side of his face like a slab of granite. Splinters of rock were thrust into his sinuses. Membranes burst with the green tons of water pressing down from above. He was upside-down, his face being driven into the stones, and the green was changing to black, the solid universe black of the hull rolling on top of him, and his legs were caught, tangled with the rigging. His back was breaking.

And then the *Kormoran* was free, moving into deep water. Beside him Tain was hauling on a rope, bringing the boom under control. The mainsail filled again and Gehan felt the whole ship grow taut. It leaped forward, running with the wind, plunging joyously into the storm. Pellets of freezing spray stung his face and drenched his clothes. He looked back and already the Vuchten and the Trundle and the scenery of his life were becoming small.

At the tiller stood the man with one hand, watching the vast skyward sweep of leather. On either shore the snow and scrub were sliding past. They passed Cobnor Point and turned southward, leaving it for ever, carried by the eager tide into the open estuary. Over Pilsey Island which he knew so well, low and flat, he saw a congregation of tiny shorebirds, flying in a cloud that changed from dark to light as with one will they changed direction and turned to show their breasts. And here, at the prow, his own cormorant, the raven of the sea, was marking his course in jet and ivory and leading him to sanctuary.

From brown water they moved into grey, into the broad ocean, and now the waves were breaking over the bows and the wind was in his face. The ship was disintegrating, its passage done. He called to his men and felt the wind under his wings and he was being lifted clear. Below him the boards were breaking and the sails shredding with the spindrift and the storm. He saw his men in the sea. Their heads were bobbing, their hands and arms clutching at wreckage. He soared on wide wings and they were drowning below, but he was free. He was no longer a raven: he was an eagle, borne in majesty to the heights where sea and sky were one, out of the blizzard, out of the clouds and into the sun.

8

Tagart was not dead. He had been lying here alone for a long time, and he was not dead. Voices had come and gone away again, but now he was not certain that he had not imagined them. Twice he had raised his head and dimly seen the snow. The first time he remembered seeing the Flint Lord. The second time the Flint Lord had not been there, and it had stopped snowing, and the sky was darker, and to keep himself alive he was trying to discover whether the voices had been real and whether they had come before or after the second time. The thread of memory was fragile and difficult to follow, dissolved by pain.

He had known pain before, but never like this.

Never like this.

He seemed to be waking, and there was a voice again. He was confused. Was this one of the voices he had heard before? Or was this imaginary too? But it was a voice he knew, and it was speaking a familiar word, a word from his old life, before his back had been opened.

'Shode! Shode!'

It was Fodich's voice, and he remembered then that he was no longer lying alone on the hillside. Fodich and another man had come for him some time before dusk and carried him to the thicket. They had laid him face down on something soft, massaged his hands and feet and covered him with furs. He had listened to them talking. Rian had been taken by the soldiers and they were worried that she might tell them that Altheme was still in the gorse. After that the furs had been removed. Someone had touched Tagart's wound and started to clean it and he had lost consciousness.

There had been some daylight left then; now it was dark.

'Shode! Shode!'

Long ago, in his sleep, Tagart had known that Fodich and Altheme and all the others in the gorse were dead, surrounded by the soldiers, burned alive. He had even seen the orange flames, black smoke drifting down the hill; but it seemed the smoke had been in sunshine and in this he was mistaken too. He had thought Fodich and the others were dead. He had thought he would have to crawl away from here by himself.

But it was not true.

He was here with them, in safety and shelter. They would help him and heal his wound.

Tagart reached out his hand.

'We want to lift you now,' Fodich said. 'We're going back to the forest.'

Tagart stretched his hand further, to confirm the sound of Fodich's voice, to confirm that Altheme was kneeling beside him and speaking too.

He felt his fingers move. He touched the hard spikes of gorse. He touched the spears and icicles, the palisade. The fort was under his fingers, black, a few lights twinkling. By his grip he could crush it, crush the Trundle, crush the Flint Lord.

But when he closed his hand they had already picked him up and were carrying him away.

The Earth Goddess

Part 1

1

In the grounds below his fortress Lord Heite, Gehan of the Gehans, had built a small pavilion by the lake. On spring mornings such as this he liked – when the burden of his duties allowed – to come here to meditate or perhaps to receive in privacy an especially favoured guest. Constructed of fragrant timber, five-sided, and with a gently sloping roof, the pavilion stood at the very water's edge and allowed the occupants to hear each nuance of the quiet surge of ripples on the shore. The sun had just come out: the ripples were being repeated as a network of light on the cedar uprights and supports, on the lintel and across part of the ceiling. A chiffchaff began to sing from the leafless sallows. Lord Heite looked down again, at the water, and breathed deeply. He was at peace. He had made the right decision.

A dry branch snapped on the path behind the pavilion. His bodyguards were waiting at a distance, on duty in the grove. They had let his guest come through.

'Please join me, General Teshe,' he said, and looked round.

The General mounted the steps and, bringing his bulky form to a halt, gave a correct but informal salute. His eyes were friendly; his broad, blond-bearded features were about to break into a smile. He had been travelling all night, but he looked, as ever, immaculate. The grey leather of his dress armour creaked softly as he accepted the unspoken invitation to seat himself beside his lord. In the regulation manner he drew about him his finely woven cloak, grey and darker grey, edged with black serpents along the hem. His kneeboots gleamed. Even when seated, he kept his shoulders perfectly square; yet he was also at ease. There was something permanent about the man, timeless, infallible. It had been the same twenty years ago, when he and Lord Heite had been boys together at the academy.

'Well, Kasha,' said Lord Heite, free now from the ears of his entourage. 'Tell me. How are you?'

'Growing older, liege.' The smile broadened; his teeth were white. 'The pagans in my care would age even Heite Gehan.'

'How did you once describe them? "Fractious"? Was that the word?'

'Let us say that their resentment of authority is second only to their idleness.'

'On the contrary, Kasha. You have tamed them remarkably quickly. The returns from your province tell me so.'

'You flatter me, my lord. Much remains to be done.'

'But not by you.' For a moment Lord Heite regarded the peaceful waters of the lake. Then he said, 'Do you remember my kinsman, Brennis Gehan Fifth?'

'Only vaguely.'

'His father tried to make the island country independent of the mainland. When he inherited Valdoe, Brennis Fifth pursued much the same idea. We tolerated the position until he, fortunately or otherwise, went out of his mind. It then became necessary to replace him.'

'With General Hewzane,' General Teshe recalled.

'Exactly. That was seven years ago. Did you ever meet Torin Hewzane?'

'Yes, my lord. He is of the Garland.'

'Well, now of course he is Lord Brennis. Unlike you, Kasha, he lets such titles go to his head. I must say he has disappointed us. A mistake was made. We misjudged him.'

General Teshe sat forward, incredulous.

'We are informed,' Lord Heite went on, 'that he has been stealing from us. He wishes, apparently, to finance the start of his own dynasty. In private he is already said to style himself "Brennis Hewzane First". We understand that next year he will be strong enough to approach the barbarian warlords in the east. There is no reason to imagine that his envoys will be received other than cordially. First to be attacked would be our eastern holdings; from there he would encroach upon the citadel itself, using Brennis as a base.'

'Forgive me, liege, but is your information reliable?'

'Yes.'

General Teshe was plainly stunned.

'Even had this matter not come to light, we should by now anyway have considered transferring him to some lesser post.

He has failed to carry out his brief. Settlement and forest clearance have not progressed at the expected rate. Only three new forts have been finished. Fraudulent or not, the harvest returns have been consistently bad. He is unable to control the farmers without recourse to the most absurd and destructive measures: at least seven villages have been burnt to the ground. As a result, a substantial number of people have returned to the mainland. More are expected to follow. The whole system of taxation in Brennis is in jeopardy. With Hewzane as their model, corruption has spread to the regional commanders, to the beilins, and even to certain officers and Trundlemen at Valdoe. Until we know how far it has gone we dare not risk a move. By the autumn, though, our information will be complete. At that time, Kasha, you will accompany Bohod Khelle and his annual commission of inspection. On arrival at Valdoe, you will publicly dispose of Hewzane and announce yourself Protector of Brennis Gehan Sixth.'

'I . . . do not understand, my lord. I thought Brennis Fifth died childless.'

'So it is generally believed.' A note of distaste had appeared in Lord Heite's voice. 'Lady Brennis, as you may have heard, was with child at the time of her husband's death. Unluckily she was lost during the siege of Valdoe, and although her body was not accounted for, the Prime is satisfied that she was killed.' Lord Heite paused. 'However, among the various aberrations leading to his downfall, Brennis Fifth contracted a liaison with his sister, the Lady Ika. The result is a boy, now six years of age. In the absence of a legitimate heir, the Prime has decreed that this child shall be designated "Brennis Gehan Sixth". Until he comes of age you are to be his guardian at Valdoe. In effect you will control the island of Brennis and be accountable only to me.'

'Where is the boy now?'

'At Valdoe, with his mother. During the siege she escaped to a village close by. On my orders she was found and brought back to the Trundle, where she has remained ever since.'

'Does Hewzane know all this?'

'Of course. But he would not dare harm the child. I had even hoped its presence might have reminded him of his true position and tempered his conduct. There are still many people in the Valdoe domain who remember Brennis Fifth, if not fondly, then at least with a certain nostalgia. At least he made things work. The farmers knew where they were. I suspect the appearance of another Gehan at Valdoe will be met with equanimity, or even approval. That is one of the main reasons the High Council has decided to confer Brennis on this boy.' Lord Heite stood up; the General did the same, still trying to absorb the implications of all he had been told. 'Shall we view the herons, Kasha?'

More than two hundred and eighty years earlier, at the foundation of Hohe and the Gehan empire, herons had begun to nest at the lake below the citadel. Overlooked by the temple, they had established their colony in the southern end, among islands wooded with alder and birch. The trees were bleached with droppings; almost every fork and crutch among the outer branches held its mattress of sticks, repaired and built upon year after year or, for no obvious reason, abandoned and allowed to disintegrate. To the priests in the temple, and then to the men of the garrison, the birds had become sacred symbols of the Gehan ideal. The grace of the heron's flight, its patience, persistence, and skill in hunting, its noble and independent nature, its courage in the defence of its young, its cooperation with others of its kind to secure the continuance of its race: all these made it an exemplar of the eternal truths. Gentleness through strength – this was the path to the highest goal of the empire and of the Prime, and as the empire grew and prospered, so did the heronry, until the trees were full and ninety or more pairs came each year to breed. On a morning such as this, viewed against the rise of the citadel, the air above the heronry was a confusion of arrival and departure: in many nests the hungry young birds, grey and fluffy, could already be seen.

But Lord Heite, one hand on the rail of the viewing platform, was more interested in observing his guest.

'You do not seem to be enjoying the spectacle, Kasha.'

On the way here, following the plankwalk through the ornamental marsh, the General had been rather quiet, and for the last few minutes he had spoken hardly at all.

'I am troubled, my lord,' he said at last.

'Duty is always onerous,' said Lord Heite. 'That is how we grow stronger.'

'I know, my lord. But I remember Torin Hewzane as a brother officer. An officer of the Garland. What I must do is not easy.' The General put both hands on the rail. 'Is there no way he can be saved?'

Lord Heite did not answer at once. Out of respect for his friend, he briefly reconsidered the decision with which he had been struggling for many weeks past.

They were separated from the trees by a hundred yards of water. Wildfowl of many sorts were lazing in the sunshine, safe in the lee of the island; bright reflections, sisters of those that had lit up the pavilion, were moving across the bare branches above their heads. It made a peaceful scene. Lord Heite allowed his gaze to travel upwards, to the herons, and then to the sheer wooden walls of the temple and of the citadel.

'There is no choice,' he said. 'Hewzane must die.'

2

'Listen, father,' Paoul had said. 'The beechmast sounds like rain.'

Tagart had not noticed, but it had been true. Yesterday afternoon, all through the beechwoods, uncountable numbers of husks had been opening to let their contents fall. As each nut fell it had struck, perhaps, one or two yellowing leaves before hitting the ground, just as a raindrop might. Tagart, for all his years in the forest, had marvelled that he had never heard the sound before.

He was thinking of it now, when his mind ought to have been on other things. With Paoul sitting here beside him, cross-legged on the gleaming boards of the Meeting House floor, the arguments of these village elders seemed infinitely less important and interesting than the sound of falling mast.

Bocher, the head man, glanced yet again at Paoul. Tagart could guess his thoughts. The sight of Paoul made Bocher dissatisfied with his own small son. It was the same in almost every village: the boy sitting cross-legged on the floor was extremely beautiful. There was no other way to think of him. Tagart tried to see him through Bocher's eyes, through the eyes of someone unprepared for his appearance.

He was seven. He might have been a year younger, or a year older, but his beauty was ageless. It came from within, from some deep source that defined and brought to life each detail of his outward form, blending him into an exact, ideal, and self-contained whole. In colouring he was dark, with brown eyes, as his mother had been; in general cast of feature he resembled his father, who, as even his victims had admitted, had been a handsome man. There the resemblance ended: Paoul's gaze was open, innocent, and sane. His limbs were smooth and clean, his skin utterly flawless. His hair had been cut very close, revealing the perfect shape of his head. The ears were neither small nor large, modestly moulded, of such delicate make that light seemed almost to pass through them unhindered. His cheekbones and the structure of his jaw made a face that was at once striking and mild, softened still more by the gentleness of childhood. His nose was straight, his mouth exquisitely formed; but something in the set of his lips was uncompromisingly masculine. So too were the repose and the attentiveness with which he sat listening to the arguments of the adults.

Trouble had come to Sturt. Besides the crushing weight of ever-increasing taxation, besides the number of people who had left the village and gone to the mainland, besides last year's drought and this year's floods, besides the diseased animals and blighted crops, the village had been singled out for especially harsh treatment at the hands of the spirits. The head man's daughter had been struck down by a horrible ailment. He was being punished. Gauhm, Spirit of the Earth, was angry. Because of all their troubles, the villagers had been neglecting the observances. It was Bocher's fault, his responsibility, and now Gauhm could be appeased only by a huge sacrifice. This the village could not afford. Many pigs would have to be slaughtered, many bushels of wheat and barley burned. Bocher had begged neighbouring villages for help; it had been refused. They too had suffered from the drought and the blight, and they too were subject to Valdoe's taxes. The taxes had always been heavy; since the arrival of the new Flint Lord they had grown intolerable – and Sturt had yet to be assessed for this year's harvest. Several villages in the region had been ruined. Others had been destroyed by the soldiers themselves, in retribution for real or imagined crimes against the Valdoe domain.

All this and more the elders were debating at length, just as if it had any bearing on the matter in hand. Tagart cared nothing for their gods. Excepting the daughter's illness, the troubles of the village, such as they were, had probably arisen from the villagers' own indolence and lack of foresight, or from the greed of the Gehans, over whom even the gods had no control. But Tagart well understood why the villagers felt the need of a supernatural explanation for everything bad, and by now, after a hundred such debates at a hundred such villages, he had learned to listen with patience and apparent humility.

He and his party had come seeking work. The crops had long been in, but one of the villagers, the councilman in charge of field-drainage, had wanted to offer payment and a week's lodging in return for clearing a blocked ditch in the south meadow. The task was unpleasant and greatly overdue; despite the councilman's complaints, nothing had been done about it all summer. Now the winter and perhaps further flooding were on the way and, like it or not, the ditch would have to be cleaned. If the villagers were reluctant to do the job, the councilman had argued, why not give it to this band of vagrants? Others on the council, though, had objected to the cost, so Bocher had convened a meeting. While most of Tagart's party waited outside the village, he himself had been brought into the Meeting House to listen to the interminable talking and to answer the council's questions.

His head ached. His eyes hurt. The room was dazzling, filled with reverberating light. The long southern shutters had been laid open, letting sunshine pour in. The walls were limed, the floor and beams highly polished. Even the altar at the far end was of glaring, spotless white stone. But the doorway, overhung by a thatched porch, was in shadow, and beyond it, beyond the village houses and the palisade, there was a wide view of the wooded, gently rising slope. The trees there had started to turn: oaks mainly, one or two maples and cherries. Their foliage formed a continuous mass, invested by the warmth of the afternoon with a barely perceptible haze. The air was quite still: he faintly heard the cry of a soaring buzzard.

Even on such a luminous autumn day as this, three weeks after the equinox, the village of Sturt might at one time have seemed to Tagart a squalid and confining place. He would have been made uneasy by the closeness of the palisade; he would have despised the way of life of those who had built it. And, even in the years before he had known anything at first hand of the farmers or their fields, he would have taken an instinctive dislike to this shifty and indecisive head man.

But it was no longer in him to have such feelings. He was too tired, too old, too weary of wandering from place to place. He had seen his own and all the other nomad tribes destroyed: the old way of life was finished for ever. Its freedom and plenty, its grinding hardships, its terrors and grandeur, everything he had lived for, everything was gone. Even had there been enough people to make a spirit group, there was nowhere left for them to go. The trees had gone from vista after vista, cut down or ring-barked and left to die. The ancient territories of his people had been laid waste, and still Valdoe's blades were at work. Once he had been angry; recently he had begun to fear that, one day, he would view it all with indifference.

By his reckoning he was thirty-three. The last eight years he had spent in pain, and now he could scarcely walk ten steps unaided. His hair was turning grey, years before its time. Often at night he longed for release. It would be better then for the others in his party, the people who still called him their chief. Including himself and Paoul, only eleven remained. They carried him everywhere on a wicker seat. He was aware that he made a strange and pathetic sight, at the gates and meeting houses of villages throughout the domain; the children still sometimes threw stones, even where he and his party had been before.

Were it not for Paoul, he knew he would have killed himself long ago.

'What do you say, then, Bocher?' asked one of the elders, when the debate came at last to an end.

Tagart stared at the floor. In his bones he knew he was going to be turned away. Once again he would have failed to find his people decent food and shelter. They all thought they depended on his ability to negotiate, but he knew they were wrong. He was useless. He was stupid, too. By letting the ever-curious Paoul accompany him like this he had succeeded only in antagonizing the head man: he had made him jealous because of Paoul.

But Bocher had yet to answer the question.

Tagart looked up and for the briefest and most extraordinary moment sensed Bocher's dilemma, glimpsed somehow the inmost workings of his heart. Bocher had recognized the source of his own hostility. His eyes were drawn to Paoul's. The room might have been empty of everyone else. The child was looking at him calmly, with complete confidence in the fairness of the outcome. He had said nothing, not a word, since the start of the meeting, but it now seemed as if he were not only a party to the negotiations, but benignly overseeing them. He was content to put his trust in Bocher. He had placed Bocher entirely at liberty: he was free to choose as his conscience and judgement directed best.

'Well?' said the elder.

'Let them stay.'

'And the payment?'

'It is little enough. Give them what they ask.'

The dawn of their last full day in Sturt brought cold air in from the north, and suddenly it seemed that winter was very near. The previous night the sky above the village had been threaded with the thin calls of migrating redwings. Tagart had lain listening to them for hour after hour, kept awake by the pain in his legs and lower back, while all round him, in the straw, the other members of the group had slept. He had heard the furtive movements of Munt and the girl Tanda; he had heard Fodich talking in his sleep; he had heard one man and then another getting up, at long intervals, to urinate. He had heard Paoul close by: the steady tenor of his breathing, the occasional rustle when he shifted or turned. And slowly, like the growing chill in his joints, Tagart had watched the grey morning light pushing back the darkness to reveal the interior of the ruined barn which was serving the group as a dormitory.

There would be one more night here. Tomorrow they would have to leave, to continue their wanderings. At this season work became hard to find. Most of the farmers themselves would be hungry by the spring: the harvest taxes saw to that. By midwinter, when the snows came, Tagart and the others would again be fending for themselves in the woods. Last year they had built a makeshift camp and subsisted on the few beasts that the able-bodied men had managed to kill. The weather then had been kind, but the preceding year two of their number, an old woman and a child, had succumbed to the cold. Perhaps this winter it would be Tagart's turn. Or perhaps the camp would be attacked by wolves again, as it had been two years ago, when three people had been lost.

The group was steadily getting smaller and weaker. Sometimes, when the sun shone and food was plentiful, it was almost like a real tribe, or a large family, but more often there were arguments, bitterness, endless jealousies and complaints.

Munt, Einthe, and his woman Igmiss had once been slaves. Except for Paoul, all the others were of pure nomad stock. That was one source of friction; and then Tanda, free of the restrictions of tribal law, had made trouble between Munt and Worley which had lasted until Worley's death.

At the beginning, when Altheme had been alive, Tagart had hoped to find further remnants of the nomad tribes, but it had never happened. The survivors of the siege, of the fighting at Valdoe, had scattered in all directions. Most had gone north, back to the forest. His own group had spent three years there, searching, visiting all the old camps and hunting grounds. They had found nothing but desolation, the results of clearance and of the Gehans' campaign of extermination. By now, after seven years, there could be little hope. Tagart's party, as far as he knew, was the only one left.

Once it had numbered nineteen. Now it was reduced to eleven. Two of the slaves had managed to join villages, and a third had been recaptured and presumably taken to Valdoe. Soon there would be too few people left to support him and Tagart knew the group would break up. At that time his life would end. Fodich would want to stay, and Maert, Fodich's woman, but he would be too much of a burden and eventually they would have no choice but to leave him. No village would take him in. Alone and crippled, he might last about a week.

He did not care. He cared only about what would happen to Paoul

Without thinking he reached for the pouch he wore on a cord round his neck, and as he clasped it saw Altheme, dying under the oaks, tormented by insects, disfigured by exhaustion and pain. Her features were blurred now. He had never so much as thought of her in that way, but her face and the faces of his women, the two women he had known in the old time, had become interchangeable and confused. The second woman had been false; the first had not, and she had borne him a son. They were dead too.

Paoul was his only son now. The boy believed him to be his father. Five years ago, on that long and terrible summer evening, Tagart had been charged with bringing him up in ignorance of the truth, in ignorance even of his mother's true name. Altheme had exacted this promise and in secret had given Tagart her pouch. It contained what was left of her valuables, the bits and pieces of jewellery she had snatched up before leaving the Trundle. They were for Paoul, she had said, whenever he should need them. Their worth, Tagart believed, was trifling; but, despite all the privation she and the others had endured, despite the almost continuous temptation to exchange mere trinkets for food and shelter, he had been unable to bring himself to sell the least part of Paoul's inheritance.

The time was drawing near when Tagart would have to do it. He did not know how. He knew only that the boy was too young, too defenceless, to be left to the mercy of circumstances. Alone, or with only Fodich to guard him, he would end in slavery or suffer some even more appalling fate. For months, years, Tagart had been worrying and wondering what to do. In vain he had examined each village with an eye to leaving Paoul as an adopted son of one of the kindlier families. Certainly there would be no trouble in finding him such a home; there had even been an unprompted offer, earlier this year. Refusing it had made Tagart realize much about himself. The family had been unsuitable, but his refusal had been immediate and instinctive, and he had seen for the first time how much he dreaded giving Paoul up. Since then he had tried to be unselfish, to look without bias at prospective homes, to be less critical and suspicious. Even here, in Sturt, he had made himself overcome a feeling of unease which formerly might have impelled him to take Paoul and leave. The head man, Bocher, seemed to be watching the boy. His own son and Paoul had become firm friends – everywhere he went Paoul made friends with all the village children and left a deep impression on their parents, but something about Bocher's interest had struck Tagart as undesirable. Perhaps not suspicious or threatening, but unwelcome just the same. Paoul's friendship with his son was unfortunate. Because of it Bocher and his wife had been able, at leisure, to evaluate the most obvious of Paoul's gifts, none of which he was old enough to know how to conceal.

Everyone in the group loved him, but only Tagart, who had spent so much time in his company, had glimpsed the full extent of his qualities. It had always been accepted that Paoul was special, but recently, in the past few months, Tagart had begun to realize that he was very much more than that.

He feared for him. Paoul made friends too easily. Tonight, as usually happened at the end of a stay like this, Tagart was due to go to the head man's house to collect the group's wages and, as proof of the council's satisfaction, a clay tablet impressed with the village seal. Because of Paoul's effect on the head man and his family, the occasion had been turned into a sort of farewell meal to which Paoul had also been invited. This had happened before, at one or two other villages. Tagart did not like eating with these people. He much preferred it when they treated him with incivility. It was safer to keep a distance. So far he had not found the heart to teach this to Paoul, but he would soon, gently, have to tell him that not everyone could be trusted.

As the daylight grew Tagart heard waking sounds and voices from the village compound. Presently, after a breakfast of oatmeal and milk, the others would leave him behind for the day. They would go out to the fields and by their labour provide his food and shelter while he, to make himself feel useful, would sit outside the barn and repair, for nothing, such broken weapons and implements as the villagers cared to bring. It was then that he chafed most harshly against his fate and wished that Brennis Gehan's spear had done its work properly and left him dead on Valdoe Hill instead of half alive. That he had been crippled was bad enough, but then to be given Paoul like this – to be unable to protect him – was unbearable. Like Paoul's father, the man who had wielded the spear, the irony of this circumstance was too cruel and complicated for Tagart to understand.

He watched Paoul sleeping for a moment longer. Fodich awoke with a yawn. Einthe sat up and stretched. Then there arrived, at the barn door, the two village girls with the pails containing breakfast, and everyone else began to stir.

3

At bedtime – especially when the evenings grew dark and the table lamps lit either side of his bed – Hothen's second self emerged. Gone were the tantrums of the day; forgotten were his cruel words and threats, his transparent, ugly little deceits. In the unsteady lamplight he looked almost like a normal child of his age, but more helpless, and sad, and Rian felt she might one day even bring herself to pity him.

She stroked the hair from his eyes and arranged his arms on the counterpane. 'There,' she said. 'Now you're nice and clean, your mother will come to tell you a story.'

'You tell me a story,' he said. 'Are you a slave, Rian?'

'Yes. I am a slave.'

'Can I have some more blackberries tomorrow?'

Rian stood up without answering: the Lady Ika had appeared at the door. Rian moved back from the bed. 'Good evening, my lady.'

'I came in too late,' Ika said. 'Was Hothen asking for anything special?'

Even his own mother had trouble understanding his stammer. 'Just some blackberries, my lady. For tomorrow.'

'Of course you can have some blackberries, dearest.' Ika felt for the bedpost and guided herself to the seat. 'You can have anything you want.'

As usual, Rian settled herself in the far corner, leaving her mistress to hold Hothen's hands and to recount in a soothing voice the tales he liked so well. Rian did not pick up her sewing; away from the bedside lamps it was too dark. Her corner, like the rest of the room and, it seemed, the rest of the world, had suddenly been banished, excluded, shut out from the illuminated scene of mother and child together. Its radiance did not even reach the ceiling; the shapes and identity of nearby furniture receded into the gloom. Ika's face was three-quarters turned away, her thick blonde hair plaited into a mass which caught the light only at its edges. But Hothen, his pillow, and the carved bedhead above him were fully lit. The bedhead was made of blackened oak. On it, within a stylized border of wreathing vines, each scale of the Gehan serpent threw its upward shadow. The original pigments of red and green had mostly flaked away, for the bed was old, a hundred years at least. It had been made for the first Flint Lord and used by his descendants and successors – five in all, the five Brennis Gehans, the last of whom had been Ika's brother. The bed had been kept in a larger, much grander chamber then, but under its covers Hothen had been conceived.

Rian looked on bleakly, reminded again of her former mistress. In this bed unhappy Altheme had also slept. Rian had worshipped her; she still mourned her loss, eight years ago this winter. Where was Lady Brennis now? What had become of her unborn baby, the Flint Lord's first and rightful child?

Dead, both were surely dead. After the siege of the Trundle, Altheme had fled into the forest with the savages – the remnants of those who had vainly tried to take the fort. In the following years the last of the savages' tribes had been systematically destroyed by Torin Hewzane, the new Flint Lord, the man installed by the Home Lord and the mainland Gehans; the man who had betrayed and murdered Altheme's husband. If she had survived, Lord Torin would have found her. She had not been found: Altheme and her child were surely dead.

Yes, they were dead. Brennis Gehan Fifth had left only a single monument to himself, perhaps a fitting one – defective, inbred, reared on a diet of lies and intrigue. How much more terrifying would be Hothen's rages if he knew the extent of his importance abroad, at the citadel? For Rian had heard that he was being kept here as a check on Lord Torin. The Home Lord, as did the whole fort, the whole of Valdoe, knew Hothen's parentage; if ever it became necessary or expedient, there might yet be a Brennis Gehan Sixth.

The stories Ika told him often concerned Brennis Gehan First, founder of the Valdoe domain, builder of the Trundle and, after her own father, chief inspiration of her brother's life. At least, the stories purported to detail the valour of the first Lord Brennis, but in many episodes Rian recognized a subtly fashioned portrait of Hothen's father, and sometimes, unconsciously, Ika gave her hero her brother's features, demeanour, and manner of dress – far removed from the ugliness and austerity that were said to have characterized his ancestor. Yet she never spoke of him directly, not to anyone, least of all to Hothen.

On her brother's death she and a servant, a certain Rald – who had also shared her bed – tried to escape from the new Lord Brennis. They did not get far. On the orders of the Home Lord, Ika was brought back and given medication for the blinding she had received in the siege. During this treatment it became apparent that she was pregnant. The priests, aware of the rumours that had been current just before the siege, questioned her closely. At first she maintained that Rald was the father. Rald, who had red hair and green eyes, was interrogated and the nature of their relationship was established. The last union that could have given rise to a child had taken place at least two months before the siege.

Hothen was born two hundred and eighty-four days after the start of the siege. He was fully formed; he had been carried for the full term. His hair, like his father's and mother's, was blond. His eyes were blue, and that was how they remained. There could be no doubt. Hothen was the son of Brennis Gehan Fifth.

To everyone but Ika, it was obvious from the start that the child was not normal. He was slow in learning to suck; in the cradle he lay inert, taking no interest in dangled toys or his nurse's fingers. He did not recognize his mother, and was nearly three before he uttered her name. About that time the convulsions began. Mercifully they had now abated, but in their place had come fits of frightening and inexplicable rage. These always followed the same course. Some tiny incident, at the meal table, for example, would be enough to spark one off. Hothen's eating habits were disgusting. Rian might reach out to wipe his chin, to offer the mildest possible word of correction; and it would start. First, with miraculous fluency, his stammer forgotten, he would say the worst and most hateful things he knew. Rian was dung, vomit, spittle. Somewhere – no doubt from the soldiers in the enclosure below his window – he had learned a variety of profanities, all of which he knew how to use with telling effect. Rian tried not to listen, but often his words struck deep and she was hurt that such things could be said at all. He seemed to have a cruelty far beyond his years. And then, without warning, in the middle of this stream of vituperation, he would slur his speech, shouting and struggling uncontrollably, upsetting dishes and bowls and platters, become incoherent, pull faces, perhaps begin to laugh. His head would twist to one side and then the other. His eyes, which always seemed slightly filmed, would become yet more opaque, unfathomable, and withdrawn. Very often he would bring up whatever he had eaten. Afterwards, much subdued, he would allow himself to be cleaned and carried to his bed: these rages always left him much exhausted. Even in his sleep he made Rian more work, for he was still not properly trained. Sometimes she had to change his bedding twice or more in one night.

Looking after him, and she had always been his nurse, was gruelling work for a woman of her age. By rights she should have had assistance, for she was also Ika's body-slave, and by rights Hothen should have had his own body-slave as well as a nurse. But Rian had to do it all. In just the same way were the quarters for Ika and Hothen dingy and cold. Their food was inferior, and their clothing had to last. They were Gehans, members of the Home Lord's clan, but the other slaves and servants, the workmen and soldiers, treated them with ill-concealed contempt. Their movements were closely regulated. Ika – because, they said, of her blindness – was not allowed to leave the Trundle on her own. Accompanied, she could go as far as the settlement fields, but no farther, and the road to Apuldram, where the ships docked, was strictly out of bounds. Ika and her son were prisoners, and that made Rian doubly a slave.

Perhaps she was lucky to have a position of any kind. At least it was keeping her alive. She might easily have followed all those whom Lord Torin had suspected of loyalty to Brennis Fifth. In the weeks after he had taken power, many, many people had been put to death – not only here at Valdoe and in the outer forts, but in the villages also. And though Rian knew she was too old and unimportant ever to be considered dangerous, still she was very guarded in what she said. She did not care so much about herself, but her own three children – who had long since grown up – were all in service here.

She leaned back, glad of this chance to rest before her duties of the evening. Tonight there was to be a banquet, and Ika had to go. Each autumn a commission was sent from the homelands to inspect the domain: it had arrived this afternoon. The custom was for a welcoming feast attended by everyone of rank. Lord Torin and his lady would of course be there, as would his two generals and their ladies, the commanders of the outer forts, and the most important priests and Trundlemen. There would be other freemen too, those who were rich and who benefited from Valdoe and the Home Lord, and everyone else whom the commission expected to see. They would be expecting Ika. Tomorrow they would probably come to check on Hothen.

Rian's eyes wanted to close. The smell of burned incense, combining with Ika's voice, had made her sleepy. The incense was used each day to purify the air in Hothen's room; his mother's voice was like the smoke, soft and warm, drifting through a story told many times before.

'And that's the end, Hothen.' Ika put a caressing hand to his cheek. 'You must go to sleep now. You're very tired.'

She kissed him and Rian forced herself to rise. 'Good night, Hothen,' Rian said, and touched his forehead with her lips. She put out the lamps and followed her mistress into the adjoining chamber.

Ika's finest white robe had been laid out across the bed. On the dressing board, on its inset rectangle of soft green leather, waited her best remaining jewels – those left to her by the exigencies of life under Torin, Lord Brennis: a jade and ivory necklace, matching bracelet, and large ivory brooch. She would wear them all, and new slippers lined with leverets' fur, but first she had to be bathed and dried, manicured, anointed with herbal oils, powdered; her lips had to be darkened, and her hair – highlighted earlier with a camomile rinse – brushed and carefully plaited with freshly picked flowers. Only then would she be fit to be dressed and brought into the presence of Lord Brennis and of Bohod Khelle, chief commissioner from the homelands.

'Send for hot water,' she told Rian, discarding her day-robe.

It was time to make ready for the feast.

Bocher's house was the biggest of all the thirty-eight dwellings in the village. Set in its own garden surrounded by a quickthorn hedge, it shared the larger precincts of the Meeting House and stood almost exactly in the centre of the compound. It was made of stone and weathered oak, with a conical roof for the main chamber and flat roofs, covered with turf, for the others. The winter shutters had yet to be fixed; all the windows were open except one, in the rear, which was his eldest daughter's sickroom. Paoul had, earlier in the week, been allowed to peep inside. The sight of a girl of fifteen so wasted and pale had affected him deeply. One skeletal arm, contorted somehow and drawn up, had protruded from the bedcovers. Her brittle dark hair, her sunken eyes and speechless mouth had been those of a corpse. 'What's wrong with her?' Paoul had whispered. 'She's dying,' her brother had said.

She had been bedridden since the spring. Now she was getting weaker. The priest had tried everything. At last he had been forced to tell her father that this was the work of the Earth Goddess. Only a great sacrifice might save her, if it was not already too late.

The girl's name was Utara. Her affliction seemed to fill the house. It had come to dominate the family; every aspect of the household had been subordinated to its needs. None the less her brother Berritt, a boy the same age as Paoul, had daily been allowed to invite his new friend to spend time quietly indoors or in the garden, and tonight, for the farewell evening, most of her family – father, mother, uncle, brother, and younger sister – had gathered and a special supper had been prepared.

Usually Paoul did not like village food, but he had never tasted anything quite like this before, succulent lamb roasted with hyssop and served on a steaming bed of tender vegetables. Sometimes in the past he had been given mutton, but it had always been stewed, gristly, and overcooked; and he had certainly never tasted such vegetables or the flavour of such a subtle and delicious herb. The hyssop was from a special bush which grew only in Bocher's garden. Paoul had seen it there, together with many other herbs, all of which were tended and propagated by Bocher's wife, Dagda. Berritt had named each kind for him and explained some of its properties and uses. The cultivated herbs were even more interesting than the ones Tagart had taught him, the wild plants of the wayside. Berritt said that sometimes the flint sellers would bring a new sort, and then the price would be high. Paoul knew that dried herbs, some very rare and expensive, were sold at the great Valdoe fairs. Dagda had told him that the priests at Valdoe grew or stored every herb ever known, including secret ones which it was forbidden for anybody else to have.

Almost every day this week Paoul had eaten a meal at Berritt's house. Here, in this room, he had begun to understand why people chose to live in villages. Life in the woods was hard; the forest only seemed beautiful if you were not hungry or frightened or cold. But if you had a solid house with a hearth, and a palisade to protect you from the wolves and bears, there was time for other things besides survival. Berritt's sister – the one who was not sick – had shown him the leather pictures she had made, and Dagda, whom Paoul did not really like, had taught him how to eat properly, with a spoon. She had presented him with his own clay spoon, fired in the village kiln and fitted with a wooden handle, but at other meals, in the barn, Paoul had been too embarrassed to use it.

When he had learned that both he and Tagart had been invited here tonight, the spoon had given him hours of worry. If he used it, Tagart would think he had been less than open, concealing from his father the acquisition of manners which could so easily be taken as criticism of the way he had been raised. This deceit, which he had not intended, would make Tagart unhappy and disappointed. But in turn, if he left the spoon in his tunic and ate with his fingers, Dagda's feelings might be hurt, and besides, she would ask him where it was. So this evening, an hour before the meal had been due to start, Paoul had made a point of showing Tagart the spoon.

His reaction had been strangely subdued. Paoul was still puzzled about it. They had never been shown such hospitality before, and yet, as the meal drew towards its close, Tagart appeared to be growing more and more anxious. Even as they had crossed the compound from the barn – even as Fodich and Uden had helped him through Bocher's gate and along the path – Tagart had seemed uneasy. His eye had been drawn to the Meeting House, where four or five young men had been sitting on the steps, indolently watching, and then, on seeing Dagda's burly brother by the hearth, he had grown more uneasy still. Paoul could not understand why. He wondered whether Tagart's anxiety could be related in any way to himself, to the incident of the spoon – to his friendship with Berritt. He realized keenly now, too late, that throughout the week Tagart had mutely disapproved of his visits to the head man's house. Paoul regretted that he had ever set foot here; he was ashamed that he had craved, even for a moment, the advantages of a settled life. For Tagart was very wise and if he disapproved there was always a reason, and if he felt threatened there would be a reason for that too. Paoul began to wish that Fodich and Uden had not been so quick to return to the barn.

The meal ended with cheese for the grown-ups. He and Berritt, who were sitting together, next to Dagda's brother, had been given fruit junket in wooden bowls.

Utara, meanwhile, was being cared for by Bocher's mother. The old woman came out of the rear chamber once again, collected a bowl of junket, and crawled back through the low, narrow doorway, letting the leather curtain fall behind her.

When she had gone, Bocher glanced at his brother-in-law, reached back and took something from one of the shelves by the hearth. 'This is our seal,' he said, handing it to Tagart. 'Your people have done a good job here. The council is pleased.'

Tagart examined the seal, holding it closer to one of the rush-lights, and slipped it into his tunic. 'We're glad to have been of use.'

Bocher wiped his mouth nervously and offered Tagart a platter of oatmeal biscuits. 'Where are you making for next?'

'I'm not sure. We might go north.'

'Up to the Weald?'

'We might go that way, yes.'

Bocher shot an odd glance at his wife. Paoul did not understand what it meant, but he saw that Tagart had noticed it too and suddenly felt alarmed. Dagda was big and raw-boned, like her brother, with red hands which she was always wiping on her smock. Her voice intimidated him a little, and he had pitied Berritt, whom she was always scolding, for having such a mother. Whenever Paoul tried to picture his own mother he always imagined someone very different from this.

No one else would know, but Tagart had become extremely tense. Paoul could tell by his eyes, by the minute changes in his expression.

Bocher reached over his shoulder once more and gave Tagart a goatskin pouch. 'This is what we owe you.'

Even to Paoul's eyes the pouch appeared much too big and heavy for a week's wages, but Tagart quietly opened the flap and looked inside. He took out the first flint to hand, a blue pressure-flaked spearhead of the finest Valdoe quality, and tested the edge with his thumb.

'This isn't what we agreed,' he said. 'You're giving us too much.'

Despite Dagda's brother, despite the young men on the Meeting House steps, Bocher was terrified. He had reached a cliff-edge, goaded there, driven by his wife, by forces stronger than himself. A moment more and it would be too late, not just for him, but for Paoul too. Paoul sensed it but did not understand how. His instinct was to reach out for Tagart, to shelter behind him, but he knew that would only make things worse. He saw Bocher pleading silently with his wife: she had fixed him with an insistent, accusing stare which pushed him and pushed him until he toppled forward into the void.

'We want to give you more,' he said.

'Why?'

'For the boy. We want the boy.'

Falling, helpless, Bocher had finally hit the rocks below. Paoul felt the impact just as if, yard by yard, he had fallen with him.

'It's like this,' Paoul heard Bocher say. 'You've seen how well he and my lad get on. Dagda and me, we've talked it over. We reckon he deserves better. Better than he can get on the road with you. It's not your fault, I know, but look at his clothes. Look at the state of his feet. What's it going to be like for him when you're dead?'

Paoul hardly dared breathe. He could see how desperately Tagart was searching for a way out: but there was none. There could be no question of a fight. If it came to that, Bocher would win. He was the head man here. There were only nine people in the barn: nine friendless, rootless people, against more than two hundred villagers. Whatever Bocher chose to insist upon, whatever he wanted, that he would surely have – if Tagart allowed it to come to a fight. But by the same token there could be no question of subterfuge. Tagart could not pretend to accept the price and then later try to rescue Paoul. Judging by the young men at the Meeting House, such a rescue had already been anticipated; and anyway, even Bocher would never believe that Tagart cared so little for his son.

The only solution was to be patient. If Tagart pretended to yield, Paoul would somehow, later, make his escape. He did not understand why these people wanted him; he understood only that this was the answer. This was the only way to get back to Tagart. But Tagart had not seen it. His face, moulded by years of pain, exhaustion, disillusionment, revealed that the final blow had been dealt to the very centre of his suffering – to his pride. A hammer blow, wielded by a stupid man who had suddenly become the focus of a lifetime's rage. Paoul had never guessed the depth of his frustration. Tagart was finally losing control, in a long, slow slide that had begun in earnest earlier this week and that was now accelerating, speeding, racing towards its ends.

'He's not for sale,' Tagart said.

'You don't seem to understand,' Dagda said.

'Keep out of this,' Tagart told her. He did not take his eyes from Bocher's face.

Paoul wanted to say, 'It doesn't matter, I'll do anything they ask, just as long as you're not hurt,' but when he tried to speak the words would not come. He was too frightened.

'Paoul,' Tagart said. 'Run to the barn. Tell Fodich we're leaving.'

'Stay where you are!' Dagda cried.

Before he could even think of moving, Paoul felt a large hand grasp the scruff of his neck. He had been seized by Dagda's brother.

Turning his head, Paoul missed the beginning of what happened next. For weeks, months, afterwards, he tried to reconstruct these few instants in their true sequence. Each time he tried it became harder, until the disparate fragments of vision and memory would not fit together at all and made sense only in his nightmares. With the flames of the rush-lamps wildly agitated, casting insane shadows across the walls and ceiling, he had seen Tagart attacking Dagda's brother, heard her husband's shouts and the piercing screams of her daughter; he had witnessed the jerky, dreamlike, flickering movements of Dagda with arms raised high, clutching in both hands what Paoul later knew to be a hearthstone, heard the sound made by a jagged edge of the stone brought down with all its weight on the side of a man's head – not just any man, but Tagart, his father whom he loved, whose dark blood was suddenly spattered in spots and streaks on Berritt's face, and, looking down, on Paoul's tunic and the backs of his hands. And afterwards, while he was being restrained, he had seen his father's body dragged heel-first through the doorway and out into the autumn coldness of the night, to lie alone in the compound till morning, till ignominiously taken away. And among the terror and screaming in Bocher's house he had heard the orders given by Dagda and then by Bocher to the young men, who had grown in number until they were a mob armed with picks and mattocks, the orders meant to forestall any further trouble from these vagrants, to prevent them from biding their time beyond the palisade, to stop them coming back for revenge. He had heard the orders sending the young men running to the barn, heard them, but remembered only one, the one that Bocher had shouted last, crazed, unhinged, like the mob, no longer human:

'Kill them all!'

4

It was one of Rian's duties to accompany Ika whenever needed, to be her eyes; and though she had attended many social functions with her mistress, she could never quite feel easy when other slaves, some much more elevated than herself, behaved as if she were a rightful member of the gathering. And even now she felt awed by the presence of Lord Torin, who tonight was wearing the black, white and grey dress uniform consistent with his rank. Something about him – his dry, bloodless lips, perhaps, his thin, spare frame, his fastidiousness – always seemed to her to be peculiarly arrogant and repulsive. He was three years short of forty; his blond hair was cropped in the formal manner; he was clean shaven, and by any standards would not be judged ugly, but Rian could not imagine how his wife managed to submit to him – if, indeed, she ever did.

'What is Lord Torin doing now, Rian?'

'He is talking to the Commissioner, my lady.'

'Tell me more about what Lady Torin is wearing.'

Rian had done her best to describe the elegance and richness of Lady Torin's green and cream robes, just as she had tried to describe the appearance of the other guests. In this one room were assembled all the most important people in the Valdoe domain: the highest-ranking officers, the wealthiest and most exalted freemen, the most influential priests and Trundlemen. They had all gathered to honour the arrival of Bhod Khelle and his annual commission of inspection. He had been brought by a Gehan ship which, flying the Hohe standard and carrying his inspectors and a nominal guard of ten men, had docked today at Apuldram. The four inspectors were here tonight as well; and most of the ten guards had taken up position among the resident Trundle guards, by the doors and along the walls.

'Did you say Bohod Khelle was wearing maroon?'

'Yes, my lady. With a sable collar.'

It was hard to believe that even Ika could not see by the

light of so many lamps. There were hundreds, large and small, on poles and stands, sconces and brackets, glaring whitely or giving off an oily yellow glow. The odour of scented lamp fat permeated the length and breadth of the Receiving Room; the rafters, even at this stage of the proceedings, had been lost to the smoke. From here, towards the back of the hall, the faces of Lord and Lady Torin and of Bohod Khelle were already becoming indistinct.

All the guests, except those on Lord Torin's dais, were seated on the floor, on bleached rush matting. Rian and her mistress had been placed near one of the side doors. Rian had thought this odd: at previous autumn feasts Ika had always sat in the centre of the hall, just behind the Trundlemen and their wives.

Although it was late in the evening, the banquet had yet to start. Lord Torin and his retinue had only just arrived; the guests were still settling in. In a moment Lord Torin would make his speech of welcome, and then, probably at length, the Commissioner would reply.

Rian felt a touch on her shoulder and looked round. A young usher, whom she knew slightly, had appeared from the shadows of the doorway. He squatted and spoke close to her ear. 'Please inform my lady Ika that she is requested to spare you for a brief errand.'

Rian was instantly apprehensive.

'What is it, Rian?' Ika said.

'I do not know, my lady. I am needed for an errand.'

'A request of Lord Torin, I believe,' said the usher, and Rian's apprehension grew.

'Request? What request?' Ika said.

'It will not take long.'

Rian put her hand on Ika's forearm. 'I ought to do as he says.'

The corridor beyond the doorway was lit by several flaming brands. The usher took one down. 'We are to fetch Master Hothen,' he told Rian, and then, seeing her expression, he added, 'Please. Don't worry. No harm will befall him, I assure you.'

'What do you want him for? He's only a child.'

'I understand he is to be presented to the gathering and

honoured in some way. That's all I know.' The usher's pleasant manner had begun to dispel Rian's doubts.

'Who sent you exactly?' she said. 'Lord Torin himself?'

'The chamberlain gave me the order. But it came from Lord Torin, or so I was told. Please,' he insisted, taking her elbow. 'We're wasting time. Lord Torin will be angry.'

Hothen's room was on the far side of the building. The usher led the way, along gloomy corridors and up dark flights of creaking stairs.

Rian woke Hothen as gently as she could. At the usher's insistence, she dressed him in the rather musty military-style clothes he had last worn some months ago, at an official audience with Lord Torin. Hothen was too sleepy to notice or object; his head drooped as she fastened the collar. Her fingers pushed against the defenceless softness under his chin. She looked up at the usher. 'Are you certain he'll be safe?'

'Yes. Quite certain.'

Yes, Rian told herself. Of course Hothen would be safe. Lord Torin would never harm him in public.

'Please hurry,' said the usher. 'We must be getting back.'

They had almost reached the Receiving Room when it happened. Coming down the stairs and along the final corridor, approaching the brightly lit doorway, Rian heard Lord Torin addressing the assembly, his high, precisely modulated voice clearly enunciating each word. He was saying something about the homelands, praising the citadel, when there was a sudden loud noise: a thud or a smack, so loud and unexpected that it seemed in its wake to fill the room with a swaying, unreal, transparent silence. Rian saw guests in profile, horrified, appalled; only Ika's face remained, for the moment, calm. Then there came, out of sight, from the front of the hall, the sound of someone falling, crashing backwards. A woman screamed. Reality rushed in and the whole hall was a turmoil of shouting, confusion, of people rising to their feet.

Before Rian could prevent it, Hothen had been snatched by the usher and propelled to the doorway. A soldier, one of the Commissioner's men, seized him and he was bundled through the throng, towards the dais.

Only then did Rian realize that Lord Torin had been shot. She could see nothing of him – the dais had been surrounded, and whether he had been killed or merely wounded she could not tell. His bodyguards were forcing their way to the back of the hall: the arrow must have come from there. But many of the other soldiers, and all the Commissioner's men, were making no attempt to help find the assassin. Instead they were forming an orderly line, pushing people back from the dais and opening up a passage from the main doors.

A prolonged and imperious roll of drums silenced the assembly and halted the bodyguards. Even Lady Torin looked on, stunned, incredulous, as the doors swung open and a broad-shouldered man of forty or fifty, his dark-grey cloak sweeping the air behind him, strode to the dais and mounted it. Rian had never seen him before. His uniform was that of a general, the highest rank below a lord's. On his breast was the green and scarlet emblem of the Garland, the elite of officers dedicated to the Home Lord, and Rian began to be aware that everything this evening had long ago been planned.

He glanced sideways and down before levelly contemplating the faces of Lord Torin's dinner-guests.

He did not choose to speak at once. The leisure of his silence charged the hall with menace, power, inexorable right; he was all these things himself, but what he represented was even stronger, more certain and implacable. He represented the Home Lord: he represented the Gehans.

'My name,' he said, 'is General Kasachie Teshe. I am commanded by Lord Heite, Gehan of the Gehans, to make known a proclamation of the Prime. By order of the High Council, meeting in the third session of the second quarter of this, the Year of the Blue Hare, be it known that Hewzane, Lord Torin of Brennis, has been tried in his absence and found guilty of the following capital crimes against the empire. One: treachery. Two: murder. Three: theft. You are to know that sentence has been executed in accordance with the decree. The traitor's corpse will be dismembered and burned. You are to know also that Balom, General of Valdoe, Abisende, General of the Coast, Crill, Commander of the Weald, and Tourse, Commander of the East, have been tried in their absence and found guilty of capital crimes against the empire. They will be conveyed to the citadel for execution of sentence.'

There were cries of astonishment and dismay. Rian looked

and saw that these men, four of the highest officers in the land, had been pinioned and rudely stripped of their weapons and insignia.

'Finally,' said General Teshe, 'I am commanded by Lord Heite, Gehan of the Gehans, to make known a proclamation of the Prime concerning the lineage of Brennis Gehan Fifth and the rightful inheritor of the Valdoe domain.' He turned to Bohod Khelle and Rian's blood ran cold. The General spoke and she heard what she prayed she would never hear. She heard the words that signalled catastrophe, for herself, for her children, for all that remained at Valdoe of human feeling. And for poor Hothen too.

For the General had said: 'Bring forth the boy!'

The system of exploitation devised by Brennis Gehan Fourth was so reliable that it had survived unchanged to the present day. Although based on the methods used in the homelands, it was more flexible and better suited to the needs of an island domain.

Most of the Flint Lord's income was gathered, not through taxes, but less directly, through trade, for he controlled the extraction and price of the flint upon which forest clearance and the production of crops depended. Fishing, the breeding of livestock, and certain other trades were taxed at source, by means of tithes and imposts – to which the harvest surpluses of consistently successful villages were also liable.

The harvest inspectors, nominally soldiers with a military rank, were experts in everything to do with the land. Many were themselves the sons or grandsons of farming families, and well understood the problems caused by the weather, by disease, and by evil spirits. Often, and this was a measure of how well the system was accepted, their technical advice was sought and closely followed. During drought or pestilence it was in their discretion to waive or reduce liability to impost, and even, through their regional commanders, to seek direct relief from the Trundle.

That was the tradition. In practice, the reputation of the harvest inspectorate had declined since the days of the Brennis Gehans. Under Lord Torin the inspectors had become increasingly disliked, and then hated, by the villagers in their control.

Their visits now gave rise, not to grudging resignation, but to dread.

Farming villages received three inspections a year, the first in spring, the next in the growing season, and the last in autumn when the crops were in. Few villages now escaped the impost. Even the meanest and most wretched settlement received its three visits each year. At the third the harvest was assessed and arrangements were made for the impost – in grain, meat, hides, or sometimes in crafted goods – to be carried to the nearest fort.

It was this autumn inspection that the farmers dreaded most. Once regarded as incorruptible, the harvest inspector and his men now saw nothing wrong in accepting whatever welcome each village had to offer. Depending on the warmth of that welcome, the assessment might or might not be revised. Some of the inspectors attached to the eastern forts had, so the rumours went, taken this practice one stage further. With the complicity of Commander Tourse himself, they were now demanding outright bribes.

Beilin Crogh had heard these rumours, and it was a source of regret to him that he had been posted to Matley fort, at the westernmost edge of the domain. The villages in this region were mostly quite new and undeveloped, offering little scope for the imaginative methods adopted by his colleagues in the east. Beilin Crogh hoped one day to be transferred there, or at least to a fort with a less conventional commander than his. He needed more than a soldier's pay; he dreamed of settling eventually at Valdoe Village, in the shadow of the Trundle, where he would live with his family and slaves and earn his bread by keeping bees.

But time was getting short. Already he was thirty-four and his eldest son was almost grown. His dream was beginning to look like nothing more than that. Younger men had been promoted instead of him; Beilin Crogh had come to realize that he was not well suited to this work, and now it was too late to change. He was too generous, too unsuspecting. His men, he felt, laughed at him behind his back. All his attempts to toughen up had come to nothing: he forgot each resolution as soon as it was made. This was not the way to achieve life's ambitions; this was not the way to eminence in the harvest inspectorate.

'You,' he said to the man walking beside him. 'Walver. Fasten that breastplate. Are we soldiers or what?'

Walver looked at him in surprise. After another two or three steps he tightened the straps of his leather cuirass, glancing for an explanation at Lorco, an equally insolent soldier who had only recently been moved to Beilin Crogh's team. Lorco's front teeth had been lost in a disgraceful brawl at the fort. He smiled at his superior, showing newly red gums, raising his eyebrows, and ostentatiously checked the straps of his own armour and leggings. Beilin Crogh suppressed a stern rebuke. What could he do with men like these, the dregs of the domain? There was not an ounce of sense among the four of them.

'Lorco,' he said. 'What is the name of this village we're coming to?'

'Sturt, sir.'

'Very good. And what is their crop?'

'Can't remember, sir.'

'Tell him, Fairmile.'

In a resigned tone Fairmile recited the tedious inventory of the summer inspection. So many roods of emmer, so many of oats, barley, lentils, millet; so many swine, goats, milk-beasts, heifers, a solitary bullock . . .

Beilin Crogh allowed his mind to wander. He liked the woods at this time of year. They exhaled a special smell: damp, rotting, melancholy, which meant the onset of another winter, the season when he had least work to do and could spend some time at home. This village today would be one of the last.

The road, leading downhill now through the oaks, became much wetter, strewn here and there with red and yellow cherry leaves. It had rained heavily every day for the past week: at the bottom, near the edge of the fields, Beilin Crogh saw to his annoyance that the mud was so deep as to be impassable. He would have to force a way round it, through the undergrowth, and, of more importance, carriage of the impost to Matley would be delayed.

This was the first matter he raised with Bocher, the head

man, who received him, as usual, in the Meeting House. Upkeep of official roads within two miles of the village was Bocher's responsibility, not Valdoe's.

'I'm sorry,' Bocher said. 'We'll see to it. More ale, master?'

The customary form of address, coming from Bocher's lips, sounded unpleasantly servile. Some radical change in his manner had taken place since the last inspection. Beilin Crogh narrowed his eyes.

'No,' he said, 'No more ale. I would like to begin at once.'

5

Between sleep and waking, Paoul heard unfamiliar sounds outside and adapted them to his dreams. He was dreaming again of the Meeting House on that first afternoon, when Tagart had answered the council's questions and Paoul had sat beside him listening. The sun was beating on the polished surface of the floor, pouring through the open shutters, bleaching the interior of all colour and yet imbuing it with its own special, ethereal light. Through the doorway he could see, with a clarity remarkable even for his eyes, each detail of the rising slope of trees. The shape and pattern and colour, the very texture of each leaf was quite distinct. His gaze lingered on the finely toothed edges of the cherry leaves, the cherry leaves beginning to change from green to yellow to red. They were real, and not real, for he could see through them and they were nothing. Coming down the path below them – the path that he and the others had walked just now – he could see nine soldiers like those he had seen at the Valdoe fairs. Four of the soldiers were carrying a tenth, their leader, on a wicker seat. This man had Tagart's face: he was Tagart, dressed, not in armour like his men, not in the clothes Paoul remembered, but in crude, grimy, and ill-fitting furs and skins. His arm was wounded and he was in pain. Paoul saw him raise his hand and the blood trickled across his palm and down the backs of his fingers.

But Tagart was also beside him here, in the Meeting House. Yet this Tagart did not have Tagart's face. He was well fleshed; his thick, curly brown hair had no trace of grey; his dark eyes twinkled. His beard had been shaved a few days since. For some reason Paoul liked this other Tagart. He knew him to be a friend.

The negotiations were over: Tagart stood up. So did Bocher, and Dagda, and the whole village council. They were afraid. They were afraid of the soldiers coming down the hill.

'It's there, isn't it?' Tagart said. 'By the stone.'

Despite Bocher's denials, and then his pleas, Tagart made him fold back the altar-mat. A large trapdoor had been cut into the floorboards. On either side, let into the wood so that it lay flush, was a white rope handle.

An unpleasant smell which Paoul had noticed earlier now grew stronger

'This will go badly with you if you're lying,' Tagart said. 'Open it.'

'But, master – '

'Open it, I say!'

Bocher and his wife each grasped a handle and heaved. The trapdoor was heavy and very stiff. As they pulled, as it juddered and creaked. Paoul knew what they would find. Floating in the bilge under the Meeting House floor, under the altar-stone, they would find, face up, the source of the sickly sweetness that Paoul alone had been aware of till now. They would find his father's corpse.

But the trapdoor would not open. Tagart spoke more harshly, threatening to bring his men. Bocher and Dagda pulled harder, forcing the door, scraping one edge against the cobbles. From the widening crack came daylight which spilled into the dank, greenish darkness of the tool-house and hurt Paoul's eyes.

He sat up, flinching and holding up his hands, and discerned the shapes of two men – one of them Bocher – standing in the doorway.

'I told you, master,' Bocher said.

The next voice, the voice of the other man, Paoul had heard before, but only in his dreams, and so he knew he must be dreaming still.

'What's that in there? Is it a child?'

'Nothing for you to concern yourself about, master.'

'Who is he?'

'A slave. We found him in the woods. My woman's brother has gone to make a price.'

'Bring him outside.'

'The tool-house contains no produce, master, and slaves do not count towards the impost.'

'I wouldn't treat a dog like that. Bring him outside at once.'

'May I remind you, master, that I am head man?'

'Do you seek to argue with me?'

Paoul remembered where he was, in the village tool-house, among the racks and stands and bundles of communal implements. This was the only securable building in the compound, with solid walls and a close-fitting door, against which Bocher had wedged a prop so that Paoul could not escape. He had been here for many days, perhaps nine or ten, grieving, remembering, lying in the darkness and listening to the rain. Until this morning the rain had scarcely stopped, if at all. It had blurred one day with another and he had lost count. Each morning he had been allowed out, for an hour or so, to keep him healthy. He had seen nothing of Berritt or the other children: the whole atmosphere in the village had changed. Accompanied by one of half a dozen different villagers, he had been made to walk inside the palisade until it was time to go back. Although they had also fed him well, kept him warm and, in the past few days, given him infusions in milk or water of centaury, brooklime, and then willow-bark, he had become more and more feverish, so that now, even though he was beginning to think that he might after all be awake, this version of reality seemed very little different from the one in his dreams, or rather, in his nightmares, each of which had flowed into the next to make a continuous and inconclusive whole. His father was dead. Tagart had been murdered for his sake. Tagart's body, and the bodies of the others, of all the people he had loved best, had been dragged away and hidden in the woods. Only Paoul had survived. He had been the cause of all their deaths – how, he did not understand – and now he was utterly alone.

He allowed Bocher to pull him to his feet and lead him out into the unbearable brightness of a fresh and cloudy autumn day. Flinching and shielding his eyes, he could not believe at first what he saw. The other man, the one Bocher had called 'master', was the second Tagart, the Tagart of the dream.

'How he stares at me,' the man said. Gathering up the folds of his cloak, he dropped to his haunches so that his face was just below Paoul's. 'What is your name, boy?'

Paoul was afraid to speak. The man's eyes were kindly, dark, precisely as he had seen them a moment ago, in the bleached, unearthly light of the Meeting House. This too was certainly a dream, the strangest dream of all: this too was taking place in sleep. If he spoke he would wake and lose even this imaginary friend.

'How long has he been in there?'

'A day or two,' Bocher said. 'He has not been well. We thought it best to keep him safe. If he tries to go back to the woods alone, he will surely die.'

'How can he go back to the woods? The gates are barred; without a ladder he can't climb the palisade.'

'He might try, master, and that too would be dangerous.'

'Can he talk?'

'Yes. But he is not well.'

'I forbid you to put him back in that filthy hole. Look after him properly. Let him have the run of the village, at least until your woman's brother gets back. He can't possibly escape.'

'As you wish, master.'

'Good. Now, I think we are more or less done. It is time to fix the impost.' He took a last, not unsympathetic look at Paoul. 'He won't fetch much, you know.'

Bocher humbly agreed.

On the man's initiative, he and Bocher set off towards the Meeting House, leaving Paoul alone, still feeling dazed, standing in the thick grey mud by the tool-house door. The man was slightly taller than Bocher, but rather round-shouldered. His drab military cloak was stained with much travel; his boots looked well worn. Paoul had already guessed that he might be a beilin, a harvest inspector, for he had seen one before, in another village. Beilins were soldiers, and soldiers came from the forts. Everything to do with the forts, according to what Tagart had told him, was to be shunned and feared. But this beilin was just a man, an ordinary man. At no advantage to himself, he had made Bocher let Paoul out. Perhaps he might be trusted: he might even turn out to be a friend.

Bocher and the beilin were about fifty paces away when Paoul began to follow. He saw them disappear behind the low, grey walls of one of the stone dwellings, then reappear, walking along the duckboards that led past Bocher's garden hedge. They entered the Meeting House precinct, climbed the steps and, removing their boots at the threshold, pulled on sheepskin house-shoes and went inside.

The rain began falling again as Paoul crossed the compound, keeping where he could to the raised walkways. He drew the surprised glances of two women at the bakery, but most of the villagers seemed to be indoors or in the fields, and he reached the Meeting House steps without attracting any great attention.

One by one, he mounted the wide, rain-soaked boards. Under the thatched overhang of the porch they became pale and dry, and here, by the ornately carved doorpost, stood three pairs of boots, two large and one small. Paoul timidly sat down and looked into the Meeting House chamber. Bocher and the beilin were seated near where Tagart had sat on that first afternoon. Between them, set out on a dining mat, were many small bowls and dishes, patterned and plain, heaped with dainties. A girl was filling Bocher's upheld beaker from a wooden jug.

The beilin, beaker in hand, noticed Paoul and turned. Paoul wanted to draw back. The unthinking courage that had brought him here had suddenly dissolved. But he remained where he was. The beilin spoke to Bocher and then beckoned. He smiled: for this was a whim, a diversion, a break from routine. And it confirmed his ascendancy over Bocher.

Paoul hesitated. He had made Bocher very angry. Later, Bocher would punish him for this.

'Are you hungry, boy?' the beilin said. 'Take your boots off and come inside.'

'Yes,' Bocher said, with a marked lack of enthusiasm, when prompted by his honoured guest. 'Come inside. Help yourself.'

Paoul found himself obeying. He felt dizzy. The floorboards were warm and smooth against his feet.

'Have some of this,' the beilin said, giving him a basket of honeyed reed-bread. 'I think you might like it. Then try the apple jelly. What would you like to drink? Strawberry juice, perhaps? Or milk?'

'Milk, please,' Paoul managed to say.

'So he can talk, after all. My young friend would like some milk. Can that be arranged, head man?'

Bocher nodded: the girl fetched a mug of cool milk and served it to Paoul from a tray. He was thirsty. As he drank he sensed that Bocher wanted to get rid of him but did not know how. Refreshed, already feeling better and more confident,

Paoul wiped his mouth and carefully set the mug in its proper place on the tray, just as Dagda had taught him.

The beilin noticed. 'If you sit quietly and don't interrupt,' he said, 'you might learn something interesting. We're fixing the impost. Do you understand what that means?'

'Yes, master.'

'Really?'

'The impost is the proportion of harvest taken by Lord Brennis. You are deciding what the proportion will be and in what form it will be delivered.'

With an incredulous glance at Bocher, the beilin smiled and looked back at Paoul. 'Who taught you that?'

'My father.'

'This is serving no purpose – ' Bocher began.

'Was your father a slave too?'

'No, master, he was not. And nor am I. Nor did Bocher find me in the woods.'

Again Bocher tried, with greater determination, to intervene: the beilin ordered him to be silent.

'Tell me where Bocher did find you.'

'I came here with my father and our friends looking for work. The villagers let us work for a week, then murdered everyone but me.'

'Don't listen to him, master! He's lying.'

'How many of you were there in all?'

'Eleven, master.'

'So you say ten have been killed.'

'Yes.'

The beilin gave a mischievous smile. 'What made you do it, Bocher?'

The dull and humourless Bocher did not understand. 'He's making it up, master. That's obvious. He's making it up.'

'I'm not,' Paoul said, becoming heated, feeling his advantage slipping away. 'I'm not. I'm telling the truth!'

'Then ask him where the bodies are,' Bocher said. 'We'll soon find out who's telling the truth!'

'In the woods! They're in the woods! Hidden in the woods! All except . . . all except my father, and he's under the altar, under the secret door – ' Paoul clapped a hand to his mouth. How could he have said anything so foolish? He had ruined his case, his attempt to win the beilin's trust and sympathy. The trapdoor, like the bilge under the floor, like the memory of Tagart's corpse, existed only in his nightmares. In reality the Meeting House was quite different: tangible, solid, ordinary. There was no smell, no strange light, no assembly of councilmen.

But his words had produced an astonishing effect on Bocher which did not escape the beilin's notice. 'Secret door?' he said. 'What's all this?'

'Nothing, master. Can't you see he's just a little liar? He's been lying since the moment we found him.'

The beilin put down his beaker and looked round, towards the altar at the far end of the room. His eye dwelt on the white stone itself, on the votive wreath of box-sprigs placed on its top, then moved to the expanse of rush matting laid before it.

Slowly and deliberately, the beilin rose to his feet.

Beilin Crogh chose another pouch at random and opened the drawstring. This one, like many of the others, was filled with seed rather than dry leaf. He took a pinch between his fingers and sniffed it. 'And this?'

Bocher was almost beside himself with fear. His denials had turned to bluster, then to pleading, attempted bribery, and finally to abject terror. At first he had merely sweated. Now he was weeping too. 'Coriander, master. I think coriander.'

'Also a forbidden herb, if I'm not mistaken.'

Intrigued, Crogh peered again into the space under the trapdoor. It was about three feet square and four deep, lined with broad shelves. Here, in trays, boxes, and leather bags, he had found enough illicit produce to have Bocher burned alive, and the whole village with him. Besides no less than three types of sacred herbs whose possession was, outside the red priesthood, punishable by death, there were several pecks of the permitted kinds – the equivalent of many bushels of grain. But far more remarkable than the value and variety of this hoard was the manner in which he had come to unearth it, and more remarkable still were the reactions of this strange young boy. The discovery of the very thing to which he had wanted to draw Crogh's attention had left him speechless. It was unlikely that the boy could have known of the trapdoor by normal means. Probably in all the village no more than a dozen people knew of its existence. How, then, had the boy known? And why had he said that it would conceal, not illicit herbs, but the body of his father?

At first, before Crogh had had the presence of mind to send him away, the boy had stood there watching, incredulous, in a sort of reverie. From his expression Crogh had seen that he now felt pity for Bocher and could understand, if not forgive, his crimes. Crogh himself found Bocher pitiable. The excuses he had made were human enough. He was frantic to cure his sick daughter and could not afford the necessary sacrifice. During the summer, at a secret clearing in a remote part of the woods, he and his wife had grown these herbs. The illicit ones they had obtained as seed, in tiny quantities, from a Trundleman's slave at the spring Valdoe fair. They were planning to barter the hoard with neighbouring villages once the autumn inspection was complete.

Crogh reached into the hole once more and drew out a somewhat larger and heavier bag. It contained a variety of crafted goods, evidently the spare treasure of the entire village, put here for safe keeping: stone buttons, pendants, combs, bone fish-hooks and needles, unusual shells, a damaged axe-head of ornamental limestone. Tipped out on the floor, this hopeless collection of rubbish came close to touching Crogh's heart.

Reconsidering, he looked up. The serving-girl was also no longer here; like the boy, she could no longer witness what was taking place. Bocher had sent her away even before the mat had been moved. Crogh and Bocher were alone.

'They're yours, master,' Bocher said, resuming his clumsy attempt at bribery. 'It's all yours, the herbs, everything.'

Crogh looked out of the window and into the rainy compound. His men were nowhere to be seen, still sampling the beer provided by over-friendly villagers, no doubt. He looked back at Bocher, into the hole, at Bocher again. He had never in his life been tempted by such a blatant or valuable bribe. If his commander got wind of it, Crogh would be finished. But then he thought of his family, his future, his dream of a leisured life. What would his commander do for him when he was too old to be of use? Nothing.

On the other hand, the price of the herbs, great as it was, would not go far towards paying for his dream. It might be better to win favour with the commander by reporting the matter fully; it might secure the promotion which so far had been denied, a promotion perhaps to another fort – perhaps even to the east!

'Then there's the boy, master. He's yours too. He's worth a lot, much more than the herbs. My woman's brother has gone to the priests about him. They'll want him, I know they will. You've seen for yourself.'

So that was it. Crogh suddenly understood and, understanding, suddenly became excited. This mooncalf Bocher was not so stupid, after all!

Crogh looked away. Earlier, he had rather liked the boy. He had felt unaccountably drawn to him. He liked him still, but now he was also a little uneasy. The boy was more than merely strange, an adult in miniature. He did not seem like a child at all.

Crogh felt a twinge of fear. It might yet be better to report this business in full.

'Here, master,' Bocher went on, fumbling to open his tunic. He brought out a doeskin wrapper and hurriedly unfolded it. 'Here, master. Look.'

'Where did you get these?'

'They belong to the village, master.'

'Impossible.'

Bocher did not reply, and Crogh saw no profit in pursuing an explanation which would anyway be tendered in the form of further lies. He was already engrossed in the wrapper's contents: the most wonderful jewellery he had ever seen, a small tangled heap of jade, amber, ivory, and, most precious of all, copper. Gently he extended a forefinger and lifted clear an extraordinary necklace made from interlocking scales of nacre and blue lapis. This one piece alone, this string of scales dangling from his fingertip, would take him at least half a year to earn. No: a year. Two. No; he would never be able to pay for such a thing. Or this, a tiny serpent, half the width of his palm, in copper, and amber, adorned with brightly coloured stones whose name he did not know.

Obviously Bocher had no idea what he was offering, for he

need only have revealed one piece and everything would have been settled.

Did the jewellery have any connection with the boy? It had to. In that case, he could not afford to leave the boy behind. He would have to question him at length about the jewellery before attempting, cautiously and unobtrusively, over the years, to sell it. Besides, the boy would indeed be worth a good deal in his own right. There would be no difficulty in getting him to Valdoe: the autumn inspection was nearly over, and soon Crogh would have time to spare.

He rapidly came to a decision. He would accept the jewellery and the boy, but not the herbs. The forbidden ones would have to be destroyed, likewise the secret field in the woods. The rest he would allow Bocher to keep. The sick daughter would get her sacrifice after all; the boy would be released from captivity and spared an uncertain fate, for, if the priests did not want him, Crogh would not sell him to Valdoe, but to a private home. He might even keep the boy himself. As to the question of the murders – and Crogh was inclined to believe the boy's version – that was a matter for Bocher, the village, and the Earth Mother.

After another moment's hesitation, Crogh reached out. He took the wrapper from Bocher's hands, poured in the jewels, and carefully began to enfold them.

6

All trace of Lord Torin had been expunged.

Lady Torin, her four children, and the principal members of her late husband's entourage had already sailed, in disgrace, for the mainland. His bodyguards had been dispersed and enslaved; his personal slaves had been put in the mines; even his hawks and his matched pair of deerhounds had been given away. His clothing had been burned with his corpse. His paintings, rugs, tapestries, and other valuables had been put in storage to await transmission to the homelands, where they would be sold or otherwise disposed of.

For the past three weeks, since the morning after the assassination, labourers and craftsmen had been at work in the private residence. On the orders of General Teshe, the main room upstairs – in which the prospective young Flint Lord was to eat, sleep, and conduct his affairs – had been completely stripped. The ceiling had been cleaned; the walls had been broken out and freshly rendered with Cornish clay, smoothed, limed, smoothed again, and decorated to the taste of General Teshe with murals of birds, bears, and dragons. The floor-boards had been torn up and replaced with seasoned maple, abraded with sandstones, repeatedly waxed and polished, and brought to a sheen. The doors, shutters, and all internal fittings had been renewed throughout the whole of the private residence. Rooms had been prepared not only for the customary domestic entourage – the various body-slaves, the cooks, the food-taster – but also for Hothen's tutor and for his nurse.

Rian's chamber adjoined Hothen's and shared its southerly outlook, towards the marshes and the distant sea. The chamber had once been Altheme's sitting-room. Leaning on the window-ledge, Rian could see beyond the inner palisade to the roofs and chimney-holes of the vansery, the priests' quarters. The vansery had not been there in Altheme's day; neither had the stone temple on the hill. Like his father, Gehan Fifth had abhorred the red priesthood and, except for a few apostate doctors and a single astronomer, had kept it resolutely out of Brennis. Soon after Lord Torin's accession, however, a delegation from the citadel had arrived to supervise work on the new vansery and temple. It had been finished within two years. The Prime himself had risked the crossing to consecrate the altar and make the first oblation, conferring on Valdoe the highest possible status. From then on, the priests had assumed more and more importance in the affairs of Valdoe and of the whole domain. Another vansery had recently been built, at Cissbury, and Rian had heard that yet another was being planned elsewhere.

She had no feelings, good or bad, about the priesthood. It existed: it was just part of the system that had placed her and was keeping her in the condition of slavery. The aims and learning of the priests were utterly beyond her grasp. As men, as individuals, she found them intimidating. Their self-mastery, the complete absence of any human weakness or failing, were as incomprehensible to her as their prayers, their rituals, or their special signs.

They wore special clothing, too: voluminous grey tunics of the finest cloth, grey leggings, kneeboots, sometimes a grey cloak and soft hat, sometimes grey robes. On entry to the hierarchy, each priest received a red tattoo on the left side of the body: three lines along the arm, flank, and leg, ending in a pentacle on the instep and one on the back of the hand. The lower priests of the villages were marked in a similar way, but in blue, and always on the right side. The blue priests were not required to be celibate. They were common people, farmers, chosen from the village elders. Sometimes the head man himself would serve. He would go to Valdoe or to one of the forts, where a senior blue priest would show him the necessary rites and observances. He would be taught how to pray, and how to divide the year so that his village would know when to plant and when to reap. Then he would take the blue tattoo and return to his home. Of the mysteries, of the red priests' world, he would have learned nothing.

About twenty red priests lived at Valdoe. Their studies here, it seemed, had much to do with the sky. In clear weather Rian had seen them leaving the Trundle and walking down to the temple, where they would remain till morning. Sometimes they lit fires on the beach or on surrounding hills; sometimes they erected great crosses, or poles marked in black and white, or stakes around which they would draw their sacred ropes. Once, at noon, she had seen them flying a kite and marking the position of its shadow with white pegs in the grass.

They studied other things also. At the settlement farm near Valdoe Village they bred animals and birds and maintained several plots where they tested different kinds of cereal crops. Nearby was a young orchard and an area for soft fruit, mostly blackberries and gooseberries. Rian did not know whether they ever ate the produce. Perhaps it was magic, like the plants in the physic garden. This was laid out between the vansery and the inner palisade, protected at either end by a high spiked fence. The garden was usually tended by an old priest named Kar Houle, a doctor who had once treated Ika's eyes; he had eliminated her pain, but had told her that her sight could never be restored. During the treatment Rian had got to know him quite well – as well as a slave could ever know a red priest – and, somewhat against convention, he now always acknowledged her and occasionally even exchanged a few words.

Yesterday he had told her that the choice of Hothen's tutor had been settled. The tutor was to be a young priest recently arrived from the citadel, a teller of the legends called Ilven Loes. On five mornings a week Ilven Loes was to take Hothen for exercise: for walks on the hill and, in warm weather, to Apuldram for boating and bathing. The afternoons would be spent in the residence, where Hothen would learn his numbers and speech. Later he would be taught drawing, writing, pottery, movement, and history. When he was yet older he would be prepared in earnest for his coming of age. Other priests in the vansery would teach him mensuration, strategy, agronomy; he would spend three years in the homelands, at the military academy, learning the workings of the empire. At fifteen he would enter the Valdoe barracks part time to be taught the control of men. On his twentieth birthday, provided the Vansard – the arch priest – agreed, Hothen would become Flint Lord in fact as well as title and General Teshe, or whoever then was his guardian, would step down.

That was the plan. Rian did not know how far Hothen would get with it. They must have known how backward he was, how incapable of assimilating such learning, but still this elaborate scheme for his future had solemnly been laid out. Perhaps it was all a charade. Perhaps the Home Lord did not intend him to finish his education or to assume control of Valdoe. The appearances, however, would have to be observed.

The first stage in this process was beginning today. At any moment now the tutor would be coming over to be introduced to his charge. The Vansard would accompany him; General Teshe had arranged a small ceremony to mark both this event and the refurbishing of the residence. Food and drink had been prepared; three musicians had just arrived and were tuning their instruments. Hothen had been ready for at least an hour. He was sitting with his mother in the main room, while the slaves, straightened mats and hangings that were already straight and Rian looked nervously out of the window towards the gate of the inner palisade.

She still could not believe that events had moved so quickly. She still could not believe that Lord Torin was really dead or that Hothen, poor little Hothen, had been propelled with such speed and force into the highest and most dangerous reaches of power. Three weeks ago he and Ika had been nothing, despised, ignored. Now Ika was important. She had new clothes, new jewellery, her own suite of rooms, body-slaves, everything she wanted. By sledge or litter she could travel anywhere she pleased. Hothen, naturally, also had his own retinue: Rian's work had been reduced to a tithe of its former amount. In three weeks her life had been transformed. It was unbelievable, but true. And for proof, she saw at last two grey-clad figures passing through the inner gate and crossing the mist-soaked turf towards the residence.

'They're coming,' she said, and hurried back into the main chamber.

'You must leave us now,' the older priest said.

Beilin Crogh stood up, turning his hat in his hands, and looked anxiously at Paoul. The younger priest took his arm and drew him to the door. 'The first examination will last till sunset. Come back then.'

Paoul did not look round. He heard the door close behind

him and felt even more afraid – Beilin Crogh was at least familiar. Paoul had begun, almost, to like him.

They had been staying in Valdoe Village, at the house of Beilin Crogh's father.

The walk from the west had taken four days. From Sturt, Beilin Crogh had moved Paoul to another village, nearer Matley fort. He had remained there for five days until collected by Beilin Crogh and two of the soldiers who had been at Sturt. In the interval, it seemed, Beilin Crogh had heard some momentous news about Valdoe, about the Flint Lord. Because of it he had been on the point of abandoning Paoul to the village; then he had changed his mind. At a rapid pace they had travelled the roads and tracks Paoul had last walked with the group. Each familiar bend and prospect, each river crossed had reminded him of Tagart, of the old life which now was over and would never come again. Paoul was bewildered as well as frightened and unhappy. Beilin Crogh had asked so many questions that he had made Paoul cry, but Paoul's own questions had been ignored or evaded. He knew that Beilin Crogh had bought him from Bocher and that he was going to Valdoe to be resold, as a slave. But he also knew that he was too small to work usefully in the mines or anywhere else, and he could not understand why he warranted this special treatment – why a harvest inspector and two soldiers were troubling to escort him sixty or seventy miles across country, or why Beilin Crogh was so anxious to know every last detail of his life. Beilin Crogh had interrogated him most closely on the subject of his parents. Paoul remembered nothing of his mother, but Tagart had told him that she had been kind and beautiful and had died after drinking bad water. Beilin Crogh had insisted on hearing about her, not just once, but over and over again. And her husband, Tagart, had he always been a vagrant, a nomad? How had he come to be crippled? Was Paoul sure that his father had never been connected in any way – especially by blood – with the important families of Valdoe or the mainland? And his mother? What had been her name? Had she ever owned precious objects? Necklaces, for example, or brooches? Was he sure? Had anyone in the group, anyone at all, ever owned or come by such things? And how had he known about the trapdoor? Was it truly a dream that had shown him, or did he have access to the spirits? How often did he have such dreams? Had he ever seen the future before? Never? What did he know about magic, or ritual words, or secret markings, or how the pentacle was made? What did he know about the heavens? What did he know about the sun, the moon, the seasons of the sky? Nothing? Was he sure?

On arrival at Valdoe the questioning had finally come to an end. Beilin Crogh had seemed satisfied, even pleased, with Paoul's answers. He had become more affable; he had promised Paoul that nothing bad was going to happen.

They had arrived in the village at noon, in drifting fog which had wreathed the base of Valdoe Hill and obscured the Trundle at its summit. After a meal, Beilin Crogh had taken leave of his father and had climbed the hill, returning very late at night. From his corner of the rear chamber, Paoul had strained to overhear the ensuing conversation between Beilin Crogh and his father. He had heard 'the boy' mentioned once or twice, and 'Dagda's brother', and he had been able to distinguish a few other words and phrases, but nothing to signify what was happening or what the future held.

Early this morning, for the first time in his life, he had been bathed in hot water. Beilin Crogh's mother had scrubbed him with a doeskin pad soaked in a sort of colourless jelly. Afterwards she had rinsed and dried him, cleaned out his ears and nose, examined his hands and feet and teeth, and pronounced him ready to be dressed – in new clothes, clothes of a quality Paoul had never seen before: a supple jerkin with braided seams, a doeskin blouse, kidskin leggings and breeches, hide boots lined with marten fur and fastened with horn-toggled straps.

Paoul had sniffed at his hand, tasted his skin. Even a summer bathe in the cleanest pool had always left him smelling very slightly of mud, of natural things; even a swim in the most dazzling surf had made his skin smell of the sea, but today he smelled of nothing, not even of himself. He could smell only the sickly odour of leather-dressing, coming from his new clothes.

'Where's that other boy you brought here, Crogh?' Beilin Crogh's mother had asked her son.

'I think you must have left him in the bathwater.'

And another boy, it seemed, had been left on the long ascent of the hill, approaching the dark ramparts and palisades of the Trundle, another as Beilin Crogh had led him through the jaws of the south-east gateway and into the enclosure, another as they had gained admittance to what Paoul realized were the priests' quarters, and yet another as the door had shut on Beilin Crogh, leaving Paoul alone with his two examiners.

'Now, Paoul,' the older and more important one said, rising from his seat. 'There is no need to be frightened. Nobody is going to hurt you.' He beckoned. 'Come to the light. We want to see what you're made of.'

Paoul had never been spoken to by red priests before. He had never seen them so close to. He knew they were red priests by their tattoos, and by their grey clothing. He had occasionally glimpsed such men at gatherings or festivals or, once or twice, when travelling on the road. Tagart had told him that they were to be feared, much more than the blue priests of the villages, much more than the soldiers or the Trundlemen, more even than the Flint Lord himself.

'Come along,' said the younger one. 'Don't keep Kar Houle waiting.'

Paoul stood up. He made himself walk to the window. The older priest, a man of great age with a shock of white hair and very clear blue eyes, laid a hand on Paoul's head and gently felt his skull.

'Why are you trembling so much, boy? Keep still.'

'I . . . I want to know why I have been brought here. Am I . . . am I to be sacrificed?'

The old priest looked highly amused. 'What makes you think that?'

'I once heard someone say . . .'

'Say what?'

'That children were sacrificed to the Earth Mother. By the red priests. By you.'

'I'm sorry to disappoint you. Here we cut no throats at all. Not even children's.'

'Then . . . am I to be made a slave? Tell me what you want of me.'

'Just be quiet. You talk too much.'

The old man continued, with gentle yet insistent fingers, to explore the shape of Paoul's head. 'That's interesting,' he said. 'Yes.' From a bowl beside him he took a small, flattened stick, squatted and, opening Paoul's mouth, pressed the stick against his tongue. 'Easy. Don't tense.' Paoul watched his eyes making a swift, darting examination. Paoul started to gag: the stick was instantly taken away. Next the old man's fingers probed under his jaw, feeling his windpipe and neck. 'Turn your head. Now the other way. Back again. Now come closer to the light.' Paoul felt his left ear being pulled, the end of a short tube being inserted. 'Yes. And the other. Yes.'

The younger priest had meanwhile left the room. From somewhere just beyond the doorway came a very faint tinkling sound, as of fragments of shell being blown by the wind. 'Do you hear anything?'

Paoul nodded.

'Hold up your hand when it stops.'

The test was repeated with a variety of sounds and whispered words, and repeated again, first with the right ear blocked and then the left. At the end, the old man seemed satisfied. He next made an extended and meticulous examination of Paoul's eyes, folding back the lids, asking him to look from side to side and up and down and, with the lids closed, lightly pressing the eyeballs in a dozen different ways. After this he directed Paoul's attention outside, into the enclosure. A black board, marked with concentric patterns in red, green, and white, had been hung from a post some twenty paces from the window. Using either eye, and then both together, Paoul had to describe the markings in great detail.

As question followed question, Paoul began to feel less fearful. He was even beginning, in a curious way, to enjoy himself.

'And inside the inner one? Is there anything else?'

'No . . . there might be. I'm not sure. Is it a dot?'

Once more the old man squatted, to share Paoul's view of the board, and Paoul noticed how lithe, how controlled, how unlike those of other old men, his movements seemed to be. Paoul allowed himself to become aware of what he had not wanted to acknowledge before: an indefinable, tingling sensation of fascination, attraction, a desire to please, to win the approval of his questioner. 'Don't strain,' the old man said.

'Blink normally. Breathe easily. Don't screw up your eyes. Just guess. It doesn't matter if you're right or wrong.'

Suddenly Paoul knew the old man did not intend to hurt him. And if the old man did not intend to hurt him, then neither, perhaps, did the young one nor any of the other priests, and perhaps Beilin Crogh's promise, that nothing bad was going to happen, had after all been true.

'So. What do you think it is, Paoul?'

'A cross. A white cross. Is it a cross?'

'You tell me.'

'Yes. It's a white cross.'

The old man rose to his feet. 'Please remove your jerkin and blouse.'

Over Paoul's head the young priest said, 'He might even do, Kar Houle.'

'There's a long way to go yet. But I agree, he might. If, that is, we decide to meet the beilin's price.'

The beilin's price? Paoul did not understand; but he dared not ask.

'Quickly, boy,' the young priest said. 'We've better things to do than wait for you.' And, firmly but not at all roughly, hc helped Paoul pull the new leather blouse over his head, deftly folded it, and laid it on the shelf.

7

Paoul was examined daily for almost a week, usually by Kar Houle, who was always present, but often by other priests too. On the first day they completed the examination of every part of his body – his frame, his muscles, tendons, the shape and feel of his internal organs – and, with a graduated rod and large and small pairs of pivoting, sharp-pointed tongs, they measured his height, girth, the length and thickness of his limbs, the size of his head, and the proportions of his face. They immersed him in a vat brimming with water and balanced him on a counter-poised beam. They made him run against an older boy, made him step up and down on a log, jump, lift stones, throw spears and bend bows. They felt his neck and counted his breaths, listened to his chest through a small tube, made him perform a number of contortions to test his suppleness.

The next day another priest, younger than Kar Houle but still very old, gave Paoul a selection of strange objects – both man-made and natural – and asked him to guess their origin and function. He then set Paoul some puzzles. At first they were simple and Paoul could answer without hesitation. Later they became harder, much harder, until, however much time he took, he remained baffled. After this the priest showed him a tray of small objects: a feather, a crab's claw, an acorn, a toadstool, a dead mouse. Almost at once he covered the tray and asked Paoul to remember what he had seen. That was easy. Paoul could name all the objects, even when more were added or some were taken away; but, by the time there were twenty or twenty-five to remember, and the time was reduced to just a few moments, his memory began to falter.

On the third day the same priest sat with him in the examining room. Much of the morning and the whole of the afternoon were taken up with a difficult series of tests, using pebbles at first, then wooden shapes, and then multicoloured cubes laid out on a large chequered board. The markers formed confusing patterns which Paoul had to study and, if necessary, complete, by moving, adding, or taking away one or more of the markers. When the tests became too complicated they began again, but this time the priests engaged in distracting conversation which made it even harder to think.

By dusk, when Beilin Crogh again came to collect him and take him down to the village, Paoul felt exhausted. He was beginning to feel angry and resentful, too: for not once had Kar Houle or any of the others told him when he had given the right or wrong answer. Not once had they praised or corrected him; not once had they indicated the purpose of all these tests.

'That's enough,' Beilin Crogh growled, when Paoul asked him for the hundredth time what it was the priests wanted. 'I'm not listening to any more. I've already told you, it's for the best.'

'But – '

'Another word and I'll wallop you. That's a promise.'

By the fifth day, however, Paoul thought he knew. The previous morning had been spent testing his ability to remain motionless; in the afternoon, Kar Houle had lit incense and, with the examining room in near darkness and Paoul lying on a couch of layered oxhides, had asked many questions about his dreams, particularly the one at Sturt in which he had seen the trapdoor. During this, from somewhere at the far end of the vansery, Paoul had heard chanting, five or six voices in unison, and in the soothing, extended music of their song he had thought he had sensed the thing that made Kar Houle different from other old men. He had sensed that Kar Houle was searching for signs of this thing in him. Last night, in the village, Paoul had lain awake thinking, and now, this morning, as Kar Houle again entered the examining room, as his assistant again bade Paoul make himself comfortable on the layered couch, Paoul thought he knew. He thought he knew and was indignant. He considered deliberately failing the rest of the examination. But then, Kar Houle would not be deceived, and besides, what else could the future hold? If he failed the rest of the examination – not that he was sure he had passed so far – he knew that Beilin Crogh would sell him as a slave, to work in the fields, in the mines, or worse. Paoul was alone; and he was lonely. He was lonely for Tagart, for the others in the group: for Fodich and his jokes, for Tanda's little songs, for the many smells of the forest, for the excitement of arrival and departure. He wanted nothing more than to lead that life for ever, but it was gone, just as Tagart was gone, just as Tanda and Fodich were gone. Of all the people he had met since that night in Sturt, there was none he could admire as he had admired Tagart; and yet, despite his tattoo and grey tunic, despite all that Tagart had said about the red priesthood, Kar Houle had come very close to earning Paoul's respect. More than once Paoul had caught himself trying to emulate the old man, wishing that he could be like him one day, wishing that he could be so calm and patient, so knowledgeable, and so wise.

'Now, Paoul,' Kar Houle said, seating himself on the floor, his assistant some way behind. 'You know you have no cause to be tense. Let the couch take your weight again. That's right. Like that. Are you comfortable?'

'Yes, thank you, Kar Houle,' Paoul said, just as he had been trained by the assistant. 'I am comfortable.'

'I would like to begin today by talking about your parents. Beilin Crogh has told us a little, but not enough. Your father was called Tagart, and your mother . . . Mirin. Is that right?'

'Yes, Kar Houle.'

'Those are ancient names. Savages' names. Was your father a savage?'

'No.'

'I beg your pardon, Paoul. Was he a nomad?'

'Once. Long ago.'

'He was crippled at the siege of Valdoe, was he not? And then became the leader of a party of itinerants. The others must have held him in high esteem.'

'He was a chief, chief of all the southern tribes. Fodich told me.'

'Fodich being another of the nomads? I see. Beilin Crogh tells us that your mother died after drinking bad water and that you do not remember her. Did your father speak of her much to you?'

'No, Kar Houle.'

'What did he say, if anything?'

'That she was kind and beautiful. That she loved me.'

'Nothing more?'

'It hurt him to talk about her.'

'Did Fodich or any of the others ever speak to you of your mother?'

'No, Kar Houle. My father did not want them to.'

'Don't you find that strange?'

Paoul said nothing.

'I ask these questions, Paoul, because we are concerned that you do not appear to be what you are meant to be. Is it possible that your mother was not a nomad? Could she have come from one of the villages?'

'My father would not have married a village woman. He did not like farmers. He was a chief. He was Shode, the first man of the spirit. He used to be a great hunter.'

Kar Houle waited delicately before speaking again. 'Forgive me for asking this. Are you sure that Tagart was your father?'

Paoul answered at once: he could not have been more sure of anything in his life. 'Yes.'

'And you were born on Crale Day, seven years ago.'

'That is what my father told me, Kar Houle.'

'You see, Paoul, unless we are greatly mistaken, you are not of nomad blood. Your bones are not proportioned as a nomad's are; your skin is too fair and your eyes are not dark enough. But, most of all, the shape of your head is wrong. If I had been told nothing about your parents, I would have said that they had come from the homelands. I would even have guessed that they had probably been born in one of the provinces round the citadel. Does this mean anything to you?'

'No, Kar Houle.'

'Do you remember at any time travelling across the sea?'

'No, Kar Houle.'

'When was the first time you saw the Trundle?'

'I was very young. We came here for the spring fair.'

'Tell me about it, please.'

With only a few breaks, the questioning continued all day. This interrogation, Paoul soon realized, was much more clever and searching than had been Beilin Crogh's. Paoul answered honestly: he saw no reason to do otherwise. By dusk, or so it seemed, he had exposed his complete stock of memories to view.

'So,' Kar Houle said, when he had finished. 'I expect you would like something to eat.'

The assistant brought Paoul a meal of fresh bread and butter, cheese, fruit, and a hot tisane, then left the room.

Kar Houle sat watching benevolently, sipping a beaker of herb tea. 'Is the food to your liking, Paoul?'

'Yes thank you, Kar Houle.'

'Good.'

After a pause, Paoul went on eating.

'The examination,' Kar Houle said, 'is almost concluded. You have already guessed its purpose, have you not?'

'Yes, Kar Houle.'

'Tomorrow is the last day. In the morning you will meet the Vansard. That should not take very long. Depending on what the Vansard desires, I shall then speak to Beilin Crogh. If, as is likely, we accept his terms, and if you agree, you will go to the citadel for instruction. When you are ready to return to Brennis to take up your duties, you will be offered the red tattoo. I think you have seen and been told enough in the past week to know what life here is like.'

So Paoul had been right. He had guessed correctly. The priests wanted to take him and turn him into one of themselves. But, now that he was sure of it, he no longer knew how to react. Part of him, the part that belonged to the old life, was resisting strongly. But the rest was more practical. If he went along with this, he would at least be clothed, housed, and fed: and he had seen that the priests were supplied with the best of everything. If he hated the citadel, if they mistreated him, he could always run away. He could do that as well on the mainland as here, for he had no one in all the world. And despite his doubts, and the uneasy feeling that he would be betraying Tagart's memory by accepting the offer, Paoul was secretly fascinated by Kar Houle and intrigued by the possibility of learning what it was that Kar Houle knew.

'Most vanseries train their own novices,' Kar Houle went on, 'but as yet we do not have the facilities here. Usually our boys go just across the channel to Raighe. However, as I have said, we propose to send you to the citadel. The school there is without equal. We have been privileged to be able to send it several pupils. All were talented in their own way, or we would not have put them forward. Some are being supported by their parents; the others we are sponsoring. I examined them all, just as I examined you, just as I have examined many hundreds more, both here and in the homelands. Now listen carefully, Paoul, because you will never hear such words again, not, at least, in this or any other vansery. I should not even be saying them now. It is the Vansard who decides who shall be offered a place, not I. But, so that you may conduct yourself properly tomorrow, I am going to tell you that, in all my life, I have never examined anyone more worthy of acceptance than you. If you attend to your teachers, you may one day make yourself equal to your gifts. I can praise you no more highly than that. But if you are lazy, or if you choose to ignore altogether this opportunity Gauhm has put in your way, you will be committing an act of great sacrilege. Do you understand what I am saying to you, Paoul?'

'Yes, Kar Houle.'

'And what is your inner wish?'

'I think you already know it, Kar Houle.'

The next morning was sunny and exceptionally clear, Beilin Crogh was sitting nervously on a bench in the ante-room next to the Vansard's chamber, wishing, more than ever, that he had not been so foolhardy. He should never have taken this chance; he should have left the boy at Sturt.

Through the open window he could hear the martial shouts and cries of the priests at their weapons practice in the enclosure.

'To you! To me! Now! Strike! To me!'

With each ferocious clash of staves, with each thud of wood on leather, Crogh wanted to cringe, to flinch, to put as much distance as possible between the Vansard and himself. But, beyond repeatedly wiping his palms, crossing and uncrossing his legs, and adjusting the position of his hat on the bench beside him, Crogh did not move. He had come this far: he would have to see things through. Besides, it was too late. He had already woken the beast.

At last the door opened and Paoul emerged, ushered by Kar Houle's assistant. Crogh sprang to his feet. From this angle little could be seen of the interior of the Vansard's room:

oatmeal-coloured hangings, the edge of a dais, sunshine on waxed floorboards. The assistant closed the door behind him. 'Kar Houle will be with you presently,' he told Crogh. 'Please resume your seat. Paoul and I will be waiting nearby.'

From Paoul's face Crogh could divine no clue as to what had happened. Paoul looked up at him, briefly and expressionlessly engaged his eyes, and was gone.

When Kar Houle came out he offered, with his customary, scrupulous, and intimidating politeness, profuse apologies for the delay. 'Would you care for some mead, Beilin Crogh? We do not take alcohol ourselves, but we like to offer it when the occasion arises.'

The chamber reserved for entertaining lay visitors was at the end of the corridor. It overlooked the herb garden and was much more richly and comfortably furnished than the rest of the vansery. On the wall hung a circular wooden plaque, finely polished and inlaid with ivory strips in the shape of a perfect pentacle. This, and a discreet but superbly made figurine of the Earth Mother in the niche below it, was the only sign that Crogh had not been invited into the private residence of some high-ranking soldier or wealthy merchant.

'The mead is excellent,' he said, but in truth he was so scared that he could hardly taste it. 'I don't suppose you make it here? No, well, it's delicious all the same.'

Kar Houle accepted the compliment with a gracious smile and sat back, making the cushions creak. 'Now,' he said, fixing Crogh with a clear blue gaze. 'To the matter in hand. Before we begin, however, I feel it will not prejudice our position if I tell you that we are deeply grateful to you for bringing this child to our notice. He is quite exceptional.'

'I thought of you the moment I clapped eyes on him. The policy of the priesthood is . . . it's well known. Even as far out as Matley.'

'Ah yes. Matley. We have been in contact with your commander. On his orders the head man was questioned and the village searched. You may be interested to know that a mass grave was found in the woods. It contained six males and four females, all adults. If we take the boy, their bodies will be sent here for examination. It seems that the good people of Sturt have devised a thrifty method of paying their debts to itinerant labourers.'

Crogh did not know whether he was meant to smile.

'That, of course, concerns us not in the least. What does concern us, Beilin, is the apparent inconsistency in your version of events in the Meeting House. The boy, truthful in all other verifiable respects, is convinced that there was a secret chamber whose contents you did not want him or the serving girl to see. You, however, have already assured me that there was not. The head man, even under duress, maintains that you and not the boy are correct. By a remarkable coincidence, the floor of the Meeting House has very recently been relaid. Thus your comrades from Matley were unable to get to the truth.'

This was the moment Crogh had been dreading. He had taken every possible precaution, but he had never dealt with a red priest before.

'You well appreciate, do you not, Beilin, the penalties for depriving Valdoe of its due?'

'Of course.'

'And the penalties for abetting such behaviour?'

'The boy had a nightmare. He wasn't himself, Kar Houle. It's not surprising when you think how they'd treated him, locked up in that shed for ten days. At least ten. Perhaps more. Then don't forget his father and all his friends had just been massacred. No wonder he was seeing things. I'd be seeing things myself in those circumstances.'

'You are a clever fellow, Beilin Crogh. Somewhat of a scoundrel, but a clever fellow none the less.'

'I assure you, Kar Houle – '

'No more assurances, if you please. Let us merely point out that our gratitude to you has precluded the further investigations that otherwise would certainly have been made. It is not every day a Paoul is brought to us. We do not wish to discourage the process by which he arrived. Nor do we wish to treat you unjustly. He may be, as you claim, mistaken about the trapdoor. But I think I need hardly remind you of the fate of those who earn an evil reputation for themselves. You need look no further than the example of Lord Torin.' Kar Houle indicated the pitcher. 'More mead?'

'No. No thank you.'

'As to price. You suggested four toles of copper. I have discussed this with the Vansard and he feels three would be more suitable. Three toles of copper, or nine thousand first-grade scrapers or their equivalent in raw celts or worked tools.'

'Copper is more portable. Yes. Copper, I think.'

'Very well. Copper it shall be.'

8

Paoul spent another six days at the vansery, but Beilin Crogh was no longer there to collect him each evening and take him down to the village; now he remained after nightfall with the priests, eating their food, absorbing their conversation, sleeping in his own tiny cell. Alone in the darkness, he would hug himself and weep, but at dawn, awoken by the sound of chanting, he would feel a little better and in full daylight his unhappiness receded almost completely. There was so much that was new, so much that was strange and that promised more strangeness for the future. Kar Houle and the others used these six days to prepare him for the journey and ultimately for his arrival at the citadel.

The last boat of the autumn, due to leave before the crossing became too rough, was the *Veisdrach*, a huge new vessel of nearly sixty feet belonging to the merchant Bohod Thosk. Paoul first saw it at mid-morning, glimpsed among the trees and between the sheds and workshops on the Apuldram quay. The sky, softly blue, promised more fine weather; a cold breeze was keeping the ship facing generally west, riding its mooring in the middle of the channel. From time to time, the wind disturbed a drooping standard, red and black, which hung from the sternpost.

'Those are the colours of the Thosk clan,' Kar Houle told him, as they came out of the trees, two hundred and fifty yards from the precincts of the sheds, where Paoul could see men busily at work. After taking formal leave of the Vansard and saying goodbye to the other priests he had got to know, Paoul had walked with Kar Houle down from the Trundle, along four miles of muddy road which ended here, at the Flint Lord's main harbour. Paoul noticed four men launching a black coracle from one of the landing stages. They began to scull towards the ship. 'Bohod Thosk,' Kar Houle was saying, 'is an important merchant. He owns at least a hundred villages and an estate near Hohe where Lord Heite himself is often a guest.

His traders cover the whole empire, even to the east. He has built many ships: the *Veisdrach* is one of the finest. You are lucky to be travelling on her.'

'Yes, Kar Houle.'

The quayside was strewn, seemingly at random, with stacked boxes, bales, cases of tools, bags, coils of rope, sacks, furled sails, bundles of pelts and furs, goats and pigs and sheep in wicker pens; two shag-haired grey deerhounds had been tied to the corner of the nearest shed. 'Those were once Lord Torin's dogs,' Kar Houle said. 'Now they are to be given to Bohod Thosk.' He held Paoul back as two men came past, carrying a spar. 'Keep by me.'

The shingle crunching under their boots, Kar Houle led him past the partly opened rear of the main building, an enormous repair shop which fronted the stone flags of the quay. Inside, looming out of the darkness, Paoul saw the stern of a small ship. A carpenter was chipping at the rudder with a curiously shaped adze. Another, on his back, was scraping at the keel.

Kar Houle found the harbour Trundleman in his quarters and was directed to the water's edge, where the ship's master, standing among some of his crew, was waiting to supervise the process of bringing the *Veisdrach* in. Three of the four men from the coracle had clambered on board; the fourth was sculling back towards the quay, trailing a length of light rope.

'Good day to you,' said Kar Houle.

The whole group looked round and immediately their manner changed. The ship's master, heavy and swarthy, with a grizzled beard and a pointed leather hat, smiled and proffered his palm, which Kar Houle lightly touched. 'Good day, Kar Houle.'

'I trust everything is going as you wish.'

'Yes thank you, father.'

'When do you sail?'

'On time. At noon.'

With a hand to the nape of his neck, Paoul was brought forward. 'This is the child I told you about.'

'Passenger for Hohe,' the ship's master recalled. 'His name is Paoul and he's to ask for Forzan Zett.'

'Just so,' said Kar Houle with a smile.

'When we've done loading I'll show you his berth.'

'Excellent,' said Kar Houle. 'Until then, we'd better leave you to your work. Come, Paoul.'

They retreated to a safe distance. The Trundleman emerged from his doorway; the overseer yelled an order and a dozen slaves came hurrying to the landing stage. Paoul watched intently as the man in the coracle flung the light rope ashore. It was attached to a heavier rope, and yet a heavier, which the slaves began hauling in. The three men on board, meanwhile, had freed the rudder and loosed the mooring cables and, gradually at first, and drifting slightly on the incoming tide, the great ship started to turn. The figurehead slowly came into view: a white dragon with half-closed wings, rising from an inferno of scarlet flame. Its tongue, protruding from jaws filled with incurved fangs, was forked and dark blue. As the prow came round the eyes swept the shore and Paoul felt a shiver of fear as he entered and left their sightless gaze. It was not just fear he felt, but anticipation, excitement. This ship, more even than the marvels of the Trundle or the workings of the vansery, embodied for him what the future held. The timbers of the hull drew their strength from the oak forests of the mainland; the precision of its curves was the product of a masterly expertise. The means to arrive at such a thing came only through total domination and through wealth: the wealth of the merchants allied to the power of the Gehans. And, as Kar Houle had told him, the Gehans were the citadel and the citadel was the Gehans. It was their inextricable heart. At the citadel resided the Prime; at the citadel lay the temple and the very centre of the priesthood, and it was to the citadel that, beginning here, today, Paoul was to be sent.

These were the thoughts of a mere moment, fleeting and instantly gone. There were no words for them, only the shiver left by the cold-eyed stare of the dragon before its head turned further and the bows were facing down the shore.

'Pull there! Pull, damn you! Pull!'

Bending long poles to keep the *Veisdrach* clear of the shallows, the three men on board manoeuvred her into place. Inch by inch, the water between the hull and the landing stage narrowed and, with a creek of fenders, disappeared. Two ridged gangplanks were raised to the bulwarks; final turns were given to the cables fore and aft, and the ship was secured. The slaves immediately began fetching and stowing, in what could now be seen as a carefully planned order, the heaps of cargo from the quay.

Close to, the ship looked even larger and more impressive. It smelled almost more maritime than the sea itself.

'Do you see how the gangplanks hinge?' Kar Houle said. 'As the tide comes in you'll see the ship rise. The gangplanks are made to rise with her.'

Paoul nodded.

'Those two men at the bollards. What do you think their job might be?'

'To loosen the ropes as the tide comes in.'

'And if they didn't, what would happen?'

'The ship would tilt over.'

'Not tilt. The word is 'list'. The ship would list.'

Paoul nodded again. He was becoming used to this continual correction.

'Now, Paoul, remember what I've been telling you. Keep your wits about you. This journey is the beginning of your training. I want you to keep your eyes open. Absorb everything you see. Everything.' Kar Houle pointed to his own eyes. 'These. These are the essence.'

'Yes, Kar Houle,' said Paoul, not really understanding.

The harbour Trundleman approached and invited Kar Houle to sit in his quarters to await the departure. A slave brought him fragrant tea; for Paoul there was a dish of warm milk flavoured with juniper berries. Neither the milk, nor the sweet biscuits which the slave also provided, did anything to suppress the growing sensation of fluttering in his stomach. Kar Houle continued to lecture him on what to expect of the journey and how to behave when he reached the other end. At Kar Houle's insistence he opened his leather bag and checked its contents – clothes, house-slippers, spare boots and boot-linings, a face-cloth and box of mucilage, a comb, a small pouch of flints for incidental expenses, and, most important of all, the Valdoe seal impressed with the Vansard's ring, wrapped in a square of tallowed skin and hidden in a secret pocket at the bottom of the bag. The seal, Kar Houle told him yet again, was to be given to no one but Forzan Zett.

As Paoul repacked his bag, as the loading of the ship

continued, he sensed that Kar Houle, despite his carefully cultivated calmness, was also beginning to feel anxious. His anxiety went further than mere concern for the investment the vansery was risking by entrusting Paoul to the waves; it was as if the old man had conceived a genuine affection for him, a feeling Paoul had not experienced since last he had seen Tagart. Suddenly Paoul felt very close to Kar Houle. He wanted to determine to do well, to please him, to justify his faith, to repay in gratitude the sensation that someone cared about him and worried on his behalf. But, even had he known how to express himself, Paoul was not sure how his words would be received; and so he said nothing, but fastened the straps of his bag more tightly and resumed his seat.

Something of the same effect had been produced in Kar Houle. He seemed to grow slightly more distant and, when word arrived that the ship's master was at last ready to receive the passenger, he led the way down to the landing stage in virtual silence. They climbed to the bleached planking of the deck. Immediately Paoul noticed, underfoot, a vague swaying, an absence of stability. He had left the land: he was already on the sea. From here, among the clutter of ropes and gear and as yet unstowed cargo, looking out over the curved bulwarks to the worksheds, it seemed the land had lost its permanence. By aligning the rail with the far edge of the landing stage, Paoul could see that the ship was rehearsing its rise, roll, and fall, being urged by the tide to slip its hawsers and be gone. The fluttering in his stomach grew worse.

His berth was a cramped cubicle, smelly and dark, below the smallest of the three deck-houses, reached by a steep, awkward ladder which the ship's master called a 'companionway'.

'We were expecting his lordship this morning,' the master told Kar Houle, as Paoul felt the hardness of the bunk. 'He was due to look over the ship. Been no sign of him, I suppose?'

'None. But he might yet come. His tutor has instructions to show him anything of interest.'

'Well, he'll have to be quick. The tide won't wait.'

They returned to the sunshine; the master, seeing something amiss on the fore-deck, excused himself and left Kar Houle and Paoul alone. Kar Houle guided Paoul to the rail, where there was the least chance of obstructing the crew, most of whom were by now on board, or the slaves, who had nearly completed the loading.

'So,' said Kar Houle. 'What do you think of your berth?'

'It is rather small.'

'If you feel seasick, do as you've been taught. Come up to the air and practise the breathing exercise. Watch the land, not the waves; the shore will be in view throughout the voyage, even on the crossing itself. At night watch the stars instead. If you must be sick, do it over the side and away from the wind. Don't fall overboard. Keep out of the crew's way, especially when they're hoisting sails or rowing. Be polite. Do exactly as the master tells you. He is a good man.'

'Yes, Kar Houle.'

Kar Houle continued in this vein until the master told him the gangplanks were about to be removed.

'Goodbye, then, Paoul. I hope to be alive when you return.' With his firm, dry, old man's grasp, he gave Paoul's hand a reassuring squeeze and moved to the head of the after gangplank. 'Remember what I've told you.'

'Yes, Kar Houle. I will try.' Paoul felt small and helpless, more desolate than ever: Kar Houle's brief and fatherly tutelage was finished.

'Above all, remember Gauhm.'

Paoul clung to the rail, no longer sure whether Kar Houle's feelings for him had been real or a clever illusion designed to make him more compliant. But he was determined not to cry – not, at least, until he reached the safety of his bunk.

Kar Houle descended to the landing stage. As the slaves took down the gangplanks, Paoul noticed movement on the road beyond the worksheds. A small sledge, green and red, drawn by six slaves in green and red livery, and with an arched leather hood, was rapidly approaching the quay. Kar Houle, following Paoul's gaze, saw it too and called out to the master. 'Lord Hothen is here! Put back the gangplanks!'

'There's no time! We've delayed too long already! Any longer and we'll miss the tide!'

With a good-humoured expression of frustration and regret, Kar Houle smiled at Paoul and turned to greet the arriving sledge.

'Cast off fore and aft!'

'Casting off!'

'Away bows!'

Three crewmen at the bows again brought poles to bear and, aided by other poles wielded by the slaves, began to push the *Veisdrach* away from the landing stage and into the current.

The sledge came to a halt. A young priest, an ilven in a cloak and hat stepped down and was followed by a fair-haired boy of about Paoul's age and size. Paoul had never seen him before, but he knew the boy could only be Lord Hothen. He was wearing very costly clothes: a blue cape and jacket and matching leggings, and boots of rich, supple hide.

Even before he had finished climbing out of the sledge, however, it became apparent to Paoul that his movements were not quite right. As Kar Houle went forward, the boy brought his attention to bear and his head turned on his shoulders in a slightly exaggerated way. When he showed his teeth they looked dirty and coated with overmuch saliva; his skin seemed dry, scaly, and pale, and his blue eyes were lacklustre and remote, unable to focus on anything for longer than an instant. The ilven took his hand and Paoul's own concerns were forgotten. He did not know why, but he felt a stab of sympathy for the boy. Despite his fine clothes and elegant sledge, he seemed to be lost, or aimless, deficient in some quality that healthy people possessed in abundance. No one had ever had to take Paoul's hand like that.

The ilven, whom Paoul had seen once or twice at the vansery, snatched off his hat and spoke quickly to Kar Houle, obviously apologizing.

'Out oars!'

Eight of the twelve crewmen, each with a long oar dipping from sockets cut in the bulwarks, lowered their blades in unison and stood, arms out, waiting for the next order. The bows had already turned away from the shore. Paoul, near the stern, was as close to the landing stage as he could be. He looked down. The expanse of green water was widening.

Flanked by his two companions, Lord Hothen had walked to the landing stage and come to its very edge, watching without great interest the spectacle of the departing ship. No more than a few yards separated him from Paoul.

'One! Two! One! Two!'

Kar Houle raised his hand in farewell.

Paoul, meaning to wave only at Kar Houle, elicited a half-hearted response from the boy as well. With a puzzled, jerky motion of his head he sought some clue from his tutor but, receiving none, looked back at Paoul. Briefly their eyes met. In that instant Paoul was reminded of the dragon's gaze. But the dragon had been carved from seasoned oak: a human craftsman had deliberately created its air of chilling indifference. The boy's gaze was not like that at all. It was empty only because he himself was empty. He was not made of oak; he was the antithesis of oak, of the dragon and its lineage, and yet he had been given his title and dressed in lordly blue.

'Raise the mainsail!'

Behind Paoul there was a squeaking of blocks and, hoisted arm-over-arm, the tall black sail slowly climbed its mast. The breeze did not wait for it all to unfurl: the broadening fabric filled at once, bellying towards the shore, and Paoul felt the ship tighten under its impetus. They were really under way, moving out towards the estuary, leaving the land behind, leaving the forest where Paoul had been born. Some of the goats on board, frightened by the growing swell, began bleating loudly.

'Ship oars! Raise for the mainsail!'

The road down from the forest, the worksheds and warehouses, the slaves on the quay, the three figures on the landing stage: the whole of Apuldram was steadily reducing in size, losing its detail. When his face was no longer distinguishable, Kar Houle returned Paoul's wave for the last time and turned aside, walking with the boy and his tutor towards the sheds and the Trundleman's quarters.

The sledge team dutifully followed. The green and scarlet body of the sledge, brilliant in the late autumn sunshine, provided the brightest spot of colour in the scene. Paoul watched it dwindling until the course of the ship, passing the first low, tree-clad headland, obscured not only the sledge, but the buildings, the landing stages, and all signs of human life.

The crewmen were busy with their work: Paoul was left alone, kept company only by a silent man at the tiller and the fluttering red and black standard of Bohod Thosk. As the ship moved effortlessly downstream, towards the broad waters of the estuary, Paoul studied the wild, wooded shore – not in hope of glimpsing anything familiar, for he knew Tagart had never taken him here, but trying to gather into his memory as much of the landscape as he could. This country was his home. He knew he might never see it again. He wanted, if nothing more, not to waste his last sight of it.

But he could not concentrate. He could not stop thinking of Lord Hothen and the peculiar, uneasy feelings he had raised in his breast. These feelings were with him still, dominating the view, colouring his last memories of the shore.

The channel widened into the brown vastness of the estuary, hazy against the sun, and Paoul knew his last chance had slipped away. Brennis, his home, the land for which he should feel only kinship, had escaped him. In all its forests and shores, in all its settlements, in all its forts, there was no one he could truly call his friend, no one who shared his blood. Brennis had killed his mother and then his father. Now it was rejecting their child.

'Look there, boy,' said the man at the tiller, pointing a mile or more across the water, almost directly into the sun. 'That's Eastoke Point, the harbour mouth. Get past that and we're into the open sea.'

Part 2

1

The origins of the Cult of Gauhm and the Gehan ethos were now the subject of legend as well as history. Like the citadel, like the empire, like the universe itself, the ethos began as an abstraction, a mathematical point representing only the potential for growth. All phenomena arose from this one point. The ideas it embodied were at once simple and capable of extension into realms of the utmost complexity. But, however complicated, all parts of the ethos conformed to the same pattern and obeyed the unified law of the central point. Even the elementary geometry taught in the lower temple school formed an easy introduction to the complete range of concepts the pupils would encounter later.

Gehan geometry was developed according to the basic law, in five distinct stages. The number five was sacred. It represented the four opposing elements of the universe – air, fire, earth, and water – with the addition of their sum, spirit. Each element was associated with its own level of spatial complexity. Air had no dimension, fire one, earth two dimensions, water three, and the spirit four.

The five levels of geometry corresponded to these increasing levels of complexity. First, without dimension, came the point. Secondly came another point and hence the line. Thirdly came movement of this other point and hence the circle. The line and the circle, variously combined, gave all possible geometrical figures in one plane. The fourth level, solid geometry, completed the description of static objects. The dynamic geometry of the fifth level, incorporating the dimension of time, described the phenomenon of change and was, like the fourth level, much of the third, and the advanced study of the second and first, so difficult that it was only lightly touched upon in the lower school.

The third level, and in particular the study of the circle, yielded the most fruitful source of basic symbolism. All life, all processes, behaved in exactly the same manner, following the same fourfold cycle of creation, manifestation, decay, and dormancy. The four parts or quadrants of this cycle each governed one of the four elements and each element was represented by one of the four deities. The fifth element, spirit, the motive power of the cycle, and the seed for it to continue indefinitely, was symbolized by the circle itself. Spirit could be taken as virtue, benefaction, love; in the higher philosophies it was identified as time, and then nothingness, the essence of being. By contraction the circle again became its centre and the cycle began anew.

Pupils soon discovered that these were more than mere abstractions. A process as basic as breathing followed the cycle and was indeed one of the first illustrations of it to be taught. The taking of breath, the inspiration, represented creation and was in the quadrant of air, ruled by Aih the Son. The hold of breath represented manifestation and was in the quadrant of fire, ruled by Tsoaul the Father. The exhalation, representing decay, was in the quadrant of earth, ruled by Gauhm the Mother. The absence of breath, the period before the next inspiration, represented dormancy and was in the quadrant of water, ruled by Ele the Daughter. The whole cycle gave existence, being: and it was being that impelled the cycle to continue.

At a later stage in their training, the boys in the lower school were gradually given to understand that the man who had mastered the cycle had also mastered himself. By observing the eternal truths, by regulating and controlling his own behaviour, he could predict that of other men and, if he so desired – if such a desire also conformed to the direction of the cycle – he could use it to his own advantage. The closer he came to living in harmony with the cycle, the closer he came to the essence of the central point. When he had reached the centre he had also reached enlightenment, immortality, nothingness. His desires had coincided with the innate spirit of the cycle: his will had become one with the will of the gods.

But, just as the lowliest plant or humblest animal lived and died, according to the cycle, so the pupils learned that even enlightenment, like mankind and all its works, and the world, its seasons, the moon, sun, and stars, the universe, and the cycle of universes expanding and contracting from and to the central point, the cycle of universes that made up the cosmos – everything was transient, fleeting, and illusory, governed by the inexorable progress of the essential mystery that had neither beginning nor end.

•

Below the lake, further down the mountainside, among lush, nightingale-filled woodland, one of the streambeds met a layer of granite and fell a few feet into a sunny pool. At mid morning the sound of the water did not penetrate far into the trees; the path, hemmed in by dense bracken, came upon it sooner than Paoul had expected.

The principal of the temple school, Forzan Zett, was leading the way. Behind him walked three other novices besides Paoul who, as the youngest, was bringing up the rear.

Although he was only sixteen, Paoul had long ago been placed in the teaching group of these older boys. They were now eighteen, some two years away from their initiation. Like them, Paoul had just passed with honour from the lower school and was ready to begin his higher training. This morning's lesson marked its start.

Slabs of rock had been placed by the pool for use as benches. They were already hot; away from the shade of the woods the heat was intense. A gaudy blue dragonfly was hawking to and fro over the water, which, after the turbulence of the fall, flowed limpidly away above a clean gravel bottom. The waterfall and its pools were sacrosanct. It was here, on this very spot, two hundred and ninety-seven years ago, that the Earth Goddess had appeared to the man who was destined to become the first Prime. She had revealed to him the nature of the ethos and the means by which the empire was to be attained.

This meeting between man and goddess, the genesis of the Gehans, formed the central legend of the entire Cycle of Songs. In its usual form the story had Atar – the man who was to become the first Prime – gazing at his own reflection in the pool and pondering on the meaning of existence. Atar was young and handsome, born into a noble family, but at twenty he had given away all his possessions, left his bride, renounced his inheritance, and withdrawn to the mountains, where he had lived in solitude for seven years. Each day he would come to the pool to drink and bathe, and afterwards he would study his reflection, searching for the answer to the problem with which he had been wrestling for so long. One autumn morning he looked up to see Gauhm, the Earth Goddess, emerging from the waterfall in human guise. Day after day she had watched the young man and had fallen in love with him. Atar, overwhelmed by her beauty, allowed himself to be seduced – or perhaps it was the other way about. Their congress was the beginning of knowledge. Atar vowed to worship her and in return she imparted the secret of being, until then known only to the gods and still their jealous preserve. He begged her to stay, to forsake her consort Tsoaul and their progeny Aih and Ele; but she returned to the pool and vanished in the fall.

Besides this central Song to Gauhm, the Cycle of Songs consisted of one hundred outer legends. The first of these could also be regarded as the last, preparing the listener for his return to the centre. To understand the First Song, one had to know that it was describing the physical setting of the genesis. Refraining from any mention of Gauhm or Atar, the Song, in apparently simple and guileless language, invoked the cycle of rainfall and used it as an example of the universal cycle. Water, rising from the sea, became combined with air in the form of clouds. Driven by fire – the sun – the clouds arrived at the land, the mountains, where they condensed into droplets which fell as rain. From the mountains the water flowed downhill and returned to the sea.

'Today,' said Forzan Zett, once they had all made obeisance and were seated, 'I wish, as you have been informed, to discuss the First Song. Buin, will you tell us what you know?'

Paoul was relieved that he had not been asked first. He knew every word of the Song; for the past week its sense had been the subject of his morning meditation, and yesterday, for many hours, he and Enco had studied its symbolism in depth. He had prepared himself thoroughly, but he knew this would no longer, in the higher school, be enough to satisfy his teachers. And he was still, even now, a little afraid of the formidable principal of the school, the man who had taught Lord Heite and who was a close companion of the Prime.

Buin launched his dissertation confidently, giving an orthodox account of the meaning of the Song. The endless flow of water in the fall represented time, the water itself the material world by which time was made manifest. The material world was composed of an infinity of droplets, weak and insignificant on their own, but capable of any achievement – even of cutting into rock – when united and allowed to function over an extended period. By inference from the Second Song, the droplets could also be compared to individual men joined together in society. Certain individuals rose, or were thrown, above the torrent as sparkling spray, making a rainbow. The droplets of the rainbow were the highest and strongest among men, those capable of transcending, however briefly, the run of white water; those who could prolong, for a moment, their passage through the world. But even the highest and strongest of them had eventually to return to the body of the stream and hence to the sea. In other words, they had to die.

Forzan Zett received Buin's disquisition in damning silence. 'If you remember, Buin, I asked you tell us what you know. You have merely told us what you have been taught. The two, you will appreciate, are not the same.'

Buin blushed deeply.

'Enco, perhaps you have something original to offer.'

Enco was eighteen, dark and sallow, with a square face and rather large, rounded ears. His modest, phlegmatic disposition concealed an incisive approach to his studies; of all the people in the school, he was Paoul's best and closest friend. 'In the first verse,' he said, 'the Song speaks of the water's roar. This may be the world-noise, the gauhm.'

'Did you arrive at that idea alone?'

'No, Forzan Zett.'

Forzan Zett glanced at Paoul. 'Very well. Continue.'

'It is significant that, in the genesis, Gauhm vanishes in the fall. This reinforces the theory that the waterfall represents the substance of earth and mankind. Because it is also moving and represents time, the waterfall may be taken to symbolize not only mankind itself, but also the condition and affairs of mankind, which are in a state of constant change.'

'That much Buin told us.'

'The rainbow is a function of light and thus of Tsoaul. The iridescence of the droplets, besides marking them out as enlightened, is therefore also a symbol of Atar's congress with Gauhm, because, by joining with Gauhm, Atar took on the role of her consort. In worshipping Gauhm, the enlightened man takes on some of Tsoaul's attributes and so approaches more nearly to the central point. A rainbow, however, may only be seen under certain conditions. When there is no sun, or when it is not viewed from the proper angle, the rainbow disappears. From below, for example, from the viewpoint of the main body of the stream, the rainbow will be invisible. To the ordinary man caught up in the affairs of the world, therefore, the higher man does not appear to be enlightened. He appears only to occupy a higher place.'

Forzan Zett restrained a smile. 'Is there more?'

'In . . . in the Fourth Song the rainbow is used as an example of illusion. If a rainbow in the sky is an illusion, the lesser rainbow of the fall is doubly an illusion. Hence enlightenment is the triple illusion.'

Now Forzan Zett smiled openly. 'Starrad, from which Song do those words come?'

'I'm sorry, Forzan Zett. I do not know.'

'Buin? Paoul, then.'

'The Fiftieth.'

'I was not aware that you had reached the Fiftieth.'

'Ilven Melchor recited it at the summer solstice, Forzan Zett.'

'So he did.' Forzan Zett turned and for a moment contemplated the waterfall. The four boys looked at each other and then at their teacher, waiting for him to speak again.

Paoul was not sure whether he had blundered. The interpretations Enco had expounded were mainly of his doing, and Forzan Zett seemed to know it. Paoul also felt unhappy about the unfavourable impression that Enco's answers would have given of Buin and Starrad. But then neither of them had made any real preparation for this lesson; they were still relying solely on their intelligence to carry them through. And Starrad, risking everything, had even been slipping out at night to visit a girl in the township.

Paoul studied the Forzan's powerful shoulders and the back of his neck. Despite the sound of the fall, an intense stillness had the morning in its grip, a stillness inseparable from the force of the principal's personality. It seemed impossible that they were less than two miles from the citadel, less than two miles from the township and the garrison. It seemed impossible that these woods were not the primeval forest, but a carefully preserved and tended part of the temple grounds. Except for the intrusive slabs of rock and the evidence of the path, this pool could have been in some region unknown to man. Its vegetation was lush and apparently undisturbed; the birds nested here in peace, and still the dragonfly was hawking to and fro.

Forzan Zett treated Paoul to a moment's cool appraisal. 'Now,' he said, addressing the whole group. 'Before your misguided imaginations carry you any further along these overgrown and hazardous paths, I feel it is time to examine this Song in a logical manner. Buin has rightly reminded us that the Song invokes the cycle of rainfall. This will be our starting-point. Paoul, to which quadrant of that cycle does a description of a waterfall properly belong?'

'To the third. To the Quadrant of Earth.'

'Because, Starrad?'

'Because the water is on the mountain.'

'And we are studying its progress downhill. We are studying its decay. Why is this appropriate? Buin?'

'The Song is about Gauhm, master.'

'We see, therefore, that the physical setting of the genesis could scarcely be more apt. It even takes place in the autumn, the third quadrant of the year. Before proceeding with this, however, I wish to summarize what you have been told in the lower school. You have been taught to perceive phenomena in terms of a multitude of concentric and interrelated cycles, each having the properties and direction of the universal cycle. Let us take an example. You are asked to describe an old widow who learns that her daughter is with child. The unborn child you would assign to the first quadrant, the daughter to the second, the widow to the third, and her late husband to the fourth. This analysis you would correctly maintain as valid notwithstanding the condition, for example, of the daughter's fortunes, which might be declining, or the state of the village or province in which these people lived. These other facts you would perceive as being governed by different, yet related, cycles. Are we agreed? Good. Now we can return to our consideration of the First Song. Buin has said that the waterfall, which, as we have seen, belongs to the third quadrant, is a symbol of the world. What may we deduce from this? Starrad?'

'The world is in a state of decay.'

'Exactly. Decay. Leaving aside all secondary symbolism, this is the theme of the song. Decay. Do you understand?' Forzan Zett indicated the fall; Paoul began to feel a sense of rising excitement. It was as if he had smoothly and swiftly been brought close to the core of the ethos. 'The waterfall is old. The mountain is even older, but not as old as the world itself. It was created and became manifest long ago. You know from your studies that there is no clearcut division between quadrants. Each succeeding quadrant has many properties of the one that went before. Decay continues into dormancy, dormancy into creation, creation into manifestation, and manifestation into decay. Yet there comes a point at which one can say with certainty that the properties of a single quadrant are ascendant. Consider the case of our imaginary family. The widow has lived a long life; she is old. Her faculties are obviously failing. Her mind and body are in a state of slow but inevitable disintegration. She is, beyond question, proceeding towards the literal decay of her flesh. We assign her to the third quadrant, even though she is actually every bit as manifest as her daughter. So with the world. It is manifest: it is all around us. But from innumerable clues we know that it is disintegrating. Even were we incapable of interpreting such clues, the mere fact that the world is manifest would alone be enough to tell us that it is either approaching or has entered the quadrant of decay. I want you to bear this idea in the forefront of your minds. I cannot emphasize it too strongly; it is crucial to your higher studies. These will include a basic astronomy in which you will learn that the cycles of the planets, the sun, the stars, and the universe itself are all passing through the third quadrant. The cycle of the universe has been in decay for an unimaginable period of time. It was decaying long before the birth of the sun, the planets, or the earth. Likewise the earth began its decay long before the appearance of mankind. The manifestation of mankind is in fact a symptom of the earth's decay, just as the manifestation of the earth was one of the symptoms of a dying universe. Greater cycles contain the lesser: this is one of the first laws you were taught.

The earthly cycle contains and dominates all the lesser cycles. Do you now begin to understand why we worship the Earth Goddess rather than the others of her Family? Do you see why it was the Mother who appeared to Atar and not the Daughter? Why was it Gauhm who betrayed her consort and divulged the secret knowledge of the gods? Because man is of the earth, and she is his goddess. Hers is decay; hers is the influence that dominates all the lesser cycles. The earth is dying. Its wonders and its treasures are transient. Soon they will be gone, no matter what use we make of them. How, then, should the enlightened man treat such a world and all it contains? Buin? Paoul?'

Paoul thought he knew, but dared not speak. The implication of Forzan Zett's words was too exciting, too vast, too horrifying and profound to be absorbed immediately. They had integrated and amplified all that he had ever felt or learned; as if in a flash of lightning he had seen illuminated the innermost recesses of the Gehan mind.

'Starrad? Enco?'

None of the boys was able – or wanted – to offer an answer.

'Let us take another example. A man has been marooned on a small island far out at sea. His only fresh water is in a single cask. When the cask is empty that will be the end of his water and he will die. The cask is leaking. There is nothing whatever he can do to repair it or to prevent the water from seeping away. In these circumstances, should he stint himself or should he drink his fill? Starrad, if you were that man what would you do?'

'Drink.'

'Of course. And so would I. So would anyone. The leak, then, decay: this is the theme of the First Song. Metaphorically, the enlightened man should drink. He should take and use the treasures of the world. This is the essence of the message transmitted by Gauhm to Atar.' Forzan Zett looked up; the sun was almost overhead. 'The secondary symbolism of the Song, although of subsidiary importance, is nevertheless extremely rich and we shall be exploring it at our next meeting, which, by the way, will take place in my chambers. Before then I want you to consider a statement made by Enco. He said that the roar of the waterfall might be compared to the gauhm or world-noise. I should not need to remind you that the gauhm is the universal sound, produced by the dynamic interaction of the elements. The noise of the river is one example. Another is the sound of wind, or of a forest fire, or indeed the pulsing of blood in your own ears. Doubtless you can think of many other examples, any of which might serve as a fruitful seed for meditation.' Forzan Zett arose and the boys instantly did likewise. 'Now I believe Kar Ander is expecting you for taug.'

Under their teacher's critical supervision, each of the novices made the signs of obeisance appropriate to leaving a holy place. Forzan Zett then made his and led his pupils to the line of white pickets which marked the boundary of the shrine.

'Paoul, shall we walk together?'

They started uphill through the green summer woods, Paoul respectfully taking the position on Forzan Zett's right. Paoul was afraid that he was going to be reprimanded for the possible irreverence with which he and Enco had interpreted the First Song; but he was mistaken. 'You may have heard,' Forzan Zett began, 'that Bohod Thosk's new hall is to be consecrated in three weeks' time, at the Crale. Lord Heite and several members of his family will attend the ceremony, which will be conducted by the Prime. It is the custom of the temple school to be represented on such occasions by two students, one junior and one senior, to act as lamp-bearers. I have already appointed the junior student; you are to be the other.'

Paoul was speechless, overwhelmed.

'I am counting on you to live up to this distinction. Remember, you will be the representative of the whole school. The reputation of three hundred boys and their teachers will rest on your shoulders.'

'Yes, Forzan Zett.'

'Rehearsals begin tomorrow. Report to Ilven Gars at the fifth hour of the afternoon.'

'I do not know what to say, Forzan Zett.'

'Then, Paoul. I advise you to say nothing.'

2

The transition from the lower to the higher school had brought many changes. Most painful of these was the ending of the close relationship between Paoul and his matron, the lay woman who had been charged with his emotional development. Her name was Erta, and he had shared her with five other boys. She had never said as much, but he suspected that she kept a soft spot in her heart for him alone. When the time came for them to part he realized how much he had grown to love her and how completely he had come to regard the citadel as his home.

He had not forgotten Tagart, but the memories of his earliest life had now become diffuse and remote, as if belonging to some former existence – which, in a way, he supposed they did. Only the flavour of the Brennis countryside had remained within him unimpaired, so different from that of the mainland, so subtle and verdant compared with the dramatic scenery of Hohe.

In the years since coming here, Paoul had almost finished growing. He had attained all but an inch or two of his adult height. This, the kars had long ago predicted, would be fractionally less than the average. Under their guidance, he was in the process of realizing in full the physical potential of his childhood. Like all the recruits and trainees at Hohe, he was being fitted for a life of service to the Gehans. In the army, emphasis was placed on physical development as the basis of the military ideal; in the priesthood, it was viewed rather as the first step towards the mastery of self which alone allowed higher mental and spiritual development. For this reason, physical culture or taug was accorded great importance in the training of a novice. Its teaching was in the hands of the kars, the doctor-priests. The taug embraced all matters of health and hygiene; the treatment of injury and disease was seen as a minor part of its discipline. Its goal was the perfection and integration of the body's natural systems and processes. A man correctly trained in its techniques seldom succumbed to any but minor or accidental ailments. In the absence of an external cause of death, exponents of the taug regularly lived to be eighty, ninety, or even older. Kar Meisch, one of Kar Ander's predecessors at the taug school, was now a hundred and three. It was rare for a farmer or slave to survive beyond fifty; the longevity of priests was in itself a matter for awe and a sign of their divinity.

In this, as in most things, the Gehans played on the ignorance of the common people, or pagans, as they were contemptuously called. The methods of the taug were kept in the strictest secrecy. Even simple medical treatment was forbidden to anyone outside the red priesthood, the ruling clan, the highest ranks of the army, and the merchant class of bohods – who had to pay handsomely for the services of a kar. The ordinary people were allowed their own healers, usually chosen from the blue priesthood, but these had to work with an inadequate range of herbs and knew nothing of the taug.

The taug derived from the basic law and thus, like the human frame itself, was divided into five interdependent sections. The first of these, characterized by the right arm, was the quadrant of flexibility and control. In this the novice acquired not only extreme suppleness in all parts of the body, but also the most refined and delicate precision of movement, especially in the hands. Each of the four fingers – and the thumb – had its own symbolism; the hands were indistinguishable from the concept of control on which the empire was based. But control also implied strength, which was the province of the second quadrant. Its training produced a coordinated development of all the muscle systems and paved the way for the third quadrant, that of endurance. In this, novices were subjected to steadily increasing workloads – in walking, running, climbing, swimming, and the carrying of weights, and were exposed to lack of food and water and sleep, and to extremes of heat, cold, and humidity. The fourth quadrant dealt with diet, cleanliness, refinement of the senses, and care of the bodily organs.

The four quadrants of the taug were symbolized by the limbs and the associated areas of the trunk. Its essence was symbolized by the head. Study of the essence was concerned with the mind in relation to the body: with carriage and efficient use of the frame, control of muscular tension and the emotions, resistance to pain, self-healing and mobilization of the vital force or spirit, and, ultimately, with excellence in unarmed combat and the use of weapons. Combat, one of the necessities of control, led back to the first quadrant and the cycle began anew. Progression on the cycle of taug eventually raised the student beyond the physical and brought him to the realm of the intellect – which was the territory of other teachers besides the kars.

It was considered best to begin the taug as early as possible: a boy of five was not too young. At that age a child's body was held to be in a virtually natural state, uncorrupted by misuse or the influence of unsuitable adults. Paoul had begun his training aged seven, rather later than Kar Ander would have liked, but he had made such good progress that he had now overtaken some of the boys who were not only two or three years older, but who had started at the age of five or even sooner.

There were four main classes of priests, or nominations, each corresponding to one of the quadrants of the cycle of knowledge: the ilvens, who specialized in the arts; the kars; the phedes, who were scientists and mathematicians; and the forzans, whose field was philosophy, ethics, theology and the law. Early in a boy's training it was clear to his teachers where his talents would be likely to take him, and the approach to his taug would be individually adjusted. Buin, for example, who had a gift for poetry, was having special training in rhythm and the voice; Enco, who was himself destined to become a kar, was making a deep study of the fourth quadrant; while Starrad, one of the cleverest boys in the school and a potential astronomer, was receiving special training of the eyesight. Paoul's taug was much concerned with the essence and with the first quadrant: he was being prepared for the duties of a forzan.

To counteract some of the disadvantages of this early specialization, teaching groups in the higher school were composed of one boy from each discipline. They shared the same dormitory, ate at the same table in the school refectory, and, whenever possible, took their lessons together.

The taug school was on the far side of the vansery grounds, adjoining the open mountain. The quickest way there from the novices' quarters would have been to cut through the cloisters and straight across the temple square. The temple square, however, was overlooked by the rear chambers of the Prime. Even when the Prime was absent, as today, it was not allowed for novices to set foot in the temple square unless accompanied by a teacher. From their quarters, therefore, Paoul and Enco had to walk past the clothing stores and laundry and – keeping strictly to the permitted paths – follow an involved route through the animal sheds and paddocks, the fruit and vegetable farm, the physic gardens, and thence into a stand of yews. Some of the trees overhung the vansery palisade, on the other side of which, from the closely built streets of the township, rose the cries of children at play.

'Do you think this is where he gets out?' Enco said.

Paoul did not know. Speculation about Starrad's nocturnal adventures was a favourite topic at the moment; Paoul preferred not to think about it. The consequences for Starrad, if he were caught, would be severe. Paoul fully shared the urges to which Starrad had given way, but it was part of his training to contain those urges and channel them into higher activities. 'Come on,' he said. 'We don't want to be late.'

This afternoon's taug, a general session, was to be attended by all of Paoul's group, together with four other groups of the same year. Most of the class had already assembled as Paoul and Enco, dressed in freshly laundered tunics and carrying their swimming gear, hurried across the sun-baked lawns and entered at the side door.

The building was cool and spacious and smelled of beeswax. The walls of the main classroom, part panelled and part limewashed, reflected the glare of the day outside: all the storm-shutters and doors to the terrace had been thrown open. Beyond the low wooden balustrade, the mountainside fell away into sheer space. There was nothing between the terrace and the next peak, Mount Sandle, twelve miles west of the river. Its very tip still bore a remnant of snow; as far down as the treeline its flanks, even at this distance, looked mostly bare, the great slabs of weathered and broken rock devoid of any but the sparsest vegetation. Then, scattered at first, the firs began, becoming densely bluish green before gradually yielding, far below, at the same level as the citadel, to the richer green of the deciduous forest which once had covered the entire Home Plain and which still covered the lower slopes of Mount Atar, up beyond Hohe and the citadel towards the fir-woods of the summit.

This view of Mount Sandle, and of its companions stretching into the farthest distance, dominated the whole vansery and lent the taug school, jutting out over the lake and the canopy of trees, a feeling of airiness and light. But it was also a constant reminder for the pupils of the harshness and solidity of the mountains. In the best weather – on a day like today – and under strict supervision, Paoul and his fellows had once reached the top, a feat that had made them all the more aware of the mountains' hostility, and conscious of the achievement of some of the senior priests, who had climbed Mount Sandle many times, and not just in summer, but in the depths of winter too.

The most enthusiastic climber at Hohe was Kar Ander, head of the taug school, a quiet and entertaining man of forty-one with very pale blond hair worn in a long pigtail, a neatly trimmed blond beard, and intensely blue eyes. More perhaps than any of the other teachers, Paoul admired, and, for a time, had even hero-worshipped, Kar Ander, trying to copy his mannerisms and appearance, even to the extent of wishing that his own hair could also be blond and his eyes blue. That phase had long since passed, but Paoul still retained a profound respect for him. Kar Ander, together with Erta, had been the main influence on Paoul's upbringing. Erta was gentle, kind, and indulgent; Kar Ander was strong, resolute, and wise, the personification of the Gehan ideal. Kar Ander's body was the living proof of the taug. At weapons practice – with the bow, spear, axe, hammer, flail, net, and shield – he made even the Vuchten, the crack, shock-troops of Lord Heite's garrison, look clumsy and inept.

Far more impressive than any of this, though, was the intangible optimism, the positive energy made manifest in his every movement and gesture. According to the ancient doctrines that predated even the taug, Kar Ander had awoken the vital force from its deepest seat at the base of his spine. It had now infused his whole being. He could never be seriously ill. Unless injured or killed, he would grow old naturally, deteriorating at the slowest possible speed, and, at the end of the maximum term his body could sustain, he would peacefully die. Until then he would experience each moment to the full, completely and thoroughly alive; and it was this vitality that he radiated wherever he went.

The atmosphere in the room changed: the class had come subtly to attention. Paoul looked round. Kar Ander had entered.

'Good afternoon, gentlemen,' he said, in his calm, even, and perfectly controlled voice. 'To the terrace.'

After an hour's exercise in the sunshine, the class descended to the lake. The northern end was set aside for bathing, with a changing shed for visitors, a small raft, and marker buoys for distance swimming. Normally the boys would have been brought here by another kar; Kar Ander's teaching time was too valuable to be spent on routine supervision, but this afternoon he wished to gauge their progress in person.

The lake formed part of the vansery grounds. It was open only to the priesthood and to members of Lord Heite's family and their guests. Overlooked on its north-east side by the citadel, the water was seventy or eighty acres in extent, with many wooded islands. The largest of these were in the southern end, and here nested the herons whose fate had become inextricable from Hohe's – for enshrined in the legends was the belief that if ever the heronry failed so would the citadel and the whole empire. The lake had become the herons' sanctuary. Much of the shore had been left wild; the northern end had been partly screened with a magnificent grove of beeches – planted, according to legend, by Atar himself. In front of this Founder's Grove a close sward, kept specially short by the early morning grazings of the lakeman's three white goats, extended to the water's edge and to a small clump of ornamental cut-leafed alders.

When everyone had undressed, Kar Ander started the class in relay. One by one the weaker swimmers reached their targets and dropped out, leaving the rest still churning through the cold, clear water of the lake. Paoul's target for today was seventeen laps of the two hundred yard course; he was one of the last to finish. Climbing out at the end of his swim, he felt again the familiar fatigue, as if his flesh had been softly but repeatedly clubbed, that meant he had exceeded his previous maximum by the required amount. The sensation was not unpleasant. Paoul liked swimming, especially at this season, even when the load was being steadily increased. Most of his classmates liked it too. Having been judged by Kar Ander and with his permission, they were now lazing on the sward or, laughing and fooling about, had plunged in again and swum out to the raft. There would be no more lessons today.

Paoul picked up his chamois leather and dried his face and arms.

'Your style is still too formal,' Kar Ander told him. 'And you are still snatching a little at your breath. Let the air come naturally, in harmony with your stroke.'

'Yes, Kar Ander.'

'Otherwise, your progress is satisfactory.'

'Thank you, Kar Ander.' Paoul rubbed at his hair, prolonging the moment before he was dismissed. All through his swim he had been unable to stop thinking about this morning and the waterfall. Could it be that Forzan Zett's words had really been such a revelation to him? Or had he invented those feelings because he so much wanted to understand, to do well? Was he deceiving himself? But, even more than the lesson itself, what the Forzan had told him afterwards had thrown his mind into ferment. To bear a lamp at a consecration attended by Lord Heite and conducted by the Prime – surely there could be no greater honour in all the school! The honour was made greater still by the fact that Paoul was so young. He did not want to admit it to himself, but this was a source of pride, and pride was specifically disapproved of by his teachers. And so, even though he was bursting to tell Kar Ander what had happened, he did not know how to do so without seeming boastful. It had occurred to Paoul that he surely knew already: as one of Paoul's teachers, he must have been consulted by Forzan Zett and the Prime.

But if he knew, Kar Ander was not letting on. Paoul's hopes that he would raise the matter were left unfulfilled. The next swimmer to finish was already wading ashore.

Before he had left the water, however, Kar Ander's attention was attracted by movement among the smooth grey boles of the beech trees. Paoul followed his gaze and saw a man and a woman on the path, being followed by two slaves carrying bags, and a squad of ten soldiers dressed in the green, red and grey of Lord Heite's personal guard. Although the man and woman were not actually touching, the way they were walking conveyed an unmistakable sense of intimacy. The man, tall, fair-haired, of middle age, and dressed casually in a pale tunic, was indeed none other than Lord Heite himself. The woman Paoul had never seen before. She was dark and young and, even from here, looked extremely pretty.

Kar Ander clapped his hands. The two swimmers still on the circuit broke off their practice; those on the raft dived into the water, and they all made for the shore. By the time the newcomers had arrived, the whole class was standing in formation behind Kar Ander.

Paoul understood little of the ensuing conversation between Kar Ander and Lord Heite. Despite the terrifying proximity of the Gehan of the Gehans, Paoul scarcely looked at him or heard a single word he said. From his position in the second rank, he could do nothing but fight the urge to stare without restraint at Lord Heite's companion.

She was the most beautiful woman he had ever seen.

3

The three syllables of her name made the loveliest sound in the world. In his bed, letting them infuse his thoughts, Paoul repeated them over and over again. Atane, Atane, the Lady Atane. Lying awake long after midnight, listening to the dogs barking in the township, he could not keep his mind from her face and her voice and the shape of her body. He could not keep his mind from the wonderful events of the afternoon.

Put logically, coldly, they were simple enough. She and Lord Heite had come down to the lake for a swim. They had arrived, inadvertently, at the end of the lesson. Kar Ander had immediately offered to leave; Lord Heite would not hear of it. Kar Ander was one of his personal friends. Lord Heite insisted that he and his class should remain just as long as they liked. Wasn't this, Lord Heite had asked, the class that had just entered the higher school? And wasn't this the class that was to provide the senior lamp-bearer for Bohod Thosk's consecration? Whereupon Kar Ander had been persuaded to point out the chosen one and, for the first time in his life, Paoul had been addressed face to face by Lord Heite. 'So this is the special young man from Brennis. The Prime has spoken to me of you, Paoul.' Lord Heite had said other things too, all equally intoxicating. Paoul still felt dizzy: he could not really remember them now. He had been intensely aware of the Lady Atane in her green-grey robe and sandals, her soft and shining dark hair worn loose about her shoulders, her amused, intelligent dark eyes taking everything in, responding to every word spoken. Then, later – after she had emerged from the changing shed in an off-white garment which had contrasted with the smooth, slightly olive, southern perfection of her skin – Lord Heite had challenged Kar Ander to a race, out to a birch-covered island and back. Kar Ander, of course, had beaten him easily, but Lord Heite had been expecting this and had merely laughed. And then Lord Heite had suggested that Atane should race someone. With an enchanting smile she had tried, in vain, to refuse. 'You must race, if only to restore honour to the military!' Laughter. 'But not Kar Ander – he's too good for anyone.' Then – who was a good swimmer in the class? No one? Surely not. What about the lad from Brennis? What about Paoul? Would Kar Ander permit it? 'He's just swum all but two miles, my lord.' 'Then the competition will be slightly more equal!'

There were two things Paoul remembered most about the race. The first was the fact of being in the water with her, of sharing the same sensuous, all-encompassing medium; the second was his appreciation of the need for delicacy in his tactics. For it had been instantly obvious that she had neither strength nor skill in swimming. Thus, rather than win by too great a margin – or, worse, shame her by deliberately losing – Paoul had contrived to finish only a few yards ahead.

'Well swum,' she had said, once back on dry land. 'I'd hate to race you when you're fresh.' She had understood his strategem and, in this exquisitely private and elegant way, had chosen to thank him. Trapped in her dark glance, Paoul had been tongue-tied, powerless, and she, sensing it, had lowered her eyes. Then she had looked up at him again, boldly, as if he were a man and not a boy. An instant later the slave had enclosed her in a wrap and she had danced away towards Lord Heite, ignoring Paoul, and in the few minutes left to him by the lake she had scarcely glanced at him again. But that look, that one look, had been more than enough.

'Enco,' Paoul whispered. 'Enco. Are you awake?'

Paoul heard the neighbouring mattress creak as Enco turned over, growling disagreeably. 'What is it?'

'I'm thinking about the Lady Atane.'

'What about her?'

'How old do you think she is?'

'Twenty. Twenty-two. I don't know. What's it got to do with us?'

'Do you think she's been at Hohe long?'

'Go to sleep.'

Starrad's quietly jeering voice came from the corner. 'Paoul's in love.'

'But not with a fishmonger's daughter,' Enco said. 'At least he doesn't sneak over the palisade every second night.'

'Who says I sneak over the palisade? And even if I do, who says I'm in love with her? If I go, it's for one thing, and one thing only. The same thing Lord Heite gets from the Lady Atane. He's probably between her legs right now.'

Paoul sat upright. 'No!'

'If not her, then one of his others. Even Lady Heite. They're all the same.'

'You'd better shut your filthy mouth, Starrad.'

'Or else what? You're young, Paoul. You don't know a thing. Why do you think those two came down to the lake exactly when they did? They knew we'd be there, that's why. It gave Lord Heite a thrill to see us gaping at forbidden fruit. She even played along with it, the bitch. Looking at that thing she was wearing. She's just a courtesan, Paoul. Don't make a statue of her.'

'They're all forbidden fruit to us,' Enco said. 'You'd do well to bear that in mind, Starrad.'

'What on earth do you mean? I've no idea, to be sure.'

With that, the conversation came to an end. Paoul resisted the impulse to say anything further. He did not want to admit it, but he felt betrayed. He knew that Starrad, the worldly, perceptive Starrad, had almost certainly been right. What Paoul, in his innocence, had taken to be the spontaneous expression of mutual attraction was now revealed as nothing more than sordid coquetry. He had forgotten, momentarily, the teaching of the taug and allowed himself to be swayed by carnal desires. Such behaviour was appropriate outside the vansery palisade – it was worthy of the common people, the rabble, the pagans. But it was not worthy of a future forzan, of someone who had been noticed by the Prime. But then – had Lord Heite's praise also been a part of his game? How much of it could be believed? Perhaps the whole episode had even been staged by the kars; perhaps it had been a test which Paoul had miserably failed. He had let himself and Kar Ander down.

For a long time he stared into the darkness, feeling cheated and confused. Most disturbing of all had been the conduct of Lord Heite. For the Gehan of the Gehans to behave in such a way was unthinkable. In the eyes of the world – including, Paoul had naïvely imagined, Starrad's eyes too – he was almost a god, the secular representative of the Prime, the enactor of the holy decrees, the leader of the army and the ruler of the empire. He was nobility itself, above petty temptation. But now he had shown himself to be weak and depraved, just as other men were.

No. It was simply not possible. Starrad was wrong. He had imputed his own values to a man beyond reproach. The Lady Atane, young and beautiful as she was, had acted naturally, in faith with her heart. In recent weeks and months Paoul had received certain glances in the street which had made him wonder whether he might be attractive to girls. Might the Lady Atane merely have shared their opinion? Yes: that was it. His first impression had been indisputably correct. None the less, it had been wrong to forget himself like that. He would learn from the incident and take it as a warning. His admiration of Lord Heite remained undiminished.

Still trying to convince himself of this, he slipped at last into a shallow and uneasy sleep.

The next morning's routine began in the usual way. Paoul and the others woke to the sound of a wooden gong. In the early twilight they sluiced themselves with cold water and dressed in the black leggings and tunics which denoted their lowly rank. After participating in the dawn litany at the temple – attended by nearly all the priests and pupils and conducted today by the Prime – they went back to their quarters for breathing exercise and meditation. Then came breakfast, of milk, steaming oat-meal porridge, ryebread, raw fish, fruit, and the soft cheese for which Hohe was renowned.

This was one of the mornings set aside each week for handicraft. In theory a part of the taug – for they belonged in the region where art and science merged – these lessons were not normally given by kars, but, depending on their exact nature, by ilvens or phedes, or sometimes by ilvens and phedes working together. The projects undertaken by their pupils ranged from minute carvings on ivory to the construction of full scale buildings. The buoys, raft, and changing shed at the lake had all been made by the school, as had various structures in the citadel at large.

In the lower school the pupils were brought to a certain level of skill; once in the higher school, the teaching became less formal, and there was more scope for self-expression. Paoul, who was both musical and had an aptitude for fine work in wood, was planning to try his hand at a scharan, a big-bellied stringed instrument with a sweetly melancholy tone of which he was especially fond.

Before starting on this, though, he was required, as were his classmates, to make a set piece commemorating their arrival in the higher school. The set piece was always the same: a circular plaque with an inlaid pentacle in contrasting wood, made to the highest standards of accuracy and finish.

The geometry of polygons formed part of the simple mathematics taught in the lower school, but the precise technique of constructing the pentagon and its derivative pentacle was shown to a novice only when he had reached the higher school. The secret was imparted by the chief phede at the confirmation ceremony. The confirmation plaque, as it was called, had a special significance in a novice's career. If good enough, the plaque would be sanctified as a talisman. If not, it would be burnt and the novice would have to try again.

For his plaque, Paoul had chosen applewood and yew. On previous mornings he had selected seasoned logs from the lumber-sheds and, with axe, adze, scraper, and finally with sandstones of decreasing coarseness, had produced two smooth, knot-free blanks. These he now took from his locker and carried to his place in the workshop, where he shared a bench with Enco.

The morning was already quite hot. The sun, beating on the timber walls and sloping roof of the workshop, seemed to heighten the smell of the bubbling gluepots and the agreeable odour of freshly worked wood. Except for the quietly authoritative voice of Ilven Gars, and the occasional comments one to the other of the boys, the room was silent but for the sound of tools.

'Ready?' Enco said. He was halfway through marking out his own plaque, and now it was time for him to help with Paoul's.

The diameter of the plaque, excluding the frame, was to equal the span of the maker's left hand at full stretch. The size of the pentacle was determined by the size of the notional pentagon at its heart: the sum of the five sides of this pentagon was also to equal the span of the maker's left hand.

Aware that he was about to take part in a symbolic tradition almost as old as the Red Order itself, Paoul laid his left hand on the clean beechwood surface of the bench and spread his thumb and fingers to their utmost extent. Enco opened a pair of callipers and meticulously measured the span. Paoul, craning over, confirmed that the measurement was correct, and Enco's part in the proceedings was over.

Using a large tablet of geometry clay, Paoul ascertained the dimensions corresponding to one half and one fifth of his span. Locking first one and then the other blank in the bench holdfast, he took his best and sharpest flint scribe, his boxwood compass and hornbeam straight-edge and, remembering what he had been told by the chief phede, marked on each blank the seven arcs and nine lines that generated the sacred figure.

When he had finished he painstakingly checked all the measurements against the original setting of the callipers and, satisfied, stood upright. The two pentacles – that on the applewood enclosed by a faintly scribed circle – lay side by side, waiting to be cut and worked and transformed by a mystical fusion of art and science into the finished piece. If Paoul had heeded his teachers, if he performed well, if he used his mind and body to control the difficult and fragile flint chisels, the yew would eventually slot precisely into the applewood, male into female, a fit so snug that Ilven Gars would be able to invert the plaque without it parting. And, having passed that test, Paoul would smear the merest trace of fish-glue on the jointing surfaces, fix the frame, treat the whole to many coats of thin varnish, then to a final, somewhat thicker, coat, and lastly to repeated waxing and polishing. And if, after all this, the Prime judged his work true, if the shine, like the surface of a still pool, made an uninterrupted and undistorted reflection, then Paoul would know that his entry to the higher school had been justified.

At Paoul's request, Ilven Gars came over to inspect his setting-out.

'You'll have to watch the grain here, Paoul. And here.'

Ilven Gars was silver-haired, of middle height, one of the senior teachers of joinery as well as an accomplished sculptor.

He was also in charge of much of the ceremonial organized by the vansery. It was to Ilven Gars that Paoul was to report later today, to start rehearsals for the ceremony at the Crale.

Ilven Gars did not mention the fact. 'Yes,' he said, nodding at the blanks in approval. 'Begin.'

When he had gone, Paoul selected a chisel. As he made the first cut, some quirk of sensation or feeling put him in mind of a half-forgotten scene from his early childhood and he remembered standing with Kar Houle on the quayside at Apuldram, watching the *Veisdrach* turn. Like a herald from the mainland, the dragon of the figurehead had given him notice of what was to come. He had watched it with a mixture of awe and fear: awe that mere men could make something so splendid, and fear of the knowledge that enabled them to do it.

Paoul now possessed some of that knowledge. In outline, at least, he would know how to set about building another *Veisdrach*. And more: his learning went far beyond the simple skills of a shipwright. He could no longer count himself a part of the ignorant, amorphous mass of ordinary people from whose ranks he had risen. He had become more priest than layman. By their rite of confirmation, by bringing him into the higher school, his teachers had in effect told him this already.

On the eve of his confirmation, Paoul had been warned to consider the consequences very carefully. Once in the higher school, he would have learned too many secrets and there could be no turning back. But he had no doubts: he believed in the faith, in the ethos, with all his heart. More than anything he yearned to prove himself worthy of his training; he desperately wanted to continue on the arduous journey towards his initiation, towards the day when he finally became a real priest. The pentacle of his talisman would then be not of yew, but of crimson pigment tattooed into his flesh.

A corner snapped off the chisel and Paoul checked his hand. In his enthusiasm he was forgetting the most elementary rule of all. He was letting his thoughts race ahead, failing to maintain the single point of concentration where all success lay.

Pausing to take breath, he discarded the broken chisel and chose another from the rack.

4

Three weeks later, just before the Crale, the fine weather came to an end. Crale Day itself, the day of the ceremony, was cloudy, with sporadic drizzle and a noticeable chill in the air: the autumn equinox was only a month away.

The Crale was a festival of the agrestic calendar of the farmers, and thus was not officially recognized by the Red Order, which divided the year into four seasons and not six. There was nothing unseemly, however, in the choice of the Crale for the consecration of Bohod Thosk's new hall; and the celebrations afterwards would be fully in tune with those taking place in the township and throughout the countryside. The festival marked the end of High Summer and the beginning of Harvest. It also happened to be the day, seventeen years ago, on which Paoul had been born.

It seemed to Paoul, standing alone and apparently unnoticed by a window, that dusk was falling quickly, prematurely, draining the outside world of colour. The tall trees, the evergreen shrubs and topiary of the formal gardens had become so many fantastic and sinister black shapes; the lawns and terraces, the stone ornaments, the lily pads on the carp pool, were now a uniform grey and becoming gloomier by the minute.

Inside, though, all was brilliance. The half hour after the ceremony and before the banquet was giving the guests a chance to admire in detail the splendour and workmanship of the new hall. Individually and in groups they were congratulating their host. Those of inferior rank were surreptitiously trying to get closer to the Prime, to Lord Heite or to members of his family. Of the Lady Atane, Paoul had noted, there was no sign. He had not seen her since that day at the lake. Instead Lord Heite this evening was accompanied by his wife, two sons, three daughters, one of his brothers, and a concubine whose name Paoul did not know. Slaves in the red and black livery of the Thosk clan were passing to and fro with trays of wine and essence. Alcohol was eschewed by practitioners of the taug; abstemious as ever, the Prime had even refused fruit juice. Paoul was also empty-handed, mainly because no one had thought to offer him anything. It was not his place to ask, or to do more than remain on the sidelines of such a glittering gathering. The other lamp-bearer, the boy of twelve who had represented the lower school, had already returned to the citadel, but Ilven Gars had allowed Paoul to stay and, as part of his education, had secured him an invitation to the banquet. Ilven Gars was elsewhere at the moment, however, and Paoul had been left to his own devices.

'Excuse me. Would you like something to drink?'

Paoul looked round to see a girl in an embroidered robe, the same rather pretty girl he had noticed at yesterday's dress rehearsal, the same girl whose presence he had been conscious of during the ceremony itself. She was about his age or a little younger, with dark blonde hair tied back, a creamy skin, and brown eyes. She seemed shy, which he found hard to understand, because she was Bohod Thosk's daughter and must have been exposed to court life from an early age. Last night he had caught himself thinking about her and wondering whether she would be here again today. Then he had heard Starrad stealthily leaving and had angrily dismissed the matter from his mind.

'The slaves seem to have forgotten you,' she said. 'They're very busy, I'm afraid. I know you can't have wine or anything, but would you like some grape juice?'

'No. Not for me.'

She shrank back and Paoul realized he had spoken curtly. It had cost her an effort to approach him; her motives had sprung simply from kindness, and now he had let down the good name of the school. 'Really, I'm not at all thirsty,' he went on, untruthfully, trying to rescue the situation. 'Besides, there'll be plenty to drink at the banquet.' He smiled and engaged her eyes. She certainly was pretty: not like the Lady Atane, of course, but attractive in a more lasting and less obvious way. In other circumstances, in another life, perhaps, he might have let himself admire the colour of her eyes, the shape of her mouth, or the whiteness of the enamel on her small, neatly formed teeth. Drawn there by the tiny pink and blue flowers of embroidered forgetmenots, he might have allowed his gaze to stray briefly over the youthful swell of her bodice. He might have noticed her femininity, the softness of her voice, the delicate make of her hands; and he might have acknowledged to himself how gentle and graceful she was. Instead he made himself smile again and said; 'My name is Paoul. I have the honour to address the daughter of Bohod Thosk, I believe.'

'Yseld. That's my name.'

Her name was modest, yet also the sort of name that a hopeless suitor might breathe to himself in unrequited passion. It fitted her perfectly. Paoul wanted to tell her so, or, at least, to say something else, but, despite what he still imagined to be the coolness of the composure bestowed on him by the taug, he found himself lost for words. He had never conducted such a conversation before.

'Was that lamp as heavy as it looked?'

He was about to say 'Not really,' but that would have been another lie. 'Heavier.'

'It made a horrible smell.'

'I know.'

'Almost as bad as the Prime's censer.'

'If the incense is disagreeable to you, my lady, please speak to your father, for it is he who imports it.'

Paoul had tried to temper this reply with a smile; he was expecting one in return. It did not come, and for the first time he realized, with alarm, how disconcerting he found her. And more: he realized that his feelings were reciprocated. 'I'm . . . I'm so sorry,' she said, still speaking, he supposed, about the incense. 'I didn't mean – '

She was unable to finish. Her father's voice sounded close behind Paoul's back. 'There you are, Yseld.'

Disturbed beyond measure, Paoul tried to calm himself, to pretend that nothing had happened. It was as if he had been struck a physical blow, taken the full impact of one of the heavy sandbags swinging from the ceiling of the taug school. What had just happened was impossible. A moment ago, before meeting her, he had been in possession of his will. Now he had lost it, surrendered it, and, it seemed, she had done the same.

He knew that on no account must he betray himself or give

her cause to imagine that he saw her as anything more than the daughter of his host. And so he moved aside, as though intimidated by Bohod Thosk's importance. Bohod Thosk was, indeed, on close terms with Lord Heite. But most of all he was father to the Lady Yseld, her proprietor and controller. For a moment he turned his smoky brown eyes on Paoul and it seemed as if he had guessed everything. But his expression remained utterly bland, concealing all emotion, all opinion, all thought and feeling. 'Ah. One of the lamp-bearers. Paoul, isn't it?'

'Yes, sir.'

Had it not been for Yseld, Paoul would have taken this as it had probably been intended, as a cue to depart. He would also have felt amazed and flattered to think that Bohod Thosk should have known or remembered his name: they had not met until now.

'Forgive me for interrupting your conversation.' There was no trace of irony in Bohod Thosk's tone. He turned to his daughter. 'Yseld, it is nearly time to go in. Do you forget that Lord Mond is here?'

This was the younger of the two sons of Lord Heite had brought to the ceremony, a well-favoured youth of eighteen who had inherited his father's looks and manner. Immediately Paoul scented the odour of a marriage contract, of politics and intrigue. For the daughter of a rich and ambitious merchant, what could be more inevitable than a union with the ruling clan? Paoul wondered at last whether he was expected to slip away: his conversation with the Lady Yseld had, after all, hardly warranted the name. But he stayed where he was, reluctant to leave her, and fascinated, too, by the opportunity of studying at close quarters one of the most famous and influential men in the empire – in the known world.

His study was short-lived. Even before another word was spoken there came, from the great doorway of the dining hall, a flourish of pipes and horns, followed by a measured beating of the drums. Bohod Thosk took his daughter's elbow. 'You will excuse us,' he told Paoul.

As her father drew her away, Yseld half turned her head and gave Paoul a parting look.

This look, all the more eloquent because she had yielded it

involuntarily, quite unlike the Lady Atane, haunted him until the guests had almost finished taking their places for the banquet. Walking behind Ilven Gars and three other priests, Paoul entered at the end of the procession and was shown to a lowly position near the door, a long way from Yseld and the main dais. Ilven Gars was standing beside him, waiting, like all the guests, for the Prime to enter and bless the meal. As the guests waited they marvelled at the blue and white opulence of the dining hall, gazing up in wonder at the intricate carvings of dragons, storks, and eagles on the ceiling. None of it registered with Paoul. He could think only of the Lady Yseld. So little had been spoken, but so much said in the language of the eyes. It was irrational, illogical, mad, contrary to all his past experience, to base such certainty on such slight apparent cause. They had been together for no more than a minute; he knew nothing about her, nothing except one undeniable fact: that, in his excitement, he was sure that he must meet her again, touch her, stay with her, and confirm beyond all doubt that she felt just as he did.

The Prime entered, larger than life in his cream and scarlet brocade, his voluminous train dragging the floor as he mounted a podium near the main dais. The hall became silent. Briefly the Prime's grey eyes surveyed the gathering with a benign yet distant expression. Grasping the rail with his lean, supple hands, he then inclined his head deeply, revealing the close-cropped, whorled denseness of the pure white hair of his crown. This was a moment for individual contemplation: the guests also bent their heads, raising them only when the Prime began to speak.

'Great Gauhm.' His voice did not seem loud, but penetrated with astonishing clarity every corner of the hall. 'From the fruits of your womb we accept now this bounteous harvest.'

The words of the blessing were familiar to Paoul. He had heard them in the refectory each day for almost ten years. As line succeeded line, Paoul, despite the presence beside him of Ilven Gars, found himself overwhelmed by the need to turn and seek out Yseld's face, certain that she would also be turning to seek out his. But she was obscured by others and could not be seen.

As soon as the blessing was over, however, the guests began

to sit and Paoul glimpsed her settling into her place next to Lord Mond, on the right side of the dais. The head of the dais was occupied by the Prime, flanked by Lord Heite and Bohod Thosk.

From here, diagonally opposite her and about forty feet away, Paoul had a clear view of her face. She cast several glances over the assembly, but did not seem to single him out, even for an instant. Neither did she avoid looking in his direction.

The fish dish was announced and brought for the food-tasters to try. While this was happening, Lord Mond leaned towards her, away from Paoul, and spoke. She smiled modestly. Lord Mond spoke again and her eyes widened. With a new and wholly unfamiliar pain, Paoul watched as she put her hand to her mouth as if to suppress a laugh. Lord Mond, the effortlessly superior rival in a contest which Paoul could not even enter, had already won his spoils. She had already been assimilated by his future: she was already part of his vast inheritance. He leaned towards her again with another amusing remark, made no doubt at the expense of those in the body of the hall. The change it produced transformed her face. When she smiled like that she was more than passively pretty. She was beautiful.

'Paoul!'

Paoul looked round. Ilven Gars was regarding him closely.

'Did you hear me? I asked you a question.'

'I'm sorry, Ilven Gars. I humbly beg your pardon.'

'Do you know the etiquette of eating capercaillie?'

'Yes, Ilven Gars.'

Ilven Gars frowned. 'Are you feeling ill, Paoul?'

'No, Ilven Gars. I am quite well, thank you.'

'Are you sure? There's still time for you to leave. You may go to your chamber if you wish.'

The prospect was tempting. Paoul had been looking forward to the evening, but he no longer had the stomach for a large and extended meal, or for giving his polite attention to the small talk of the guests. Most of all, he no longer wished to sit here in plain view of Lord Mond's companion. To leave now, though, would be an intolerable admission of defeat.

'Thank you, Ilven Gars, but I'm quite all right.'

Paoul consoled himself with the thought that he would not have to stay for very long. At midnight or thereabouts, soon after the food had been eaten, he would be able to withdraw to his room upstairs. Because Bohod Thosk's residence was some distance from the citadel, too far to be safely traversed in the dark – it was situated near the Lower Township, the river port – and because the gates of the citadel were anyway locked at nightfall, accommodation had been provided for the guests. Paoul had been given a tiny room, barely large enough to take a bed, next to the chambers occupied by Ilven Gars and the other priests. They too, like the Prime, would be leaving the banquet at midnight. Only then, Paoul guessed, would the true celebrations – the ancient, unruly observance of the Crale – begin.

The food, in small portions, was exquisitely prepared and served, and Paoul made himself eat every scrap, as good manners required. As course succeeded course and toast succeeded toast, he managed to keep his eyes as much as possible away from the main dais. But, when the Prime and with him the whole assembly arose, when it was time for the priests to leave, Paoul's concentration lapsed.

He turned and in that instant she did the same. When she saw him she hurriedly looked away, at Lord Mond, at her father, at the Prime, and, with an embarrassed intentness, watched and listened as the Prime took his leave.

Once Paoul had escaped from the dining hall – his eyes fixed firmly on neutral territory – and once he had washed himself and was in the privacy of his room, he climbed straight into bed, unable even to consider starting the routine of breathing exercises which preceded the nightly meditation. For once he would be undisciplined and let his meditation go. The exercises would calm him, he knew, and let him examine his experience more objectively, but that was theory and the Lady Yseld was fact. And so he immediately snuffed the lamp and pulled the sheepskin cover across his shoulder, lying not on his back, as he had been taught, but on his side. The mattress felt lumpy and prickled his naked skin; the bedclothes exuded a stale, faintly nauseous smell. From below, through the thick planking of the floor on which his mattress lay, came the sound of the banquet. He was not directly above it, but at a slight remove. Nevertheless he could hear the music and, by using his hearing as the kars had shown him, by narrowing its field and singling out individual sounds, he could distinguish several of the feasters' voices: he could hear Lord Heite proposing a toast. She would be hearing it too, not as thin, distant abstraction, but loudly and with all the richness of presence.

In the next chamber Paoul heard Ilven Gars moving about. Soon the noises ceased and Paoul knew he had assumed the meditation posture. He had begun his breathing, counting in heartbeats for each phase of the fourfold cycle. The first three cycles were performed to the count of three, the next five by the count of five, on through the series of sacred numbers: seven, nine, and, for the experienced, eleven. In the adjoining chambers, the other priests would be doing the same. Then, for half an hour or more, their minds would empty. Sitting very still, breathing very quietly, eyes half closed, they would no longer be here, now, in Bohod Thosk's hall, but everywhere and nowhere, set free from their bodies and the constraints of time. Paoul wished he shared their ability. He wished his training had already taken him further. He wished he were older and able to exert total self control. Then he would not be so weak and vulnerable and uncertain.

By the time he again heard slight sounds from the next chamber, Paoul had relived the evening over and over again. He could remember each word she had said, each inflection of her voice, each nuance of meaning, and he realized that, by complaining about the smell of the incense, she had spoken of the Prime with a hint, however veiled and guarded, of disrespect. Her behaviour had been forward; had she not approached Paoul and spoken first? Starrad would see no difference between her and the Lady Atane or the fishmonger's daughter.

Paoul knew so little about girls, however, that he was prepared to accept that he had read her wrongly. He thought he had sensed in her manner something forced, uncharacteristic, almost desperate, overlying a deeper sincerity to which he had intuitively responded. Even before the exchange of names, it now seemed, their eyes had confirmed and begun to explore a mutual attraction which yesterday had existed only in Paoul's wildest conjectures. But he was already betrothed, and to the sternest possible bride. The Lady Yseld had acted, as he had, without thinking. Their instincts were dangerous and misplaced. She had understood this, but too late. Her remark about the Prime might have been an attempt to bring their encounter on to safer ground.

All that, though, however much he wanted to believe it, was contradicted by her demeanour at the banquet. There she had shown him quite plainly that she found his reaction embarrassing. Her approach had been meaningless, empty, and flippant. Lack of contact with young women had made him over-serious and too susceptible to their charms. That final glance had told him everything. Her prank had misfired. What fun to flirt with a trainee priest! How entertaining to giggle about it with her friends tomorrow! Starrad, after all, was right.

And because he was right, Paoul could not help thinking of her as he had thought of the Lady Atane. What would it be like to touch her, to caress such skin, to receive a kiss from such a mouth? To . . .

Abruptly he threw back the cover, glad of the chilly night air on his body. In the darkness, impervious to the sounds from below, he faithfully executed the cycles of breathing and, much calmed and comforted, managed to achieve a few minutes' peace.

He returned to bed and lay supine, relaxed. Before composing himself for sleep he put into concise terms the lessons of the evening. He saw that he belonged here, above the music, side by side with Ilven Gars and the others. This was his life. Not only was he reconciled to it: he loved it. There could be no greater privilege than acceptance by the Red Order. Temptations put in his way served merely to strengthen his resolve and teach him how worthless and transient were the treasures that ordinary men held dear.

Paoul shut his eyes. His relaxation deepened and he purposely fragmented his thoughts, darting from one unconnected image to another, inducing the state that was already drawing him down. The last thing he knew was the sound of a whisper. It had nothing to do with him, it came from beyond, from outside; but, in the instant of falling asleep, he knew the whisper had also been the sound of her name.

5

At the end of the next morning the novices went back to their quarters to get ready for the afternoon session. They had just endured a long tutorial with Forzan Zett. Even though it was the Crale and work in the rest of the citadel had come to a halt, the schedule of the vansery was continuing unchanged.

Earlier, on returning from Bohod Thosk's estate, Paoul had gone straight to Forzan Zett's chambers. He had apologized for and explained his lateness and, taking his place, had thought little of the fact that Starrad was absent. Very soon, though, he had sensed that something was badly wrong.

'No one knows anything,' Buin had said, on the way here through the rain. 'No one dares ask. All we know is that he didn't come back last night.'

Water was dripping sparsely from the wooden canopy above the window. The damp and the midday gloom made the dormitory seem even smaller than it was; Starrad's tidy locker, his bed – straightened in his absence by Buin and Enco – and the neatly appointed shelves above it all appeared to be waiting in vain for their master's return.

'Buin thinks he's been caught,' Enco said, taking out his best tunic.

'Or robbed. He might have been attacked.'

To Paoul's ears this sounded most unlikely. Inside the citadel robbery was almost unknown, and anyway Starrad knew how to defend himself, as did all the higher school pupils.

'They must know where he is,' Paoul said, 'otherwise they'd have asked you questions when he didn't show at the litany. Whatever else may have happened, we can take it he's been found out.'

There was little time for further discussion. They had to get changed, and quickly. In a few minutes the whole class was expected at the temple, for this was the day of their first confrontation with the Prime: this was the afternoon when he was to examine their confirmation plaques.

Somehow Paoul had been expecting such an important day to be sunny. He had awaited it eagerly, but the news about Starrad had overshadowed his pleasure and now all that remained was a dread of failure, tinged with a fear of facing the Prime. And there was something more: a residue of unease from the events of the previous evening.

Buin straightened his cap and they were ready to depart; but, at that moment, the curtain at the doorway was pulled aside and Ilven Fend stepped into the room. One of the least strict of the teachers, Ilven Fend was relatively young, in his thirties, with reddish hair and freckles. He was a favourite of most of the pupils. There was no smile on his face, however, as he said, 'Which is Starrad's locker?'

'That one, Ilven Fend.'

The contents of the locker and the objects on the shelves were alike tossed on to Starrad's bed and, with the bedding, gathered unceremoniously into a bundle which Ilven Fend took in his arms. He turned to go. 'I am permitted to tell you,' he said, addressing the three boys equally, 'that Starrad has, by his bestial conduct, brought shame to the school. He has defiled its reputation and you will not be seeing him again. He has left Hohe. From tomorrow it will be forbidden to utter his name anywhere in the citadel. Until then you may pass this information on to your fellows.' Ilven Fend moved to the doorway, treating Buin to an especially withering glance. 'The complicity of his room-mates in this matter has not been overlooked.'

Buin respectfully held back the curtain: the ilven pushed past him without another word.

The three boys looked at each other, stunned as much by the force of his anger as by his revelation that the worst – the very worst – had befallen their friend. To be expelled at this stage of the training was unimaginable. After so much work and self sacrifice. Starrad, for a trifle, had thrown away the chance of life as a red priest – in his case, as a high-ranking phede, perhaps even an astronomer. He had been ruined, dishonoured, ignominiously thrust from the gates of Hohe. His punishment was appalling, yet each of the three was also privately fascinated to be involved, however peripherally, in such a serious affair; fascinated, and relieved and thankful that it was not he who had shared Starrad's fate.

Buin had known him best. 'Where did he come from?' Enco said, already speaking of Starrad, Paoul noted, in the past tense.

'I'm not sure. A province in the east. His father is a bohod.'

'I didn't know that,' Paoul said. Once inside the citadel, it was considered irrelevant and ill-mannered to talk about one's origins.

'So he's not sponsored?'

Buin shook his head. 'He can't ever go back. What could he say to his father? What could he possibly say?'

'We'd better get moving,' Enco said, reminding them sharply of the next session, of the temple and the Prime. 'You heard what Ilven Fend said. We're in enough trouble as it is.'

'Your plaque is now a talisman,' the Prime had told Paoul quietly, under the echoing vault of the temple, the rest of the class sitting in ranks on the far side of the floor, either waiting to be judged or already knowing the verdict. Most had looked elated; some, their plaques rejected, had looked downcast. 'Like most of your work, it is of the required standard. However, the Principal tells me your progress recently has been giving him concern. He had intended to speak to you personally, but the events of this morning are so grave that he has asked me to intervene. Buin and Enco I shall deal with in due course. As for you, come to my chambers tomorrow at noon.'

Paoul arrived early, having left a mathematics lesson part way through to spend half an hour grooming and dressing. His state of dread could not have been more complete. He had hardly slept; nor had Buin and Enco, whose interviews were to take place later in the day. At breakfast he had been unable to touch his food, and in class he had been severely reprimanded for his lack of concentration.

The chambers of the Prime formed part of the upper storey of the temple and were reached from the cloisters by an enclosed staircase which Paoul now climbed for the first time in his life. At the top was a small landing and a pair of elaborately carved doors. He paused before raising the knocker, shut his eyes, and tried to swallow. He could not. His mouth was too dry. Beside him, set deeply in the wood and clay wall, a circular window gave a view over glistening roofs towards the herb gardens and the vansery palisade, beyond which he could see the rain-soaked streets of the township. A few stray particles of drizzle blew in and clung to the sleeve of his robe.

He was admitted by an attendant – a young forzan in the cream robes of the Prime's personal staff – who took him through one door and then another, along a dark corridor, and showed him into a waiting room furnished with a low, padded bench.

Paoul was too agitated to sit. He went to the window. To keep calm he tried to identify some of the roofs, shingled or merely boarded and caulked, which spread out below. He had never seen the vansery like this before, or realized how big it was; higher up the mountain, looking down on the citadel, the vansery tended to merge with the township and the barracks. The view from here was much like that from the landing, except that more of the gardens could be seen. Paoul noticed that one or two of the yew boughs, where they had overhung the palisade, had been freshly lopped. In his imagination he saw Starrad dropping from the branches in the darkness, landing badly, perhaps spraining his ankle, unable to climb back, trapped in the township. Or perhaps the lopped branches were unconnected with Starrad's disgrace: perhaps he had been betrayed by one of the townsfolk. The girl's father? The girl herself?

The midday gong sounded dolefully in the temple square.

Paoul turned from the window, deciding to use his remaining moments more sensibly. Fully expecting to be interrupted, he sat down, closed his eyes, and began a breathing routine. He was able to finish: no interruption came. The Prime, it seemed, was keeping him waiting, either deliberately or, much more probably, because Paoul and the matter in hand were so insignificant.

In the corridor outside he could hear the continual passage to and fro of the servants and officials of the Prime's staff. To this suite of chambers were directed scores of messages, inquiries, and petitions a day. Some were relatively trifling; others raised profound questions of religion or state with far-reaching consequences on the lives of tens of thousands of people. Each petition had to be carefully considered and an answer sent to the offices of Lord Heite for enactment. For, although the Gehans controlled the army, the real power lay with the Prime. He was the very hub of the empire, the still point at the centre of the circle: through him came divine guidance from the Earth Goddess. He was her mortal representative, in absolute command of the empire – through the two priesthoods, the Gehans, and the merchant class, which depended for its survival on his favour. The common people regarded him as a god. With very little encouragement, Paoul reflected, they would also worship him as such.

Paoul looked about him. In the Prime's suite even a humble waiting-room was finished with matchless skill. The walls were panelled to chest height with bas-reliefs of the four seasons which, continued in fresco, rose to the ceiling where they merged with a subtly clouded sky. The door, varnished and veneered with reed-leaf laminate, hung on five hinges and made a flawless fit with its frame. The copper-lined oak lever and hook of the latch had become worn, but still engaged sweetly and were probably original, installed over eighty years ago. The whole temple, of which the Prime's chambers formed an integral part, had been rebuilt then, following a fire. Its site – and hence the site of Hohe, the 'High Place' – had been decreed by Gauhm: easily defended, easily reached from the Great River, and surrounded by the rich farmland of the Home Plain. The precise position of Mount Atar also had symbolic properties with respect to the earth's surface and the celestial dome. Its latitude and its relationship with the solstitial positions of the five major constellations and the paths of the five planets produced a unique web of coordinates which fixed Hohe as the only possible location for the temple. The distance between the temple altar and the waterfall, furthermore, was exactly one five thousandth of the equatorial axis or, measured in standard bars, three thousand one hundred and twenty-five – or five raised to the power of five. Paoul had also been told that the temple altar, suspended as it were between heaven and earth, was exactly one fifth of this height above sea level.

For those sensitive to such influences, the citadel had a

special, spiritual feeling about it, weakest in the outlying parts of the township, stronger in the vansery, stronger still in the temple, reaching its purest concentration at the altar stone itself. The Prime dwelt directly above the stone, sharing its focus of coordinates, absorbing Gauhm's power. This power he radiated outward and downward through the ranks of his priests. Paoul could feel it even now, just as he had felt it yesterday in the temple, and just as, to a lesser extent, he had felt it in the Prime's presence at Bohod Thosk's hall.

The door opened. The attendant had returned. 'The Lord Prime will see you now. Quickly.'

Paoul followed. After being made to pause in a panelled antechamber, he was escorted through a pair of tall doors and found himself in the Prime's huge day-room. The doors shut behind him: he and the Prime were alone.

'Be seated,' the Prime said, indicating a broad, leather-covered stool in front of him. 'I shall not keep you waiting very much longer.'

Wearing a cream and dark-green robe, he was sitting at a walnut writing-table, his back to an alcove on the right-hand side of the room. On a smaller table beside him was a sheaf of swan quills, and several parchments covered with columns of neat black hieroglyphics.

Most of the far wall was taken up with a line of deeply canopied windows which overlooked the formal gardens and, beyond the billowing tree tops of the Founder's Grove, the greeny-grey water of the lake. As Paoul crossed the room he noticed a heron far below, gliding over the trees.

He sat down, his eyes irresistibly drawn by the quiet scratching of the Prime's pen. With rapid, confident strokes, the Prime was adding comments in red to the columns of black. Upside-down, and from this distance, Paoul could make out none of the words but, observing the movements of the nib, he was able to guess at some of the characters being formed. 'Borders.' 'Province.' 'Blue priesthood.' 'Gehan.' 'Petitioner.' And again, 'Gehan.'

Despite his terror of the approaching interview, a corner of Paoul's mind was left free to be intrigued by the sensation of sitting here in the sanctum of the Prime, of being able to observe closely the weave of his robe, the pattern of the braid edging on his cuff, the shape of his fingernails and his neatly manicured cuticles, the way the veins on his left hand were just beginning to distort the shape of his tattoo; and, most intriguing of all, displayed on the polished surface of the table, two small objects which were evidently personal possessions: a flint penknife in an ivory holder and, no more than three inches high, a limestone figurine of the Earth Mother. For these few seconds Paoul was privileged to witness what none of his friends had ever seen: the Prime at work, attending to the minutiae of his awesome office.

'Now,' he said, setting down his pen, and Paoul felt his heart in his throat. 'Tell me what you know of this Starrad business. From the beginning.'

'Last spring, my lord, I understood he met a young woman in the township.'

'Do you know her name?'

'No, my lord.'

'Then do you know anything else that would serve to identify her?'

The Prime's tone was so ominous that Paoul made the mistake of hesitating before answering.

'Your reticence does not please me.'

'She is a daughter of one of the fishmongers, my lord. I do not know which.'

'Continue.'

'Starrad . . . Starrad was conducting improper relations with her. Once or twice a week, sometimes more frequently, he would visit her at night. We believed he was getting over the palisade near the physic gardens.'

'By climbing the yew trees?'

'That is what we thought, my lord. But we were never certain. He always denied everything. I never saw the girl or heard anything but rumour and speculation. That is all I really know, my lord.'

'You were aware of his absences, of course.'

'Yes, my lord.'

'Then why did you not report them to your teachers?'

Paoul was unable to reply.

The Prime sat back, subjecting Paoul to the full force of his searching grey eyes. 'Tell me, young man, why do you think you are attending the temple school?'

'To . . . to learn the ethos, my lord.'

'And what is the ethos? How do we describe it?'

'Gentleness through strength.'

'From where does that strength derive?'

This was a line from an elementary catechism. 'Perfection of the self, obedience, and loyalty.'

'Loyalty to whom?'

'To Gauhm, my lord.'

'Yet you prefer to give yours to a liar and a fornicator.' The Prime paused, allowing his words their maximum effect. 'Did it never once occur to you that you were going Starrad a disservice by failing in your proper duty? If this matter had been brought to light at the start, the outcome for him may not have been so serious. By your connivance you contributed to his weakness and must be held partly to blame.'

'Yes, my lord.'

'You understand, do you not, the damage that such an incident can inflict on the Order? What may appear to you as no more than an infraction of vansery law may have profound and unforeseeable consequences. If we are to serve Gauhm, our reputation must remain unassailable. Do you understand?'

'Yes, my lord.'

The Prime's gaze relented slightly and he seemed satisfied that the lesson had been taken to heart. 'It is customary,' he went on, 'for offending novices to be dealt with by the Principal. However, in order to impress upon you and the whole school the gravity of what has happened, Forzan Zett has asked me to conduct the investigation myself. That is one of the reasons you are here. Another is the question of your recent progress, which, as I informed you yesterday, has been giving him cause for concern. He wished me to have an opportunity to speak to you in circumstances which would arouse neither the suspicions nor the curiosity of your fellows, and nothing I am about to say is to be transmitted by you to any third person.'

Paoul did not know how to respond to this enigmatic statement and could do little but nod in compliance.

'Your part in this Starrad affair is perhaps indicative of

what the Principal means when he tells me your work is disappointing. Since you are no longer a child, I can speak to you bluntly, without fear that you will mistake my words for praise or derive from them any grounds for conceit. I trust you will bear this in mind when considering what I am about to say next.'

Again Paoul could only nod.

'Judged by normal, commonplace standards, your work has always been excellent. In the ten years you have been at Hohe you have developed well. Your progress has been so rapid that you are now at least two full years ahead of your age and on course to becoming one of the youngest initiates the order has ever known. By commonplace standards, you would be considered an exceptionally able pupil. In your case, however, the commonplace does not apply. Your gifts are such that you cannot be measured against your peers. For your work to be merely excellent is not enough. It should be exemplary. You should not be two years ahead, but three, or even four. Do I begin to make myself understood?'

'Yes, my lord.'

'The decision to advance you into the higher school was taken some months ago. Since then, Forzan Zett has had occasion to question his own wisdom. He sees that you are becoming content to adopt the pace of your fellows. He sees that you appear to defer to them, that you seek at every turn to spare their feelings, that you thereby waste time on tolerating inferior debate. Perhaps this is understandable. You are unassuming by nature. The age difference inhibits you still further. But, while making full use of the advantages your teaching group has to offer, you should not become subservient to it. You must be more assertive. Do not be afraid of making yourself unpopular. Such unpopularity is the product of small and envious minds and must not be allowed to hold you back. This is what the Principal fears, Paoul, that you are holding yourself back. Gauhm does not choose her servants lightly. You have no right to squander her gifts in this way. They are not yours to dispose of as you see fit.'

For a moment Paoul remained silent. He could see that Forzan Zett was right: he had been failing his teachers for some months past. Quietly he said, 'I am very sorry, my lord.'

'You are resolved to take your rightful place in the school?'

'Yes, my lord.'

'Good. Well and good.' The Prime contemplatively reached out and made a tiny adjustment to the position of the figurine. Gauhm's broad hips and narrow shoulders were inverted and vaguely duplicated by the reflection that descended into the illusory depths of the tabletop. Her face could not be seen from here: she had her back to Paoul. 'More may hinge on your resolve than you might guess. You have eighteen months more at Hohe. Then, of course, you will embark on your six months of travel. If you acquit yourself well you will return here to take the pentacles. You will then leave us and go back to Brennis. That is only proper, for Brennis is where you began and you have a debt to repay to the vansery at Valdoe. It is not, however, a foregone conclusion that you will spend the rest of your life in Brennis. As you must be aware, the Order is constantly searching for men of special promise. For such men, the opportunities are almost without limit. I trust this is something else you will bear in mind.'

An air of finality in the Prime's manner hinted that the interview had come to its end. The Prime's expression confirmed it: Paoul stood up, his head swimming.

The Prime remained seated. 'Do you have any questions, Paoul?'

'No, my lord.'

'Good.' The Prime picked up his pen. 'Do not forget what has been said here this afternoon.'

As if anyone could forget such words! 'I won't, my lord.'

'The attendant will escort you to the stairs. Good day, Paoul.'

'Good day, my lord. Thank you, my lord.'

Paoul found himself crossing to the doors. He opened them and, turning to back out, looked up, half expecting the Prime to be watching; but he had already taken another parchment from the small table beside him and, his pen held ready, was again immersed in his work.

6

The mathematics lesson would be finishing by now: there was no point in going back there. And besides, he needed a few minutes on his own. He needed to think, to compose himself.

Scarcely aware of the treads beneath his feet, Paoul descended the staircase and entered the cloisters, slowing only in deference to the three or four priests he passed. From the cloisters he went straight to his dormitory and pressed shut the door.

Too stunned and excited to think of changing his clothes or preparing for the next session, he made himself sit down on the edge of the bed and tried to make sense of his feelings.

His world had been shattered and remade. He had suddenly been freed from the many small doubts, each insignificant on its own, that he now realized had been weighing him down. At their root – which the Prime had so perceptively uncovered – was a doubt that the horizons of Brennis were broad enough to contain his future. From slight beginnings a sureness had been growing within him, a confidence that he would one day be of service to the Order and thus to the empire and his fellow man. How, he was not certain, but he knew he could not serve best in isolation, and Valdoe was no place for an ambitious forzan: it was for phedes, astronomers, an observatory of a very high standard, but of little interest to him. Whatever nostalgia he had felt for Brennis itself, he believed, had long since glimmered and died. His life there had ended with Tagart's death, with the horrible scenes he still sometimes relived in his nightmares, with Dagda and Bocher and Beilin Crogh. Without even being aware of it, Paoul had been assuming that he was somehow sentenced to a lifetime in Brennis, and that he would soon have to leave for ever the place where he felt he belonged. The citadel had become his home, and the Order had become his family; more than a family. It had been better and kinder to him than any parent could have been. And all the time, while his doubts had been growing and proliferating and bearing strange fruit – such as his encounter with the Lady Yseld – his teachers had been planning for him and wisely guiding his course.

They wanted him for something more than a provincial forzan. It all seemed to fit into place: first, his early elevation to the higher school; second, his selection as lamp-bearer; third, the remark that Lord Heite had made at the lake – 'the Prime has spoken to me of you, Paoul'; and fourth, most important of all, the circumstances of the interview and the things the Prime had said.

He would have to spend some time in Brennis, the Prime had made that clear. But after that? Would he be coming back to Hohe? It seemed likely, perhaps even certain: why else should the Prime have spoken as he had? Why else should he have told Paoul, in so many words, that his opportunities were 'almost without limit'?

Paoul could not imagine what form those opportunities might take. Just to be in service here at Hohe would be more than enough. Would he be offered a post in the temple? Or in the school, as a teacher!

But then it struck him that he was meant for an even higher position than that. Perhaps, after many more years' study, he would be put in charge of a minor vansery of his own, become a vansard! Or would they train him for the High Council? Would he sit with Lord Heite and become an adviser on the Prime's staff?

It was all too dazzling to contemplate. The Prime, indeed, had tried to slow down this line of reasoning, to reduce its final impact, by explaining his motives for conducting the Starrad inquiry in person. It was inconceivable that the Prime, even by the subtlest omission, should ever be guilty of falsehood; but nothing could get away from the fact that, in the past, breaches of school discipline, however serious, had always been dealt with by the school Principal. There was surely a reason for the Prime's intervention on this occasion, and Paoul could think of only one. Was it possible? Was it possible that the Prime – the Prime himself, and not just the Prime acting on behalf of the Principal – could have wanted an opportunity to speak to Paoul alone, arousing 'neither the suspicions nor the curiosity' of his fellows? Was it possible that the Prime thought so highly of him, was so interested in his career, and was so anxious to impress upon him what was at stake? Incredible as it seemed, there could be no other explanation. The rest naturally followed. And it also followed that, in the plainest terms available to him, the Prime had warned Paoul that he was in danger of risking whatever it was that had been planned for him. 'More may hinge on your resolve than you might guess.' Were those not the very words the Prime had spoken not half an hour since?

Paoul arose. He had decided, as a man decides. His determination to heed the Prime's golden advice would not be sudden, dramatic, or flimsily contrived. It would be slow to build, strong, immovable. There would be no immediate or superficial results. His reform would come from within, from the core of obduracy at his centre, a gradual change in his habits and outlook that would slowly but irreversibly increase his capacity for work. His mind was made up. He would not fail his teachers or the Prime; he would not fail Gauhm.

Calmly, unhurriedly, he took off his robe and hung it in its place. From the wicker basket by his bed he selected a clean taug tunic and his swimming things. As he was washing, Enco and Buin arrived.

'Well?' said Enco.

'Yes,' said Buin, also fearful about his own interview later in the afternoon. 'What did he say?'

Paoul told them all they were allowed to know.

During the next eighteen months each of the boys spent progressively more time in specialist classes: Paoul with the forzans, Enco with the kars, Buin with the ilvens, and Relle – Starrad's replacement – with the phedes. As their basic training drew to a close, they were being prepared for their vows and for the years immediately after initiation.

They were also being prepared for the six months of travel which completed every novice's training and gave him a chance to see at first hand the way the empire worked. The novices, in pairs, were always accompanied by a teacher to act as guide and mentor. The exact itinerary was left to his discretion. There was not time to see more than a small part of the empire, which, counting the extensive tracts of uncivilized mountain and forest outside the settled regions, covered some three-quarters of a million square miles. Of this vast area, only a fraction was under the direct administration of the Gehans or their subordinated, blood-related clans – the Abendgehans, the Felsengehans, the Nordengehans, and the others. The remainder, especially in the south and west, was the original territory of a legion of chieftains large and small who had been conquered by the Gehan clans and paid them yearly tribute. This process of expansion was still continuing, with the fiercest wars being fought in the chiefdoms of Iberia. Along the borders of the north and east, however, there was no expansion, only an unremitting struggle to hold back the invasive tribes of barbarians whose warlords, if ever they became united, would be a formidable threat indeed.

Such regions were not visited by touring novices. They kept to the heartlands, to villages where they were sure of a suitable welcome. Journeying between the villages could itself be hazardous enough. Even today, in the marshes and mountains and unclaimed forests, there were plenty of bandits. Some, perhaps, were the remnants of the aboriginal tribes of hunters; most were disaffected or dispossessed farmers and their descendants. The novices would learn to deal with other hazards too – with wild animals, the vagaries of the weather, and all the other hardships of the road.

There was a certain amount of freedom in the boys' choice of travelling companion, and when Paoul and Enco expressed a wish to travel together this was not refused. Their mentor, traditionally chosen from another discipline, was named as Ilven Fend. A week before they were due to leave, when muddy torrents of meltwater were already roaring down the mountain and the ice in the lake had largely broken up, Ilven Fend decided on the final route. On a cloudy afternoon, with a cold east wind blowing sleet across the temple square, he called Paoul and Enco to his chambers.

Opening cylinders and scrolls, spreading skin and reedpaper maps on the floor, he took up a hazelwood pointer and indicated the course of their journey. It was to be a thousand miles long, beginning with a river passage north from Hohe, through the home provinces and thence into the country of the Felsengehans. At the port of Coblenz they would leave the river and head generally west, moving towards the channel coast. From the important seaside settlement of Raighe they would turn south, exploring the farming villages of the Kluh and the Courfen Plain and, eventually, by following the River Loire for part of its course, descend into the valley of the Rhône. After a brief stay in the fort at Chaer they would, by skirting the High Peaks and following the course of the River Doubs, make their way back through the homelands and so to the citadel.

'We will visit only three vanseries and a single fort, the one at Chaer,' said Ilven Fend. 'I want you to see as much of the country as possible and to spend your time among the simple people. Our route will not be easy, and we shall have to maintain a good speed if you're to be back here for the equinox. But I think you'll enjoy it.' He glanced at the earthenware kettle which, on its bed of heated rocks, had nearly come to the boil. 'I've elderflower and spearmint, nettle, or thyme. Enco, will you make the tea?'

Paoul sat quietly as Enco prepared the three beakers. He felt subdued. He was pleased, very pleased, that Ilven Fend was to be their mentor, but he was still slightly in awe of his teachers and could not get used to the way they were beginning to regard and treat him almost as an equal. To be invited informally into the chambers of an ilven still had a flavour of novelty and privilege.

And there was something else on Paoul's mind. This morning he had accidentally heard, from another novice, that Lord Mond was soon to be married. The bride was to be a distant cousin from a subordinate clan. 'Not Bohod Thosk's daughter, then?' Paoul had asked, as casually as he could, for the news had affected him strangely. Quite often in the past eighteen months, ever since their first and only meeting, he had been unable, despite the most rigorous efforts, to stop remembering the Lady Yseld. He had long ago forgiven her for her conduct: such behaviour was implicit in the mysterious and unattainable symbol she had become. For Paoul she represented everything his vows were designed to help him renounce. She was the alternative to his calling. Whenever, among his friends, the subject of women arose, it was her face and form he put to the hypothetical example being discussed. But so soon as the talk became coarse, as it occasionally did, he protected her image from defilement, replacing it with a composite derived from a dozen girls he had seen in the township. The same was true of his dreams. Her rare appearances there were invariably fleeting and innocent. Sometimes, to his alarm, he suspected that he also dreamt of her in other ways or, perhaps, more frequently than he knew. It was as though, deliberately excluded from his waking mind, she was managing to surface elsewhere. Yet he was convinced that he had no real feeling for her – how could he, after such a brief and unsatisfactory meeting so long ago? Had he not been a trainee priest, had he been exposed in the normal way to any number of marriageable girls, he would surely have soon forgotten the Lady Yseld, just as, without question, she had forgotten him.

Not that she concerned him anyway. Her only function was to serve as a symbol. None the less, it had helped to know that she was betrothed to Lord Mond and thus truly out of bounds.

Perhaps their betrothal had been called off long since. Or perhaps it had never existed, except in Paoul's imagination. Perhaps she had already married someone else. That was more than likely. To be unwed and eighteen and the daughter of Bohod Thosk was an improbable combination. Yes: she was already married. Paoul knew next to nothing of court life. Its events only touched the vansery when ceremonial was required. He would not have heard of her marriage. It had undoubtedly taken place; and, even if it hadn't, what possible difference could that make to him?

Irrational as it was, the matter had been intruding on his thoughts all day. He had not been so disturbed since the ending of the Starrad affair, when another boy had told him that, shortly after Paoul's interview with the Prime, one of the fishmongers in the township had disappeared. The fishmonger's wife and two unmarried daughters had disappeared also, and when soldiers had come to dismantle his shop and empty his house of possessions, his neighbours had been told that he had been ejected from Hohe for evasion of the tithe.

Nobody had known the name of Starrad's conquest or which of the three fishmongers in the township was her father. There was no more than the flimsiest circumstantial evidence linking the two events. It was both profane and ridiculous to suggest that the Prime, using the army to distance himself from the affair, should have stooped to punish a guiltless girl and her family – for they had committed no recognized offence. Rumours even arose that the family had not merely been expelled, but executed. Execution was the normal punishment for evasion of the tithe, but always in public and before a large crowd. If the rumours were taken to their logical conclusion, it followed that the authorities had not dared to expose the fishmonger to an audience and so had secretly murdered him and his family.

Naturally, no one believed this for an instant. The rumours were idle speculation, supposition, the kind of extravagant gossip which circulates in the wake of any drama. There was no cogent reason for the girl to be silenced, even less for her family. But Paoul had still found the rumours distressing, because it had been he, and Enco and Buin, who had given testimony which could conceivably have been used to identify the girl. For a short time the rumours had even threatened to shake his faith in the Prime and weaken his resolve to work harder.

Like all such affairs, though, this one had soon been forgotten, and Paoul had emerged from it virtually unchanged. He had kept his resolution. A fortnight ago, in the academic tests which qualified a novice for the tour and marked the end of his formal training, Paoul had surpassed the highest standard in all but two subjects, and in those he had been commended with honour by his examiners. Together with Enco, Buin, Relle, and most of his friends, Paoul had been pronounced fit to enter the Pathway of the Tracts. The next morning, therefore, attended by an ilven and a kar, the first stage of his tattooing had begun.

The tattoo of a red priest was applied with needles of blue flint, fashioned by the phedes and heated to boiling in vessels of sanctified water. Elaborate ritual attended the preparation of the pigment, which was sent from Hohe to all vanseries where priests were trained. The pigment base, found only at one site on the slopes of Mount Atar, was a red earth yielding a deep crimson when mixed, in aqueous solution, with the fresh pulp of ripe barberries – fruits sacred to Gauhm and gathered for this purpose only on the day of the autumn equinox, from a consecrated grove below the citadel. To this was added an infusion of marjoram in water from the shrine falls, and, to promote healing, a decoction of madder-root. The whole was reduced by heat to the consistency of blood, and stored in airtight jars until needed.

The symbology of the tattoo was extremely complicated. The pattern consisted of exactly three thousand puncture-marks, forming a pentacle on the left instep and another on the back of the left hand, connected by three lines, or tracts, extending up the leg and flank and down the arm. The pentacle on the foot symbolized contact with the earth, source of the power which was channelled through the tracts to the hand. Of the three tracts, one, the major, was thicker than the paired minor tracts; the position of the major, whether to the right or left of the minors, varied according to a priest's nomination. A major adjacent to the outer edge of the forearm denoted a phede or ilven; one adjacent to the inner edge denoted a forzan or kar.

The apex of the pentacle represented spirit. Each of the four lower points, proceeding sunwise from the apex, represented one of the four quadrants – creation, manifestation, decay, dormancy – and hence one of the four nominations: ilven, kar, phede, forzan. The major tract ended at the point on the hand corresponding to the priest's nomination.

The pentacles of phedes and kars were upright, with the apex pointing towards the digits, while those of ilvens and forzans were inverted. Thus the three tracts began and ended in a different way in each of the four types of tattoo. The arrangements and connections of the tracts and pentacles formed a kind of language, intelligible to the initiated, which could be read as an account of the unifying and distinguishing characteristics of the four nominations. And there was a fifth nomination, that of the Prime. In his tattoo all three tracts were of the same thickness, the minors being reworked as a sign of the new Prime's accession.

A novice's tattoo was applied in stages. First, before the tour, he entered the Pathway of the Tracts. The Pathway began at the instep and ended at the hand. On each day save the last, over a period of eleven days, he received fifteen times fifteen punctures; each set of fifteen had its own special prayer, song, or chant, forming a narrative, recited by the attending ilven, who also marked out the course for the kar to follow with his needles and pigment. On the last day there were only thirteen sets of fifteen. Then, six months later, on returning from the tour, the two pentacles – each of two hundred and fifty punctures – were made. Lastly, at the full initiation ceremony, the pentacles were connected to the tracts with a further fifty-five punctures.

Paoul had almost finished the Pathway and heard the whole narrative: he had been tattooed as far as the upper arm. He was finding the process more uncomfortable than painful. A herbal styptic, a fragrant white powder sprinkled by the kar from a perforated box, stanched most of the residual bleeding. At night the most recent punctures pained him slightly, but it was a pain of which he was intensely proud, and he was studying with fascination the regular, beautifully even progression of the three tracts towards his wrist, each evening comparing his tattoo with those of his friends.

Sitting here now, sipping nettle tea and listening to Ilven Fend making plans for the tour, Paoul was pleasurably conscious of the ache which from time to time made him adjust the set of his upper sleeve. Only three sessions remained before his Pathway was complete. Each session was carrying him further towards his goal. With today's news about Lord Mond, Paoul saw that each session was also carrying him further away from the danger posed by his image of the Lady Yseld. He was glad. Soon he would be safe for ever. And he was glad that next week he would be leaving on the tour. His departure was coming just at the right time: travel would remove him from her in person as well as thought.

Paoul finished his tea and, asking a question about the route, sat forward and gave Ilven Fend his undivided attention.

7

Arriving at Chaer Fort in the cool of the evening, Ilven Fend made himself known to the sentry high in the gatehouse. A minute later Paoul heard first one bar and then another and another being pulled back: a small doorway, just wide enough to admit one man, opened in the heavily timbered expanse of the gates, and Ilven Fend, followed by Paoul and Enco, stepped through.

They were met by a soldier wearing the braided wristband of a unit leader. 'Good evening to you, father,' he said, with the same note of deference that Paoul had found everywhere so far on the tour – in all the villages and settlements, at the ports and ferry stations, and in the tone of almost everyone they had encountered on the road. 'And to the young men, of course. Welcome. I'm sorry the gates were locked, father. There's been some trouble today.'

'What sort of trouble?'

'Brigands, father. Please come with me. I'll take you to the commander.'

The settlement at Chaer was the largest in the province, with extensive field systems in the fertile soil of the river valley. The road to the fort passed near the village, which was one of the more prosperous Paoul had seen, its people apparently healthy and its thatched houses and barns in generally good repair. The fort stood on level ground a quarter of a mile or so from the village, guarded by a high palisade and a deep double ditch lined with a fearsome array of spikes.

Except for the citadel and the Trundle at Valdoe – which he could remember at best only indistinctly – Paoul had never been inside a fort before; neither had Enco. This visit was intended to improve their knowledge of the day-to-day administration of the provinces, a process in which the forts played an indispensable part. Paoul had already seen at first hand something of the function of the forts. Their main purpose was to supervise the farming population, keeping order, enforcing the edicts and the judgements of the provincial commanders. They also controlled the labour-gangs of slaves who maintained the roads, bridges, ferries, and other communal works. Their third duty was to defend the empire's interests from those who refused to recognize its authority – barbarians beyond the border, or bandits within. Paoul had seen little of this aspect of provincial administration, except, and the scene remained disgustingly vivid in his mind, at a village farther north where the mutilated remains of three robbers, caught stealing livestock, had been hung from a gibbet outside the gates. This sight, more perhaps than any of the harrowing scenes of poverty and neglect he had witnessed on the tour, had brought home to Paoul how vast and how puzzling was the discrepancy between the plenty of the countryside and the lot of its inhabitants, all its inhabitants: for it seemed to him that the bandits and robbers were themselves only people who at some stage in their history had been displaced or dispossessed. For reasons he was not sure about, Paoul had decided to keep these feelings private. At the gibbet Ilven Fend had declared that there could be no room for weakness when dealing with such criminals.

The physical structure of the fort spoke of anything but weakness. The palisade, ramparts, and the buildings of the central stronghold were all constructed of dark timbers, more or less massive, and the roofs, unlike those of the village, were not of reed-thatch, but of overlapping planks – perhaps a precaution against fire attack. From a slanting pole above the gateway of the commander's quarters hung the familiar green and red pennon of the Gehans: a few days ago, Ilven Fend had led his two charges out of the country of the Abendgehans and back at last into the territory of the ruling clan. The few soldiers on the ramparts were clad in Gehan armour and helmets; those in the enclosure or visible at the windows of the barracks were, like the unit leader, wearing hot-weather tunics and leggings. A smell of new bread was coming from the long, low building Paoul took to be the cookhouse, and he wondered how much longer he would have to wait before eating. Since dawn, when they had left the village of Vinzy, he and his companions had covered thirty-five or forty miles. Ilven Fend had insisted on reaching Chaer by nightfall. Paoul was footsore, thirsty, and hungry: the food the head man had given them on leaving had not lasted long, and Ilven Fend had not allowed them to stop to catch or pick anything from the wild, as was their custom on the road.

The unit leader showed the group into the official receiving room, a ground-floor chamber four yards square, furnished more to civilian than military standards. The window overlooked a little limewashed courtyard where, on the far wall, a trellis was laden with a profusion of honeysuckle foliage and blooms. Darkness was approaching: the unit leader fetched a taper to light the oil lamps, and made as if to close the shutters.

'Leave them open, please,' said Ilven Fend.

'Gladly, father, but the insects – '

'Yes, of course. Do as you must.'

Commander Yahl came in. He was a spare, resilient-looking man of early middle age, with brown eyes, greying hair and beard, and a nose that looked as if it had been broken long ago. 'Please be seated,' he said, once the introductions had been made. 'Kuber, take these bags to the guests' quarters and see that fresh water and bedding are made ready.' He turned back to Ilven Fend. 'Was your journey uneventful?'

'Should it have been otherwise?'

'Perhaps. I am surprised but also very thankful to see you all safely here. I sent smoke to Vinzy, warning you not to set out. Was the message not received?'

'It merely warned us to be on our guard.'

'Then, somewhere along the way, it was misread. You were lucky, father. Several travellers have been attacked by brigands on that stretch of road. Did you see anything unusual, anything at all?'

'No, Commander. Nothing.'

Yahl sat forward. 'Yesterday the brigands became more ambitious. They burned a village three miles upstream. This morning we finally managed to locate their camp, but the patrol was discovered. Two of my men were brought back dead, one has died since, and another is dying even now. One of my best.' The commander gave a harsh smile in which Paoul detected great anguish and bitterness.

'Would you like me to attend him?'

'No, father, I cannot ask you that. You must be tired and in need of refreshment.'

'Not so.' Ilven Fend stood up. 'Take us to him.'

The wounded man was in a small chamber in the barracks. The first thing Paoul noticed, even before entering, was a strong smell of excrement. That, or the smoky light of the rush-lamps, had attracted an assortment of insects: lacewings, beetles, flies, small moths, dashing themselves against the lamps and the freckled limewash of the low, uneven ceiling.

The man had been laid on a straw-covered pallet by the far wall. Behind his head, keeping watch, was another soldier, and beside the pallet, offering water from a wooden bowl, was an old man in coarse garments, a civilian. Paoul did not realize at first that the old man was a village priest, not until he saw the tattoo on his right hand and forearm, the blue tattoo with its three thin, wavering tracts and its crudely drawn pentacle. The old priest, noticing the newcomers, arose and moved aside.

The room was silent but for the insects and the congested passage of the man's breath. Ilven Fend squatted by the pallet, allowing Paoul and Enco to take a closer look. Paoul felt his stomach twist. The brigands had used an axe.

'What is his name?' Ilven Fend asked the priest.

'Reisen, master.'

'What prayers have you said for him?'

'All the prayers for the dying, master.'

The man was still conscious: he could understand perfectly what was being said. He recognized Ilven Fend's robes and tattoo and the agony in his eyes were relieved for a moment by gratitude. His mouth opened more widely, but no sound emerged.

'No, my son. Be quiet.'

He seemed to be about Paoul's age, no more, dark and strongly made, his skin deeply tanned and his hair streaked with grime and blood and with fragments and stalks of straw-coloured vegetation. The stump of his left arm had been clumsily wrapped in chamois. The terrible wounds in his chest and abdomen had been uncovered and thickly sprinkled with what looked like fine wood-ash.

'What is this?'

'From the altar in the village, master. A sacred offering.'

'Burnt bone?'

'Yes, master.'

Ilven Fend lightly shook his head. Bone ash: useless, worse than useless, an ignorant, stupid, pagan superstition. Paoul felt his pity turning to bewilderment and then to anger. He had seen wounds before, and pain, and corpses: it was part of Ilven Fend's brief to show him and Enco these things. He had seen suffering before, but never quite like this. Here, in this squalid room, on this red-soaked pallet, was the reality of the administration that Paoul had previously learned only as lofty and distant theory. This foul, mangled mass of flesh had this morning been the noblest pinnacle of the earth's creation: a man. He had been strong and healthy and vibrantly alive, the same age as Paoul, with the same scantiness of memory and experience and the same hope and eagerness for the future. And now, through his trusting service to the Gehan ideal, to Lord Heite and the bohods and all the frivolities of the court, to the Atanes and the Yselds and all their kind, he was finished, cut down; his life was almost over.

This morning, perhaps, the moment he had been brought in, he might have had a chance. If instead of this old fool he had been attended by a kar – by Kar Ander – he might have been saved. But now it was too late. Enco offered to clean his wounds; Ilven Fend refused. The young soldier was already slipping away.

Ilven Fend began to recite the beautiful words of the Seventy-fifth Song, the Song of the Voyage, the song of death.

Commander Yahl bowed his head and the others did the same. Paoul bowed his head too, but as he listened to the verses unfolding they began to take on a horrible and unfamiliar aspect. They began to sound like something hollow and contrived, a clever piece of mummery to beguile the credulous and keep them subservient to some ulterior cause. Paoul remembered the starving villagers he had seen; he remembered the gibbet; he remembered the luxury of Bohod Thosk's new hall; he remembered Lord Heite with Lady Atane at the lake, and it seemed to him in this moment that the words of the Song were meaningless, a travesty of the brutal truth of this young man's death, robbing it of its dignity: and the worst part was that the dying man was deceived to the very last. He was wrong to be comforted by Ilven Fend's presence, wrong to be reassured and grateful that a red priest should have appeared, as if by divine intervention, at the scene of his final agony.

'He is dead.'

Paoul was unsteady on his feet, light-headed and close to collapse. Suddenly, eagerly, he realized that this was more than enough to account for his hallucinatory perception of the Song. He was faint from hunger, from exhaustion, from the heat. He was in no state to think, to form opinions, or to withstand such profound emotional distress.

None of this could he reveal to Ilven Fend. As much as anything else, the tour was a practical test of endurance and fortitude. If he failed it, Paoul would not be accepted for his initiation. And so, as Ilven Fend shut the soldier's eyes and rose to his feet. Paoul imperceptibly braced his shoulders and assumed the impassive, self-contained expression of strength that was second nature to any man who belonged to the Red Order, who was dedicated to it and served it body and soul without question.

'Will Reisen be buried here?' Ilven Fend asked the commander.

'Yes. Tomorrow morning.'

'I will officiate, if that is your desire.'

The retaliatory raid on the brigands next day was described by Commander Yahl as a complete success. Of the two hundred soldiers in the fort, a hundred and eighty took part, led by the commander in person. The brigands' new camp – two miles from the last, which, as expected, they had vacated following its discovery by the patrol – was surrounded and each of its sixty-three occupants, women and children as well as men, was captured or killed. Children under the age of about nine were routinely dispatched as worthless; the others, and all the surviving adults except one, who, being lame, was therefore dispatched also, were bound and fettered and brought back to the fort.

They arrived late in the afternoon. Once the prisoners had been sorted they were interrogated. As a result of the interrogation – which had involved torture with burning brands and with tourniquets wound round the forehead – Commander Yahl decided that two more of the men, leaders and trouble-makers who would anyway be unlikely to make suitable slaves, should be given to the soldiers for disposal as they saw fit, bearing in mind the murder of Reisen and his comrades the previous day. Lastly, most of the younger women, and some of the older ones, were taken to the barracks for the evening to be used in any way the soldiers pleased.

'You were very quiet at supper, Paoul,' said Ilven Fend, studying him closely.

They had just left Commander Yahl and had returned to the guests' quarters. Before retiring, as was their habit, Ilven Fend and the two novices had sat down to discuss the events of the day.

'Yes, Ilven Fend. I was.'

'Nor did you eat very much. That was a discourtesy.'

'I am sorry, Ilven Fend.'

For the instructive experience it had promised, Ilven Fend had accepted the commander's invitation to take Paoul and Enco out with the soldiers on the raid. There had been little danger, for both the novices were proficient in the use of weapons and had gone armed; and Ilven Fend had in any case kept them well back from the fighting. They had been close enough, though, to observe everything that had happened; and afterwards, at the fort, they had watched the interrogation and seen the execution of the two leaders. And, during supper, Paoul had from time to time heard laughter and vile shouting from the barracks.

He knew in theory the justification of the policy that countenanced the soldiers' behaviour, just as he had known the theory that had brought Reisen to his death. Gentleness through strength: that was the key. By the application of strength, peace was maintained. In this peace, this 'gentleness', the empire was able to flourish. It was the same in nature. The weak submitted to the strong, resulting in beauty and harmony. The empire was indeed not to be distinguished from nature: it was merely one part of the manifestation of the universal and therefore continuous with Gauhm's will. Any and all actions taken in defence of the empire were thus a form of worship. Had the brigands not been stopped, they would have burned another village, and another, until the whole province was in ruins and its people without food.

This was the irrefutable proof of a theory which was easy enough to understand in the safety and comfort of a tutorial chamber, but a different matter entirely out here. The brigands' ramshackle tents and shelters had been inexpertly concealed among dry scrub on a hot and barren hillside; the camp had seemed to Paoul less like the stronghold of dangerous criminals than the pathetic refuge of a tribe of frightened destitutes. The brigands themselves, most of them, had been pitiful creatures, like vagrants and outsiders almost anywhere. If they had met the same hostility in the valleys as had once been shown to Tagart and his group, then it was not surprising that they had been reduced to such straits of evil and despair.

What Paoul had seen here had also affected him in another way. Until today, the existence of slavery had been a fact of his life which he had not thought to question. Nor had he wondered about the source of its raw material. If asked, he might have said that the slaves had always been so, and surely, replaced themselves in the usual manner.

Now he knew otherwise. And, since he himself had once been part of a band of vagrants, since he had in effect been captured by the ruling clan, what was he if not a special and unusual kind of slave? And if that were so, to whom exactly was he enslaved, when it was the Red Order that, by guiding and confining the actions of Lord Heite, was in reality the controller of the empire?

And further: it appeared to Paoul that the controller of any system must be responsible for the conduct of all those in its administration. If the soldiers committed atrocities in the name of Lord Heite – and hence in the name of the Prime – then surely the Prime, by failing to punish or forbid these acts, was equally if not more to blame. And, because it was the Prime who made the laws, who ultimately controlled the apportionment of land and titles and favour, then it was also the Prime who was to blame for the conditions which produced the misery of such people as the brigands.

Paoul felt he had not yet comprehended the full implication of these thoughts, but already he knew they must be wrong. The idea that the Prime could ever be considered blameworthy in any way was clearly a preposterous contradiction in terms. It had to be. The reason Paoul felt so shaken, so disturbed, he told himself, had nothing to do with the Prime. It was the simple result of heat, fatigue, and exposure to scenes of violence and brutality. On the hillside it had taken all his strength to prevent himself from being physically sick. It had been the same during the interrogation and the executions that had followed.

He had tried to keep his feelings hidden from Ilven Fend, but without, it now seemed, much success.

'And you, Enco,' said Ilven Fend. 'You too are guilty of discourtesy to our host.'

'I am very sorry, Ilven Fend.'

Ilven Fend straightened the folds in the front of his robe and laid one hand upon the other in his lap. 'I must say I had been expecting greater insight and self-control from you both. Have you already forgotten the most basic principles of your training? In a few weeks you are due to be taken into the Order. To all intents and purposes, you should already be behaving like red priests. Yes, Enco?' he said, even more sharply. 'Do you have a comment to make?'

'No, Ilven Fend.'

'Doubtless you imagine that what we have seen today is both monstrous and wrong. By the standards expected of a man of refinement, it is monstrous. Of course it is. But not wrong. The conduct of Commander Yahl and his men has been in complete accord with the teachings. That is why I am so glad we came to Chaer when we did, for you have been allowed to observe what few of your fellows will ever see: the most extreme example of the ethos at work.' He lifted his hands. 'Well. You are young. Perhaps I am being harsh. I remember my own tour. I too had never been beyond the citadel, not, at least, with intelligent eyes. But I think you are old enough now to understand the ethos not as an intellectual abstraction, but as an emotional reality. I think you are mature enough to understand why the soldiers act as they do. Enco?'

'I confess to being shocked,' Enco said, and Paoul watched, fascinated, as his friend seemed to swell with the pride of being able to accept Ilven Fend's compliment. 'I had never seen such things before, but now I understand. I meant no discourtesy to Commander Yahl, nor did I mean to criticize him.'

Ilven Fend nodded, pleased with Enco's answer. 'And Paoul?'

In all his years of training, Paoul could not remember ever once having told his teachers a conscious lie. Falsehood was wrong, contrary to the ethos. And besides, he had always imagined that lies were instantly found out, that the liar always betrayed himself, if not by blushing or stammering, then by some change in voice or expression that would be apparent to his elders. He had not guessed how easy a lie could be, especially when it was a lie only by omission: for what Ilven Fend had asked him was whether he understood the ethos as Enco did, and to this Paoul could give what was in fact a truthful answer.

'Yes, Ilven Fend,' he said, 'I understand.'

But, no sooner had he spoken, no sooner had his lie, so glibly framed and delivered, found its mark and done its work of deception, than Paoul realized he had taken an irrevocable step towards alienating himself from everything he had aspired to be. With these few words he had begun to set himself apart, to dissociate himself from the Order. A cold and yet enticing feeling rose within him that had lain dormant since his early childhood, since the time when he had been orphaned and sold and sent across the sea.

It was the feeling of being alone.

8

The vessels plying the Great River between Coblenz and Hohe were of many different kinds and sizes. Larger even than the seagoing ships of the Gehans and bohods were the sturdy, blunt-prowed riverboats, designed to carry heavy cargoes of merchandise and passengers from port to port and from landing stage to landing stage along the way. They carried little sail; going upstream they were drawn with long ropes wherever there was a towpath, or propelled by their crewmen with poles and oars.

It was on a boat like this that Paoul and the others had begun the first stage of the tour, alighting at Coblenz. Now, for the last twenty-five miles to Hohe, Ilven Fend had decided, with uncharacteristic leniency, to take passage rather than walk. He had said that they all deserved a rest, and at first light they had boarded at the village of Imber.

The ordinary passengers travelled in the open, among the goats and sheep and sacks of grain, and were expected to lend a hand with the towropes when required. For the others, though, there was usually a cabin, which provided a degree of comfort and somewhere dry to sit. On the first trip, nearly six months ago, Ilven Fend had chosen to travel on deck; but today, on hearing that the cabin was vacant, he had gone to the expense of hiring it.

The cabin on this boat was built high on the after-deck, and was about eight feet square, with bench seats giving a view of the river to the rear and to either side. The flag at the sternpost, Paoul had noticed, was red and black: the colours of the Thosks, and he reflected that it had been a Thosk ship that had first brought him here from Brennis. Rain had been falling for much of the afternoon; Paoul had watched the flag gradually becoming darker and more soaked, and now, as the light began to fail, it was no longer even moving with the breeze, but hanging dejectedly against its pole.

They were nearly at Hohe. Already, once or twice, they had

glimpsed the citadel; after three more bends, three more bluffs of grey, fir-grown rock, the lamps and smoke and jetties of the landing place, the merchants' sheds, and the houses of the Lower Township would come into view. Staring out across the water, he could see several rafts and black coracles trailing nets and lines, and beyond them the huts and houses of one of the outlying villages. A cormorant was fishing too, its back almost awash and its neck and head protruding from the water at an angle, like a bent piece of burnt wood. With a shallow leap the cormorant dived: Paoul saw its webbed feet and the oily, dark feathers of its rounded tail, and it was gone.

'Not far now,' said Ilven Fend. 'We should be up at the gates before locking-up. They usually wait for the last riverboat.'

Enco was eating raisins. He offered the bag to Paoul who, for Ilven Fend's benefit, accepted a few and ate them. It would be better not to stare at the river any more, better to make a more convincing job of hiding his despondency. So far he had been very careful to give no grounds for suspicion. He had applied the techniques of the taug, and since Chaer had learned to be more guarded, even with Enco; he was sure that neither Ilven Fend nor Enco had guessed what was going on in his heart.

Not that Paoul himself really knew. Looking back on the tour, he could not truly name the point at which he had realized that he no longer felt the same about the priesthood. Since Chaer he had wanted, several times, to broach the subject with Enco and more than once with Ilven Fend. His inner counsel, however, had cautioned him to keep silent. He had already received most of his tattoo; he was not fitted for life outside the Order. The only practical course now would be to accept the rest of the tattoo, to take his initiation, and to wait and see.

This was logic speaking, the voice of philosophy and of the mind, his own special field. His emotions spoke differently. With each passing mile, with each yard gained against the river current, he wanted less and less to return to Hohe.

'Look there!' cried Ilven Fend. They were rounding the second bluff, the crewmen straining at the oars, while the rain slanted down across the deck-passengers and the animals and the bales of skin-covered cargo, making the planking gleam.

An area of thinner cloud, a rift of brightness, had appeared in the south-east, behind the lower flanks of Mount Atar, spreading its watery light down into the valley and across the river, illuminating the inside of the cabin. At its apparent heart, at its source, lay the familiar silhouette of the citadel gates and palisade, the township, the barracks, and, above them all, the roofs of the vansery and of the temple.

'Farewell, then, Enco. Or "Kar Enco", I ought to say.'

'No. Let me always be plain "Enco" to you.'

There was very little time left. Paoul looked once more round the small dormitory room that had been his home for almost two years. All but Enco's shelves and locker were bare; all but Enco's bed had been stripped and the bedding neatly rolled and tied. Buin and Relle had already left Hohe, gone to vanseries in the south, and this afternoon Paoul was due to board the Gehan ship taking the annual commission of inspection to Brennis. Only Enco, at the special request of Kar Ander, was staying on: he would soon be given his own chambers in the kars' quarters, where he would be employed as an assistant to the Chief Herbalist. The announcement of this honour had come as a surprise to nobody but Enco himself.

A week had passed since then, since the day of the autumn equinox and the last in the series of solemn ceremonies that had transformed Paoul and eighteen others into initiates of the Red Order. At the final ceremony Paoul had been allowed to touch the Vessel of the Forzans, and the Prime, as vansard, had supervised the completion of his tattoo and heard his vows of obedience, celibacy, loyalty, and faith. Then the Prime had touched his forehead and he had arisen as a priest.

After the rite of initiation, Forzan Zett had called each new priest to his chambers to tell him what and where his first post was to be. The vansery at Valdoe had sent word to say that, if Paoul's initiation were confirmed, and if his services were not required at Hohe, then he would be expected to begin his duties with a period of one year as a teacher in the school at Valdoe Village. His pupils, Forzan Zett had explained, were to be the sons of the military and civilian officers at the Trundle. When the year was up, he would either have to continue at the school, or, more probably, he would join the astronomers working under the new Vansard, Phede Keldis, whom he would eventually serve as a theological adviser. 'However,' Forzan Zett had added, in an oddly cryptic tone that had immediately put Paoul on the alert, 'However, I doubt whether you will spend much longer in Brennis than is needed to repay Valdoe for their sponsorship. In something less than five years you are likely to return to the citadel. This is a delicate and strictly confidential matter to be discussed with you by the Lord Prime, and you are invited to present yourself at his chambers tomorrow at the third hour of the forenoon.'

The substance and import of that interview had thrown Paoul into a turmoil from which he thought he might never recover, a turmoil of conscience in which, by the cruellest irony imaginable, his doubts had become deeper and more numerous. And yet, even if he had not been ordered to keep silent – he had been empowered to divulge only the details of his duties in Brennis – he would still have felt unable to discuss the least of his doubts with his best and closest friend.

'I must be going, Enco.'

'I could come with you as far as the gate.'

'Better not.'

Enco held out his hand. Paoul took it.

'Farewell. Paoul . . . I hope this is not the end of our friendship.'

'So do I.'

Paoul walked alone to the vansery gate. He had already taken leave of his teachers, of Erta and the other lay staff, and of the rest of his contemporaries. There was nothing left but to summon the gatekeeper and say goodbye to him also.

Once through the township, once through the main citadel gates, Paoul hefted his heavy leather bag on to his shoulder and started down the steep road to the river and the Lower Township. The afternoon was warm and bright, with a solid azure sky above the yellowing birches that lined this part of the road. Each twist and turn kept him facing more or less towards the south-west, and as he walked, passed now and then by respectful peasants and townsfolk heading uphill, he knew exactly how the appearance of the citadel behind him was changing. With the sun on his back, the darkness of the palisade would just be visible through the trees, and above it, to the right, the south face of the temple and the balconies of the Prime's quarters. There would be smoke rising from the township, perhaps three slate-blue pigeons circling in the air. And here, further down the road, the temple would have disappeared, its place taken by the twin towers of the western gatehouse, each bearing at its pinnacle a tall staff flying the personal standard of Lord Heite – an emerald green serpent on a scarlet ground. These two flags, brilliant against the autumn sky, would be the last of the citadel that he would see before reaching the river.

The temptation was to turn and look, to permit himself a trace of sentiment. But that presupposed his continuance as a priest, his adherence to an order which he now felt he had entered dishonestly, with fraudulent vows of loyalty and obedience. And it presupposed he could live with what the Prime had told him almost a week ago.

No. He had to look. He would never see this place again.

But when he turned, he saw that the two standards had also disappeared. The citadel lay completely hidden, like Paoul's falsehood, like his reaction when he had been informed that, five years from now, he was destined to be brought back from Brennis, brought back, and entered on the long and gruelling course of preparation that, one day, might end with him becoming Prime.

Part 3

1

'Forzan Paoul! Are you here to take tea with me again? What a delightful surprise! Do be seated. Yes, there. Tell me, are they working you too hard down at that school? You mustn't let them, you know.'

'I won't, Kar Houle.'

It was Paoul's free afternoon. Bringing a gift of Kar Houle's favourite oatmeal-and-hazelnut biscuits, he had left his lodgings at the settlement farm and, well protected against the snow falling on Valdoe Hill, had climbed up to the vansery to visit once more the priest who, twelve years ago, had first examined him. Even then it had seemed to Paoul that Kar Houle was impossibly ancient; but, although now becoming rather frail, the old man was still quite active, taking regular walks on the hillside, practising his daily routine of martial exercises, and working each morning in the physic garden or in the herb room indoors. His skin was liver-spotted and beginning to acquire the texture and colour of the finest parchment; he had lost two or three teeth and his white hair was not quite so thick, but his eyes were just as clear and perceptive as ever. He was in his ninety-seventh year, the oldest inhabitant of the vansery, and indeed of Valdoe and perhaps the whole domain.

Paoul liked him. But there was another reason for today's visit. On the way up here, Paoul had been trying to find the words that would enable him to seek Kar Houle's advice without seeming to do so. He wanted above all just to talk freely, to find a listener who might shed light on the paradox that had taken control of Paoul's life: the paradox of distrusting the aims of the priesthood and yet revering its individual priests. Until this was resolved Paoul could not decide how to deal with the astounding revelation that they were planning to prepare him for the highest office of the empire. He did not know how many other candidates there would be, or how many different posts would intervene before the final question of his accession. But, given the opportunity, given that he was spiritually suited to such a position – and this, surely, they already believed – then he knew he had the ability to succeed. This was a fact he had demonstrated to himself over and over again. If he chose to become Prime, if becoming Prime depended solely upon himself, then, no matter how long it might take, he felt he could do it.

The Vansard, Phede Keldis, should have been the recipient of a young priest's questions, but Paoul, living as he did away from the vansery, had only conversed with him twice. Besides, to ask fundamental questions of that kind would surely be regarded as an act of heresy.

Yet Paoul had to unburden himself. He had to talk to someone. Kar Houle, with his slightly irreverent manner, his vast experience, his wisdom, and his apparent special fondness for Paoul, would be unlikely to report the contents of a dubious conversation to Phede Keldis: Kar Houle was himself the senior kar at Valdoe and a member of the vansery board. And, alarmed, fascinated, and also peculiarly reassured to discover in himself a self-protective streak of chilling and ruthless realism, Paoul had not overlooked the fact that Kar Houle did not have much longer to live.

As the servant brought the tea and arranged Paoul's gift of biscuits on a carved willow platter, Paoul framed his opening remark and decided he would speak as soon as the man had shut the door.

At last the door closed; the peg of the latch dropped into place, and Paoul felt his tenseness giving way to the act of forming the first word.

Suddenly, one of the logs in Kar Houle's hearth, whitish grey and all but consumed, collapsed and projected a smoking cinder on to the mat. Kar Houle rose and quickly threw the cinder back, and, pulling fresh logs from the basket, made up the fire. 'One of the few privileges of age,' he said, once he had sat down again, and nodded at the hearth. This chamber, on an outside wall of the vansery, was one of the few private rooms to have a fireplace rather than the customary cradle for heated rocks or, what was more usual still, no heating at all. 'Have your lodgings improved Forzan Paoul? Last time we spoke I sensed you were not entirely comfortable.'

'I did not mean to give that impression, Kar Houle.'

The old man smiled. 'Well, the least we can do is give you a hot cup of tea.' He handed Paoul one of the two beakers and proffered the biscuits. The gesture, the faintly sweet smell of oatmeal and honey and chopped nuts, the aroma of clover-blossom tea, reminded Paoul of the Kar Houle who had waited with him in the harbour Trundleman's quarters, who had sipped the same kind of tea and eaten the same kind of biscuits while the *Veisdrach* had been loading. For an instant Paoul was transported back there, to the moment on the ship when he had doubted Kar Houle's affection for him, and he realized that he was still no nearer knowing whether Kar Houle or anyone else in a priest's tunic was to be trusted. That providential little cinder might have spared him from what could have proved a fatal mistake.

'Tell me, Kar Houle,' Paoul said, once they had drunk their tea, 'how thorough is the archive we keep here? At Hohe everything that is written is put into store.'

'The same applies at any vansery. Is there something specific you wish to know?'

'Not really. I was just curious.'

But later, as darkness was falling and Paoul left Kar Houle's chamber, he decided to make his way to the library, not quite sure what it was that he hoped to find. From the sleeping-quarters he passed through narrow corridors lined with polished wood and lit by stone cressets, through the refectory and past the taug room, and came to the double doors of the library. After a moment's hesitation, he went in.

On the day of his arrival, Phede Keldis, conducting Paoul round the vansery, had given him the freedom of the library and had briefly shown him how the shelves and pigeonholes were arranged. The shutters had been open then; it had been sunny, and three or four priests had been at work at the low, sloping tables; another had been illustrating a copy of one of the legends, adding clustered berries to the honeysuckled border of the scroll with deft strokes of a fine squirrelhair brush dipped in crimson ink.

This afternoon there was only a single priest present, on the far side of the room, a young phede who Paoul remembered was one of the leaders of Phede Keldis's team of astronomers. His table illuminated by two free-standing lamps, he was engrossed in the uppermost of a heap of large parchments, a sky map showing the celestial dome as a circle and the stars and constellations as points of black, red, yellow, green and blue. A measuring-rod and pair of compasses lay across the parchment and he was busily making notes on a small tablet.

He looked up as Paoul entered acknowledged him in the informal manner, and, after making an offer of assistance which Paoul politely declined, went back to his work.

Lighting a portable lamp, Paoul approached the end of the room devoted to the archive, twenty racks extending from floor to ceiling and almost from wall to wall, so closely spaced that there was barely enough room to pass between them. Either side of each of the first fifteen racks was divided into five hundred compartments, each a hand's-width square. Many of the compartments were as yet empty; in each of the rest, tightly and concentrically rolled, were stuffed several parchments. The other five racks, differently divided, held clay tablets, sheets of wood or reedpaper, and the more precious parchments, which were stored in capped cylinders.

Some of the hieroglyphs labelling the rows of compartments were flaking away; it took Paoul a while to deduce their meaning and to trace the section containing the records of induction. These were arranged in chronological order. Finally he found the parchments covering the Year of the Blue Hare, the two hundred and eighty-seventh of the Gehan era, and pulled them out.

Of all the secrets preserved by the priesthood, writing was one of the most powerful and the most arcane. In its higher forms it was even denied to the ruling clan. The notation was based on pictures of the object to be represented, refined and augmented with a stylized version of the smoke-signalling system evolved by the army. The characters were written with a pen or brush, vertically, in columns from left to right. Paoul had been taught the latest Hohe script: Kar Houle's hand, full of old-fashioned flourishes and lacking many of the contractions that Paoul used, was nevertheless very neat and readable, and Paoul had no difficulty in finding the parchments relating to himself.

Kar Houle's report was exceedingly thorough. Paoul read it to the end. The part describing himself at seven was uncanny, so unfamiliar and yet recognizable was the embryo of his adult self. It was curious to see how much and how little he had changed, and how incompletely the boy he had known himself to be had been perceived by the kars. But the account of the search at Sturt, the interrogation of the villagers, Kar Houle's interviews with Beilin Crogh, and, most of all, the detailed examination of the ten corpses recovered from a grave in the woods and brought back to Valdoe, all this – and especially the description of an 'aboriginal male in fourth decade, subject's putative father, incapacitated by old spear wound, killed by severe blow above right ear', the impartial, clinical, inch-by-inch dissection and measurement of the body of Tagart, Paoul's father, Shode, leader and chieftain of the southern tribes – all this he read with a surge of pain and adult understanding, realizing now something of what Tagart must have endured and trying to imagine him as he must once have been, in the days when he had been whole and proud and free. The knives and probes and note-taking of the kars were not the last indignity he had suffered, nor was the callous disposal of his remains, like so much refuse, 'by fire': for, throughout the report, Kar Houle again and again expressed doubt that Paoul was Tagart's son. Only at the very end did he relent. 'Without confirmation of these suspicions, the child's word has been accepted on this matter.'

The library was empty when Paoul had finished reading: the phede, leaving one of his lamps burning for Paoul, had gone. Paoul slowly rolled up the parchments and returned them to their place. The rest of his personal records, dealing with his career at Hohe and his arrival at Valdoe, would be in the Vansard's quarters. Even if he had been free to see them, he was sure they could have told him nothing, any more than he had learned from the archive here. He still did not even know what he had wanted to find.

From the common-room he could hear a five-voice chant, the contrapuntal Benison of the Night, a chant he himself had sung at Hohe. The words then had seemed moving and profound. Now they seemed to have no more warmth or solidity than the snowflakes falling so thickly outside.

Resolving to go back to his meagre lodgings at the farm

rather than take supper here, Paoul left the library in darkness and quietly shut the doors.

Paoul had been at Valdoe for just over three months, and he had yet to settle in or feel himself at home. The place, or his memory of it, had changed almost beyond recognition. Under the firm administration of General Teshe, the domain had prospered. Valdoe Village had grown in size, with many new buildings; but the house where Paoul had once stayed, the house of Beilin Crogh's father, had been taken over by another family. Both the father and the mother, however, were still in the village, living, Paoul discovered, with their son, who had long since left the army and built a commodious dwelling on the outskirts, with a large plot in which he kept sixty or seventy beehives. He owned more beehives in surrounding villages; Crogh had become the foremost producer of honey in the district. He was now an important freeman, with a place on the village council. This entitled him to send the youngest of his sons, a lad of thirteen, to the school where Paoul taught each day.

Classes were held in the schoolroom, part of the ornate Meeting House, and attended in all by forty or fifty of the sons of notables from the Trundle and from the village. The pupils varied in ability as much as they did in age, from five to fifteen. The curriculum, determined by Hohe, was strictly limited to the simplest treatment of practical subjects – craft, agronomy, applied mathematics, language, a little of the more accessible philosophy as it directly affected the blue priesthood and the beliefs of the farmers. Paoul's two fellow teachers, a middle-aged phede and the old ilven who was in charge, seemed content with the drudgery of their lot, but, for Paoul, only the knowledge that his position was temporary enabled him to continue. Often, though, when he was able to treat the boys as children rather than pupils, when he was able to forget that he was equipping them to perpetuate the rule of the Gehans, he derived enjoyment, even delight, from his work. The ilven had hinted that he was pleased with Paoul's influence on the school.

One afternoon almost a month after his visit to the archive, Paoul was approached between lessons by the ilven, who, vaguely alluding to the fact that he would be 'sorry to lose him', handed Paoul a sealed note from the vansery. The note ordered Paoul to report to the Vansard the following day. No reason was given for the summons, but from the ilven's reassuring manner Paoul guessed that there was nothing much to fear. On the contrary, it looked as if his promotion had come sooner than he dared have hoped.

The course of the interview, though, soon took an unexpected turn. 'I have received impressive accounts of your aptitude as a teacher,' the Vansard said, once the formalities were over. He was seated at his high-backed chair, the raw light of a late winter morning falling across the neatly ordered parchments and tablets on the broad surface of his desk. His brown eyes, more than ever, seemed to be inquisitive, assessing, secretly ironic, watching Paoul from deep sockets set under a wide forehead and closely cropped black hair. Today he was wearing his official tunic, with a stiff, high collar which, each time he moved, rasped against the freshly shaved skin of his chin and throat. The collar was fastened with a copper pin; on his breast was a minute copper brooch, the emblem of the phedes, a serpent devouring its own tail. 'The boys are better behaved,' he went on. 'The older ones, in particular, are less unruly. They look up to you and have become keen to learn.' He held up his hand. 'No, Forzan Paoul, do not protest. I speak no more than the truth. You have shown yourself an asset to the vansery, and I am most reluctant to deprive the school of your services. A week ago, however, I received a request from the Protector and, in subsequent discussions with him and with the vansery board, your name emerged. You are ideally qualified by age as well as temperament for the delicate and difficult task that General Teshe and I would like you to undertake. So uncongenial is this work that we think it only fair to offer you the chance to decline it outright as well as at the end of a probationary period.' Phede Keldis gave what Paoul could only interpret as an awkward smile. 'Have you been introduced to Lord Hothen?'

'No, Phede Keldis.'

'I thought not. Have you seen him?'

'No, Phede Keldis. At least . . .' Paoul began, remembering once again the pathetic, deficient child he had seen all those years ago from the rail of the *Veisdrach*. 'At least, not since we were small boys, and then I only saw him once and at a distance.'

'What stories have you heard about him?'

'I know that he comes of age next autumn, and that some doubt attaches to his chances of being allowed to accede.'

The Vansard grunted. 'Have you heard about the latest incident?'

'Very little news reaches us in the village, Phede Keldis, especially where the inner enclosure is concerned.'

Choosing his words with care, Phede Keldis then proceeded to explain what he wanted of Paoul. Ten days ago, Lord Hothen had beaten one of his servants so badly that he would never be able to work again. It was partly an accident: the servant had fallen down some stairs. In the normal way, of course, this incident would not have given rise to undue concern, but it was only the latest, and the worst, in a long series of outbursts. Lord Hothen was developing very badly. Becoming even more circumspect, Phede Keldis implied that a large measure of the blame belonged to Lord Hothen's mother, the Lady Ika. She had continuously undermined General Teshe's efforts to provide him with a suitable education. She had so spoiled her son, so indulged his whims, that now General Teshe could scarcely exert effective control. But it was not as straightforward as that. Sometimes Lord Hothen could be remarkably cunning. He had manipulated his mother just as much as she had encouraged him. He was playing her off against General Teshe, perhaps in a misguided and futile attempt to have General Teshe sent back to Hohe. It was still the desire of Lord Heite that Lord Hothen should, eight months from now, be declared Brennis Gehan Sixth. Unless there was a profound change in Lord Hothen's behaviour, though, Lord Heite would be disappointed and – just at a time when the domain was achieving peace and prosperity – some degree of political upheaval would be sure to result. This would reflect most unjustly on General Teshe, who was an able administrator and had borne his responsibility towards Lord Hothen with prodigious patience and restraint. In desperation, then, General Teshe had sought the Vansard's help. The idea of a new tutor for Lord Hothen, a companion, a calming influence, someone his own age who would not be seen as a threat, had come from the General himself. Paoul was the youngest priest in the vansery, only two months older than Lord Hothen, with whom he had had no contact; and his flair for teaching suited him perfectly for the job. In addition, he had been warmly recommended by Kar Houle.

The post would last only until Lord Hothen came of age. It would necessitate taking quarters in the residence, so that Paoul would be on call at all times, though one day a week would be left free for his private use. After one month – assuming, of course, that Lord Hothen had not already taken a dislike to him, or that the arrangement had not failed in some other way – Paoul would have the right to resign if he wished, without any recriminations whatever.

'Indeed,' Phede Keldis continued, 'you can turn it down here and now. I would not blame you if you did. It is likely to be thankless work. You only have to say.'

'No, Phede Keldis,' Paoul said, astounded that he should have been chosen, and already wondering what it would be like and how he would manage to deal with the delinquent Lord Hothen. He was also thinking how relieved he would be to get away from Valdoe Village, from the school, and from his lodgings at the settlement farm. 'I am truly flattered. If you feel that I can be of service, I will do my very best.'

'Splendid!' The Vansard put his hands together. 'That is just the way Kar Houle said you'd react.' He stood up. 'I believe General Teshe is in his chambers at this very moment. Let us go there at once and introduce you to him. Then, this afternoon, we can go and meet your charge.'

2

Rian had no idea why, but she felt a great and immediate affinity for this gentle, quietly spoken young priest. He was almost absurdly good-looking, she thought, and, it seemed, completely unaware of the fact. Even at her age she still felt a weakness when regarded by such a pair of dark eyes, and his beautiful manners, his impeccable politeness, noteworthy even by the standards of the priesthood, had won her approval from the first moment he had stepped through the threshold this afternoon. The contrast between him and Hothen could hardly be more pronounced; but – and Rian could not rid herself of the sensation that something mysterious was at work in her imagination – it also seemed that Forzan Paoul and Lord Hothen shared an uncanny, shadowy, physical resemblance.

'I'm relying on you to guide me through the first few days, Mistress Rian. I don't want to upset any customs of the household. You must tell me what is expected.'

'You should not call me "Mistress", Forzan Paoul,' she said, unable to bring herself to address him as 'father': he was simply too young, barely older than Hothen himself, and not the least bit like any of the other priests she had met. 'I am a slave.'

'But are you not the Lady Ika's companion?'

'I was once her body-slave, and my Lord Hothen's nurse, but I have no title now. I just belong to the household.'

'I see,' he said, brusquely, for the sake of a servant who was passing them on the corridor, but from the earnest way he looked up at her again she saw that he wanted her help still. She saw that he made no real distinction between a slave and a free woman, a servant with the right to the courtesy title 'Mistress', and Rian felt herself becoming more drawn to him than ever. She could not remember when she had last been accorded the dignity of being treated not as an object, but as a human being: not since the old days, not since the days of the Lady Altheme.

It was early evening, an hour after dark, and his baggage had just arrived from Valdoe Village. He was unpacking, laying out his clothes and his few possessions in the room he had been given, a small chamber on the north side of the gallery, between the guest quarters and one of the pantries. The room, allotted to him earlier by the chamberlain, had been used as a temporary store for some of Ika's unwanted things. Rian had been in the process of removing them when Forzan Paoul had arrived. She had offered to unpack for him, but, declining, he had engaged her in conversation instead. Now she was standing in the doorway, in her arms a bundle of embroidered robes.

'Would Forzan Paoul like some flowers?'

The room seemed very bare and cold; his possessions, thinly spread on the shelves and on top of the cupboard, made it appear bleaker yet.

'Surely, at this time of year . . .'

'Dried flowers, I mean, and teasels and grasses.'

'You are very kind, Rian, but please do not trouble yourself.' He pushed his leather bag out of sight, under the bed. 'What I would like, though, is to know what sort of dress is worn at the night meal.'

'Formal, Forzan Paoul. General Teshe makes it a rule.'

'Will he be there?'

'This evening I believe the General is entertaining guests in his own suite downstairs.'

'And you, Rian, will you be there?'

'Yes, Forzan Paoul. I am always with my Lady Ika when she needs me.' Rian suddenly remembered the weight of all the robes in her arms. 'I think I ought to go to her now.'

'Of course,' he said, reverting to a sharper tone, for another servant had just emerged from the kitchen door farther along the gallery, releasing the odours of cooked food reaching the final stages of preparation.

The night meal was always served in Hothen's quarters, in the Flint Lord's Chamber. At one time it had often been attended by General Teshe, but no longer. Nowadays he ate there as seldom as his long and ingenious list of excuses allowed. This did not worry Rian: she feared and disliked General Teshe, and without his presence there was a better chance of surviving the meal without a tantrum. As it was, there were quite enough hidden difficulties to consider, quite enough uncertain and constantly changing likes and dislikes to remember and keep in check. Rian wondered how Forzan Paoul would fare. She had lost count of Hothen's tutors. Most had lasted only a few months, some only a few weeks, and one, whom Hothen had deliberately wounded at archery practice, had lasted only four days. All the other tutors had lived in the vansery. Forzan Paoul was the first to be given quarters here. Perhaps he was more than an ordinary tutor; after all, Hothen was getting beyond the age when there could be hope of his responding to conventional teaching.

Watching Forzan Paoul as he took his place by the dais, however, Rian began to fear for his chances. He looked too innocent, too inexperienced, despite his red tattoo and his spotless tunic of priestly grey. In the suffuse light of the pole-lamps, the resemblance between him and Hothen seemed yet more marked. It even extended somehow to Ika, who, this evening, an avid listener to her slaves' gossip about the new young priest, had made a ludicrous effort to present herself at her best. At forty-three, with the tops of her arms beginning to sag, with a lifetime's inactivity recorded in the laxity of her flesh and on the coarsening grain of her skin, she should not have put on that robe; nor should she have worn those earrings or told her body-slave to apply quite so much powder to the wrinkles round her blank, deformed, and sunken eyes. In fact, Rian realized with a start, Ika had made herself grotesque. Until tonight Rian had not noticed how stealthily and persistently the years had been destroying Ika's youth. It had all gone: Ika was middle-aged.

'Are we to be kept waiting yet again?' she said, as the three servants, having spread out the cloths and distributed the spoons and bowls in readiness for the meal, went out once more to the kitchen. Ika was sitting in her usual place, near the door from her chambers – from the suite reserved for the Flint Lord's lady, the rooms that Ika had no right to occupy – and Rian, as always, was sitting beside her. Hothen, the nominal head of the household, was sitting with his food-taster at the dominant place, his back to the east window. Forzan Paoul was on his right. The place opposite Forzan Paoul was still vacant.

'I cannot imagine what Forzan Paoul must think of us,' Ika said.

'It is early yet, my lady,' Rian said quietly, hoping that Hothen's interest had not been aroused: he was sitting in his slumped, disagreeable way, making a minute and prolonged examination of the intricate carving on the handle of his spoon. Forzan Paoul was watching him calmly, as if deciding on a course of action. Hothen had virtually ignored his new tutor. 'And there was no water for her bath,' Rian added.

Ika pretended not to have heard. 'I believe, Forzan Paoul, that there is still one of us whose acquaintance the kindly General spared you this afternoon. She was indisposed, was she not, Hothen?'

At this moment the door from the gallery opened and, to her relief, Rian saw that Yseld had finally arrived. She looked harassed and upset; the skirts of her stone-coloured robe were crumpled and a few tendrils of her hair were still damp and dishevelled from her late and, undoubtedly, lukewarm bath.

Forzan Paoul rose smoothly to his feet.

'My daughter of sorts has deigned to join us, I take it,' said Ika, turning towards the noise of the opening door. 'Forzan Paoul, allow me to present you to the Lady Yseld.'

'We have already met, my lady,' he said – and Rian was not sure which one he was addressing, for his eyes were fixed on Yseld. 'Two Crales ago, at the consecration of Bohod Thosk's hall.'

'You have the advantage of me, I am afraid,' Yseld said. 'I don't remember.' But, from the faint reddening of Yseld's cheeks, from the dissembled expression of alarm and astonishment with which she had set eyes on the young man, it was plain to a woman of Rian's experience that she remembered him very well. 'I must apologize. My father introduced me to so many people on that occasion.'

'We spoke only for a few moments, my lady. I was merely one of the lamp-bearers.' And it seemed to Rian that Forzan Paoul's memory was also better than he pretended. His expression, though, remained utterly unperturbed.

Two Crales ago: that must have been shortly before the

Thosk clan had begun negotiating the purchase of Yseld's marriage into this branch of the Gehans. She would have been sixteen then, and Forzan Paoul about the same, or a little older. Looking at him as he sat down again, Rian could still not believe that anyone so youthful could be a red priest, with all the knowledge and wisdom that the title implied. Yet he had the composure of a full grown man, and the way he had acquitted himself so far was leading Rian to suspect that he could easily be underestimated. And there, on the back of his hand, was the proof, the five-pointed star that showed he had been accepted into the Red Order; and not at any vansery, either, but at Hohe, at the citadel itself.

Yseld had come from somewhere near there: her father's estate, she had once told Rian, on one of her more confiding days, was often visited by Lord Heite. Presumably she and Forzan Paoul would have known several people in common and might have been expected to exchange polite inquiries and reminiscences, but, although sitting directly opposite him throughout the whole course of the meal, Yseld preserved a cool, disinterested aloofness which, while confirming Rian's suspicions, also made her feel even more sorry for the girl. The 'few moments' during which the two of them had spoken had clearly left a lasting impression on the young Lady Yseld. She had recognized him immediately. And if it had been impossible then for her to show her feelings – and not just because he was of the priesthood, although that in itself was more than reason enough – how must she be feeling now, under these circumstances, when she knew she would be seeing him every day?

As for Forzan Paoul, Rian could not deduce what he was thinking or whether he had even noticed Yseld's odd behaviour. During the meal he had managed to parry Ika's remarks in such a way that each one had fallen spent before it could do any harm. As a result, Hothen had been unusually quiet and tractable. He had eaten consistently: crab soup, whiting with juniper sauce, roast woodcock, venison, raspberry clabber, dried fruit and cheese, and as he had eaten his skin seemed to have taken on a complacent gloss which extended to the blond roots of his hair. His glittering blue eyes, set in his somewhat fat, pink face, had darted occasional glances at Forzan Paoul in which Rian had detected a combination of admiration and fear. Was it possible that, at last, Hothen was trying to win the approval of one of his tutors?

After the meal, once the dishes had been cleared and all but one of the servants had retired, Hothen, reviving a custom he had let lapse for some weeks, called for his scharan and began to play a tune. His tongue protruding wetly from the corner of his mouth, he crouched over the instrument, supporting it in his lap, and clumsily fretted the long neck of the fingerboard while his other hand drew mournful notes from the strings. Then, softly, he began to sing. He had learned the song from the under falconer, the story of a peregrine that had 'raked away' and escaped. The words were maudlin and sentimental, and, although Hothen took them quite literally, it was not a peregrine the song was about, but the singer's wife.

Hothen was not very proficient at music. This attempt to show off in front of his new tutor was making Rian feel embarrassed and uneasy. It was the certain forerunner of trouble. She knew the signs of old. Yseld knew them too. She was looking down at her hands, her teeth lightly pressed into her lower lip. Forzan Paoul, however, was unabashed. He was watching Hothen, studying his technique, on his face an expression of guarded approval, as if for the effort rather than the performance itself. Strangely, while he was singing Hothen never stammered, and while he was singing Ika was always entranced.

At the end of the song her praise and applause were, as usual, the loudest and the most extravagant. Goaded by a defiant stare from her husband, Yseld quickly joined in, as did Rian, the food-taster, and the serving-maid. Everyone in the room was discovering new ways to congratulate the future Lord Brennis on his artistry and skill. Everyone, that is, except the one person for whose benefit the song had been performed.

He had neither moved nor uttered a sound. He was sitting quite still, on his face exactly the same expression as before.

Becoming aware of this, Hothen turned to him and the room fell silent; even Ika had sensed that something was wrong.

Forzan Paoul waited a moment longer before speaking. Then, pleasantly, he said: 'If you want my opinion, my lord, I think your playing leaves much to be desired.'

The silence in the room suddenly grew to tremendous

proportions. Rian felt herself pinned to the floor, helpless, horrified, and yet also curiously intrigued and detached, like someone who was both the witness and the victim of an impending natural disaster, a disaster of inconceivable ferocity and power – an avalanche, an earthquake, the end of the world. Hothen's face was registering the difficulty he was having in comprehending the enormity of what had been said. As the play of emotion intensified, as it approached and rapidly passed through all the stages she knew so well, as it gathered momentum and entered a new and most dangerous region whose existence Rian had never even suspected before, she looked away and mentally braced herself, preparing for the onslaught of his rage.

Just at the very instant she expected it to break, she heard Forzan Paoul speaking again. His voice was reason itself, blandly courteous and kind, seamlessly impenetrable to any suggestion of bad feeling or hurt pride. 'If my lord will permit, I will show him where he is going wrong.'

Hothen had been disarmed, dumbfounded. Rian could not believe her eyes. Neither, it seemed, could Yseld. As for Ika, she was too surprised to react.

Forzan Paoul was holding out his hand, ready to receive the scharan, which, meekly, and to Rian's continuing amazement, Hothen passed across the dais.

The young priest easily and naturally adapted the long-necked, big-bellied instrument to his grasp and, producing a few sample notes, adjusted the pegbox to his satisfaction. In this he was quite absorbed: it was as if the other people in the room had ceased to exist. Then he looked up. 'The first thing, my lord, is to make sure it's in tune. Next, you must hold it properly, not bent over it, not crouching or tensed, but like this. Your scharan should be part of you. Its music should come as easily as thought. You cannot think straight if you are uncomfortable. So: left hand like this, the elbow free, the right hand held here. Do you see?'

Hothen nodded.

'Let us take the first phrase of your song. You were careless with your fingering. You must touch the strings lightly, but precisely. I'll play the opening chords slowly so you can see.

There. And again. And again. Now a little more quickly. Now more quickly still.'

In Hothen's eyes was growing an enthusiastic light Rian had never seen before. He was following the instruction with an intenseness of which she had not imagined him capable. Until now his scharan-playing had been regarded in the household as yet another bad joke. No one had suspected that he might have a real feeling for music or that through music he might be reached. And yet it already seemed that Forzan Paoul had discovered Hothen's vulnerable point. The notes he was playing bore only a skeletal resemblance to the sounds Hothen had made. This was a fragment of real music, pure and serene, and Hothen knew it.

'Now you try.'

Hothen's first eager effort, however, although an improvement, was not good. Forzan Paoul moved to his side, took the instrument, and demonstrated again. He corrected Hothen's grip and posture and, at the second attempt, Hothen managed to produce some chords that were a passable imitation of his teacher's. He grinned in delight, and Rian was fleetingly reminded of the little boy she had once sat up with and cared for. Her vigils then had occasionally been rewarded with just such a flash of pleasure. 'That's good,' he said, as Forzan Paoul resumed his place.

'You've made a promising start, my lord. I'll show you the next phrase tomorrow, and with it the rest of the tune.'

'No. Show me now. I want you to show me now.'

'You are forgetting the ladies, my lord.'

'What?'

'This is not the time for a music lesson. I fear we have already trespassed on their patience more than we ought. We have been most discourteous.' He turned to Yseld. 'Do you accept our apologies, my Lady Yseld?'

He had deliberately addressed her first, naming her, giving her precedence – the legal precedence to which she was entitled – over Ika. There could be no doubt about it. He had thrown down the challenge. He was prepared to make an enemy of Ika, if that was what it was going to take to help her son.

Yseld did not appear to know how to answer.

Rian had already decided as much, but now she was resolved

to do what she had planned earlier: to put a beautiful arrangement of dried flowers in the Forzan's room.

'And my lady Ika?' he said. 'Do you forgive us?'

'Yes, of course,' she said, harshly. 'What is there to forgive?'

'Never mind about them,' Hothen said. 'If they don't like it they can go to bed. I want you to show me now.'

As if he had not heard, Forzan Paoul arose. 'I have had a long day,' he said. 'With the permission of the company, I will go to bed. It is very late, my lord, and I suggest you do the same. That is, of course, if you want to be up in time for the morning's music lesson.' With that, acknowledging Yseld, Ika, and the speechless Hothen, and nodding in turn to Rian and the two servants, he retired.

3

'I beg your pardon, my lady,' Paoul said, on finding Yseld alone in the ground floor day-room where he was accustomed to giving Hothen his morning lessons. 'Is my lord not yet here?'

Until this moment Paoul had kept alive the hope that he was mistaken about her. He had hoped that her avoidance of him, which during the last four weeks she had developed almost into an art, was engendered by dislike rather than by a reciprocation of the feelings which, although he had tried to deny the fact to himself, he now realized had been growing steadily in his heart. Since that first evening, when he had been all but struck dumb by the shock of seeing her again, he had thought of little else but Yseld. She was no longer the Yseld he had met so briefly and inconclusively in the homelands and on whose image he had built such a flimsy and elaborate construction of adolescent ideals; but each addition to his sparse stock of seconds and minutes and hours spent in her company – from chance meetings on the stairs, in the corridors, in the gallery, or, where he could drink his fill of her presence, at the nightly meals – had confirmed that, at their first meeting two and more years ago, something had been exchanged that was in essence both durable and true.

She was seated by the window, where she had been looking out into the early spring rain, listening perhaps to the blackbird that was pouring out its song from a wayfaring tree in the garden of the inner enclosure. In her lap, forgotten, lay a small frame containing a half finished embroidery in muted colours. Paoul guessed that she had been sitting here for some time, anticipating his arrival, deciding what she would finally say to him. She looked round. Her face, pale and anxious, divulged everything and he knew there could be no further hope of self-deception.

'He has gone hunting, Forzan Paoul. He did not ask me to, but I have come to offer apologies on his behalf.'

Paoul came farther into the room, the floorboards creaking. His hearing told him that no one was about. This was a rare moment in the residence, rare on the ground floor, and virtually impossible upstairs, where slaves or servants were always present and there could be no such thing as a truly private conversation. Yseld had picked her time and place most carefully. Paoul thought he already knew what she was going to say, to imply, to demand of him, and he was already prepared to give it.

'I am afraid you are not helping my husband very much,' she began. 'At first it looked as if you were, but just lately he appears to do exactly as he pleases. This is the second time in three days that he has gone hunting without your permission.'

Still she was avoiding him, avoiding his eyes. Her hands, demurely holding the embroidery frame, peeping out from the sleeves of her ochre and russet robe, could, on scrutiny, be seen to be minutely trembling. These were not the reactions of the flirt he had once imagined her to be. Her behaviour at her father's banquet had anyway become understandable when viewed from the perspective of her marriage to Hothen. Evidently her father had been unable to snare Lord Mond, but she had seen it as her duty to help him try. She was not free, but a marketable commodity; her conversation with Paoul, the lamp-bearer, had been a mistake, a lapse, a foolish impulse to which, for one reason or another, she had given way. The attempt to buy her into Lord Heite's immediate family having failed, Bohod Thosk must have been compelled to set his sights lower and her dowry had ended up here.

In theory she was the future Lady Brennis. In fact, as Paoul had observed, she was subordinate to her husband's mother, and had been relegated to the guests' quarters. At first Paoul had believed – listening at night from his own chamber, which nearly adjoined hers – that she was Hothen's wife in name only and that Hothen was content with the services of the two concubines who singly or together visited his bed. On the fourth night, though, Paoul had heard her summoned to his room.

Paoul had never really known jealousy before. Despite all his training, it must have affected his attitude towards Hothen: there could be no doubt of that. To begin with Paoul had found Hothen a pitiable creature, dominated by a mother who only made his difficulties worse. He had seemed more stupid than cruel, constantly baffled by the workings of a reality he would never be able to understand. Within a week, however, Paoul had come to understand the view of the slaves and servants. Rian, in particular, had unwittingly revealed how much she detested Hothen and sympathized with his lady. What Rian would never know, and what Paoul had not been certain of until now, was that his own continuing presence here would make Yseld's position not just worse, but intolerable.

'This afternoon, my lady,' he said, sparing her from having to broach the subject further, 'I am due to see the Vansard and General Teshe. We will be discussing my place as Lord Hothen's tutor. Today marks the end of my month's probation.' This, he was sure, she already knew. The subject had arisen the other night at the meal. Although she had appeared inattentive at the time, she must have been listening: why else would she have come here this morning? 'If I so request,' Paoul went on, 'I will be relieved of my duty and sent back to teaching at the village school. I can tell you now, my lady, that I have already decided to make that request.'

'Indeed.' She did not raise her eyes to his. 'That is rather a shame, Forzan Paoul, but in the end I think it is probably for the best. My lord is getting too old for a tutor. He has never responded well to discipline.'

The blackbird stopped singing. In the unexpected silence, unbroken even by the soft descent of the rain outside, Paoul realized he was in all likelihood speaking to her for the last time. In the future, if he saw her at all it would be in company, at some official function. He would never have the opportunity to be with her like this again.

But, as she had said, it was probably for the best. He was a red priest, and a red priest was not allowed to feel this way. He was not allowed to ache when he looked upon the girl whose memory he would for ever carry in his closest thoughts. He was not allowed to long to touch her or even simply to call her, just once, by her unadorned and birth-given name.

'Does my lady know where he has gone?'

'To the woods at Lavant, I believe. They left about an hour ago.'

'If you will excuse me, then, I ought to go and seek him out.'

With a small and somehow fatalistic movement of her head she indicated her acquiescence and Paoul, trying to remain outwardly calm, passed through the door and left her alone, still sitting at her place by the window.

'Kar Houle is worse,' the Vansard said, from behind his desk. 'Did you know?'

'No, Phede Keldis. I did not.'

Paoul could not really comprehend what was being said. It was all he could do to maintain his composure in front of the Vansard and General Teshe. His request to leave the residence and get away from Yseld, to leave her and go back to the village, had just been, in so many words, flatly refused. They had said that the remarkable improvement in Hothen was directly attributable to him and could not be allowed to end. They had praised him and urged him to reconsider. Then, when he had pressed the point and tried to insist on his right to resign, the Vansard's manner – veiled, as always, with the punctilious correctitude that was one of the most effective weapons in a red priest's armoury – had become rapidly less pleasant. He had all but accused Paoul of acting against the interests of the empire. The penalty for that was invariable and swift.

Paoul was shocked. He could not believe that such a trifling dispute should have immediately called forth the full weight of the Vansard's authority. But he was even more surprised by the Vansard's lack of scruples. He had not imagined any red priest, least of all a vansard, capable of this kind of behaviour. The Vansard had been supported in his dishonesty by the silent, worldly approval of General Teshe, massive in his grey armour and cloak, legs crossed, fingertips meditatively raised and touching, observing Paoul and from time to time pursing his lips as if mildly amused. Cynicism, lies: these were his stock in trade. He cared nothing for the integrity of the Order. If one of its priests did not willingly bend, he would have to be forced, no matter what damage that did to him or to his future development.

In these few minutes, Paoul had grown up. Just as he had

clung to the belief that he was mistaken about the Lady Yseld, so had he been clinging to the last remnants of his vision of the priesthood as something noble and rare. Between them, General Teshe and the Vansard had broken his hold. They had revealed the Order for what it was, an integral part of the world of politics and expediency. The laws of that world applied to him too. Somehow he had believed himself immune. Somehow he had not expected to give an account of all the years and resources they had invested in his training. They had made him. Now, for the sake of the few remaining months of Hothen's education, they were prepared to destroy him. No matter that Hothen would never be what they wanted: it was the will of Lord Heite that the effort should be made. No matter that Paoul was capable of higher service, no matter that he had been selected as a potential Prime. If he were ruined, disillusioned, rendered unable to aspire, there would be plenty of others to take his place.

'Kar Houle?' said General Teshe. '"Worse"? Do you mean he's ill?'

'He has been ailing for some time. A fortnight ago he collapsed in the refectory. Kar Vever diagnoses no particular cause; the real culprit is age. Kar Houle is a very old man indeed.'

Paoul said, 'Is he still comfortable?'

'Yes, I believe so.'

'Is he receiving visitors?'

'Certainly, Forzan Paoul. He would be pleased to see you, I'm sure. But check with Kar Vever first.'

'Yes. Yes of course.'

As Paoul was about to rise from his seat – for, plainly, he had now been dismissed – a fanciful idea which had occurred to him after a difficult morning with Hothen a week ago, returned to him in a more serious guise, not as a means to deal with Hothen's problems, but as a chance of being reunited with the only person in whom Paoul felt he might, at least, be able to confide, and whose advice, for the sake of friendship, would perhaps be impartial and sound.

'Phede Keldis,' he said. 'I have been giving further thought to the question of Lord Hothen.'

The Vansard raised his eyebrows. As far as he was concerned, the whole subject was closed.

Paoul prepared himself for a rebuke, but pressed on anyway. 'Before leaving the citadel, Phede Keldis, I chanced to hear about some remarkable work the kars are doing now. I have a friend who has been appointed an assistant to the Chief Herbalist. We took the tattoo together.'

'And?'

'He told me about a new treatment they are developing for disorders of the mind. It uses new herbs, brought from the east. In certain cases, the results are said to be spectacular.'

The Vansard glanced at General Teshe.

'I do not know whether Lord Hothen might benefit, but it seems possible, even likely. I wonder if Kar Vever . . . I wonder if he is aware of it.'

'We receive all the usual bulletins from Hohe. I imagine Kar Vever is fully conversant with the latest developments in his art.'

'The treatment is very new, Phede Keldis. It may not have reached the bulletins yet.'

'What is the name of your friend?'

'Kar Enco.'

'Are you suggesting that I ask for him?'

'He is very highly qualified, Phede Keldis, but the final choice would of course be Hohe's.'

Phede Keldis gave an icy smile and Paoul wondered whether he had gone too far. 'I will speak to Kar Vever about this.' Paoul arose. 'Thank you, Forzan Paoul. Your suggestion may well prove helpful – whomsoever Hohe chooses to send. And thank you for agreeing to continue with Lord Hothen. It will not be for ever.'

Not for ever: but it might as well have been. Hothen would be twenty, officially, on the first day of the eleventh moon, seven months hence. That meant he would not come of age until at least two hundred more days had elapsed, or, as Paoul calculated on the way to Kar Vever's door, some one hundred and seventy working days, each of which might produce any number of encounters with the Lady Yseld. He did not know how he would manage even the first. What could he tell her?

How could he explain what had happened? She would surely never believe that the Vansard had gone back on his word.

But, once he had gained permission to see the patient and was on his way to Kar Houle's room, Paoul became aware that the source of his agitation was not simply anxiety for Yseld's sake, but this mixed with pleasurable anticipation and fear. He was ashamed to discover that he was secretly glad to be returning to the residence.

Of course, absolutely nothing could come of it. Not the slightest hint of his feelings could ever be allowed to escape. It would be too dangerous, disastrous for them both, a crime not only of the grossest and most unthinkable impropriety, but a treasonable offence. And they would be certain, eventually, to get caught.

And yet – was it not possible, even now, that he was wrong about her feelings? Was it not a great presumption and a conceit to imagine that his presence or absence could make any difference to her? What, after all, did he know about the matters of the heart? What had he learned about men and women, except for the austere, factual teachings of the kars and the ill-informed sniggerings of his classmates at Hohe?

Even so, he felt ashamed. He had broken his promise to her. Through cowardice, he had not resisted the Vansard as strongly as he ought. For the sake of honour, he should have refused outright to continue, no matter what consequences that brought on himself.

4

As the spring advanced towards the summer, Kar Houle's condition correspondingly declined. Paoul visited him as often as his duties with Hothen allowed, and so was not fully conscious of the magnitude of the changes that less frequent visits would have made plain: the wasting of his flesh, the dulling of his eyes and their gradual withdrawal into the sockets, the worsening pallor and greyness of his skin. At an earlier stage in his illness, Kar Houle had been able to get up for short periods, to sit by his fire or even, on sunny afternoons, to bask in a sheltered corner of the physic garden among his beloved plants; but recently even that had been denied to him and he now remained permanently in bed. His old hands lay limply for hours on end in one place on the counterpane. The colour of his tattoo seemed itself to have dulled as much as his gaze, which was usually directed at a point some scores of yards or miles or years beyond the whiteness of the far wall. Whenever Paoul had come in, though, he had always managed to greet him, however feebly; he had always managed to absorb and enjoy Paoul's titbits of harmless gossip; and, before he tired, he had always managed to smile at least once.

Until today. Today it had taken him some time just to recognize his visitor, and Paoul knew at last, for himself, that what Kar Vever had first said six weeks and more ago was right: Kar Houle was dying. At breakfast, interrupting his own preoccupations, Paoul had received a message from Kar Vever and had come straight from the residence to the vansery. 'He's been asking for you,' Kar Vever had said. 'I don't think he can last much longer.'

'Is he in pain?'

'No. But I suspect the end will come as a relief.'

A week ago Paoul had been told that the Chief Herbalist had granted Phede Keldis's fraternal request: Enco had been released to treat Hothen. He would arrive by the next merchantman from Hohe, the ship following the one that had brought the news.

Enco was coming. Any day now, he would be travelling the road from Apuldram up to the Trundle. He was coming, and Paoul had made it happen. By tweaking the Vansard's vanity, Paoul had managed to manipulate the organization of the Order to suit his own ends. The thought filled him with astonishment, with disbelief in his own impudence.

Much more than this, though, was occupying his mind. Deny it as he might, he was now certain of Yseld's feelings. After two more months in the residence, two more months of night meals and conversations in which only the words spoken were superficial and impersonal, he was certain. Worse: he was afraid that some of the entourage – particularly Rian – were beginning to suspect how matters lay.

His growing certainty about Yseld had been matched by his growing unhappiness with the Order and what it stood for. His qualms had started long ago – as far back as that night after seeing the Lady Atane at the lake, when Starrad had explained Lord Heite's motives for taking her there. His misgivings had greatly increased on the tour; the steady accumulation of disturbing sights had finally overflowed, perhaps, in that small room at Chaer where Reisen had died; or, if not there, then at the brigands' camp and during the ensuing scenes at the fort. And, here in Brennis, Paoul had found his doubts crystallizing into something which, for want only of proof, would become a firm conviction. If that happened, he would no longer want to be a priest. He would no longer wish to be part of the conspiracy of religion and military power that fed upon the weakness of the common people and kept them in a permanent state of deprivation. The tour had taught him that the empire relied for its continuance on a single truth: that farming, demanding a relatively settled way of life, alone created a fixed population which could be cheaply dominated and controlled. The farmers got very little back for their taxes; it seemed to Paoul that the Gehans were nothing but a highly successful version of what those brigands had tried to be. The Order bestowed on the ruling clan a spurious sheen of rectitude, of divine right springing from a deity that the Gehans had themselves invented. Like much of the faith, the Gehans' place in the scheme depended on circular argument. They were the ruling clan and hence occupied the dominant place; because they occupied the dominant place, Gauhm had fitted them to be the ruling clan.

This was heresy of the first magnitude. Except in his bleakest moments, Paoul still could not bring himself to believe it might be true. Yet, in recent months – especially since his visit to the archive – he had found himself thinking more and more often of Tagart and of the stories Tagart had told him about the old times. Although Paoul had been so young, he knew that Tagart had loved him with a father's love, perhaps the only genuine love he had ever received. He was beginning to see how important it had been. Tagart had laid the foundation of Paoul's character and given him an independence of spirit that now threatened to be his undoing. Paoul recalled that Tagart, who had been right about so much else, had condemned the farmers and farming itself as intrinsically unnatural and therefore evil. And had not Tagart also warned him to beware of the priests, the red priests with the five-pointed stars on their left hands? Had he not called them worse than the soldiers, worse even than the Flint Lord himself?

Paoul was profoundly perplexed. It would be so much easier to forget his doubts and hold to the faith as a true ideal, to accept that it was the only conceivable way of describing and explaining the world. Indeed there was much in it that was undeniably true. It would be easy and safe to accept it all and play his allotted part in the hierarchy. He could never hope to leave: they had marked him for life. His tattoo announced to the world that he had taken his vows and was to be regarded as a servant of the Earth Goddess. But, by doubting, he had already broken those vows and forfeited the right to wear the red pentacle.

He did not know what to do. He was young and inexperienced; he was prepared to believe himself mistaken. More: he was eager to believe himself mistaken. He longed to receive some evidence of it. That was what he wanted from Enco, and that was what he wanted from Kar Houle, but had always been afraid to ask.

Above Kar Houle's bed, hanging from a peg against the roughness of the wall, was an oak and boxwood plaque, perhaps his own confirmation plaque, made seventy-five or eighty years before. This was the only permanent decoration in the room; but on a wicker table beside him, next to Paoul's chair, someone had placed a patterned bowl containing a cluster of freshly picked moon-daisies.

'Kar Thurman brought them,' Kar Houle said. 'That was kind of him.'

The heat of the morning sun, falling on the canopy at the window, was making the timbers expand and gently creak. From the outer enclosure, beyond the vansery grounds, came the irregular clinking of the flint knappers at work, the sound of parading soldiers, the bleating of goats, and, from somewhere nearer at hand, the repeated cadences of a singing chaffinch. All these sounds, the commonplace sounds of an ordinary day, seemed to stop short at the window and enter in a more respectful form, as if reluctant to intrude; but the light, the intense, wholesome sunshine of late spring, entered fearlessly and found itself transformed by the white walls and ceiling into a diffusion that found its way among the pale shadows cast by the petals of each daisy and penetrated even to the recesses of the yellow disc of florets at the heart.

Paoul felt as if he were standing at a threshold. Behind him was the cold and desolate room where no one could be trusted. Ahead was another room which might be different. He had no way of knowing, except by taking one more step. With that step he might begin to learn the truth, but taking it might alarm and distress Kar Houle, and that would be unforgivable. Unless he spoke now, though, Paoul knew he might never be presented with another chance.

The bowl of flowers had become the exaggerated focus of his attention, sparing him from looking at Kar Houle. The daisies had become strangely peaceful and sharply defined, at one with the natural world. In a few hours they would begin to wilt. Tomorrow they would be thrown away.

'Is something troubling you, Paoul?'

There was no expression in Kar Houle's eyes, no clue to his feelings. Surely he knew he was dying. What thoughts were passing through his head, what memories of his long years of rich yet abstinent life? What did he see when he looked at Paoul? Himself as a young man?

'Kar Houle, I would like to ask your advice.'

'I am listening.'

'Kar Houle . . .' he began, and then the words were coming of themselves, 'is it right that one should question the faith?'

Still there was no expression in Kar Houle's eyes. 'We should always question. Questioning is all we ever do.'

'Then . . . is it right to question the aims of the ruling clan?'

'Be more specific.'

'Is it right to ask whether the Gehans exist as a force for good?'

Kar Houle did not answer; his eyes registered no reaction, but he moved his left hand on the counterpane, opening it towards Paoul in an invitation which Paoul instinctively accepted. Kar Houle's grasp was feeble. It was no longer the firm and confident grasp with which he had bade Paoul farewell on board the *Veisdrach*. Now it seemed to convey an urgent warning that could not be put into words, a fear for Paoul's safety.

Kar Houle turned his head on the pillow. 'How beautiful they are,' he said. 'The flowers. You would not think we use them as an irritant. They promote the flow of blood. In the skin. Everything has its place, you see.' He looked back at Paoul, and for a moment it seemed as if he had said as much as he dared.

Then, suddenly, his whole expression changed. Yes, he knew he was dying: there was no longer any reason to keep silent or to let anything artificial remain between Paoul and himself.

The grip of his hand tightened. 'They're evil,' he said, almost in a whisper. 'All of them. I'm sorry for what I have done to you.' He let Paoul's hand go. His head seemed to sink deeper into the pillow.

'Kar Houle – '

'No.' Kar Houle weakly shook his head. 'No more talk. I am feeling very tired, and you must return to your duties.'

'Shall I come to see you later?'

'Yes. Please do. I would like that.'

The temple at Valdoe had been built not in the vansery, but on a slight and partly man-made eminence on the southern slope of the hill, between the Trundle and the flint workings.

The temple doors, facing south towards the sea, commanded a panoramic view from the newly built fort at Bignor in the north-east, right round to Bow Hill in the north-west. The structure, thirty-four feet across at the widest point, was of imported stone, with a pitched and deeply eaved roof. In plan view it occupied an unequal pentagon with its long axis running from east to west. The altar ran the length of the west-facing wall. It consisted of a wide slab bearing the four figures of the Family of Gods. On the right, on the northern side, stood Tsoaul the Father, the spirit of manifestation and of summer. On the left was Ele the Daughter, ruling spirit of winter and dormancy. In the centre, the largest and most striking of the sculptures, Gauhm the Mother, was depicted in the act of giving birth to Aih the Son.

On the hill forty-five yards away to the east was a curving stone wall, the height of a man and with a small aperture at its centre. The aperture aligned exactly with a vertical slit in the eastern corner of the temple at the junction of the two longest walls, in such a way that, at the moment of sunrise on the day of the equinox, a beam of light illuminated the figure of Gauhm. The two ends of the curving wall were also aligned with the slit, and defined the further travel of the point of sunrise between the summer and winter solstices. Thus, in the absence of cloud or fog, the altar was illuminated four times a year, the beam striking the figure associated with the forthcoming season.

'Yes, my lord,' Paoul said. 'I saw it myself, at the spring equinox.'

Hothen was peering through the slit. 'What about the winter solstice? Did you see it then?'

'No. That day was cloudy.'

Paoul had brought him here this morning as part of a lesson illustrating the potential of accurate construction. The visit was not going well. It had been specially arranged in advance through Phede Keldis; otherwise, Paoul would have cut it short and gone back to the residence. Hothen was in an awkward mood, and Paoul felt in no condition to control him. Since leaving Kar Houle's room, Paoul had been in a kind of daze. There was no unusual sound in his ears, but his thoughts were immobilized as though by a deafening roar of surf. He could not comprehend, not yet, not really, what Kar Houle's reaction meant to him.

Hothen raised his hands to shield either side of his head. 'It's very dark in there.'

They were standing on the glaring shingle that extended from the temple walls to the surrounding yew hedge. The hedge was now waist-high, consisting of seedlings taken from hallowed ground on Mount Atar and grown along four of the five sides of the temple court. The rest of the temple precincts, two acres in all, were enclosed by a line of chalk boulders. On the south side the turf had been marked out for a new tumulus; the old barrow of the Brennis Gehans had been destroyed by Torin Hewzane. On the north side was the vansery burial mound, already occupied by three priests who had died in service here. In the precincts and beyond, across the face of the hill, were many pairs of notched posts, short or tall, temporary or permanent, which the phedes used for the study and measurement of the heavens. A few of these posts had even been planted among the spoil-heaps and shaft-heads of the flint mines, farther down the hill. Paoul had once wondered what the luckless slaves there made of them or of the ceremonies enacted at the temple itself.

Hothen said, 'I want to go inside.'

'I am afraid that is not possible, my lord. The doors are locked.'

'Unlock them, then.'

'I do not know how. Besides, we have no business inside. We should not even be looking through the slit. Phede Keldis gave us permission only to examine the exterior.'

'Phede Keldis, Phede Keldis,' Hothen said, becoming ominously more fluent. 'That old turd. He doesn't own the hill. I do. That means I own the temple as well.'

Paoul said nothing.

'Open the doors.'

'My lord, that is impossible, as I have explained.'

Hothen looked over his shoulder, towards the place where his bodyguards – a team of five men in black and grey armour, hand-picked by General Teshe – were waiting outside the hedge. 'Are you disobeying my orders, you stuck-up little bastard?'

This was the way he usually addressed his slaves, or anyone who displeased him; he had never spoken to Paoul like this before. He had always treated Paoul with a certain timidity, deferring to his person as well as his rank. That had now vanished: in its place was a hot, sudden surge of resentment. Impossible as it seemed, Paoul could not help but think that behind it all was Yseld, as if Hothen unconsciously knew what had happened and remained unspoken between his wife and his priestly, supposedly incorruptible tutor. For a curious moment Paoul thought Hothen was going to throw a punch. Hothen was taller and heavier, but he was also clumsy and soft, and he would know that Paoul, that any red priest, was adept in an invincible and exasperating system of self defence that turned the adversary's every move against itself.

Hothen unclenched his fists. He looked over his shoulder again. 'Guards!'

The five bodyguards, each armed with a shield and a short spear, jumped over and through the hedge and, boots crashing on the shingle, ran to Hothen's side. The team-leader, Hace, a dark, powerfully made man of thirty, gave his crispest salute. 'My lord!'

However good his unarmed combat, no single man was any match for a team of spear-wielding soldiers, least of all a team chosen in person by General Teshe. Paoul was unable to quell a twinge of fear. The way they had leapt the hedge showed how little they cared for his authority or the sanctity of the temple. Hothen was so unpredictable that he might order these men to do anything, and there was no absolute guarantee that they would not obey.

But he did not tell them to attack Paoul. 'I want you to go to the flint workings,' he said. 'Get an axe. Better still, get something heavy. Really heavy. A tree-trunk, or something. Then break down the temple doors.'

Hace managed to conceal his surprise, but let slip an apprehensive and questioning glance at Paoul which filled Paoul with relief.

'There's no need to look at him! You get your orders from me!'

'I'm sorry, Team-leader,' Paoul said. 'Lord Hothen is jesting. He knows it is more than your life is worth to damage the temple. We just wanted to test your readiness and see how you would react to such an impossible command.'

Hace visibly relaxed. 'Very good, my lord. Will that be all?'

Without making himself seem ridiculous. Hothen could say nothing more. He had been thwarted. His anger, thus turned in on itself, became more heated than ever, and Paoul saw a flash of genuine hatred in his eyes.

'No, Hace, that will not be all. I'm going back to the residence. Without him.' He turned obliquely towards Paoul, but took care not to address him directly. 'I've had enough of this shit for one day.'

At Hohe, whenever one of the newer pupils had thrown a tantrum, he had been appropriately chastised by his teacher. The technique had proved effective. Not a few of the boys, those perhaps from wealthier homes, had at first shown signs of being spoiled which had been quickly eradicated. Hothen was not too old to benefit from the same treatment. Indeed it was remarkable that he had escaped it for so long, remarkable and strange, even suspicious. For, although Phede Keldis had outwardly given Paoul wide discretion in his approach, Paoul sensed that a request to use the most obvious form of control would be refused.

As Hothen turned his back and walked away, Paoul considered bypassing the Vansard and acting on his own responsibility. But this was not the time to do it, when Hothen was with his bodyguards, and nor was it the place. The temple had already been defiled enough, by Hothen's intrusive inspection of the interior, by his behaviour and bad language, and by the boots and weapons of his guards.

Watching Hothen and the guards climbing the slope, letting them go, Paoul acknowledged that there was something else making him hold back. He saw that he wanted to punish Hothen not from any high-minded motives of correction, but from personal animosity that had its origins with Yseld. Had it not been for her, Paoul would have been able to view Hothen and his failings properly, with detachment. That was no longer possible.

At the flint mines, a quarter of a mile away in the opposite direction, under the midday sun, he could see soldiers and overseers standing about. One lifted a water-bottle to his lips and drank. Other figures, slaves, were busily carrying timbers to and fro, or hauling baskets and leather buckets of spoil away from the shaft-heads. Down below, in the claustrophobic darkness under the hill, many more would be at work, digging, prising from the native rock the flint that had made Valdoe wealthy, that had paid for Paoul to be trained and put the clothing on his back.

Paoul could not make the mistake of envying the slaves the simplicity of their lives, but at least the duties of a miner were well defined. He worked his shift, returned to his quarters, ate, slept, worked again. Nothing was required of him but to dig flint. His thoughts and beliefs were his own affair; his prison was made of tangible things – wooden bars, the clubs and spears of his overseers. The Gehans deprived him only of his physical liberty. He wore no tattoo: if ever he escaped he had a real chance of remaining free.

Turning his eyes from the flint workings, Paoul looked more to the west, where a finger of forest yet remained between Valdoe and Apuldram. Starting there, it would be possible, travelling almost entirely under the trees, to find a way beyond the Weald, to the ancient uncut forest farther north. There were no tribes of hunters left, no one who knew, as Tagart's people had known, how to thrive in the wild, but an existence of sorts might be found there. In his childhood, in the group, Paoul had learned the names and edibility of the animals and birds. He had learned how to make a trap and light a fire. The rest he could teach himself.

No. He would never be able to survive alone. Tagart had taught him that. It was the first and most important law of the forest. And if Tagart or Fodich – men who had been born and bred to the life – had been powerless to circumvent that law, what sort of chance would Paoul have?

The sun was very pleasant here. So was the feckless feeling of having nothing to do. But already Paoul knew he ought to be getting back to the residence, in case Phede Keldis or General Teshe discovered Hothen on his own; and he knew he ought to let as little time as possible elapse before finding Hothen again. It would only make his job harder if he allowed Hothen's resentment to simmer for too long.

But it was with an effort that Paoul started across the temple precincts, towards the narrow gateway in the hedge and the fortress at the top of the hill.

5

Besides the four great Valdoe fairs there were smaller, monthly markets, set up outside the south-west gates and consisting of fifteen or twenty stalls under broad awnings of coloured fabric or skin. Their proprietors were mostly pedlars, itinerant traders; a few were more ordinary folk, farmers from nearby villages with seed or produce for sale.

This month's market was officially due to open the following day, but already several stallholders had arrived and were unpacking their wares.

Paoul, returning from the temple engrossed in thought, felt his throat constrict. The subject of his thoughts was there, walking by the stalls with Chreo, her companion; and she had seen him. She waved.

Her wave was perplexing. He had been expecting her to ignore him, to pretend, as usual, that she had not seen him, to avert her eyes. He could do little but wave back. His line to the south-west gatehouse would take him to her; he could not very well proceed without stopping to acknowledge Lord Hothen's wife.

'You're the very person I wanted to see,' she said. 'Look. That vase over there. The little blue one. What do you think of it?'

The vase, of classical proportions and patterned with great artistry in two shades of sea-blue, looked out of place among its neighbours, the clumsy pots, pitchers and bowls that were the usual denizens of such stalls.

She did not wait for Paoul's reply. 'The man wants thirty scrapers, but Chreo says it's too much.'

'Then Chreo is wrong, my lady.'

'Exactly, Chreo. What did I tell you?'

Paoul felt again the ache that was inseparable from her presence and the sound of her voice. Today she was wearing the fine grey robe edged with maroon in which she looked, he thought, at her most beautiful. Her hair had been brushed until it shone. It had been tied loosely at the nape of her neck, in just the way he loved it best. In this moment, while her head was turned and she was teasing her staid, middle-aged companion, Paoul was able to study her freely. Then she turned back.

'Does my lady want the vase?' he said.

'Why, certainly.'

Her eyes, her brown eyes which until now had always entreated him to keep away, looked directly into his and it was as though a soft barrier inside him – inside her, inside them both – had just been breached. Something had happened. Something had changed. Something reckless was taking hold of him that he did not want to resist. It had to do with the long chain of events beginning with Dagda and Bocher, leading, through his years of training, to the Lady Atane, to the tour, to Kar Houle and the feeble grasp of his hand. It had to do with Tagart and the forest and the miners under the hill. But most of all it had to do with Yseld.

'I'll see what can be done,' he said.

The dealer was a swarthy fellow who looked none too honest. At Paoul's approach, however, it seemed as if he suddenly repented of his past triumphs. After a little haggling, Paoul acquired the vase for twenty-five scrapers, which he took from the wallet at his belt.

'Please accept it as a gift, my lady.'

'I couldn't. Thank you, but I really couldn't.'

'Then you will have offended me and made a mortal enemy.'

She laughed. 'That wouldn't do, would it, Chreo? We need Forzan Paoul on our side.' She took the vase. 'Thank you. It's lovely.'

He could not understand the change in her. He was seeing a different Yseld.

She said, 'Shall we walk together? I'd like to talk privately with you about my husband's schooling.'

At this, Chreo dutifully dropped several paces behind, and she in turn was followed by two bodyguards in red and grey, men of the group detailed to accompany Yseld or Ika whenever they left the safety of the inner enclosure.

'My husband gave me his version of what happened at the temple, Forzan Paoul, and now he's sulking. He's such a fool,

I don't know how you put up with him. At least his guards had the grace to look embarrassed.'

'What did he tell you?'

'Enough. It sounds rather funny as well as stupid. He's not amused, of course, but then he never is. I only wish I could have been there to see it.'

'He is sick, my lady.'

'What, in the head? That's one excuse, I suppose.'

They walked a few yards in silence. Paoul had the feeling that she wanted to take his arm: he would gladly have offered it. He would have renounced everything for a chance to touch her, to remain in contact with her, to feel her body come closer to his. As it was, this experience of walking beside her would feed a thousand dreams. He did not want to spoil it by calculating how many yards were left to him, but the gatehouse was already drawing near. Once across the outer enclosure, once through the inner gate and along the path to the main door, they would have to part.

'You wished to talk about his schooling, my lady.'

'Yes. His schooling. Forzan Paoul, do you think he will accede? Will Hothen be the next Flint Lord?'

'That is not for me to say.'

'But you must have some idea.'

'The Vansard and General Teshe will decide. I am not party to their decisions. If I knew, my lady, I promise I would tell you.'

'It is very important to me.'

Now Paoul understood her change in mood. The incident at the temple had made her realize that there was a possibility Hothen might not accede. If he did not accede, then her marriage might be declared void, contracted as it was on the understanding that her husband was to be the future Lord Brennis.

'Do you see why it is so important to me?'

'Yes.'

'The law of Hohe is complicated and difficult. But you know it. You have been trained in it. You are the only one I can trust.'

'If there are precedents, they will be in our library. I can find out.'

'When?'

'Immediately. Once I have placated my lord.'

Paoul did not know how all this had happened: his resolutions had been set aside. In the space of a few yards they had become conspirators. She knew his secret. She had known it from the start.

They passed under the gatehouse and ahead he saw the single gate of the inner enclosure. Their time together would soon be up.

'Could you meet me?' she said. 'Once you've been to the library.'

'In the rest-hour after the noon meal. It is quiet then. Would that suit my lady?'

'Yes. But where?'

'In the downstairs day-room.'

'No. Not in the residence. Outside.'

'In the garden, perhaps.'

'Yes, in the arbour. Will you meet me there?'

'At the second hour.'

'I'll be waiting.'

'And in that case too?' she said.

'Yes. Nullified. The husband was made to yield to the cousin's claim. His wife and issue were entailed on the cousin.'

'What does that mean?'

'His wife and children were given to the cousin as part of the title.'

'When was this?'

'Over a hundred years ago. But it makes no difference. Once the Prime has ruled, his precedent must always be followed. That is the basis of the law. Only the Prime himself can change it.'

She looked down at her lap.

Paoul gazed at her, listening to her breathing. He could smell her perfume, the same that she wore sometimes at the night meal, only now it was much stronger, as if its fragrance were an integral part of her, brought to life by the heat of her body. She had not changed her clothes, but as a concession to the warmth of the afternoon she had loosened one of the minute fastenings at her neck, revealing the side of her throat.

At this time of day no birds were singing; the only sound from the garden was the drone of the bees, visiting bloom after bloom on the branches overhead. The shrubs of the arbour were so thick that only a sprinkling of sunlight penetrated the interior of the flagged floor and the quaintly formed stone bench. The bench was not long: she was seated close beside him, on his right. He had never sat this close to her before. He had never sat this close to any girl. In all his imaginings he had never dreamed of anything as vivid or stultifying as this. He wanted to break out of his dream, to touch her, but did not know how to begin.

'Was there ever a case of a wife going free?'

'Not that I know. In law, a wife is regarded as property to be disposed of as the owner wishes. But if a man does not want a wife he has inherited as part of a title, he is bound to offer her in the first instance to her former husband. The same goes for children. Their father may buy them back, provided he has the funds. The price is set by the High Council, and a third is paid into their office.'

'That's barbarous.'

At one time Paoul would have been shocked to hear such a term applied to the methods of the Prime. But now he made no comment.

'So,' she said, 'if Hothen does not accede, I will be given to the next Lord Brennis as part of the Valdoe domain. If he does not want me, I will be offered back to Hothen. And if Hothen can't or won't pay the price, I'll be sold to the highest bidder. Is that right?'

'That's my understanding of the law.'

'But what if my father pays the price? Can he do that?'

'There is no reason why not.'

'So he could buy me back from Hothen.'

'Provided Hothen fails to accede. Otherwise, the marriage contract is binding and cannot be revoked.'

'But there is a faint chance, isn't there?'

Paoul nodded.

The rest-hour was nearly over. In a few minutes he would have to return to the residence for the afternoon's lessons. He did not want to go but, by shifting slightly on the bench, he must have reminded her of the passing time, for she stood up. He too rose.

'Forzan Paoul,' she said. 'I am so grateful. I did not mean to burden you with my troubles. Especially when you yourself always look so sad.'

'Surely not.' He was genuinely surprised: an ability to contain the emotions was a stated object of the taug.

'The others might not notice. In fact I'm sure they don't.'

'But you do.'

'Yes. I do.'

There was a light breeze blowing, the lightest imaginable, barely enough to stir the leaves. It was coming in off the calmness of the sea, a stream of pure, sweet air like the first breath of summer. In the pause that followed before she spoke again, Paoul became aware of its subtle sound in the foliage.

'Are you very unhappy, Forzan Paoul?'

He gave assent with his eyes. In a low voice he heard himself saying, 'Do you know the reason?'

'I think so.'

Her whispered reply was like the breeze, the secret sound of acquiescence. The final restraint of his yearning had been removed. His equilibrium, hers, had gone: the space between them was melting away. He felt her arm round him, her fingers on his neck, and under his own hands was the weave and texture of her robe and beneath it the incredible reality of her body. Endlessly rehearsed in his imagination, this was like nothing he had ever known before. His face was against her cheek, buried in the fragrant softness of her hair. 'Paoul,' she said, 'Paoul,' repeating his name until it became a sigh, a command to hold her with all his strength, just as she was holding him. 'Forgive me. Forgive me.'

Her words had no meaning. What was happening was beyond meaning. Too close to focus, he saw her eyes wet with tears; as the first strength of their embrace gave way, her face turned further to accommodate his, and the pressure of her arms on his neck brought their mouths almost into contact.

'No,' she said. 'No. We mustn't.'

For a hopeless moment he tried to insist; but she was resolute. She gently pushed him away.

'Please, Paoul. It's enough that we know.'

'Yseld – '

'Don't say any more. Paoul, we are who we are. And you are a priest. There can be nothing for us. Nothing but pain. They will catch us, and you will be killed.'

'My love – '

'No, Paoul. This must never happen again. I should never have asked you here.'

He reached out for her hand: she withheld it.

'I must go. I must go, Paoul. Please let me leave.'

To let her go now was impossible. She was part of him; he could as well tear himself in two. But there was no choice.

With a last look back at him, she fled.

6

At the end of the afternoon, when Hothen's lessons were finished for the day, Paoul received a note from Kar Vever. Much sooner than Paoul had expected, Enco had arrived, and Paoul was to go to the vansery common-room to meet him.

Paoul was glad to have an excuse to leave the residence. The afternoon's lessons, at Hothen's request, had been conducted in the garden, in the pavilion. On warm days the ladies of the retinue often took refreshments there, and Paoul did not trust himself to face Yseld so soon in company. In the event, though, she did not appear. She was keeping to her quarters, just as fearful of betraying him as he was of betraying her. Tonight, at the meal, would be soon enough to begin the pretence that nothing had passed between them today.

But more than this, Paoul was relieved to get away from Hothen's company. Although he had managed to achieve a sort of resolution of their quarrel, and had even elicited a grudging and half-hearted apology, Paoul knew the incident was not likely to be forgotten. For the first time this morning he had seen the depth of Hothen's resentment, which was matched only by Paoul's jealousy and dislike. Eventually there would come a violent confrontation, after which Paoul feared he would be unable to carry on. To be free of Hothen would be a blessed release, but Paoul was dreading the day. His only concern now, mad and dangerous and forlorn as it was, was the prospect of no longer sharing Yseld's roof, of being prevented from seeing her again.

The vansery common-room, in the south-western corner of the main building, was filled with early evening sunshine. Paoul recognized Enco at once, although half a dozen other priests were present and, sitting with his back to a window, Enco's features could scarcely be made out: as he rose to his feet with an exclamation of greeting, he became a silhouette against a dazzling background of gold.

He clasped Paoul's hand. 'It's good to see you again.'

Kar Thurman, with whom Enco had been talking and who had also risen on Paoul's entry, acknowledged Paoul with a subdued smile. 'Shall we continue our discussion later, Kar Enco?' he said. 'For now, I must ask you to excuse me. I have many things to do for the ceremony this evening.'

'Of course,' Enco said, with an easy confidence he had not possessed at school. 'I am most grateful to you for your interest, Kar Thurman.'

'Ceremony?' Paoul said. 'What ceremony is that? Something unscheduled?'

'Have you not yet heard?' Kar Thurman said, and immediately Paoul understood why his smile had been subdued; and why the conversation in the common-room, he now noticed, was rather quieter and more restrained than usual. 'I'm sorry. I thought you knew. Kar Houle is dead.'

Momentarily Paoul's composure deserted him. He had been expecting this blow, but he found himself, after all, unprepared for it. He shut his eyes. 'No one told me,' he said.

'He died this afternoon, in the fourth hour.'

Just at the time Paoul had been with Hothen in the pavilion, toiling through a lesson in arithmetic that should not have taxed a twelve-year-old. 'How did he . . . how did he die?'

'Quite peacefully, Kar Vever says. I was not there myself.'

'Is he still in his room? May I see him?'

'Of course.'

Paoul turned to Enco. 'Do you mind?'

'Not at all.'

'Perhaps Kar Enco would also like to see him,' Kar Thurman said. 'Kar Houle was much loved and admired here.'

Despite his friendship with Enco, despite his eagerness to talk with him again, Paoul would have preferred to go alone. He wanted to spend a few minutes in private with Kar Houle before the grand obsequies began: the rites this evening were likely to be attended by most of Valdoe. But it was too late. Enco had already accepted Kar Thurman's invitation.

The rush blind at Kar Houle's window had been let down. A second wicker table had been introduced and on either side of the bed burned a small scented lamp. The aroma in the room was of resin, of pine trees or firs, a smell Paoul had not known since leaving Hohe.

Kar Houle was still in his bed, but the bedding had been renewed, he had been dressed in a fresh nightshirt, and already, in preparation for this evening, his head had been shaved of all hair: only his eyelashes remained. Without his beard, and with his hands placed in the classical position, left upon right, above the solar plexus, he looked somehow more serene, but nothing could disguise the awfulness of his appearance. It was a marvel that this skeletal frame could have endured for so long, a tribute not only to the human body but also to the doctrine of the taug.

Enco moved to the foot of the bed, and suddenly Paoul was reminded of another room, far away, where they had stood in contemplation of a corpse. The smell then had been of excrement, not the clean air of the pines; of heat and suffering and the barracks, not of laundered robes and the cool detachment of the citadel. Which room, which body, could be explained by the teaching Paoul had received? The answer came to him: neither. There was sense in neither. What had that young soldier died for? And why should the life of this old man have been prolonged to its maximum term? What had he achieved in all those extra years that the soldier, through his premature death, had not?

Enco spoke. 'How old was he?'

'Ninety-eight.'

The tenuous idea that Paoul had been pursuing slipped away; his train of thought had been broken, leaving him only with a sense of isolation and loss. If they did hold any secret for him, Kar Houle's remains were unlikely to yield it up when another was present.

Paoul turned aside and was followed by Enco to the common-room. They sat down in the same seats; the room had almost emptied.

Paoul tried to smile. 'I'm sorry, my friend. This has not been an easy day. You must tell me first about your journey. Was the crossing smooth?'

Enco talked; Paoul, only half-listening at first, preoccupied as he was with thoughts of Yseld, Kar Houle, his own precarious future, gradually began to perceive in Enco a profound but indefinable change. This was not the same Enco Paoul had known at Hohe. This was a qualified and practising kar, mature, purposeful, sure of himself and his abilities. In only eight months of life in the mainstream of the Order, he appeared to have lost whatever it was that Paoul had once valued. Or perhaps, Paoul thought, it was he himself who had changed, and Enco who had remained the same. Whatever had happened, his closest friend had become a stranger. He saw that there could now be no question of seeking advice.

Paoul asked, 'When will you want to see your patient?'

'There's no hurry. Indeed, it's better if he doesn't even know he's being treated. The powders go straight into his food.'

'He has a food-taster.'

'That makes no difference. The doses are minute, and they're quite tasteless.'

'But won't the food-taster be affected?'

Enco grinned. 'Not unless he shares his master's symptoms, in which case he can only benefit. But let's not talk about that. There'll be plenty of time for Lord Hothen later. I want to hear what you've been up to since you returned to your native land.'

Enco was evidently impressed that Paoul had been chosen as tutor to the future Lord Brennis. He accepted with equanimity the obvious but unspoken fact that Paoul had used his position to effect a reunion with his friend, a procedure that, in the idealism of their schooldays, would have filled them both with horror.

After giving an account of his own career, Enco brought Paoul abreast of the latest comings and goings at Hohe. Among these were the retirements from the school of the Chief Reciter, whose place had been filled by their mentor on the tour, Ilven Fend. Since his initiation, Enco had got to know Ilven Fend on a more informal basis, as an equal, and he repeated to Paoul some of the stories Ilven Fend had told him about the tour, about matters which Ilven Fend had thought it best to conceal from his charges. At Vinzy, for example, he had chosen to disregard a late but ambiguous correction of Commander Yahl's smoke signal, a correction warning them not to set out for Chaer. They had been behind schedule, and a detour would have been difficult. 'Makes your hair stand on end to think of it now, doesn't it?' Enco said. His manner became more serious. 'There's another thing I think you ought to know. It concerns Starrad. He wasn't expelled, as we were led to believe. He was killed.'

Paoul endeavoured to keep his expression as matter-of-fact as Enco's. 'What?'

'Of course, they couldn't tell us at the time. We were only novices. But it had to be done: it's standard procedure. After all, Starrad was already in the higher school. He'd been warned there was no going back. We all had. They couldn't just let him leave.'

'How did you find out?'

'It's no secret. Ilven Fend told me. If you remember, he was on dormitory duty the morning Starrad was caught.'

'Yes. Of course.' Paoul's mind, already numbed by the events of the day, could barely take this revelation in. It made no new impact; it was almost as if he had been expecting something of the sort. But, although numb, his mind was still able to function. 'What about his paramour?' he said, adopting the very tone that Enco had used. 'The fishmonger's daughter. What happened to her?'

'Killed too, I imagine.'

'And her family?'

'The same. The reputation of the Order was at stake. Who knows what he'd been telling them? The Prime had no alternative.'

Paoul looked up. The senior ilven had entered and was coming across the room.

'Forzan Paoul,' he said, with a gesture of acknowledgement for Enco. 'May I have a word? We're finalizing the arrangements for the funeral.'

All red priests were trained in ceremonial: the funeral had been organized quickly and efficiently, without need of rehearsal. The torches, firebrands, and banners and been ready for days; the musicians and choristers had known in advance the sequence of dirges and laments. During the late afternoon the bier had been set up and a tomb prepared in the vansery barrow, for it was considered proper to inter a body as soon as possible after death, preferably at the onset of night.

The rites began at sunset. After a service in the vansery, Kar Houle's body, wrapped in a green and vermilion grave-robe and suspended on three richly embroidered straps, was carried in procession to the temple. At Kar Houle's request, Paoul was one of the bearers. The column was led by Phede Keldis; at its rear walked General Teshe and Hothen, behind them Lady Teshe and Yseld, and then Ika, guided by a liveried page. Behind them came the General of Valdoe, all the higher Trundlemen, the leader of the Village Council and his wife, and representatives of the barracks and of the freemen's guilds. The passing of the senior kar was an occasion for solemn and spectacular ceremonial: the first stage of the interment, the Celebration of the Earth, was witnessed too by most of the soldiers and freemen in the Trundle, who had gathered at a respectful distance on the hill. Even the returning day-shift from the mines, and then the arriving night-shift, were allowed by their overseers to pause and watch for a few moments.

The rest of the ceremony was for the priesthood only. The laymen retired; the hill was cleared, and even the sentries on the distant ramparts were instructed to direct their eyes elsewhere. And finally, after the temple had been opened and the Rites of Gauhm enacted, Kar Houle was buried and the tumulus remade. The sacred semicircle of thirteen torches was left blazing in the night breeze; taking their banners and firebrands, the priests followed the flag-marked path back to the summit.

The second part of the interment had lasted for over three hours. When at last Paoul returned to the residence, the household had long since gone to bed. He was admitted by the guard and, still in his ceremonial robes, began to climb the winding staircase to the gallery. The stairs were illuminated merely by two dim cressets; most of the lamps in the gallery above him had been doused, leaving barely enough light to show the way.

As he slowly mounted each tread, he delayed his progress by grasping the rail and using it to draw himself on. He was both reluctant and eager to reach the top; he felt exhausted and yet also infused with a lucid determination he had never known before.

The funeral had been for him the final release. As the ritual had unfurled, so Paoul had been reborn. He had accepted Tagart's inheritance and become a man who was free, capable of discerning the ceremony for what it was: a spectacle to impress the pagans and keep them in their place. This was how the priesthood kept its power, and nothing was too precious to be subordinated to that purpose. Kar Houle had given his life to the Order, and his passing had been made a mockery, an excuse for that nauseating masquerade. But, unlike the soldier at Chaer, at the very end Kar Houle had not been deceived. For his final month, or days, or hours – or even from the time he had clutched Paoul's hand in warning – he too had been free.

Watching his wasted body going into the grave, Paoul had been conscious of Enco standing nearby. Enco had become just what they wanted. He had survived the selection process that Starrad had failed; in eighty years from now Enco, like this other kar, would be lauded and inhumed. He too would have devoted his life to the Earth Goddess, and already Paoul knew what his reward would be.

And so, as the congregation had retreated, leaving the thirteen flames roaring softly in the breeze, Paoul had made his choice. He had chosen freedom. He had abdicated safety, comfort, and the security of the Order. He had renounced his calling.

Whether he lasted another year, or only a week, he would exercise within himself the freedom that was his birthright. They had tattooed him: there could be no physical escape. He would continue the outward life of a priest until such time as they became too clever for him and he was caught.

He reached the top of the stairs. As his eyes came level with the gallery floor he noticed, to the left, a faint strip of lamplight under Yseld's door. The other rooms were all dark. His own room, two doors along from hers, was to the right. That was where he had intended to go.

Paoul found himself stopping, one hand on the carved serpent's-head of the newel. He listened: there was no sound save the quiet lapping of the cresset flames.

At the funeral he had seen Yseld again and known that his longing for her was right. The vows he had taken were wrong: wrong in Tagart's terms, because they denied what was natural and true.

The obstacle of his vows had disappeared. All that mattered now was her safety.

He listened again. The household was silent, as silent as his movement away from the newel and towards the left, as silent as his return would be later, to his own door.

The handle yielded to his touch. Before he really understood what he was doing, her door was open and he had slipped inside and locked it.

She was seated at her dressing board, in a pale cream nightshift. She had unravelled and was brushing out the formal and elaborate plaiting of her hair. Startled, she turned and in bewilderment rose to her feet.

No words were spoken; he held a finger to his lips, afraid that she might yet protest or cry out in surprise. In the arbour she had been resolute, but that was then, and this was now, and as he crossed the floor she moved to meet him. He could not believe how beautiful she was, more beautiful even than before; and in her eyes, her dark and lustrous eyes, he saw not only fear but daring, the triumph over danger, acknowledgement, and desire.

They resumed their embrace, but now it was different. Now began the exploration and merging of their senses. The rapture and sweetness of this, his first kiss, dissolved imperceptibly into others. As his arousal grew, the material of her shift became an intolerable hindrance and she, understanding, immediately reached behind her and it fell away. Dazed, he beheld for the first time a living woman's body.

She delayed extinguishing the lamp until he had stepped free of his ceremonial robes, leaving them in a crumpled heap on the floor. And then, in the darkness, she took his hand and drew him towards her bed.

7

'Master Crogh!' Rian called out, as, her heart pounding, she started after him across the lawn. He had just made one of his visits to the residence, bringing samples of specialist honeys for the chief cook to try and, having secured his usual handsome order, he was heading for the gate.

Rian had seen him many times over the years. He liked to call in person, so important did he consider the patronage of General Teshe, in whose name all purchases were made; and indeed, Master Crogh's reputation as sole supplier to the residence had done him no harm. His increasing wealth had brought increasing girth, and his dense brown curls, like his rather elegant, squared-off beard, were here and there beginning to turn grey. His eyes were humorous. On the few occasions when Rian had spoken to him, she had found him, for a freeman, approachable, friendly, and easy-going. He liked to joke with the servants and slaves, and sometimes even brought them little gifts of beeswax or honeycomb.

But she had awaited today's visit with terror. As the date had approached, she had doubted her ability to see her plan through. It went against all her instincts: she would be risking death to address a freeman like that, especially a freeman of Master Crogh's rank. Just now, loitering by the kitchen door, she had actually decided to abandon her intention and take the way to safety. What difference could it make now, after all these years? Who cared about the feelings of an old woman, a slave? No one. But that was the very reason why she knew she must speak. Her life was almost over. They had stolen it; they had done their worst. She had nothing left to lose. Thus, at the last possible moment, she had decided after all to risk everything, to seize this chance to uncover what above all else she yearned to know.

It had begun eight weeks ago, when Ika had acquired from a dealer in curios and precious objects, a tiny brooch in copper studded with amber, opal, and coral. The brooch was in the form of a serpent: not quite the Gehan serpent, but a variation on its theme in civilian style and colouring. The opals were uniquely and ingeniously cut, the work of a supreme craftsman: there could not be two such pieces in existence. Although she had not seen it for almost twenty years, Rian had recognized the serpent at once. The first sight of it, in Ika's quarters, had almost made her cry out in astonishment. Beyond all doubt, the serpent had once belonged to Altheme. It had been among the pieces that Rian herself, in the final, panic-stricken moments of the siege, had scooped from her mistress's dressing board and crammed into a hidden pocket in her travelling bag. When Rian and she had been parted, when Altheme had gone off to the forest with the savages' leader, then, as far as Rian knew, the travelling bag and its contents had gone with her.

The serpent was the only clue that Rian had ever found to the fate of the one mistress whom, alone among all her owners, she had loved; the one mistress who had treated her kindly and loved her in return.

Cautiously, reluctantly, Rian had enlisted the help of her younger son, the slave of a former Trundleman who had retired to Valdoe Village. Her son was friendly with the house-slave of the dealer, Master Iorach. It transpired that Iorach had bought the serpent from Euden, the grown-up son of Master Crogh. Euden had tried to make Iorach promise not to resell in Brennis, but Iorach had refused. Even so, Euden had taken the price. It was rumoured that he was in trouble, being pressed to pay a gaming debt. Of more interest to Rian, it was believed by the house-slave that Euden had stolen the serpent from his father. In the past, at long and irregular intervals, Crogh had sold Iorach a few items of good but not exceptional quality: a necklace, a pair of earrings, a coral collar-clasp. These, the house-slave had always assumed, had come to Crogh by way of legitimate trade. But no order for honey could be worth as much as the serpent, a piece so fine that it could have been made only for a noble, a high noble – almost certainly a member of the ruling clan.

Rian had not dared ask her son to inquire further. Necklaces, earrings, a coral collar-clasp: all these had been among Altheme's effects. Somehow it looked as if Master Crogh had acquired them. But when? Where? From whom? And what knowledge did he have of Altheme's fate?

The idea of tackling him directly had not come easily. She knew the gossip about Crogh. He was a former harvest inspector who, through what now began to look like suspicious circumstances, had been able to leave the beilinry and set up at the Village, and in some comfort too. He had risen to a position of prominence on the council, and Rian knew that any man who could do that, easy-going or not, was a man to be feared.

But it was too late to change her mind. She had already called out to him and, puzzled, half-smiling, he had stopped on the pathway and was looking back. Rian forced herself on, becoming breathless. Out here, in the middle of the lawn, there was no shade, nor shelter from all the overlooking windows of the residence. She was completely on view. What she was doing was insane.

'Master Crogh, I must speak with you.'

His half-smile vanished; it displeased him to be accosted thus by a slave. 'You? With me? What about?'

'It's important, Master Crogh. We ought to speak in private. Over there, in the arbour –'

'Get out of my way.'

'It's about your son, Master Crogh. About Master Euden, and the brooch he sold to Master Iorach.'

'Brooch? Brooch? What are you talking about?'

'The serpent brooch. Your son sold it to Master Iorach, but he had no right. It was stolen from the ruling clan. If General Teshe finds out, your son could be executed.'

This was a lie, but a convincing one, and she prayed he might suspect it to be true. If he didn't, or if he knew nothing about the affair, or if his son had come by the serpent honestly, then she was lost. This conversation would be reported to Ika, to the chamberlain: she would be punished, tortured, put to death. And to begin with, at the very least, Crogh would strike her down, here on the lawn.

She was waiting for the blow. It did not come. Crogh remained still, and she saw that the first part of her plan had worked. And if the first had worked, so would the second. By threat of exposing Euden – the threat disguised as an attempt to save him from discovery – she would be able to find out whatever Crogh knew about the serpent, its history, and the fate of Altheme.

Crogh glanced uneasily towards the residence. 'It's Rian, isn't it? That is your name?'

'Yes, master.'

'Since you seem to have something to say about my son, I suppose I ought to listen.' He made a show of reaching inside his tunic. 'Wait a minute,' he said. 'I appear to have mislaid my purse. I'll have to go back and fetch it.'

The purse was hanging round his neck: Rian could clearly see the cord. This was just a ploy, a ploy with a double purpose: to forestall questioning in case they had been observed, and to give him a face-saving way of agreeing to meet her in private. His next words came as no surprise.

'Go over to the arbour, Rian. I'll join you there presently.'

There was only one place where it could possibly be: among the confidential parchments in the Vansard's quarters. Paoul had unearthed everything else. He had found the provenance of the serpent, the original bill of sale, and the inventory of the Lady Altheme's other jewels. He had found the inventory of the Trundle taken after the siege and the list of missing valuables, among them the serpent and all the pieces Rian had remembered. He had consulted again Kar Houle's record of his induction and, to his unspeakable relief, and with a prayer of gratitude for the Order's pedantic insistence on thoroughness and precision, had found every one of the essential details faithfully noted in that flowery, old-fashioned hand: the repeated doubts about Paoul's parentage, the exact date of his birth, Tagart's name and physical description and his identity as Paoul's 'putative father'. He had found everything but the vital scroll relating to the Lady Altheme, the deposition that Rian had given to Torin Hewzane's men. In this she had described the circumstances of her mistress's departure from the Trundle, naming Tagart as the leader of the group of nomads among whom she had last been seen, giving an account of the missing jewels, and, most important of all, and substantiating any other reports that the Lady Altheme was with child, Rian distinctly remembered mentioning the time at which the pregnancy had begun.

Paoul was still unable fully to take in the news Rian had broken to him just before the night meal. Perhaps he never would be able to adjust to it, not completely. If her excited suspicions were proved correct, then he was not what, all his life, he had believed. He was not the son of Mirin and of Tagart, leader of the southern tribes. He was instead a member of the ruling clan, son of the Lady Altheme and of Brennis Gehan Fifth, Lord of Valdoe. He was Hothen's half brother, Ika's nephew. During the meal he had seen them with new eyes, comparing their features with his own. The resemblance, now that he was aware of it, was too great to be coincidental. It was a horrible and unwelcome sensation to feel himself suddenly so close to them, severed from the father of whom he had always been so proud. Yseld was rightfully his. But for an accident of birth, he would already have been married to her.

The meal had demanded enormous self control. Even Yseld, during their customary polite and neutral exchanges, could not have guessed what was going on inside him. He had longed to tell her; but after the meal there had been no safe opportunity to talk, and anyway it was too soon. Before telling her, he had to be sure. He had to visit the library.

The search had taken longer than he had anticipated. By the time he had finished, it was too late to return to the residence. At midnight his free day began and, as far as the household knew, he would be spending the night in the vansery. He had practised this same deception last week. It was one way of reducing the risk.

Since that first night, he and Yseld had been together eleven times. Her room was much too dangerous to use again. There was nowhere safe inside the residence, and guards were kept posted at the entrance and at the gate of the inner enclosure. But, by using a circuitous route, it was possible to reach the downstairs day-room and from there, climbing through the window, they could escape into the garden unseen. And so, almost every night, for the two or three hours before dawn, they had met in the pavilion.

Tonight they had met here again.

After leaving the library, retrieving a length of rope he had left hidden in the vansery grounds, Paoul had skirted the palisade of the inner enclosure until he had reached the darkest and quietest spot. There, not far from the shrubbery, he had climbed over and made his way to the pavilion. He had waited for several hours before hearing her footfall on the path, and then, on their improvised bed of cushions, she had joined him.

Their passion was so intense that until now she had put all thought of the future in abeyance. She had refused even to let him speak of it, but tonight he insisted.

In the long hours he had spent waiting for her, Paoul had decided, much against his natural inclinations, not to disclose any of what Rian had told him or what he had so far found out. Without the final evidence there could be no effective claim; to raise and then dash her hopes would be more than he could bear.

So he merely said that this was to be their last secret meeting. He could not yet tell her why, but it involved finding a certain parchment. If he found it, there would for ever be an end to these furtive assignations. They could be together openly, as man and wife; they could have it all. But they had to be patient. They could not afford to jeopardize the future. Their happiness was at stake.

'But you are a priest,' she said, 'A priest can never marry.'

He did not tell her why she was wrong. He could not tell her that membership of the ruling clan took precedence over all else, even the priestly vows. It was the one, the single, the sole escape from the Order. And further: if his claim were upheld, he would inherit Yseld automatically as part of the Valdoe domain. Her dowry had purchased her the position, not of wife to Hothen, but of consort to the future Brennis Gehan Sixth, whoever that turned out to be.

Although she tried to question him, he refused to be drawn. 'You once said you trusted me,' he told her. 'You will have to trust me still.'

'Of course I trust you. I trust you with my life.'

'Then let's have no more questions.'

With that he kissed her. Fighting his own as well as her desires, he made himself break away. It was nearly dawn. They had to get dressed.

He helped her find her things, and fastened his tunic and

leggings and drew on his boots. While she finished tying back her hair, he picked up the cushions and replaced them on the bench seat that ran along the inner wall.

Together they went to the step. The east was already faintly grey; a robin which had been singing in the darkness was now joined by a wren. Over the hill, in the distance, came the first calls of a carrion crow.

'When will I next see you?'

'Soon,' he said. 'Very soon.'

'Paoul, be careful.'

'I will.'

'I cannot live without you, Paoul. Do you know what I am saying?'

'Yes. I have thought about that too.'

'If you don't find this parchment, how much longer do you think we'll have?'

'Yseld, it is time to go.'

They descended to the path. In the deep night under the cherry trees, they kissed again before parting. 'Take care,' he said, as she vanished into the dark, moving towards the lawn.

Within minutes he was back at the vansery. No one saw him come through the gate or enter the main building at the rear.

His excuse, his reason for being here, was that he wished to spend the morning of his free day in private study in the library, starting before the residence was awake. Rather than disturb the servants and the guards, he had told the chamberlain that he would sleep in the vansery, as before, in one of the small chambers reserved for visiting priests. These chambers lined a short corridor near the common-room. The one in which Paoul was meant to have slept was at the end, next to Enco's

Before leaving to meet Yseld, he had disturbed the bedding on the narrow, hard-based cot. There was a negligible chance that his absence would be discovered: once he had retired for the night, a priest's privacy was strictly respected, for the hours of darkness were an important time for meditation. Disturbing the bedding had been a needless precaution, but one that would give him the basis of an explanation if the unexpected had happened. He had also pulled three short lengths of stalk from the rush matting and left them bent in such a way that, if the door were opened widely, to its normal extent, they would be moved and their relationship with each other destroyed.

They were still in place. The room had not been entered. Paoul silently shut the door and went over to the cot.

He made himself lie down. He needed sleep, but sleep was impossible. Already he could hear the first sounds of the vansery coming awake, and he had yet to devise a means of getting access to the confidential archive. He knew where it was kept, in the inner chamber of Phede Keldis's office. He would need no more than a quarter of an hour to pick out the appropriate scroll, read it, and return it to its compartment. The problem was to find a time when the office would be unattended during daylight.

In the next room he heard Enco rise. A moment later Enco's door opened and closed as he left to perform his ablutions. What were his plans for the day? How would he react if told how his friend had spent the night? Would that shake his confidence, his smugness and self-esteem?

The treatment of Hothen had so far yielded no results. Already Enco had confided that he was beginning to doubt it ever would. He had said that Hothen's defect were congenital, the result of inbreeding. If nothing could be done for him, Enco would soon be going back to Hohe.

Paoul shut his eyes. How weary he was, how sick of it all, of the priesthood and its values. To think that he had once dreamed of nothing more wonderful than a career at the citadel!

The dawn gong sounded and the solution came, and with it a surge of new energy and excitement. Paoul got to his feet, straightened his clothes, and hurriedly made the bed. Phede Keldis almost always conducted the dawn litany himself; his assistant would also be there, leaving the office empty just long enough for Paoul to enter the inner chamber and consult the archive. Then he could join the service at its end, standing near the door at the rear of the hall, and no one would ever have to know.

8

Paoul had found it. He had found the scroll. He had seen Rian's deposition, among a sheaf of private documents relating to the ruling clan, and in it the essential framework for the successful prosecution of his claim. He had had to delay before leaving the vansery, but now, overjoyed, he was hurrying back to the residence.

The dealer Iorach was now the key. He was an honest man, Rian had said; his testimony would prompt General Teshe to interrogate Euden, Crogh's son, and then Crogh himself. There might well be some difficulty here, although Crogh could not deny his son's possession of the serpent and would be hard put to explain how he had acquired it unless he admitted the truth: that the serpent, together with the other pieces he had subsequently sold to Iorach – for which Iorach would also have bills of sale – had indeed come from Bocher's village. There was no evidence that Crogh had come by the jewels illegally; he could easily have bought them, just as he had told Rian, and just as, in Kar Houle's report, he claimed to have bought Paoul. It was not a crime to benefit from the ignorance of the farmers. Far from it: the only crimes recognized by Hohe were crimes against the empire. And even if, as seemed likely, Crogh had accepted both Paoul and the jewels as a bribe, there was no possibility that Bocher, presuming he was still alive, would ever condemn himself by admitting it. All Crogh had to do was stick to his story, the one he had given Kar Houle, and he would be safe. In protecting himself he would substantiate the link between Paoul and the jewels; between Paoul and the Lady Altheme.

The evidence was essentially flimsy. After all this time, how could it be otherwise? In different circumstances, Paoul knew his claim would not get far. Minds like his own would rip it to shreds. But, with Hothen as he was, and his coming of age now only five months away, the claim stood an excellent chance. Paoul fulfilled all the requirements of Lord Heite, and more. Not only was he the son of Brennis Fifth, but he was the legitimate son, the first-born. The claim would receive support from all quarters of the High Council: the Order, ever anxious to extend its influence, could not wish for a more pliant Lord Brennis than one of its own. Knowing the way the High Council worked, there was little doubt in Paoul's mind what the ruling would be.

He still could not believe there was every chance he would have Yseld for life, with the freedom to be with her just as he chose. He could not believe that he, Paoul, might soon be the Lord of Valdoe, the man who held sway over the whole domain and whose influence could, in time, be brought to bear on the citadel. What slow and subtle changes there would be! Secretly, subversively, he would work for reform. He would seek to free the slaves, to reduce the taxes, to diminish and divert the power of the Prime. But above all he would work for the golden dream: to extend the control of self beyond the priesthood, to pass this priceless gift to all. 'Pagans', they were called; but who were the real pagans, the heathen criminals who abused the greatest faculty of man? There could be no going back to the forest. It was too late for that. The marvels of Tagart's age had gone. Man was coming to another age, not of decay, as the Order said, but of potential unfulfilled. But it never would be fulfilled if he were deprived of the single faculty on which the world's welfare hinged, the faculty indivisible from that which Paoul loved and worshipped most in Yseld: the human spirit.

They had talked of all this; it seemed as if they had been talking for ever. Lying together in the pavilion, he had told her all his doubts and dreams, and she had told him hers. She had never been under any illusions about the Order or the Gehans. What he had taken years to realize had for Yseld been the hateful background of her life. Since birth she had been exposed to it; her own marriage was an example of her family's greed.

Very soon now, her unhappiness would be at an end. Paoul would tell her first, and then he would find Rian, the kind and faithful Rian, a woman who deserved none of the treatment that Valdoe had meted out. When she had told Paoul of her discovery she had wept with joy, saying again and again what a miracle it was, again and again how much he reminded her of his mother, her former mistress, the Lady Altheme. She had made no mention of it, but he was sure she had guessed the truth about him and Yseld, and he was equally sure she would never give them away.

Yes, he would find Rian and take her to the Vansard, and immediately begin his claim.

The guard at the residence gate was a new man Paoul had never seen before. His unsmiling face was completely at odds with Paoul's euphoric mood; so too was the greyness of the day. Crossing the sheep-cropped lawn, traversing the irregular granite stepping stones to the porch of the side entrance, Paoul noticed a wizened old gardener, a slave, morosely at work near the arbour, picking spent blossoms from the shrubs and tossing them into a wicker bin. To reach the higher blooms he was using a crook, bending down the branches, stripping them, letting them spring back. As one of the stouter branches sprang back a dark cluster of leaves was torn off and fluttered to the ground.

They touched the lawn and Paoul felt the first painless stab of premonition. Something had changed here. Something was wrong.

The side door opened and Rian appeared. She did not come out; she remained anxiously in the porch, her hands clasped. She must have been standing by the window, watching for him, awaiting his arrival.

Then, somehow, Paoul knew that Yseld had been caught returning to her room. He knew. The porch and door, approaching with unreal slowness, Rian's face, her anxiety, the cloudy morning, the swish and slap of the tortured foliage, everything confirmed it.

'Forzan Paoul,' Rian said, pulling him inside, into the gloomy darkness of the lobby. 'I have something terrible to tell you.' The lobby smelled of stale milk. A bucket had been spilled here a week before. There were many garments hanging on the rack: the servants' robes and mantles, the gardeners' leather aprons. She was holding his arm, as a mother holds her son's. 'Forzan Paoul, you must promise me you'll stay calm. You must do nothing sudden, nothing foolish.'

Still it was unfolding at the same unreal rate; but now he

realized that the stab of premonition had gone much deeper and left a widening wound, a wound filling with agony and disbelief.

'Sometimes, Forzan Paoul, my Lady Ika cannot sleep. This morning, very early, she called out to my Lord Hothen. She had heard the Lady Yseld. I think she must have stumbled at the foot of the stairs and hurt herself. The light there is very bad.'

His wound was worse, even worse than he had feared; his last hope of life was crushed by the look in Rian's eyes.

'If it hadn't been for my Lady Ika . . . if you'd heard her questions . . . Forzan Paoul, she put ideas in his head. She wanted to know where the Lady Yseld had been. She accused her of seeing the kitchen-boy, just because he's handsome and the Lady Yseld was once kind to him. Hothen called his guards. They dragged the kitchen-boy out of bed and beat him. They beat him with clubs. Then Hace . . . Hace burned him. He burned him till he screamed. He confessed to everything my Lady Ika said, foul things, disgusting things, and then they killed him. And then . . . then . . . then Hothen . . . Forzan Paoul, I am so sorry. I loved her too. Pity him, Forzan Paoul. Pity him. He has killed the Lady Yseld.'

9

Today, two months and more after Yseld's funeral, Paoul felt able at last to visit her grave alone. This morning Hothen had been removed, pronounced unfit and sent to the mainland with his mother: his place would be taken by one of Lord Heite's nephews. By the autumn there would be a new Flint Lord at Valdoe.

Paoul had lost all interest in his claim. Without Yseld, it could serve no purpose. And, although he had not yet summoned the courage to admit it, he had a bigger aim in view.

The temple and its precincts were deserted when he arrived. The sky had cleared after an early morning squall; the rain had softened the turf and wetted the grass on the tumulus. She was buried at the western end. No fragment of her wreaths remained. Only a small stone marker, bearing the single beautiful character of her name, distinguished her grave from the vacant soil.

Standing there, Paoul realized that his craving for death, for peace, had changed. It had become secondary but intrinsic to that chilling design which he was still afraid to contemplate. At first, in his guilt and despair, he had wanted to join her. He had wanted to complete the pact at which she had hinted in their final moments together. He had wanted to kill himself by killing Hothen.

He had almost done it. He had almost rushed upstairs. Without Rian, he would have been unable to contain the first access of his rage, but she, the slave, had been wiser than a priest. In the crucial instant she had checked him and given him back his self control. He would never lose it again: her words had revealed to him the course of his future purpose, if only he were strong enough to take it.

'He's not worth killing,' she had said, and she was right. Hothen, his half brother, was not the cause of Yseld's death. Nor even was Ika, nor the negligent Teshe. The cause was not even here in Brennis. It was at Hohe, at the centre of the

Gehan's circle, the same circle that had made Rian a slave, Rian and all the others, the same that had made a slave of Paoul.

The empire's goddess, Gauhm, had killed his Yseld. The true Earth Goddess had been murdered by the false. But Yseld had been much more to him than that: it was to her gentle spirit that he should build her monument. He would have to remain alive, submerged in all he loathed. He would have to remain alone, completely alone, until, working from the centre, he had done so much damage that the Gehans' empire could not survive.

Death would be easier. Death needed no resolve.

But they had fitted him perfectly for his task. They had taken an innocent child and made him into a future Prime.

Facing across the tumulus, towards the sea, Paoul turned his eyes south-eastwards, towards the citadel, and knew he had no choice.

Thirty-eight years later, almost to the day, Forzan Paoul, former Principal of the Temple School, Surveyor of the Vanseries, Honour Companion to the Gehan of the Gehans, and now Moderator of the Supreme Board of the High Council, was unanimously declared successor to the ailing Prime.

His accession took place in the winter. In the spring it was noticed, first by the lakeman, and then with increasing alarm by the men in the temple and in the barracks, that fewer pairs of herons had returned to breed. The heronry, for over three centuries the symbol of the continuance and prosperity of the Gehan empire, had in large part been unaccountably abandoned.

The following spring, no pairs at all were seen to build. The islands were deserted: the birds had gone elsewhere.